Copyright © 2025 Lisa Askham
All rights reserved.

This is a work of fiction. Unless otherwise indicated, all the names, characters, businesses, places, events and incidents in this book are either the product of the author's imagination or used in a fictitious manner. Any resemblance to actual persons, living or dead, or actual events is purely coincidental.

Cover design by Action Design Artwork
from an original photograph of the Suffolk
countryside by Lisa Askham

ONE

"I can't." He shook his head as she held it in her hands, and they stood in the car park with the rain falling and the bonnet on the car open. "I can't marry you."

"*Why?*"

He stared into her eyes. "It's a long story."

She stared back at him; she could see he didn't know whether to laugh or cry as her hands cradled his face. "Well, maybe you'd better tell it to me."

He had agreed to return with her. That was a victory as she had feared he would not want to return to the village or her house, but he had nodded against her shoulder when she had asked him. They stood in that car park, in that frantic embrace, in the rain for an age. After he had slipped out of her bed and disappeared three weeks ago, she did not mean to ever let him out of her grasp again – and that showed in her fingers clutching tightly to him. He sighed shakily and turned his head to press his forehead against hers.

"OK." She whispered. "Let's go home."

But Jacob, being Jacob, nodded to the car.

"We can't leave her stranded here. I can't fix it here – it's dark and I don't know what's wrong with it ..."

"Maybe I can help." Bella suddenly said, stepping forwards out of the shadows.

"Bella!" Jacob exclaimed, acknowledging Marelle's oldest and most loyal best friend.

"I pulled some wires off ...it's OK, she's my friend ..."

He looked at Marelle and then back at Bella. Marelle watched his eyes flicker; she felt his body tense.

"It's OK." Marelle said, taking his hands in hers. "Bella was here with her friend Freya. She saw you and called me."

"I pulled those wires out ..." Bella walked forward and pointed into the engine bay. "Here."

"Why?" He asked.

"To keep you here! I was under instructions!" She winked at Marelle.

He sighed, shook his head a little and turned back to the car. "I can bodge it; it will get you home, but it needs to be fixed properly."

"I know. I'll sort it." Bella said.

Minutes later the car started.

"We'll leave you to it." Bella grinned, getting into the car beside Freya. "Call me." She mouthed.

Then it was just them. In the car park with midnight upon them; in the dark and the pouring rain. Her car was still running and the door still open, lights still on. She turned back into him, kissed his wet face gently.

"We'd better go. Have you got any stuff?"

'The bike. It's over there. I can't leave it here."

She hadn't noticed it but now he nodded to it she could see the motorcycle parked close to the pub. His crash helmet was on the seat and a rucksack beside it. The confounded motorcycle that had no M.O.T., no tax, no number plates that he had rescued out of a ditch and plagued her with ever since. The one that he had slipped away on that night.

"I'll follow you back."

"Oh no you won't!" She exclaimed. "You're coming in the car with me … we'll get it home tomorrow."

"It'll get nicked … or reported to the police if I just leave it there …"

"It will be fine."

" It won't."

Three weeks at large hadn't changed him. Marelle sighed.

"Come with me." She said.

Not wanting to let go of him she led him by the hand to the door of the pub, now closed. There were still lights on inside. Marelle banged on the door. No-one took any notice, so she banged again.

The face of a fat, balding man appeared at a window to the right. Marelle saw him and waved. He opened the window.

"We've just shut up for the night love; if you've left something behind, you'll have to come and pick it up tomorrow …"

"No, no!" Marelle smiled. "Is it OK if we leave that motorcycle there until tomorrow? We'll come and pick it up then?"

He glanced out of the window at the bike. "I don't see why not – put it round the back though. It'll probably get nicked if you leave it there …"

"OK, thank you." Marelle smiled, still holding Jacob's hand.

"No worries." He replied out of the window with a knowing smile, then added. "You need your own band, mate. The crowd loved you in here tonight…" With a grin he closed the window.

Marelle turned to Jacob. "I'm not even going to ask about the karaoke!" She said.

Everything now sorted to his satisfaction they began the hour or so drive home to her house. She felt the need to keep one hand on his thigh as she drove and could not help but to keep stealing a glance at him. Against all odds he was here, in her car, returning home with her. She felt a growing sense of relief and elation; like she had seen someone resurrected from the dead.

"Where were you staying tonight?" She asked him. He'd adopted that normal silent manner, but it did not disturb her.

"I hadn't planned on anywhere."

"What? Were you sleeping rough?!" Marelle exclaimed. He didn't look like he'd been sleeping rough – apart from being wet he was clean and as well-groomed as usual.

He shook his head.

"Where have you been staying?"

"Cheap hotels." He replied. "One or two nights then moving on ... I hadn't booked anything for tonight. I didn't figure I'd need it."

For a second, in the dark she looked across at him with one of her hands placed on his knee. Bella had been right; he did have leather trousers on. He must have sensed her glance as he turned to look at her and gave a quiet smile. "I had plans."

"What kind of plans?"

He bobbed his head, fought thoughts for a moment then made the decision to speak. "I was going to jump off the Orwell Bridge."

For a split second, Marelle actually thought he was joking but the forthrightness with which he had said it and the absolute conviction in his voice speared her cleanly right through the heart. Her foot slammed on the brake and the car halted against the kerb. She turned back to look at his pale face in the eery dash-lit darkness of the car. He'd meant it.

Her whole spine tingled with a chill of fear and terror. He could not do that; never in a million years could he ever do that! Momentarily she shook her head; she felt sick and stupid, blinkered yet blindsided.

"No." She gasped in a whisper then in reflex, reached out to him, across the car, held onto him. "Jacob no! Don't even say that ..." She took his face in her hands and stared right into it. "No!" She cried, looking into his eyes and touching his face, tears coming together with thoughts that could not even comprehend themselves.

He cried and lay his head against her shoulder.

"It would never have been the answer Jacob. You had to come back to me! You *had to*! You can't throw everything away – when it's gone, it's gone ..." she sobbed, touching his face again, touching his hair, his body as if she was trying to gather him up right now. He had tears running down his face as he looked at her.

'Truth is, I had a go earlier, but I was spotted and the police turned up. I decided to slip away and try again later."

"Fuck, why?" She sobbed, trying to look at him.

"It was the decision I had made."

She sobbed as she looked at him, she reached out and touched his face, grabbed his hands in hers "*Why?*"

He shrugged a little flippantly. "Because I can't go on living a lie like this ... I told you ... my whole life is a lie ... I can't keep ducking and diving and hiding. I made my bed years ago ... just for myself ... just to keep my head down and get on with it ... I made my own bed and was prepared to lie in it ... I just didn't expect anyone to join me ..."

She leaned forward, placed her forehead against his, still holding his hands across the car, still sobbing. "You blame me?"

"No, no, no ..." He sighed. "I blame myself for getting into this situation. I thought finding Frankie would bring closure, but it laid me wide open. I didn't think I could hide anymore, and I couldn't face up to it."

"To what?"

"It's a long story ..."

He stared at her. Marelle was scared; she was sitting in a car with someone who had been prepared to throw themselves off a bridge tonight, to certain death because there was some complicated issue in his life that appeared to be irresolvable to him. An issue which she had no knowledge of. How did you deal with that? She wanted to take him home, wrap him in cotton wool and hold on to him forever.

He gave a small smile. "It's OK though. I'm over it. When you slammed into me in the car park back there, I realised I was wrong. I found my God there at that moment and their name is Marelle Buckleigh."

Marelle smiled; her lip trembled; she averted her eyes away then back again. His words warmed her, touched her, pleased her but they were weird. He was talking in poetry again. She didn't always believe him when he did that.

"I'm one fucked up individual." He said.

Marelle stared at him. He still had a faint smile on his lips. He was here, in her car and that was all that really mattered. She leaned across and let her lips find his, she kissed him in a way that she had longed to do for the three weeks he had disappeared, and he responded.

"I don't care." She finally replied, breaking the kiss and looking into his eyes again.

She drove them home, taking him back to the place that she felt had driven him away. It was twenty past one in the morning, a little under three hours since Bella had called her to say she was in a pub and Jacob was there, singing karaoke.

It was a chance encounter and a chance phone call. Bella had not known he was missing – no-one had – but she had been up on the east coast at one of her beloved music weekenders. She had described as 'shit', so she and Freya had ventured out to find something more fun. They had ended up in a local pub that had a karaoke night and there she had spotted Jacob. Quiet, timid, socially inept Jacob – singing karaoke! Thinking Marelle might also be there with him Bella had called her. Marelle had been at home, mulling over a possible poster campaign and search to find him. Now here she was – after a tense dash across the county to the pub car park where Bella had sabotaged her friend Freya's car in order to entice him to help her and keep him there until Marelle had made it.

Now he was here, back with her where he belonged but now going by his words on the way home Marelle guessed she still had a lot to learn.

They walked into the house. She switched lights on as they went. He walked slowly, scratching the back of his head and looking around as if it was all new to him. He had been so comfortable here before after all the time she had spent gently, gently coercing him to trust her and to be part of her life – but now after three weeks in the wilderness some of that seemed to have vaporised into the atmosphere. It was almost as if he had come home a different person.

He followed her through to the kitchen, then stood with both of his hands placed on the back of one of the kitchen chairs. Marelle filled the kettle and switched it on; just as if nothing had ever happened and they had just come in from a stroll around the disused airfield that this house adjoined. She turned her back to the worktop, folded her arms and smiled at him. He stood there as tall and slim as ever, hair still too short but getting better – in a black long-sleeved T-shirt and those leather trousers she had first discovered in his wardrobe that he had tried to hide. He looked good in them. She smiled but could not push the thought aside that he could well be dead by now if fate hadn't conspired and she had not run up to him in that car park.

Marelle teetered; shuffled; felt need tremble through her fingertips. Then she acted, leapt forwards and threw her arms up around his neck, pulling his face down to hers.

"Don't you ever leave me again." She said, tears in her shaky voice. "Ever Jacob!"

He looked into her eyes with his deep brown velvet ones – a fleeting second of intense eye contact – so rare for him – then he averted his gaze away again.

"I'm sorry." He replied.

"Don't be sorry. You are here now ... and you're staying here." She looked up to him. His eyes were away but when she stared, he flicked them back. "Some good news." She said. "Your friend called. He's got a delay on the development in the airfield ... they're going to consider it as a heritage site. I think they've stopped work for now ..." She nodded behind her towards her back garden, the disused airfield that it backed on to and where Jacob had lived in a caravan for the past ten years. Always under threat of development he had stayed on as a "watchman" for the site, on a retainer from the developer. It had afforded him a home and the chance to act as custodian of the airfield that had meant so much to him as a child and which had also been caught up in the disappearance and subsequent death of his childhood best and only friend. That was until a few weeks ago when the developers had moved in, and his perfect universe crashed down around him.

"Oh, good." He replied, unconvincingly.

It was at that point that Marelle suddenly remembered that his caravan was now in her back garden following the developers fencing everything off. He would not be happy about that.

She bit the bullet. "They've fenced off the airfield now though, so ..." She maintained the embrace they were in. "So I got them to move your caravan into my garden ... it's out there. I checked it. It's all OK ..."

"In your garden?" He asked. "Out there?"

She nodded. "Sorry, but it was that or leave it over there with them working all around it. We can't just walk onto the airfield anymore ..."

"It's not really my problem now." He said. "I'll have a look tomorrow ..."

She kissed him again. He obliged but felt tense. The kettle boiled and she made tea. Passing him a mug, she asked:

"So, why can't you marry me Jacob Frost?"

His eyes flickered, he shifted his weight. "I just can't."

"Are you already married?" She questioned.

He shook his head. "– No."

"Then why? I'm not giving up until I know why. And any reason you give me for 'no' I will have a solution for. I promise!"

He gave a small laugh with a lopsided grin that dimpled his cheek.

"Mmmm." He said.

"Jacob." She stated. "I'll ask you again. Will you marry me?"

"I can't." He shook his head. "I want to, but I can't."

"Why?"

"It's a long …"

She interrupted. "I know. It's a long story! Well, you had better start at the beginning and tell it to me!" She stared at him. "I love you Jacob. You know that. I thought I had lost you – God by all accounts I nearly did! You're the person I want to spend the rest of my life with. Just you Jacob." She felt her emotions get the better of her. He had to say 'yes'; she would not take any other answer from him.

"Sit down." She said and pulled out a chair herself.

He obliged.

"You ran out on me three weeks ago – you left me a note that broke my heart. You said you would try to come back – but you didn't. I didn't know where you were, and I had no way of contacting you. I was about to start a search for you – I'd just found that picture you left on the phone – I was going to make a poster …"

"A poster!" He laughed.

"Yes." She stated. "Then Bella rings – says you are in this pub singing karaoke. I drive over there to find you, only to have you tell me you had tried to throw yourself off a bridge and were about to go back for a second attempt! What the fuck Jacob?! So what is so fucking terrible that you can't marry me now?!"

He swallowed and stared at her. That face which she loved – which she had made opportunist, angry love to, that she'd kissed so often, which she'd held in her hands and wiped tears away from, the face she had wiped blood away from and had rolled in the long grass of a warm, summer meadow with. Now she just wanted him to say 'yes'.

"OK." He finally said. "OK." As if bargaining with himself. "I told you this was a one-way street; I told you once I start down it then there'd be no turning back again …"

She sighed. "Jacob, stop talking in riddles. I get it OK? I get it. Whatever you are going to tell me is the deep, dark secret that rules your life – *I get it*! Just tell me. It can't be that bad."

"It's possible I could go to prison for what I've done ..."

Marelle tried to keep any expression from her face with that remark even though it pierced her deeply. Just what had he done? All along she had suspected *something* and by all accounts the rest of the village did too. Her mind flicked to the discovery of his childhood best friend's body. Finally, after thirty odd years Jacob had been faced with the grim realisation that his own father had been responsible for the child's death and that the body had been secretly buried in his own back garden. Jacob had been but a child himself at the time and – even if he had known – would not have borne any responsibility for that tragic accident. Then the discovery of the second body in the same plot – another child – as yet unidentified but nonetheless also buried in what had been his garden. The finger of suspicion was pointing at his father – long dead from an alcohol-soaked existence. But with Jacob's reputation in the village anger had subsequently vented towards him and he had fled right after the discovery of the second body. Marelle raised her eyes to him; she would defend him to the hilt; he had been a child at the time that both bodies had been concealed there – he held no responsibility. His dark eyes studied her then darted away again which didn't fill her with confidence. What else did he know?

"What have you done?" She asked.

Jacob stared at the floor, shook his head a little. She really didn't like his hair the length it was now – it made his jaw too square and as he stood there with his head hung, he looked like a young boy himself – but with the shame of a lifetime carved on his face.

"Let's take a step back a minute ..."

She stared at him. This was not what she was expecting. In Marelle's world this homecoming would be long hugs and kisses, cuddling up to each other and sleeping until the new day dawned and they could get on with spending the rest of their lives together. Instead, what she had brought home seemed to be so different.

"You asked me why I can't marry you?" He asked, raising his eyes to her again.

She nodded.

He sighed. Looked to the floor then raised his face back up as she watched him take a breath and check with himself in that last safe moment.

"I can't marry you because I'm dead."

He swallowed again after he said that and stared into her eyes. The words had left his lips, and he had released that statement into the world; it would stay there forever.

Marelle widened her eyes, let a little smile pull at the corners of her mouth.

"You're not dead. You're here – right in front of my eyes!"

"Physically, yes but technically I'm dead."

Marelle exhaled a little snort; she turned her face away then back to him.

"Jacob, I don't understand. Have you ..."

He interrupted, held up his hand. "Stick with me. This is where it starts ..."

She swallowed her words and shut up – she was about to ask if he had been drinking – although up to now he'd seemed as sober as a judge.

"I died ten years ago – nearly eleven – technically I ... me ... no longer exist."

She stared at him. She didn't understand but he told her to bear with him.

"I am not Jacob William Frost. I was not born as Jacob William Frost, but I have stolen his identity in the event of being declared dead."

"You're not Jacob?" She asked, a tentative worry on her face.

"No." He stated.

Things had suddenly turned very surreal here in her kitchen and she did even wonder for a split second if she was really awake and the preceding three hours had even taken place.

"So, who are you then?"

"My real name. The person I was born as is Nathaniel Ezekiel Frost."

She stared at him. "Your brother!"

He nodded. "I'm Nat. Not Jacob."

"But your brother committed suicide ..." She said, quietly, warily. He'd told her about his brother drowning himself, disappearing for three weeks and then being found dead in an intertidal area of a river. He'd said they weren't close; he'd said his brother was 'someone else' and took a different journey in life. It looked like he certainly had.

"I did not commit suicide." He said. "My brother did not commit suicide."

"Well ... 'She began, totally confused.

"Somebody else did and they were identified as Nathaniel Ezekiel Frost. I was declared dead, but it wasn't me!"

"Then who was it?"

He shrugged. "I don't know. It doesn't matter ..."

"Why didn't you say something? Why didn't you tell them you were still alive?"

He turned his head slightly. "Well ... I was here. My father had just died ... I kind of liked the idea that I could start again and be someone else ... so I accepted it ... decided to keep my head down here ..."

"And started calling yourself Jacob?" She added.

Then a thought struck her. She knew from her initial research into his family when she had first looked into him – as you do – that there were two children – Nathaniel and Jacob. "So, what about the real Jacob?"

"He's dead."

That kind of hit her somewhere in the centre of her chest. She was, to be honest, feeling a little odd right now anyway.

"Jacob died a few days after being born ... just after my mother died. I don't remember, but I know – only ..."

Her mind was flirting with the concept of Jacob actually being dead – even though he was, as she knew him, standing right in front of her.

"... only ..." he continued. "My father never registered his death. I don't know why ... probably due to his grief for the loss of my mother coupled with the death of the child as well ... she died giving birth. I don't know why but realised this when I started sorting his stuff out."

True. Marelle had only ever found a death certificate for Nathaniel in her sessions of online stalking of her prospective new boyfriend. Now he told her otherwise.

"So, I decided to be him. I took his identity. I started a new life here. I became Jacob."

Marelle swallowed, her mouth was dry, and her head was spinning. She felt that the floor had been pulled from beneath her.

"Shit." She said, half to herself. "So what? I mean ... why ...?" She tutted and looked into those same beautiful deep brown velvet eyes she had fallen into so many times. Her heart fluttered and she wanted to hold him.

"So what shall I call you?"

He gave a laugh. "Arsehole?" He asked. She didn't smile. "I don't mind if you want to keep calling me Jacob ... I'm kind of used to answering to that now."

"So, for the last ten years you've been living here – pretending that you are Jacob – didn't anyone around here realise?" They knew you from before, didn't they?"

"They knew me, but no-one ever took any notice of me. They don't know their arse from their elbow – nobody knew any different – even at the farm."

Marelle remembered her conversations with old Mrs. Avison when she had first moved here. In her desperation to learn more about the elusive and magnetic Jacob she had asked if there was anywhere she could 'research' the village and had been pointed in the direction of a dear old lady called Mrs. Avison who had a wealth of knowledge on everything here – right in her head.

"Well Mrs. Avison. knew. She spent ages trying to convince me you were Nathaniel, and it was Jacob who had died. I thought she was a confused old woman ... but she *knew*."

"She probably did – being the eyes and ears of the village that she was – but, like you, most people treated her like some rambling old fool – people generally don't look and listen ... they just like the sound of their own voices."

Marelle sighed. Closed her eyes, opened them and he was still there. Tall, dark and handsome, here in her kitchen fresh from telling her he had intended to throw himself off a bridge earlier and now also having revealed he was not who she thought he was. She smiled and walked across the kitchen, outstretched her arms and wrapped them around him. She lay her head on his chest and he held her tightly close to him. Gently he kissed the top of her head just like he always had. Marelle closed her eyes and lay against him hearing his heart beating. No matter what, it was the same heart she had held so dearly for the past few months.

"But I still don't understand why you can't marry me! Marry me as Jacob. No-one knows, only me. What does it matter?"

"Well, there's more to it than that."

"More!" She lifted her head away and looked up at him.

He nodded and held her again, swaying to and fro.

"It got very close to me being found out. It's got *very* close quite a few times lately but right now it's probably heading that way."

"Why?"

He sighed. He'd told her so much, but this next part was sticking in his throat a bit.

"The second body ..." he said. "In the garden ..."

Marelle closed her eyes and hugged against him as the words came.

"I'm pretty sure it's Jacob."

The silence was visible, deafening. Her own breath stopped, the clock was silent; she could hear his heart and nothing else except a loud silence in her head like a vacuum.

She looked up at him again. He appeared upset.

"I can't be sure but it fit's. I know he died – I was three, so I don't have a memory of it – but my father did tell me about him – he always mentioned Jacob when he still used to put flowers on my mother's grave. I had never really thought about where he was buried ... I assumed he was in my mother's grave but not marked. But now, I don't think he was. To be buried there his death would have had to be registered. It wasn't... I think he died and he was buried in the back garden. A few years later he followed suit with Frankie ..."

Marelle almost gasped.

"DCI Catchpole was here a few days ago." She said. "He said he needed to speak to you. I told him I didn't know where you were ..."

"If they manage to identify that body then this will all unwind ... It's a criminal offence not to report a death."

"But it was your father's job – not yours – you were *three*!"

"But they can say I knew ... like some people do with Frankie."

"But you were *three*!"

He shrugged one shoulder.

"But how would anyone even put two and two together – if he's never been registered as dead?"

"It just takes one person to remember something or makes some casual remark that sets cogs turning – like you said Mrs. Avison knew."

"Yeah, but she's dead – who else in the village would remember or know?" Marelle continued.

"Might not be in the village ... people moved away ... Frankie's father for instance ..."

Marelle thought about the elderly very frail man at Frankie's funeral. "Well he didn't look like he's going to last long anyway."

"You don't know who's out there that might know ... Catchpole was hinting at asking questions the last time I spoke with him, wasn't he?"

Marelle recalled the conversation where Catchpole had interrogated Jacob quite fiercely about his family – his father and his brother. She hadn't realised at the time but now she knew the truth and could see that rising suspicion.

"But how would they identify him – as Jacob?"

"DNA testing." He said. "If they were suspicious they could test me – and test him. I don't know if you can refuse a DNA test but that in itself would look pretty suspicious."

She lay against him for a second, thinking.

"The thing is, if they check me out – which they probably have done, then there's no trace of me from the day I was born until ten years ago. Nothing – no doctors, dentists, school – anything. Then ten years ago I appear – although I have fastidiously avoided doctors, dentists and the police …"

He had. He had refused hospital treatment when he'd needed it on more than one occasion and had tried his hardest to avoid the police too. Marelle felt pangs of guilt now. She had insisted the police were involved when he had unearthed Frankie's body – he had wanted to do it on his own – she knew why now.

"But…" She began again. "What is wrong about what you have done? Just come clean – say you had a mental breakdown – you've not gained anything by being Jacob, you've not defrauded anyone have you? What's the worst that could happen, hey? You might get a slap on the wrist – but probably not much else, surely?"

He gave another small laugh. "Well … therein lies another tale!"

"What?"

He smiled and held her to him; he looked to the clock.

"I've been awake for more than twenty-four hours – lets sleep on what you know already – I'll tell you the rest tomorrow."

"You think I'm going to sleep after that? Christ, I don't even know what to call you!"

"Does it matter?"

She cuddled him and closed her eyes. "No." she said.

TWO

So, in the early hours of that morning when she had learned the man she truly loved had not only contemplated leaving this mortal coil a few hours ago – but also that he was not the person she thought he was; that he had lived a life of covertness for ten years under the fear that he always *just may* be found out. She climbed into bed beside his warm, naked body just as she had done so many times in the preceding months. Only this time it felt different,

Marelle lay beside him, stretching her toes down against his legs, laying her head on his smooth, taught chest. Ever since she had known Jacob, he had never offered conversation easily; it had taken her a while to even get eye contact from him. But tonight, he had been more forthright than she had ever seen him. He had never before spoken so lucidly or so lengthily to her in one episode. It *was* different; he was different. Maybe he was right when he had said when she had run into his arms in the car park he had experienced a moment of epiphany.

All night long she slept against him with one hand curled around his arm. Before they had retired to bed, she had locked all of the doors and taken the keys with her. Never again would she give him to opportunity to slip away while she slept.

And in the morning she awoke and climbed on top of him, sitting astride his body, bending forwards and kissing his lips. He opened his eyes, smiled and gently pulled her down against his body.

"Did you miss me?" she asked.

He nodded, quite solemnly.

Marelle still didn't like letting him out of her sight but she went downstairs first, leaving him in the bathroom. The kitchen was how they had left it last night, dirty mugs on the table, Jacob's bag against the wall. It was a strange feeling; she'd nurtured her relationship with Jacob so carefully; she had gained his trust and enveloped herself so intrinsically within his life but today it felt new. Today she felt like she had to start all over again – it was almost as if just by telling her what he had that he had switched to a different person; a different personality. But she knew – she could see and she could feel – he was the same person.

There was an admission of relief inside her when he finally came down the stairs and wandered casually into her kitchen as he had done many times before. She smiled at him and he returned the gesture as he walked, barefoot over to the window and looked out to the garden. He looked at his caravan that had been his home for the past ten years– now in her garden – and the metal fencing closing off their access to the airfield.

"It's going to be stuck there forever you know." He commented – nodding to the caravan. "You won't be able to move it out of there with the airfield closed off."

"I knew you would say that! It's not a permanent fence yet – I'm sure we could move it if we wanted to ... but it's probably better there ..."

"I'm not leaving the fence closed – not if they've stopped working." He stated.

"Toast." Marelle announced, placing a plate piled high with toast on the table. Jacob turned and sat down. "We'll need to go and get the bike."

Marelle sighed. She had hoped that wouldn't be at the front of his mind this morning. Getting it back would not be the easiest thing to achieve.

"We'll get someone to bring it back on a trailer ..."

"Who?" He asked. "And when? I don't want to leave it there too long – it'll get vandalised, or stolen."

"It's not roadworthy Jacob!"

"It got me where I wanted to be over the past three weeks." He retorted.

She bowed her head for a second and did not reply immediately.

"Well you're not riding it back."

"Why not?" He laughed.

"Because you could disappear again!" Marelle answered quickly, her thoughts escaping through her mouth.

"Of course I won't!"

She gave him a glance.

"You've got to trust me. I promise."

"I trusted you before and you got up and just ran away in the middle of the night. I trusted you then – I trusted that you were going to come back like you said in your note to me – but you didn't." She sniffed as the thoughts entered her head. "You were going to kill yourself."

He lowered his eyes and chewed on a piece of toast for a second. Jacob shook his head and got up, walked around the table then stooped to fold his arms around her. He held her, stopped from behind, putting his face next to hers.

"Yes but I was wrong. It squared the circle. Jacob lived; Jacob died. Nathaniel lived; Nathaniel died. It was simple. It was the answer and I didn't have to face the wreckage I was leaving from the life I'd left behind. You saved me –it's over. I'm past that now. I promise."

Marelle sobbed, she turned in the chair, put her hands up and around his neck and closed in on his body. She held this man; this angel that had returned to her.

"I love you." He whispered in her ear.

She sobbed more.

"Ssshh." He soothed. "Come on. It's not a time for crying now."

Marelle sniffed, wiped her eyes, looked at the floor then up at him. "You're still not riding the bike back!" She told him with a smile, stroking the side of his face.

He laughed.

"I'll come with you. I'll ride on the back of the bike." She suggested.

"No you won't!" he exclaimed. "I've only got one crash helmet … anyway, how would you get there?"

"Will it fit in the back of my car?"

"No!"

"But I think it would, with the seats down …"

"Even if it did, it would leak oil and crap all over the car. We can just drive up there and I'll ride it back – you can follow me."

"What about the rest of the stuff you were going to tell me?"

"Get the bike first. I'll tell you later."

"That's bribery!" she exclaimed.

Her phone rang, lying on the table. She turned her head and looked.

"Bella." She said.

He released her with a smile and she answered the phone.

"Hi Bella!"

"Hey!" Bella greeted. "How's it going?"

"All good." Marelle replied, looking at Jacob as she spoke.

"Got home OK?"

"Yes, fine. How about you? Is Freya's car still together?"

Bella laughed. "Yes, it's fine. Her brother is a mechanic – he'll fix it … he's standing there with you, isn't he?" She referred to Jacob's presence.

Marelle gave a smile as she stared at him. "Yes!"

Bella laughed. "Well …?"

"What?"

"Well … what you asked him?"

Marelle drew a breath in realisation. "We're getting there!" she grinned.

"Fuck's sake Marelle … you're just about the slowest worker I've ever come across!"

"Well, it takes time …" She answered.

"Well as long as you are happy? Are you happy?"

Marelle laughed "Yes." With a smile she'd wondered if she would ever feel again. "Yes! Thanks Bella!"

"Oh shush!" Bella remarked.

Jacob walked forward, he gestured towards the phone. "Oh, hang on. I think Jacob wants a word …" A little bemused by his actions, she handed the phone over.

"Hi Bella." Jacob said.

Marelle watched the smile crack across his face before he spoke again and after Bella's obviously over the top greeting to him. "No, I just wanted to say thank you." He told her. "You just might have saved my life last night."

Marelle choked a tear back again, but Bella must have made a joke of it. Jacob laughed.

"That's a guarantee!" He smiled. "See you later – here's Marelle." And he handed the phone back.

Marelle smiled at him as he stood by the window. He was hanging around. She suspected she knew why.

"Oh Marelle, he's so sweet!" Bella gushed. I'm so glad I found him for you last night."

"So am I!" Marelle replied.

"And ..." Bella added. "I've got the video on my phone of him singing! I'll show you next time ... in fact we'll have a full premier viewing of it!"

"Oh, well , we'll see ..." She answered looking at Jacob standing there and finding it hard to imagine him singing karaoke in front of anyone – let alone a pub full of drunks that he didn't know! "Hey, do you want to drop in on your way back tonight? I can cook dinner – as a thank you?"

"No, I think Freya wants to get back early – sorry. But I'll give you a call during the week and we can sort out a weekend. And you don't have to thank me! Just make sure I get an invite to the wedding!"

Marelle laughed. "I'll do my best!"

"Well Jacob was more positive than that! He said it was a guarantee!" Bella remarked with a laugh.

"Well in that case, I guess it is then!" Marelle answered, eyeing Jacob looking at the caravan. "I'll give you a call."

"OK babes!" Bella replied. "Take care of yourself – and Jacob!"

She ended the call and looked at him.

"So you are guaranteeing invites to weddings I know nothing about, hey?" She asked, staring up to him.

He shrugged playfully. She kissed him.

"We'll see." He said. "You might not want to marry me when you know everything!"

"There is nothing that would stop me!" She stated.

"Nothing? Not even letting me ride the bike home?"

So, that was how she found herself in her car, driving him back to the exact same spot where she had run into his arms last night. It was against every ounce of sense that she had to let him do this, but she had eventually conceded going along with it anyway. He wanted to drive; she wouldn't let him.

"By the way ..." She started the conversation. "Mr. Wright dropped by – about you working at the farm."

"Oh yes?" He asked, trying not to show any interest when Marelle knew he was secretly waiting for news.

Jacob had been ingloriously 'suspended' from his casual labouring at the local farm when the other members of the small team who worked there had refused to work with him following the discovery of Frankie's body and the village gossip mill was spinning up the tale of Jacob's father being a murderer and consequently tarring him with that same brush. Jacob had worked at the farm since his early teens – initially helping and filling in for his alcoholic father to ensure they kept the tied farm cottage. He had worked for the current farm owner and his father before him but had never been afforded full employment status due to an incident when he had 'disappeared' and let everyone down. However, over the past ten years he had calved himself a niche as the farm mechanic and fallen in well with the current Mr. Wright who had a penchant for collecting old commercial vehicles. Jacob's casual farm labouring had grown more into being a mechanic and he had just been promised a permanent position working with vintage vehicles in order to service Mr. Wright's hobby. But that had been before all hell broke loose and the gossip had begun to bite. One particular employee who had a long standing problem with Jacob began to ostracize him and cajole everyone into doing the same.

In Jacob's absence Mr. Wright had returned from an extended visit to relations in Australia to relieve his 'good as useless' son from the task of running the farm while he had been away. Adam, his son, had failed miserably and ended up with a mutiny on his hands in which Jacob had been suspended.

"He said he's going to move the workshop to the other side of the farm. Once he's done that he will honour his offer of employment. But he'll let you know when …"

Jacob made a small sign of acknowledgement.

"But until then you are out on your ear. And I don't think he intends to keep paying you."

Jacob exhaled. "OK. If that's what he said. What do I care?"

"He did speak highly of you though Jacob – even if he did dismiss all of the trouble with Sam as 'banter'."

Sam. The young thug son of an old thug. Spent his time looking for any opportunity he could to cause maximum distress to Jacob – and lately Marelle as well.

"I told you he's an opportunist."

"He's a wanker!" Marelle added. "So it's just wait until Mr. Wright contacts you."

"Whatever." Jacob remarked. "Who knows what may happen anyway?"

She side-eyed him at that remark. Reading into every comment he now made like that, picking it apart for any veiled threat. This time she satisfied herself that there didn't seem to be one.

"Just thinking about what I told you last night." He suddenly announced, staring ahead of himself in that long 'Jacob' stare she knew so well. "It's best I just carry on as Jacob for now … you know … it's just you and me who know … for all intents and purposes I'm Jacob."

"Of course you are. I won't breath a word – you know you can trust me," She replied with a smile and a hand on his thigh. "Jacob!"

She drove on, on the roads she had rushed along in the dark and the rain last night. Today the sun was shining.

"Where did you go?" She asked. "Were you always close by?"

He sat back for a moment and thought before he answered. "Not always. I ran first and came back later."

As they approached the Orwell crossing point and the road began to rise in front of her' she sensed Jacob become slightly uneasy. She had driven over the bridge in the darkness twice but it was not until now, on a sunny day when she rose into the heights of the clear blue sky, one hundred and fifty feet above the water below that she realised the scale of this structure. She could *feel* the space below her. There was a low grey concrete wall running it's length – not high enough to see over in a car but tantalizingly low enough to climb onto and jump off. Marelle didn't say a word, just sat deeper in her seat and gripped the steering wheel a little tighter. As they cleared the bascule of the bridge, she crept a hand across and placed it on his thigh again. Without a word he place his hand on top of hers and squeezed it. He imparted nothing to her on the subject.

Fifteen minutes later she watched him put the crash helmet on as she stood beside him and the bike in the car park of the King William. She looked across to a puddle that had been just beyond the very spot where she'd slammed into him and locked her arms around him last night. There he was now, with the black crash helmet half on, balanced on his head, standing next to the bike he had just checked over.

"Don't go too fast!" She said to him.

He smiled cheekily and walked round to the back door of the car. As he leaned in the landlord came out of the pub and walked towards them. Jacob ducked back out of the car holding a leather jacket she had not seen before.

"Everything OK?" The landlord asked.

They had already waved to him when they had arrived in acknowledgement.

"Yes. Thank you." Jacob replied. "For letting me leave this here. Got me out of a hole."

"No problem." He answered.

Marelle watched Jacob slip into the leather jacket. It was nice. It was a proper motorcycle jacket – black with white stripes down the sleeves and a high collar which he zipped up.

"Karaoke here every Thursday." The Landlord smiled. "And once a month on a Saturday."

"Oh, I'm not a regular." Jacob said. "That was a one-off performance!"

"Are you from around here?"

"About forty miles that way." Jacob pointed.

"You riding all the way on that?!"

"Yeah ... I've done a lot further!" Jacob remarked.

"Is it legal?" The Landlord nodded to the bike.

"Not entirely." Jacob replied, looking away from him.

The Landlord gave a small chuckle. "Well take care. Have a safe journey." He said and turned to go back into the pub.

"I'll try." Jacob nodded and pulled the crash helmet down.

Marelle tapped his arm.

"Where did this come from?" She patted the leather of his sleeve, raising her voice so he could hear her.

"Oh I've had it a while. Thought it would be safer. Right, I'll go in front, you stay behind me." He announced. "I'll go on the smaller roads, we should be OK."

She sighed and made a face at his choice of words. He got on the bike and kicked it into life. It didn't seem to want to start. He tried again and this time it exploded into the familiar sound she had learned to listen for when she had been waiting for him to come home.

He nodded his head to her to get in the car and she did so hurriedly, worrying that he would disappear if she did not get going quickly. Marelle pulled away, still putting her seat belt on.

He did not take off at speed but stuck rigidly to the speed limits. Taking a different route to avoid the larger roads he led her down lanes and streets she had never seen before. Marelle kept as close to him as possible with him glancing at her over his shoulder now and again. After a few minutes travelling through a slightly more urban area of a large village and moving into open country, he turned slowly as he rode along and gestured to her with his hand. He made a signal whereby he appeared to be pushing her back. She didn't understand and felt a little perturbed that he was telling her to keep away from him. On a wider piece of road, she accelerated alongside him and made an 'I don't know' gesture from the car. Jacob slowed immediately, falling behind her and coming to a halt in the gutter. She tutted to herself and stopped the car too, watching in her rear view mirror. He'd stopped with both feet down and shrugged to her.

With a sigh she got out of the car but left it running. She walked back to him.

He took the helmet off.

"What?" she asked.

"Keep back from me a bit." He said with some exasperation. "If you drive that close and I have to stop quickly you'll bump into me. At worst you'll run over me!"

"Oh sorry. I just didn't want you going too far ahead." She apologised.

"I won't, I promise." He answered, replacing the crash helmet.

They continued. The area became slightly more hilly in nature – quite unusual for here but in the autumn sunshine there were some fantastic views across the fields and landscape of the Suffolk countryside. The roads were quiet, and they travelled along swiftly but steadily. She watched Jacob on the bike. He rode with comfort and confidence which suggested he was so used to this mode of transport. She felt that he would be going considerably faster if she were not behind him but at the same time he had a precision and carefulness about him. At times he would ride along with one arm hanging at his side; now and again he would glance around. Soon she began to recognise place names and realised they must be getting closer to home. They travelled through a long stretch, through a gentle green valley, now leading into a more built up area. The odd house here and there turned into a group of ten or twelve dwellings on a new development. A larger swathe of houses looked to be up ahead on the other side of the road and Marelle could not help but think that this landscape had once been fields and meadows too; now under concrete and tarmac. Engrossed in her thoughts and now settled behind Jacob she did not see the white van coming out of the entrance road to the new houses on their right. She didn't actually see it until it had pulled out right on top of Jacob; obviously not looking left as it turned. Jacob's brake light came on sharply and she saw the back of the bike bounce violently but her eyes moved quickly to take evasive action herself as the white van made a sharp turn and almost bounced off her front wing. Marelle closed her eyes and gritted her teeth, waiting for the crunch but it did not come, much to her surprise. It must have missed her by millimetres. She stopped her car, jolted forwards and placed both hands firmly on the wheel. The van passed by her window, not overly quickly but she watched nonetheless as it continued on and made no attempt to stop.

"Hey!" She shouted in her car, but it had already gone. Adrenalin kicked in and she felt that wave of painful anticipation course through her. Marelle looked forwards; left; right.

"Shit!" She said to herself. She had taken her eyes off Jacob for a second and he'd disappeared.

"Shit Jacob! You promised!" She sighed, then her eyes moved to the motorbike, on it's side on a grass verge, twenty or so metres in front of her.

She sprang from the car, remembering what he had just said to her. Had she been too close? She panicked – what if she had run over him?

Outside the car she tentatively looked around it. It still looked pristine. Walking to the front she glanced at little pitifully under it. There was only road, a hot smell and a ticking of hot metal. Still half stooped and looked at the bike.

A slight movement beyond that caught her attention. There was a road sign denoting a nearby tourist attraction of an 'Aviary Centre' and beyond that a yellow sign saying 'Diversion' pointing to the left. Beside that she saw Jacob, getting onto his knees on the path.

"Jacob!" She screamed and ran forwards, sprinting along the pavement, past the bike on it's side. She didn't look at it but focused on Jacob, sitting back on his heels on the path.

"Shit!" She gasped, one hand on his shoulder as she got to him, bending down, "Christ! Are you OK?"

He still had the helmet on, but it was scratched on the top. As she stooped to him he made a noise that may have been a gasp of pain or was just him swearing inside the helmet.

"Did it hit you?" She asked, flustered and shouting. "He nearly hit me!"

Jacob leaned back on his heels in a kneeling position – he snapped his head back for a few seconds then looked forwards again. He lifted his right arm, went to flex his fingers but in doing so was obviously in pain. He gasped.

"What is it?" She asked. "Can you move it?"

"Give me a minute." He said.

She looked into his eyes. They looked strangely urgent from behind the helmet. He reached up his left hand and unfastened it, awkwardly, then pushed it up, off his head. He struggled slightly, not really using his right arm. Marelle assisted and took the helmet off for him, putting it down gently on the ground. It was scuffed now and no longer pristine. His face looked pinched.

"Shit." He gasped. "Did the van stop?"

"No!" She replied. "Did it hit you?"

"Caught me – sent me out of control onto the path. I thought that road sign was going to decapitate me! Fucked that up ..." He nodded to the crash helmet.

"What about you?"

"Smacked my arm on that 'Road Closed' sign over there. It'll be ok in a minute."

"You're not moving it."

"No – it hurts too much!" He replied, making a move to stand up. Lunging from his knees into an upright position. Marelle rose with him and held onto him.

"Steady." She said.

He had a rip in the knee of his jeans and clutching at his right arm with his left, he started forwards to look at the bike.

"I think it's less damaged than I am." He suggested, looking at it. "Can you help me get it up?"

Marelle assisted but once they had the machine upright and he was looking at it while clutching his right arm she was suddenly struck by a voice in her head asking her what she was actually doing! He had just been knocked off his bike by a hit and run driver; he was obviously injured and she was helping him to pick the bike up!

"Jacob you're hurt ..."

"It's OK." He answered. "Give me a minute and it will be OK."

"Move your fingers." She instructed.

He did so but by the hesitation and the look on his face he appeared to be in pain.

"Jacob, I don't really think it's going to be OK. I think it's broken."

"Of course it's not!" He laughed, then winced. "I've just clouted it on that road sign –it's just like a dead arm!"

She sighed. "Well is everywhere else OK?"

"I think so." He half groaned which certainly didn't convey that message.

He walked a couple of steps and leaned against the upright of the road sign. There didn't seem to be anyone about who had witnessed the incident. A couple of cars passed through but nothing would have looked untoward to them.

He sighed. "I'll be alright in a minute."

"That bike is too dangerous." Marelle commented, ruffling his lengthening hair in her fingers.

"It wasn't my fault!" He exclaimed.

"I know, but ..." She was realising he could have been seriously hurt here.

"Maybe I'm getting too old for this!"

Marelle smiled, kissed him on the lips and gently rubbed his good arm. Looking down she saw him flexing his fingers but also noticed a small patch of blood on the pavement, right under his hand.

"You're bleeding!" She exclaimed.

He looked down at his blood on the path then lifted the injured arm as best he could. His hand and fingers were now streaked and dripping with blood. He looked tentatively, unhurriedly. Marelle took his bloodied hand in hers. It was cold. She looked sternly at him.

"Jacob I think you need to go to a hospital. Get in the car!"

"No, no. It's OK." He replied. "It looks worse than it is, I'm sure. Look ..." He raised the injured arm slightly, pointing to a slice through the leather sleeve of the jacket which he pulled apart to expose a gash on his arm. "It's just a small cut. I can wrap something around it. Have you got a hanky or something?"

"Jacob no!" She protested. "It needs more than a hanky wrapping around it. God, you haven't changed have you?"

"Why should I change?" He asked, a little bemused by her remark. "Just wrap something around it and it will stop bleeding. I can use my t-shirt if you haven't got anything."

Marelle sighed, left him and went back to the car. She had left the door open when she had leapt out, engine running and keys still in the ignition. The back was full of rubbish – there had to be something in there. On the back seat she found a pale pink scarf, dragging it with her she also switched off the engine and took the keys and closed the door.

There was still blood dripping off his fingers but he directed her to wrap the scarf tightly around his arm.

"Jacob, you need to go somewhere ... this doesn't look good." She moaned.

"It's fine. Honestly. It will have stopped bleeding by the time we get home."

She looked up at him, tying a knot in the pink scarf. "You are not riding the bike back!"

"Of course I am! How else will we get it back?"

"For God's sake. You're not!" She exclaimed. "How can you ride – you can't even move that arm properly?"

"It's fine." He could move it a bit more than he could a few minutes ago but it was nor normal.

"Please!" she pleaded. "Don't."

"It'll be OK." He reassured her, placing his left hand on her arm. "We'll just take it steady and it'll be fine."

"Well, what about the bike? Is it damaged?"

"Not enough to stop me riding it back." He replied. "Pass me that." He nodded to the crash helmet, sitting on the grass where she had placed it. It's pristine finish now ruined by the scuff marks across the top of it.

Jacob took it and went to put it on, single handedly.

"Jacob?" She asked. He stopped, looked at her. She stepped forward, onto tip toes and kissed him. "Just be careful."

So Marelle continued the journey with him. Following him the last six miles home on the scratched but functioning motorbike, her pink scarf wrapped tightly around his gashed arm. She failed to understand his reluctance to seek medical help – even with what he had told her. If he went to casualty they would not ask questions or grill him; he would get the treatment he needed – but she knew she could not persuade him otherwise. She just hoped whatever injuries he had sustained were no more serious than a few cuts and bruises. He seemed reluctant to use his right arm properly but he may have just been safeguarding the wound on it. Marelle had watched him ride home from the driver's seat of her car, watching his every move, her eyes flicking to and fro at every junction this time.

When they pulled into her drive she felt shattered; not only from the late night last night but from the drive back now. She felt she had called upon all of her reserves to get back here. She finally stopped the car in the drive in front of the house, watching him dismount from the bike. He was hurt; she could see by the way he was moving. She had the keys in her hand as she watched him, sitting in the car for a moment. Why would he not admit he was injured – what difference would it make? As Marelle looked on him, slowly flexing himself as he got off the bike, she thought about what he had told her. Until now she had not allowed it to infiltrate her brain – just glad to have him back. But now she watched him – this man whom she had known as Jacob for the best part of the last year; this man whom she had unashamedly flung herself at and whom she had cemented into her life and her future. He had told her he was not Jacob; he was in fact the older brother of Jacob who had supposedly committed suicide ten years ago and that the real Jacob was long dead and had probably been buried in his childhood back garden – unbeknown to anyone.

Marelle didn't think she could ever get used to calling him by a different name – he was Jacob and would always be Jacob to her. It did mean that he was also three years older than she thought he was. Right now, by the way he was moving he looked it.

He gestured that he was going to take the bike round behind the house, and she nodded, watching him walk slowly up the passage at the side, pushing the bike painfully.

Marelle followed him. She left the car and walked up the narrow space at the side of the house where he had gone. Behind the house he was standing the bike near his caravan. She smiled and walked forwards to him. He'd parked the bike by the caravan and was standing looking at them both.

"It'll be safe there." She smiled.

He nodded. "We'll take one of those fence panels down tomorrow."

"Will that be OK?"

"Of course it will! I still need to get over there – I'm still caretaker – nothing's changed ... I just went away for a bit. They didn't know I wasn't planning on coming back ..."

She sighed. "Oh Jacob, stop saying that!"

"But that's all changed now. I'm back, and I'm staying!"

Marelle touched his arm gently, there was blood starting to seep though the pink scarf that she had wrapped around his arm. She nodded her head for him to go with her into the house.

"You shouldn't have put that there." He said again, looking at his caravan.

'I know." She said. "But I did!"

THREE

She had to remove the pink scarf so he could get the leather jacket off. The blood had soaked right through all of it on the way home and she unwound it carefully while he sat on a kitchen chair watching her.

"Jacob, this is still bleeding – a lot." She commented once she had removed the scarf. She briefly examined the hole in the leather which was now wet with blood around the edges. He seemed to be able to move his arm a bit more now but it looked swollen around the wrist area. His fingers also looked a bit blue.

"God, you bleed a lot, don't you?" Marelle commented remembering a head wound he'd sustained when she had first got to know him.

He shrugged his left arm out of the jacket and she helped him extricate his right, taking the jacket and placing it on the back of a chair. She was not sure how, or if, the blood could be removed or the hole repaired. It weighed a ton! When she turned back he was looking at his arm. He had his elbow on the table with his arm bent up towards himself, looking down at it.

"Oooh!" Marelle remarked.

It was an ugly, dirty wound. Maybe a couple of inches long, gaping open at one end like a slack mouth. The resulting hole had filled with semi-congealing blood. As she reached out, it overflowed and a trickle ran down his arm and off his bent elbow onto the table.

Marelle gasped and grabbed a handful of kitchen towel, made a pad and patted it to the wound.

"It should have stopped bleeding by now."

"We just disturbed it by taking the jacket off." He added.

"It looks like something has stabbed into it – it needs cleaning and stitching."

"No!" he laughed. "It's fine. I'll go and have a soak in the bath in a minute – it'll clean it out. If that's OK, of course?"

"Yes, you know it is. You don't have to ask!" She answered. "But won't that make it bleed more?"

"A bit probably, at first."

She sighed and looked at him. "Oh Jacob! The van didn't even stop!"

"I didn't exactly want it to stop!" He laughed. "The bikes not really legal – and neither am I!"

She tutted. "Maybe it's time to get yourself a car?"

"I don't need a car!"

"Well you've had a few too many scrapes on that bike."

He laughed. "It's part and parcel of it. I've ridden bikes more than I've driven cars. I *like* bikes – they keep your reactions sharp!"

"Well, they didn't look too sharp today."

"Hell they were. If I hadn't have moved over I'd have been under his wheels."

"Don't!" She raised her hand. "Stop scaring me – you're not convincing me to let you keep riding it!"

"I've got to mend it first ..."

"You've got to stop bleeding first!"

He decided to have a bath and got up.

"Are you hurt anywhere else?" She asked.

"Probably." He replied. "It's not the first time I've come off." He said as he started to make his way towards the hallway.

"Leave the bathroom door open." She said, raising her eyes to him. "Please?"

"OK." He limped stiffly across the kitchen.

"Hey?" She called. "This is not distracting you from the rest of the story you were going to tell me, is it?"

He grinned. "No – but I'm not going to tell you – I don't want to be there when you hear that. I'll let you find out for yourself!"

She looked puzzled.

"Open up your computer and google Ezza Frost – Yellow Son."

"What?"

"Google just that. I'm in the bath. I'll see your face when I come down."

"Ezra Frost?" She asked. "What?"

"Ezza, not Ezra!" He replied.

"Ezza." She repeated. "There was a t-shirt with 'Ezza You Cunt!' written on it in your caravan."

"Was there?"

"Yeah, stuffed in a hole in the back of the wardrobe."

"What were you doing going through my wardrobe?"

"Looking for clues as to where you were!" She replied looking up at him as he stood in the doorway holding his arm against himself. He wanted to run – he'd just given her the key to the door. He gave her a little smile then turned and walked away towards the stairs.

Marelle watched the empty doorway for a few seconds like he had been an apparition, now disappeared. *He* wanted *her* to google this to find out about the rest of his story? Did he even know what Google was? Why would this be on Google? Who was Ezza Frost? Her heart began to drum. If he didn't want to be here when she found out, then it had to be on the wrong side of good. Ezza? The name that the woman in a restaurant had first mentioned to her. A strange, attractive woman who had spent an entire evening in a quiet restaurant gazing at Jacob and had ultimately asked if he was 'Ezza's brother'. At the time Marelle had made the same mistake as she had just now and misheard her as saying Ezrah. Jacob, of course had denied any knowledge of a brother called Ezrah.

Marelle moved to her computer. God, did he have another brother who *was* Ezza? She knew there were no other brothers registered as being born to his family but there was also one who had died and his death had never been registered – so anything seemed possible. As Jacob had said to her "*I am one fucked up individual"* and right now it seemed that the whole family fell into that category.

As she waited for the computer to come to life she heard the bath start up in the bathroom. There was a tangible feeling in the air, a fear, a rush of anticipation and anxiety at what waited on the other side of the Google wall. The screen came to life before her and as instructed she typed *'Ezza Frost Yellow Son.'*

The page that flashed up before her showed six or seven photographs; some portraits, some in-concert photos – all of someone who looked identical to Jacob. Marelle leaned in closer to look. The first, largest picture was obviously a professional press head shot. Black and white, younger – hair very similar to how she had cut Jacob's when she first knew him and which she liked so much. He wore a dark denim jacket, dark t-shirt beneath with something written on it in white. His face was straight on to the camera, high cheekbones, dark eyes staring right into the lens– a slight wry smile just playing on his lips.

The second picture was of five people – mean, moody, posed. Looked like a band. One member dead centre, round face, very short hair, orange t-shirt, arms folded defiantly. He had gas flame blue eyes. Three others slightly behind him – one with shoulder length hair pushed back from his face and tucked behind his ears; another, shorter, quite feminine features – blonde spiky hair. The third in a vest, more muscular and pumped than the others, neat short dark hair, soulful eyes. Then, at the far right of the shot, one that looked remarkably like Jacob, staring down at the floor, his head turned slightly away. In contrast to the rest of them wearing standard t-shirt and jeans he wore a dark suit jacket and faded skinny jeans with Cuban heeled boots.

The third picture was a close up of Jacob-look-alike holding a microphone – appeared to be on stage in a concert – laughing and looking out to the audience. Another photo showed him with the guy in the orange t-shirt from the second picture – he was hamming it up in true rock style, playing a red and white guitar with 'Jacob-look-alike' hanging over him while swinging a mike stand in the air. The other pictures were similar with the final one being the Jacob character in a crouched position on stage, in front of the band, microphone to his mouth, his eyes closed.

Marelle stared at them and realised she had stopped breathing. She took a breath; scrolled down.

"Ezza Frost, lead singer with Yellow Son found dead" was the headline which grabbed her straight after the pictures.

'Ezza Frost, charismatic lead singer with the rock band Yellow Son is believed to have taken his own life following the discovery of a body. Ezza (35) disappeared from a sell-out concert in South West England three weeks ago and has not been seen since. His disappearance followed his walking off stage mid performance after recent episodes on stage described as 'panic attacks'. He remained untraceable until a discovery of a body near the River Severn yesterday. It is believed that the singer committed suicide following a drink and drugs fueled binge after on-stage arguments with other band members.'

Marelle's blood ran cold but her face flushed hot. So 'Ezza' was Nathaniel – was Jacob? Not even allowing her mind to fully process the thoughts she read on, hungry for whatever else she could read about him. There were several news stories, all pretty much along the same lines. Pictures of Ezza – Jacob – in various performances – far different to how she had ever seen him. This master of a singer, captivating his audience with a massive and warm on-stage presence. Marelle skipped over the video for now, reading the articles, getting the picture, bit by bit.

Yellow Son were a formidable rock band with – at least ten to fifteen years ago – a massive and loyal following. The band had been founded by Chas Symonds – a renowned, and some said, the best rock guitarist in the business. He was older than Jacob and by all accounts had been round the block musically – splitting a successful group to form Yellow Son with a collection of musicians whom he deemed thought and performed like him. Then Jacob – Nathaniel – Ezza had been drafted in following a chance local TV appearance with the lowly band he was already messing around with while at University. Chas had hand picked him for his looks and the latent ability he could see in him to perform on stage. As Chas had said in the article she was now reading – which had obviously been published after Ezza's demise – "*he wasn't a great singer but we could fix that – but he was a great performer. The new band needed his charisma and charm.*' Seduced by the call of bright lights Nathaniel had signed with them.

Marelle looked at the pictures – a very young Jacob, tall and impossibly skinny, perfect hair, perfect teeth – always dressed most impeccably while the rest of the group sported jeans and t-shirts. In most of the pictures Jacob was the one who never smiled, but in a few, mostly while performing, he was smiling and laughing and she could see he was truly happy in that situation.

Apparently, they had managed a few minor hits and one massive one which was now an iconic tune. Their prowess had been in live performances and in album sales. After Ezza's death they had continued with Chas as lead singer and had enjoyed a continuing career with a loyal fan base supporting them following the tragedy of Ezza's suicide.

Finally Marelle clicked 'play' on the video. It looked like a fully packed concert, audience jumping up and down to the rhythm of the music and there, centre stage was Jacob. Smiling and communicating with his audience as the intro played in, taking his place behind the mic stand then throwing the lyrics of the song in a voice which she would never have believed could come out of him. He could sing; he could work the stage and everyone on it to perfection; he could hold the audience on his every word but never came across as arrogant. The crowd loved him and reached out for him to touch in complete adoration.

Jacob. Nat. Ezza. The man she so desperately loved had lived a life she would never have imagined but which had woven consequences into tight knots she did not know could ever be unravelled.

Now she understood. If he stopped being Jacob and somehow managed to revoke his rightful existence as Nat then he would also have to be Ezza and Ezza reappearing would have wide reaching consequences. If he remained as Jacob he stood the chance of being found out if they identified the body in the garden. If they didn't then he still had to live his covert existence and a life of lies.

Nonetheless, the second part of his 'long story' was equally, if no more, fantastic than the first half. So, for ten years he had lived here – kept his head down, lived a simple life – after being part of what she had on the screen in front of her right now. He'd walked away from all of that and chosen to stay away.

She read on voraciously. Found an article from an old music magazine. It was mostly Chas speaking about an upcoming tour but she read down until certain paragraphs piqued her interest.

'At that point Ezza wanders into the room and starts making himself coffee in the background. Chas looks around, slightly annoyed at his intrusion. We had been told that Ezza was not available for the interview. He cuts a tall and striking figure dressed in black but doesn't say anything as he sits down.

"He's on suicide watch." Chas explains. "He is so fucking morose. Just wants to write songs about drowning himself ... what are you fucking doing here Ezza?"

Ezza shrugs, drinks coffee, crosses his legs. Chas continues.'

The date of the magazine was twelve years ago. The article was littered with standard shots of the band – some of which she had seen a few times this evening – one of Chas and one of Chas with Ezza – both looking moody.

The more she read the more it actually sounded like the Jacob she knew. Like the Jacob who walked up behind her now and placed a hand on the back of her chair. She had been so engrossed that she had not heard him approaching and jumped in the air with a gasp.

"Shit Jacob!" She exclaimed, turning to him. He had jeans on, nothing on top and the injured arm bent in to himself, holding a pad of tissue to the wound.

Marelle looked up at him, looked into his eyes and felt the depth of his existence – felt the pain. She smiled.

"Why Ezza?"

He laughed. "That's an easy one. It's not the question I was expecting you to ask but I can answer it." He sat down, still holding the arm. "Chas said we should all have a 'nickname' rather than use our own names. That way, he said, you could be that person – or you could be yourself. Plus, it sounded better. His suggestion was to use our middle names as the base for that. Mine is Ezekiel so it became Ezza. Chas' middle name was Charles, then there was Jem, Luc and Marty."

"Oh, I see." She replied, nodding her head, a grin on her face.

"I was always Ezza from that point. Everybody called me Ezza, nobody ever called me by my real name."

Marelle smiled, coyly at him. "So this is what you have been hiding all of this time?"

He smiled.

"What happened – in the end – you just walked away from all of that?"

"Yes, I walked away but I had intended to go back – when I was ready. Despite what was said about me I had no intention of killing myself that night or in the days after. I just needed space."

"Did you walk off stage?"

He nodded. "There is video of it – not that I want to see it!"

"Why?"

He made a face, raised his head. "It had all started a while back. It had actually started during a few gigs we did around Christmas." He started to talk then paused. Obviously he had never spoken about this to anyone, ever before. He drew a breath in through his nose.

FOUR

"I *loved* being on stage. I absolutely loved that feeling, being cut-loose and just *performing*. It was a revelation to me as well. When I started singing with the other band at Uni it was a case of 'oh well, I'll give it a go ...' and pow! I suddenly found my calling. But with Yellow Son it was bigger and louder and just *more*. God, I loved it!" The look on his face backed that up and Marelle smiled for him as he continued. "But for some reason, about a year or so before I ... walked off ... I started to 'forget' the opening lines – or 'forget' when to come in. No, it wasn't 'forget' – I just couldn't get the words out ... it was strange. They were songs I'd sung for years and years. A couple of times Chas would keep it going until I got started or he would start and I would pick it up. That *annoyed* him! You've got to know Chas to understand ..." He paused. But he had started now; it was going to be a long story. "Don't get it wrong – I loved Chas; he's a great bloke – he's older than me, knows the ropes, knows all the tricks and pitfalls. He guided me, taught me. He was my mentor and despite the image he likes to give out he always looked after me. But you were never allowed to forget it was *his* band!" he smiled slightly. "As lead singer you tend to get all of the attention – I was younger than the rest of them, I was the focus of attention, of course – but he made sure I was never allowed to be the centre of attention. He always led interviews, actually didn't let me take part most of the time and God forbid it if I got singled out to do a solo interview or photo shoot! I don't know how he did it but off stage he always managed to keep me behind him! To be honest I didn't actually mind that – just so long as he let me take the lead on stage ... which he did ... but that Christmas it all started to go wrong."

For a moment he dabbed at the cut on his arm with the tissue. It was still bleeding. He pressed on it and continued.

"Chas strived for perfection. If anything was a bit scrappy on stage we would know about it – sometimes publicly! And when this happened to me, I could see him slowly boiling over beside me – he'd be swearing at me, moaning at me. I had always had a slight issue getting on stage – especially in front of the larger crowds. Once I got going I loved it but it was getting onto the stage and getting started each time that was difficult. I never used to drink – after my father I said I would never drink but Chas knew I was a bit of a nervous performer and he told me to 'have a couple of beers before' just to relax – they all did it. So, that's what I did ... and it helped. I didn't touch alcohol any other times and just used to have a couple of cans with the rest of them before we went on stage. That was fine, and I did this for years but that Christmas it suddenly got worse. I got on stage and froze. Chas always watched me like a hawk anyway but he was right on it – started me off and I was fine. But it happened each time – he got annoyed with me and I started getting paranoid about it happening.

Marelle had turned in her chair and was listening intently to him, her head resting on her hand. He continued.

"So, the following year we already had dates in. We had a series of gigs in Germany before we returned to the UK. For the very first one I was a complete mess the night before. We hadn't performed for a couple of months – we'd rehearsed and I was fine then – but that afternoon I started drinking at about 3 – we wouldn't go on stage until about 8.30. I had been sick a few times but managed to stumble onto stage on time. I didn't miss the first line and managed to get through that whole night by the skin of my teeth. I didn't enjoy it and I didn't remember it. The second night was a repeat of the first. I got on stage pretty drunk but got through it. Chas went with it because it was an improvement! Then the third gig I did the same but was really sick just as we were about to go on. I couldn't find the toilet at the venue so went outside to a public one. I was not around when we were meant to be on stage. Chas came out and managed to find me – called me every name under the sun and practically dragged me by my ear onto the stage. Then he had me by the back of my shirt, actually holding me up to the microphone." He grinned. "I remember it so well – I had this white shirt on – big cuffs and quite long. It had been meant to be worn under a navy blue jacket with the cuffs and tails hanging out – it had looked good. But I had already discarded the jacket because I was sweating like a pig. Chas had the back of this shirt so tight it popped a button on the front! I eventually got going but spent the whole gig worrying about that button!"

"So couldn't you get help?" Marelle asked.

"I probably didn't want to. Chas took me to one side; said he didn't want to lose me; he said I was too good; he'd seen it before and he would not let that happen to me – but I had to start by helping myself. I didn't know how. On the fourth gig I started drinking spirits – less volume, more impact I figured. Hmm!" He laughed. "I got on stage, hung on to the mic, looked at Chas and decided I could not do it. I walked off. Chas followed me leaving the others to improvise and play along to the baying crowd. Chas grabbed me, hugged me, Christ he would have kissed me if he thought no-one was watching! He did not get angry with me. He sang the first line into my face until I had it in my head. He asked me if I was OK and if I was coming back on. I nodded and said I was. He told me to take two minutes, he'd go out there and explain – which he did at my expense by telling the crowd I had the shits due to eating too many Bratwürst and I'd be back in a second! He made everyone laugh, he'd diffused the situation, started it all up again. I came back on, hit it spot on and did the gig." He pointed at the computer, it still had images of him all over it.

"There's a pic from that gig on there somewhere – and one with the white shirt – it looked like he's just giving me a brotherly hug but believe me ... he wasn't!"

"You always look like you are enjoying it." Marelle commented.

He nodded, smiling. "Once I got going I did." He paused for a second before continuing. "Then we started the UK tour. Forty dates – not huge venues but forty dates is a lot. I was in a state two weeks before – plus my father had just died during this period. Chas did offer to postpone the first couple of dates but I said no, I could deal with it. His death was expected and to be honest I wasn't too bothered by it. Anyway – by this time the press were picking up on this; we weren't huge but we'd had a few hits, done some stuff on TV etc – so we were known and believe me they like nothing more than a spiral dive! That started to kick in too – press reports said we were arguing on stage; said I was doing drugs and the like. To prove them wrong, I did the first night of the tour totally sober – completely cold turkey – I got on stage and had what I suppose could be termed a major panic attack. I couldn't breath, I couldn't speak – I couldn't sing, no matter what. I had to be virtually carried off. Chas sang – I came back on for the last two songs but I was fucked and I knew it." He shook his head. "The thing is, I'd done nothing wrong – this had just started out of the blue. I didn't know why! OK I'd made some bad decisions trying to get over it but I didn't know the root cause... what could I do? It was like I was being squeezed into a smaller and smaller space, just to cope, just to get through each night. I wanted to just turn up, get on stage and *perform*. I wanted nothing more but I could not get out of this spiral of panic attacks, drinking and paranoia. I should have stopped; I should have taken a break then – before it was forced on me. That third gig was always going to be a disaster. I drank all afternoon – on my own – but I didn't feel any effect from it. I tried spirits too, but they did not kick in as I expected them too. I made it to the venue and was having a fag with one of the crew just before. I often did that – he was a wise old roadie, spoke a lot of sense – always calm – always wanted to sit and smoke a fag. He said this happened all the time, even to the really big names – he'd seen some really big stars have the same issues. He'd said I just had to work through it and *want* to work through it. Then he handed me some pills and suggested I try those. Said he used them and so did a lot of people he worked with. Now I was wary. I'd never done drugs as such – I'd smoked pot now and then, didn't like it – but I'd never taken pills or anything like that. He'd said they were just herbal things which would calm me down. Said he took them all the time. I figured they couldn't make things much worse so I took them from him and I took them. Now I don't know what I took – I don't know if it was them or the result of everything else kicking in but I walked out on stage no problem, waved to the crowd, walked up to the microphone and then this explosion just went off in my head. It was as though I couldn't hear anything and everything around me was happening in slow motion. I had Chas right in my face but everything I looked at was kind of fractured, distorted. I was standing there on stage, mic stand in hand, five or six thousand people in the audience but for all I knew was completely on my own in the middle of nowhere, holding onto a tree! I just wanted out, turned around and walked off. No-one followed me and I heard Chas start singing as I left. Even he had given up. I walked off, out of the venue and along the street. I was sick in a waste bin and remember discarding clothes as I walked. I ended up in a t-shirt and trousers – no shoes – on a train and I came back here. I didn't buy a ticket – somehow I got away with it and ended up walking from the Station about eight miles away back to here. I sobered up the next day and started sorting my father's stuff out. No one contacted me but to be honest no one knew where I was. I actually did some work on the farm and then on a Friday afternoon I was in the farm van when I heard on the radio that Ezza Frost had been found dead in a river!"

"Oh wow!" Marelle exclaimed.

"At first I didn't know what to do. I wanted to pipe up and say '*hey, hang on. I'm here!*' but what for? I'd be expected to go back, to continue with that downward spiral until I did end up killing myself. No. I wanted out and I had just discovered that Jacob's death had never been registered. So it was handed

34

to me on a plate. A month later I was chucked out of the house so I bought the caravan, moved out there and went by the name of Jacob. The rest you pretty much know ..."

She looked into his eyes. Telling her this had been a release; she could see a liberation in them.

"So didn't anyone around here recognise you?"

He laughed. "Here? No! They never had – no-one gave a fuck about me so I could just keep my head down and slip around. I said I was Jacob so they called me that – most probably wouldn't have known my name anyway. Time passed. I established myself here – tried not to look like Ezza – dressed down, shaved my hair off in the summer, let it grow long in the winter. Got away with it." He raised his eyes to her with a smile. "Then along came Marelle!"

It was nice to see him smile; properly smile and mean it. Marelle gave him a grin back.

"Oh Jacob!"

He dabbed at the cut. "I think it's stopped bleeding." He commented. "And you haven't run a mile!"

He continued. "You see I'm caught both ways. If I stay as Jacob I run the risk of being found out – believe me it's come pretty close now and again! If I say that I'm Nat then the question of Ezza is going to present itself. When I stood on that bridge the other night, jumping off was the easy option. I didn't have to make a decision – I could jump off and it would all be over. People could continue to ask whatever questions they wanted and I wouldn't have to be involved with the answers. That was it; it would be over. But when you ran into me in that car park and I felt you against me – I realised that I did have a life to live; I did have someone who wanted and needed me purely for me being me – and to jump off that bridge would be a total waste of life when life was all I really had. One life, one go, one try. As we said when we were kids – there was nothing before and likely nothing after it – this was the single, beautiful, sweet chance of happiness we would be given and I was throwing that away." He lost his words in a sob, which caught Marelle unawares as he had been so composed up to now. She reached out to him, took his hand in both of hers. "And in that second I made the decision. I was no longer going to end it; I was no longer going to spend my life looking over my shoulder – or wearing sunglasses, or a hoodie – I was no longer going to pretend to be my dead brother. I was going to be Nat, I was going to be Ezza and I was sure as hell going to walk out on that stage again!"

"And I'll be right behind you." She said with a grin before she leaned in and kissed his forehead.

"You know ..." He began again. "When you first turned up I didn't want to know. I helped you out of pure courtesy. I treated you like everyone else – a few words here and there – no emotion or acceptance – it was usually enough for people to just move on. But you – you wouldn't leave it. You just kept turning up, trying so hard to be friendly. I hoped you would go away, or a boyfriend would turn up. But you were still there – still trying – and I found myself thinking about you all of the time even though I told myself you would just shit on me from a great height lust like everyone else!"

"Oh, hey!" She exclaimed.

"Well you didn't." he smiled. "And then you cut my hair and you made me look a lot like Ezza – and I liked it. And I wanted to be like him again!"

'Then you made me cut it all off ..."

"It'll grow. It's getting there." He smiled.

She stared into his eyes, held his hand in hers. "So, are you going to marry me?"

He gave her that lopsided grin, that cheeky handsome look that moved her heart. "Yes, I'll marry you –it's just a question of who I marry you as!"

Marelle hugged him; stood up and hugged him from behind, kissed the top of his head. She felt happiness, in herself and between them. Happiness that she had always dreamed would be there. Like a warm, safe cloak wrapping itself around them. She'd never felt that before and she knew now that both of them had turned the same corner.

The images on her computer screen remained there as they embraced. Captured moments of Jacob as Ezza, as Nat – seconds when he smiled and performed alongside Chas and the rest of the band. She could see a friendship there – one which had ended with the identification of Ezza's body.

When she moved back to the computer, intending to turn it off she clicked on another page from the ones her search had yielded which brought up more images. She smiled and scanned them. Jacob slid alongside her and looked on too. She heard him give a little laugh.

"I haven't seen some of those." He remarked.

"It's endless!" Marelle said. "How many pictures are there of you on the internet?"

"A lot."

She looked at them with him beside her. In some he looked very young – in others pretty much how he looked now.

"How come the body was identified as you? You said Chas allegedly identified it?"

He nodded beside her. "Yeah." He was looking at the pictures on the screen, remembering.

"Well *how* did he?"

"I don't know – I never found anything out about it ..."

"Well as far as I know they normally make an identification by dental records, medical records, fingerprints etc ... how come his matched up with yours?"

"They probably didn't." Jacob said. "I've never been to a dentist, or a doctor or given my fingerprints to the police either. I guess it was a visual identification."

"You've never been to a doctor or a dentist!" Marelle exclaimed.

"No, I've got perfect teeth – well I did have perfect teeth" He explained. "Never been to a doctor or hospital – when I was a kid if I got ill I just had to get on with it same as if I hurt myself. I only had a drunken father to go to and he would just tell me to stop howling and deal with it!" He told her. "There probably were times when I needed medical attention but, well, I'm still here!"

That explained a lot to her – not including the fact that he was sitting here now with a nasty hole in his arm and several other injuries he would not confess to.

"So the dead man looked exactly like you?"

Jacob shrugged. "Must have done. I guess if he'd been in the water for a while he didn't look his best... probably same age, height, weight – clothes ..."

She thought about that for a moment. Jacob took the mouse and clicked onto another page of pictures. He chuckled. Jacob actually *chuckled*!

"I did read somewhere at some point that my wallet and car keys were in his jacket pocket ... the only explanation is that he picked up my jacket that I discarded and then ended up in the river. Impossibly unlikely but still entirely possible ... you know I've always wondered in the back of my mind if Chas knew it wasn't *actually* me and identified it as me out of spite – no spite is the wrong word – out of a want to kick me up the back side. I may be wrong – he may have genuinely thought it was me. I don't know but that's a question I would like to ask him someday ..."

"Do you think he would speak to you?"

"I hope he would." Jacob replied.

"So what's the plan?" She looked at the screen, a picture of Jacob with his feet up on a table drinking a can of beer caught her attention. It wasn't a professional shot but a candid one. He was dressed all in white and looked really relaxed.

"I want to put the cart before the horse. I want to turn up at a Yellow Son gig and I want to see Chas's face when he sees me there!"

"Wow! Is that wise? Won't that put you in hot water?"

He shrugged. "I just want that moment when he sees me standing there!"

That night she slid in bed beside him – a different person not just by the fact that his name wasn't the one she had actually become used to but by the fact that he was now completely relaxed and happy. The weight of ten years of hiding had been lifted from his shoulders – at least with her. And that confirmed to her that he did actually care about her in the way that she had always hoped he would. Ten years ago he had made the decision to live that life – he had thought he could and for ten years he had but now all that had changed.

Two nights ago he'd decided to take his own life by jumping off a bridge because he could not see a way forwards. Tonight, he had given her the final piece of the jigsaw and freed himself from that burden.

God, he was happy! Jacob happy was something to behold and it thrilled her. Tonight, she cuddled up to the man whom she'd studied in those photographs online – the man who had led a pretty formidable rock band – who had strode the stage with a confidence even Bella would have struggled to muster! But it made no difference to her who he was or what he'd done. Tonight, she wrapped her arms around the Jacob she always knew he was deep inside.

"So." She said, laying entwined with him in the bed. "The woman in the restaurant who asked if you were Ezza's brother?"

He grinned. "Yeah." He said. "I think that was Chas's sister – she did recognise me, and probably told him. If he knows he mis-identified me then that will pique his interest; if he genuinely thought it was me then he'll probably discard it ..."

She lay her head against his chest.

Sometime into the night Marelle awoke. The bedroom was filled by moonlight and was washed in a pale blue tone. She lifted her head and looked down at Jacob. He was sleeping soundly, his arm laid across his chest next to where her head had been. Gently she pushed herself up in the bed so as not to wake him and sat there looking at him. He was half covered by the sheet, his top half bare and his skin pale blue and smooth in this light. She observed his profile, the prominence of his cheekbones, the straightness of his nose, the push of his collar bones against his skin – the leanness of him. He was the most beautiful thing she had ever seen and he had come back to her. He had chosen her over death; that was something she would never forget yet the sheer intangibility of that sent fear fleeting from her fingertips as she guessed that thought always would from now on. The lover who had once, momentarily belonged to many now here, in her bed, on sheets she had bought. She placed a hand on his arm, gently. He did not wake but a flicker of acknowledgement passed across him. Marelle felt the warmth of his skin, felt the pulse beneath it; sensed the blood running in his veins. The blood that gave him life and made him what he was. She looked at his face. Suddenly she felt overwhelmed by him, by who he had been, who he had chosen to be – what he'd chosen to do – and by the sheer fact that he was here now.

A tear ran down her cheek. She was immensely happy yet endlessly sad all at the same time. Her eyes filled with tears and she choked back a sob. Slowly she slid herself down again beside him and wrapped her arms around him, holding on to him, stretching her legs along his and closing her eyes as she buried her face into him.

He awoke, finding her clinging to him crying. He turned and enveloped her in his arms, albeit it slightly gingerly with the right one.

"Hey." He whispered.

Marelle pushed herself closer to him, hugged him to her tightly.

"Don't ever leave me again." She cried. "Please don't ever leave me like that again. I nearly lost you forever Jacob ... life is short and I want to spend what I've got with you. I don't care about any of your past – I only care about us and the future ..."

"Sshh." He soothed. "It's ok. I won't leave you. I promise. I'm back now and I'm staying here."

Making a mental list the following morning, staring out of the kitchen window at his bike and caravan, Marelle thought on the things she needed to sort out, or at least talk about. If they were going to make this life together then there were items on her list that required resolving. She could hear him in the bathroom and as her mind wandered and collated she felt safe in the knowledge that she knew exactly where he was and what he was doing.

She needed to tell him about the vandalism to his mother and father's grave in the churchyard. Someone had taken it upon themselves to smash his parents headstones in a sheer brutal act of violation – either against Jacob or his father. It had shocked her that someone could be that callous. Jacob needed to know; she would pick a moment and tell him.

Then there was the whole situation with this house – jointly inherited – and now owned by her and her older brother Sebastian. The absolute animosity between Seb and Jacob was borne out of an unfounded suspicion that had led to a rift between her and her brother. He had ultimately pushed her to choose between him and Jacob. That was a no brainer and her decision had resulted in Seb giving her a six months deadline to see sense. He had offered her a 'proper job', working with him rather than her working from home on an ad hoc basis as his researcher – or she could sever all ties with her brother and find a life on her own with Jacob.

She knew she could either buy Seb out of this house or leave it and take her half. That all depended on Jacob.

Which led to problem number three. Sam – and the rest of the village. From the initial discovery of Frankie's body there had been a burgeoning hatred and persecution of Jacob. The fact that he himself had been a child when Frankie had tragically been killed and that it was an accident did not matter. Jacob's father had taken the life of a child and Jacob was being ostracized for it. The discovery of the second body had poured more fuel on the fire. As yet the intensity of that conflagration was unknown. And Sam – work colleague at the farm; son of the village's hard man – bully – call them what you will. Half Jacob's age and twice his weight. Sam had always treated Jacob as the butt of his bullying. Singling Jacob out as the village weirdo and making sure everyone knew. Taking any opportunity to inflict harm on Jacob by any means. Marelle had also come to be included in this. It had surprised her that Jacob had never raised a finger to fight back – she knew he was more than capable. Now she knew why. Any altercation may have led to the police being involved which may have ultimately led to his true identity being discovered. So, time after time Jacob had taken the beatings; some dreadfully and dangerously brutal. Right now, he still had a tooth missing from that last ambush on the airfield the night before he had disappeared.

Marelle doubted the hatred and persecution would ever stop, no matter what he did. As Jacob said – people see what they want to see and believe what they want to believe – you can never change that.

Was Jacob prepared to stay here with that chasing him? Did he want to move away? Marelle would be prepared to move; she had no ties – only Jacob. She just wanted to be wherever he was.

He arrived in the kitchen and interrupted her thoughts, but she had made a mental list and would have to find a good time to broach them without overloading him this early on. Marelle turned around, smiled at him; he returned the smile albeit with the broken tooth gaping at her.

Another thing for the list.

Marelle liked seeing him smile; especially now when the providence of it shone through. He was wearing a navy-blue v neck jumper with a crisp white tee shirt underneath. The sleeves were too long and covered his hands.

"I'm sorry but there's blood on the sheet – my arm must have started bleeding again ..."

"Don't worry." She replied. "Has it stopped now?"

"I think so."

He sat down at the table. Marelle had been adventurous today and placed a bacon sandwich down in front of him with a smile.

"Ta." He said.

She sat herself down, sipped tea staring at him. A smile broke cheekily on her face. 'I thought that toast isn't really fitting for a rock star of your caliber!"

He laughed dryly. "Don't be fooled. I've lived on cold baked beans straight out of the tin many times!"

Marelle smiled, watching him eat and taking pleasure in it.

"How's the arm?"

He shrugged. "Oh, a bit sore." He pulled the sleeve of his right arm up as he had it laying on the table. "It's a bit swollen."

It was. Puffy and swollen across the back of his hand and past his wrist. She'd noticed he was still using his left hand and resting the right on the table.

"Are you sure it's not broken?"

"Nah, it'll heal ..."

She sighed inexplicably and stared at him.

"I've done it before. And I had to carry on working that time!" He added, "But doesn't it hurt?"

"A bit. I can take pain. It's OK."

She sighed again. "If it gets any worse then you're going to the hospital. No ifs or buts. OK?" She asked. "Is that a deal?"

He grinned. "OK." He replied resignedly, pulling the sleeve back down.

"Can I borrow your car?" He asked.

She looked up at him. "No – you can't drive with your arm like that."

"Of course I can!"

"What for?"

"I need to go somewhere."

"Can I come?"

"It's OK. I'll go on my own. I'll only be an hour."

"Then no. But I can take you ..." She stated; Marelle was not letting him go anywhere on his own for a long time.

"Well I could go on the bike ..."

"And you're not going on the bike!" She exclaimed. "Jacob! I'll take you." She repeated. "And if you want to keep driving my car then I'll put you on the insurance – you do have a driving licence, don't you?"

"Of course I have!" He replied.

"What name is it in?"

He raised his eyes to her. "I've got both but obviously Nat is dead."

"Did you take a driving test as Jacob again then?" There was a smile on her face.

He nodded. "Passed both first time. Did the bike test again as well."

"Have you got everything in Jacob's name?"

"What I could. I had to. It was easy – I had all of the documents – just no record of his death."

She stared at him as he looked down at his plate, finished the last mouthful of bacon sandwich then stirred his tea.

"So – when you walked off stage and came back here – didn't anyone try and contact you? Like before the body was found in the river?"

"No." He stated. 'Who would?"

"Well, Chas?" She asked. "Surely you had a manager?"

"Chas' wife managed us. He probably wanted to let me stew for a while – and anyway, I don't think they knew where I lived down here. I rented a flat up near London where they usually contacted me – we didn't live in each other's pockets. They had no idea I was here. Six months later a letter turns up from a solicitor saying that they had identified me as the last and only living relative of Nat and I would be the sole beneficiary of his estate. I never met them, spoke to them on the phone a couple of times, exchanged documents then they gave me all of my stuff back... well, most of it. Some things had gone missing."

So, you inherited back everything that was yours anyway?" She laughed. "Wow!."

"Minus solicitor's fees."

"Yeah, well. I know all about that as well." She commented." ... and you've not heard anything from anyone since?"

He shook his head. "I was dead. No one knew I lived here. No-one tried to contact Jacob after the event. Why should they? It was game over."

"And you never wanted to go back?"

"No. I was pretty happy – just had to keep my head down and my hands clean. In time I kind of forgot about Nat. He became another person and I became Jacob ... till someone crossed my path." He gave her a grin and a cheeky wink.

She smiled back at him. Still seduced by his charm.

"So, where do you want to go?" She asked.

"Oh, it's ok. I'd rather go on my own."

"I will take you and I don't want you to keep secrets from me. I won't keep them from you, I promise."

"It's not a secret ... I just wanted to ..."He raised his eyes to her and shrugged.

"What?"

He thought for a moment. "Ok, you can take me." He sighed.

After her promise of no secrets she immediately thought of the smashed headstone of Jacob's parents but still decided to broach it later. It wasn't a 'secret', she just needed to find the right time to tell him.

Climbing into the car with him today, she was like an excited child. Today was different; today she had a totally different Jacob alongside her and she felt a new course of pleasure running through that he really, truthfully, absolutely was the person she had always hoped he would turn out to be.

"So, where to?" She grinned at him from the passenger seat.

"Drive towards town. Come off at Rousham." He instructed.

Marelle obliged and he directed her to an industrial estate – to a large unit at the back that had a huge red and yellow sign across the front that said 'RFL Storage.'

"Park there." He pointed to a marked parking bay at the front. Marelle parked and looked up at the building.

'What's this?' She asked.

"I'll show you." He said and got out.

Marelle noticed he was clutching his right arm but said nothing. She would have to keep an eye on that as he would not tell her if it was getting worse.

He walked in through the yellow door, holding it for her as she followed. Jacob had obviously done this many, many times.

Inside was a neat reception area which was unmanned and another yellow door with a pin pad at the lock. He entered a six digit pin and pushed against the door. It opened and he went through, again holding it for her. Marelle walked through and they both entered what was a large warehouse space lined with what looked like row after row of individual, windowless, partitioned rooms. Each had a yellow door with a red number painted on it. Maybe she looked a little worried, or confused – or both but he grinned and nodded for her to follow him.

It was quiet in here except for the noise of a forklift moving something somewhere and the constant bleeping at it reversed. Jacob walked off to the right, along behind two rows of rooms until he came to another row at the end, perpendicular to the others. Three doors along he stopped in front of 122. Once more he entered a pin code and placed his hand on the door handle. With a look back to her he pressed it down and opened the door. Reaching in he switched on a light and walked inside. She followed and the door clicked shut behind her.

FIVE

It was a four metre by five metre space she guessed. At the far end was shelving and on both long walls there were stacks of boxes and a long rail hung with clothes – all in plastic wrapping. Marelle looked up at him, eyes wide and wondering.

"Is this all of your stuff?" She asked,

He nodded. "Well, Nat's stuff."

Marelle looked around herself.

Everything was neat and tidy – each box was numbered and all of the clothes on the rail were orderly, clean and ready to go at a moment's notice.

Jacob went to the shelving, reached up and took down a blue and red crash helmet. It looked brand new and had the image of a snake's head on it; the jaws forming the open face of the helmet. On the shelf were two others. One white with a tyre track print on it and one black, open faced with an American flag on the front.

"For when I ride the bike again." He said.

Marelle glared at him.

"Are these all of the clothes out of the caravan?" Marelle asked.

"Yep – and some more." He went to a small box on the shelf but noticed something else. With a smile he picked it up and placed a hat on her head. He laughed.

It was a bit big for her, she took it off and looked at it as he turned back to the box on the shelf. It was a black trilby type hat with 'kiss me quick' on the front in white.

"What the hell ...!?" She laughed.

"We had a load for a tour once. I can't remember why!" He had taken something out of the box and put it into his pocket then continued along the shelf, tipping up the small boxes and looking inside them. Then he turned to the clothes rail and started going along it; selecting items and putting them to one side.

Marelle watched him, looked around the room at all of the boxes. He rifled in one labelled 84 and took out t-shirts and jumpers, making a neat pile next to the crash helmet and the other clothes in plastic covers. On the floor at the far end stood two guitars; one in a black case, the other on a stand, red and white. Marelle looked at it.

"Can you play?" She asked.

"No." He laughed. "Not seriously – I can strum along if needs be but that's it!" He placed a neatly folded pile of clothes down carefully with his left hand. "Grab that." He nodded to a green holdall standing on one of the boxes. She picked it up, took it over and began placing clothes into the bag.

"I'm kind of a bit short of clothes at home. I brought them back here, I didn't think I'd need them." He explained.

Marelle smiled and raised her eyes to him, catching their reflection in a large full length mirror standing in amongst the boxes. She looked at herself next to him; it struck her that she had not seen them together like that before and she stared. Jacob, tall, square shouldered, long limbed, beautiful face and the short dark hair that was gradually growing back to a length she preferred; and her there beside him. Marelle looked into her own eyes in the reflection. He wasn't looking, distracted by something in a box. But she saw a look of pride in her eyes. A deep, soft atonement that she'd finally achieved what she'd wanted so much. Today she'd put on make-up and done her hair. She only wore jeans and a cute red sweatshirt, but she looked good; good against him and as though she belonged there – except for the kiss me quick hat still on her head. He was six foot, six-one maybe and she stood with her head just about at his shoulder, straight on to the mirror. He was behind her in profile, looking in a box when he suddenly noticed her intense staring and his eyes moved to her.

They connected with her eyes in the reflection, he gave a smile and turned to stand straight on. At that moment Marelle wished she could take a snapshot; a beautiful picture of them both together but as soon as that split second in time had arrived, it went as Jacob turned her to him. He lifted the hat from her head and put it back in a box.

"I don't think we need that." He said as he leaned down to her and kissed her full on the lips.

Marelle slid her arms beneath his and behind his back, pulling herself to him gently and holding him. Cherishing every inch of contact her body had with his for every second it lasted.

"Come on." He said. "There's CCTV everywhere in here plus, I want to show you something else."

Jacob slung the holdall on his shoulder and carried the clothes on hangers slung over his left arm. He handed Marelle the crash helmet to carry and just as they were about to leave and close the door he reached back inside and grabbed a black baseball cap, placing it on his head. She gave him a raised eyebrow and a smile. She'd not seen him wear a baseball cap and to be honest it didn't suit him, but she let it go and walked out of the building with him.

"Let's put this in the car then we'll go round the corner." He instructed.

"What's round the corner?"

"I'll show you." He winked.

With the car locked they walked around the side of the building where there were a dozen or so yellow roller doors to what looked like garages, but smaller and closer together. She followed him to the second one where he undid a padlock at the bottom and rolled the shutter door up.

This unit did not have the finish of the one inside but was nonetheless clean, tidy and neat. Again, he flicked on a light switch and a bright, cold fluorescent strip clicked into life.

This space was mostly empty but right in the middle of it was something quite large, covered with a pale grey sheet. It looked almost the size of a small car but Marelle could see you would not have got even a small car through the yellow shutter door. Jacob walked forward, gripped the edge of the grey sheet by the corner and pulled it slowly off what it was covering.

There, in the centre of the space stood two pristine, sparkling, large motorbikes. Close together but not touching, both looked brand new and as if they had never seen the light of day.

"Oh wow!" Marelle exclaimed. "I take it they're yours?"

"Well. Nat's. "He replied. "But mine now. I thought they had got pilfered as well but I managed to prise them away!"

"Why haven't you been using these – if they are technically yours?"

"Too conspicuous." He remarked. "What would it look like if Jacob started riding around on these? Maybe one day ..."

Marelle laughed. "And I worry about you hurting yourself on the one you've got. What the hell could you get up to on either of these?"

"Oh, quite a lot!" He grinned. "They are getting on a bit now but they've had a pretty quiet life!"

"Do you come up here a lot?" She questioned, sensing this was probably where he went when he disappeared sometimes.

"A bit." He answered. "I pop in now and then, pick up clothes, check these out. I did take the blue one out on the road a couple of months ago – but I have to be careful ..."

"I don't know anything about bikes, as well you know." She commented. "But they're beautiful. I just don't like the thought of you riding them!"

"I haven't ever done any serious damage yet! Scared myself a few times but no major damage."

"Well keep it that way! You came pretty close yesterday." She warned.

He walked around them, looking longingly at them for a moment or two before carefully replacing the dust sheet.

'I wouldn't consider you a 'biker'". Marelle smiled.

"I'm not! I just like the speed." He replied, taking one final look and reaching up to switch the light off before they walked out and he closed the door again.

"So you've got all this stuff stashed here! What else are you going to surprise me with, hey?" Marelle laughed, walking back to the car.

"Nothing." He said. "Everything I own is in here ... a lot of stuff in the first room is my father's stuff out of the house. Most of it should probably be binned but t's one of those things I haven't ever got round to. This is the sum total of everything I managed to keep hold of. I nearly lost the bikes. See, I *knew* of them, knew where they were but they weren't being included with everything else. I made up some cock and bull story about finding a storage invoice and finally managed to get hold of them."

"So your life is packed up in all of those boxes?"

"No, that's Nat's life packed up in all of those boxes. Jacob's life is at home, on the airfield, at the farm. There have been times when I have come here and just sat in there, listening to echoes of lives once lived."

Marelle slid into the driving seat, pondering on his words. In all the time she had known him he had spoken to her more in the last two days than he ever had before. She sensed that should stand for something to her. With that in mind she smiled to herself as she pulled out of the parking space and headed home. Jacob seemed happy and relaxed so she decided to tell him about the headstone in the graveyard.

"Jacob, I went down to the churchyard the other day ..." She began. "And, well someone had vandalised your parents' headstone. I'm really sorry ..." she sighed. "We can go there together, now if you want."

He didn't respond for a moment. Looked straight ahead of him and tightened his mouth just like he always used to do.

"I know." He finally said. "I did it."

She almost braked, almost stopped the car as she spun her head to him in surprise. "*You* did it?" She exclaimed. "Why?"

"I got angry – his stupid actions were taking away a chance at life again – what he had done was causing all of the mess before I left; his actions were giving me no choice. It was wrong, and I'm sorry ... but I was angry." He said quietly. "I shouldn't have done it."

That shocked her. The idea that he had violated that space himself coupled with the thought of him getting so angry that he could undertake such an act. She reached out a hand to him and placed it on top of his.

"It's ok. I am sure we can get it repaired. I was worried you didn't know and it would upset you."

"What's done is done." He said.

As they drove through the village, past Derek and Patricia's house Marelle suddenly saw DCI Catchpole, just about to get into his car as they passed. He looked right at her and consequently right at Jacob. Marelle sighed.

"I think we may be about to get a visit." She exhaled, watching in the rear view mirror as they continued along the road. It sprang a little fear into her – firstly because she had told Catchpole that Jacob was missing but had not told him when he had returned and secondly because it would be their first encounter with anyone since Jacob's return, revelation and subsequent transformation. Marelle didn't want to upset that delicate balance and push him back into the state he'd been in previously. He seemed so happy and so totally different but even she knew that could likely disappear in the blink of an eye.

"What? Catchpole?" He asked. Seemingly not worried about any further imminent interrogation.

"Mmm." She said, still watching as he started off behind them.

"I did tell him you'd gone missing – I thought he might be able to help me find you. I'm sorry. He came round and caught me off guard at a bad moment."

"That's ok." He replied. "I've got nothing more to say to him anyway."

Sure as eggs were eggs he pulled into the drive behind her and got out before they did. He was walking up the passenger side of the car when Jacob got out.

"Good afternoon." He greeted, first to Jacob then to Marelle who was watching him from the driver's door, over the roof of the car.

She pre-empted his question. "I'm sorry – I was going to call you and let you know that Jacob was here ..."

"When did you get back?" He asked Jacob, looking at him.

"Day before yesterday." Jacob replied.

"Where have you been for three weeks?"

Jacob shrugged. "I just had to clear my head, you know? It's ok now, I'm back."

Marelle darted her eyes to him across the car. He was being Jacob. And she realised anything he now said had a double meaning; suddenly she was filled with a sense of the twisted and intertwined threads his life was and hers to become. The chaos inside his head was now apparent and also in hers.

"Glad to hear it." Catchpole commented. "This young lady for one will be pleased – she was convinced you were going to do something stupid. But I told her that the note you left was not a suicide note." He eyed Jacob through narrowed eyes as Jacob stooped his shoulders and held himself inwards.

"I need a quick word – if it's convenient?" Catchpole asked.

Once again Marelle invited him into the kitchen. He seemed to be eyeing Jacob with a suspicion today. Catchpole refused tea but sat down without being asked this time. Marelle remembered the last time they had all sat here and Catchpole had been interested in the circumstances around Nat's death. Jacob had become quite upset at this and now she could see why.

"So, how are you?" He asked Jacob.

"I'm fine."

"What happened to your tooth?" He asked.

"Got into a bit of an altercation with one of the farm boys." Jacob replied. "It's what happens when you are getting falsely accused of being a murderer!"

"Marelle did mention that. Is that why you left?"

"No!" Jacob exclaimed. "I told you. I needed space to think. I'm not scared of that idiot!"

Marelle held her breath. Did Catchpole know more than he was showing? Had Sam pitched up and claimed assault? If he had then she would step up – it had been her that had smashed a bottle into his head – not Jacob – and she would not let him take the rap for that.

"We have now searched the whole garden of the house over there." He explained. "We have not found anything else."

Jacob remained staring at the table as Catchpole stared back at him. He paused, waited but got no reaction. So he spoke again. "Have you had any further 'recollections' – any new memories that may help us identify this poor, unfortunate individual?"

Jacob shook his head. "No."

"Forensics are still examining the area and the remains which were found. Due to the nature of the deceased they may wish to use DNA testing to identify the body."

Jacob didn't say anything but Marelle saw his eyes flicker, just a tiny bit.

"Would you be happy to be part of that – to have a DNA test?"

Jacob raised his eyes "Why?"

"We feel the remains could be that of a stillborn child. I am not saying it is the case but if the DNA test on the remains, and yourself – should you agree – were to be a match then we could assume that the deceased may be a stillborn sibling of yours."

"No!" Jacob exclaimed. "There is no conceivable way that my parents would have done that! They were church going people. They would not have buried a stillborn child in the garden for God's sake!"

Catchpole stared at him for a moment. "Grief and fear can often drive people to do strange things – believe me. And I am sure you as well as anyone know that there were often what could be described as 'strange' traditions being upheld in remote villages in the past ..."

"Christ man! We are not talking about the dark ages you know. You'll be calling us six -fingered and web-toed next!"

"It's ok, Calm down Jacob. No one is accusing you of anything. I just wanted to check if you would be willing to take a DNA test – if it comes to that?"

Jacob lifted his eyes to him, shuffled in his seat a little, stared right into Catchpole as he could if he set his mind to it. "I've no objections to it, no. But I am not sure if I can take finding out there is a stillborn sibling. I don't know if I can live with that – I'm willing but I would have to consider my own mental health – should it be requested."

Catchpole stared at Jacob as he finally looked away again. He gave a very small nod in acknowledgement of Jacob's carefully chosen words.

"I just wanted to put the idea past you, so if we do decide to ask it isn't a shock."

Jacob nodded, looked agitated. "My parents would not do that." He said quietly. "My father may have buried Frankie there but he was not acting rationally and was a hopeless alcoholic at that stage ... but for both of them to bury a stillborn child ... no."

"It may have happened before your birth – even before your brother's birth. You may well have never been made aware ..."

Jacob looked at Catchpole with the velvet brown eyes of a child.

"I'm sorry if that has upset you." Catchpole said.

Jacob lowered his eyes and remained staring at the table. Marelle was behind him, arms folded, leaning against the worktop.

Catchpole raised his eyes to her then back to Jacob.

"Well it's good to see you back. I will let the powers that be know. I will be in touch if we need to take this further." He stood up. "I'll see myself out."

And he left.

Marelle waited until she heard the door close. Then she got up, went through to watch him get in his car and drive away. Then returned to Jacob. He was sitting at the table still but looked to her as she walked in.

"Why did you agree to a DNA test?" She asked.

"Because he wanted me to refuse. What would it have looked like if I'd said I wasn't willing? Anyway, it'll probably never happen – he's sounding me out. Watching my reaction."

"It sounds like he's on to something?"

"But he's barking up the wrong tree. He might just be trying to rattle me."

"Has it?"

He shook his head. "I can stall it if I want to. I don't think he can force me to take it unless I'm under arrest."

"But – "Marelle mused. "If you did the test and it came back positive, as a match, he has handed you a scot-free way out."

"How?"

"Well, say it's positive ..."

"Which it will be."

"Yeah. Say it's positive. Well, he thinks that it would prove it was an unknown stillborn sibling – who died and was buried long before your birth. They may have buried it in the garden but it wasn't known to you – a long lost sibling which will be identified by the DNA. Catchpole knows who it is, you're off the hook and can carry on being Jacob without the fear of getting found out. If they identify that body as some relation of yours then you're clear. Jacob is not going to crop up again, is he?"

"No." he said. "I'm doing it properly or not at all. I don't want that always hanging over me like some sword of Damocles."

Marelle didn't know who Damocles was or what the implications of his sword were. "But it's a way out of this. You could remain as Jacob. We could get married."

He gave her a small, warm smile. "I know – but – things have a habit of coming back and biting you. I would always know and I don't want to live with another twenty odd years of that!"

"Twenty years!" She raised an eyebrow.

"Well. I'm no spring chicken you know!"

She moved towards him, stooping and placing her arms around his neck from behind. "I should hope you've got more than twenty years – I at least want my life again with you or I'll feel I'm being short changed after all this effort!" She studded a kiss on his cheek, leaning her head on his.

SIX

Things seemed to be turning towards normal as he started tinkering with the bike outside in the sun. Marelle now found it hard to understand why he insisted on constantly repairing the broken, unroadworthy machine when she knew he had two pristine examples wrapped in cotton wool in a lock-up. But he had stated his reason– he didn't want to be too flashy – and, she supposed, especially right now. Marelle grinned to herself watching him out of the window. She quite wanted to see that side of his personality.

Right now though he looked far from flashy. Standing, staring at the bike, worn jeans, white t-shirt, untucked, hanging out from beneath a baggy blue jumper. He still looked good though. Clothes loved him, no matter what they were. She watched him; he looked calm today, relaxed – God forbid – happy. Now and again he cradled the injured arm and she had seen him grimace a couple of times but he was never going to admit it to her. She clutched her arms around herself and felt a chill pass through her. How could she have almost lost him forever? How could she have taken her eye off that – even for a split second? Now she knew, that could never happen again – she would never let him slip through her fingers like that.

She remembered the broken and shattered ghost of a man she had sat with on that bench in her garden the day before he had disappeared. She felt ashamed she had assumed that he was ok; ok to just be left; not to wrap him tightly in cotton wool and keep a hold on. All the signs had been there but she had not read them correctly. She vowed he would never, ever return to that as long as she lived.

He looked up at her now and again and gave her that genuine smile which was so full of warmth and happiness. Tt soared right through her like an ascending lark and she smiled too.

Late afternoon Jacob came in. The sun was already quite low in the sky and the air was cooling. In a couple of hours the early autumn evening would be dark and another day would have been claimed.

"I'm just going for a wander round the airfield." He said. "I've pushed one of the fence panels out of the way."

"Oh, ok. Hang on, I'll come." She smiled, getting up from her computer, grabbing her phone and wriggling into her shoes.

"I'll just get my jacket." He said and ran upstairs.

Marelle slipped into her own lightweight quilted jacket and preened herself in the mirror while she waited for him. He skipped down the stairs in the olive green military style jacket he'd started wearing. On his head he had sunglasses.

"Ready?" He asked.

He had completely moved one of the fence panels to the side, opening up the old gap they used. Lowering the sunglasses from his head he turned to take her hand as they stepped over the fence and onto the airfield again. They walked hand in hand up the runway. There had been no-one on site today – it did look as if work had stopped although there was a lot of idle machinery standing around. Jacob glanced at it all but didn't comment. The gates were closed but as far as she could see, not locked. He looked across to where his caravan used to stand, and she turned to look too – it was strange with it gone; a sense of imbalance and loss came to her.

They had dug a couple of holes and heaped up soil in two piles but apart from that there didn't seem to be much change. Some of the grass was flattened and muddied with the traffic that had passed.

"How long do you think it will remain on stop?" Marelle asked.

"I don't know really. The order will only apply to the actual Thor site and a small apron around it – I don't know why they can't carry on here but – they're a law unto themselves. Let's go on up to the Thor site and see if anything has been going on there."

The last time they had been at the Thor site had been the night when Sam and his father had set about Jacob and she had feared they were going to kill him. He had lost the tooth and suffered numerous cuts and bruises after she herself had managed to ward off Sam with a bottle of sparkling rosé smashed into his head! Marelle remembered that run back to the house, dragging a bleeding and bruised Jacob with her for – what she had not realised at the time – was that it could have been her last hours and minutes she had with him. It instilled apprehension in her as they rounded the trees, and the Thor site came into view.

They walked towards the central wall, the one that had the clearest view due west into the sunset. It was already setting and they were bathed in a warm amber light as they stood by the wall, staring into the quiet of the sunset.

The skeleton of a long dead tree was silhouetted against the sky. During the day it looked pale and bleached, just like bare bones bleached in the sun. It's bark had long gone, and the remaining wood was almost silver in daylight. She had asked about it once and Jacob had explained that it used to be alive; it was an oak tree. He guessed it had been struck by lightning at some point and had died as it stood there.

"It's like a hanging tree!" She had remarked, with a wry smile.

Jacob had looked at her oddly. "What!" he had asked.

Marelle smiled. "Oh when we were kids, we watched some programme on the telly about America where they hung the slaves from a tree. Bella became a bit obsessed with it for a while and every time we saw a dead tree we used to say it was a Hanging Tree!"

She laughed softly at the memory, not the subject.

He hadn't replied to that as far as she could remember. It had been in the days when she accepted, he wouldn't always answer her.

This evening the tree was a sinister black silhouette against the amber sky.

Everything had happened here. That thought struck her for the first time. From her birthday picnic when she had made him kiss her for the first time; where he had finally taken the lead and made love to her here; it was the place he often came to when he wanted 'space', when he wanted to think; and the place where he had been involved that last battle before he left.

"Not much changed here." She said, quietly, not wanting her voice to taint the beauty of the sunset.

He hitched himself up onto the low wall, so he was sitting and patted the spot next to him for her to do the same. She sat close to him as she had done so many times up here. Her thigh touching his, leaning into him, dropping her head against his shoulder. The sky was a deep coral pink, the sun a sticky, translucent neon red. It lit their faces with a luminescent glow. Marelle sat beside him; she sought his hand.

As she gripped it, he stood up, sliding himself off the wall so he stood on the ground in front of her, still holding her hand. For a second, he stood and smiled at her, his back to the sun now, his face in shadow but his sunglasses still catching the light. He held her hand in his right hand, gently. With his left he pushed the sunglasses up onto his head then fished in his left-hand jacket pocket.

"Now, you know me." He spoke. "I like things to be done properly – or not at all. I don't do anything by half measures ... so ..." He took his hand from his pocket.

Marelle watched him. He did not make eye contact but gently dropped to one knee.

"I'm not experienced but I believe this is how you do it?"

In the late and gradually fading light of the autumn evening he took the ring he had in his left hand and held it to the third finger on her left.

"Now if this doesn't fit, or you don't like it we can get something else but – Marelle, will you marry me?" He asked, putting the ring onto her finger. It was a little snug but with slightly shaky hands he pushed it up past her knuckle then raised his eyes to her.

Marelle couldn't find the right expression between laughing and crying. She looked into his eyes and even in the fading light she could see tears in them. She had truly never been so touched by emotion in her whole life, nor the feeling that was inside her right now. The second or two that passed seemed like forever – there was stillness around them, the breeze had stopped, a blackbird elevated its song before returning to roost and the falling sun just reflected off the sunglasses on top of Jacob's head and left a radiant glimmer of light like a halo.

In silence she just fell forwards and hugged him as he stood up to catch her in his arms. Marelle couldn't speak, she couldn't do anything except hold him so dearly and so tightly, clutching at his clothes in fistfuls and trying to find a breath amongst it all.

He hugged her, one hand against the back of her head, rocking her gently.

"Come on, you're not going to say 'no', are you?" He whispered with a laugh in his voice.

Marelle lifted her head, looked up into his face. She shook her head, tears streaming down her cheeks.

"No Jacob. I'm not saying no." she sobbed. "I'm saying yes! You know I'm saying yes, I asked you first!"

He grinned and hugged her to him. "I know but I wanted to do it properly!" He rested his head against hers. "Out here, while it's still here."

She gave a little sob of happiness, then looked at the ring on her finger.

"It's beautiful." She said.

"It's a bit plain and we can get another if you want but ... it was my mother's engagement ring – my father always kept it in his wallet."

She cried even more at that. "Oh Jacob, that's special. It's perfect!"

"Don't cry." He whispered.

"It's happy crying." She said, still tearful.

"I know." He hugged her tightly to him and rocked from side to side. "But as you know, there are things I need to sort out first so it might be a slightly prolonged engagement."

Marelle smiled. "I know. That's ok. I can be patient – it took me long enough to capture you in my butterfly net!"

He laughed and squeezed her. "It's getting dark. We'd better walk back."

"Hang on!" She said, taking her face in his hands. "One thing."

"What?"

"You've got to promise to let your hair grow back and let me cut it into that style again – no more number ones!"

Jacob laughed. "Oh I think that's a fair deal!"

Marelle did not walk back; she floated. Which in itself was a miracle because the weight of that ring on her finger was immense. The fact that it was his mother's engagement ring made that burden of love even greater. Almost back to the garden she stopped him and gave him a kiss.

"Can I tell Bella?"

'Tell her what?"

"About this!" She held her hand up.

Jacob laughed. "Of course if you can withstand the screams of pure delight that will ensue."

Marelle grinned. "Yeah – there will be that!"

"But don't tell her anything ... else ... will you?"

"No, of course not. I promise."

"Do I have to ask your mother – or Seb – for your hand in marriage or is that taking a step too far back into ancient history?"

"Oh for God's sake no! I'm thirty-four years old – I think I can make my own decisions!" Marelle held on to his upper arm and looked up into those dark, velvet eyes.

"Thirty-four?" He asked, musing.

"Yes! Why?" She replied, cheekily.

"You're a baby." He spoke.

"Well I know how old you are. I know your date of birth!"

"My *real* date of birth?" He asked.

"Yes, both of them!" Marelle stated.

Jacob seemed oddly pleased that she made a joke about that. He actually laughed, patted his hand on her shoulder then continued their walk back to the house. For her, seeing him so relaxed and unburdened was a dream come true in itself. She had the man of her dreams right here in the palm of her hand and the connection between them was cemented by the knowledge they both now shared.

It was dark outside, but she did not consider it too late to call Bella. She picked up her phone in the kitchen, dialled then looked up at Jacob.

"Hi Bella!" She smiled.

He gave her the lopsided grin which never failed to weaken her knees and with a nod walked off into the living room.

"Hi Marelle." Bella answered. "How's it all going? I was going to call you ..."

Marelle heard him turn on the TV She smiled to herself and leant against the worktop.

"Well Bella. It's great!" She said.

"You didn't call me to say that though, did you?" Bella picked up on her tone, her mood – the words she had not said.

Marelle laughed. "I'm just standing here, in the kitchen, with a ring on my finger ..."

Bella screamed. She actually screamed so shrilly down the phone that Marelle had to take it away from her ear for a moment. She was sure Jacob must have heard it too. She laughed.

"Oh my God Marelle! You did it – you really did it! When's the big day then? Oh my God – I will need to make sure I am free that weekend!"

Marelle chuckled.

"So tell me about it?" Bella asked. "When did it happen? What did he say?"

"Well, I asked him, didn't I? In the car park and he did tell me 'yes' – in the end. God, we sat up talking all night Bella – things have happened to him in his life you would not believe but the man is a living Saint, Bella ... and to think I nearly lost him; I actually let him slip away – I almost lost him. He would have been gone forever this time Bella ..." She stopped herself rambling into tears. "He said he wanted to do things properly and he got down on one knee this evening and asked me to marry him." She choked back a sob that this time was happy but still bore the sadness of what may have been.

"Where?" Bella asked. "Where did he ask you?"

"On the airfield."

"On the airfield! Oh my! The guy is weird!"

"No, no ... on the airfield ... where I first met him, where I first kissed him – where we've – well made love in the grass – we have shared so much out there on the airfield Bella – it's a special place – it was the *right* place!" She sighed. "It couldn't have been more perfect ... and I didn't even see it coming!"

"He sounds too good to be true."

Marelle laughed. "I know. He is – but he is!"

"What about the ring! Did he buy a ring?"

"No, but the ring he's given me was his mother's engagement ring! It's beautiful ... and it means so much to him. I feel like, I feel like we've got each other's blood running in our veins now! Oh Bell – I feel like I've been touched by an Angel!"

"Are you drunk?"

"No! I just can't explain how this feels or what he really is, or what he means to me ..."

Bella laughed. "Shit girl! You fell – you fell hard but you landed on your feet in those ruby slippers!"

Marelle laughed, cried, laughed again.

"What about everything else? What about a date? Seb? *Your mother*?"

"Oh don't! Seb doesn't even come into it. I'll call Mum sometime ... and, well there are a few things we need to 'sort out' first ... but that doesn't matter, nothing else matters now. He's mine, I'm his!"

"Oooh – *sort a few things out* – I don't like the sound of that. Is he already married, got kids or something?" Bella questioned.

"No!" Marelle exclaimed. "It's nothing. It's just *admin* – nothing to worry about – forget I said it. It doesn't matter and we'll set a date soon enough."

Bella sighed. Then laughed "Congratulations! To both of you! I'm so happy it's worked out – and that I actually played a tiny part in it!"

"You played a massive part in it Bella – believe me. I am eternally grateful."

"Don't gush Marelle. I don't like it when you gush." Bella warned playfully. "So, I think this calls for a visit at the weekend – what do you reckon?"

"I think that could be an idea – let me just check with my future husband, just to make sure he doesn't have any plans ..."

"Jacob! Plans!" Bella scoffed.

"Oh well, you never know. He's changed a lot!" Marelle grinned, walking through to the living room where she found Jacob in the armchair, one bare foot crossed over the opposite knee, TV on a music channel.

"Jacob?" she called his attention as she walked in. "Bella is planning to come down at the weekend – is that ok or have you something on?"

"No, that's ok." He answered. "I did want to ask Bella something actually, so that will be handy."

"Oh?" she replied to him then went back to the phone. "Yes Bella, all good. He wants to 'ask you something' apparently – so be prepared – I've no idea what it is!"

Marelle said her goodbyes to Bella shortly after with a promise that she would be there for lunch on Saturday.

"So, what do you want to ask Bella?" She had questioned Jacob with some intrigue, flopping down next to him on the arm of the chair.

"Well – she goes to these concerts, doesn't she?"

"Yes?"

"Well she said she'd seen Yellow Son a little while ago."

"Did she?"

He nodded. "I thought maybe we could go along to one when they were playing again."

"Really?!" Marelle exclaimed. "Is that wise? Won't they see you?"

"Not if I don't want them to. I want to just observe them from a distance. WFindout how the land lies and how my plan of attack needs to work …"

She eyed him for a moment in silence. Then she gave a little laugh. "You want to go to one of these weekender things that Bella goes to?"

"No, *we* are going to go." He pointed a finger." She is always trying to make us go – it is the perfect opportunity … only we have to make sure it's when they are playing – I don't want to sit through a weekend of inane bands for nothing."

Marelle bit her lip and smiled. "Really. I just can't imagine you there …"

He shrugged. "To be honest neither can I, but, well, it's an easy starting point."

"So, what is the plan?"

"Just go and see what they're doing now – what they're playing. For God's sake they're playing in a disused holiday camp out of season to drunken adults … it's not exactly stadium rock anymore, is it? They're all quite a bit older than me as well … I'm just *interested.*"

"Ok." She nodded. "Don't freak out on me though."

"No, I'm fine now." Jacob replied. "Then I'll pick my time. We'll find a gig they're doing at a suitable venue, and I just want to stand there and let Chas see me. I want to see his face when he sets eyes on me!"

"Wouldn't it be better to resolve the issue with being dead first?"

"No, then he would know. I want to see his face when he sees me standing there."

"Wow!" She commented. "Are you sure? This may be a rocky road?"

He nodded. "I'm not hiding anymore. This is mine … and I want it back."

Marelle was sitting at her computer in the kitchen when he came in through the back door with a bucket.

"Gonna wash your car." He announced.

"Oh, ok. "She replied, looking up at him as he began to fill the bucket in the sink.

"I normally take it through the car wash."

"I know. I can see. It's filthy." He answered. She watched him as he filled the bucket and lifted it out of the sink with his good arm.

"Are you washing it in the front garden?" she asked.

He nodded. "Of course I am!"

She smiled, didn't say anything. That worried her slightly. There was no obvious boundary between him and the whole wide world if he was washing her car in the driveway. He went out of the back door with the bucket; she got up and carried the laptop through to the living room. Where had he found the bucket? She didn't even think she had a bucket. Marelle put the laptop on the coffee table, but it was too low for her to be able to keep an eye on him and work. She moved to the arm of the chair nearest the window, balanced the laptop on her knees and watched him.

He started at the roof, moving quickly, working methodically from top to bottom. He looked agile; sprightly. She smiled. He was still guarding that arm, but it didn't seem to be impeding him. Marelle admired him, his long legs, his square shoulders, his solid back. She giggled to herself. It seemed like he had been an icon once and still could be now – she hadn't really dwelt on that thought – not until it entered her head right now. His past didn't matter to her at all but, he had actually been someone in the public eye – once. Someone who people may have recognised on the street, someone who may have actually stirred a few teenage dreams. She had looked at all of the pictures the other night but since then had not delved any further but right now, watching him washing her car, she wanted to.

Marelle hit google and typed in 'Ezza Frost'. Immediately the screen filled with his image – albeit from ten plus years ago. There were literally thousands. Some she had seen the other night, some were new. She scrolled through them, covering her mouth and giggling for the most – sometimes out of pure joy of the images she found but sometimes because he was wearing something pretty indescribable or just looked like he was posing *so* much. There were some great shots of him performing on stage – where he looked so animated and at his best. She could still see that person outside in the pictures, albeit somewhat softened. Then she came across one picture that she had not seen before.

Jacob was kneeling on a stage, surrounded by a forest of hands reaching out to him. He had the most glorious smile of warmth and genuine humility on his face as he reached and touched those hands – almost as if he could not believe the adoration he was on the receiving end of. It was a beautiful picture – probably not to anyone else who did not know him like she did, but to her, it melted her heart. She clicked on it, and it took her to a music magazine website archive and an article titled 'Losing Ezza'. It piqued her interest and emotion. The article had been written seven years ago; three years after Ezza's death and as she read it, she realised it was a heartfelt tribute to him from a music journalist who had also obviously been a huge fan. Marelle read on.

'It's been three years, three months and twenty-two days since we learned of the death and apparent suicide of Ezza Frost, charismatic and iconic lead singer of Yellow Son.

I was a fan. I am not ashamed to say that. He strode the stage and delivered a performance that bristled with talent and emotion entwined with an innocent humility and humble reaction to all those who adored him.

Yellow Son made records; they had hits, but their strength was their live performance and their fans never let them down. Formed fifteen years ago from the shattered remnants of Kullinane with Ezza drafted in after a chance performance on an early evening music programme which band leader Chas Symonds watched – Yellow Son were born.

Chas never denied that Ezza was brought in as eye candy. As a frontman to carry their appeal further than he could on his own. 'I am a singer" Chas said. "I've been a singer all my adult life – why would I bring a new singer in? Ezza was a clothes horse; he's the poster boy who just happens to have a pretty good voice and he gives 200% on stage."

The rest is history. A success story. A group of guys who worked together so well, never lived in each other's pockets; always delivered and had time for their fans.

I've seen them many, many times. I've watched Ezza stride across the stage with long legs in leather pants. I've touched his hand and shaken it many times.

So how did it all go wrong? He was adored he had the world at his feet and the crowd right behind him. I watched Ezza's demise, and it's taken me three years, three months and twenty-two days before I could find it in myself to document that fatal fall.

There was a picture of Ezza here she had not seen before. He had a long, white, untucked shirt on, cuffs over his hands. The camera had been at his eye level, looking down. His hair was very long on top, very short at the sides, slightly spiky but pulled forwards into a long fringe over his forehead. His eyes looked huge at that angle, looking up into the lens. His expression strong, mouth straight and tight. Marelle knew that look and that expression. She looked into his eyes in the picture and saw the same Jacob inside.

"Have you got any wax?" He suddenly asked, looking through the living room door.

It caught her unawares and she jumped, instantly closing the lid of the laptop as if she had been caught looking at something dodgy.

"Wax?" she asked, a little absently, feeling slightly odd about reading the article.

"Yeah, wax – polish." He made a polishing motion with his hand. "

"There's some Mr. Sheen under the sink ..." She replied vaguely.

"No! Car polish!" He laughed. "I had some, but it's run out."

"There should be a bag of cleaning products in the back of the car – came with it Seb said but I've not used it. There may be polish in there?" She stared at him, comparing what she had in front of her with the pictures. It was hard to believe the man on the stage in leather trousers was the same person she had washing her car right now.

"Ok, I'll have a look. What're you doing?"

"Nothing!" She exclaimed. "Just research."

She had been so intrigued she had even failed to see him leave the task and come inside; she had sat here to keep an eye on him – he could have disappeared in that time. For a second or two she watched him look in the back of her car, find the bag then take the contents out bottle by bottle until he selected one and began shaking it.

Marelle continued reading.

"*I watched him on three of the four nights in Germany. Both for work and for pleasure. I missed the first night which, by other people's accounts was where it all began to go wrong.*

The second night I watched a failing confidence about him; he struggled with lyrics and had lost that spark. However, two or three songs in it seemed to click and I thought maybe everything would be alright after all.

Over the next two nights I observed Ezza perform on stage drunk. I saw fear and bewilderment in his eyes for the first time and I knew something was going wrong.

It was subtle but real fans of his would have noticed. 'Solitude' was performed like an out-of-control express train with the other band members trying to keep up with Ezza's rushed and improvised performance. Other songs fell victim to the same choice new lyrics and questionable gestures throughout. I watched and saw the initial detonation and felt a sadness that life was going to take him.

With trepidation I took my place at the first of the UK shows, surrounded by eight thousand other people. I had told myself that it would all be fine; he'd had an off day or two and the break between dates would have helped. The support act finished, and Yellow Son were late on – eventually heralded by Chas doing nothing less than dragging a disheveled Ezza on stage. My heart sank into my feet, and I knew the end was nigh.

From my front row position, I could look Ezza in the eye but after looking at his sweat stained bewildered face and cold, dead eyes throughout a haphazard performance of 'Too Close' I felt exactly that – bewildered.

Part of me expected the second night to be cancelled; part of me wished for that but I, with the thousands of other fans, stood on the spot and once again awaited the entrance of our hero, our icon. He appeared battle scarred and weary. Ezza walked on with a tiredness and hesitance I had never seen in him before. When he walked up to the mic stand, clutched it in both hands and rested his head against them I knew this was over.

But what did we do? What did all of us do when we stood shoulder to shoulder in front of this shattered individual. We beyed for more; we clapped and chanted and urged him on. The chant rose as the rest of the band played the opening bars to 'Out of the Dark' – prolonged it until Ezza raised his head, looked blankly into the crowd then turned and walked off.

We all cheered, shouted, urged and looked at one another as we watched Chas step up to the mic and start singing. He remained there for the whole gig and raised a mighty cheer at the end.

Why though did not one person follow Ezza? Why did not one single person there take a moment to reach out a hand to him? I bear that burden of guilt as should every person who was in that place. We urged him on when we should have told him to stop, we let him slip away when we all had the chance to help him.

I interviewed Chas a while after and although he did not want to speak too deeply about it, he did say "We feared this for Ezza right from the start – he was brilliant but he could be unreachable – he liked simple things and liked to be left alone. He often disappeared but over the years we realised he always came back. He loved the adoration of an audience but pretty much hated everything else. Ezza was unique and I don't think he knew his full potential – sadly we never will."

Yellow Son continues. They are still successful and still sell out venues. There is talk of a new album but there are no plans to replace Ezza.

No one ever will.

RIP Ezza Frost.

Marelle looked up. There were tears in her eyes and a discomfort of emotion in her chest. She turned her head and looked at him, out there, furiously stretching across the roof of her car to polish it. Jacob, Nat, Ezza ... loved, adored, dead. Never before had she cared about what he had done in a "previous life" – she didn't bother whether he was indeed a rock star or a farm labourer – she had always said that. She wanted Jacob for herself not for what he had been or what he'd had. But the words of that journalist and the picture of Jacob kneeling and reaching out to an adoring audience brought it home to her. This was bigger than she had imagined. Even the other day when he showed her the first pictures of him as Ezza – it had not occurred to her how much of a 'thing' this was, or could be. So he'd been in a band, he'd played a few gigs, he'd had a few fans. Marelle just hadn't thought it had been that big or that important. But obviously it had. And now he'd said it "was his – and he wanted it back"; and he seemed to think he could just slot right in where he had left a large Ezza shaped space. Marelle watched him; there he was – ten years older – ten years spent in perfect isolation, with an identity he could tentatively hide behind – but now he wanted to rip that flimsy veneer away and expose himself once again to what had taken his life the first time around. She took one last lingering look at that photo then closed the laptop and stood up.

When she walked out into the driveway he had moved on to the back wing of the car. The bonnet was unbelievably shiny with a real depth to the red she didn't think she had ever seen before. Marelle smiled and walked up behind him. He had his head down and his bottom in the air. She stopped, grinned to herself and walked up behind him, firmly placing both of her hands on the cheeks of his bottom.

She wasn't expecting the reaction she got but he flew round so quickly he nearly knocked her flying.

"Woah!" She laughed. "Didn't you know I was there?!"

He mumbled. "No!"

"Whoops, sorry!" She laughed. "I didn't mean to surprise you like that!"

He sighed, rag in hand. 'I was engrossed in what I was doing – I wasn't expecting to be fondled."

"Fondled!" She giggled. "Fondled?" She said again and continued laughing while he looked slightly disheveled and embarrassed. "Come here! Let me 'fondle' you some more." She wrapped her arms around his neck, and he pulled her to him. Marelle held in her arms the person she had just been reading about on the internet – he *was* that person, alive, here – polishing her car and now holding her tightly. She kissed him, once – quickly on the lips just as a siren began to wail in the distance. It soon became louder and was obviously heading down the street.

"God, what's that?" She asked. "Hope it's not heading over there." She nodded in the direction on Derek and Patricia's.

"So do I." he remarked as they both turned their heads to watch as the siren approached. It was not a police car; it was an ambulance on full blues and twos speeding past their house and up the main street.

"It's ok." She said. "It's an ambulance."

They watched it drive past then turned back to the car.

"Looks good." She commented. "Looks better than it did when Seb bought it!"

"I haven't waxed a car in years!" He smiled. "She's come up well. I'll check the oil and water when I've finished."

"I'll get you added onto the insurance – 'I'll probably need your driving licence – Jacob's driving licence – when I do."

"No problem." He replied. "I'll dig it out sometime."

SEVEN

Marelle returned indoors having fulfilled her need to touch him again and just remind herself that all this was real, and the ring was still on her finger. Now, with an apprehensive hovering finger she hovered, paused and then dialled a number on her phone.

The international dial tone initially worried her – as it always did – but then she remembered it was normal and waited.

"Marelle!" the familiar yet strangely unremembered voice answered.

"Hi Mum." She smiled.

"Oh, hang on! My second child I believe – what, must have been thirty-two, thirty-three years ago now?"

Marelle laughed. There was no malice intended in her mother's voice. "Thirty-four Mum."

"Did I miss your last birthday?"

"No –!"

"Oh well, obviously too much going on in my life to remember I remembered!" She quipped. "So, which of the big three is it then?"

"What?" Marelle's mother was normally quick witted, outspoken – fun. But today Marelle had immediately failed to keep up with her.

"Hatched, matched or despatched? Are you pregnant, married or dead?"

"Oh." Marelle smiled. "Well, none – yet anyway!"

"So this is just a call for a *chat*? The first time in thirty-four years you have ever called me for a chat! What's the weather like there then?"

"Fine! No, Mum – listen." She began.

"Oh I don't like '*Mum listen'* conversations ..."

"I'm not married yet, but I wanted to let you know – I'm engaged!" she said it with a smile in her voice.

"Oh that's wonderful!" Her mother laughed. "And I always said you weren't the marrying type. That's why you never married that last one ... what's-his-name ... you were with him for years."

"Mum, you make me sound like I have a trail of them!"

"Well, don't you?"

"No!"

"Who's this one then? The one Seb told me about?"

Marelle's heart sank in her chest. Of course Seb had got his pound of flesh first, she might have guessed.

"The local who Seb thinks is a paedophile?" Her mother regretfully continued.

"He's not a paedophile!" Marelle protested. "Please Mum, don't listen to Seb – he's jumped to conclusions and he's all wound up in this!"

"Oh I know what he's like – just like his father – there's only one opinion – and it's his!"

Marelle sighed and smiled. "Thanks Mum."

"Does he make you happy?" Her mother asked.

"Yes – very!"

"Is he kind?"

Marelle grinned to herself. "Yes, he's wonderful – he is *so* kind and gentle."

"Is he good looking?"

"Extremely!"

"Well then, what's the problem?"

She laughed. 'Oh Mum, you would *adore* him!"

"Curious as to how Seb jumped to the paedophile thing though ..."

"We went to Abbi's birthday party – a disco at the Hall. Well, Jacob ..."

"Jacob? Is that his name? Biblical name ..."

"Yes, Jacob ..." Marelle continued as her mind thought that it could also be Nathaniel – another Biblical name – or Ezza – also derived from a biblical name. "Well Jacob does have ... did have ... an issue with crowds, social situations you know, and he was just taking a quiet moment to himself in the toilet. Seb walks in and finds him in there and because it's a kid's party Seb jumped to conclusions and won't let go of that notion."

Her mother laughed. "I can see where he is coming from – your choice of words is a little dubious too ..."

Marelle tutted. "He is adorable Mum. He would not hurt a fly. I love him and he proposed to me – on one knee – last week. He gave me his own mother's engagement ring!"

Marelle's mother chuckled. "Sounds like he's a bit of a romantic – you're like me – sort of a free spirit, more interested on what's inside than the packaging."

"But the packaging is pretty good too Mum!"

"Send me a picture. I may need to judge for myself ...:"

"You'll love him Mum!"

"So does that mean I've got to come over to that shite hole for a wedding?"

"Well, yes ... but not yet. We're not in a rush – and there are a few things to sort out first!"

"Sort out! Is he already married or got kids in tow?"

"No!" Marelle exclaimed lightly. "He's 100% single with no dependants."

"Well don't waste too much time; the good ones have a habit of getting away!"

"Oh he won't get away Mum. I'll guarantee that." Marelle stood up and walked to the window. He had the bonnet of her car open and was leaning inside it. It reminded her of the night in the pub car park when she had run into his arms. She smiled to herself and felt that warm feeling pass over her again while she gazed at the ring on her finger.

"Look, do you want to say Hi to him?"

"Is he there?"

"He's actually cleaning my car for me right now!" Marelle laughed.

"Well he's sounding better by the minute! Doesn't he work?"

"Oh, yes but he's off today – he works at the local farm but he's also a caretaker for the airfield that backs onto the house – well for the developers actually." She moved through the house to the front door. "Hang on."

Carefully she placed a finger over the microphone and called to Jacob from the doorstep. He looked up.

"Hey, do you want to say Hi to my Mum?"

He looked a little blank for a second, a little apprehensive for another one but walked forward.

"Talk about putting me on the spot" he said, then held out his hand for the phone.

"Hi." He said in a familiar voice to her, made her think of the times she had called him, and he had answered with "Hi".

He raised his eyes to Marelle as he spoke. "Yes, it's Jacob ... and I'm sorry but your daughter did not tell me your name."

"Vicki" Marelle mouthed but her mother was already explaining. He had a sort of conversation with her, didn't look awkward or weird in any way and eventually he handed the phone back to her after saying

"Bye Vic, see you soon."

Marelle raised her eyes to his. With a smile to her he turned and walked back to the open bonnet of the car.

"See, he exists, he's normal and he's lovely!" Marelle said as she too went back inside.

"Seems perfect!" Her mother replied. "Sexy voice – speaks very eloquently."

"You should see his arse!" Marelle quipped then laughed as she realised with some embarrassment what she'd just said to her mother.

"My dear, I would love to."

"Well you will. I promise." Marelle stated. "Thanks Mum – don't take any notice of what Seb says – Jacob is truly an Angel on earth, and he has a heart of gold."

"I take things as I find them Marelle, as you know. I don't let other people make my mind up for me. Congratulations – he makes you happy and that's all that matters. Love will always find a way."

Sometimes her mother could be outspoken and quite annoying but equally she could say just the right things at just the right moment – and she had certainly done that today. Still smiling after the conversation she went back out to Jacob.

'That was a low punch." He said.

"What?"

"No warning and suddenly I'm on the phone to your mother."

"Well you made a good impression."

"Did I?"

She nodded. "What did she say to you?"

"Not a lot. Just asked me to make sure I look after you as you are her only daughter."

"Did she?" Marelle seemed a little surprised.

"And said her name is Victoria but she like to be called Vicki with an 'i' as it makes her seem younger!"

Marelle laughed. "I'll need to watch her around you – she'll be stealing you away."

"Mmm, wouldn't mind being a toy-boy." He said, then grinned.

Marelle grabbed a handful of his t-shirt and pulled him playfully towards her. "Hey, you're going nowhere – not now that I've got this ring on my finger!" And she kissed him, roughly and longingly, in the driveway next to her car. She laughed and made a joke of it, but she knew what she said was true. He was here now, and hell nor high water would ever separate them again; for *whatever* reason.

Bella's arrival on Saturday was always going to be loud. Marelle had seen her car pull in behind hers and braced herself. She waited, watching her best friend walk up to the front door with a holdall, a shoulder-bag and a bottle in her hand. Bella rang the doorbell. Marelle took a deep breath and opened it.

Bella screamed in sheer delight, bags on the floor and arms outstretched with the bottle still in one of them. Marelle laughed as the two of them hugged furiously for a number of seconds.

"Let me see! Let me see!" Bella gasped, fumbling for Marelle's left hand, pulling it flat and examining the pale gold ring with a single stone set in it.

She squealed again. "Oh my! It's beautiful – and it fits, ok?"

Marelle nodded. "It's a little bit tight but at least it won't fall off easily."

Belle looked back up into her eyes. She squealed again and bobbed up and down out of pure delight.

"Oh I'm so happy!" She laughed. "Well, where is he?"

Marelle took her through the house – Jacob was in the back garden; he'd got the caravan door open but seemed to be fiddling with the fence at the end of the garden. They both stopped at the kitchen window and looked out.

"Aaah!" Bella sighed. "Look at him. He's OK after last Saturday then?"

"Apart from coming off the bloody bike on Sunday and probably injuring himself more than he's letting on – yeah – he's fine. Now."

Bella laughed a little then caught Marelle's change of expression and emotion. She turned back to her.

"Marelle, what?"

Marelle gave a quick glance to Jacob then moved away from the window. Bella followed.

"Do you know what he told me when we got back home?"

Bella shook her head.

"His plan on that Saturday night was to leave that pub and jump off the Orwell Bridge."

Bella truthfully did not know what to say to that.

"If you hadn't kept him there then he would be dead. Truth was he had apparently tried it earlier but there were police around so he ended up at that pub with the intention of going back later. I so very nearly lost him Bella."

Bella stared at Marelle, her brown eyes filling as she did so.

"Oh my God Marelle, I didn't know – he was in the pub, singing karaoke! He looked happy and enjoying himself so much – and he was so calm and friendly with Freya afterwards – I didn't know!" She reached out and took Marelle in her arms. "I am so sorry!"

"Nobody knew Bella – the signs were all there – he would have just gone off and taken his life – alone – with no-one even thinking he was going to do such a thing ..."

"But he's here – and he's asked you to marry him!" Bella whispered. "Is he OK now?"

Marelle nodded, sniffed, moved away from Bella. "Yeah. He's OK. He's fine. Says the moment I ran into his arms in that car park was the moment that changed everything – made him realise it would have been the wrong decision."

Bella still held Marelle's hands in hers. She smiled.

"He's never going out of my sight ever again Bella – I will make sure of that!"

"But he loves you Marelle – he's done it in the sweetest way, but you know that now."

Marelle nodded. "I feel like I've been on a massive journey, and I've finally found what I was searching for at the end. And I'm never letting go of it!"

Bella squeezed her hands.

"He's different Bella. He's really changed – he's happy; he's relaxed. He's told me a lot more about himself – I understand him even more now – and I love him even more!" She looked into Bella's eyes and wanted to say that Jacob had a past; that he had lived a previous life that no-one would believe but she knew she could not breath a word of that to anyone. Not even her oldest, truest friend. One day it would be sorted and then everyone would know.

"And it's a time to be happy, not sad! Bella grinned. "And he's here and he's alive. Plus I've brought Champagne, and I've got a cake! So let's celebrate!" She laughed and wheeled off, grabbing for the back door handle and exploding though the door.

"Hey Mister. I want a word with you!" She shouted.

Jacob looked up, turned then smiled. He'd only just stood up straight as Bella ran down the garden path and threw herself at him. Marelle smiled, if anyone else was hugging Jacob like that she would be defensive. She watched as Bella embraced him warmly then took his hand and pulled him back to the kitchen with her. Jacob smiled to Marelle as he was led in through the back door.

"Come in, come in!" Bella ordered, bringing them both into the kitchen.

"Marelle – glasses!" She exclaimed, taking hold of the bottle of Champagne again.

Marelle cringed as she anticipated Bella letting the cork go in her kitchen, but she held on to it and popped the cork sensibly as Marelle reached up into the cupboards and Jacob stood there with his hands in his pockets and a smile on his face. For a second, he raised his eyes to Marelle in a fleeting warm glance as Bella filled the glasses. With a toothy grin Bella thrust one into his hand and one into Marelle's. before she picked up her own.

"It's a bit early Bella!" Marelle exclaimed.

"Sssh Marelle! It's never too early for Champagne and this is a very, *very* –"She raised her glass to Marelle then turned to Jacob. "Special occasion." Bella paused. "To two of the best people; the two people who were meant to be together – forever." She toasted.

"Amen!" Jacob said with a grin. Marelle smiled but the word reminded her of that agonised day in the church at Frankie's funeral when she should have realised that she had lost him already. She grinned now but tears still pricked the back of her eyes.

"For that you can give us a speech too!" Bella exclaimed at his quip. "Well ... husband to be ... say something ..."

Jacob had a sublime little smile on his face, he waited a second then raised his glass. "To Marelle ..." He turned to Bella ... "and Bella ..." He paused again then looked right into Marelle's eyes "... the two ladies who saved my life."

It wasn't what Marelle was expecting and following the earlier conversation with Bella – raised the emotions even higher in her throat.

"Ladies!! Fuck what, Jacob? *Ladies* – well ..." Bella made a 'maybe' gesture with her hand. "Marelle may be a lady – sometimes – but me – I'm no lady Jacob!" She laughed. "But I'll take it – just cos you're so sweet!"

She'd saved Marelle from tears; she gulped a laugh before she took a sip of Champagne.

"Hang on!" Bella exclaimed and grabbed her bag which she unzipped and lifted out a box. "Cake! You *have* to have cake!"

It was a rather large, chocolate frosted cake which said 'serves 16' on the box but which Bella proceeded to cut huge slices off with a butter knife she found on the draining board. She dished them out on plates which Marelle grabbed from the cupboard.

The three of them stood in the kitchen at midday, drinking relatively warm Champagne and eating chocolate cake like three children at a party. The giggling started as Bella helped herself to more cake and more Champagne; she topped up Marelle and Jacob's glasses.

It was a haphazard but ecstatically happy moment. In it, Marelle smiled at Jacob, and he held out a hand to her. She took it and moved close to him.

"Come on Jacob – there's a lot of cake to eat!" Bella exclaimed, pointing to it.

"I don't really eat cake." He replied.

"No, I can see that!" Bella laughed, leaning across and poking his tummy. "Look at you! He needs fattening up Marelle."

"Oh I don't think we'll ever fatten Jacob up." She smiled. "He's got hollow legs!" Just as she turned to him and smiled the doorbell rang.

It was no small wonder they had actually heard it over Bella's laughter, but Marelle sighed and stood up from her leaning against the worktop position.

"If that's Catchpole …" She sighed under her breath.

"I'll go!" Jacob piped up.

"No, it's OK. I'll go …" she gently raised a hand as she walked past.

"Who's Catchpole?" Bella asked.

Marelle didn't hear Jacob's reply but just as she opened the door there was an almighty shriek of laughter from the kitchen. She swung the door inwards and there on the doorstep was Mr. Wright. In her drive behind Bella's car was a new looking Audi.

"Oh, hello." He greeted. "Is Jacob there?"

The laughter coming from the kitchen sounded like an out-of-control kids birthday party.

"Erm, yes. Hold on a second."

She turned back to the hallway. "Jacob!" She called.

Bella was still laughing; Jacob did not appear. Leaving the front door open she walked back to the end of the hallway where she had direct line of sight into the kitchen. Bella had Jacob cornered up against the worktop with cake in hand which she was thrusting into his face – they were both laughing. Marelle smiled – mostly to see him so relaxed and doing frivolous things.

"Jacob."

Bella laughed as she stood aside. Jacob walked towards her.

"It's Mr. Wright, for you." She said, looking up at him. "You've got cake on your face."

He rubbed at his face but in the wrong place – he walked towards the door while Marelle hovered between the hallway and the kitchen door. Jacob leaned across the doorway so he blocked a lot of her view of Mr. Wright, and she couldn't completely hear what was being said. Bella was standing in the kitchen, making faces at her while she ate a huge lump of chocolate cake. Marelle looked at Bella then back at Jacob; she wanted to go and stand nearer to him but didn't want to appear as if she was trying to listen in. So, she continued to hover in the background until Jacob finally closed the door with a nod to Mr. Wright and walked back towards her. He looked serious and still had a smear of chocolate cake across his face.

"What?" She asked.

"He wants me to 'fill in' for a couple of weeks if I want to. Seems like Sam's father has had a stroke, and it doesn't look good – it was probably the ambulance we saw the other day. He is very ill, and Sam is taking a couple of weeks off. One of the other guys has left to join the Navy so that just leave shim with Adam and Ryan. Ryan's not really experienced enough, and Adam is going to work in Australia for a year – so came to ask if I can fill in until Sam comes back."

Marelle stared at him, reached up and brushed the cake off his face. "What did you say?"

"Well, I said yes." He shrugged.

"What about everyone not wanting to work with you? Has all of that gone out of the window now?

"Well, by what he's saying it's only Ryan ... he's ok. I'll help them out."
"When?"

"Monday." Jacob replied.

Marelle looked at him in a slightly disconcerted fashion. "What, for two weeks and then what? Tell you to fuck off again?"

"Well, – we'll have to see ..."

"Jacob! Why did you say yes so easily? I don't ..."

"Sssh." He interrupted in a whisper. "It's fine. I want to. We'll talk about it later – OK?" He said gently then as she looked up at him with a look on her face which was verging on disappointment, he leant forwards and kissed her, once on the lips. "OK?"

"OK." She replied with a faint smile.

Late afternoon, after they had all been on a walk across the airfield a conversation took place about buying fish and s and whether either Marelle or Jacob would be served in the local chip shop following Jacob's exclusion from the village shop and Marelle's subsequent argument with them. Jacob would have boldly walked in there and taken the consequences now, but with the issues Marelle now knew about, she had dissuaded him from doing so.

"Well I'll go in, but I may get told to get straight out – I haven't technically been barred but word travels around and I probably have ..." Marelle explained.

"Oh for God's sake!" Bella laughed. "It's like two kids trying to pass off a dodgy pound coin in a sweetie shop! I'll go – they won't know me."

So she set off, walking up the road with a list and money that Jacob had insisted on giving her.

"I may be some time. "She quipped with a fake salute.

Marelle closed the door and walked through to Jacob who was in the sitting room.

"It's gone quiet." He remarked.

Marelle laughed.

"So, are you going to work at the farm on Monday?" Marelle gestured, that point was playing on her mind.

"Yep." He replied.

"Is it wise Jacob – and in the circumstances?"

"It's fine ... and 'in the circumstances' it's exactly the right thing to do. Sam won't be there. It'll be fine."

She sighed. The truth of the matter was that she did not want to let him out of her sight. But he would be off at six in the morning and be gone all day –

probably out in the van or some other farm vehicle. Out of her sight and grasp. Marelle did not feel ready to deal with this yet, but he obviously was.

Bella was longer than they expected and as usual returned with too much food and a carrier bag of alcohol to boot.

"You two – honestly!" She commented. "The guy in the chip shop was lovely – and so was the lady in the shop."

"Well you're not us" Marelle commented. "They won't serve us!"

"Well – "She began, "I did probe them a bit – said I was down here on holiday and asked about recent goings on that I'd read about ..."

"What did they say?"

"Wouldn't really talk about it. Just said that yes, there had been some things happening that had been in news reports, but they didn't want to dwell on it as it painted a bad picture of the village and, as usual, it's just one *bad apple* in the box..."

"Who said that?" Marelle sighed.

"Woman in the shop, but I felt she had been told to say that as a set piece, you know?"

"Fuck's sake." Marelle sighed.

"Well at least they're not saying anything awful ..."

"Bella, the 'one bad apple in the box' they are referring to is Jacob. "She pointed. "It's him." As he stood there looking as innocent and bewildered as he had the ability to. Tall, dark, handsome and as innocent as the day was long.

Bella gave a doubtful little smile. "But they didn't blame it on him specifically."

"They don't need to!" Marelle sighed, then felt tearful. It was exactly this which was what had almost robbed him from her, and it was still prevalent.

"It doesn't matter." Jacob stated. "As I've always said people will see what they want to see – you won't change that ... we're here; we're fine ... forget them."

Bella smiled. "Well said Jacob. Now let's get this eaten before it gets cold."

They ate in the living room, Bella sat herself on the floor. When they'd finished and she was dishing out a second bottle of beer to Jacob and herself she gave a wicked little grin.

"Right. It's premiere time! Good, I can see you've got a DVD player ..." She grinned, grabbing her bag from the seat of one of the armchairs. "Look, see what I've got." She produced a DVD in a clear jewel case form her handbag.

"What is it?" Marelle asked.

Bella laughed. "It's Jacob singing, in the pub!"

Marelle looked to Jacob as he went to say something, but nothing came out. His colour paled significantly.

Bella crawled forwards on her knees to reach the DVD player.

'It's not plugged in." Marelle said. You'll have to unplug something else."

"Hang on." Jacob finally said. "Where did you get that?"

'I filmed you!" Bella laughed. "I knew Marelle would never believe it!"

"You filmed me?"

"Yes! You were in a pub full of drunken idiots – anyone who stands out is going to get filmed at some point. *And* I wasn't the only one filming it either – so chill – "

"On your phone?"

"No! On a bloody full size TV camera that I drag around with me – you ninny!" Bella exclaimed with a laugh, pulling out a plug and putting the plug from the DVD player in that socket as the lamp on the cabinet extinguished.

"But you've got a DVD." Jacob pointed.

"Yep. Geeky son of my neighbour – thinks he's a bit of a film producer. I got him to get it off my phone and put it onto a DVD so we're not all pressed around the screen on my phone trying to watch it – you can keep a copy."

"Well how many copies are there?"

"Two. I've got one and this is the other."

"What about the geek?" Jacob questioned.

"Well I don't think he really wants a copy of some forty something year old bloke in leather trousers singing karaoke!" Bella laughed. "It's OK! I'm not broadcasting it."

Jacob sighed. He looked slightly concerned but not enough to raise any adrenalin in Marelle.

"Don't worry." Bella added. 'You're good."

There was a sideways glance between Marelle and Jacob that Bella did not see as she inserted the DVD and closed the tray.

"Right." She said, remote control in hand as she sat back against the armchair. She looked across at Marelle and Jacob, both sitting forwards on their seats, earnestly looking at the blue TV screen. Bella smiled to herself and pressed 'play'.

The geek had gone to town. There was a red screen up front with the name of the pub on it, followed by the date spinning in from the right. Then it opened with some general shots of people in the pub; close-up and quite grainy with what sounded like overly false crowd noise put over the top. Bella giggled. Marelle looked slightly amused but Jacob was stoic and expressionless.

Then a yellow screen appeared which said, 'Jacob performs No Way Home'.

"How did he know the name of the song?!" Jacob exclaimed.

Bella shrugged. "Maybe because in a few seconds you sing it?" She asked sarcastically. "Perhaps he knows the song. I don't know."

"Jesus." Jacob whispered under his breath, but Marelle heard it. She placed a hand on his thigh.

"He's done a good job hasn't he? Considering he only had what I'd filmed on the phone." Bella commented.

Then there he was. In a black t-shirt with some or other symbol like a star on the front in white – he had still had it on when she had run into him in the car park and brought him home … and the leather trousers with a belt that had a fancy silver buckle. He'd had those on that night too, but she hadn't commented or asked why. It was a small point in a precious moment.

Jacob took the microphone out of the stand, looked slightly sheepish, looked at the crowd then turned to the guy hosting the karaoke as he put the track on.

"Ok guys – it's a classic. "The host said over the microphone he was holding. "Go on mate, give it some!"

The music started, Jacob took the microphone in his hand, swished the lead out of the way like he'd done it a million times then looked out over the crowd with a look that might have been commanding a Roman legion. Then he looked to a couple of people at the front and cracked a smile. Slowly raising his left hand until his finger was exactly the same height as the top of his head, reaching it at the very point the lyrics cut in. Jacob began singing. His voice was clear, and he had the ability to project it and cut through the crowd noise; it was strong and broken at the same time – holding the lyrics like they were his own words, sung so often. And he had a presence; commanded attention just in this little pub at a simple karaoke, he exhibited that craft of holding the audience in his hand, not needing to look at the karaoke screen; knowing the song so well and so true.

Marelle watched him switch into the performance she now knew he was totally capable of.

The crowd was egging him on, encouraging his flamboyance up a notch further as Marelle watched Jacob on the TV screen – singing and performing this song with the full intention of walking out of that pub and jumping off a bridge.

The crowd loved him. Marelle knew the song now – she had heard it before. Seb had played it in his feeble excuse for a band when he had been at college; Jacob had heard a recording of it in her car. He had played it with a chuckle and a by-the-way comment at the time. Now it made sense; now it all fell into place. She looked briefly at him now sitting beside her – watching intently.

The crowd cheered, adored him, touched him, high-fived him.

"Well the guy's a professional!" the host exclaimed. "We'll get him back in a bit to do another one ..."

Then the film just stopped, and the screen went blue again.

Bella chuckled. "Told you he was pretty good." She turned and smiled at them. Marelle smiled back; Jacob was still straight mouthed.

"Didn't know you had it in you Jacob!" Bella continued, ejecting the DVD.

He gave a little laugh.

"You haven't shown this to anyone, have you?" He asked.

"No!" Bella laughed. "Only the geek kid but he's not bothered."

She replaced the disc in the jewel case and held it aloft. Jacob went to take it, but Marelle beat him to it.

"Don't let him have it, he'll destroy it!" She exclaimed with a grin. I might want to watch it again!"

"I think he's done that before." Bella remarked. "And I think he ought to give us a private performance right now."

"Oh no. I'm not doing that!" Jacob shook his head.

"Ah go on." Bella teased.

Jacob shook his head with a grin.

"Nope!" he insisted.

Bella went to say something but decided against it. She looked pensive for a moment then smiled, "but all good fairy tales have a happy ending – don't they? The girl marries the prince, and they all live happily ever after!" She grinned but Marelle looked into her eyes, and she knew that Bella was thinking of what she had told her earlier.

With that smile Bella placed a hand on Jacob's knee, levered herself up from the floor before sitting herself back down in the armchair.

"So what's the plan?"

"Plan?" Marelle questioned.

"Yeah – for the wedding. You must have a plan?"

"Not yet Bella." Marelle chuckled. "One step at a time."

"You've got to have a really big bash – with *everything*!" She exclaimed enthusiastically. "I really need a mega party!"

"You're on a constant party!" Marelle commented.

"Yeah – one weekender after another." Jacob added, surprisingly joining in with the conversation. "When's the next one?"

"Only one more this year." She said. "Then no more till next year. This last one is usually pretty good though – they normally have some better acts on." She explained. "It's up on the north Norfolk coast ... wanna come?" She raised an eyebrow cheekily.

"Might do." Jacob replied, equally as cheekily.

His response animated Bella. "Really! Really!? – Oh, go on – it would be great with both of you there. The last one is normally totally mental. They had a foam party last year!"

Marelle laughed and shook her head. "I don't think so."

"I wouldn't mind seeing some live music – kind of reincarnated the student in me with the karaoke ..." Jacob mused, and Marelle suddenly got his drift.

"Oh there will be some great bands." Bella enthused. "Better than the last one; they were scraping the barrel there. Your performance at karaoke topped anything we saw and that's the truth!"

Jacob smiled. "Who's there at the next one then?" He asked.

"I don't know without checking. I want to go but no-one else can come on that weekend – but if you two will – well that will be epic!" She turned to Marelle. "Have a look on your computer – to see who's there."

"I don't even know what to look for Bella." Marelle commented.

"We'll let me then!"

Ten minutes later they were huddled around Marelle's laptop.

"Here you go." Bella gestured. "It's a Friday night, Saturday and most of Sunday. They'll have the best acts on Saturday – most people go home around lunchtime on Sunday ..." She scrolled around on the laptop and then began reading. 'Ultra, DJ Wyx, Snack Dragons. Gollo, The Glow, Yellow Son, Supertastics and Four Point Two." She announced. "Oh I like Four Point Two ... they're pretty good."

Marelle looked at Jacob, but he did not acknowledge her.

"Sounds good." He said.

Bella lifted her eyes to him and gave a breathy little laugh. "Hey, just listen to him, one karaoke song and suddenly he's an expert!"

It was just under six weeks away. Marelle really didn't fancy it but knew Jacob had his reasons.

"Are you coming then?" Bella grinned. "We can book it right here, look ..."

"Jacob turned to Marelle. "What do you think?"

"Oh wow! Marriage has changed you!" Bella remarked.

"If you want." Marelle shrugged back to him.

So, with Bella's fingers moving deftly on the keyboard she went through the booking process with the ease and speed of someone who had done this a hundred times.

"Now shall we all share one room?" She asked. "If we book a 'family room' it's for four people sharing –it's cheaper."

"Erm, I'm not sure. Maybe separate ones?" Marelle replied.

"Oh, why? It's more fun with us all in together!" Bella exclaimed.

"Maybe a couple of doubles?" Marelle managed to catch Bella's gaze as she also nodded knowingly towards Jacob with a look on her face that reminded Bella that he could well either have nightmares or go walk about during the night. Bella pursed her lips as she looked away – "Oh, ok. Two rooms then –it's more expensive and there's a surcharge if we want them next to each other – we normally have just one room so I'm not sure how much more it will be ..." She scrolled.

"I'll pay." Jacob piped up. "My treat – for you – for being a good friend to Marelle and me."

Bella turned quickly and glared at him, quite taken aback at his words. She swallowed.

"No, it's..." She swallowed again. Marelle looked to her; she'd been touched by his words. "It's OK. I'll pay for me."

"No. I insist." Jacob stated. "Or we're not coming."

"You're good at giving ultimatums, aren't you?" She smiled. "OK. Give me your credit card then..."

"Debit card." He added.

"Debit card is fine."

He leaned forward slightly and pulled out the wallet that Marelle had seen many times. As he handed Bella the card Marelle asked:

"You were going to let me have your driving licence – so I can add you onto my insurance ..."

There was a look on his face that kind of said he didn't want to do that right now, but Marelle knew it was right there in his wallet. Reluctantly he took it out and handed it to her while he looked earnestly over Bella's shoulder.

Marelle took the licence, looked at it briefly then turned it over in her hand. She laughed suddenly, without holding back which, maybe, she should have done but it was too late, she had let out the laugh in exclamation and Bella had turned to look at her. Jacob was still staring at the screen, a look of resignation on his face.

"Oh. I'm sorry!" Marelle giggled. Her hand over her mouth. "But Jacob – what is *that*?"

The photo of him was awful – driving licence photos along with passport ones – were always bad – but this was an exception. He looked like a seventies thug – extremely short hair with a thin moustache and beard combination. You could see it was Jacob, but it was not a good look!

"Let me see!" Bella scrabbled for the licence which Marelle showed to her and she laughed too.

"Oh my God! Who got you ready?"

"Sorry Jacob." Marelle grinned. "But – what possessed you?"

"Alright! I know." He sighed. "I was 'experimenting' with different looks at the time." He explained with a wink to Marelle, and she immediately understood.

"Oh, I see!" she replied, still smiling.

"That's not good. I hope you never get asked to produce that!" Bella laughed.

"Well you're forgiven but please – don't ever experiment with that look again!" Marelle said.

He sighed with a smile. "I'll try not to."

That picture fueled their mirth for much of the rest of the evening. Jacob took it in his stride and didn't seem to be bothered by it. He was relaxed and happy and as long as he remained that way, Marelle was happy.

EIGHT

With Bella in the back-room, Marelle slid into bed with Jacob that night and straight into his arms. She had spent the evening slightly worried about the fact that they had just booked onto a weekender finale at some God forsaken old holiday camp on the North Norfolk coast – with Bella. Jacob had instigated it due to the presence of Yellow Son as part of his plan he had revealed to Marelle. But she was concerned that firstly, he didn't know what he was letting himself in for and secondly, if he could cope with it all. Yes, he was changed but while he was Jacob, he still courted that vulnerability. Marelle huddled to him.

"Was there just a tiny bit of Ezza in that performance in the pub" She asked.

"A bit." He replied. "Hopefully not enough for anyone to actually recognise me – I didn't realise it was being distributed!"

"It'll be fine ... Bella has it on her phone and some geek kid edited it – he won't have had any interest in it – probably only interested in whatever Bella bribed him with!"

"Mmm. You don't know." He mused. "If someone starts pointing a finger prematurely I'm scuppered ..."

"Well why did you do it if you are worried about someone recognising you?"

"Because on that night I didn't care. I wasn't planning to be around to face the consequences." He replied, his chin against the top of her head.

Marelle winced. Her comment had been flippant – she had let that fact slip her mind for a moment. She wriggled against him a little in an uncomfortable response.

'This weekender thing ..." She began. "Do you really think it's a good idea?" You don't know what it'll be like."

He laughed gently. "It will be fine. I just want to see what they're doing."

Marelle sighed, not tired, she stared into the darkness ahead of her with bright, open eyes.

'What if he sees you – Chas? Is it?"

"He won't see me. Not till I want him to."

Somehow, she totally believed him. She lay her head against his chest and listened to his heart beating. Marelle had always said there were many layers to Jacob – all of which she had worked hard to peel away one by one to slowly reveal what she had now. But with that came the realisation that there were still many more and what she had now was still a long way off the final article.

Waking up curled next to Jacob, her head against his shoulder, she lifted it to look at him. He was sound asleep, and she smiled to herself as she gazed at him in perfect slumber. For a few seconds she stared at his sleeping, relaxed face; his chest gently rise and fall. Marelle pushed herself up, onto her belly and rose up the bed slowly. Jacob took a deeper breath and stirred slightly at her movement. With a cheeky grin Marelle lowered her face to his and kissed him on the lips. Jacob responded then opened his eyes as she looked down on him with a smile. He grinned.

"Are you two decent?" A voice called with a simultaneous knock on the bedroom door. "Cos even if you're not I'm a coming in anyway!" Bella sang.

And she did. Literally seconds after the handle and opening the door wide, backing into the room. Marelle turned and wrapped the sheet around her, Jacob pushed himself up on his elbows.

"Morning!" Bella smiled. "I've brought you two breakfast in bed."

Bella breezed in, a tray in her hands, pushing the door with her hip. She was fully dressed and came in with a huge smile. Marelle twisted herself around and sat up, pulling the sheet against her. Jacob sat up, yawning and scratching his head.

"Oh God! You two are just so adorable!" Bella giggled. "Champagne breakfast in bed!" She enthused, putting the tray down on the bedside cabinet. "I would have done smoked salmon, but I know you don't like fish Jacob – so it's bacon sandwiches and Champagne!"

"Oh Bella!" Marelle said, "You didn't have to."

" did! This weekend is a celebration." She grinned, then added. "Of many things."

"Well join us ..." Jacob said, sitting up a bit more.

"No, I'll leave you to it ..."

"No. Join us I insist!" Jacob mocked.

Bella smiled. "Well, mine is downstairs. Hang on, I'll go and get it." She gave a little grin. "Thank you." And she dashed down the stairs as Marelle grabbed a t-shirt and knickers which she slipped into. Picking up a t-shirt from the chair beside the bed she could just reach, she tossed it to Jacob.

"I'm ok." He said.

"Put it on. I get jealous if you're naked in front of my best friend!"

He grinned and slipped the t-shirt over his head.

Bella thundered up the stairs and returned with a plate of bacon sandwiches and a glass of Champagne.

"I've never had bacon sandwiches and Champagne together." Jacob commented.

"Me neither!" Bella laughed. "But I could get used to it!"

"This will go straight to my head." Marelle added.

"Then eat the bacon sandwich – it'll soak it all up." Bella advised.

Jacob laughed.

There were a few minutes silence as they all ate. Bella sitting cross-legged at Marelle's end of the bed, Jacob staring down at his plate and Marelle glancing at both of them in turn. She smiled quietly to herself and washed the doorstep of bread down with a mouthful of Champagne.

Bella suddenly looked up. She raised her glass. "Hey! Hey!" She exclaimed. "A toast."

They both looked at her.

"To the two most beautiful people who were both meant to be together – forever and ever!" She smiled.

"Oh Bella!" Marelle smiled softly.

"No. I mean it! She stated. "I have never seen you like this Marelle – I've never seen you this content – or this focused. It's as if you were always meant to be together but fate had to bring you here. And Jacob – you are so perfect for Marelle! You are so sweet and kind and lovely. I've watched you change into the person you were meant to be. Marelle has made you complete and you two together are like pieces of a jigsaw!" She proclaimed. "I love you both! I really do!"

She smiled but there were languid tears in her eyes. She lowered them and drank the Champagne she had in the glass. 'Now." She continued. "We need to get the wedding planned!"

"Not yet Bella!" Marelle laughed.

"But promise I can be there – I don't want you two to go off and do something in secret then turn up and just say 'we've got married'. You're not doing that – I'm not letting you."

"We won't do that." Marelle confirmed. "Will we Jacob?"

"No, we won't do that." He sighed. "But if I'm honest it does sound appealing!"

Later that day after Bella had left ,Marelle was in the bedroom gazing at the engagement ring on her finger. There had been a lot of hugging when Bella had gone but ten minutes before she had taken Marelle to one side in the kitchen and said

"You know it might just be worth seeing if Jacob needs a little help. What you told me – he may be over it but it's not something you should gloss over – keep an eye on him?"

"Of course I will." Marelle had replied. "But I think he's OK now."

Now she stood in the bedroom, looking at the ring. It had been Jacob's mother's engagement ring; given to her by his father. By the account that Mrs. Avison had given, Jacob's father had been besotted by Jeannie – this was the ring he had given her to seal that love. This very ring. Marelle had often wondered what it actually meant to die of a broken heart. Now she understood. She knew she could never love anyone the way she loved Jacob; if he was taken away from her, she knew she would not be able to carry on. She had never felt like this with her previous partner – never – not even remotely close. If Jacob was taken from her then her own heart would fail, and she would too. Now she understood why Jacob's father had turned to drink to get him through the years he faced without the one person he truly loved. And now the mark of that true love between Jeannie and Ezekiel was on *her* finger, passed down to continue that bond and seal *their* love. The sheer weight of that was on her finger now and she felt the pull of it – yearning longing from the past – and the push of it forwards – into a new time in its life.

It was all so perfect, and everything fitted into its place. Except for Jacob's place in this world, who he was, who he wanted to be and what the future held for him. But no matter what, it was a ride she was with him on until the bitter end.

Letting Jacob leave the house alone in the morning to go to work was the hardest thing for her to do. Marelle guessed it must be like a parent letting their child out on their own for the very first time and being bombarded with every scenario of every hazard they could probably encounter. He had been back a week and in that week, he had not gone out of her sight – now he was leaving the house and she would have no vision of him until he walked back in that night.

"I'll take you." She offered.

"No, it's ok. I'll walk." He'd replied and even that filled her with dread. Jacob walking through the village on his own. God! She could imagine he'd be pelted with eggs or rotten cabbages; or whatever else they did in medieval times.

"I'll be fine." He reassured, a hand on her shoulder.

"Take the phone then ..." she bargained. "So we can at least talk."

He gave a resigned smile.

"Can I call you?" She asked.

He nodded. "I don't know what I'll be doing but I'll answer if I can."

That was normal Jacob but not what she wanted to hear.

"If you can come home for lunch then do, won't you?" She questioned even though she had fastidiously packed him sandwiches, crisps, chocolate and a couple of cans of cola like any good wife would have.

He smiled. "I'll see. I'll call you."

She nodded but was about to cry and he could see it.

"I'll be fine!" He stated. "And I'll be back later ... that's a promise." He kissed her and she took the opportunity to throw herself around him.

'It's only for a couple of weeks then I'll be told to sod off again." He remarked with a small laugh.

"You should have said no." Marelle sobbed against him.

"I like working at the farm." He added. "Be nice to do it for a bit."

She sniffed.

"Tell you what – take my driving licence and get me added on to your car insurance today ..." he fished in his pocket, and she stood away until he handed her his licence again. She looked at it and laughed, even if a little tearfully.

"See!" He smiled. "Knew that would have a use one day!"

Being on her own in the house again was even worse than it had been when Jacob was missing. She felt the emptiness more; she felt his absence more. Then she had always had the hope that he would return, now she had the fear that he wouldn't and the overwhelming rawness of what might have happened if she had not found him when she did.

But as she sat down at her computer to try and start some work, she had the distraction of the internet and the whole wealth of stuff she could search and watch of Jacob as Nat, as Ezza, which she did. Furiously googling his name with different words – Ezza Frost video; Ezza Frost performance; Ezza Frost singing ... the list was endless and the images she was presented with were also infinite. Videos of Jacob on stage; a couple of actual official videos made for their songs which were questionably cheesy! The more she watched, the more she was in awe of his ability to be Ezza on stage and Jacob off. For someone who she always saw as quiet and socially timid he could sure switch it all on once he was on the stage. She had seen a glimpse of this in Bella's little film – a glimmer of the old character, still there, still wanting to reveal itself. But then she found a film titled "Ezza Frost, last performance". It was a grainy, poor film, before phones had the ability, maybe it was filmed using a camcorder – she did not know. It was filmed from the audience, looking directly onto the stage, initially waiting for the band to come on.

There was a backdrop which looked like mountains, lit in shades of purple. She could hear the crowd noise, and it rose in volume when the band started to walk on stage. The lights were still low, and they were in silhouette. The music started, the guitars and drums kicked in. It seemed to go on forever and the crowd, getting restless, began to stamp their feet and clap until another figure appeared in silhouette and wandered slowly up to the microphone in the centre of the stage. The crowd went wild, the music burst, and the bright lights came up, picking out each member of the band in their own spot. But there, in the centre of the stage was Jacob – Ezza – in a white shirt – half tucked in, half out; open sleeves hanging over his hands which were clamped in tight fists around the mic stand, his head resting against them, and his eyes closed. He looked truly awful. His skin was grey and sweaty, almost puffy. Chas moved close to him, said something to him that appeared to go unheard.

Marelle got the impression that he should have started singing by now, but he did not move. Then he looked up, looked out into the crowd for a second as they bayed for him. He wiped his mouth with the back of his hand then turned and strode off again. The crowd whipped up at his exit, but Chas stepped in quickly and began singing. That was it; that was the end of Ezza.

The video stopped but she kept staring at the screen for a moment or two. That had upset her; that brought home to her how he must have felt. the despair and confusion that he could not control or hold back anymore.

And from there he had walked off, into the night, alone and unchallenged and he'd come back here – to a place he called home that he was soon to be evicted from and a life where he would become Jacob.

The more time she spent thinking about it all the more she realised how completely it all ran into one another. How everything he'd done had an impact on everything else – and how he could not just simply walk away from it. Marelle could understand his process but to achieve what he wanted to, one day he would have to let Jacob go.

At the moment he lived that lie with the vestiges of a previous life squirrelled away in the storage unit. Remnants of a life that was both his and not his.

She suddenly felt tearful and sat staring into space, thinking about him. In her mind she removed him from Ezza – that was too much to bear just now. She'd read the outpourings of grief at Ezza's demise; the anger, the utter sense of loss some people had felt. She'd read things online and knew there were still fans who mourned the day he died, who remembered him on that day and what he had meant to them – people he did not know and would not ever know.

Marelle picked up her phone and called him. She was already panicking that he would not answer but, surprisingly, he did, quite quickly.

"Hi" She breathed, relieved.

"Hi." He said. "Are you alright?"

"Yeah, I'm fine." She said, overly cheekily – so much so that it sounded false.

"You sound upset."

He'd noticed and that made it worse.

"No, it's OK. I'm just being stupid, just being emotional …" She half composed herself.

"Why?"

She almost gasped that he actually had to ask *why* but perhaps it was better that he did.

"Oh, I don't know." She shrugged. "Are you ok?"

"All good." He replied.

God! She loved his voice on the phone.

"Where are you?"

"Lambs Lane." He answered.

"Where's Lambs Lane?"

"On the left-hand side, behind the church."

"Oh." She replied. "What are you doing?"

"Rolling."

"Rolling?" She asked, perplexed.

He gave a little laugh. "Yeah, rolling a field – just driving a tractor with big rollers on the back."

"Oh I see." But she didn't. "Are you coming home for lunch?"

"No, it's too awkward to stop right now …"

She sighed. "Ok."

"What are you doing?" He asked.

"Oh, erm … just been doing some research." It wasn't a lie. "Missing you!" She added.

He laughed. "Missing me! I'm nothing but trouble!" He joked, but she wondered.

"But you're *my* trouble!" She smiled.

"I'll be back later." He said.

"Ok." Marelle answered. "Be careful."

She *heard* him smile. He sounded happy – how much was attributable to him having found his new freedom or being back at the farm, working. She was not sure, but Jacob was happy.

Each new day was difficult when he set off in the morning but each day, she felt a tiny bit of that painful anxiety melt away. Not enough to allow her to relax about him being at large all day but enough to dampen that deep intrusive ache brought on by the adrenalin coursing through her when he left the house each day.

At the beginning of the second week she had walked into the kitchen first thing to find him there – in his black ripped jeans and fleece, tapping a spoon on a mug and quietly singing to himself. Marelle smiled.

"One of yours?" She asked.

He grinned with a sigh. "No – just something I came up with, but we never actually ever played it."

"I need to hear more of your stuff." She commented.

"Oh, I'm sure you will, in time – hopefully live!" He said.

"Haven't you got anything – like a CD or something?"

He shook his head. "No."

Marelle poured boiling water into the mug he was tapping.

She remembered the day she'd walked up to his caravan and found him burning stuff. He had played her a CD on a Walkman – they'd shared the earphones and listened to it together. It was beautiful. Then he'd tossed it into the flames when she'd finished.

'The CD you played me ... the one you burned when we sat up at the caravan that day ..." she asked. "Was that you?"

He nodded, a little sheepishly.

"That was beautiful." She said.

'That was me, on my own – aspirations of a little solo project – once ... a long time ago. But I'm not good enough on my own."

"I'd say what I heard was pretty fucking fantastic!"

"You're biased!" He said. Smiled to himself. "Chas didn't like it. Said it would ruin the reputation of the band if I put out shit like that!" He laughed.

"Charming!"

"No, he was probably right. We were a rock band. If I started singing more ballady stuff it would cause all kinds of chaos."

"Seems like Chas was a bit *controlling*?"

"No, no – not at all. Just ... focused." He replied after a moment's thought. "Straight talking – calls a spade a spade and not scared to put you straight." Then he turned to her with a smile. "You'll like him."

And off he went to work again. Marelle kissed him goodbye and held him tightly as she always did; looked into his eyes and gave him a smile even though inside this ritual broke her apart every day.

Jacob spoke of reclaiming Ezza in a positive tone; in a way that felt like he had already made the initial steps and with a confidence that Chas would welcome him with open arms. That remained to be seen – she realised that but wasn't sure that he did.

Marelle was working later that morning when the doorbell rang. Immediately, she looked at the clock then got up; it was almost lunchtime – she would call Jacob shortly. By the shape of the body through the frosted glass in the front door as she approached Marelle knew it was Catchpole. She opened the door.

"Hello." She smiled.

"Morning." He returned. "Is Jacob here?"

"No, he's at work. He's back at the farm."

He nodded. "Ok. Is he back later?"

"Yes, he'll be back about six. Do you want me to get him to call you?" She offered.

"Erm, yes, please – if you could. I need to have a chat with him."

"What about?"

"Just some questions about the discovery in the garden over there."

"Have you identified the body?" Marelle questioned.

"No further developments as yet." He replied.

Marelle raised her chin a little and stared at him. She swallowed.

"You said about a DNA test before?" she asked.

"Yes, it may come to that … if he is willing to. He did say he was."

"Well …" she began. "I know he said he was willing, but I think it may not be the best idea …"

Catchpole tilted his head slightly. "No? Why is that?"

Marelle took a breath through her nose, she didn't really want this conversation on her doorstep but then again, she didn't want to invite him in.

'If I tell you then this is in confidence." She stated. "Ok?"

"Ok." He nodded but she only had his word and did not know how much she could trust that. "He tried to take his own life a couple of weeks ago …"

Catchpole raised his eyebrows a little in reaction but did not look shocked.

"He did?"

She nodded.

"How?"

'The whys and wherefores don't matter – luckily we got to him in time …"

'Has he spoken to anyone? Is he getting help?'

"He's fine, but I'm not having this conversation with you to speak about that." She stated. "But if he takes a DNA test and he *is* related to that second body … how will that affect him? He does not know anything about this – he has told me that and I truly believe him – what will that do to him if he suddenly discovers that there are remains of another person buried in his childhood back garden and that those remains are related to him? How would that affect him given his already pretty fragile state of mind?" She asked – not liking her words or actually discussing this with the DCI. 'And anyhow, if he knows nothing about it then why does it matter?"

"I understand what you are saying." He nodded. "Taking a DNA test may not be the best course of action and, at the moment, it's not something I am going to push for ... but the point of a DNA test is that it may enable us to identify the body."

"But it won't, will it? It won't *identify* the body – it will just say if it is related to Jacob or not. It is then going to lead to a million more questions he cannot answer. If it's not, then there will be a million different questions no one will ever be able to answer. It's just stuff he doesn't need to know."

Catchpole sighed. "It's my duty to find out what happened to that person – that *child*."

"I know. I know." Marelle replied. "But it's *my* duty to keep him alive – he's ok at the moment but I'm not sure a DNA test and its implications won't push him over the edge."

Catchpole stared at her with a tired gaze. "But he did say he was willing – he may *want* to know – it's his wishes we will go along with."

"That may be so, but I'm just giving you the heads up. I don't think it will be wise to pursue that just now."

She looked into his grey eyes. He stared back. "Is that a new ring on your finger?" He asked.

That question took her aback, she immediately broke her stare and fumbled, sheepishly, with the ring.

"Yes." She smiled. "Jacob proposed to me."

He smiled. 'Congratulations!"

Marelle gave a small, almost embarrassed, smile in return.

"I'll bear your words in mind." He said. "On second thoughts I may not be around later so I will try and catch Jacob later in the week. Is he working every day?"

She nodded.

"Ok, I will see if I can pop round when he's here then.

Catchpole left. Marelle breathed a long sigh – she had thought about this, and her words were true. She did not truly know how a DNA test may affect him – even though he had verbally agreed to it. She knew he had called Catchpole's bluff in doing so – never in a million years would he agree to that but his upfront casual agreement to comply was a shield to fend its propensity away, together with her attempt this morning. If she was confident Catchpole would not press for a DNA test, then she could relax a little about it. Also, at the back of her mind was the thought that a positive test would be bad enough, but a negative one would be worse.

She did not mention Catchpole's visit to Jacob when he returned home. There was no point, and he would be apt to worry about it. Things were, for the moment at least, on a pretty even keel and she wanted to keep it that way.

Jacob was happy; he liked working at the farm without Sam to cheerlead the others. He was left alone. Sometimes Marelle believed that there had been a massive sea change that night in the pub car park when she had finally found him after his three-week disappearance. Jacob had changed so much. He was the person she had always wished he would become – not only was he the Jacob she had nurtured and loved but he was also *happy.* He often had a smile on his face; would often joke and play with her until they fell about in laughter, and when he *let* her look into his eyes now there was a calm and walm solace within them.

The autumn evenings were pulling in quickly and despite the days still being fueled with the cooler sun of the turning season the days were ending sooner and the nights were coming quicker. It was too late in the year to wander around the airfield in the evening, so they left it to the barn owl, the hares and the deer for now.

This evening he had gone out to the caravan in her garden. At the moment it had no power connected to it, so he took a torch. Marelle followed him out there and stood on the top step in the doorway.

"What are you doing?" She asked.

"Just opening it up. It stinks if you leave it all closed up for ages."

"You can connect it up to the power in the house if you want to, you know."

"Can do, but I don't intend using it at the moment." He turned to look at her over his shoulder, his face half lit by the torch, a grin on it.

She smiled.

"I'll just leave the door open for a bit." He sighed, turning his back against the worktop in the kitchen area and holding the torch in front of him. Marelle came up the steps and into the caravan. She walked in and sighed. "Where did it come from?" She asked, looking around herself.

"I bought it from a guy in the next village."

"So they chucked you out of the house, but you still kept working for them?"

He nodded.

She smiled and walked up to stand next to him, close to him, her thigh touching his, her shoulder against him.

"How come you were so fucking cool about it all?" She shook her head.

He gave a small laugh. "I had to be. If I was going to carry on with being Jacob, I had to turn it all down. Nat could be up to eleven sometimes."

"Up to eleven?"

"Yeah, over the top, too loud ... not all of the time. Looking back, it was either off or on – nothing in between Jacob had to simmer between a one and a two."

She smiled. "Can I handle Nat?"

"He's gone." He whispered. "At least *that* Nat has. The real Nat is mostly Jacob .... You can handle him."

She smiled. "Can I?"

He turned to her, took her around the waist and pulled her to him. "Yeah." He said in a soft voice.

With a laugh they moved to the partitioned off bedroom, through the concertina door and onto the perfect, pristine, made-up bed.

He'd left the torch on the worktop, so the bedroom was unlit. The curtains were drawn but a gap let in the moonlight from the airfield. With a laugh he swung her round and let her down on to the bed, hanging himself above her, suspended on his outstretched arms. She giggled. He had a serious look on his face as he bent down to kiss her. It wasn't a playful peck on the lips; it was full on and flourished rapidly into a passionate embrace that had intention. Marelle could feel him against her, his mouth against hers he undid his jeans and slipped them down. Marelle had yoga pants on so she could easily slip them away with one hand, her other hand around his neck. His open belt jangled against the floor with his jeans around his ankles and the caravan moved with them until the torch crashed off the worktop in the kitchen area. But the background noises were just that as she heard both his and her own breath loud in her ear and head. Her heart was beating its wings to be set free, and her teeth grazed his cheek as he gave her what her body was now yearning for.

Jacob lay himself upon her, kissed her forehead then lay his head next to hers, breathing slowly and deeply. Marelle placed her arms around him and squeezed him to her.

"You've really never had a proper relationship?" She whispered. "I can't believe that!"

"No." He said "Never – been living here for the past ten years ... resigned myself to that."

"... until I came along!" She giggled.

"I guess you've had a few boyfriends?" he asked.

She laughed and slapped him on the shoulder. "Hey! What do you think I am?!"

"I mean – "He stated, his voice muffled as he turned his face against her. "You are being such an attractive young lady!"

"You did not!" She slapped him again. He laughed against her. She pushed him off, laughing. He sat up, pulled up his jeans and hitched them under his bottom.

"No shame in it." He said, "We're all human. I've been a naughty boy in the past!"

Marelle wriggled back into her own leggings in the moon washed twilight. "... and what does that mean?" She smiled, curling herself around him from behind.

"Well, I was a singer in a group – we had groupies ..." He trailed off.

Marelle tensed; she felt a pang of jealousy spike within her. This conversation had gone in a way she didn't really want it to but despite the avarice she felt, she wanted to know.

"Did you ...?" she asked.

He paused, yawned. Rested his elbows on his knees and lowered down. "Yeah. Couple of times – in the beginning – until I learned."

"Learned what?"

"Keep a distance!" he said quietly in the darkness. Jacob sighed. "Sorry."

"It's ok." She whispered, still curled around him. "I'm jealous but I understand. We all have a past."

"Yeah, but sorry – I shouldn't have told you. It's not something I'm proud of.

"We're not keeping secrets any more Jacob, are we?" Marelle asked in the dark.

"Aah it's not a secret." He sighed. "It's just inconsequential; it doesn't mean anything."

She sat up behind him, leant her arms against his back and hung her head over his shoulder.

"Good because I was waiting for you!"

"Oh, were you?" He laughed. "Were you!" Turning and grabbing her around the waist to pull her onto his lap. She lay across his knees looking up at him with a grin.

"Yeah." She said. "You won't find anyone else like me!"

NINE

Two weeks on Marelle had grown used to Jacob going to work and being apart from her each day. She still caught her breath every now and then however, still stopped and had a minor panic about the distance between them. But each night he'd come home with a smile and a gentle kiss, and her heart had beaten slowly again.

On the second Friday, two weeks in, he came home and wandered into her kitchen. He had come across the airfield tonight; sometimes he let her pick him up; most days he walked. He gave her one of those rare and beautiful smiles when he stepped into the kitchen.

"So, are you finished now?" She asked, "you said two weeks, didn't you?"

"Not sure. Wright said he would call me if he wanted me in next week..."

"What, with Sam back?" She asked, a little disturbed that the cycle would begin again. Jacob shrugged. "Not sure. We'll see".

With nights getting darker there was less opportunity to be outside and Marelle thought this may have a detrimental effect on him. Surprisingly however he was happy to settle down on the sofa and watch TV. She liked it when he did that, and she could pull her legs up and cuddle next to him. He amazed her that he liked to watch a film – or documentary on TV; he seemed to have a knowledge of films that she had not realised, thinking such things would be too trivial for him. When she commented on it, he replied

"How else do you think I passed ten years of winter nights alone in the caravan?"

His comment had made her smile but at the same time made her sad. He could still be in that position and would have been forever.

He spent Saturday in her garden. Cleared the caravan out again and cleaned it then ended up with the bike in bits in the relatively warm sun of an autumn afternoon. Marelle sat on the bench with a can of drink in her hand; they'd been sharing it up to now.

"I may bring one of the other bikes home." He said, thoughtfully." If I think I can get away with it ... I think this girl has probably had her final fling."

"You can use my car. You're on the insurance now." Marelle told him.

"Oh, OK. Thank you." He smiled. "Still like one of the bikes to have a blast on though!"

That remark did not please her and neither did his suggestion on Sunday they should go for a walk up to the weir. It was a place, if she was honest, that frightened her. From the initial time when Jacob had said he often swam there; when he told her that he came close to drowning there as a child and memories of the night he had sleep-walked there, with her in tow, and scared the life out of her when she had thought he was about to jump into the raging and broiling waters. The idea of re-living that place did not fill her with the joy that a pleasant walk on a bright and sunny October day should have done. Still, she got the sense he would go alone if she did not go with him – so she went.

They wandered along the tracks towards the weir. Everything looked more overgrown than before, and the autumn bounty of hedgerow fruits was burdening the brambles and shrubs with its weight. Jacob walked along, picking blackberries and eating them.

"Is that safe?" She asked."

"Of course it is!" He replied with a grin." Try one!"

She stopped and tentatively picked a blackberry from the clingy fingers of the bramble.

"Used to live on those this time of the year when I was a kid." He smiled.

Marelle wasn't overly impressed, even though he explained she chosen a red one when a black one would have been riper and sweeter! Shortly after he went up through the damp, wooded part, rising with the ground to the ridge.

The drop on the other side of the ridge led down to the weir and the so called 'calm pool' where Jacob admitted to swimming sometimes. She could hear the rush of the water below – it sounded much louder than she had remembered from previous visits.

"Been a lot of rain lately." Jacob commented. "It will be pretty strong down there."

"You're not planning on going in, are you?" she asked, slightly shocked, looking at the side of his head as he focused on the sound and the weir below.

"No!" He said. "It's a bit too cold this time of the year."

"Oh, I thought you said it was fine! When you made me get in there you thought it was so funny that I was so cold!"

Marelle remembered the evening he had somehow persuaded her – against all of her better judgement – to skinny dip in the calm pool on the other side of the weir. The coldness of the water had completely taken the breath out of her, and she had floundered until he had grabbed her, hugged her in the water and placed her feet on the upslope of the bank.

"Well that was in the summer – it *was* reasonably warm then ..." He said with a laugh.

They started down the bank. Jacob walking confidently while Marelle kept a hand on the flexible trunks of the young trees – only too aware of the sudden vertical drop into the water at the bottom of the slope. Jacob was ahead of her, and she could not help but think of the night she had followed him down this slope – unbeknown to her sleepwalking – with a fearful hold on the back of his t-shirt.

Now he approached the gate which proclaimed 'Danger. No Entry. Deep Water.' And cocked a leg over it. Marelle negotiated it too by climbing carefully over and followed him down the last stretch of the slope to where he stood on the flat facing bricks of the top of the wall, above the twenty-foot sheer drop of bricks beneath them into the angry, raging white water.

Jacob stood there, looking down. He'd played here as a child and had a fascination with it.

"It's a bit lively today!" He commented. "There's a lot of water in there ..."

Marelle stood back a bit, glanced down too. She did not like Jacob standing there looking down like that. The roar of the plunging, diverging water was loud; as mesmerizing as it had been before, instinctively, she placed a hand on his arm.

"I don't like it here." She said.

"It's ok. If you're careful." He reassured.

Jacob stood there too long looking down at the water. She wanted him to move away and was glad when he did, stepping to his left.

"Let's have a look at the calm pool." He suggested.

Just as he turned a small rock came crashing down the bank, bouncing slightly, between the two of them. Marelle scuttled sideways and made an exclamation as the rock flew over the edge and fell into the turmoil below with a sound that was not heard above the roar of the water.

She was laughing at her own nervousness, reaching out a hand to Jacob as he turned his head to look along the bank where the rock had come from. She mirrored his action and there, on the incline stood Sam, dressed in camouflage clothing with a shotgun. Marelle gripped Jacob's sleeve as Jacob stared at Sam; and Sam stared at Jacob.

"Let go." She said.

He did not hear her or chose not to, or to challenge her plea.

"Sam?" He said instead. A single word. An utterance of his name which had compassion in it and a tentative call to ascertain his mood.

Sam did not answer him. He stopped his descent and stared at them. His face red and blotchy, solemn. As he held the shotgun across himself it was hard to determine whether it was anger or sorrow across his face.

"What are you doing up here?" Jacob asked.

"Could ask you the same." He replied succinctly.

"I'm always up here. Not seen you here before." Jacob continued the conversation.

"Shooting squirrels." He said.

"Oh they won't hurt you – leave them be." Jacob replied."

"I could shoot you. Both of you. No-one would know then I'd be gone ..."

Jacob laughed but there was a nervousness about it. "Don't be silly Sam. You don't want to do that. They would find us and that would be your life ruined. Honestly, I'm not worth it!"

Marelle clutched his arm as they stood between the crashing water of the weir and Sam with a shotgun.

"I've always dreamed of this moment." Sam said, quietly.

"Hell Sam. You don't want even be considering this ... all's not lost. We can talk about everything – I don't bear any grudges." Jacob offered.

"I do." Marelle whispered. Jacob ignored her.

Sam lifted the gun away from himself. It was a shotgun, it had two cartridges in the barrel or none at all.

"There's nothing I want to talk about with you." Sam said.

"Sam." Jacob laughed. "You don't want to be pointing that gun at us like that – do you. Think about how your Mum and Dad would feel if you did anything silly – "

"You don't know me! You don't know my family!" He exclaimed, suddenly inflamed and holding the gun in both hands. "Get out of here! Go! I want to be by myself!"

Marelle tugged at Jacob. "I think maybe we should go Jacob." She urged.

"Go!" He exclaimed again, pointing the gun. "I don't want you here!"

"Jacob!" She urged.

Jacob half turned to her, flattened a hand as if to halt her. Turned back to Sam with his hand still flat.

"Leave me alone!" Sam shouted, starting forwards he slipped on the slope. With the gun in both hands he did not reflexly reach out to grab a tree, but his feet slid on the sloping, loose surface.

It happened so quickly. Sam slipped, lost his footing; the gun went off. Marrelle ducked and screamed, letting go of Jacob's arm. Sam pitched past them, grabbing at Jacob, pulling him with his weight towards the edge of the wall and the sheer twenty-foot drop into the water. Marelle, realising Jacob had been ripped from her grasp, spun round on her knees in the dirt, screaming *"Jacob"*. He was holding onto a small tree, right at the edge, looking down into the turbulent waters. Sam was nowhere to be seen.

Before she even got to him, Jacob was kicking off his boots.

"No!" She yelled at him. "Jacob no! Please - you will kill yourself – please - you *promised* that dream would not come true!" She cried before she scuttled to him but before she managed to place her outstretched hand on his arm, he dived into the water below.

Marelle grabbed a young tree; stopped herself mid lunge from following the both of them. She cried and looked down to the water. If it had not been so cold it looked like boiling, angry, rolling waters. Pounding itself against the wall of the river and the outlet to the stream below. Recoiling back on itself in white, foaming explosions of water. The roar of it all filled her ears.

"Jacob!" She screamed in a sob with so much force it felt like she had scraped the lining from her throat with the mere sound of it.

Twenty feet below both Sam and Jacob had entered the water, but she could not see either of them and in that moment she could sense death looming above her. So close and yet so far; she had finally achieved what she wanted so much but now the dream she had endured, with Jacob being on the slab in the morgue after drowning, seemed to be coming true.

He could not swim in that; he could not save Sam from that. As a child he'd almost drowned in there only to be saved by his best friend Frankie. Now he was facing that again and she was the only person here who stood a chance of dragging him from the water this time. The conclusion of that dream, that nightmare, was now solely in her hands.

She held onto the tree and looked down into the raging torrent. Marelle could swim, but was not a strong swimmer, Jacob had also said the water was too cold. Maybe she could summon some superhuman courage and strength. Both of their lives depended upon it.

Not really knowing what to expect or what to do, she poised herself on the edge. One hand still clutching the tree looking down the sheer drop below. She would die alongside him or save him. There was no middle ground as she did not want to stand here and watch him die. Marelle took a breath and braced herself, looked down, still with one hand on the tree. Then she noticed a dark shape in the water and realised it was Jacob. He was thrashing in the current, trying to keep his head above water but managing to move very arduously back towards the wall where the flow of the river plunged to the lower level. Marelle clung to the tree and watched him. He was struggling; she could tell. The water battered him pushing him closer to the wall and the edge of the weir where the water dropped from the higher level. He would not get out from there; the sheer slippery wall was twenty feet high. If he came back towards her there was a lower wall and a grassy bank to her left, back towards the calm pool. He was a long way off that and moving further away from it as the seconds passed. Marelle cried to herself and clapped a hand over her mouth in horror.

Then she made out the second shape – not as clearly visible as Jacob was in his dark clothing. There, right up against the wall at the side was the camouflage clad shape of Sam. His body was flailing in the flow of water but not swimming and not fighting it. He seemed to be caught on something which was holding him there in that position. His limbs looked flaccid in the water and his head was flopping. Jacob was flung into him with the power of the water – both bodies now in the full wrath of it; raging water surging around and over them.

"Jacob." She yelled." Jacob!" But he did not hear her. He struggled with Sam's body using it to hold himself up and in place, obviously taking breaths between the pounding motion of the water. Constantly being rammed into Sam against the wall, over and over again until, suddenly, Jacob managed to free Sam's body and they both disappeared under the water. Marelle screamed as she watched. It seemed like seconds – minutes –longer than she could ever hold *her* breath.

"Jacob." She called, crying, sobbing, her face covered with snot and tears. Imagining their bodies trapped in a whirling and macabre ballet in the currents beneath the water as their breaths were ripped from them. Jacob told her this was dangerous; told her he had nearly drowned here as a child before he really understood what the danger was.

"Just leave Sam and get *yourself* out Jacob." She whispered to herself.

The time ticked by; there was no sign of either of them as the water below ravaged and boiled. She teetered on the edge gripping the tree staring across and into the water, shaking her head in disbelief it would end like this. Just as in her dream she would be looking down on Jacob's cold, lifeless body in the morgue.

"Jacob!" She screamed again, down towards the water, almost willing her voice to lift and drag him to the bank.

Then he appeared again, just beneath the water, thrashing to the surface, managed a fleeting gasp of air before the surface broke over his head again. Something was dragging him down, but he surfaced again, pushing Sam's body in front of him through the water. Jacob was exhausted; she could see that and having to swim against the wall of water, with Sam, was rendering him almost static. He made hardly any headway, appearing to stay in the same spot – probably only twenty feet from the grassy bank, but it might as well have been a mile.

Marelle let go of the tree, ran headlong across the slope towards the grassy bank between the calm pool and the weir.

"Jacob." She called as she went " – Jacob – here!"

She tried to watch as she ran but had to be careful about her own footing. Once she glanced and he disappeared beneath the water again – only to resurface quickly this time. Her feet reached the flat top of the grassy bank, and she looked down to see him, now swimming on his back with Sam in tow, making his way to the bottom of the bank. Marelle ran into the water, to her knees, grabbing out a hand to Jacob as he struggled towards her. He turned and pushed Sam in front of him, onto the bottom of the bank, shoving him out of the water just enough to make him stay there. Marelle ignored Sam; not caring if he was alive or dead – hands grabbing at Jacob in desperation as he let go of Sam and fell into the water onto his hands and knees.

Marelle grabbed him, dragged him, pushed him and manhandled him onto the bank himself as he gasped and paddled his feet in the grass. He lay on his back, his eyes closed, mouth open, his chest heaving in panicked breathing. Sam was on his front, but not moving. Marelle kneeled beside Jacob, touching him, patting his face, trying to hug him.

"Please "He gasped and pushed her away pretty gently as he had no strength left. She sat back and stared at him, crying.

" Is he –?" He asked.

"I don't know, and I don't care." She sobbed.

Jacob mustered strength and sat himself up, crawled around her and went to Sam. As he got to his prostrate form Sam stirred, kicked one leg then rolled onto his side. He coughed and spluttered, pushed himself up on his elbows. Jacob touched his arm

"– Sam – " He gasped in a raspy voice and coughed himself.

Sam recoiled away from him, found strength and scrambled to his feet, still coughing. He stumbled slightly, righted himself with a hand to the ground but stood unsteadily upright.

"Take your fucking hands off me. "He coughed, stepping backwards a couple of steps before he turned and stumbled off through the undergrowth.

"Sam!" Marelle yelled. "He's just saved your fucking life."

Jacob collapsed down on his back again and lay there; still gasping, coughing – his chest still heaving, eyes closed.

Marelle took his arm. She could feel his hands shaking – seconds later he began to tremble all over. Finally he sat up, shivering and shaking. Marelle held him.

"It's OK." He whispered. "It's the adrenaline and the cold. Give me a minute."

Marelle kneeled beside him, wanted to hug him but he was wet through.

"Take this off..." She tugged at his freezing cold sopping wet fleece.

He sat there, shaking, with his eyes closed. So she unzipped the neck and undressed him. He was too exhausted to fight and eventually she peeled the T-shirt beneath off him too.

"Put my jacket around you." She advised, slipping out of it and placing it round his shoulders.

"No, I'm OK. You'll be cold." He whispered; eyes still closed. He coughed a couple of times.

"I'm not cold. I've got enough panic running through me to keep me warm." She said, pulling her jacket around his bare torso as best she could. It was far too small, but he clutched it around him until his teeth stop chattering and his breathing slowed down.

"Are you OK? Marelle asked.

He nodded.

"You should have left him. You can see how grateful he was!"

He shook his head. "He would have died. Sam can't swim. Even if he could the gear, he had on was way too heavy." Jacob breathed for a bit, through his nose now. "He got caught on the grille – if he'd gone under and been caught in the cycle of the weir, I wouldn't have been able to save him – I couldn't walk away leave him to die in there."

Marelle wrapped herself around him, he was still shaking slightly.

"You're too good Jacob. I thought you were going to die!"

"There was a point when I wondered..."

She tutted. "I was going to jump in and try and save you."

He shook his head in disbelief. "Christ I'm glad you didn't. I would have had to save you as well!"

"I would have done. I figured I'd rather die with you than be left alone."

He swallowed and lay his wet head against her, one hand clutched hers as she felt his body still crave oxygen.

They both breathed together; her own breaths in panicked gasps alongside his, until their heartbeats slowed, and he finally stopped trembling beneath her hands.

"You saved his life." She stated, eyes open, her head against his as she stared at the grass they were sitting on.

It was over a mile walk home. She'd never seen Jacob this exhausted or unable to recover quickly. His legs were wobbly and he could not summon the strength to stand for a good fifteen minutes. Eventually he stood, looked shattered, soaked through – with her jacket around his bare shoulders.

"Should I go and get the car?" She asked.

"No, it's OK." He replied. "It's half a mile walk around to the parking spot anyway. I'll be fine by the time we've walked that far."

Marelle crooked an arm through his and they walked slowly.

"Where did the gun go?" She suddenly questioned as they made slow progress.

"In the water somewhere – along with his rucksack and whatever he had in it..." Jacob explained. "It can stay there."

"Where did he go?"

"Home, I suppose. God knows why he was wandering around up here with a shotgun ... I've not seen him up here before."

"I thought he was going to shoot us." Marelle said with a chill in her voice.

Jacob walked slowly beside her, her arm in his in support. "So did I." He confessed.

Normally it took them fifteen minutes at a steady pace; today it took them an hour at an ambient wander – which was about all Jacob could manage at the moment.

They finally crossed the airfield from the farmland and made their way to her back garden and back door. Jacob stood leaning against the wall as Marelle unlocked the back door. She glanced briefly at him; he had his eyes closed again.

"You, OK?" She asked.

He nodded but did not open his eyes. Marelle turned the key in the lock; she paused.

"What's that smell?" She sniffed the air, looked accusingly down at the drain just by the back door. "Is the drain blocked?"

Jacob shuffled his feet slightly but otherwise did not respond.

"Oh God I hope there's not a blockage in this sewer – we had that at the other house –took weeks to sort out and it smelled just like this."

She turned and looked around herself as if to look for further evidence of any blocked drains.

"Can't you smell it?" She asked, looking at him. "Jacob?

He hadn't moved still leaning against the wall, eyes still closed. Marelle almost thought he'd fallen asleep right here, but he opened his eyes slowly at her calling the name he had used for the last ten years.

"That might be me." He said, quietly.

"What?" Marelle asked, thinking she understood what he meant but seeing no meaning to it.

"I shit myself." He replied solemnly. "When I was trying to get Sam out of the water, I thought most of it had washed away but it's obviously drying out a bit now with the walk home".

Marelle stared at him as the back door swung open. She stood there. He was deadly serious – and he wasn't laughing. The door opened fully, she just stood there looking at him. He said nothing else.

"Oh, well... You better go and clean yourself up then." She muttered, quietly and stood aside for him to enter first.

She watched him walk in not really knowing what to say. He kicked his boots off just inside the door left her coat on the back of a kitchen chair before he walked slowly through the kitchen to the hallway, and she heard him go upstairs. Marelle stood in the open doorway just inside the kitchen. She was finding it hard to believe that he'd said what he just did. Was he not going to say anything – until she rattled on about blocked drains! Had she forced him into that confession? She closed the door behind her with a gentle click and went a couple more steps into the kitchen.

A smile suddenly broke on her lips. He'd shit himself! And he wasn't going to tell her! It suddenly struck her as funny – his words and straight-faced delivery made it even more so as she giggled to herself at his words, which she heard over and over again. She stood at the sink, laughing hysterically to herself; her shoulders shaking as she tried to keep it quiet.

"Oh Jeez!" She laughed to herself. What the hell was he like? Her own shoes and jeans were wet where she had waded in, and she bent down to unlace her shoes and slip them off; still laughing – she wiped a tear from her cheek with the back of her hand.

"Oh Jacob." She laughed. Why the hell had he shit himself? She collapsed into giggles again, so much so that she had to sit down on a kitchen chair. He'd said it's so matter of factly, so seriously, so without any hint of humour ... then she stopped; still stooped over her wet shoes and trousers as the laughter suddenly faded.

It hadn't been a laughing matter. It hadn't been an unfortunate accident by a misplaced bodily function. It had been a reaction by his body to the abject fear he must have felt in the water – feeling that his hold on life was tenuous and that he was unlikely to survive this. It was no laughing matter – it was a reflex reaction to life's imminent end which he had felt fast approaching out there. She sat up. Cold. A shiver passed over her. Marelle could hear water running upstairs. She felt guilty and bad for laughing now – his words played in her head, but they were as solemn as he meant them to be now. A new tear ran down her cheek but there was no mirth behind it this time. Marelle stood up, kicked off her trainers and stood there, barefoot on the cold kitchen floor. Her jacket that she had draped around his shoulders was neatly placed on the back of a chair and his wet t-shirt was wrung out on the draining board. Marelle looked at both of them in turn and then walked slowly through to the hallway. She took the stairs in an unhurried manner. One careful step at a time, with each careful thought, she reached the top and stood by the banister looking at the closed bathroom door. The shower was going, and she heard the toilet flush. The house around her was silent, suspended in that moment of vacuum between breaths as she stood at the top step and waited. The shower stopped; she heard him moving about. Marelle willed him to open the door, but he remained in there for an inordinate length of time.

Then the door clicked, opened up – he stepped out – naked except for a towel wrapped around him. She raised her eyes to him – he had anticipated seeing her waiting.

"OK?" She asked.

He nodded.

Marelle stood there; Just staring at him. It was awkward for a second or two.

"I'm so sorry." She finally said.

He raised an eyebrow to her – "Sorry, what for?"

She gave a little shrug, felt her lip begin to tremble and tears begin to push out from behind her eyes. "Just for..." She began but emotion took her voice away. "Just for everything... Just for the way life has treated you..."

He sighed, made that grin.

"You could have died!" She sobbed.

He walked back to her, took her in his arms and held her close to his warm, naked body.

"People need to be told what you just did there – it's not right it just gets swept under the carpet. You saved his life! *Sam's* life for God's sake!"

"No, they don't need to know." He whispered to her. "It's a happy ending – that's what matters. He's still alive and I'm still alive. And remember... I'm still Jacob... I need to keep my head down."

"It's not fair". She cried. "You're an Angel..."

He laughed. "I'm not, I never have been."

"I need to wrap you in cotton wool and keep you close to me". She cried against him. He laughed and wrapped his arms tighter around her.

TEN

There was a quietness between them; Marelle felt a humbleness brought by Jacob's actions. His unthinking dive into the water after Sam somehow pasted a fuller picture of him than the fractured pastiche of him, she currently had in her mind. And shown with a backlit Halo she had not seen before. He was standing in the kitchen late afternoon, mug of tea in his hand, staring out of the back window. Marelle was looking at her computer, sneaking glances at him. She'd just dropped into Google while she sat there and had been presented with yet more images of the charismatic Ezza which she compared to the man standing in her kitchen right now – a cheeky little smile on her face. Jacob, standing there now, looking like an average family man, mug in hand, staring out of the window. And there on her computer, ten years or more ago admittedly, striding across a stage; throwing out lyrics; smiling; laughing; speaking to the crowd; receiving their adoration. But with the same heart beating within him.

There was a knock at the front door. A solid tap- tap. Jacob turned slightly to look; Marelle raised her head then got up as she clicked the screen away on her computer.

As she walked through, she hoped it wasn't Catchpole turning up right now, Sunday, early evening– she could do without that!

Marelle reached up to the latch and opened the front door, suddenly aware of Jacob right behind her too like an inquisitive child. It was Mr. Wright. Standing on their doorstep with his Audi parked in their drive again. He smiled.

"Good evening, dear... good evening Jacob. Have you got five minutes?"

Jacob stepped around her, he still had the mug in his hand; She watched him lower his eyes to the floor.

"Yes, Of course." He said

Marelle looked to him as he turned the volume up on being 'Jacob' right in front of her She wasn't sure how he kept that act up so impeccably over the years, but he had managed to fool everyone; including her to some degree. Or, he simply had become Jacob through fear, desperation and loneliness and now the new sunlight that he had allowed into his life was allowing the real person to nurture and grow again.

Her phone began ringing back in the kitchen and although she desperately wanted to hang around and hear this conversation she turned and went back to her phone buzzing on the table with Bella's face on it.

" Hi Bella. She smiled.

"Hi Marelle." Bella answered. "I've got the tickets – they arrived yesterday!" She laughed.

"Tickets?" Marelle's mind was elsewhere.

"For the weekender! You and Jacob are coming? Don't tell me you've forgotten – or hell – that he's decided he's not coming now – you can't get a refund you know."

"No, no, it's OK. Sorry – I was thinking about something else. We're coming, I promise it – in fact Jacob is more enthusiastic about it than me!"

Bella, laughed a sarcastic little laugh. "Only they've changed the line up slightly – not that it will bother us a great deal."

"Erm, have they?" Marelle added, hoping to God they were not going to have to endure this for nothing.

"Yeah – Four Point Two have had to pull out so Yellow Son will play the headline slot on both days now. It won't bother you – you don't even know who I'm talking about!" She laughed.

Marelle laughed.

"Everything OK then?"

"All good Bella." She smiled, electing not to impart today's events.

"Great!" Bella said. "Where is he? Standing there naked staring at you?"

"No!" She grinned. "Speaking to his boss at the front door."

"Oh, yes! Did work go ok for him?"

"Yeah, should have been his last day today but because his boss has just turned up on the doorstep, I suspect that changed again."

Bella laughed. "You know I can't believe he works on a farm – he's such a cool dude! Then I suppose that's what keeps him so *fit*!" She stated the word *fit* in a way which had a more conducive meaning.

"Well probably!" Marelle grinned.

"You'd better make sure you hold on to him at the weekender you know!"

"What do you mean?"

"Well there's likely to be a lot of drunken females there and they'll be all over him." Bella laughed.

"Have to fight me off first!" Marelle smiled but inside she sighed to herself. Not only would she have to endure a weekend of hell, on tenterhooks about Jacob's motive and possible behaviour, but she would also have to keep a tight hold on him.

"Not, of course that I am suggesting Jacob would even be interested in them – not with you around of course..." Bella added.

"Nice save Bella!" Marelle commented.

Bella laughed. "Chill Marelle. It'll be fun."

Marelle wasn't sure what it would turn out to be, but she kept that thought to herself and said her goodbyes to Bella; turning to Jacob as he walked back into the kitchen.

He walked in slowly, one hand scratching the back of his head; his face looked slightly troubled. Jacob walked a couple of steps and stopped.

"What?" she asked.

"Apparently Sam's father passed away this morning..."

"He came to tell you that?"

"Well no, he wants me to do another couple of weeks. He's given Sam some compassionate leave because he is apparently pretty distressed, and his mother is beside herself."

"So you are at work tomorrow then?"

"Yeah." He said at some length, walking a couple more steps and staring pensively out of the window. "But shit! What was he doing up there with that gun? And imagine if I hadn't have pulled him out – his mother would have a dead husband and a dead son."

She saw it. There was a look of confusion and bewilderment in his eyes, like he could not understand why fate had taken that idea and twisted it into his guts with the smile of a reptile. Right there, in front of her now she could plainly see the part of him he had always called on to be Jacob.

She walked over and stood chest to chest with him, taking his free hand, looking up into his eyes which would not gravitate to hers right now. He was still fragile.

"Well it's a good job you saved him them, isn't it?"

"It's something more than that." He said, quietly. Marelle sensed the detachment of his mind starting to fashion this into an episode.

"Hey!" She reached up and turned his face to hers. "There's nothing more than that. He was there; he slipped and fell in; you jumped in and saved him. Happy ending."

He finally looked into her eyes. "Not entirely. His father died."

"Why are you feeling emotion for this? They should mean *nothing* to you."

"But what if we hadn't been there? What would he have done..." he asked.

"Shot a few squirrels, not fell in and probably gone home to his mum again once he had vented his anger because his father had died."

"I don't think it's that black and white."

She sighed. "Jacob. Just leave it. It has nothing to do with us. You saved his life, but he swore at you and ran off. He shouldn't even be entering your thoughts – you've never been in his."

"No, I know – but... it kind of makes me feel a bit funny! It's like seeing and feeling fate working."

"Or maybe it was fate giving you a chance for revenge – he and his father were intent on seriously maming you that night on the airfield – I know you are too benevolent but remember, I was being held by his father and had to watch Sam beating you up – what was *fate* doing then, hey? Things happen... and on both occasions you could have been seriously hurt – or worse..." She stared into his eyes; he still looked troubled by it. Pursed his lips a little and stared down at her.

"Stop being so *Jacob*. She said. "Start being more *Ezza!*"

"You may not say that in six month's time!" He said.

"Jacob, I've handled you ignoring me, I've handled finding Frankie with you, I've handled the aftermath of that, I've handled your nightmares – and mine – I've handled you disappearing and confessing you were about to throw yourself off that bloody bridge and I've handled you telling me you're not who I think you are... I think I can handle anything Ezza can possibly throw at me!"

Maybe he had his reasons, but Marelle could not quite understand why this affected Jacob as much as it did. Nonetheless it was on his mind for the rest of the evening and into the night when she slid down into the bed and coiled her legs around his. She held him to her. What tonight would bring remained to be seen. As usual the doors were locked, and the keys pocketed away. She fell asleep with her head on his chest and her fingers around his arm.

In the circumstances it could have been a worse night – remembering some of the ones she had endured with him in the past. Tonight, he had just been fitful, restless. Probably didn't sleep a great deal but did not wake up screaming at any point.

In the morning he got up, dressed and came down into the kitchen with her. He ate toast and drank tea while standing up. Black jeans, black fleece – boots unlaced as he stood with his long legs crossed at the ankles, his backside against the worktop. She smiled at him; his hair was growing longer. If he let her cut the sides, it would make the top look longer. Marelle wanted to get it back to how it looked when she first cut it – when she had unknowingly made him look like Ezza – when she now knew that initial tiny spark had suddenly ignited in him. Right now, she didn't want him to leave; as she looked at him standing there like that, she felt the urge to force herself up on him again, discard clothing through the hall and up the stairs like they had on that very first time. Marelle sighed internally. He turned and rinsed the mug in the sink. Marelle handed him the rucksack with his lunch then raised herself up on tip toes and kissed him. Her hands reached around and gripped his bottom.

"Oh I do love you." she smiled.

He laughed. "I'm glad somebody does!"

"Let me cut your hair." She raised her hands and pushed the sides back flat against his head – "At least get one step closer to how it was."

"Not yet, leave it a bit. I'll tell you when you can cut it again." He smiled.

"You're not growing it long!" She exclaimed.

"Oh I don't know; I could have a ponytail!" He grinned.

"You have a fucking ponytail, and I'll cut it off in the night!" She scolded, playfully.

Jacob laughed. "No, I don't want to go to this thing with Bella looking too much like Ezza."

Marelle drew a breath through her nose and felt the cold air run through her. She smiled up at him. "Need to get that tooth sorted too!"

He made a little face. "I know, but I don't have a dentist."

"We'll have to find one. You can't go meeting Chas like that, can you?" She grinned, straightening the collar on his fleece.

He smiled in return, "see you later."

"Be careful!" She called after him.

The waters seemed to have levelled. The next few days Jacob got up, went to work at the farm and Marelle did Seb's work at the house. Jacob was living a life, and it was suddenly very normal. He was happy and settled; he did actually enjoy working on the farm and the development on the airfield seemed to have crashed to a halt again. Sometimes, she went for a walk across it; sometimes she would go for a wander around it at lunchtime but now he had no real cause to constantly patrol it Jacob let it be while the changing season made its mark.

Marelle was thrilled to see him like this; thrilled to see him happy in the way he was. At times she felt the ten years spent hiding from himself ,leave him as he played the part of a besotted teenager with her – playful, coy, uninhibited. There was so much life and love in him that could have been so easily destroyed in an instant and lost forever. Jacob was what she'd always known he could be – sweet, gentle, loving, perfect – but he was also cheeky, and fun, and smart – no longer ducking behind the facade of Jacob when he was with her. She had his ring on her finger now and that filled her with a love and pride that no words could ever describe but she could also see the real Jacob – Nat – Ezza –poised and ready to explode from him at the first real opportunity.

A week and half later he walked in as usual but with a solemn and slightly perplexed look on his face. He'd clenched his jaw, and it had narrowed his cheeks and made his already high cheekbones more prominent.

"What?" she asked; knowing every expression he made and what they meant.

"Sam's gone." He said.

"Gone?"

He nodded. "Left the farm, moving away. His mother wants to go and live nearer her sister apparently, and Sam is moving with her."

"What, permanently?".

He nodded again. "Yeah. For good. She had been with his father since their early teens –can't bear to be without him..."

Marelle wasn't sure whether this was a time to smile.

"Who told you?" she asked.

"Wright. Sam went and spoke to him yesterday – left immediately. They're not even having a funeral here..."

"Really?"

He shook his head. Thinking for a moment.

"Grief is a horrible thing." He suddenly said. "It follows the life of one lost then takes others with it."

Marelle stared at him for a second, blankly. She still didn't quite know how to react when he got poetic, but knowing his past a little more now, it concerned her less.

"Like it did for my father." He added.

"Like it would have for me... if you had ..." Marelle's words came out fully before she even thought about them leaving her lips. She shook her head. "It's not grief – it's love." He looked up to her. Nodded slowly. He looked slightly saddened by the thought of it. But then he said, "I've been offered a permanent job there."

"What, Sam's job?"

He shrugged. "I suppose so."

She smiled, eventually. "Well that's good news, isn't it."

"Yeah." He said at length. "But, well what if my plans work out and Chas lets me go back?"

"Well you could hand your notice in just like Sam has just done. Anyway that's probably a way off, isn't it?"

"Not too far." He said, quickly.

Marelle smiled at him, almost like a parent humouring a child. "Well, we don't know how that is going to go yet – do we?"

The look he gave her at that remark was less than forthcoming. "Well how can he not let me be part of it again?"

Marelle felt that stab of fearful pain she thought had gone from her life for now on hearing those words. Jacob actually *believed* he would be welcomed with open arms when he exposed his presence to Chas.

"Just be careful Jacob; it may not go down well... he identified the body as you – it might not fill him with the feelings you are expecting if he sees you."

"But you don't even know Chas!"

"I know, but I *do* know what people are like. It might be a bit of a shock for him ... I want this thing to happen for you more than anything but, well ... it might not be as easy as you think."

He paused for a moment, looking at her.

"He'll love it; He'll think it's funny..."

Jacob accepted the job offer. Three weeks in, he had to ask for a Friday off for him to go to the weekender with Bella. It seemed to be the first time in his life he'd ever had to actually ask for a day off! During that preceding three weeks they had endured another visit from DCI Catchpole. They both knew he was fishing, and they both knew he was suspicious. Jacob maintained the hard-shell exterior of indifference, but Marelle could see him sweating from across the room now when he spoke. Catchpole imparted those forensics had deemed the remains to be that of a very young child; probably newborn or at best two or three days postpartum. She watched Jacob take in the information he already knew and react as if it was all a revelation to him. It was so different now she knew what he knew, and why he couldn't rush it getting discovered until, or if, he was ready.

There were so many questions she wanted answered – just what was his plan? Was he going to tell Catchpole the complete truth; a part truth; nothing? Or was he actually going to stumble over the cliff edge and then try to catch himself on the way down? Marelle didn't ask him – she was not sure he knew the answers himself. For now, she chose to enjoy what she held in her hand.

Bella called the night before they were due to set off to the north Norfolk coast.

"I'll get to you about midday?" She asked.

"OK." Marelle nodded.

"We'd best be there by about four – it gets a bit chaotic on the Friday if you're any later than that. I want to be at the bar with a drink in my hand by five!"

Marelle swallowed. "Shall we go in my car?"

"If you want – it might be more sensible- – it's bigger than mine..."

"OK, Jacob will drive. I've put him onto my insurance now so it's all above board."

"Just hope we don't get stopped with that dodgy driving licence then?" Bella laughed. "What dodgy licence?" Marelle asked, rewinding in her head, fearful she'd said something.

"The driver's licence with that hilarious picture of Jacob on it. He better bring a disguise to make him look like that or we'll be having some trouble explaining it to the coppers!" She laughed. "That was fucking hilarious!"

Marelle smiled. Yes! That photograph on Jacob's licence! Nevertheless she was sure he was planning on bringing plenty of disguises!

Marelle was more nervous than Jacob as they packed that night. She hated anything like this – had never been a concert or festival goer and did not tolerate pushing and shoving crowds easily.

Bella arrived, threw her case into the back of Marelle's car and stood there with her hands on her hips.

"Do you want a coffee?" Marelle asked.

"We'd better get going babe!" Bella checked her watch. "It's best to get there early – avoid the rush..."

Marelle sighed. "OK, I'll give Jacob a shout..."

Five minutes later they were in the car; Jacob driving, Marelle the passenger and Bella laying across the back seat.

"This is going to be *epic*!" She laughed. "Never ever thought I would get you two to come along."

"Oh why is that?" Jacob asked, looking at her in the rearview mirror.

"You're usually scared of your own shadow!" She exclaimed. "But now; now you're different. I guess it's the *Marelle effect*."

She did air quotes fingers. "I'll give you a tip – pace yourself with your drinks. Most people get very drunk very quickly and they don't make the second night."

"I don't plan on getting drunk." Marelle piped up. "... and I don't think Jacob does either."

"Oh what! You can't come to a weekender and not drink – it's what it's all about!"

"Well we can."

Bella sighed. "Yeah – we'll see. We'll get there and you'll start getting the wine down your neck..."

Marelle gave a little laugh and looked out of the window at the Suffolk countryside.

"Hey! Hey!" Bella exclaimed from the back seat – "look what I've got just to *get us in the mood.*"

She leaned between the front seats with a blue and yellow CD in her hand. "And you like these, don't you Jacob?"

"What is it?"

"It's a Yellow Son CD – I found it in a record shop last week." She strained forwards and pushed into the CD slot.

Marelle looked at Jacob, but he kept staring straight ahead.

The music started. Marelle didn't recognise it – she had not paid much attention to the music she had to admit; most of the time she had been concentrating on *looking* at Jacob when she trawled the internet. She may recognise some of the lyrics, but she could not identify or even place the song.

"Turn it up then!" Bella ordered from the back seat. "You like these, don't you Jacob?"

"Er – yeah. A bit." He said, convincingly, glancing briefly at her again in the rearview mirror while casually driving with one hand on the wheel. His voice blasted out of the speakers. Marelle recognised his vocals now, but Bella had no idea.

"Jesus!" She said. 'This is over twenty years old." She was reading the sleeve notes on the CD. "It says Yellow Son were formed in the early 80s by Chas Symonds ... they must all be pretty old by now." She laughed. "Hey look, there's a picture – bet they don't look like that now!" She hung through between the seats, laughing. "Look, Marelle ..." She held out a small, narrow black and white picture of the band from the insert of the CD. Marelle studied it – there was Jacob, far right, in profile but for some reason with half his face behind a guitar and with sunglasses on. Luckily Bella had not recognised him. "Bet they're all fat and old now!" She grinned.

Marelle gave Jacob a little look, but he was not responding.

" Mmm." she said.

"I saw them last year. They were quite good." Bella continued, reading the sleeve notes some more. "Loud."

Jacob kept staring straight ahead as Bella mulled over the sleeve notes. Marelle stole a couple of glances at him as his voice filled the car but he did not acknowledge her or allow any expression to cross his face.

"Oh, hey, hey ...!" Bella exclaimed as a new track started. 'I know this one ... this is good." She reached between the seats again and turned up the volume. Bella began singing along. Marelle instantly recognised it too – she'd heard it many times – but had never expected this to be Jacob. With a flick of her head she turned to him.

'This is the one that Seb's band played!" She laughed, remembering her playing him a recording of her brother's truly awful band that he had been in with a group of friends in his teenage years.

Jacob turned to her and nodded with a quiet smile.

'Oh my!" She exclaimed to herself when she realised how close to the truth she may have been when they had discussed that in the past.

Bella was going for it as they approached the chorus – she tapped Jacob on the shoulder. "Sing Jacob! You must know this one – even Marelle knows this one!"

Jacob laughed, raised his left hand which was in his lap as he drove with the right one on the wheel. "No, it's ok ..."

"Shut up and sing! You know this one! It's the one you sang on karaoke ..."

Marelle suddenly realised that it was, the same song he had sung in that pub while Bella had covertly filmed him.

"You're going to have to do a lot more singing this weekend so you may as well practice!"

She extolled to him and began singing the chorus right into his left ear until he shook his head and joined in.

It was a bizarre situation to say the least. All three of them in the car, singing along to an old CD – but with the huge white lie hanging blatantly over both Jacob and Marelle. As they drove, he did relax into it, once Bella had stopped reading the sleeve notes and looking at pictures. Now he was relaxed, laughing and singing along – suspiciously on time with all of the adlibbed "heys!" and "ows!" that the song came with. Bella laughed when he hit the spot and hammed it all up.

"See... I told you... you're a closet rock star!" She laughed.

"Oh yeah." Jacob replied with a grin, to the music.

Bella laughed and looked to Marelle as she tapped her arm and nodded to Jacob. Marelle smiled, laughed. This was how it was meant to be!

They listened to the whole album. Bella knew one or two songs, Marelle only knew the one, but Jacob knew them all, word perfect. As Bella egged him on, complete with air guitar from the back seat, Jacob sang along, word and action perfect on each and every song.

"Wow! I think he's a fan." Bella laughed to Marelle. "We will have to watch him this weekend – he'll be moshing down the front with the rest of them!"

Marelle laughed. "Don't worry he'll be under control!"

They arrived at the venue mid-afternoon. It had been an uneventful but informed drive and Jacob pulled into the entrance to the holiday park and rolled down the window to the guy in the orange vest who walked towards the car.

"Good afternoon, Sir. Have you pre booked?"

"Yes, we have."

"Could I please see your tickets Sir."

Bella reached a hand through next to Jacob's head. "Here." She called.

The guy took them, examined them then handed them back to Jacob.

"Very good." He said. "You're in Sundowner Way, block E, straight ahead, first right, then down to the end where you can park."

Jacob nodded his thanks and pulled away. Marelle looked across to him, smiling at the sight of his tanned, toned arms on the wheel. He looked so happy today.

ELEVEN

Their chalets were next to each other as planned.

"Go in and make sure everything is working and – if it's not we can complain straight away, and they'll move us or put it right." Bella advised.

Marelle and Jacob walked into theirs. It was light, quite airy but cold and damp. Marelle was not impressed, standing with her arms wrapped around herself on the grey carpet in the middle of the small lounge area. Jacob walked around, into the bedroom, the bathroom and the small kitchen area.

"Well it's bigger than the caravan!" He remarked with a smile.

"It's cold." she said.

"We'll soon warm it up!" He replied. "I've been in worse!"

Bella suddenly burst in through the front door.

"All, OK?" she asked. "Toilet flushing, taps working?

She breezed past them both– into the bathroom. They heard her flush the toilet and turn all of the taps on. She came out to the kitchen and did the same with the taps in there.

"Make sure there's hot water... we spent a weekend a while ago where there was no hot water all weekend!" She turned the taps off. "You're fine!" She announced.

Marelle and Jacob were still in the middle of the room, looking at her.

"Right." she smiled. "Time's getting on. Let's get down to the bar!"

"What? Right now?" Marelle questioned.

"Yes!"

"I'm not ready..."

"Nobody will be. Get here, get down to the bar have a few drinks, check the lay of the land and then come back and get changed to go out tonight. That's what you do. "Come on!" Marelle laughed. "Really , we've only just got here!"

"I know. And we haven't paid to just stay in the chalet and admire the decor... come on!"

Marelle looked to Jacob; he shrugged, she sighed.

"Oh come on then." Marelle answered, looking to Jacob again.

"Hang on!" Jacob suddenly said and went back into the bedroom. A few seconds later he emerged with sunglasses and a baseball cap in his hand.

"It's not *that* sunny!" Bella laughed. "And we'll be inside!"

"I'm on holiday!" he grinned to her and put the cap on his head as well.

Marelle stared at him. She'd never seen him in a baseball cap, and it looked odd. It was a black one with a white Mercedes logo on the front. He was also wearing a black t-shirt with lightwash jeans – it didn't look like his usual attire – which Marelle had noted to herself earlier. Now with the cap and sunglasses on he did not look at all like Jacob but, she guessed, that was the idea.

The bar was massive with purple and orange carpets. A large, open plan space with seating around the sides and a small, raised stage area with a compact dance floor on the far right hand side. There were a few people already in there, scattered between the bar and the tables. Marelle looked around like a rabbit in the headlights; Jacob stood there with his hands in his pockets; Bella walked straight past them towards the bar until her attention was grabbed by the stage in the corner.

"Hey!" She exclaimed, turning back and touching Jacob's arm. "Look, they've got karaoke!"

Jacob looked, turned to Bella then shook his head. "No."

"Oh go on! Look there's nobody doing it yet…"

"No." He laughed. "What do you want to drink?" And he managed to detract her from the karaoke with that question.

They had just got drinks when the karaoke fired into life. The host announced his presence and encouraged people to come up and sing but it did not appear that anyone was drunk enough yet, so he began to sing himself.

Marelle wanted to sit down so they found a table inconspicuously out of the way of the karaoke and sat themselves down. Jacob was drinking coke which pleased Marelle, and it didn't appear that Bella had noticed that fact yet either. She was too busy staring around at everyone else who was there and fulfilling her urgency to get into the spirit of the weekend as prematurely as possible even though it was only mid-afternoon on a Friday.

"So, is this where they have the bands as well?" Jacob asked.

"No, no!" Bella laughed. "This is the bar. The bands are all on in a big theatre type place over the other side. They won't let you in there until about six. The first band is normally on about seven, the second about nine and then there's a disco until the early hours…" She explained.

Half an hour and at least another glass of wine later Marelle was watching the bar fill up. It was, without question, more women than men. Lots of small groups of females, giggling and shrieking as they made their way to the bar; some couples who looked more controlled and getting prepared to enjoy the show; and a few lone males. The age range was also considerable – some of the groups of girls looked very young – would probably not have even been born when some of the music covered over this weekend was around. A lot of them were close to her and Bella's age and a handful were older. Jacob seemed relaxed and as she constantly checked on him with a quick glance, he seemed happy enough – but still with the sunglasses and baseball cap in place it was hard to tell his true feelings. Nonetheless he did not look remotely as uncomfortable as he had at her niece's birthday party when it had all gone so horribly wrong. He caught her smiling at him and grinned back.

"I feel pretty underdressed." She commented. "Not that I'd feel much more suitably attired in the clothes I've bought but, should we go back and get changed?"

"Wait a bit." Bella said. "Let's see how full up it gets in here first."

It *was* filling up and it *was* getting loud with the constant chatter and female shrieking. The groups of girls were already dressed for the night in multitude of gaudy colours, all heels and hair. Micro mini skirts and high heels, stumbling about in front of the three of them while constantly trying to pull the mini skirts down.

Jacob grinned and shook his head. "Were you ever like that?"

"No!" Marelle exclaimed.

"Oh yes you were! You should have seen her at eighteen! She was a right little cockteaser!" "Bella! *I was not!*" Marelle exclaimed.

Bella laughed. "Oh yes you were!" She stood up. "I'm just going to the loo."

Marelle watched her go then looked at Jacob. "I was never *that* bad." She explained.

"No?" He asked.

"No!" She stated the vehemently.

"Still a cockteaser though, aren't you?" He smiled.

"I hate that term!" she laughed, slapping his arm, but shifting her chair closer. She reached over and took his hand in hers. "I think it's going to be a bit of a long night..."

Jacob gave a little laugh. "I'm only here for one thing."

"Oh, I know that!" She smiled. Marelle looked at her watch. "But that's four or five hours away yet... I feel like I want to go and lie down already!"

"What does Bella do when she's here then? I feel we're cramping her style. I suspect she would be stumbling around shrieking if we weren't here?" Jacob commented.

Marelle laughed. "Probably!"

At that point Bella lumped down beside them again, a little out of breath. "Right, my round." She said. "Same again Marelle?" She pointed to Jacob. "And you're not drinking coke all night either. You might need something stronger in a minute anyway!" And she got up again to go to the bar.

"What does she mean by that?" Jacob asked, for the first time looking slightly worried.

"Don't know." Marelle answered. "Probably planning on getting you on the dance floor later!"

The bar was busier, and it took a while for her to come back, she had a bottle of wine and a bottle of beer for Jacob.

"Cheaper by the bottle." She advised.

"Hey Bella!" Somebody suddenly called from behind him and all three turned to see a tall, blonde woman, impossibly slim but with a perfect figure – dressed in a mid-thigh, close fitting, black sparkly dress. Over her shoulder she had a small, silver shoulder bag hanging by her side.

"Hey babe!" Bella greeted standing up. They embraced each other as Marelle and Jacob looked on.

"Mae, this is Marelle and Jacob."

Mae smiled. "Hi." She seemed too quiet to be one of Bella's friends. "Bella has mentioned you – nice to meet you."

"Hi." Smiled Marelle. Jacob raised his hand in a casual wave.

"You can join us." Bella gestured.

"Thanks but I was just speaking to some people at the bar – I'll catch you later – be at the front when the bands start up."

"OK, I'll be there – hopefully with these two in tow. They're newbies so we'll have to teach them the ropes!"

Mae smiled, clutching a glass of wine to her just as the 'host started speaking again.

"Let's get this party started guys and we have our first victim – er – singer right here. Classic song, right with the vibe this weekend as this band is here later would you believe it? Let's see if he can give them a run for their money! Where are you, Jacob? Come on give us your rendition of *'No way Home'*."

Bella grabbed Mae's arm. "Oh my god. You've got to watch this. Jacob... go on... go on. It's you – I put your name in!"

"What!" He exclaimed.

"Go on!" Bella ran forwards and tried to pull him out of the seat.

"Bella. No!" He replied. "I'm not singing karaoke here!"

"Shut it Jacob and just get up there!"

"Jacob. We're looking for you!" The host announced. "Don't you go getting cold feet on me with a song like this."

Jacob looked at Marelle. She could feel his expression, but he didn't look pleased. Bella tugged at him.

"Come on!"

Marelle stared at him. He put down the beer bottle and turned his face to Bella. "You're doing it with me!" And he stood up.

Bella whooped, jumped up in the air, and grabbed his hand before she pulled him through the gathering crowd towards the karaoke. Mae looked to Marelle, smiled sweetly then followed.

"Shit Bella!" She said to herself, indecisive about whether to follow or stay here.

"Jacob where are you? You're not being a chicken on me – are you? We're all friends here and no one's going to pelt you with rotten vegetables!" The host was continuing.

The crowd began to clap and cheer up ahead. Marelle closed her eyes for a second and stood up. From here she could see Jacob and Bella climbing onto the stage. Jacob looked so tall – although she would hardly have recognised him in the cap and glasses. He had the microphone in his hand and looked totally relaxed about it. Bella was laughing, clutching her microphone like a weapon, dancing and fooling around. Marelle watched; felt her heartbeat inside her but did not hear the crowd or the shrieking anymore as she focused in on Jacob. He looked over and said something to Bella. She laughed. He looked so at home and relaxed out there. Almost as if he was just fooling around on the airfield and there were only the sounds of the birds and insects to trouble him. The host spoke to him, Jacob nodded and walked over to look at a computer screen. Jacob pointed to the other equipment and said something; they both laughed, and he walked back to Bella as the music started. It was *that* song. The one they had all sang along to in the car; the one Seb had played; the one that everyone knew. Cheers and shouts came from the crowd as Jacob swung the microphone lead out of the way almost innately, took a step forwards and hit the first line with perfect timing and voice.

"Shit!" Marelle said again and felt the compulsion to stand on her chair so she could see better. Bella wasn't singing; she was clutching the mic, laughing and pointing at Jacob – but Marelle could see he wasn't taking any notice of Bella; of where he was or exactly what he was doing. He had a crowd, he had lights, and he had a microphone in his hand.

She was watching Ezza.

He worked the stage; he worked the crowd. His previous performance in the pub had been static – this time he *performed*. He paced the small stage, he sang to the audience, stooped to them, gave someone in the crowd a high-five; strode back and forth; knew every step he made to every beat of the song. The crowd were with him – if they had been ambiently interested to start with they were now engrossed by this – held by his magnetism, his charisma.

Marelle closed her open mouth and realised she felt abnormally cold; snapped herself back into the room as the song came to an end and he finished with one hand in the air and his legs astride at the centre of the stage. The crowd went crazy; Bella hugged him and for a moment, in all of this, Marelle saw Jacob kiss her on the cheek. Still holding the microphone he handed it back to the host.

"Wow!" The host said. "Looks like the professionals are here early! Hey, are you in a tribute band or something?"

Jacob shook his head, holding out a hand to the host in reply, making his way from the stage. Marelle strained to see now as he came through the sea of people; hands touching and high fiving him on his way.

"I think he's a dark horse. I think he's someone in disguise!" The host continued to a drunken crowd who were taking very little notice of his words. Marelle heard them but realised she was probably the only one that did.

It seemed to take forever for him to return. Marelle waited and suddenly became aware that she was still standing on her chair when he walked through the crowd, looking at her. People were still patting his back and saying things to him as he approached her. She climbed down from the chair.

He smiled at her, held out his arms as she walked forward two steps into them. He held her; squeezed her tightly as she placed her hands on his back – the t-shirt felt warm and slightly damp as it clung to his body. She could feel a tremble within him; a tightness that wasn't tension. It was release. Marelle hugged him, laid her head against him and closed her eyes. There was a horrible, clenched knot in her own chest for which she was seeking an explanation. She did not know whether it was fear, love, anger – but as she clutched tightly at him and hoped it would go quickly.

"You were good." she eventually said, raising her head and looking up to him.

"I'd rather have a band behind me!" He laughed.

She lay her head back against him. There were tears rising which she held at bay. "Where's Bella?" She asked.

"She was talking to that blonde girl up there."

Marelle sighed and held her body close to his; trying to gather him to her; trying to hold back the piece of him which he'd left on that stage.

"Hey lovebirds!" Bella suddenly exclaimed, walking up. "Jesus fuck Jacob. You are a fucking superstar! What the fuck Marelle!" She laughed shaking her head.

Jacob smiled and shrugged as Marelle finally unfolded herself from him but immediately clutched at his hand.

"Should we go back to the chalet?" Marelle asked, finding her voice incredibly small among all of this.

Bella looked at her watch. "I suppose so, but we'll need to be back soon if we want to be up the front tonight."

Once out of the bar with the buzz of the crowd and the music gone Marelle found it strangely silent. She kept her hand crooked through Jacob's arm as they walked the short distance back. He didn't say a lot, almost as if he had not just done what he had. Bella had a spring in her step and laughed to herself every now and then.

"I'll come into you when I'm ready." Bella grinned at their door and slipped into her own.

The chalet, for some reason, seemed that little bit colder and damper when they returned. Jacob closed the door behind him, but Marelle stood there, her arms clutched around herself, just standing in the silence for a few seconds.

Jacob smiled and walked back towards her.

"OK?" He asked.

She nodded.

"The crowd loved you." she said.

He grinned. "A bar full of drunken people; they'll react to anything... they will be the same to the next person up there..."

Marelle smiled. "But you enjoyed that, didn't you?"

"Yeah." He grinned. "I did. I probably shouldn't have done it but yeah, I did enjoy and... It's just giving me a heads up I could still get up there and do it!"

He smiled wholly, completely, *ecstatically*. So much so that she eventually smiled broadly at him as the knots inside her began to unravel and with it she felt that absolute change sparking her emotions and skinning her soul.

Bella had got changed and was bursting back through their door while Marelle was still dithering, and Jacob was in the bathroom. Bella had a toilet brush in her hand.

"Look at this!" She exclaimed, holding it up to Marelle.

"What?" She wrinkled her nose and made a face with the toilet brush being so close to her.

"Look!" Bella waved it.

"What?!"

"It's got lumps of shit all over it ...it's disgusting! I'm going to complain!"

Marelle shrugged. "Who cares? Who even uses a toilet brush anyway?"

"That's not the point! It's someone else's shit!"

Jacob came out of the bathroom, t-shirt in hand, stripped to the waist.

'Look!" Bella exclaimed, thrusting the brush towards him.

"What?" He backed away from it a little.

"It's got someone else's shit on it!"

Jacob made a face Marelle had not seen in his repertoire before. It almost made her smile. She bit her lip and giggled to herself.

Jacob gagged, reflexly, uncontrollably and backed away from Bella.

"What Jacob?" She laughed. "It's only shit!"

"Take it away!" He exclaimed, still gagging and finally having to turn away and clasp his hand over his mouth.

Bella laughed. Marelle smiled. Bella walked into their bathroom, still holding the offending toilet brush aloft and came out with theirs as well.

"Yours is fine!" She announced. "Dirty bastards! I might complain ..."

"Just take it away now Bella." Marelle advised with Jacob still gagging noisily in the kitchen area.

"Are you ready yet?" Bella asked.

"No."

Bella sighed. Replaced their toilet brush then headed back outside with hers.

"Oh dear. Are you ok?" Marelle asked Jacob with a slight, latent amusement.

He nodded, still recovering himself.

"I hate toilet brushes! Most disgusting thing I can think of – especially in hotels and places like this." He said – then gagged again before he finally composed himself and walked back to the bedroom. "Don't let her bring that back in. here again for God's sake!"

Bella returned a couple of minutes later. Despite how quick she had been and the close encounter with the toilet brush, Bella had put on make-up, put her hair up and changed into a slinky red dress and heels.

"Come on!" She urged. "What are you two doing? I want to be at the front! – I hate being at the back."

"I don't particularly want to be at the front." Jacob said, pulling a navy blue, long-sleeved t-shirt over his head.

"It's much better at the front." Bella continued. "Come down there with Mae and me."

"No, it's ok. I'll stay back a bit." He smiled to her.

She sighed. "You *are* a strange one."

There was a disco playing background music when they walked into the large space that was called "venues". It was huge, with a bar at the back but the front of the area was a raised wooden floor with a large stage at the front. There was no crowd barrier, but the stage was quite high. Bella went up to the front. There was still plenty of room and she selected a spot where she wanted to be. Marelle went to get drinks, and Jacob joined her as the area began to fill.

Bella had her back to the stage, watching the crowd. Jacob was staring at the stage; absent mindedly sipping at the pint of what looked like lager in a plastic tumbler. Marelle asked for coke; she had already drunk a couple of glasses of wine which were fraying the edges a little but she felt she should at least try to keep a clear head for tonight's events.

"No drum kit." Jacob said.

"Pardon?" She asked, deep in thought about what other people were wearing and the drunken behaviour of a group of very young girls to their left.

"There's no drum kit – some of the stuff on stage is theirs but there's no drum kit ..."

"What does that mean?" Marelle questioned.

"No drummer." He replied.

'There's another group on first, isn't there?"

"Yeah, but the drum kit would be on stage already."

Marelle shrugged. "Dunno." She said.

Mae came through the crowd, walking up in the way she had glided across to them before. Bella gave her a hug and made space for her alongside. Mae turned to Marelle and Jacob,

"I'm not pushing in, am I?"

"No!" Jacob replied with a smile. "We're moving back in a minute anyway."

"Oh, aren't you staying up here with us?" Mae questioned, blinking her huge blue eyes, almost seductively.

"No, we'll leave it to you and the old hands." Jacob said in reply.

Mae smiled sweetly. "Awesome singing earlier." She said.

"Stop making his head bigger than it already is!" Bella exclaimed. "They're newbies – still think it's better to be at the back!" She laughed with a wink, staring at Jacob.

It was a lot fuller now and people were all gathering at the front.

"Let's move back." Jacob leaned down and whispered to Marelle.

She in turn indicated this to Bella and then placed a hand on Jacob's back as she followed him through the crowd. Finding a spot by a railing on a slightly raised area at the side.

"Will you be able to see here?" Marelle asked – they were far right of the stage, slightly behind a pillar.

"Yeah, it's ok. It's a good place for tonight."

"Are you worried?"

"Worried? What about?" He questioned as if she had asked something decidedly odd.

"Well – seeing *them*? Seeing Chas – him seeing *you*?"

"No! He won't see me, not here. When you're on stage with the lights, you can't see anything much in the crowd beyond the front row – and I'm *interested* to see what they're like now …"

"Without you?" She grinned, coyly.

"They've done OK without me." He answered, taking another sip of his drink. Jacob was still wearing the baseball cap, the sunglasses were folded and tucked down the neck of his t-shirt. Marelle wrapped her arm around his and pressed herself to him. She didn't believe what he'd said, he *was* worried.

The first act came on about forty minutes later. Now full, the venue was loud, buzzing and warm. Groups of people were dancing to the disco that was still playing; there was much shouting and laughing – drink was being spilled on the floor. The space they stood in was also now filling but they maintained their position against the rail. Eventually the stage lights dimmed, the crowd cheered and the act's walk on music pumped from the stage. Lights blazed in a rainbow of colours, and three over-tanned, sparkly dressed girls strutted onto the stage; in complete co-ordination, cordless microphones in hand. The crowd whooped, everyone started to dance and jump up and down. They sang some pretty, poppy little tunes but their performance, although polished to perfection, was very predictable and over-rehearsed. Marelle jigged along to it against the rail as Jacob watched intently. He gave a little laugh.

"What?" She asked, feeling him more than hearing him over the music.

"Wholly inappropriate support act for Yellow Son."

"Yes, but it wasn't meant to be them, was it? They've stood in at the last minute apparently … you're going to get to see them twice!"

"Not sure they'll play the same set both nights … they usually have a pretty rigid set if Chas has anything to do with it – not as rigid as this though!"

"Oooh critical!" She grinned. "Mr. rock star!"

"I think they're miming." He said.

"No!" Marelle exclaimed. "Really?"

"It takes more effort than that to sing." He nodded.

"Will Yellow Son be miming then?"

He laughed. "I doubt it. We did it once for a TV show and Chas said he would never do it again. We looked – and felt – like idiots!"

"These are going down well with the crowd …"

"Mmm"

He said.

They performed eight or nine songs. If Marelle was honest, they all sounded the same and ran into one another but they left the stage to huge applause and screaming from the crowd now in full party mood.

Jacob looked at his watch. Bella suddenly appeared through the crowd; she had a huge smile on her face.

"Hey, you two ... come over there with us – it's a bit crazy but it's better than over here – you can't see anything!" She had two empty plastic tumblers in her hands.

"I don't think I can cope with all that shouting and jumping up and down over there." Jacob said to her in a raised voice above the music. "I'm not as young as your lot."

"Give over! You could give anyone in here a run for their money – you're fit!" Bella laughed, poking Jacob in the chest. "Weren't they good?" She nodded back to the stage.

"Jacob thinks they were miming." Marelle piped up.

"Of course they weren't!" Bella scoffed. "Yes, I'm afraid old man – they really were that good!"

"Really?" Jacob asked, one eyebrow raised. "Who were they?"

"Oh for God's sake! Sugarush ..." Bella laughed. "Maybe you are a bit older than us! Everyone knows Sugarush!"

"I don't." Marelle said.

"Well you don't listen to music! Only Seb's old shit."

Marelle made a playful face at her.

"I'm going to get Mae and me a top up – you want anything?"

"No, I'm fine Bella." Jacob said. "Think I'll keep a clear head."

"I'll get you drunk tomorrow." Bella pointed.

He smiled at her shaking his head.

"Marelle?" She asked.

"No – I'm fine ..."

"Well see you in a bit. Come down there if you want to – I'll fit you in."

"I'll be here." He stated again. "Maybe next time."

Bella made a face as if to say, "oh yeah!" and moved off towards the bar.

Marelle looked up to him and smiled. It was far from bright in here – the lights had come up a bit for now, but she could not see his eyes as clearly as he flicked to her with a smile and snapped them away again. Marelle knew that look. Outside he was calm, but his eyes showed some kind of latent worry – it wasn't fear – it was *worry*; anxiety. She cuddled close to him; he lifted one arm off the rail and let her stand between his arms, in front of him. He wrapped one arm around her waist and rested his chin against her head, still leaning forwards slightly. Marelle could feel his heart beating against her shoulder. It was fast and racing.

People began to return to their places, held for them by friends, shimmying through the crowd with drinks in hand; groups of girls in sparkly dresses, laughing, clustered together like excited children.

Suddenly Jacob jumped, stood upright, nearly spilled his drink and turned over her.

Marelle had no idea what was happening and turned with him. A group of girls were passing, and one had decided to pinch Jacob's bottom as it protruded prominently into her path. She stood there now, in a short blue velvet dress, laughing, obviously tipsy to say the least.

"Sorry! Couldn't resist – sexy arse." She giggled, clinging to another girl who stood beside her. "I'll see you on the dance floor later ..."

Jacob gave a tiny smile and turned back. Marelle ducked over his arm and went to say something, but he turned her back to him.

"Leave it." He said.

"But she ..." Marelle protested.

"They're drunken girls!" He said with a grin.

"You would or you *have* probably done the same."

She looked to him with a sigh and an exasperated look on her face.

"Remember?" He asked, raising an eyebrow.

She wasn't sure when he meant. "But you were not with someone else!" She finally said.

"When you're drunk things like that don't matter!"

"If she does it again, I'm giving her a piece of my mind." Marelle moaned, still staring in her direction. "If she starts on you later, I'm not having it."

"She's drunk. She'll forget all about it and pick on someone else ... forget it ..." He turned Marelle back towards him and placed his arms around her.

'They're not allowed to touch you." She said, "You're mine!"

He gave her a little squeeze. "Shh ... look out ..."

The lights began to dim again, and the crowd's clamoring buzz turned into a cheer.

Marelle felt him move his weight from one foot to the other behind her. His arm was just touching hers now and she could feel a slight tremble within him.

The crowd began to clap and cheer louder until figures began to walk onto the stage. Three people, walking on and taking their places. People she had seen in the pictures on her computer but this was ten plus years on. Fatter, older, greyer or balder. The guy un the centre of the stage waved with a friendly smile then picked up a yellow guitar and put the strap around his neck like he had done it a million times. He was stocky, looked shorter than Jacob and wore a pale orange t-shirt, untucked over dark blue jeans. His face was quite round, his hair extremely short. He had a grin on his face as he looked to the other guy to his right who was also now holding a guitar in a fiery red colour. With a nod he looked to the bass player on his left as he started to play a funky bass rhythm.

"What?" Jacob laughed behind her.

"Is that Chas in the middle?" She asked.

"Yeah." Jacob replied quickly. "What the hell are they playing?"

Marelle shrugged.

She felt him give a nervous laugh and shake his head. "What the hell?"

"Who are the other two?"

"That's Jem on the left and Marty on the right. Luc the drummer isn't here. I don't know why – "

Chas started singing. He had a pretty strong voice; he sounded good. Chas looked to be enjoying what he was doing, and Marelle found herself tapping her foot. He already had the crowd at the front dancing and bouncing up and down. The first track finished with a flourish.

"Do you know that one?" She asked.

"No – yes – I know the song but it's not one of theirs and not one I'd expect them to do!"

"Hey?" Chas spoke, holding up one hand in the air. "Hey guys. You didn't come here to see us tonight. You all came to see four point two but, unfortunately, they're not here. So we said we'd step up and do this slot ..." A small cheer rose from the crowd. "So ..." Chas said, taking a breath. "So we'll try to play what you came to hear. We've not got Luc with us tonight so we have no drums, but we can still party and get funky and have some fun here with these tunes." He looked around the others as he spoke. "We've spent the last week rehearsing these songs for you, so I hope you enjoy them. We'll do a couple of four point two songs and then have a bit of a party – cos that's what we want tonight, isn't it?"

As he spoke, he playfully strummed the guitar. The crowd whooped. "Right Marty. Let's get funky!"

The bass player struck up again to the cheers of the crowd.

Marelle moved her body back against him; he felt very static. She turned her head to look at him, his face half in silhouette in the darkness.

"This isn't Yellow Son." He said, next to her, almost to himself. "What do you mean. "

"They're playing covers ... very well ... but they're playing covers."

Marelle looked at him for a second, then turned back to the stage. "But the crowd are loving it." She commented .

They were. They had the crowd bouncing, clapping and cheering.

"Chas is trying too much. He's nervous; he always talked to the crowd lot when he was nervous.""

Marelle watched. They were better than the previous lot by miles; she could see what Jacob had meant when he had said they had been miming. This music felt real. She could feel it, almost touch it as it touched you. There was an energy about their performance; a harmony and she could see the physical effort etched on their expressions and running down their faces as sweat. All of them looked older than Jacob - but they are mature group giving a performance that a younger one would have been proud of.

Jacob sighed fitfully behind her. Somehow, she could feel his dreams shattering. She placed a hand over his on the rail in front of them. He felt hot but she kept her eyes on the stage and the performance. The song seemed to be ending, approaching a crescendo. Chas stopped playing and raised his hand.

"Are we having a party?" he shouted.

The crowd replied with a cheer, and someone shrieked down at the front.

"Well we're going to slow it down for a minute so you can get a bit sweaty with the person next to you – if you want to …" He laughed. Beside him the one with the red guitar plucked at the strings and fiddled with the instrument.

"Ok." Chas sighed, adjusting his guitar. "We don't play this one very often … in fact we've never played it live before in front of a crowd like you lot. So, bear with us …" He laughed again. "This was written by a very dear friend of ours who is sadly no longer with us – but I think he would be happy to hear us playing it tonight. God bless you Ezza."

She physically felt Jacob gasp. She felt him tense and shuffle. Chas started playing and within seconds Marelle recognised the song. She turned to Jacob.

"It's *that* song." She said. "The song you played me."

It was. It was the song he had made her listen to as they'd sat by his caravan burning stuff on a bonfire in his final act of 'tidying up'. He'd put a CD into a Walkman, letting her listen through one ear piece and she had heard this song. It had captured her. It was a beautiful said song; a beautiful voice. Had he expected her to know it was him back then – had he expected her to put two and two together? She hadn't and he had thrown the CD into the fire, and she thought it had gone forever. He had hinted; he had said you could find it again if you really wanted to – had he wanted her to? For a second, she felt a twisting pain inside herself at what that moment had really meant and what he'd really been doing that day. Things could have been so different, and that fact still brought tears to her eyes. She gripped his hand as Chas sang the words, she had originally heard Jacob sing on that CD. Chas did not have the finesse or depth of emotion that Jacob's voice had mustered but listening to it being sung – even by Chas – touched her.

"Sneaky little bastard!" She heard Jacob say under his breath.

The whole feeling on stage had changed and the crowd were listening, quietly swaying or dancing together. The song finished with the last few haunting notes on the guitar. Then there was a moment of silence before the crowd clapped – slightly stunned at the intensity of the song being slotted into an otherwise pretty lively set.

"Can we have the lights up guys?" Chas suddenly asked, reaching skywards and pointing to the lights. Beside him Marty strummed quietly on the bass.

"Lights up …" He gestured with his hands as the lights slowly brightened and everyone could see each other again.

"Right, right, thank you." He said. "If you can give me two minutes here." He looked out into the audience, hand outstretched in front of him as he surveyed the crowd. "Now a little bird has told me that there is someone very special in the crowd here tonight …"

Both guitars were tinkling along in the background as he spoke.

Marelle felt Jacob stiffen behind her at Chas' words. She suddenly realised what he had said and turned her face to Jacob in question. He was staring straight ahead, frozen in some emotion; she wasn't sure which.

"Someone who we go back a very, very long way with ..." Chas continued. 'Someone who means a lot to us ..."

Jacob swallowed. First, they had played that song that she had listened to with him – now Chas was looking out into the crowd, saying these words, looking for someone.

Marelle looked to Jacob; to Chas; back to Jacob. He was tense, on the verge of shaking; worried. She gripped his arm; he stood upright and looked very uncomfortable.

"Ellen, where are you?" Chas asked – pointing to someone right at the front and laughing.

"I've been told it's Ellen's birthday today and she is one of our oldest fans – she was a fan when she was a baby!" He grinned, exchanging gestures and laughs with the person at the front. "Hey Ellen! Happy Birthday to our number one fan!" He clapped and the crowd clapped.

Marelle felt Jacob exhale slowly; his body leaning slightly forwards again, just touching hers.

The lights dimmed and they struck up a loud and energetic introduction to another track. She felt Jacob move a little against her and Marelle began to wonder just what this was all doing to him. She was sensing the rollercoaster ride he was on.

She turned to him, reached up to his face gently. "OK?" she asked, looking right at him in the dim light.

He nodded but she could see the wet track of a tear on the side of his face as the lights caught it. Turning back, she took his hand in hers again, pulling his arm across and around her. His fingers clasped her gently and pulled her to him.

"We always used to open with this one." He spoke. 'This is the one I walked off to."

Marelle stood there with his arm around the front of her, he was feeling this music more; she could feel a sense of excitement in him – a need to get up on the stage and perform.

The song finished with a flourish from Chas. He looked to Ellen in the crowd again and smiled. "That was for Ellen. Happy Birthday!" He announced.

She shouted something back from the crowd; he stooped down to speak; stood up, laughed, walked back to his microphone.

"Security – get her onto the stage for a moment – Ellen..." He pointed to her and gestured to the side of the stage.

As the bass player continued with a funky beat it was thirty seconds later that a short, plump blonde woman scurried onto the stage.

"Aaah here she is!" Chas said. "Come here!"

He obviously knew Ellen, although Jacob claimed he did not know her. Chas walked over to her and placed an arm around her shoulders.

"Ladies and gents this young lady has been to more gigs than anyone else I know. She has followed us everywhere from the very beginning."

The crowd responded with a drunken sounding cheer.

"She knows more about us than we do!" Ellen was beaming with excitement at having Chas' arm around her.

"And she turns up tonight in a t-shirt with Ezza on the bloody front!" I feel like he's fucking haunting me!"

Ellen leaned across to Chas' mic. "We can't forget Ezza!" She said into it.

There were some cheers from the crowd, albeit minimal. Most of them had probably been toddlers when Ezza had last sung with the band.

"No, we can't." Chas replied. "But go and get yourself a proper t-shirt. Merch will give you one for free for your birthday ..." He laughed, taking his arm away from Ellen. "Fucking Ezza!" He smiled under his breath as Ellen was helped down from the stage by security.

Marelle looked round at Jacob again. His mouth was tight, and it looked like a fresh tear had rolled down his cheek. She smiled and turned fully into him, hugging him protectively.

"Couple more songs guys then we'll hand you over to the disco so you can boogie your little backsides off till the sun comes up." Chas said behind them.

She turned back to look at the stage with Jacob's arms wrapped around her. They watched the final two songs in that embrace: still, with Jacob resting his chin on her head. Both songs were not theirs; but both were crowd pleasing, sing-along tunes which everyone enjoyed and went totally along with. There was no denying it, the crowd loved it and were screaming and shouting for more when Chas announced

"That's all folks. Thank you and goodnight."

The disco kicked in exactly at that point with the lights on the stage going off and the rainbow of strobing and sparkling disco lights filled the room. Over the booming music the DJ said:

"Thank you to Yellow Son for that truly stupendous performance and for stepping in to cover for Four Point Two who sadly could not be here tonight. Thanks guys. Let's dance!"

As the crowd immediately changed their focus to the bright lights and the DJ Jacob sighed.

She turned back to him. "OK?"

He nodded.

"Want to go and get a drink?"

He nodded.

TWELVE

There was a bar at the back of the room that was not as crowded as the one in the thick of it. It didn't have so many bright lights or glowing display fridges behind it and was a bit less busy. Marelle and Jacob walked in that direction.

"I'll get them." She said. "What're you having?"

"I guess I'll have another plastic glass of what they are calling lager!" He said.

She smiled.

"I'd rather have a bottle ... but ... I know the rules as well as anybody." He added.

It didn't take long to get served and Marelle handed him the pint in a wobbly plastic pint glass. She had a glass of white wine, also in a plastic tumbler.

With him sipping the lager they stood off to the side, Jacob backed up against a wall with her standing next to him.

"Well?" she asked cheekily flicking her eyes to him as she sipped the wine.

He shook his head. "Wasn't what I expected."

"Good or bad?"

"Bad." He said, taking a mouthful of lager, pausing then downing the whole pint in one go.

"Jacob!" She exclaimed, worrying slightly that this may not end well from past experiences.

"I needed that!" He said.

'*That* bad?"

"They were playing cover versions. They played two of their own songs, one of which was mine which Chas told me they were *never going to play that soft shit*!" He drained the tumbler. "It's like some two-bit tribute band."

"The crowd loved them!"

"They're all drunk – you could stand someone up there shaking a tambourine and the would still go wild!"

"'Ellen' looked pretty happy." Marelle grinned.

"She's just one of those creepy '*number one fan*' types!"

Marelle laughed.

"Well maybe they'll be better tomorrow. I mean they didn't have a drummer tonight, did they?" She offered.

"Probably do exactly the same set tomorrow night as well."

"You seem disappointed?"

He made a face. "I was expecting better." He said. "I wouldn't want to be with them singing cover versions."

"There you are!" Bella suddenly shouted, striding up to them and sliding an arm through Jacob's. "What're you doing over here, the party is over there!"

"We were getting a drink." Marelle replied. "It's quieter here."

"Do you want a drink?" Jacob asked, gesturing his empty plastic glass towards her.

"Erm, yeah, ok. Thanks." She smiled. "Hey! They were good – weren't they? I can see why you like them!" She laughed. "Playing the Two Point Four Stuff was a stroke of genius, wasn't it?"

"Er yeah. They were OK." Jacob replied, slipping away from her and walking back towards the bar.

Bella followed him and Marelle followed her. Jacob placed himself at the bar.

"What are you having?" He asked Bella.

"I'll have a lager please."

"Pint?"

She nodded.

Jacob requested the pint, turned to Marelle who shook her head and pointedly put her hand over her glass.

"... and a double JD and coke please." Jacob asked.

Marelle heard him and flashed him a look but when he did not acknowledge it, she leant forward and took his arm. He turned to pass the lager to Bella and Marelle leaned into him.

"Jacob? Really?" She asked; haunted by memories of the day of Frankie's funeral when Jacob had also tried to drink himself into oblivion and plunged into belligerent stupidity as a result.

"It's fine." He said. "I just fancy one."

"But a double?"

"It's OK." He whispered to her.

She sighed, looking up at him but catching Bella staring at her. He paid and walked away from the bar.

"What now?" He asked Bella.

"We dance until dawn!" She laughed, holding the lager aloft.

"Oh no, I'm not dancing." He replied with a grin.

And that was why, an hour and a half later, Jacob was still on the dancefloor with Marelle, Bella and Mae. All four of them in a tight little group on a packed dance floor. At first, he had looked awkward, scared to dance but with Bella fooling around and Marelle dancing, if only with him, he soon began to relax into it. He didn't go any further than the one drink he'd worried her about at the bar. For the rest of the night, he drank coke which pleased her and assuaged any fears of a repeat of what he'd done before when a situation had stressed him out of his comfort zone. There on the dancefloor, in the middle of a crowd with the dancing lights on his face Marelle saw in him someone she never would have believed could have existed. He laughed with her, fooled around with Bella and even formed some kind of bond with the enchanting but slightly aloof Mae.

Towards the end of the night there was a moment when Bella playfully shoved Jacob and he went to shove her back, but he slipped slightly on someone else's spilled drink and had to catch himself.

Bella laughed at him, playfully. "Oooh! Nearly!" She exclaimed.

In the process he had half body slammed the male in a couple who had been on the dance floor beside them most of the night. The guy was probably about Jacob's age but bulkier and stockier. His immediate reaction was to shove Jacob back again and when he did Marelle caught him and took his arm.

"Just watch it fella!" The bloke warned. "You've been giving it large all night and I don't know who you think you are but if you do that again I may find it hard to stop my fist from connecting with your jaw ... wanker!"

Jacob backed away; his hands raised in apology. "I'm sorry." He said. "Sorry."

Marelle pulled him to her and took him in her arms as the music slowed down just at the right moment. Marelle hugged into him, her head in the crook of his shoulder. She closed her eyes and felt every inch of him against her. Then before she knew it Bella joined it, wrapping her arms around both of them in a group hug.

"I love you two. Thank you for coming." She said. "Mae, come and join in." She called and suddenly all three of them were wrapped in a hug around Jacob. Marelle raised her head and looked up at him. He smiled down at her and leant in to place a kiss on her lips.

"Uh-oh." Bella said, looking to Mae quite theatrically. "Think it's time to let these two go to their room – I can see something coming on!"

She stood away from them, an arm loosely around Mae's shoulders.

Jacob gave a cheeky grin. "Well, I know when we're not wanted." He took hold of Marelle's hand. "I'm ready to knock this on the head anyway ..."

"Well, it's pretty much finished." Bella added.

"Are you coming back with us?" Marelle questioned.

"Erm, no. I think I'll make the night last a little bit longer. Might just get another drink and chill a bit – you go on though ..."

Marelle smiled. "OK."

"Hey, I'll bring breakfast in the morning, so be decent when I come in!" She laughed, pointing at Jacob. "I've seen a bit too much of you at times!"

"Yeah, and you got it for free. Most people would have to pay!" He quipped.

"Man! He's on fire tonight!" Bella sighed with a grin. "Go on – you two, get outta here. I'll see you in the morning."

With a laugh they walked off, arm in arm while Bella walked towards the bar with Mae.

They walked the five minutes back slowly, wandering across the site towards their chalet. There were other people going back too; some alone, some in pairs, some still in drunken, shrieking groups.

"Somebody has got to clear all of that up before tomorrow." Jacob commented.

"As long as it's not me." Marelle remarked. "Bella will probably end up helping them!"

"Who's this Mae then?" He asked.

"Don't know. Someone Bella has met at other shows I suppose. Seems a bit quiet for Bella ..."

"Nice looking girl." Jacob commented.

"Hey, you're not supposed to notice – I've got your ring on my finger! Remember?" Marelle exclaimed playfully; she knew he'd only said it to wind her up.

He laughed.

"I thought your 'groupie' Ellen was more your type. Is that the fan demographic for the band now?"

"Ow! Touché." He replied.

Marelle laughed and waggled a finger at him as they reached the door to their chalet.

She made them a hot drink with the minimal kitchen facilities. Bella had said to bring a few essentials and luckily, she had remembered to do so. Jacob was oddly quiet but seemingly happy. Now in the space of the chalet he was absorbing the night. They must have sat up for an hour; Marelle had expected a visit from Bella on her way back, but it didn't appear.

"Maybe she's just decided to leave us alone and slip quietly into bed?" Jacob suggested when Marelle expressed a mild concern.

"I hope she's OK. Bella doesn't generally do anything quietly and with alcohol inside her I am surprised she resisted the urge to bang on this door ..." Marelle sighed. "Still, she's been to a million and one of these type of events – she should know what she's doing!"

He smiled. "Maybe she is leaving us alone; maybe she thinks we want to be left alone?"

"Oh yeah?" Marelle smiled. "And why would that be?" She cocked her head to him seductively.

The bed was cold with inadequate covers as far as she was concerned. Between them however, they soon made it warm, and she fell asleep with her head on his chest and his arm around her.

She was stirred by movement in the bed a while later – it could have been minutes; it could have been hours. Marelle felt Jacob move from under her and she reached after him as the last warmth of his body left her arms. Sleepily she stretched out to regain the warmth but awoke with a breathless start when she realised, he wasn't there. Instantly, she sat up in the bed, still trying to work out where he was.

"Jacob!" she shouted, taking her mind back to the night he'd left her and fearing an echo from the silence.

"What?" His voice replied from the bathroom.

Marelle breathed a sigh of relief and willed her heart to slow.

"What are you doing?"

"Going to the toilet." He replied.

She drew a breath to herself and sat there, her knees drawn up under the covers until he returned to the bed. He climbed in and slid down on his back with a sigh.

"What?" She asked.

"I can't sleep." He said.

"Well, that's not unusual, is it?" She smiled in the semi darkness. He probably couldn't see it.

"No, but ... I feel like I used to after we'd done a gig. I never used to go to bed; I'd stay up and sleep the next day."

"Why?"

"Adrenalin, I guess."

"But you haven't done a gig tonight." Marelle said.

"And I'm glad I didn't do that one!" He sighed. "I was really disappointed by them tonight. They're just like a tribute band of what they once were." His words were quiet in the darkness, almost to himself. Marelle sensed a sadness in him. "And ... "He continued. "If that's how they are, I don't want to be part of them."

"Well, they were very well received by the crowd. Surely that's the most important thing, isn't it?"

"Maybe, but they were playing cover versions – other people's songs – there's no passion in that; you didn't write them; their words mean nothing ..."

"They played your song."

"I know. After Chas said it was something they would never perform; said if I wanted tossing shit like that, I'd best get a solo career!"

"Chas seems a bit of a grumpy person really." Marelle commented.

"No, he wasn't. Just liked things done his way ... he may have changed; may have got complacent. They weren't even that tight tonight."

She lay down and rested her head against him. Silence prevailed for a bit. She thought; he thought.

"What is your plan?" she sighed, at length.

"My plan was to watch them tonight, and tomorrow then make a move at a gig in a couple of weeks.'

"Make a move?"

"Reveal myself."

"What, publicly?"

"No, just let him see me. Hopefully he will see me right at the front and then he'll want to speak to me afterwards."

"What if he doesn't see you?"

"He will." Jacob stated.

Shortly after Jacob began snoring softly and Marelle smiled to herself with her head against him again.

Marelle was woken by her phone in the morning. It made the sound of a text coming through and stirred her from a relatively light slumber. Sliding up in the bed, the room half lit by sunlight through the scanty orange curtain, she reached for the phone.

"RU up yet?" It said.

Bella. She smiled to herself. It was ten past seven. A second text popped through.

"I'm coming round in 5."

Marelle replied. "Just woke up. Come in ten and we'll be decent."

"Ok. Bringing brekkie."

Jacob had also woken beside her. He lay on his back and yawned, running his fingers through his hair. It was getting longer.

"What was that?" He asked.

"Bella." She smiled. "She'll be over in ten minutes. You'd better get yourself decent. She says she's bringing breakfast."

When Bella banged on the door he was still in the bathroom. Marelle was dressed but had no make-up on and her hair was not done. She was twisting it into a high ponytail as she opened the door.

Bella stood there, Pale pink jeans and a white cropped sweatshirt top. She was in full make-up and was sporting a pair of large sunglasses. In her hand she held up. A brown paper carrier bag with the word 'Valentinos' printed on the front.

"I hope you've got coffee going. I've been to a fantastic little bakers just down the road. I discovered them last time. Croissants and pastries to die for!

Marelle stood aside for her to come in.

"I didn't hear you come in last night. I was expecting you to bang on our door!" Marelle said as Bella made for the kitchen and switched the kettle on.

"I had a drink with Mae then went back to hers for a little while. I didn't want to wake you – I thought you might be *occupied*!" She winked theatrically.

Marelle smiled, knowingly.

"What's with Mae" She asked. "Do you know her from here?"

"Here and there. I usually hang around with her and her partner, but they've just split up so she's here on her own."

"Thought as much. I've caught her fluttering her eyelashes at Jacob a couple of times."

Bella laughed. "She's not. I can guarantee Jacob is not her type; you've got nothing to worry about. She's just trying to be friendly! But to be honest with those big blue eyes she looks like she's coming on to everyone!"

She was looking at the jar of coffee as she spoke and making a face at it.

"Don't worry yourself about Mae."

"She's very quiet." Marelle added.

"She's better when you get to know her – where's Jacob?"

"In the bathroom."

"Well, these are still warm – will he be long?"

"Probably not. He didn't sleep well."

"Oh, why? No nightmares?"

"No – just couldn't sleep. I think he was buzzing a bit afterwards."

"He wasn't even down at the front! I thought he would be … he likes them, doesn't he?"

Marelle shrugged.

"Well, he keeps singing their song on karaoke!" Bella exclaimed.

"He doesn't like being in a crowd."

"Nonsense! We'll get him well and truly *buzzed* tonight! Mae and I will make sure of it!"

At that point the bathroom door opened, and Jacob appeared. He wore dark jeans but no top; Marelle smiled to herself. He'd pushed his hair up on his head in a vague attempt to recreate the old style.

"Oh, hello Prince Charming." Bella said, with a smile.

He smiled in return. "You're up early."

"Have to be … to catch the worm – or warm croissants in this case!" She pointed to them. "Anyway, maybe I haven't been to bed!"

"Haven't you?" Marelle exclaimed.

Bella shot her a glance. "Of course I have! You don't get to look like this with no beauty sleep!"

Jacob walked past her into the kitchen area. Bella looked him up and down with a grin. "Have you brought those white jeans?" She asked, with a wink to Marelle.

"No." He replied, dryly.

"Oh man!" Bella mocked. "I was looking forward to seeing you in those … what about the leather ones?"

"No." He repeated, his back to them both.

Bella laughed. "No, I suppose either of those options may be a bit more than inebriated women around here could take! Damn near blew my mind!"

He knew she was playing with him and purposely didn't rise to it as he looked inside the carrier bag she had put on the worktop.

"It'll be crazy tonight." Bella continued. "Saturdays are always crazy. There will be a lot more people here – a lot come on just a Saturday ticket … you'd better come down the front with us; it'll be the safest place." She explained. "And I can look out for you."

"I'm not coming down the front." Jacob said. "Don't worry about me – I can look after myself." He took a croissant out and bit into it. He made a face of appreciation.

"What are you two planning today then?" Bella asked. "There's lots to do but the music doesn't start until this afternoon. We were thinking of going to the water park if you fancy coming along?"

"We?" Marelle questioned.

"Mae and me; It's usually quite a laugh – you up for it? You like swimming, don't you Jacob?"

"Not in a bath of other people's piss – thank you." He replied.

Bella laughed. "You have such a way with words Jacob! Love it!" She chuckled to herself. "So, we're not going to get you in swimming trunks this morning then?"

"I don't own any swimming trunks." He replied, finishing the croissant while standing in the kitchen area. "Where's the beach around here?"

Bella shrugged. "I don't know. I've never been to the beach here …"

"Fancy a walk along the beach?" He asked, mainly to Marelle but included Bella with a glance to her.

"No – not with my hair – all that wind and salty air." Bella stated. "I'll take my chance with the chlorine and piss!"

"It's meant to be a nice beach here, isn't it?" Marelle commented.

Bella shrugged, making coffee.

"We'll go and take a look." Jacob suggested. "I need some fresh air."

"I'm going swimming with Mae. Meet you here about three? We can get ready and get over there early?"

"OK." Marelle replied. Jacob nodded.

"… and we can get right at the front. You really needed to be down there last night. We were right there – right in front of the lead singer – what's his name?"

"Chas." Jacob said, almost too quickly.

"See!" Bella grinned. "You're a bit of a closet fan, aren't you? A bit too shy to be right up the front near your hero, hey?" She nudged Jacob. "We were going to Google them to see what his name was."

Jacob looked quickly to Marelle then away again before Bella noticed.

"I thought they were really good last night. To be honest I've not taken much notice of them before, but they were superb." She added. "Mae really liked them too." She laughed. "Let's get right at the front later."

Jacob didn't say a lot; Marelle chose to steer the conversation in a different direction to stop Bella circling Yellow Son, Chas and all that came with it as she was catching glances from Jacob that conveyed a slight discomfort at the conversation. They ended up laughing about the groped bottom incident while they finished the croissants and pastries with Bella downing a third cup of coffee. Their plans were to meet back here at three after Bella and Mae had been to the water complex and Jacob had found the beach with Marelle. Bella said she thought the beach was only a few minutes away, so they set off and were directed by a helpful signpost which said, "to the beach."

Marelle clutched Jacob's arm as they walked. It was pretty cold today and there was a stiff breeze. She had put a coat on but only had a t-shirt beneath so was feeling the bite of the sea air. Today Jacob wore a black hoodie and had pulled the hood up, partly to keep himself warm.

The beach was wide and golden. In the height of summer, it would have been an idyllic setting of the quintessential English seaside but today it was windy and cold. The sun was out and if you had taken a snapshot, it would have looked perfect. The colours sharp; the layers of sand, sea and sky were defined in bands of co-ordinating colours; the sea flat and pretty calm despite the chill wind coming off it. There were sandy cliffs which dropped gently down to the beach via a tarmacked walkway. The narrow road above had a few shops and scant amusements but the beach below with just sand and sea.

The sand was soft and not easy to walk on. She kept close to Jacob, huddling against the stiff breeze, walking first across and then down towards the foaming fingers of the grey blue sea as it lapped continuously at the land. Down there the sand was damper and firmer, and they could walk more easily, leaving their footprints in the sand as brief testament that they had spent time here.

There were other people on the beach, but it was practically empty. Just ahead of them was another couple walking towards them, arm in arm like they were. They had a small tan coloured, terrier type dog with them that was playing tag with the water as it advanced and retreated, ducking, diving and barking. It ran towards Jacob and Marelle as they approached the other couple then turned and ran back to it's owners before diving at the sea again then running headlong at Marelle.

'Chip! Here!" the owner called, his voice gruff and commanding. Still probably fifteen or twenty metres apart, his voice covering the distance sharply to call the dog. "Chip!" He shouted again as they came closer.

Marelle laughed as the dog ran circles, playfully, around them.

"Chip!" He yelled again. "I'm sorry." He apologised as they neared each other, an apologetic smile on his face as he grabbed for the dog – and missed it as it began another circuit.

Beside her Marelle suddenly felt Jacob's step falter, almost stumble. She kept hold of his arm and looked briefly at him. Maybe he'd slipped on the sand. He was looking earnestly at his feet and the ground he was about to walk on.

"Sorry!" The guy with the dog said. "He's a little bugger sometimes – been couped up all night now he's like something let loose!"

Marelle laughed. Felt a slight pull on her arm again from Jacob.

"That's alright." She smiled to the guy with the dog, looking straight at him and the white-blonde haired, well-dressed woman with him. Jacob was definitely pulling her forwards – she wondered for a second if he was scared of the dog – maybe he was. Once past, she turned slightly towards him in order to ask but just as she did the dog returned running around and around them, barking playfully and wagging its tail in pure delight. Marelle stopped, keeping hold of Jacob's arm as the guy with the dog came stomping back.

"Chip! Get here!" He shouted. The dog ignored, so she stooped, caught its collar as it did another circuit then picked it up as it wriggled in his arms.

"You little fucker!" Marelle heard him say to it as he walked away.

She gave a little laugh, turning back to Jacob.

"Are you scared of dogs?" She asked, half sympathetically, half surprised. He was still turned partially away as if he didn't even want to look at the animal.

"No." He answered. "No, I'm fine with dogs but that was Chas."

"Chas?" Marelle questioned, not immediately putting the name with the figure. "Chas!" She exclaimed, turning to look at him, still walking along the beach away from them.

"Yes, with his wife Mya."

"Chas from the band?"

He nodded.

"No!" She exclaimed. "He's very unassuming!" She watched them walking away in the distance now. He had set the dog down and it ran to the sea again.

"Why don't you say something?"

"No!" Jacob exclaimed. "Not here. It's neither the time nor the place."

"Catch him unawares ..."

"No!" Jacob stated again, this time slightly more forcefully.

"Does he live here then?"

"No – probably staying in a hotel nearby. It's a two-night gig so I imagine he would probably stay here."

"And that's his wife?"

Jacob nodded, still not totally wanting to look in his direction. Marelle watched them – just a couple on the beach with their dog.

"You should say something. Do you want me to?" Marelle mused.

"No! I'll pick my time, but I'd better keep my guard up a bit better."

"Is he staying at the holiday camp?" She questioned.

"I doubt it ... God! I hope not. I could bump into him at any time ..."

"Do you reckon they're all here then?"

He shrugged.

Marelle was still standing watching Chas. She wanted to shout "*Chas!*" and see if he turned.

"Well, he didn't seem to recognise you." She finally said to Jacob, taking his arm again.

Jacob didn't reply, he just walked on in silence for a good few strides. Marelle felt a tenseness in him as Jacob perfused through his veins beneath her fingers.

"So he's got a dog then?" She asked.

"Looks like it."

"Well, he wouldn't be allowed to have the dog in the holiday camp, would he? It said no pets."

Jacob shrugged. Marelle sensed that apathetic, anxious unease in him that she thought had passed forever. She held his arm but turned her head to look back down the beach to the two small figures and a dog moving into the distance and away from them.

"Maybe that would have been a good time to say something – catch him off guard ..."

"No! This is not the right place and especially when Mya is with him."

Marelle sighed, turned back and walked alongside him.

"He's taller than I thought." She commented.

"But shorter than me."

"How much older is he than you?"

"Dunno really. I suppose he's in his late fifties, early sixties ... most of the band are. I think Marty is the oldest."

"Which one is he?"

"Drummer."

"Were you as close to any of the others as you were to Chas?"

"Probably Marty. He had his head screwed on the right way round!"

Marelle smiled at his phrase. She still felt he should have confronted Chas there and then. It was a chance meeting that he should have reached out and taken hold of. But he hadn't and Chas was now a tiny figure receding into the distance, disappearing with that moment which she felt should have been seized. Jacob had his reasons and his plan which Marelle knew he would not be swayed from. But right now, she sensed a tension in him which she did not welcome or even like and knew she had to somehow make it go away.

They walked up the wide golden beach which stretched eternally into the distance until Chas had completely disappeared – at least from view. Marelle changed the conversation, laughed, joked about Bella, talked about the sea, the sky, the seagulls. Jacob joined in but a large part of him was elsewhere. Eventually they turned and walked back, found a fish and chip shop and ate whilst sitting on a low wall around a modern church. It was warmer off the beach, but Jacob insisted on keeping the hood on. He sat astride the wall, slouched, looking down at the sausage and chips as Marelle sat beside him, furtively watching as he ate. She liked watching him eat – he ate with a mission – completely absorbed in the action until he had finished. He didn't hurry, just did it in his own time but with absolute resolve. Unless, of course, he was too distracted by some or other issue to even consider food – which unfortunately, she had also observed many times too.

He folded the paper the food had been wrapped in and crushed it into a ball between his hands. Then he raised his eyes to her. Deep. Dark and intensive – like she knew they could be but often never were. Marelle smiled; she saw Jacob; she saw Nat and she saw Ezza; all in one, right in front of her. He was none of them as individuals – he was the sum total of all three.

When they walked back to the holiday park it was buzzing. There was a queue of cars coming into the park and far more people around than there had been earlier or yesterday. Groups of girls, women, groups of blokes, wandered around – excited and loud. Jacob was still carrying the burden of coming face to face with Chas together with his disappointment at last night's performance and walked through them all, dressed entirely in black, arm in arm with Marelle. A couple of months ago she would not have got him near this place let alone in. rowdy crowd. But now he was here enduring it, and Marelle felt a tiny stab of fear that by the end of the night he may end up freaking out on her. And she did fear that, knowing just how bad he could be – he had been. Marelle didn't like the tilt of his mood; she didn't like the crowds, and she didn't like the very narrow line he was walking. He appeared in control, but she knew how good he was at hiding everything. Her heart was beating faster as they made their way back to the chalet.

They had just got in the room when Marelle's phone rang.

"Hi Bella." She answered.

Are you at the chalet yet?"

"Yes, just got back."

"Where did you go?"

"We walked up the beach. It's a lovely beach …"

"I've never been up there … listen, I'm going to go back with Mae, get changed and then we'll come to you? Is that, ok?"

"Sounds fine."

"Have you eaten?"

"Yes, we had some very nice fish and chips."

"Oh that's good. We've just grabbed a burger – reckon we can all survive on alcohol for the rest of the night!"

"Er, no, I'm not drinking Bella … I need to keep a clear head in case …" She stopped, not wanting to say anything else more.

"In case what?!" Bella exclaimed.

Marelle sighed. "In case I need a clear head – for any reason."

Bella tutted. "Marelle, it's party night – *no-one* needs a clear head!"

Marelle did not respond to that.

"Gonna be frantic. I suggest we get to the front and stay there." Bella said.

"We'll see." Marelle answered.

"Just get in there and let it all go!" Bella laughed. "Act like you're still seventeen."

Marelle gave a small laugh. She almost said that she wished she was still seventeen but did not speak her words because that would mean she would not know Jacob and their paths may never have met in that parallel universe.

"– and …"Bella began again. 'Tell him not to wear that bloody hoodie – it gets hot in there and he'll melt if he does. Best to be a bit cold to start with and we'll soon warm up!"

"Bella's on her way." Marelle commented to Jacob when he came out of the bathroom after her call. "With Mae, so make sure you are dressed before they get here. And Bella said don't wear the hoodie – you'll be too hot!"

THIRTEEN

He wore the hoodie, over a white t-shirt with dark wash jeans and the sunglasses. Bella banged on the door.

"Come on, let us in. We need to do a full orifice inspection!" She yelled, laughing then bursting into the room with Mae in tow when Marelle opened the door.

"Are we ready to party?!" She announced, flamboyantly – one hand in the air. Mae right beside her – and both of them wearing what looked like brand-new Yellow Son t-shirts.

"Ta-da!" she laughed, pulling the t-shirt tight across her and pointing to Mae as well.

Jacob, who was standing in the doorway of the bathroom gave a little laugh.

"We just bought them – why don't you two get them as well – we can stand right at the front and keep shouting at – *Chas* – is it?" She winked at Marelle. "Go on – it'll be fun!"

Jacob shook his head. "I really don't think so." He said with a grin. "And I'm not standing down the front either."

"It's ok. We'll look after you. Come on, it'll be a blast! Just let yourself go for once!"

He looked at her and raised his eyebrows in question as the tiny dimple in his cheek considered making an appearance.

"What's the point coming here if you're just going to hover at the back like a spare prick? Hey? Come on Jacob – you're here now – everybody is just having fun – just let yourself go – stop acting so *old*!" Bella protested. "You will come with us, and we will make sure you have a great time – even if it kills us!"

She turned and winked at Mae, who smiled in return.

"Right, are we ready?" Bella asked.

'Yeah, we're ready." Jacob answered dryly.

"You going like that?" Bella asked.

Jacob looked at himself. "Yeah?"

Bella sighed. "Where are your tight, white jeans, or your leather trousers?"

Jacob widened his arms in gesture. "Take me as I am!"

Bella tutted. "Why don't you get a t-shirt?" As she reached for the door.

"I don't want a t-shirt." He replied, following her and Mae out.

Marelle locked her arm into Jacob's and with a grin Bella did the same on his other side; Mae took hold of Bella's arm and all four of them walked in line across the site with Bella's excitement bubbling over enough for all of them.

The doors of the main hall had just opened when the four of them walked up. A few people were inside but most of them were gathered around the bar.

"Right! Top tip!" Bella turned back to them. "You two go down the front and find a good space. Mae and I will get the drinks."

"But I don't want ..." Jacob began.

"Just go!" Bella exclaimed, pointing them in the direction of the stage.

"Well, I'm not staying there once you get there." He said, with a grin, walking across the floor.

"Stop being a baby!" Bella shouted back.

Jacob walked casually up to the front of the stage with Marelle still arm in arm with him. There was a tubular steel barrier about three feet from the edge of the stage which he sauntered up to and leaned his elbows upon. Marelle stood close beside him, her hands resting on the cold steel of the barrier. To their right were two, middle aged, balding guys in Yellow Son t-shirts like the ones Bella and Mae had bought. Jacob was staring at the stage. There were instruments and speakers, amplifiers, microphones and a whole array of equipment set up on the stage which Jacob was staring at.

"Why is there a barrier?" She asked.

"Well God forbid we don't want any fans touching us, do we?" he stated. "Security." He added, matter of factly.

"But I've seen pictures of you reaching right out into the crowd before."

He nodded. "Yeah, sometimes."

She stood beside him. Some more people arrived to their left – again all in Yellow Son t-shirts. Jacob didn't look or move. Marelle stared back at the stage.

"Why are there two drum kits?" She asked.

"One for the support, one for Yellow Son." He explained. "Luc's kit is the big gold one at the back I would have thought. At least it looks like he's here tonight."

"Will they take all of the other gear away then when Yellow Son play?"

"Yeah." He replied with a sigh. "Where's Bella got to?"

He turned and looked hard as a road crew member walked onto the stage.

"Oh ..." Marelle looked to the bar. "I think she'll be a while."

He sighed again, stood upright and placed his hands on the barrier just as three people occupied the space between them and the bald guys in Yellow Son t-shirts. There was a woman and two blokes, they had drinks and were chatting.

Jacob sighed, stretched, then turned back.

"Hi!" the woman now next to him smiled. "Big fan?" She asked.

Jacob stared at her for a second. "Erm yeah." He replied.

Marelle leaned forward to make herself seen.

"Should be good tonight." The woman smiled. "Were you here last night?"

"Yeah." Jacob replied.

"What did you think? Wasn't one of their best performances but they were standing in at short notice and they made the effort to play some of the other band's songs – trying to be someone they're not. They did a good job though. They're awesome!"

Jacob didn't reply. Marelle could tell he was hoping she would go away but chances are she wouldn't; she wanted a front spot too.

"I must just about be their number one fan!" She continued. "I've been to virtually every gig!"

Jacob nodded.

"Right from the start." She exclaimed.

Jacob sighed. Marelle clutched his arm and moved closer to him.

"I still love Ezza though! God! He was so good – they'll never be the same without him."

Marelle felt a bolt of tension pass through Jacob and remain in every muscle.

"Don't you think?" She was carrying on. "Do you remember Ezza? Did you ever see him live?"

"Er ... yes ... I have, did ..." Jacob stuttered.

"Well, you'll know then. He was a God!" She sighed. "But Chas is brilliant; he's so funny and he has done so well to keep it all going – and all the fan's loyalty ..." She smiled.

Jacob smiled in return, nervously.

The woman turned to face them both directly. Marelle thought that straight on, she seemed vaguely familiar but couldn't place her.

"That's why I'm wearing this!" She exclaimed with a cheery smile. She opened her jacket to reveal a t-shirt with an image of a full figure portrayal of Ezza on it, printed in white on a black t-shirt.

"Oh! Wow!" Jacob said with some genuine surprise and uncertainty in his voice.

"I know it winds Chas up, but it's only friendly banter and we don't want to go forgetting this superstar, do we? They wouldn't be anywhere without what Ezza did!"

Jacob shook his head. "Er, no."

"I'm Ellen." She suddenly held out a hand.

Jacob took it and shook it, limply. She did the same to Marelle.

Ellen.

"It was my birthday yesterday – did you see? Chas got me up on the stage! He's such a joker – he's done that loads of times – always call me their *'number one fan'* – which is a real compliment – they're like family to me!" She chuckled.

Jacob shuffled, looked for Bella again, threw a glance at Marelle.

"Hey, look, look!" Ellen took out a phone and showed then pictures of her with various band members. Jacob maintained a banal grin, Marelle tried not to look concerned. "And this – this is my favourite picture!" She held the phone out to proudly show them an image of her, obviously some time ago, arms wrapped around a very sweaty looking Ezza – red shirt wet and stuck to his torso, hair slightly tousled and flopped over his forehead but a smile on his face. "This was about fifteen years ago – I scanned in the photographs to get them on my phone – Ezza was always shy about having his picture taken with fans, but he let me!"

"Shit! I remember that shirt!" Jacob exclaimed in amazement as his brain was completely taken over by the situation, he found himself in.

"Yes, he wore it to a few gigs!" She smiled. "That picture is so precious!" Ellen sighed. "What I wouldn't give to have him back."

Jacob turned and faced front again, leant onto his arms again, moved slightly closer to Marelle.

Ellen continued beside them. "You know ..." She began, stuffing her phone back into her pocket. "I don't think he's dead."

"What?" Jacob suddenly turned his head to her.

"No – I don't think he died. I think it was a cover up to get him away from everything. It doesn't add up. There was no funeral, no memorial – nothing."

"Do you really think that?" Jacob asked.

Marelle shook his arm as if to tell him not to pursue this conversation.

"Well ..." Ellen began.

"Come on! Get these down your necks! I got two so I don't have to keep going backwards and forwards." Bella exclaimed, walking up with a handful of drinks which she carefully stood down on the floor in front of them. "Budge up!" she said to Ellen, squeezing in between her and Jacob until she was against the barrier then nodding for Mae to join her. Bella smiled at Ellen as she did so. "Hey, you're the one they got up on stage last night?" Bella asked.

Ellen nodded, with a certain smugness.

"Cool!" Bella laughed. "Do you think I might be able to get up on stage tonight?"

Ellen gave a little laugh. "Oh, I doubt it. I am a personal friend of Chas, so he made an exception."

Bella glared at her. "Really?"

Marelle slid an arm around Jacob's waist and leaned in to look at Bella as she pushed, very subtly in front of Ellen.

"Yes." Ellen replied then with a smug grin added "Tt's nice to see younger fans coming through. It's what the band needs – I was just having a conversation with – is he your father...?"

Bella laughed explosively. "What?!" She looked round at Jacob then back to Ellen. "No, he's not my father – he's my best friend's fiancé! How the fuck could he be my father?"

Jacob made an open-handed gesture towards Ellen but Marelle felt a ripple of unease pass through him.

"I'm sorry ... it's the hood ... I can't really tell, and I assumed ... it makes you look older."

"See!" Bella said to Jacob. "I told you not to wear it – she thinks you're my Dad ! Take it off!" She reached up and grabbed at the hood, but Jacob ducked out of the way. Bella took it as a game and grabbed at him again, but this time Jacob had his hand on his head.

"I don't want to take it off, leave it!"

Bella laughed, pulling at the edge of it as he held tight onto it."

"Come on! You ashamed of how fucking good looking you are ... let Ellen see, I don't want her thinking you're my father!"

"No." He repeated, still trying to fend her off.

"Bella. Leave him be." Marelle added, with a wink to her.

Bella continued to pull at his hoodie, laughing and batting at his head with her hand. Jacob had playfully pushed her away, but she came back at him again. They were like a couple of Bella's six-year-olds that she taught in school, but it was light-hearted. Ellen stood watching with her eyebrows raised at the scuffle until Jacob pushed at Bella with one hand, but she moved out of the way quickly and Jacob ended up flinging his arm out uncontrollably8u8-= and smacking it into the cheek of a passing guy who was walking behind them. He immediately grabbed at Jacob, clutching at a handful of his clothing at his chest. Marelle stood upright and felt her knees weaken; Bella stepped forward and started shouting at the guy on the receiving end of the misplaced slap.

"Leave him, it was an accident!" She exclaimed. "It was my fault ... I'm sorry."

"Fucking ignorant pisshead. You touch me again and I'll knock your fucking head off your shoulders! Whoever's fault it is!" He grimaced right into Jacob's face.

Bella grabbed at Jacob's arm, pulling him away before the bloke released him from his grip. She pulled, he let go. Jacob staggered backwards against Marelle. He raised his hands plaintively.

"I'm sorry. It was an accident." He said as he stepped back.

"Fucking dozy prat." The guy spat and walked away.

"Phew, sorry!" Bella exhaled, taking Jacob's arm.

"You ok?" Marelle asked.

"Yes, yes, I'm fine!" Jacob nodded, exhaling a held breath himself.

"Look – Bella – you go there." He pushed her gently to the front and Mae joined her. Behind them he wrapped his arms around Marelle, holding her in front of himself, looking at the stage again and avoiding eye contact with Ellen who was still staring at him. He took a long drink from the plastic tumbler Bella picked up from the floor in front of her feet and passed to him with a smile.

"Ooh that tastes odd!" He moaned after downing half of it one go.

"It's the plastic glasses." Marelle said with a grin. "This tastes weird as well."

"What is it?"

"Coke." She replied. "But it's probably some cheap replacement ..."

"Why are you drinking coke?" He asked.

"Because ..." She answered. "Someone's got to keep an eye on you! It's been pretty bizarre so far and you've nearly got you head smashed in as well!"

"I believe that was your good friend Bella's fault." He remarked, taking another drink.

Bella looked round at him with a grin when she heard her name.

"I may not stay here." He said. "I might move to the back."

"Oh no you're not!" You stay right there!" Bella turned and pointed.

Jacob stayed under duress. Half of him wanted to remove himself and go to stand at the back but half of him wanted to remain there – Marelle could see that. As the place filled however, moving anywhere seemed to be quite an impossibility. It failed to stop Bella shimmying off to the bar on a couple of occasions however despite Jacob's insistence that he would go.

"No, no, you stay right there. I'm not giving you any excuses to disappear! You need to be there to help me wind Chas up!"

"Wind Chas up? Why" Jacob asked.

"Because it's fun!" She laughed. "Same again? I'll be back in a moment."

It was both manic and frantic even before the support band came on to the stage. There was so much screaming, shouting and laughter – with Jacob and Marelle in the middle of it all, his arms around her protectively.

"If it gets too much then I am moving." He said quietly to her.

"Ok." She replied. "It's your call."

As the lights finally began to dim Marelle looked around herself. It was much, much fuller than it had been last night. They were pretty much shoulder to shoulder with the people next to them. Was it because it was a Saturday or were all of these people here to see Yellow Son? She suspected it may have been the latter considering the number of Yellow Son t-shirts she could see.

Then with a crescendo of music the white lights came up on stage and the band playing before Yellow Son walked on. A projected screen commented "The Glow" in large red neonesque letters and the four members walked or ran onto the stage. The was a buzz from the crowd if not a cheer as they gave the impression they were not here for this group. Marelle watched Bella and Mae whoop and start to jig about with their hands in the air, much to the dismay of Ellen and the guys to their right. The music was very loud and very 'pop'. It was made for a much younger audience and its intent was probably lost on ninety percent of the crowd. Bella and Mae were obviously enjoying it and being right at the front, had the sole attention of the lead singer who fancied himself like crazy. He was a better dancer than a singer and homed in on them as the focus of his attention. Marelle felt Jacob swaying slightly to the music behind her and she smiled to herself. It was hot in here and if she was honest, she felt a little lightheaded.

"She's good." Jacob said, leaning in to speak in her ear but ended up shouting.

"Who?" She shouted back.

"The drummer. I like her ..." He said.

Marelle turned to look at him in question. He had a weird smile on his face. "She's good." He said again.

Yes, they had a female drummer – dressed in a sparkly blue strappy jumpsuit, her long, straight, blonde hair in a high pony tail which swished playfully as she gave her all to the drumming with a natural energy that the rest of the band did not match.

"Musically." He finally added, shouting into her ear again, Then he laughed. "Not in any other way of course – she's far too young!"

Marelle took another drink; she could have done with another but guessed now wasn't the time to go and get it.

Then suddenly Bella grabbed her hand, pulled her forward – it was strange, she didn't want to go but found it hard to resist. Bella slid an arm around Marelle as she jumped up and down. Marelle glanced back at Jacob who grinned as he finished his drink and shrugged as she got dragged into dancing with Bella and Mae. Half a minute later Bella dragged him forwards too, he stumbled and dropped the plastic tumbler and crashed into her. There was a bit of a frustrated exclamation from those next to them as he fell against them but with the music and the lights it soon got lost.

"Come on you two – time to start dancing!" Bella ordered. "Come on!" And she wrapped her arms around Jacob and began jumping up and down with him, singing to the song. Marelle laughed – he smiled. He looked happy!

He didn't look intimidated by the crowd or fearful of his surroundings, so Marelle let her mind go where it wanted to. Soon she was seventeen again, laughing and singing with Bella. Shortly after Jacob was right behind her, his hands on her and his laughing, smiling face right next to hers. Bella put her arms around both of them with a grin.

After forty-five minutes or so, The Glow finished their set and walked off with a wave and a kiss to the audience. The lights came up a little and Bella turned to Marelle and Jacob.

"Wow! They were good!" She laughed.

Jacob had his arms wrapped tightly around Marelle, his chin resting on her head and a grin on his face. "They were ok." He said. "I need a drink, who else wants one?"

"I'm getting drinks tonight – I promised!" Bella exclaimed earnestly. "Come with me Mae – you two come here and keep our place."

As Jacob moved back to the barrier, Ellen next to him spread herself a little until her elbow touched his.

"Your friends are quite excitable, aren't they?" She asked.

"Seem to be." Jacob answered, not looking at her.

Marelle squeezed in beside him, feeling a little ragged around the edges as she leant her head against him. Right now, she wanted to be alone with him; she didn't want to share him with all of these people – with Bella, Mae – or Ellen. She looked up and gazed at him.

"What?" He asked, smiling at her.

"You're beautiful." She replied with a little grin.

He wrapped his arms tightly around her then kissed her in an open display of affection that was not entirely appropriate for the situation.

"Hey! Hey!" Bella suddenly shouted, making her way through the crowd with drinks, to a few protests. "Put her down!"

Marelle giggled. Jacob smiled and swayed to and fro with her as they parted and stood side by side.

Bella handed Jacob a. pint and Marelle a coke then turned to Mae for her own drink. She took a couple of mouthfuls then signalled that she was coming back to the barrier. She and Jacob swapped places as Ellen beside them took out her phone to take a shot of the stage now set up for Yellow Son. Jacob stood watching her for a second, took a sip of his drink then reached out a hand to her phone. She wasn't expecting that to happen so without much of a fight he took it out of her hand.

'Hey!" She exclaimed, reaching back for it. "What do you think you're doing?"

"Sorry." He said, with a grin, then leant in towards her with her phone up at arm's length to take a selfie. "Don't you want a selfie with me?" He smiled as he took the picture, and she leaned away from him. He laughed. "You'll regret that!"

"I don't want a bloody selfie with you – you're drunk!" She spat, taking her phone back from him angrily.

"Don't delete it." He said, pointing to the phone.

"Just leave me alone ... you're an idiot." She moaned, turning her back on him.

Marelle and Bella were both staring at Jacob – almost aghast at what he'd done. He just laughed and moved back behind Marelle.

"Don't delete it!" He called again to Ellen with a grin and finished his drink, an arm around Marelle. She smiled to herself; in the middle of all this crowd she had a warm, fuzzy feeling at being so close to him. Bella grinned back at both of them then turned back to the front with Mae.

It seemed to take forever until the lights dimmed and with an enormous cheer from the crowd the band members of Yellow Son began to walk on stage. First on was the drummer. He held a hand in the air to the buoyant cheers – climbing behind his drum kit he immediately thrashed out a rhythm as the other three came onto the stage. The bassist and a guitarist who immediately took up their instruments and picked up the tune, smiling and laughing as the crowd bellowed. It was louder and much fuller then last night and you got the sense most people were here to see Yellow Son alone. Then on walked Chas, slowly, calculatedly, moving into the central spotlight which was waiting for him. Casually he took hold of his guitar and with a nod to the others launched into the first track of the set with a power and an energy that had been very tightly packaged away the night before. The crowd went wild; Bella was screaming with her hands in the air in front of them and Jacob had fingers in a tight grip, digging into her shoulders as he stood behind her.

"Wow! They're loud!" She turned to exclaim to Jacob, but her words were lost in the noise and the look on Jacob's face would have blocked them anyway. Marelle felt a shiver inside as she looked at him, a crinkle in time, space and perception. Jacob was transfixed; he had a grin on his face and tears in his eyes. Marelle watched and smiled sublimely to herself as he could contain himself no longer and he began to sing along.

Despite not wanting to be at the front he made no attempt to move back and was going with the flow of the crowd. Behind Bella and Mae, he still had the hoodie on and was singing along with perfect timing. His hands trembled as he wanted to emulate the moves he always used to make to the music, his music. He still had one arm around Marelle, almost protectively – or supportively, she didn't know as she felt his body moving against her and his voice singing above her.

The first song was loud, fast and powerful. Chas proved to be a better singer than she had expected when he sang his own songs with the full band behind him. They moved seamlessly into a second track to which Jacob actually whooped – so loud that Bella looked round at him with an astonished grin on her face. She laughed to herself and looked at the people on both sides of them – all guys – all completely absorbed in the performance and to the front Ellen – transfixed by Chas; clapping and shouting. Every single one of them completely unaware whom they were standing next to. Marelle laughed at that thought, sought and gripped at his hand, squeezing tightly when she found it. Now she could feel his pulse, his heartbeat, the vitality that had now risen and was running through him. She knew now where Jacob belonged.

The second track came to an end and this time Chas held up a hand, smiling broadly. The band stopped, the crowd noise rose.

"Thank you." Chas said. He adjusted the guitar around himself. "Who's come just to see us tonight?"

There was a massive cheer. He laughed.

"That's good. I hear there was some two-bit group here last night playing covers ... don't know who they were!"

The crowd laughed and cheered.

"We'd better please our fans then, hadn't we!" He grinned, looking down at the front row. "I can see a few familiar faces here." Beside him Marty played a rhythm on the bass as Chas spoke. It seemed that most of the crowd recognised it immediately and a rumble of a cheer crackled through them.

"Too Close." Chas said, quietly, before the drums kicked in and they were in full flow again.

Behind, holding her to him, Jacob laughed. A laugh of recognition and acknowledgement. This was obviously what he had been expecting last night. The crowd started bouncing, Bella and Mae joined in, hands in the air, shouting and singing. Marelle recognised the song from the CD on the journey there and Jacob also started singing to it, loudly. Bella turned around, grinning – pointed at Jacob and laughed, then turned back. Marelle twisted round and looked at him. He had bis eyes closed, knowing and singing every word with more meaning and intensity than even Chas. She could see the adrenalin bristling through him as he acted out every word of the song, taking it to the very last note. After which he leaned forward and said something to Bella. She laughed, said something back then nodded and turned around again. Then he stood back and hugged Marelle tightly.

As the song faded and there was a slight lull, Chas moved over to speak to the other guitarist – Marelle couldn't remember who Jacob had said it was – she heard Bella shouting.

"Chas! Chas! Play Fickle Finger!" She yelled, straight up at him.

He may have heard her; probably didn't but as he walked back, she shouted it again, right at the correct moment between quietening crowd and the music beginning.

"Play Fickle Finger!" She shouted.

This time he heard her, stopped, gestured down. "Really?" He laughed. "I'm not playing that." He shook his head, counted one, two then started into a new track.

At her next chance Bella tried again. In a quieter part she shouted out.

"Play Fickle Finger!" Again, twice, until Chas looked directly at her. He pointed a finger.

"I'm not playing fucking Fickle Finger … you weren't even born the last time I played that … what's the game? Hey, young lady?"

Bella laughed. "He told me to say it –" Pointing to Jacob behind her. Chas raised a hand to shield his eyes. Bella turned with a grin but Jacob was not there. She looked around for Marelle who shrugged.

"Fucking Fickle Finger." Chas sighed, taking a step back to the mic. "What shall we do with them Ellen, hey?"

"Throw them out. They're idiots!" Ellen shouted back but Chas didn't seem to hear.

Bella looked immediately at Marelle as Jacob stood up from his ducked down position in the crowd. Bella laughed and playfully thumped him. He grinned and wrapped his arms around Marelle again as all eyes around them had been locked on him both suspiciously and contemptuously. The band launched into another tune.

Ten songs later they had played ninety minute set. The crowd were buzzing and the band were dripping with sweat. Jacob was wired and unusually ready to leap into whatever was coming next. The crowd booed playfully.

"We're old guys now – we need to go home to Horlicks and bed!" Chas laughed. "One more tonight. This song …" He picked an absent minded note on his guitar as he spoke, looking out into the crowd. "As many of you know, we used to have a great singer called Ezza …" A whoop went up from Ellen. "Who – bless his soul – we sadly lost a number of years ago now …"

Marelle felt Jacob's arms tighten around her his chin rest on her head.

"If you want to know what he looked like …" He grinned and pointed to Ellen "There's a young lady down here who insists on wearing his ugly mug on a t-shirt just to make sure he fucking haunts me!" He smiled. "Ezza sang this song much better than I do – but – here goes – ladies and gents, our last song tonight – Sleep No More. It's from the final album we did with Ezza."

Chas stood back from the mic and began playing a melody on the guitar as the others remained silent for a few moments. Then, one by one they joined in with the weaving, building melody until the song crashed into life and Chas began singing. It was a powerful, full on track with everyone playing as though it was their last ever performance and Chas' voice rising above it all. In the middle was a pause where Chas got the chance to play quite an involved guitar solo that the crowd cheered for. Jacob gave a little laugh with his body pressed against Marelle which made her smile too. The song wound down with Chas playing the same melody that he had started with as he sang the final words of the song '*and I will sleep no more*' followed by him smiling and announcing. "That's all folks. Goodnight."

The crowd were clapping and stamping their feet, shouting for more. Marelle watched Bella and Mae join in. She turned her head against Jacob to look up at him.

"They'll come back on again." He said. "Wait a second ..."

And sure enough they did. The crowd's cheer rose to a crescendo as all four of them came back onto the stage and picked up their instruments again. Chas smiled and stepped up to the mic.

"You know." He said. "I always worry that one night you won't shout for us to come back on!" He smiled. "But you did – so here we are. One more then we are taking these tired old legs to bed. No Way Home."

The crowd erupted. There was no other word for it. The cheers rose; the crowd rose. The whole atmosphere in the venue felt electric as that song started up. The song which Jacob had sung on karaoke – in the pub that night and here yesterday. Obviously Yellow Son's signature song – it soared and pulled the crowd with it.

Jacob sang along, words she'd heard him sing a few times now – words that to him were still so ingrained in his brain – waiting to be released again. He was animated behind her; she felt him feel and live every moment of the music as the cells within his body came awake one by one.

And at the end of the song, when Chas was saying 'thank you' – thanking the other band members and giving each one a round of applause – Jacob clapped and cheered too. Then as they walked off stage, he folder his arm around Marelle and rested his head on hers. Behind them the disco kicked into life and half the crowd suddenly turned their attention to that. Bella was laughing and talking with Mae, still at the front near the barrier. Marelle turned and looked up into his face.

"Was that more what you were expecting?" She asked, a smile breaking on her face.

Jacob smiled too and nodded but she could see a tear just crossing his cheek in the dancing coloured lights. He pulled her to him.

"It was awesome." He said quietly into her ear." They're still as good as they used to be. Just one thing missing!"

Marelle laid her head against him, lifted it then kissed him cheekily as she wrapped her arms around his waist and looked up into his eyes.

"Oh any excuse!" Bella suddenly exclaimed beside them. "Look at them! They can't keep their hands off each other."

Mare stood there beside her and smiled sweetly. Marelle laughed.

"You know, of course, you're not real fans – I've never seen any of you at a gig before – so don't tell me you are! Behaviour likes yours isn't appreciated." Ellen's voice unexpectedly chimed in as she leaned in to them in passing. "You don't know them like I do."

With that she turned and walked away. Jacob stared at her for a moment but said nothing.

"They've got some weird fans." Bella commented, watching her go. "I have seen them before, but they were on fire tonight!" She laughed to Jacob. "And you enjoyed it, didn't you? See I told you – no need to go hiding at the back! Right what shall we do – dance the night away in here?"

"Well to be honest, I'm a bit tired." Jacob replied. "I might leave the dancing the night away bit to you two."

"No. I'll probably head back if you're going … could do with a coffee to be honest." Bella smiled.

Marelle squinted at her. Bella – leaving a party before midnight? Bella smiled back at her; Marelle thought she winked but before she could be sure in the dim yet hideously flashing lights Bella took Jacob's arm in one hand and Mae's in the other. "Come on, let's head out."

Once out of the hall the air felt cold and damp. It took all of ten seconds to hit Marelle and she felt oddly giddy. Staggering a little, she held on to Jacob's arm.

"Woah!" Bella laughed at her. "Think it might be bedtime for Marelle!"

"I'm fine." She grinned.

Bella chuckled.

There were a few people milling about; some leaving having only come to see Yellow Son's performance – some going back to their chalets, some hanging around outside between the hall and the food kiosks.

"I'm hungry." Jacob announced. "Who wants a hot dog?" And he veered towards a garishly lit up little shack to his left.

Marelle and Mae declined but Bella and Jacob ended up with two enormous hot dogs covered in the full works. Rather than walk and eat, which looked like it would probably be messy, Jacob elected to sit on a low wall around a flower bed. Marelle smiled at him and sat down by his side, leaning in to him and feeling the warmth of his body against her. Bella parked herself with Mae on her left..

"Well, we've finally managed to winkle you out of your shell tonight, haven't we?" Bella grinned. "What was all that 'Fickle Finger' business, hey? I thought you were getting me into trouble there!"

Jacob grinned with a mouthful of hotdog. "It's a joke." He finally said, when he could.

"A joke! On whom?" She exclaimed, smiling. "You're a dark horse Jacob. You've seen them before, haven't you?"

He chuckled. "Maybe I have." He replied.

Bella shook her head to him and laughed. She leaned forward and looked along at Marelle. She had her head against him, her eyes closed.

"You ok Marelle? Being a bride-to-be knocked you out?"

"No!" She laughed, opening her eyes. "I'm just tired, my head's spinning a bit. I'm not used to this."

Bella laughed. "Aaah – *lightweight!*"

She leaned back, looked up at Jacob as he took another bite of the hotdog. "And you!" She continued. "You really are a dark horse, aren't you? Hey?" She exclaimed.

They sat there together on the wall for a bit, finishing the hotdogs, watching people in varying stages of inebriation mill about; going between the venue and their accommodation, Bella informed them it was open until three am.

"Well, I'm not staying here until three o clock." Jacob yawned.

"Have you had it old man!" Bella laughed.

"Yeah." He stated with a subtle smile.

"I'll just walk back with Mae then I'll come to yours." Bella said, standing up. "Leave the door open and put the kettle on."

"Well, you can both come back if you want?" Jacob suggested.

"No, it's ok." Mae smiled. "I need my beauty sleep!" And she smiled to Bella.

"Ok, see you tomorrow then." Jacob answered, Marelle smiled beside him, her head still against his shoulder.

"Be over in a bit." Bella nodded, taking Mae's arm as they walked off in their Yellow Son t-shirts.

"Hmm." Jacob mused with a smile.

Marelle allowed herself to close her eyes for a second. There was a lot of noise, like a continuous buzz in the background – people talking, laughing, shouting, music playing. She missed the silent buzz of the airfield. Jacob's hoodie smelled of smoke, alcohol and sweat. She sighed.

"Come on. I'd better walk you home too." He smiled to her.

FOURTEEN

Jacob walked in and took off the hood straight away. He yawned. Marelle's head was spinning, and she still felt a little dizzy. She sighed, maybe she should have eaten something. Jacob went into the bathroom, and she found the kettle, filled it then switched it on. Then sitting herself down at the small table she closed her eyes for a moment again.

"Marelle! Marelle!' A voice was calling her from a long way away. She knew the voice and it sounded happy, so she did not worry or panic. It was fine; she would answer in a minute.

"Marelle!" Someone was shaking her shoulder. She didn't want to wake up yet, but they persisted. "Marelle!"

With a sigh she lifted her head and opened her eyes.

"`Bella." She said, staring at her best friend – a moment of pure confusion still passing over her then she woke fully.

"What's wrong with you?" Bella laughed. "Jesus! It's not even midnight yet!"

"I'm tired." Marelle replied. "Sorry."

"You're not tired. You're drunk!" Bella grinned, walking over and flicking the kettle on again.

"I'm not drunk! I've been drinking coke all night." Marelle exclaimed.

Bella laughed then fished in her bag. She paced a nearly empty bottle of vodka on the table in front of Marelle.

'Well, you two had that between you tonight so I'd say you've pretty much had a skinful."

Marelle stared at the bottle then up at Bella who was smiling.

"Bella! For God's sake!" Marelle exclaimed.

"I was determined you two – and especially Jacob – were going to have a good time tonight. None of this hanging around at the back in the shadows!"

"– but, Bella!"

"And you did. He did. Jacob loved every minute of it. It was beautiful to watch ...!"

"Where is he?" Marelle suddenly panicked, sitting up straight and looking about herself.

"Asleep in there by the sound of it." Bella smiled.

Marelle got up, felt giddy, grabbed at the chair back then stumbled to the bedroom. Sure enough she could hear him snoring softly. Bella stood close behind her as she stood looking into the doorway.

Jacob was asleep on the bed. He lay on his side, legs slightly bent up, relaxed, happy – asleep. Still fully clothed and almost a smile on his face in the semi darkness. Marelle sighed. She turned back to Bella who gave her a grin and stepped back towards the kettle.

"For God's sake!" Marelle sighed. "I didn't want him getting drunk ... what if he kicks off on one during the night, hey? You know what he can be like! If he does then I'm coming to get you. You're only next door!"

"He won't."

'What if he does? Hey?"

"I thought he was fine now. I thought it was all rainbows and butterflies now!"

"Christ Bella!" She hissed, whispering in case he woke. "He's still ... he's still someone who tried to kill himself ... he's still Jacob! Yes he's been great he's been a changed man but ... it will be all rainbows and butterflies but there's a hell of a shit storm to get through first!"

Bella stared at her. 'Hey, ok ... what shit storm?"

Marelle realised what she'd said in the heat of the vodka filled moment. And she'd said it to Bella. "Just shit that's got to be sorted before we can get married." She said, still in an elevated whisper.

"Marelle, what shit? I thought it was all good?" Bella questioned, moving closer to her as Marelle sat down again.

She shook her head. "I can't tell you. I promised."

"You can't tell *me*? Your *oldest* friend, your *best* friend! I thought we told each other everything?"

Marelle drew a breath. Her head was fuzzy; she didn't need this. Bella sat down, staring at her.

"... but if he starts tonight, because of this I am coming next door to get you!" Marelle changed the conversation, awkwardly.

Bella lowered her eyes to the table, then back to Marelle.

"I may not be next door." She said.

"Why? Where are you going?"

Bella looked serious, gave a little shrug, looked serious again. She took a breath and Marelle watched her shoulders rise and fall beneath the Yellow Son t-shirt. "I was going to spend the night in Mae's chalet. I came over here first to make sure you and Jacob were ok."

"With Mae?" Marelle questioned, in confusion.

Bella nodded, looking into Marelle's half open mouthed expression. "I'll admit I'm not sure what I'm doing but I've found myself attracted to her for a while. She's been to a few weekenders, but she had a partner. But they've split up and she called me the other day to ask if I was coming here ... she was on her own ... and I thought I'd just see what happened ..."

Marelle stared at her. "Like a couple?"

Bella nodded. "I slept in her chalet last night too ... I've not felt like this about anyone – boy or girl – before. You and me, we're like sisters but I'm sexually attracted to Mae. It's probably nothing, it's probably a flash in the pan ... but ..." She spoke quietly and shrugged her shoulders a little unsurely.

"Are you telling me you're gay?" Marelle questioned, her head still half stuffed with cotton wool and this whole conversation seeming so bizarre.

"I think so." She stated. "I wanted to tell you – I didn't want you to *find out* or work it out. I think Jacob has twigged it."

"He has!"

Bella nodded. "I think he has."

Marelle was quiet. Bella had always been a tomboy. She had messed around with boys rather than had relationships with them ... and now Marelle thought about it she could not recall Bella ever getting 'serious' about a boy. Marelle had always thought it was because she was so much of a flirt; so much of a live wire – maybe it had been for other reasons.

'It doesn't change our friendship of course." Bella added.

It didn't. Marelle smiled. "Of course it doesn't. As you would say to me – you go for it girl!" She laughed. "Mae seems sweet. And she's pretty."

Bella smiled, she laughed then reached out a hand and wrapped an arm around Marelle. "Give me a hug. I was so scared about telling you!" she smiled.

Marelle hugged her, like sisters, like best friends.

"It's fine." Marelle told her. "You can bring her to the wedding."

Bella laughed. "If it lasts that long!" Then she sat away again, raised an eyebrow and stared at Marelle. She drew a breath. "So what shit storm, Marelle?"

Marelle shook her head. "Forget I said that."

"I can't. Tell me ..."

"I can't. I promised Jacob. It's fine. We'll sort it out."

"Sort *what* out? You've got to confide in me ... you always have ... what's changed now? Don't keep secrets from me! If you had told me when he disappeared before I might have been able to help you find him before ...." Her voice trailed away.

"I can't tell you Bella. I'm sorry. Shit!" Marelle exclaimed in a whisper, feeling the whole situation getting the better of her. "I shouldn't have said anything."

"What is it? Does he have kids? Is he married – hey?"

Marelle closed her eyes, shook her head. "No. It's not that."

"Is he a criminal?"

"No!"

"Tell me Marelle ... I can help."

"You can't. It's ok."

Bella sighed. Made a little face but just sat there. Marelle sensed her disappointment that the friendship they'd shared for so long was now being tested by her refusal to confide in Bella. She had just bared her soul to Marelle – told her something that was personal and probably controversial. Bella had trusted Marelle; she had probably jeopardised what they had by imparting that secret. Bella had even said she had been scared to tell Marelle. Bella – *scared*! Marelle thought of all the secrets they'd kept between them; the promises they'd made to each other – and kept. Marelle raised her eyes to Bella.

"Well you know that group we've just seen? Yellow Son?" She began. The words came easier than she had expected. "Well Jacob used to be the lead singer." She said.

That second those words left her lips she knew she had done wrong; broken Jacob's trust – allowed those words out into the world and as they flew around the room and bounced off the walls in their liberation she felt like Pandora and wished she could immediately close the box with them trapped back inside.

Bella was staring at her at the end of that long, vacuous tube of betrayal. Bella smiled.

"Really? I knew there was something going on!" She gave that little giggle of delight she always did when she found something out. "Why didn't you say something. I knew he had some sort of history with them! Oh my God – does that mean he's famous?" Bella had a grin from ear to ear.

"Bella." Marelle whispered. "Bella. Ssshh!" She pleaded. "I should not have told you, ok? Ok?" She gasped at Bella. "Please Bella, don't tell him I told you ... please!"

Bella smiled, shook her head, took Marelle's hands in hers. "Sssh! Of course I won't. I won't breath a word – I *promise*. And you know I will keep my promises!"

Marelle sighed, felt tears welling up. "Shit. I shouldn't have told you."

"It's ok." Bella soothed. "You know you can trust me. I won't breath a word ... to *anyone*." She explained. "But tell me, surely that's a good thing, isn't it? Why is it a shit storm?"

Marelle took a deep breath through her nose and stared at Bella with glassy eyes. "It's only a very small part of it. I can't tell you more."

"You can't tell me a tiny piece and then back off."

"I can." She whispered, listening with one ear to hear Jacob still snoring in the bedroom.

"It's not a bad thing, is it? Why is it a bad thing?" Bella questioned. "So what? He was a singer in a band – does that matter?"

"No. That doesn't matter. It's not that ..." Marelle shook her head.

"Well, what then?" Bella grinned. "I don't understand – you've kept this secret that he used to be the lead singer of so-and-so band ... why is it a secret and if it's so much of a secret then why the hell is he here? Watching them play?"

"Ssshh!" Marelle exclaimed. "If he hears this, I don't know what he'll do. He asked me not to tell anyone yet."

'When did he tell you that?"

"When he came back. That night, the next day. He's confided in me – no one else knows – he told me not to tell anyone."

'But I don't understand why? Surly it's something to celebrate?" "It's not that simple." Marelle whispered.

"You're worrying me now Marelle – what's so bad that you can't tell me? If you're getting yourself into something, then you need to tell me – I knew all of this was too good to be true!

"Fuck sake!" Marelle exclaimed, still in a whisper. "You sound like Seb now."

"Well tell me! Whatever it is I won't breath a word and I won't let him know I know."

Marelle shook her head.

"You're worrying me. It must be something so bad if you can't tell me …"
"It's not *bad* … just *awkward*."

"It gets worse! Tell me Marelle. Just remember. I can walk out of here and go have a conversation with Mr. Google and draw my own conclusions from what I find. What will I find?"

Marelle sat there. Tight lipped.

Bella sighed. There was silence for a few seconds. In the bedroom Jacob was still snoring.

"Is he a paedophile?" Bella suddenly asked in an even quieter whisper.

Marelle drew a breath; she wanted to scream but Jacob asleep, not feet away, stopped her.

"No he's not a fucking paedophile!"

"Well, I thought maybe an underage groupie or something – you know, nothing sinister as such, just a mistake …"

'Bella!" Marelle scorned. "Stop it! It's nothing like that; he's done nothing wrong." She spat. "Well. Not wrong … as such."

"What did he do?"

"Nothing!"

"Why did he leave the band then?" Bella questioned.

"He didn't leave the band." Marelle replied, continuing her whispered argument.

Bella looked at her in a perplexed way. "But you said he *used* to be lead singer – he's not now, so he must have left." She nodded her head in question.

Marelle shook hers.

"What did he do? Why did he leave?"

Marelle stared down at her hands.

"Marelle. What?"

This was Bella. Bella wouldn't let go of this. She had never broken a promise to Marelle. Eventually, she raised her eyes to Bella.

"Not here." She said.

"Come to my room …" Bella stood up.

"No, I'm not leaving him on his own."

"Outside then. There's no-one out there."

It was not the place Marelle would have chosen – standing with one hand on the door handle with one ear on the sounds coming from within in case he stirred. Bella standing in front of her with her arms folded, she tilted her head slightly and looked to Marelle to begin this tale.

Marelle sighed, choosing to still speak in a whisper. "If I tell you any of this, I want you to swear on your life that not a single word of it ever gets spoken to *anyone*, *ever*. Or you don't sit there making knowing little faces whenever you are in front of Jacob!"

"I don't do *knowing little faces*!" Bella exclaimed, equally in a whisper.

"Yes, you do! Promise me!"

"I promise. Not a word. Not a single flicker of my eye – on my life."

Marelle closed her eyes and sighed. "I don't know where to start."

"That doesn't sound good."

"It's not that bad ... it's just ... complicated!" Marelle explained. "Right. I'll start here." She took a breath, braced herself, then began. "Jacob used to be the lead singer of Yellow Son – ten or eleven years ago he had some kind of mental breakdown and walked off stage in the middle of a gig. He went back home, holed himself up with a plan to just keep his head down here for a while. Then he hears the news that a body has been found and it has been identified as him. The whole world thinks he committed suicide." She looked to Bella who was listening intently.

"But he didn't?" Bella asked.

"No. He was back at home, in the village. For some reason the body that they found was identified as Jacob ..." She paused, realising this was not entirely true.

"So why didn't he say anything?" Bella interrupted, quite surprised that someone could be accidentally identified as being dead and not speak up about it.

"Because he wanted to walk away from it; because he wanted to be someone else ... he saw it as an opportunity to begin again."

"So, technically he's dead?"

"Yes." Marelle said. "Well, no ..."

Bella stared at her.

Marelle sighed. It was one of things she wished she had never started, a path she regretted stepping on.

"Look, it's far, far more complicated than this – I'm trying to give you a summary. But while he was there, he decided to take on the identity of his brother who died at birth. He had all of the paperwork as his father had also just died. You see, Jacob is not really Jacob. Jacob is his brother – Nathaniel – who was known as Ezza in Yellow Son."

Bella was still staring at her, a little blankly as Marelle held on to the door handle.

"You've lost me." She said.

Marelle sighed. "I shouldn't have started this and I don't want to be standing out here talking about this longer than I really need to."

"Hang on." Bella offered. "So Jacob is not Jacob he's this other person who was the lead singer in Yellow Son – but he faked his own suicide?"

"No!" Marelle exclaimed. "He didn't fake it. He went back home but they found a body that was identified as him ... he didn't fake anything – he just saw it as a way out and took it, but to do so he pretended to be his dead brother, Jacob."

The way Bella stared suggested she was still confused. Marelle tutted; it wasn't difficult to understand.

"So who is he?"

"His real name is Nat – Nathaniel Frost."

Bella was still just staring blankly at her.

Marelle shook her head. "I shouldn't have told you any of this – you must promise you will not mention this to *anyone* ..."

"No. No, I won't. You know I won't. I wouldn't know where to start to be honest – but – do you believe him?"

"Of course I believe him!" Marelle gasped. "It's all on the internet – that's how he told me. He told me to google Ezza Frost ... it's all there."

'Then how come you hadn't come across it before – or anyone had?"

"If you don't know what you're looking for then you won't ever find it." Marelle replied.

"Shit Marelle. I don't get it ..."

"You don't need to. Just forget it. He's Jacob, nothing's changed. Ok?"

She had filled Bella's head with what was in hers – it wasn't easy to put it simply and there was no beginning to the story. It was a continuous circle ... wherever you jumped in was a good place to start.

Of course, she knew Bella would go off and google. Who wouldn't? She may understand more, she may understand less in doing so but either way she would be faced with what Marelle had first seen that evening. She hugged Bella before letting her walk off into the night to go to Mae – another free radical now in circulation with the knowledge that Jacob had trusted to Marelle – and only her with. She trusted Bella; she knew Bella would keep quiet, but it was with a crushing uneasiness that Marelle went back into the chalet and walked in to stand looking down at Jacob, still asleep on the bed.

Her head was clearer now; being outside trying to get the words out in a comprehensive yet concise way had cleared it miraculously. She had told Bella enough – but not all of it. Standing there in the doorway she now drew a breath in which became shaky as she realised what she'd done; realised just what level of betrayal she had stooped to. Shame and regret both came to her now with the heart beat she felt passing through every single tiny blood vessel within her being. Watching Jacob in pleasantly ignorant slumber – now fully, painfully awake herself, a silent tear ran down her cheek. Bella had departed into the night; taken that knowledge with her – within her – to Mae. Marelle hoped that whatever occupied her that night now moved all of her thoughts away from the tale she had just listened to. In the circumstances Marelle believed it would and by tomorrow maybe some of the sharp edges would have dissolved away.

She sighed. Walked into the bedroom and with a lingering gaze at Jacob, lay down behind him and wrapped an arm around his torso, spreading her fingers wide across his rib cage. She could feel the steady, rhythmic beat of his heart within and willed hers to slow in harmony.

He awoke her, throwing himself up from a prone position to sit on the edge of the bed in one movement. Drawing a noisy breath, he placed his head in his hands. Jacob sat there for a few seconds in the darkness, breathing noisily. He was still fully dressed, as was she, and as he realised, he undid his zip on the hoodie and ripped it off himself, sighing and throwing it into the corner of the room in the dark.

Marelle lay still, watching him. She was not sure if he was awake or asleep – he seemed slightly agitated but not distressed. Marelle could hear voices outside in the distance, laughing.

"Ok?" she asked, tentatively into the room, disembodied words in the blackness.

His reaction to her question was unexpected. Jacob flew around with a fear filled start, towards where her voice had come from, towards her, still on the bed behind him. He gasped in exclamation.

"What the fuck?" He muttered, reaching out to feel her legs. His breathing increased and he took a couple of noisy breaths in quick succession.

"Hey!" She sat up, feeling for his hand in the dark.

He gripped her hand and turned fully to her.

"Hey, it's OK Jacob." She repeated, taking his hand and pulling him to her.

"Fuck." He said, at last releasing the breath and losing some of the tension. He exhaled slowly, then gave a little laugh.

"What?"

"Shit!" He said again. 'Sorry ... I've done that a few times. Woke up and didn't have a clue where I was."

"Shit, I thought I was with the band; thought I'd just done a gig and woken up in a hotel room!" He explained. "Sorry, I thought I was alone."

Her mind was contemplating what to say in view of the fact that he had 'forgotten' she was there.

"Aah come here." He eventually sighed, turning to her in the dark room; still pretty much fully clothed and reaching out to her. Marelle crawled into his arms.

"Jesus! I haven't dreamt about being in the band for years." He laughed. "Must mean something." Hs voice sounded unusually gruff for him.

"Means you forgot about me." She said, quietly.

"No – no, I didn't forget about you!" He exclaimed. "I was dreaming – and thought I was somewhere else – ten years ago! How could I forget about you?"

He held her tightly.

"What time is it?"

"Dunno." Marelle replied, reaching out for her phone and switching it on. The light from it illuminated their faces crudely in the dim light. Jacob was smiling.

"Ten to five." She replied as the light extinguished. And they were plunged into the dark again.

"Must be getting old." He mused. 'Fell asleep as soon as I sat down on the bed."

"I did the same. Nothing to do with age – Bella spiked our drinks all night. Apparently, we consumed nearly a bottle of vodka between us. She has been suitably reprimanded." Marelle told him.

"What?" He asked. 'Why?"

"To ensure we had a good time." She replied. "That's why she kept getting the drinks – she had a bottle of vodka in her bag – I did wonder why my head was so thick."

"Wait till I see her!" He laughed. "But it was a good night."

"Better than last night?"

"Hell yes!" He exclaimed. "You saw them. They've still got it. When I saw them last might I was worried. I thought they'd turned into a cabaret band and – I'll tell you now – I wasn't impressed. But tonight! Wow! They were shit hot!"

Marelle smiled. "They were loud!"

He laughed.

"So what's next? Marelle questioned.

"Go to their next concert ... I might allow myself to be seen ... I think they've only got one date left this year so if I don't make a move I'll have to wait until they post new tour dates next year. I don't really want to wait that long!"

"Do you think he'll recognise you?"

"Of course he will. Just need to let the hair get a bit longer!"

"Hallelujah!" Marelle smiled in the darkness.

He squeezed her to him. "Do you fancy a walk down to the beach?"

"What, now?"

"Why not?"

They hurried like kids, changing clothes and pulling on shoes. Jacob picked up his hoodie from the corner of the room and slipped it on again over a clean t-shirt. It was still dark when they left the chalet and walked briskly down towards the beach.

"Had you better text Bella?" He questioned as they walked.

Marelle gave a little chuckle as she put her hand in his. "I think Bella is pretty occupied at the moment ... at least after what she told me last night."

"What?"

"Bella thinks she might be about to embark on a gay relationship with Mae." Marelle said, just like that, no secrets there.

Jacob gave a small laugh in acknowledgement. "I thought as much."

"She said she thought you had twigged it!"

"Yeah, well … it was a bit obvious … and anyway Mae didn't seem to fancy me, so I guessed there was more going on there!"

"Hey!" Marelle reprimanded him. "You're not fair game for everyone … especially if you're planning to get up on that stage and flaunt yourself."

"Flaunt myself!" He exclaimed. "Oooh I've never had a jealous girlfriend before!"

"Fiancé." She reminded him.

He laughed, wrapping an arm around her. "Come here!" Hugging her to him as they walked and she realised that he was a joker, that he had a sense of humour that had been hidden away for years. He made *her* smile.

The air was quite cold and a sharp breeze was carrying in off the sea up ahead.

"You don't want to go worrying about things like that – I'm an old man now. I'm not in the flush of youth I was when young girls liked to fall at my feet!"

"Don't you count on that!" She scoffed. 'You've got the likes of Ellen to contend with!"

"Jesus! Ellen! Stood right next to her idol and didn't even notice. I bet she deletes that photo and she'll regret that for the rest of her life."

"Do you remember Ellen? Seems she's been around for a long time."

"No. Not that I would. You don't remember people – you pretend you do, but you don't. I don't, anyway …"

They reached the beach and the darkness was just lifting to a veiled early sunlight. They could see each other clearly now – either due to the approaching day or the fact that their eyes had adjusted. They slipped hand-in-hand down the inclined walkway and onto the soft golden sand. The sound of the waves crashing into the shore filled their senses and Marelle remained amazed at its relentlessness. Twenty-four hours a day, three hundred and sixty-five days a year the waves reached out for the land, gripped their salty fingers into its fabric for a fleeting second before gravity pulled them back. Day in, day out; they never conceded. There was some naïve notion in her head that at night they stopped; that the seal also slept; became quiet and still in slumber. This proved to her now, that they did not.

In the gently lifting light they walked down towards the shoreline. They were alone on the beach, no sound or sight of anyone else here right now. Behind them to sun would soon rise.

"It's the only place on the east coast that faces west." Jacob said but his words were consumed in the noise of the waves and the breeze. Marelle heard what he said but did not reply as she stood and held his hand with the waves only inches from their feet. The wind whipped her hair across her face and she felt the breath held with Jacob as he stood alongside her. Marelle wanted to turn to him, to hug him and confess that she had told Bella but there was a part within her which feared doing so. She feared admitting her betrayal of his trust.

"Imagine this was it." He said, his voice raised so she could hear him. "Imagine we were the only two people left on earth, just standing her where the sea meets the land … wouldn't that be good?"

"Just us?" Marelle asked.

He nodded, now more visible in the breaking dawn. 'I'd like that. In the past I have wished it was just me. Now I wish it was just us."

"Have you really wished you were the only person left on earth? All alone? She asked him.

"I have, yes. I've wished for a lot of inconceivable things. Most don't ever come true ..." He answered, staring out at the sea, rising and falling in the blackness before them. "Some do."

Marelle rolled her head against his shoulder as they stood there staring at the ocean. She could feel Ezza filling him pushing at the edges of the envelope that was Jacob; but at the same time, she could sense Jacob still reinforcing the borders.

Jacob sighed, twitched slightly and began to shuffle before he kicked off his boots beside her.

"What are you doing?" She asked, looking down at his feet.

"I'm going in." He said, beginning to take other items of clothing off.

"In the sea! It'll be freezing! It's quite rough – Jacob – no!"

"It'll be ok." He laughed. "Come in too ..."

The last time in the river had been enough for her not to want to re-live the experience.

"No." She replied. "Jacob please, don't!"

"It's fine ..."

He was a strong swimmer, but this was the sea with its relentless pounding and pummelling of the land – not a calm little pool in a chalk stream. Jacob had an obsession with water and a never-ending connection to drowning that had haunted her since that awful nightmare when she had visited his dead body in a morgue. It chilled her now.

He was down to his jeans, undoing the button and unzipping the fly. "Here, hold my clothes." He thrust what he had taken off into her hands, completing the bundle with his jeans. 'I'll keep my pants on – don't know who's about!" He quipped.

"Jacob!" She called as he ran towards the water, his body pale in the morning twilight.

"Jacob, no!" She shouted but he had gone, up to his knees, up to his waist then he dove into the water.

It was darker towards the sea than the land and once he had submerged himself in the water she lost sight of him.

"Jacob!" she called into the sea which took her voice before it was heard. His clothes, still warm from his body, clutched to her chest. Just her now and the crashing sea which had enveloped him.

Marelle strained her eyes, looked for movement in the water; a glimpse of his pale skin in the dark, broiling water but there was no sign of him and thoughts turned full circle in her head; stopping at stations she had stood on the platform of before. She sighed, half gasped to herself, wanting to pace but not daring to move from that spot.

"Fucking hell Jacob!" She cursed to herself, feeling tears behind her eyes as that dull pain of fear suddenly began to eat away at her insides. "Jacob." She called towards the dark sky and black water.

She took. Step forwards, peering into the ocean as the waves claimed ground and brushed her feet with their fingers.

"Shit." She said to herself, stepping back. Her heart was racing and her breath was shallow – she could feel the chemical advance of adrenalin within her as it took hold of her knees.

"Jacob!"

FIFTEEN

Then her phone rang in her back jeans pocket and began to vibrate. Not knowing why so she thought for one second that it just might be Jacob, she angrily extracted it and the light from the screen lit up her face with a blue glow.

It was Bella. She answered.

"Where are you?" Bella exclaimed. "Your door is unlocked but you're not here!"

"I'm at the beach." She replied, her voice hurrying and her words almost breathless. "I can't find Jacob!"

"At the beach! Why? Did he sleepwalk? What's happened?" Bella replied, panic now clutching at her voice too.

"No, we slept fine then woke and he wanted to come for a walk down the beach – he's gone into the sea for a swim and he's disappeared!"

"It's dark!" Bella remarked.

"It's just getting light." Marelle interrupted. "I've got his clothes, but he ran in, and I can't see him anymore."

"Oh shit Marelle! Why did you let him do that?"

"I couldn't stop him!" Marelle answered, tears in her voice. "He just went into the water – it was dark – now I can't see him anymore!"

"How long ago?"

"I don't know." Marelle replied, distracted as she looked into the movement of the ocean before her.

"Shall I call the coastguard? We'll come down there ..." Bella offered.

Marelle sighed. 'I don't know what to do – the sea is rough – it's cold ..."

"You stay on the phone to me. I'll get Mae to call the coastguard ... there's been chaos here – someone set a fire alarm off ... that's why I came round to make sure you were ok – but your door was unlocked ..." Bella explained. "Hold on, I'll just speak to Mae."

Marelle took a shaky breath. She wasn't being stupid. Bella was concerned too.

At that moment, as she clutched his clothes to her with one hand; her phone to her ear in the other and her eyes still scanning the deep, dark ocean rising before her – she was unexpectedly body slammed from behind – unsteadying her, almost losing her balance in the greyness. Marelle screamed.

"What?" Bella exclaimed in her ear as she was greeted with fearful gasping and heavy breathing. "Marelle!"

As she regained her footing the cold damp arms wrapped themselves around her. She felt his wet hair against her face and his innocent little laugh in her ear.

"Oh God!" Marelle gasped.

"Marelle!" Bella yelled again.

"It's ok. He's here ... he's here!" Marelle cried as he hugged her, cold and damp, laughing at her reaction.

"He's there?"

"Yes!" She replied. "It's ok. We'll see you when we get back." Marelle said quickly then she cut the connection, turning in towards him and pushing her face into his cold, bare chest.

"Hey?" he laughed. "What's wrong?"

"You disappeared. I couldn't see you!" She sobbed. "God Jacob! Why did you do that?"

"Hey ..." He hugged her to him. "Who were you calling?"

"Bella called me. She wondered where we were ..."

"She should come down too, with Mae. We could all go in." He said with a grin."

"I don't think even Bella would be *that* stupid." Marelle retorted. He made a sad face to her.

"I swam along a bit, got out then ran up the beach to warm up." He explained. "I knew what I was doing."

"Well I didn't!" She protested. "For all I knew you had planned to run into the sea, lay right down and drown! I couldn't see you ... you didn't answer me when I called to you!" She almost cried but managed to suppress it with her anger.

He sighed. "Why would I do that? Why?" Jacob questioned. "When I have so much now; when I am on the brink of reclaiming something I thought I had lost forever. When I have you ... here with me?"

She shook her head and laid it against him again.

"Look – you've got to believe in me now. It's different – I believe in me so you've got to as well." He wrapped his taught arms tightly around her. She felt his muscles tense and twitch as he did so. "It was fun! It was exhilarating!" He enthused as she closed her eyes and wondered if her fear could ever be construed as excitement as long as Jacob was involved.

"Can I have my clothes?" He asked, breaking into her thoughts.

He dressed, pulling on clothes quickly, balancing on one leg while he removed wet underpants and pulled his jeans back on. The dawn had skimmed the land and now touched them with its infant light. They were both visible on the beach and as the light finally caressed the sea it somehow did not look as threatening.

Marelle sighed and looked back at him as he was pushing feet into boots. He brushed his hair with the flat of his hand. Jacob's eyes caught hers. He smiled, that little, warm smile that was so 'Jacob'. It made her smile too, but it was tentative and began to tremble. He sighed at that and reached out to her, taking her in his arms again, clutching her warmly to him in the same way she had held him many times.

"It's ok." He said. "Stop crying."

'But I thought you'd gone – I couldn't see you – I thought you'd swam out to drown yourself – like my dream – *nightmare*." She said, her face against his neck.

"I wouldn't do that. I told you, why would I do that?"

"Because you tried to throw yourself off a bridge a few weeks ago!"

"But it's different now. I've got you now. You're the very reason I'm still here!"

"And Bella ..." She added.

"No, just you. It was your body against me in the car park *that* was my epiphany. Even if Bella had found me it did not mean that I was saved. If that self-destruct button remains pressed it remains on. Someone may be able to pull me back from time to time, but it's engaged – it is always engaged and will always override anything else. I still had every intention of going back to the bridge and throwing myself off it, even when I was in the car park with her and that car. Only one person can switch that button off and it's me. I alone have the power to disengage the self-destruct button – and to have the wish to so do. And I did, when you ran into my arms in that car park. It's off, as long as you are here it's never going on again." He kissed her neck, her face gently, then her lips. "Trust me."

There on the beach he held her tightly with the cool breeze rising off the sea and blowing her hair across their faces as he kissed her. Their embrace was as if both their very lives depended upon it, her fingers clutching at his back; standing on the land where the sea extended its own open fingers to them across the beach and as the dawn rose fully behind them Marelle felt like she had finally reclaimed him from the clutches of impending danger.

As they made their way back to the appropriately named 'Beach Road' they met various 'morning 'people – walking dogs, jogging, coming home from the night before. Jacob held her hand. He said 'good morning' to people they passed with a cheeky expression on his face and a healthy glint in his eyes.

They were nearly back to the holiday park when her phone rang. Holding on to Jacob she stopped and pulled it out of her pocket.

"Bella." She said to him, answering and at that moment remembering their conversation last night. A tiny stab of guilt pierced her side.

"Where are you?" Bella asked, almost as if she was speaking to a wayward child.

"We're just about back at the main entrance." Marelle replied.

'So, is it all ok now? Jacob, ok?" Bella questioned.

"Yes." Marelle smiled as if it had been nothing. She heard Bella sigh. There was a short pause before she continued. "We fancied going to the restaurant for a cooked breakfast – do you want to come with us?"

"Er, yeah – we could do." Marelle replied. "You go ahead, and we'll meet you there ..."

"Well, we're at my chalet as you left yours unlocked and I didn't want to leave it like that with your stuff inside ..."

"Oh, ok, well we will be there in a few minutes ..."

"Righty-ho, we'll wait for you then." Bella responded. "It's still early but everyone is up due to the fire alarm, are you ok if Mae comes along?"

"Of course it is!" Marelle answered.

"You on speaker." Bella asked.

"No, why?" Marelle laughed but shot a guilty looking glance at Jacob as she spoke.

"Is he ok?" I mean you were pretty distraught earlier …"

"It's fine." Marelle stated. 'We'll be there in five minutes …"

"I've never had breakfast with a rockstar!" Bella said quietly with a cheeky edge to her voice.

"Bella! No!" Marelle warned. "Is Mae there?"

"Not in earshot." Bella replied. 'Don't worry. Scout's honour and all that."

Marelle wanted to tell her to stop pissing about but didn't want to raise any suspicion in Jacob. She ended the call and carried on walking hand in hand with him. She glanced up at his face; he had a curious little smile on his lips. Half of her felt like he knew she had told Bella – somehow like he had got inside her head and unearthed her thoughts.

"They're going to the restaurant for breakfast." She told him.

"I said we'd go along too."

'Mmm." Jacob replied. "Not a bad idea. I'm pretty hungry, actually."

Bella and Mae were standing leaning on the wall outside their chalets when they walked up hand in hand.

"Well good morning!" Bella grinned in greeting. "Don't hurry yourselves or let me know if you're planning on skinny dipping in the middle of the night!"

Jacob laughed. "I believe you were otherwise occupied!"

Bella huffed; exclaimed a little playful gasp at his audacity then shook he head with a smile. "I wondered where you both were – fire alarms were going off everywhere. I thought you two had run off to Gretna Green or something!"

"Now there's an idea!" Jacob mused with a cheeky wink.

"You left your door unlocked too!" She continued. "You can't go doing that; you can't trust people around here – well – except for me." She shot Marelle a glance and winked.

Marelle very slightly raised one eyebrow to her but no-one else noticed.

Jacob grabbed his wallet then locked the door. Bella led the way with Mae. Today Mae looked plainer; she had no make-up on, and her long blonde hair was pulled into a high pony tail; she was wearing faded jeans and a white sweatshirt and looked incredibly young in the cold hard light of day.

The restaurant was busy but not packed. They found a table for four over by a window and sat down Marelle was reminded of the pub she and Jacob had stopped at on the way home from Frankie's funeral and the consequences of that made her uneasy. But she looked up at Jacob, sitting back with the laminated menu in his hand, a little grin on his face.

"I always think ..." He said. "That when a menu has pictures instead of words then they just expect you to just point to what you want!" He stated.

Bella laughed. "But some of us are not used to the high-end dining that you obviously are!" she replied.

"*Moi*?" he asked, his hand against his chest. "I'm a cold beans out of the tin kind of guy!"

"Well, I'm sure they can accommodate that here as well." Bella smiled sarcastically but playfully. "And how long have you been able to speak French too?" Mae laughed sweetly beside her.

A waitress who looked even younger than Mae took their orders. She was a bit nervous and it would have been easy to be a little belligerent with her, but Jacob exercised a side Marelle had not seen before and put her at ease and was gently considerate to her.

"It must be a nightmare working here." He commented after she had left. "Dealing with the likes of us."

"Oh, I think she'll be ok with us." Marelle replied.

"I think she thinks we're a family!" Bella said feigning seriousness but from the tone of her voice Marelle knew the punchline was coming. "She thinks it's Mum, dad and two kids!" She smiled.

"Hey Bella! I'm younger than you!" Marelle exclaimed, pointing at her.

"Only by a month."

"It's still younger." Marelle defended.

"And I'm not your bloody father!" Jacob added. "I'm not old enough to be your father!"

"You're old enough to be Mae's father." Bella stated.

"Well, maybe, just? Depends on how old she is." Jacob continued the thread of conversation, raising an eyebrow to Bella and Mae.

"I'm thirty." She said. "Just."

"See, you're well old enough to be her father!" Bella laughed.

"You're a cheeky little mare, aren't you?" He pointed at her again, grinning.

"Moi?" She mocked him, her own hand to her chest.

"Did you really go swimming in the sea, in the dark, this morning?" Bella asked after the mirth and merriment had died down a little.

He nodded.

"Yes, he did." Marelle added, rolling her eyes.

'Why?" Bella asked with a shrug.

He shrugged in return. "Just felt like it."

"Woh! Impulsive Jacob! That's a new one." Bella exclaimed, mocking shock and horror.

Marelle gave her a hard glance. Bella smiled.

"You're mad." She grinned to Jacob.

"Yeah, I've been told that before." He said, sitting back on his seat as he saw the waitress approaching.

"Not to mention ..." Bella pointed a finger. "I had her ..." She pointed the finger to Marelle. "Screaming down the phone at me because she couldn't see you in the dark."

"Bella!" Marelle sighed.

"Well, I did. You've got to stop this rockstar behaviour Jacob you're turning Marelle into a nervous wreck!" She made a face of question and stared at Jacob with an open hand as the waitress walked up to the table with a couple of plates and Marelle took the opportunity to stomp on what she hoped was Bella's foot beneath the table. It must have been as Bella made a little face and glared back at Marelle. The breakfast had somewhat distracted him from the full impact of her comment. Moments later everyone was eating so the conversation was all but forgotten. Jacob's appetite had obviously been piqued by his dip into the ocean and he happily tucked into a huge full English breakfast with his usual focus. Bella did likewise, Mae ate but looked embarrassed about doing so; Marelle chewed at a piece of toast and washed it down with coffee.

Midway through Bella paused, drank a sip of coffee then asked

"Did you enjoy last night then Jacob?"

He took a moment, nodded then looked up at her, still eating.

"Friday was a bit of a let-down but last night was right on form." He said. "But I gather my opinion was probably coloured by your little *enhancement*?"

She laughed, beginning to eat again. "Only a little ... you enjoyed it ... that's what matters."

"They were good." He added.

Bella looked at Marelle, flashed her eyes back to Jacob but back to Marelle again when she sent her *'don't you dare'* gaze burning into her. Bella grinned.

"Good!" She said.

Marelle was finding it hard to eat with the ping pong comments Bella seemed intent on rallying. She knew Bella would not say anything, but she would push it as far as she dared and enjoy teasing Marelle in the process, Bella finished eating and sat back. Jacob was just behind her; he looked up to Marelle sitting beside him, still holding the same piece of toast.

"What?" She asked him.

"Are you eating that?" He asked, nodding to her plate.

"Er, probably not ..."

He reached across and took the rashers of bacon on his fork, lifting them to his plate. Seconds after he reached across with his hand and took the sausage too.

"Gonna come again then?" Bella questioned, smiling at Jacob.

"Maybe." He said biting at the end of one of the sausages.

"Good." Bella remarked, "It's been fun with you, you sure knew how to wind the singer up last night! It's almost like you knew him ..." At that point Marelle kicked sharply into Bella's leg again, she caught bare skin with the toe of her trainer.

"Ow!" Bella mouthed involuntarily.

"What do you do Mae?" Marelle asked just as Mae nudged Bella and nodded to the sausages left on her plate. Bella shook her head,

"Jacob – sausages!" she pointed. He reached across and took them from Mae's plate with his hand. Bella laughed. "Jesus Jacob! You're packing it away today – you eating for two or something!"

"Swimming in the sea." He grinned. "Gives you an appetite!"

Marelle smiled.

"What did you say you did Mae?" She continued the thread of conversation she had started earlier. "Are you a teacher as well?"

"No – she's a nurse." Bella spoke for her, leaning towards her and putting her head against Mae's shoulder.

"Really!" Marelle smiled. "I would never have guessed."

At which point Jacob had stuffed both sausages sideways into his mouth beside her. Bella suddenly laughed in exclamation as he then made a stupid face with both sausages in his mouth. Bella screamed with laughter at him. Marelle turned to look at what was causing such hilarity – she laughed too.

"What's he on today?" Bella grinned.

"High on life." Jacob mumbled through the sausages – it was hardly intelligible and he almost as he said it which Bella laughed at even more. He coughed and one of the sausages flew out of his mouth and landed right in the mug of coffee in front of Mae.

Bella shrieked so loud that most of the tables surrounding them all turned to look, Marelle covered her mouth with her hand, grinning behind it.

"I'm a theatre nurse – mainly working with children." Mae said, quietly.

They all made the decision to leave around lunchtime. There were events on today, but people were already leaving and Bella decided they weren't worth hanging on for. While Marelle and Jacob got ready to leave Bella went back with Mae. Half an hour later she was ready too and climbing into the back seat of Marelle's car.

"I'll drive." Jacob announced, holding out his hand for the keys.

The drive home was happy. Jacob was singing along to random tunes on the radio. Bella was talking about the weekend, reminiscing on moments where he had made her laugh.

"You're so much fun Jacob! It's just took you a while to come out of your shell!" She'd said.

Marelle smiled, bit her lip a little then looked to him. He had a smile on his face, a new hope in his heart. He tapped the steering wheel as he drove, his face in profile to her, his eyes bright. There was a warm feeling within her – no longer the cold, biting anxiety that had festered for so long. There was a sense of destination, of homecoming. Marelle settled into the seat, driving her bottom deeper and stretching out her legs. Quietly Bella tapped her arm. She turned her head to glance at her, but Bella was no longer half between the front seats as she had been. She had sat back, her phone in her hand. She turned it to Marelle, showing her the picture on it. Marelle turned to look; for a second a fleeting smile passed across her lips then she realised Bella was showing her one of the pictures she had seen on-line of Ezza – full theatre performance on stage. Bella grinned, pointed to the phone, winked then blew a kiss towards it.

Marelle shook her head a little, trying not to alert Jacob to this. Bella giggled quietly, swiped the picture and another appeared; she grinned and then made an open mouthed 'shocked' face pointing at it.

Marelle turned away from her, stopped fuelling the fire but Bella tapped Marelle's arm again and held the phone out so she could see another picture – one she had not seen before – Ezza bare chested with red and purple lights playing on him, one hand running up through his hair and smiling. Bella made a face of "wow!" and licked her lips theatrically. Marelle sighed, half looking at her, half looking at Jacob who was, thankfully, still oblivious.

Marelle pushed herself back up in the seat, twisted to reach behind herself and try to bat the phone out of Bella's hand.

"Bella!" She mouthed silently. "Stop it!"

Bella laughed. Scrolled another picture. Marelle reached backwards, flailing at her as Bella laughed and dodged her hand, holding the phone away. Marelle aimed another backwards swipe at her and connected with the phone. It flew from Bella's hand and clattered across the top of the dashboard to stop, teetering on the edge right in front of Jacob; his picture right there for all to see.

The whole of the car suddenly seemed very quiet. Bella was leaning between the seats with one hand resting on Marelle. Marelle was staring at Jacob, her eyes wide and expectant. The radio was suddenly quieter, it's sound diminishing into the vacuum. Jacob looked briefly at the phone, looked at the picture then without a word picked it up and handed it back to Bella. As his hand returned to the steering wheel, he indicated left and drove off the dual carriageway they were travelling along. As that road split from the one they'd moved onto he pulled the car over into a lay-by and stopped.

He looked to Marelle, his eyes no longer mellow and carefree as they had been earlier.

"You told her." He said, quietly.

"No!" Bella exclaimed from the back seat. "She didn't tell me. I googled Yellow Son and that's what I got – put two and two together – it all makes sense now!"

Jacob continued to stare at Marelle; she could hear him breathing.

There was a tangible vacuum in the car that was consuming everything – the air; the sound; the light. Marelle stared at him, looked into his eyes as deep as she dared.

"She didn't tell me Jacob." Bella stated again from the back seat, a disembodied voice in a dream; a commentary to the scene they found themselves in.

Jacob sighed.

"But it's not that *bad,* is it? It's incredible! It's fantastic." Bella enthused. "I'm sitting in the car right now with someone famous – I'm being driven home by someone famous!"

"No, no …" He said quietly "You're not. I'm not Ezza."

Bella laughed.

"I'm not Ezza, I'm Jacob."

"But from what I gather you *are* Ezza. You may call yourself Jacob, but really *you are* Ezza!"

He sighed. Marelle stared at him.

"Ezza didn't die, did he? You went and hid and called yourself Jacob … you're still Ezza … aren't you?"

He looked straight ahead of himself, one hand still on the steering wheel. That happiness had gone from his face – washed away like snow in the rain – the tension had returned.

"I can sit here and deny it, just like I have done many times, but you have found it, you can see it. You were always going to be one of the first to know I guess … but I didn't want it to happen this way. I knew putting my head above the parapet would always be a risk but it's a chicken and egg situation and I had to pick a starting place somewhere in the circle. I guess it's here, now."

There was a silence, not as intense as a vacuum, but still a silence. From the moment a couple of hours ago in the restaurant with the sausage to now was an epoch. Even Bella didn't immediately have anything to say but eventually she spoke.

"Jacob. This is fantastic. Live this moment; live this life – don't hide from it. When the moment is right just go out there and smash it! It's brilliant! It's just incredible … and to top it all you're going to marry my bestest friend!" She reached through and placed a hand on his shoulder.

He sighed, breathed noisily through his nose.

"But this goes no further than us three here … not a word, to *anyone* … I want – I *have* to do this my way."

"Of course! I won't breath it to a soul. It's just you, Marelle and me …"

He sat there for a moment then re-animated himself., started the car again and pulled away from the lay-by.

"Shit." He said to himself.

Back at the house Bella had put her stuff in her own car. Marelle was out there with her, watching as she closed the hatchback. She turned to Marelle with a smile. There had been a certain anxiety about her since they had returned home, fuelled by Jacob's silence on the rest of the journey back. He was now out in the back garden, staring across the airfield. Bella slipped an arm around Marelle and hugged her.

"I won't tell anyone. You know I won't."

"No, but you had to push it, didn't you? You covered for me by saying you found out for yourself but now he's worrying about that," Marelle sighed.

"It's better for you if I know ... you don't have to keep weaving little white lies with me now – we can talk about it – if you need to."

Marelle nodded. "What about Mae?"

Bella laughed and shrugged. "I'll probably see her next time – I get the impression she would rather be back with her ex – she's sweet but I don't think there's anything likely to happen between us."

Marelle gave a sympathetic smile.

Bella smiled broadly in return. "Can't wait for your wedding ... it's going to be epic!"

Marelle grinned. "We'll get there eventually."

"Come on!" Bella nodded. "Let's go find him. I need to give him a hug and say bye ..."

Today, watching Bella hug Jacob in the back garden was a moment when Marelle was touched by the fact that the three of them were bonded by that secret. Soon, if Jacob executed his plan, it would be common knowledge and this moment they had now would no longer exist.

Bella hugged Jacob, leaning back and looking up at him, a grin on her face.

"I love that mischievous side to you." She laughed. "Can't wait to see you again ... what's next, hey?"

"Oh, I don't know. We'll see..." He smiled. Jacob now in his voice and his stance.

Bella smiled sweetly. "Well look after yourself. Take care – and look after madam there." She nodded to Marelle.

"Oh, I intend to." He said, making eye contact with Marelle.

SIXTEEN

With Bella gone and Marelle checking emails on her computer in the kitchen, Jacob walked in. He had his shoulders slumped this evening.

"What?" She questioned to his sigh.

"If Bella managed to work it out then plenty of other people will as well ... we might need to move a little faster."

Marelle turned and stared at him. "Oh I don't think people will work it out ... Bella knows you pretty well now and she was right next to you all weekend in that situation, totally immersed in the whole thing ... I don't think anyone else will put two and two together just as she has."

He shrugged.

Thankfully, Marelle knew that Bella had not '*worked it out*', it had been a lie to save her but now that lie was playing on Jacob's mind because, to him it was a very possible truth.

"Hmmm." He said. "Don't you count on that! We have the likes of the wonderful Ellen!"

"... yes, and you took a selfie with her! Marelle reminded him. It had been slightly drink fuelled, slightly adrenaline fuelled behaviour, she knew now.

'She will have deleted that by now! She had her idol right next to her but thought I was just a drunken idiot!" he replied.

"Do you actually remember her?"

"God no!" He exclaimed.

"Chas does."

"Well she's obviously been right there, night in and night out. No, it's a good thing ... if it wasn't for the likes of her then Yellow Son probably wouldn't still be going, and I wouldn't have the band to go back to."

Marelle sighed.

"... but it's out there ... and if people can find it then we need to make a move sooner ... can you have a look on there ..." He nodded to her laptop.

"What for?"

"Their next gig." He replied, matter-of-factly.

She sat herself down at the laptop, Jacob hanging over her shoulder as she did so. Marelle tapped in 'Yellow Son' and eventually found their website. Jacob sniggered when it opened on her screen. The landing page was wide picture of the group as they were now, looking moody against an orange background.

There was a bit of a bio which they both began reading. Ezza got more than one mention and there seemed to be a love and respect for him in the words. After a moment's silence as they read, Marelle clicked on the 'upcoming gigs' tab at the top.

The list was long but most of the dates were passed. Marelle scrolled down to the bottom of the page. Jacob leant over her shoulder as she studied it. "It looks like there are only three left." She remarked. "And it says that one of them is cancelled."

Marelle clicked on the date. "We regret that due to issues with the venue's public liability insurance this event has unfortunately been cancelled. This was beyond our control. Full refunds will be issued to all ticket holders. Please check our website for alternative gigs."

"So only two left." He said. "That's not ideal but I can work with it. When are they?"

"One in three-weeks and one a couple of weeks later."

"Unusual. They normally do two or three gigs a week ... but ... I suppose, it is the end of a long tour. Probably more dates fallen out too. OK." he read the details. Gave a little sigh.

'Looks like we'll be going to Guildford."

"Where's that?" Marelle asked.

'Surrey.' Jacob replied. "Couple of hour's drive – could be worse ... can we book tickets?"

Marelle clicked on the 'book tickets' link and went through the process with Jacob hanging over her shoulder. When it came to payment, he handed her his card.

"There." She said, once payment had gone through.

He gave a little laugh, like an excited child as he took his card back.

The next morning he had stood in her kitchen at a quarter to seven, ready to go to work – looking totally delectable, even in the lowly fleece and ripped black jeans – but the relaxation and the smile on his face were what thrilled her the most. That smile she had longed for; a new glint in his eye that she had only ever dreamed of. Marelle walked up to him and placed her hands on his shoulders, looking up into his face as he gently placed his hands around her waist.

"Do you want a lift to work?" She asked.

"No." he laughed. "I'll walk, I'll go across the airfield."

She slid her arms around his neck, pulled him down to her.

'Love you." She said, looking into his eyes.

They smiled back; they danced in his face and showed her without any words how he in turn felt about her. Those eyes that had flicked themselves away from her own so many times – fastidiously avoided contact – strived to focus on everything and anything except her eyes. He pulled her to him, and she buried her face in his fleece. It smelled of washing powder and fabric conditioner – and him.

'And you know I love you too!" He whispered. "But I'd better go ..." He kissed her gently. "I'll see you later on."

Marelle nodded and let him go.

Everyday this departure was painful, and she knew she would never feel comfortable with him going away from her. She smiled and the look on his face filled her with warmth; it was an expression she never thought she would see portrayed on Jacob's face. A whole new expression in his eyes told her that he had finally found somewhere he felt he belonged.

Marelle worked all morning. Completing whatever Seb sent and feeling no need to communicate any further with her brother than the formally polite minimum. He had no hand in her life despite what he thought. He said he would give her three months to come to her senses and realise her life with Jacob was going nowhere and go running back to eat humble pie under the security and protection Seb could offer her. Marelle grinned to herself; she told him that last time she had seen him that one day she would show him that he was wrong to treat Jacob with such disdain and contempt – and the time in her life where she could claim the laurels of that sweet victory was close.

"Fuck you Seb." She said to herself.

She didn't need him now; she had never needed him. He had always been there, interfering with her life – 'helping' when she didn't need help. The inheritance of this house had thrown them together even more and just for a second back there she had very nearly been blinkered enough to let him decide what she should do with her life. Marelle did not need his advice or his surveillance in hers anymore. The only bond they really had now was this house and that meant one thing; she didn't want him with that hold over her anymore.

For a moment she sat staring into the space of the kitchen around her and nearly, very nearly, picked up her phone right now and demand that he sells his half to her. Somehow, she would find the money. The house would be hers and Seb would have no right or reason to be part of her life anymore.

But what did Jacob want? Did he want to stay here? Whenever she talked about buying the house he had always back pedalled, always dismissed the idea. If he wanted to stay here and wanted her to buy the house, then she would. Maybe he wanted to buy it with her? But she knew that in itself would be an issue as she knew Seb would refuse to sell it if he knew Jacob was part of it.

Maybe Jacob wanted to move away? She doubted it – he had always returned here – his heart was here – some deeper foundation always drew him here. He would never leave permanently. She was sure of that.

And what if she did buy the house? What if Seb did agree – he would make it as difficult as possible for her to reinforce her life with Jacob. But she also knew that what Seb said and what Seb did were often two different things; she could weave him a sob story and in the end, she could probably get what she wanted out of him. She would certainly try if she had to.

At lunchtime she called Jacob. It was a routine which helped her get through the day and one which he didn't seem to mind. His voice on the phone still thrilled her every time she heard it.

"Hi." She smiled when he answered. "What're you doing?"

"Just going out in the van." He replied.

"Oh, where?" There was worry in her voice even though she tried to hide it.

'Just to the parts place. Need a hose …"

"Oh." It meant nothing to her, but he sounded happy. "Have you had lunch?" She asked.

As usual he had gone off with a packed lunch she had prepared for him. Marelle liked picking and packing food for him – he never complained and at least she knew he was eating properly – and when she thought about the slice of toast she had slathered in butter and eaten half an hour ago she realised he was probably eating better than she was!

"Some of it." He answered. "Going to eat while I drive ..."

Marelle didn't like the thought of him eating and driving but there wasn't much she could do about it.

"Had yours?" He asked.

"Yeah ..." She sighed, wondering whether to say anything about the house right now but deciding not to. "Work's boring. Might just start googling you if it gets too tedious!"

He gave a little laugh.

"Send me a picture!" She suddenly said. "Take a selfie and send it to me."

"Why?" He laughed.

"Go on. I miss you!"

"Well you haven't forgotten what I look like, have you?"

"Of course not! But I don't have many pictures of you."

"There are thousands on the internet!" He said with a little chuckle.

"But they are not of you." She said. "Ellen has a picture of you!"

He sighed. 'That will have been deleted by now." He replied. 'Long gone ... alright but I hope to God Ryan doesn't see me posing for a selfie!"

Marelle giggled.

"I'll send it in a minute, ok?"

"I'm waiting." She answered. "Be careful."

"I'm always careful."

"Oh no you're not!" She quipped. "See you later – or in a minute when you send me a selfie ..."

"... alright!"

"Make it a nice one!" She laughed.

A couple of minutes later her phone pinged and she opened the message with a grin. The day was cold and bright; he had taken the picture alongside the white van, his image clearly displayed against it. He had the camera high, at arm's length, leaning into the shot, half squinting at the camera. His hair looked very dark in the light – it was longer now; she could do something with that! His eyes were happy, and he portrayed that cheeky lopsided grin that looked so natural despite the fact she knew that, on occasions, it had been fabricated. Today it wasn't; today it was genuine and that was a picture of someone who looked truly happy with his life. Marelle smiled widely to herself; he was beautiful; he was amazing, and he could pull a shot like that while just stepping out of work for a moment. And he was hers – mind, body and soul. No one could deny that or take it away from her now.

She texted him back '*Love you*'.

Seconds later he replied with a smiley face. The sheer frivolity of his reply made her laugh, made her cry all at once. Six months ago, that would never have happened, and that tiny gesture marked the distance they had travelled together.

And how much further they still had to go.

The look in his eyes fortified her mood through the afternoon. The smile on her face was strong and unwavering even when the doorbell rang unexpectedly. Marelle presumed it would be Catchpole as usual, trying to read between any lines, trying to catch her off balance for that split second that counted. Through the frosted glass however she could see a fluorescent orange jacket. Perplexed, she opened the door.

A guy stood there with envelope in hand, which he was turning constantly through his fingers as he waited. He had dark hair which reminded her of how she had been forced to cut Jacob's; his eyes were dark and beady, but small.

"Hello." She said.

"Good afternoon. I was looking for Jacob Frost?"

This time his voice and the question in it portrayed an uncertainty. She wasn't sure who he was or what he wanted, On the right hand breast of his hi-vis jacket he wore it said 'Devorah.'

"Why do you need to see him?" She asked.

He held the letter forwards, "I need to pass this to him."

"What is it?"

He shrugged. "Don't know. I have just been asked to pass it to him. He used to be in the caravan, but I can see it's in your back garden now."

"Yeah, well ... it wouldn't be ... if work hadn't started on site."

He gave a small smile, a slight apology but held out the letter to her. She didn't want to take it; not knowing what it was.

"Is he here?" He asked., offering the letter again.

"What is it?" Marelle asked once more.

He laughed. It's not a summons or a court order. It's just a letter. I asked in the shop where he was living, and it was like getting blood out of a stone!"

Marelle pursed her lips. She sighed, held out her hand and took the envelope from him.

'He's not here at the moment – he's at the farm. He'll be back later and yes, he is living here, with me.'

He smiled. "Thank you. Can you pass it on to him?"

She nodded.

"Did he move the fence panel at the bottom of your garden?"

Marelle gave a guilty little shrug. "May have done ... he's lived on the airfield for a long time ... I guess he feels a bit lost being shut off it."

"Well, I suppose there's not going to be much going on for a while anyway ..."

"Why?" Marelle questioned.

"This heritage site thing happens all the time – if it's not newts it's archaeology, or heritage sites. We'll be back." He answered. "Ok, make sure he gets that."

"I will." She replied. "Thank you."

He waved a hand as he left. There was a white van parked at the road which he got into. Marelle closed the door and looked at the letter. It was a white A5 envelope with a window. In the window it read

'Mr. Jacob Frost, c/o Groveham Parfield Site, Groveham Parfield, Suffolk'

He would have to change that to *'Valspar, The Street'* she thought as she stared at it. Why would Devorah be sending him a letter? She had a good idea and suspected it wouldn't be good news.

Leaving the letter on the worktop in the kitchen she resisted opening it. Marelle knew she could possibly 'shake' the address out of the way a bit and say she didn't look at the name on it – the way she had many times with Chris when a suspicious letter arrived. But this hadn't come in the post and would be a bit of a stretched white lie in this case. She guessed it was just telling him that his time as custodian was up – which they both knew anyhow. A few weeks ago, she would have feared giving it to him. Now she doubted he would care.

Marelle was still working in the kitchen as the clock moved towards five thirty. She had one eye on the time and decided to stop in five minutes and start to think about dinner. The nights were drawing in more each day and it would be all but dark by six thirty – maybe a little later due to the day being bright and sunny. She sat up and looked across the airfield through the window, remembering the time she had moved in here – it had been winter then. The days had been short with the nights long and dark. Just like the first time she had met Jacob. They had shared the year and the summer and melded themselves together as the year returned to the prospect of winter. Marelle sighed – thinking about a winter wedding but doubting it would happen that quickly. As a child she had seen a picture of a winter wedding dress, trimmed with white fur and a large draped hood; it had fascinated her but given the chance she liked that idea now.

The sound of a vehicle in the front drive alerted her away from her thoughts. It was loud and sounded like a truck or something. Not expecting a delivery of any sorts, she pushed the chair away from the table and went through to see who or what was in her drive. Through the glass she could see a white vehicle, looked like a large van. On opening the door, she was greeted with the large white van from the farm, right up to her front door and Jacob climbing down from the driver's seat.

"Hi." She smiled. "What're you doing?"

'Said I may as well bring the van home to use – because I'm working there properly now and no-one else is using it."

"Oh, that's good, isn't it?" She questioned.

He gave her that lovely little smile, dimpled his cheek, grinned.

"Yeah." He replied as he locked the door and began to walk towards her.

There he was just a regular guy returning home from a manual job; a farm labourer – but his dark hair his dark eyes and his beautiful face telling her a different story. Here he was Jacob; inside he was Nat; in his head he was Ezza. He stepped up the steps to the front door and she fell into his arms.

'Nice picture!" She commented, closing her eyes and burying her face against him.

"Oh I take a pretty good selfie!" he laughed.

Marelle squeezed him, buried her face in him, closed her eyes and breathed in every sense of him – home again, safely back in her arms.

"Not used to you coming in the front door." She laughed as they walked through the house to the kitchen. "I'll give you a key ... looks like you'll be coming in that way more if you are bringing the van home."

He followed her through.

"I've been thinking about the house." She began. "What we ought to do."

"What's this?" He asked, having spotted the envelope on the worktop and seen his name on the front.

"A guy from the site brought it to the door this afternoon – been trying to find you apparently, He wouldn't say what it was."

Jacob picked the letter up and ripped the flap open. She watched him swallow as he did so.

"I didn't want to take it – in case it was some kind of legal letter ... but the guy assured me it wasn't." she explained but he was unfolding the piece of paper and reading it.

Marelle could see Devorah's blue logo at the top of the page as she watched Jacob read. When she had first met him, she had shamefully wondered if he *could* read and write! He'd just seemed like some local recluse who had probably never been to school or read a book. Now she knew how totally wrong that was and the absence of such boundaries in his mind.

His dark eyes scanned the text and the letter, reading quickly, moving sharply from left to right. "What is it?" She asked.

"Hmm." He made a little noise. She wasn't sure which emotion was behind it.

"Well." He said, still looking at the letter. "Due to unforeseen delay, and a revised commercial position by the owners, the work on site is currently suspended until further notice." He raised his eyes to Marelle.

"So?" She shrugged.

"So they are asking me to remain in place as custodian of the site for the time being." He gave a little smile.

"Move your caravan back?" Marelle exclaimed, a little worriedly.

"Well, no ... I don't need to ... but probably can if I want."

"Are you going to?"

"No." He laughed. "I'm here anyway, aren't I? They want me to be the gate keeper again – keep an eye on the site ... just like the past ten years." He smiled broader. "It's just us and the airfield again."

Marelle smiled. Mirroring his smile. Inside he was leaping with joy but Jacob kept it contained.

"... because of the Thor site, do you think?" She asked.

"Part of it ... but I read more into it ... there's obviously some other issue too, might be money? Maybe we've got another ten years!"

That thought was in her head as she curled herself around him in the bed that night. She was still thrilled to place her hands on his warm, bare skin and sense the blood running in his veins and the beat of his heart. She still wondered at him being here with her and still found it hard to believe that he had chosen her she had opened her heart to him and, despite the barbs and spears he came with, he had accepted refuge in her and she was so completely grateful for it. She said his name to herself and still felt the exhilaration of excitement run through her. This was Jacob; *her* Jacob; she was his and he was hers. Every cell in their bodies were now linked and to break them apart would destroy them both.

And now, knowing what she knew, knowing his past and what – *who* – he had been ... what if he had never suffered that mental breakdown, what if he had carried on as Ezza. Ten years on he would still be singing with them she supposed he would not even know of her and she would probably have not even known of him or Yellow Son. Their paths would never have crossed and she would never have been given the chance to spread her fingers across his ribcage and feel it expand with every vital breath nor run her fingers through his hair.

"I need to sort this tooth out." He suddenly said, in the darkness when she thought he was asleep. Obviously at the end of a thought process that he had not shared with her.

"Why? Does it hurt?"

"No. Just don't really want to place myself in front of Chas looking like a gap-toothed gypsy!"

She smiled and nestled her head against him. "It looks quite cute ...!"

"No, it looks like a gap-toothed gypsy!" He insisted.

"You haven't got a dentist, have you?" She asked,

"No. Never been." He replied.

"I've got a dentist down where I used to live ... there must be one around here. I probably ought to change too ..."

'I don't know where to start, no idea." He said.

"Well I think you will probably have to go private to get that sorted properly ... it won't be cheap either ..."

"Want someone to do it without asking too many questions ..."

Marelle laughed. "It's a tooth – and a dentist! Nobody's going to ask questions!"

'You know what I mean. Someone who doesn't want a full history – just sort it and go."

"I would imagine it will be more than one visit. Chris had a bridge, and it took weeks."

"I'd like to get it sorted before the concert – can you have a look tomorrow?"

"I can." She answered. "I'll see if I can get you an appointment, somewhere."

Marelle went to sleep with her head against his gently rising and falling chest thinking on today. On that day he had been afforded the work's vehicle, found he could remain in his position on the airfield and made a move to repair the broken tooth. She was content with a feeling that things were at least moving forwards in a positive way.

S

SEVENTEEN

It was a strange feeling when he climbed into the van in the morning. She had seen him driving it many times but this morning, when he sat in the driver's seat with the door open as she kissed him goodbye, it seemed odd. She tiptoed up to kiss him as he leaned down, one hand on the steering wheel. The van was old and pretty untidy inside – it didn't look as if it had ever been washed or cleaned out. She wondered how long Jacob would tolerate that now it was in his custodianship.

She watched him reverse the van out onto the road and turn right. With a wave and a smile, he disappeared.

Marelle had wanted to broach the subject of the house with him last night but with the good news from the day she didn't want to dampen any happiness with a serious discussion. But it was still on her mind today so, to placate herself, she decided to look at similar properties close-by to see what the market value of this house might be. That way she wouldn't be talking out of her arse when she decided to lay her cards on the table.

In the meantime, she had the question of a dentist to sort out for him. Where to start? Where everything now started she guessed, and she tapped 'dentists in my area' into her computer.

There were a few dental practices in the local town, and she began by calling the first one on the list. It was not a good choice. The woman she spoke to was not really helpful; initially she said they were not taking on any new patients but then asked what the problem was. Marelle ended up discussing Jacob's teeth and she realised she didn't totally know the extent of the problem.

"He's broken a front tooth." She explained.

"Is he in pain?"

"No, no – I don't think so ..."

'I may be able to fit him in in about four weeks."

'Four weeks! I don't think he can wait that long."

"Well, is he in pain then?"

"No." she said again. "It's more of a cosmetic thing – he has an 'event' in a few weeks. He wants to have it sorted by then."

"Well, if it's just cosmetic then he may have to look for private treatment."
"Oh I know that." Marelle answered. "I did explain that to him he is prepared to go private."

The receptionist sighed. "He would need to have a private consultation first and the dentist would then decide which treatment he would need. It may not be a procedure we can offer ..."

Marelle cut the conversation after that. It didn't seem to be going in any direction, and she didn't like the sound of the practice if she was honest.

The next one asked too many questions which she didn't know the answers to. He had broken a tooth – why so many questions about it – and him. Part of her understood his reluctance to seek any medical treatment when their questioning was so invasive. She also wondered if it would be more sensible for him to speak to them he could explain exactly what was missing, if it was loose and how much was left of it when she didn't really know, The third one was much more amiable – friendly, and talked her through everything without firing questions at her or not giving her a chance to try and answer. They said they could help but he would need to speak to the dentist to make a decision as to whether a bridge or an implant would be the best solution. There was an appointment available in a couple of days if he could attend their Cambridge surgery.

'It's a Saturday appointment." The receptionist said. "This will be slightly more expensive, but it will give him a less hurried appointment and time for him to decide what he would like to do.

Not knowing what she was getting into or how much it was likely to cost, Marelle booked that appointment for him.

With her newly gained knowledge she imparted it to Jacob when he came home.

"You can have a bridge or an implant." Marelle explained. "But it will depend on the state of the broken tooth and what your gum is like."

"I don't want to know what they are going to do; I just want it sorted ..."

She looked up at him, surprised that he wasn't interested in the technical aspect of it. "Are you scared?" She asked.

"No!" he replied with a nervous laugh. "Just don't fancy having it done – but it's got to be done. I guess I would have left it but ..." He shrugged. "But I'm vain!" He answered with a tight little smile. "It's got to be sorted. Ezza is a vain bastard – he wouldn't walk onto stage with a tooth missing!"

Marelle smiled at his quip, along with him but her guts began to knot inside her at the thought of the road he was setting out upon and indeed, his expectation of the outcome.

The night before his initial consultation she could see the anxiety building in him minute by minute. In a way it made her smile she had watched him worry over many things, she'd seen like a moving shadow in his eyes and sensed it's creeping anxiety running through him on numerous nights – but tonight she saw it in him over a trip to the dentist!

He drove her car to Cambridge the next day. His appointment was ten o clock, so they had left the house by eight thirty. It was a bright, breezy morning that possible had promise for later in the day as they moved west, leaving the flat landscape of Suffolk for the slightly rolling hills of Cambridgeshire.

"I've never been to Cambridge." Marelle remarked, settling herself into the passenger seat. "How far is it?"

"About forty miles – each way." He answered. His mind still turning the upcoming appointment over and over.

"It's a university, isn't it?" She asked.

"There is a university there ..." He said. "It's a nice city. Terrible place to park though."

"My first time there today."

"I've played there." He suddenly said. "A few times."

Marelle stared at him. She smiled. "Really?"

He nodded. "Used to like playing there. Nearest decent venue close to home."

Marelle looked ahead, smiled to herself for a moment. He wasn't elaborating right now.

"The lady on reception said they had two parking spaces in front of their building. We might be lucky." She looked back at him. His jaw was very tightly clenched. "It's only a consultation today you know. There's nothing to worry about!"

He sighed, driving on. "I know, but it's the combination of the thought of someone drilling a hole in my mouth and having to let the system get its hands on my details – once they've got you, they've got you. I'm still Jacob."

"It's a dentist!" She laughed. "A private one at that – as long as you pay, I doubt they'll care what your name is. Give them a false one."

"But you've already told them my name."

True. She had.

'Well say I got it wrong!"

"Oh yeah! My wife doesn't know my name!" He laughed but his humorous little remark suddenly filled her breast with pride and happiness, she smiled to herself and lowered her eyes to her hands. A short while ago, she hadn't truly known his name.

"Don't worry about that." She smiled, "Worry about the hole in your mouth instead then."

He laughed. "Oh shut it!"

Cambridge was busy on the bright autumn day. They travelled in, past an airport and through the bustling outskirts of the renown seat of learning. There seemed to be an inordinate number of roundabouts, all of which were a bit dog-eat-dog. They would have flustered her, but Jacob took them in his usual stride; calm; unhurried; perfectly.

"I think it's up here." He commented, taking a third exit and turning up a tree-lined avenue of what she guessed would have been Victorian town houses; many of which now appeared to be commercial premises with their front garden's tarmacked for client parking spaces. Halfway along they found the dental practice, two parking spaces at the front, one taken. Jacob glided her car into the vacant one.

He cut the engine, paused, sighed then looked at her.

This was the moment. All that he had told her; all of those years he had kept his head down and been Jacob were now condensing into the single black point which was the place where it all changed. Today his fears were not just of physical mutilation and pain; today his fears were of the future and of that very first step that was the starting point in freeing Ezza from the place he had been locked away in for the last ten years.

She elected to go in with him. Her choices had been to sit in the car, take a walk into the centre or go in with him. It would have been pointless sitting in the car; she didn't fancy walking into the centre as her mind would be elsewhere. She would sit in the waiting room for him and in that event, she would be there, just in case he freaked out. He was nervous as hell – she could see that – and she was unsure if that amount of anxiety would set off any other reaction in him.

Watching him walk into the dentist's room was like watching a child being taken away for an operation; handing that precious being over to someone who was ultimately going to cut into their flesh. He looked so skinny and lanky as he stood up and walked to the door which the dentist held open for him. Today he looked older, time ragged at the edges.

The dentist was blonde and built like a rugby player. You could see he was pretty muscular beneath the green scrub top he wore. There was something cartoonish about his perfect, chiselled appearance and Marelle felt she wanted to plead with him not to hurt Jacob! But the door closed, and she was left alone with her thoughts and the receptionist.

It was so quiet. The receptionist kept her head down; in the background Marelle could just about hear very quiet music playing but otherwise it was silent. Voices from the dentist's room just about audible but she could not make out any words they were saying. She looked at her watch. It had only been five minutes and she was already feeling him missing from the empty space beside her.

Jacob was only feet away from her, on the other side of that door but what was taking place in that room signified the very first steps in his metamorphosis from Jacob to Ezza. He had commented that Ezza was a vain bastard; this was for Ezza. It was not something she supposed Jacob would have done. As she sat there, staring at the top of the receptionist's head she unexpectedly felt overwhelmed by sadness. She didn't want Jacob to go; she didn't want the world to know he existed. Marelle wanted it just how it had been this past year – just her and Jacob. But this was his dream – his driving ambition, part of his reason for still being alive and she could not, or would not stop him from making that transformation. Her heart was beating fast, and the back of her throat began to constrict. She didn't want to share him with the world and the likes of Ellen!

Marelle shuffled, lifted her eyes from the back of her hands, sighed. Then her phone rang, it was in her bag but turned up to full volume so she could hear it ringing from virtually everywhere at home in the house – just in case Jacob ever called her unexpectedly,

The noise of the phone ringing shattered the silence in the waiting room, Marelle panicked, fumbled to find the phone and eventually drew it from her bag. With it in her hand she hurriedly stood up. The receptionist was staring at her; clutching her bag and the ringing phone she walked outside.

"Hi Bella." She finally answered, glad of the distraction.

"Hi." Bella replied. "What are you doing? You took a long time to answer – up to no good with lover boy?"

"Not exactly." Marelle laughed. "I'm in Cambridge, at a dentist."

"What?"

"With Jacob, getting that missing tooth fixed."

"Cambridge! Don't you have a dentist closer than that?"

"Yes, but they didn't want to know – we eventually found a private practice in Cambridge that can sort it out."

"Fuck! How much is that going to cost?" Bella gasped.

"I don't know. Jacob wanted it sorted properly …"

"Is he having it done right now?"

"Yes, well no … he's having a consultation first. He was really worried about it; he's never been to a dentist before!"

"Never been to a dentist!" Bella exclaimed.

"No …nor a doctor, or a hospital … apparently."

"How?"

"Just didn't when he was a kid and hasn't since he's been an adult."

"Wow! He never ceases to amaze me!"

"Me neither!" Marelle grinned. "What're you calling for anyway?"

Bella gave a little laugh. "Well – Mae called me last night … she's invited me up to hers – *tonight*." Bella said and Marelle could sense the grin on her face.

"Are you going?"

Bella paused " – Yeah!" She laughed in exclamation.

Marelle smiled. "Well don't go doing anything I wouldn't do!"

"I'm hopefully going to do lots of things that you wouldn't do!" Bella quipped.

"Hussy!" Marelle giggled.

"Well, you only live once. You've got your man … I may have well found my girl!"

Marelle smiled. Now she was here listening to Bella gush on about an object of affection when for so long it had been the other way around.

"Probably a flash in the pan." Bella was continuing. "But I wanted to tell you – it doesn't change us though."

"Have fun Bella." Marelle told her, with a smile. "We can have a double wedding!"

Bella laughed. "Now that *would* be fun!"

"If it ever happens …"

"It will happen Marelle. He won't let you down!"

"No, I know that." Marelle stated, thoughtfully.

"I've been looking their stuff up you know, listening to a bit of it this week. You know they are really, really good!" Bella said. "But at the end of the day he's just Jacob to me and always will be."

When Marelle returned to the waiting room nothing had changed. She sat down again. This time however, she smiled. Bella had called to tell her about

Mae; that she was about to drive to Mae's and stay the night. Although Bella shared everything with Marelle, she rarely provided such an update on a relationship – in fact Marelle could not recall her ever treating any relationship she had been involved in like this. Normally, with Bella, it was flitting from one encounter to the next with no commitment in between. This time Mae seemed to have made an impression and Marelle knew, despite what Bella had said when they had come home from the weekender, that this mattered to her.

The dentist's room was silent. Marelle turned her head to the closed door. Now she couldn't hear anything; she looked up to the receptionist, but she was still looking down. Maybe Marelle should have gone in the room with Jacob; maybe he had wanted her to insist? He had been scared enough but he wouldn't have asked. She fidgeted, strained her ears, raised her eyes to the girl behind the desk again. Maybe he had come out while she had been outside. Maybe he was in a toilet or something maybe he had become so overwhelmed? Surely the receptionist would have said?

The she heard voices from the room again and a click like something being switched on, or off. She looked at her watch again. Her phone was still in her hand so as a means of a distraction she began searching Ezza on the internet again, making sure she had muted her phone before it blasted out Yellow Son at a high volume! He said they had played Cambridge, so she typed in '*Yellow Son live in Cambridge*'. The first video was dated thirteen years ago; the still showed Ezza standing holding the microphone with a smile on his face; his hair was very, very short around the back and sides – almost a number one – but the top was long and very spiky. It seemed to have a purplish red tinge to it, but it could have been the lights. He wore a fairly baggy, white, cap sleeved t-shirt with some weird black and yellow print on the front. He was grinning. She pressed play and checked the sound was off again. The video came to life and Ezza appeared to be speaking to the crowd; he wasn't singing. His impossibly long legs were in black jeans over cowboy boots with long, pointed toes. He spoke for ages holding the mic in the stand in one hand, smiling and laughing. He turned his head to the side and spoke to Chas as the camera had taken them both into the shot. Chas said something in return then walked forwards, playing his guitar. Ezza opened his arms and Chas walked into a brotherly embrace with him. They parted laughing as Ezza gestured that the music was beginning, and he animated himself to sing. The caption that came up said '*Out of Here – Yellow Son*' Live. Cambridge and the date just over thirteen years ago. It wasn't a song she recognised the title of and by the way Ezza was now singing it didn't look like it was a fast one. Marelle desperately wanted to know what he had said and listen to the song he was singing. Maybe she would save it for later – she bookmarked it and flicked back to the images.

There was one that she had not seen before which had appeared today. It was a portrait and he looked so young! His hair had not yet found his trademark style at that point and looked a little hacked about. Marelle smiled slightly to herself – then she looked into those deep, dark eyes and even then, in that picture on her phone she sensed a sorrow. There was not a single line etched on his face as yet in that image and there were flecks of residual acne on his cheeks. He must have been in his very late teens or early twenties at most. His mouth was small and tight. The faded denim jacket he wore had the collar turned up over a white t-shirt. Marelle tapped the picture, and a page opened up with a number of pictures she had not seen before either. A black and white one showed a very young Jacob with who she assumed was Chas. He had more hair than he had now and was thinner – looked a lot older than Jacob in the photo. She tapped it again and a page opened up from an old music magazine. It was tiny print and black and white, but she zoomed in on her screen to read. The masthead said, *'Diamond in the Rough'*.

'Chas Symonds has a vision.' It began. *'He has travelled a long road with Kullinane and now wants to put his feet up from singing duties and hand the reins over to a younger candidate.'*

'It's just time to change.' Chas explains. *'I had good times with Kullinane, there is no animosity but I'm not getting any younger, but I do still have ambition. I have decided to disband Kullinane and sit in the back seat while a bright new thing fronts the new band.'* Chas speaks in his autonomous east end accent. His voice is roughened at the edges from obligatory cigarettes and alcohol, *'I'm a guitarist.'* He adds. *'I want to play guitar.'*

And who is the bright young thing?

Sitting next to Chas is the new lead singer of the new band. The red v-neck jumper he is wearing looks like it is part of a school uniform – teamed with a grey shirt and a striped tie. He is certainly young, sporting a schoolboy haircut and a face fresh out of puberty. Shyness seems to be a problem and his eyes flit away from mine. A nervous smile appears on his face to order as he says *'hello.'*

This is Ezza, Chas' secret weapon to keep his music alive and entice a whole new bevvy of younger fans.

'Don't be fooled. He's a fucking God on stage.' Chas informs me but as yet, I see no proof of that.

Marelle smiled to herself. The thought of a shy, spotty-faced Jacob drafted into Chas' remit made her smile and as she looked into those innocent but troubled young eyes in the photo she asked if he had any idea at that point what those eyes would see and what would happen inside that brain. Even at that stage she could see 'Ezza' had not been a completely blank canvas; there were already outlines of a previous sketch, just visible.

Marelle stared into those eyes a little too long and she saw a pleading; she saw a cry for help that no-one had before – even at that early stage in his life. But no-one else had. And as those eyes pleaded with her now, she felt that smile falter from her lips and begin to waiver away.

She started reading again.

'So which obscurity was Ezza plucked from?

Chas explains.

"I saw him on the TV with his band on 'The Remedy' (a local Friday teatime music show) – they weren't meant to be on there and had literally got called in with an hour's notice, was it Ezza? Cos the band that should have been featured pulled out at the last minute. Someone knew someone who knew the band and they got

invited on to fill a gap on live TV. I often watch The Remedy – it's "yoof TV" – lets me see what is current – what I'm up against but he blew me away. I instantly knew he had to be the lead singer with Yellow Son'.

Yellow Son is the name of the new band – more on why that name later.

'Took a while to track him down but I eventually found him. He's a fucking scientist you know – a fucking geek – he was at University!'

So, this man, ok boy, pulled from the classroom due to a chance appearance on TV. Now he has a reputation to fill and uphold.'

This was right at the very beginning she realised. Right at the point where Nat became Ezza and started out on a path which would lead to Jacob. And she would have been a child; barely aware of her own consciousness and memory while Jacob had still been Nat and had sat alongside Chas for this interview. Marelle was suddenly aware of this life he had led before they had met, long before he had hidden himself away from the world for years. She had known but until now she had not felt the breadth of it, now it felt 'real;' to use a word which his childhood friend Frankie had in his letter and which Jacob had hooked onto so strangely when he had read it on finding it years later. Now she understood what he meant, and she felt the jetsam of his past trailing behind her as well as him – now part of her life as well as his past and her legacy. Looking back into the eyes of that boy in the picture now; teetering on the edge of the rest of his life. She could feel the years and she could see that transformation into Jacob.

That picture had been the beginning of what she had now. Marelle stared into his eyes on her phone. Lost in them; lost in the story she was reading; lost from where she was and what she was doing in the vacuous silence of the waiting area. Marelle was suddenly transported back to the here and now when the door of the dentist's room opened with a click, and she looked up.

The dentist held the door open for Jacob and he walked out. He looked briefly into her expectant eyes as she clutched her phone in her hand and then back to the dentist. Marelle looked to the picture on her phone again and back to Jacob. Some twenty plus years between the two. Yes, Jacob looked young for his age, but those twenty odd years had gently etched themselves into him.

"Thank you." Jacob nodded to the dentist.

"No problem. We can soon get this as good as new for you ... shall we see if we can book you in?"

Jacob's jaw was tight; she watched it tighten more. 'When would you be able to do it?" He asked.

"Let me see ..." The dentist smiled, pushing past Jacob and going behind the reception desk. Jacob walked over to it, glancing at Marelle.

She stood up, picked up her bag and went to stand next to him.

"It will need to be a weekday appointment. I only usually do consultations at the weekend." He smiled. "You may also want to take a couple of days off work. What do you do?"

"Erm, I work on a farm."

"Manual stuff?"

Jacob nodded.

"Then I suggest we look for a Thursday appointment then you can take the Friday off too – that way you also have the weekend to recover …"

Marelle placed a hand on his bottom, sliding it round to his thigh. Jacob felt hot, tense; he looked pale. He was terrified.

"Will it be that bad?" Jacob laughed, nervously.

"No, no … but well there may be a bit of discomfort for twenty-four hours or so … it's only one implant so it will be minimal. If it were any more then I wouldn't be prepared to do it in one hit." The dentist explained, giving Marelle half the story – but enough. She gently slid her hand up and down against Jacob's leg.

"I have space in two weeks' time– if you can get here for nine am?"

"How long will it take?"

"Probably two to three hours. I would block the morning off as there is some setting up to do as well. I would prefer you not to drive home either." He looked up at Jacob. "But you'll be fine!"

Jacob drew a breath, bought space. 'Two weeks?" He asked.

"Yes, the seventeenth … I would need a deposit today – we usually ask for ten percent."

"Ok." Jacob said.

He booked the appointment. Marelle stood with her hand against his thigh. She could feel the tension in the muscle of his leg, and she was sure she could feel a tremble where his arm was just touching hers as they stood side by side.

"Shall I drive?" She asked as they walked out into the bright autumn sunshine. A breeze had begun to rise and it was beginning to trouble the leaves on the trees that already had a nod to autumn approaching along the avenue.

"No, it's ok. I'll drive. I need something to take my mind off this."

Marelle slid into the passenger seat. "Why? It's not *that* bad – they are just mending a tooth."

He laughed sarcastically. 'Well, that's the end result but the whole thing sounds pretty barbaric!"

"Of course it's not! What's he doing?"

"I don't really want to go over it."

She stared at him as he drove. "It's the dentists! Oh Jacob, it will all be fine … tell me what he said. If you talk about it a few times it won't seem so bad. If you keep it in your head, it will get worse."

He smiled, a little.

"Go on. What's he going to do?"

Jacob sighed. "Well, he's going to remove what's left of that tooth – says I am lucky that the nerve hasn't been exposed or I would be in agony! He reckons it's pretty close though then he's going to drill a hole where that one has come out and put in a titanium implant that the replacement tooth will be screwed into."

"Ow!" She replied. Wrinkling her nose.

"Ow, yes!" He repeated. He doesn't normally do extractions and implants simultaneously but it's one tooth and because he has done x-rays and whatever else he's done today, he is happy that I've got good bone density, strong teeth and no problems going on in there. So, he's prepared to put me through hell for two or three hours and charge me a small fortune for it." Jacob stated

Marelle wasn't sure if he was expressing sarcasm or fear.

'That's how much I suffer for my art!" He said, gave her a lopsided grin and raised an eyebrow.

"It'll be fine!" Marelle smiled. "People have stuff like this done every day. Christ it can't be worse than a root canal!"

"Well, I'll tell you afterwards."

EIGHTEEN

That evening Marelle climbed astride his naked body under the sheets on her bed. He lay back, against the pillows as she sat astride his torso, his skin warm against her inner thighs. She pressed her hands on his chest and smiled down at him; scooting herself deeply against his body, draining the residual moments of stimulation that remained from orgasm as she did so – she sighed, warm and happy.

"You're special." She said.

"I know." He replied.

She screwed her mouth and stared down at him, cocking her head. "Modest too!"

He nodded, grinning.

"Is that Ezza out of the box?"

"Might be?"

She smiled, she lifted one hand and gently lifted his lip with her finger, so she could see the broken tooth.

"It's quite cute." She smiled. "The gap."

"It'll go rotten, could get infected – won't be so pretty then."

"So you will have a screw-in tooth?" She smiled.

He nodded. "If I can stand the procedure ... otherwise I may be running out of there with a bloody hole."

"You'll be fine. You won't feel a thing."

"I hope not."

She took his face in her hands. "I was reading an article – while you were in the dentist's room – about you." She began. "It was when you first started with Yellow Son. You looked so young."

"I was young." He said.

"How old were you?"

"Twenty-one, twenty-two?" Jacob replied.

"You looked younger." She laughed. "Still had a spotty face and a schoolboy haircut!" She grinned. "You were so cute!"

He smiled. "With Chas?" He asked.

"Yeah." She looked down into his face, she could see the same eyes, the same darkness in them, even now.

"You'll like Chas." He said.

Marelle leaned forwards and kissed him. Those same lips that had been in a tight little pout in those pictures on her phone – a worried, tortured, tense expression on the face of that boy in those photographs. The question was would Chas like him? Would Chas welcome him with the open arms Jacob was expecting? After ten years believing he had walked out of the gig and taken his own life. Would Chas be happy to see *him*?

It was, therefore, ten days later that they walked into the dentist's surgery again. Jacob had driven; the traffic had been awful which had stressed Marelle on the way there. She had panicked they would not make it in time, but as usual Jacob maintained a calm exterior even though she knew inside he was in panic mode albeit not about the traffic. They made it with time to spare, pulling into the same parking space in front of what had once been a grand Georgian townhouse.

After being asked to take a seat and told the dentist would be with him in a few minutes Jacob sat, not looking at Marelle, not looking at anything just staring at the floor. Wrung out so tight right now Marelle could see the trickle of sweat squeezed out and running down his temple. She could sense his heart racing and feel the heat coming off his body next to her.

"Ok?" She asked in a whisper.

He nodded that quick little nod which said he was, but which Marelle knew really meant '*No, I'm in pieces, but leave me alone.*'

He sighed, shakily, clasped his hands in front of himself, arms resting on his knees. It was five past nine and he wanted to be getting on with this.

"Why don't you go for a look round Cambridge?" He suddenly said. "You'll be sitting here for a few hours."

"It's ok. I'll wait for you." She smiled.

"It could be three hours ... it's a long time to sit here."

"I'm fine." She stated, placing a hand on his thigh.

"You sure?"

She nodded. "Why don't you want me to wait?"

He shrugged his shoulders but didn't move. "Don't want you to hear me screaming!"

"Oh come on. You'll be fine. You won't feel a thing!" She whispered and laid her head on his shoulder. "Do you want me to come in the room with you?" She asked quietly.

'No!" He laughed just as the dentist appeared from a door to the right. Marelle felt every muscle fibre in Jacob's body go solid. This was it.

Marelle relinquished him, holding on to his cold, clammy fingers until the very last second and they finally released so the air moved between them.

"Ok, are we ready?" the dentist asked, breezily. 'We've got a bit of paperwork to complete then we can get underway." He nodded. "If you would like to come this way – we are upstairs today – my surgery is upstairs – I only use that room for consultations." He explained. Jacob didn't say anything, just followed blindly and the door closed behind them Marelle could hear their footsteps ascending a staircase. She listened until they had gone, and the silence resumed. It was the very first time in his entire life that he was about to place his body in the trust of a medical professional.

Marelle sat there, looking at her fingers. She had watched him recently, tentatively stepping out of his comfort zone day after day, inching away moment by moment; still donning the vestiges of Jacob but gently and quietly beginning to cast them away when no-one was looking. But now, with this, he was way out of that zone; he was a mile away from her over the far side of the fold as she stood on the edge of the circle, he had long ago drawn for himself. And she feared that he would not hold his composure; that was why she was sat here now. Despite everything she feared he might freak out in the middle of treatment, and she wanted to be right here when he did.

People came and went while she sat there. Patients, some almost as scared as Jacob; some chatty; some with too much to say for themselves. They sat on the chairs, stared at her, looked around themselves, took a book out and started reading. Marelle adopted Jacob's tactics and did not make eye contact. She did not want someone else's conversation to break into her thoughts. Other members of staff came in and out, whispered conversations together, greeted their patients – said goodbye to their patients. A couple of times people had come down the stairs behind the door which Jacob had ascended a while ago – each time she hoped it was him, but it wasn't. The longer it went on, the more she worried. It was one tooth for God's sake why was it taking so long? And who had he put as next of kin on the contact form? What if he hadn't completed it? What if something had gone wrong up there ... would they tell her if he had not entered her as next of kin? She sighed shakily, feeling those same thoughts that had fuelled agony in her many times before. The same thoughts that she knew would be there for the rest of her life, thoughts of love, loss and fear. If you loved so intensely; you feared loss so intensely.

And at that moment when those thoughts were in her head, she felt that intense, rendering, burning pain start to stir in her chest once more; the pain of loss and grief that she had endured many times during her relationship with Jacob. The rise and fall of emotion as her heat beat fast and her mind wandered back to the occasions when she thought she had lost him forever. Marelle felt her eyes begin to fill with tears as that whole wave of emotion fuelled by the threat of loss overwhelmed her. She stared at the floor, tried not to think about the dream of the morgue, or Jacob about to throw himself off the bridge. There was such a fine line between life and death. So tenuous that it could break and be gone forever in the blink of an eye. And she had so very nearly lost him like that – lost that body, that soul, that character, that existence – thrown into oblivion and snashed to pieces. A world without Jacob now could simply not exist and the tears fought their way out of her eyes as she stared at the floor. Pain in her chest and her throat, her heart racing as one solitary tear dropped onto the blue carpet. There was a sob climbing its way up her throat, clutching up hand hold by hand hold to lift its head and bellow out of her mouth. She would not let it; she would not cry in here.

Squeezing her fingernails into her palms she fought it away, forced it back down into the pit of her stomach where it writhed and complained bitterly while concentrating her mind on that smile he could muster at her when he wanted to. That sublime, beauteous, cheeky smile that she loved but which had not graced his face nearly enough times. Marelle drew a breath through her nose; felt hot and lightheaded. She raised her head, and another tear took advantage and escaped down her cheek. Her head was swirling, and she needed air. Standing up clutching her bag, she walked across the reception area and stepped out of the vacuum. The receptionist did not look up.

Marelle sighed as the sun and the breeze touched her face. She walked to her car and leant against the side of it, resting her elbows on the roof and placing her head in her hands. Right at that moment she knew what Jacob meant when he had said he needed to find space. Right now she needed space. She wasn't running away from anything ≠ she just needed to take a breath; just needed air. For a few seconds she stood and looked across the roof of her car, watching traffic in the street, groups of people walking by. There was the sound of a bird singing in the bright autumn sunshine. What kind of bird was it? One she did not immediately recognise; one that frequented the city, not the airfield. Once that would have been her too but now, she had changed within the warm embrace of Jacob's influence. Marelle took her moment; drew a breath then turned and walked back into the surgery.

She had just walked in and closed the door when the door to the stairs clicked open right in front of her. She heard the dentist's voice – very buoyant and jovial – in front of him was Jacob. The dentist had his hand on Jacob's elbow, almost as if to assist him. Marelle looked up at Jacob, locked into those eyes and let a smile break across her face which she could not control. Every impulse in her body wanted to throw herself at him; just as she had in the car park on the night she had finally found him following his disappearance before – but he was pale, he looked fragile, and he looked as if he may fall over at any moment.

'Ok?" She asked, reaching out a hand to him and grasping his.

He nodded, very gingerly.

'Yes, all went well. Nice job." The dentist smiled, leaving Jacob and walking round the receptionist's desk where he hung over her shoulder and tapped some keys on the keyboard before her.

Marelle gripped Jacob's hand. He took a step forwards but faltered a little as she tightened her hand on his to steady him.

"Hey, ok?" She asked quietly.

Jacob stepped towards the desk and placed a hand on the edge of it as he stood there. Marelle slid her hand around his back and cradled an arm around him. The back of his black t shirt felt clammy and damp. She could feel the heat rising off him. Gently she patted her hand against the small of his back as the dentist went on to explain do's and don'ts to him, made an appointment in ten day's time and took payment.

"You may get a little bruising and swelling in the next couple of days – some people do, some don't. There might be a bit of pain or discomfort when the numbing wears off – probably in a couple of hours but you can take over the counter pain killers regularly for a couple of days and you should be fine. Any problems then give us a call – especially for any bleeding, fever or anything untoward but I'm pretty confident you will be fine!" He explained. "As I said, we have a 24/7 emergency line of you need us."

Jacob nodded. Not speaking at all so far.

"We will see you in ten days when we can fit the bespoke crown and you will be good as new!" He smiled a toothy, wide grin.

Jacob smiled and nodded, turning to leave

'You're not driving, are you?" the dentist asked. "I'd advise you not to drive for a couple of hours at least ..."

"No, I'm driving." Marelle piped up, turning back, taking Jacob's arm.

"Good." The dentist replied. "Take care."

Jacob squinted in the sunshine, but he looked pale. He felt wobbly walking she kept a hold on him. She watched him intently as he got into the car. He had not uttered a word since he had come down the stairs. She watched him get in then put herself in the driving seat as she pulled the seatbelt around herself, she smiled.

"Go on then - let me see!"

He looked shattered. Marelle leant across and put a hand on his thigh. Jacob sighed, slowly he raised his hand and carefully lifted his lip so she could see the gap, now filled.

"Oh wow!" Marelle grinned. "You really wouldn't know, would you?"

He let his lip down and then let out a long sigh as he closed his eyes and lay his head back against the headrest.

"I am never doing that again." He mumbled, slurring slightly.

"Was it that bad?" She asked, half humorously, patting his thigh.

He nodded. "I can't feel my face." He said, obviously struggling with the anaesthetic effects. 'And it feels like it's out here." He gestured a foot away from his cheek with his hand.

"It's not." She replied. 'It doesn't look any different. The numbing will wear off soon ... it usually takes an hour or so afterwards."

"I should have left the gap." He muttered.

"What have you got to go back for?"

'This is a temporary crown – they'll make one up that matches my other teeth perfectly. He says this one is a bit small ..."

"Oh – so will you have to go through all of this again?"

"Fuck no!" he sighed. "He will just screw the new one in."

Marelle made a face, staring at him but he still had his eyes closed.

"I could do with a drink."

"I don't think that's a good idea. He did say no alcohol ..." Marelle remarked.

"I mean water!" He sighed. "I'm sweating like a pig."

"I know you are." Marelle smiled.

"Why? Do I smell?" He asked.

"No!" She laughed. "Your t-shirt is wet at the back ... here ..." She rummaged in her bag and produced a plastic bottle of water. She open sit and then held it out to him, nudging his arm.

"Ta." He said, taking it from her and finally opening his eyes.

'Be careful ..." She began, thinking of what it was like to have a numb lip after a filling, but he had already chugged a mouthful in only to find most of it dribbled out again. Marelle laughed.

"Shit! I am not liking this!" he cried as angrily as he could with no feeling in his face.

"It's ok. Give it an hour. Have a sleep on the way home – you'll feel better then." Marelle smiled, reaching out a hand for the open bottle which he held back to her as he closed his eyes again. Marelle took the bottle and was about to replace the top when she noticed the water left in the bottle had a rusty brown hue to it.

'Hey, are you bleeding?" She asked.

He opened his eyes, looking at the water she was holding up. "I don't know." He said, "Is it?" He opened his mouth barely enough for her to see, Marelle lifted a finger and looked at the tooth. It looked fine, not bloody anywhere around it. "I don't think so ..." She replied. "But there's definitely blood in here ... open a bit more ..."

He did, minimally, but enough for her to see fresh blood gathered in the cusps of a couple of his bottom teeth.

"Let me see." She said, lifting her finger again to pull his bottom lip away. "Oh shit." She said.

"What?"

"You've bitten into your cheek down there – it's bleeding quite a lot."

"Where?"

"" Just down the side there. I've done it when I've had a filling. You can't feel your mouth and you end up biting into it when you talk ... ooh that's going to be sore ... do you want some more water to wash it out?" She held up the plastic bottle which contained blood and water now.

"No. I'll leave it." He answered. "Shit. Should have left the gap. Why am I so fucking vain?"

Marelle laughed. "You'll be fine. I'll get us home – you can spend the rest of the day recuperating!"

Jacob was not a good patient. He had never been a good patient, just generally got up and tried to carry on wherever he could. If he couldn't, from experience, he would just go to sleep and remain asleep for hours. She didn't know if he slept all of the way home or just sat there with his eyes closed but he opened them when they came to a halt, and she pulled on the handbrake.

It was mid-afternoon and the sun had moved to the back of the house, so the front was left in shadow. Marelle gave Jacob a smile, a pat on the thigh then she climbed out, grabbing her bag and the bloody bottle of water as she did so. Jacob did likewise, gently closing the car door and walking around to follow her to the front entrance.

"Ok?" She asked, going inside, turning to him.

He nodded, gently.

Inside, the hallway light was on – Marelle hit the light switch as she passed. They had left in a bit of a hurry so it was no wonder it had been left on! She waited for Jacob to walk in and she closed the door behind him. Placing a hand on his back she momentarily paused then with a smile, tiptoed up and placed a tender little kiss on his other cheek.

He gave an even more lopsided smile than usual. "I'll return that when I can feel my face!" He mumbled.

She smiled. "And make sure you do!" She started off down the hallway towards the kitchen at the back of the house. As she passed the door to the sitting room she glanced at it. The door was shut. She had never seen that door closed since she had been here. For a second she stared at it then depressed the handle and opened it as she walked by. Maybe she had closed it; maybe Jacob had – she couldn't remember. This morning had been a bit fraught!

"Right." She said, in the kitchen with Jacob standing behind her. "Let's get the kettle on. Are you hungry?"

He shook his head.

"Is it still numb?"

He nodded, standing by the table. All four chairs were neatly pushed beneath it. Had she left it like that? Normally they were pulled out and scattered wherever they had ended up last time they had been sat on.

"Did you do that?" She asked, gesturing to them.

"What?"

"All of the chairs neat"

He shrugged.

She continued to fill the kettle as he pulled one chair out and sat down.

"Go and have a lay down." She suggested.

"No, it's ok."

"Do you want painkillers?"

He shook his head. "It just feels like my head is about to explode!"

She glanced at him. He had his eyes closed. Was it meant to be like this? She was expecting it to be like having a large filling done – which surely that was essentially all it was? But he seemed to be suffering. His first experience of a dentist so far would not compel to go back she feared.

"Do you want tea? I can make it cooler for you."

He shook his head.

"Can you eat on it?"

"He said not for the first few hours – and to be careful afterwards. There are stitches in the gum."

"Ow!" She winced standing with her back to the worktop as she waited for the kettle to boil. He sat there on the kitchen chair, eyes closed, breathing through his nose. Marelle smiled and stepped towards him. She reached out a hand and ruffled his hair. He did not move but leant his head into her hand. Marelle grinned, slid her arms around his neck and leaned down to him.

"You're still beautiful." She whispered in his ear.

By mid-evening he was in pain. It took him a while to admit it but eventually he did.

"Have you got any painkillers?

They were sitting in the settee, she had her head against his shoulder, watching TV and he had been sighing and fidgeting for a while. His speech was less slurred, so she guessed the anaesthetic was wearing off. Marelle hadn't said anything, but his face did look slightly swollen on that side now. She pushed herself up.

"Yes, of course." She replied, sitting forward looking back at him. "You should have said earlier if it hurts – they'll take a while to work."

The night was hard and long. He didn't sleep. It reminded her of how he used to be before it had all come to a head. He was up and down all night, sighing, wandering about the house, going into the back room and staring out at the moon washed airfield. Marelle stayed with him, placed hands on him, hugged him and made sure he took painkillers regularly. He had not eaten and had only drunk sips of water. Jacob had not been like this for ages – she hoped it was not a trigger for worse to come – leading a path to those nightmares she had endured with him screaming beside her.

It was three in the morning and he was up again. He had gone to the bathroom but not come back to the bedroom. Marelle was awake and still tense when he was not in bed beside her; too tortured by the night he had got up to go to the toilet and flown; left her alone and taken himself off into the world alone, to contemplate the unthinkable. Marelle rose, too tense to remain even though she had heard him go into the back bedroom.

Her feet strode softly across the room and along the landing. There was a full moon capturing the sun's rays from the other side of the world and reflecting them down onto the airfield tonight. It was dark, kissed by the moonlight, but entirely possible to see everything in a hundred shades of blue. She walked up to him.

"Ok?" She whispered, putting a hand lightly across his bare backside. The window was open, and he was leaning on his elbows on the sill. His skin looked perfect and pale, just like it had done in the awful dream Marelle had experienced of him being dead in a morgue. It still sent a chill through her but when she touched his skin now it was warm and vital; not cold and plastic as it had been during that nightmare.

He was looking out over the airfield, silent and subdued in moonlit beauty. Many times he had stood here and many times Marelle had joined him. Always reminded that this was the very window his childhood friend Frankie had climbed out of, never to return. It was still in his mind, she knew, despite everything and that this window and this house would forever be part of his life and part of who he was.

A plane flew across the night sky, a tiny speck in the distance. She placed her hand on his back.

"Some people have a whole mouthful of these. I don't know how they do it." He said quietly.

"In a couple of days, you'll be fine."

"I'll be better off going to work tomorrow – it would take my mind off the pain."

"No. You can't. You don't want to go risking anything going wrong – do you? You're staying here with me, all day ... doing nothing."

"I'd be better off. I'd be in less pain."

"No Jacob." She whispered.

"It's swelling up now."

"I know. I can see." Marelle replied. "I can get you something cold to hold against it ..."

"Will that help?"

"It's what it said on the piece of paper he gave you."

"If you want.' He sighed.

Marelle went downstairs to the kitchen. The moonlight was flooding in the kitchen window in a bright, white shaft. She walked across it's spotlight. The empty, quiet kitchen reminded her of the nights when Jacob had not been here; the chairs pulled out and left where they had sat, a used mug on the table. She still locked the door and still had the key in her pocket.

There was no ice in the freezer except for that which was starting to encrust the top drawer. After a few seconds contemplating chipping some off she finally opted for frozen sausages instead. Carefully, she wrapped them in a plastic bag and then in a flannel. It was cold – it would do the job.

Jacob had not moved when she returned. His gaze was still on the airfield.

"It's a hunter's moon." He commented. "Clear and bright. Like daylight."

She handed him the wrapped sausages. It was beautiful. The silent calmness of the airfield was majestic beneath the full moon. Every fleck and highlight picked out by the its touch. The trees still, the long, drying grass and aging flower heads bowed beneath its milky white light.

"And it's all still here." He added, holding the cold package to his face as he spoke.

"And so are we as well, thankfully." Marelle reminded him. She looked out and sighed. "What do you think will happen with it?"

"Who knows." He answered.

NINETEEN

He was asleep beside her when Marelle woke in the morning. At her suggestion he had pulled the pillows behind himself and fallen asleep collapsed back into them in a semi-sitting position. She didn't want to wake him so pushed herself very gently into a sitting position. His head was slightly to one side but his face was definitely swollen this morning – he would not like that and he would also be less than impressed with the bruising she could see developing over the area and just beneath his eye. Marelle stared at him and gently smiled to herself.

She managed to get out of bed without waking him and tiptoed around the house while he slept. It didn't last long however, and it was only a short time until she heard him get up and go to into the bathroom. She heard the toilet flush, and the shower start up, so she boiled the kettle.

Jacob arrived in the kitchen twenty minutes later. His hair was wet and still tousled from being rubbed with a towel. It reminded her of how he had looked when she had first cut his hair – he looked adorable.

"Morning." She smiled. "How are you?"

"Alright." He said. "I wasn't expecting quite so much swelling or bruising."

"I have had both from a filling so it's quite normal – I think – how's the pain?"

"Still there. Not quite as bad. Maybe I'm getting used to it. It all just feels so *tight*." He explained. "I'd better take some painkillers."

Marelle guessed he must have looked like he did after that fateful night on the airfield when Sam and his father had set about him. She had never seen his wounds; he'd taken off into the night and had healed in the three weeks he had been gone. All she had seen was the missing tooth – and now that was gone too.

"Well, we'll just relax here today. By tonight you will have turned a corner, I'm sure."

He refused breakfast, tea and coffee which frustrated her. However, she chose not to argue but instead waited and eventually said

"I'll make you an omelette."

He looked at her, raising his eyes but not lifting his chin. It was not a '*no*', so she continued.

"I make a cracking omelette. It's almost as good as your fish finger sandwich!" She remembered fondly the night he'd cooked her his 'signature' fish finger sandwich in his caravan. For a moment she smiled but the events after that were still a sword in her side.

Marelle carried on before Jacob began to protest that he did not want an omelette, throwing the ingredients together quickly, then whisking furiously.

"I could go to work really." He stated.

"No – you need to stay here. What if you end up knocking that tooth – or getting an infection in it? Just one day – let it heal up properly." Marelle sighed.

He picked at the food; almost scared to put anything into his mouth and eat but she could see he was hungry. After a while he gave up.

"Does it still hurt?" She asked.

"A bit. Just feels strange – feels really tight and as though my face is going to explode – but you can make that again when I can eat it!"

She smiled. "Was it good?"

"Pretty good." He replied, attempting a smile but most of his mouth was being dragged in a different direction.

He got up and went to the sink, ran a glass of water then stood looking out of the window. Marelle could contain herself no longer and got up; she wrapped her arms around him from behind and buried her head against his shoulder. He placed a hand on hers, clasped around his chest.

"I still pinch myself every morning when I wake up and see you there. She whispered close to his ear.

He gave a muted little laugh. "Why?"

"Because I can't believe you're mine!"

'Me? I'm nothing special – you know that – I'm a liability – I'm just – I don't know …" He shrugged.

"Don't." She said sternly, squeezing him. Don't say that. You're special. You don't know what you mean to me."

He sighed dropped his head forward and held on to her hands.

"Well I just hope I can live up to that expectation." He said.

Right now she wanted him. Like that first time when she had been so fuelled up by Seb's remark and alcohol that she had thrown caution to the wind and literally knocked him off his feet as soon as they had got into the house. An angry, messy, aggressive union that she had yearned for then – just to prove she was totally serious about her intentions. And he had not resisted; he had nor rebuked her assault upon him. It had not been the sweet and passionate way a relationship should have blossomed but on that night she had taken what she'd wanted, and he had been only too willing to give it to her.

Right now, despite her longing, she knew she could not release that aggression again – even in passion. Right now, she couldn't even kiss him like she wanted to. Marelle damned that tooth.

"I love you." She said, her words coming out almost involuntarily. She suddenly felt sad with that love flowing within her, overwhelming – filling her breast and tingling her fingertips. "But I get so scared when I think what might have happened." Marelle closed her eyes and pressed her face into him. He smelled of shower gel and fabric conditioner.

"But it didn't, did it?" He said. "And it never will."

They had finished breakfast and Marelle was trying to look at the new tooth. Jacob was sat on a kitchen chair, and she was stooped over him as he lifted his lip to let her see. There was quite a significant swelling today and the part he had bitten had turned into an ulcer. The bruising beneath his eye looked angrier now.

"You could hold something cold against it again." She suggested, wondering where the sausages from last night were.

The doorbell rang down the hallway. It was just after ten as her eyes wandered to the clock. She sighed and stood up.

"I can guess who that will be." She muttered, moving towards the hallway and the front door. As she reached up to open it, she sensed Jacob behind her. He guessed he knew who it was too.

Marelle swung the door open, expecting Catchpole but instead was met with her brother, standing there – sandy hair flopping over his forehead, wearing a tan leather jacket.

"Well good morning, Marelle, glad I've found you at home today!" He said.

"What do you want?" She asked, coldly. "And if it takes more than ten minutes I've got to go out."

"Oh, it needn't take that long." Seb replied. "Can I come in?"

She stared at him. Jacob was still behind her, a short way along the hallway. "No, you can say it there." She replied.

"I would rather come in and have a civilised conversation."

"I don't want you in here."

"But it's half my house … remember?"

"Yeah, and you said you would give me six months – remember?" She reciprocated sarcastically, reminding her brother of the six-month deadline he had threatened her with a couple of months ago. Essentially for her to forget Jacob and move back in with him – he had offered her a 'proper' job, she had taken it as an insult but had not expected to see his face for at least six months.

"Well, the situation has changed. I hear there have been *developments*."

"What the fuck do you mean?" She sneered.

Seb looked at her, stared at her in that condescending way he had mastered so effortlessly in his life. Marelle stared back, said nothing.

"That ring on your finger for a start." Seb finally said, nodding to her hand, surreptitiously folded across her chest.

"Fuck off Seb. That makes no difference to this."

"I'm afraid it does." He stated, taking a step and extending a hand.

"Can I come in? I'd like a chat in private …"

He moved closer to her. Touching her.

'No!" She exclaimed, shoving him away so he staggered and nearly had to step down a step again. "I don't want you in here!"

'This is the very reason I am here." Seb continued. "Because you don't know how to behave anymore – you've just been dragged down to his level like some spoiled little brat."

"Well, if you want to see a spoiled brat – and exactly what I *can* do – I suggest you look me right in the face!"

"I am." Seb said with a sarcastic smile.

"Fuck off." She spat.

"Don't start." He held a flat hand to her. "We need to speak about this."

"About what? About me? About Jacob? Then speak – say what you've got to say right to his face." She yelled, half turning, gesturing to Jacob who was still hovering a couple of steps away. "Go on … tell him to his face; tell him what you told *me* before … there are no secrets between me and Jacob."

"Jacob and I." Seb said, quietly.

That sparked off a higher level of anger in her. Something was released which froze her in consummate rage for a second. "You cruel, fucking, sarcastic wanker." She exclaimed, releasing a breath. "Just – just fuck off!"

Seb grinned. "I can. But if I go any decisions made will be mine alone … I won't involve you … but you had better start looking for somewhere else to live …"

"Half of this is mine!"

"And half isn't." He said back.

"Marelle." Jacob suddenly spoke behind her. "Marelle, let him come in, at least hear what he wants to say."

"Jacob!" She turned but sighed when he raised an eyebrow to her. Marelle turned back to Seb. "He can say it here."

"It's better if he comes in. We don't want any more dirty washing in the street." Jacob said behind her.

Seb laughed, sarcastically, raised a hand and placed it on the door post of the front door, Marelle stared him in the eye. He stared back with a grin on his face that was far from humorous. She controlled her anger but her heart was still pounding in her chest. Eventually she stood slowly aside. Seb paused, looked at her then walked up the steps, brushing past her and into the hallway.

"In the kitchen." She said without looking at him.

He went on and into the kitchen. Stared blankly and coldly at Jacob as he stood there. Marelle closed the front door and walked back, raised her eyes to Jacob but said nothing.

Seb was hovering in the kitchen, his hands in his trouser pockets.

'I'll be out here." Jacob said, passing through and reaching for the back door handle.

"No, stay here Jacob!" Marelle protested. "This is as much to do with you as it is me!"

"I'd rather it was a private conversation." Seb stated, raising his chin and staring at Jacob.

"Don't worry, it's fine." Jacob replied to Marelle quietly. "I'll come in if you need me."

Seb laughed to himself and shook his head. Marelle sighed, watched Jacob go outside then turned he head to Seb.

"You really are a bastard." She told him. "Why do you hate him so much? You don't even know him!"

"Oh, I know enough."

She stared at him. He knew nothing! For a split second, Marelle sensed the words in her mouth – if they flowed from her lips, they would truly put Seb in the picture and wipe that sarcastic grin off his face. Oh, how she wanted to let those words rip from her mouth but, she knew right now it would be the worst possible thing she could do.

"What's he been up to this time hey? A drunken mishap – someone slap him in the mouth, a general beating up for being a closet sex offender – or a paedophile?"

She made a face. "Your little world must be such a cruel place."

He laughed. "My world is called reality – yours is called pure fucking fantasy with your head in the sand." He smiled. "Every time I see him, he looks like that."

"He's had surgery. Yesterday."

"Surgery! What the hell for?"

"He had dental surgery. He had a tooth repaired. He's in pain."

"You don't get a face like that from having a tooth repaired." He answered.

"He had an implant. They put screws into your jaw."

"An implant! How the fuck did he get that done? Do you know how much they cost?" He laughed but then suddenly turned back to her. "And I suppose you paid for that too …"

"No. I don't know how much it costs and I didn't pay for it." She snapped almost over his words.

"Probably sells kiddie pictures online – is that it?"

Marelle wanted to hit him; she wanted to scream and beat his face to a pulp with her bare hands.

"He's not a fucking paedophile – just fucking leave it …" She spat, anger screaming from every pore. She'd raised her voice and seen Jacob look up from outside. She turned her back to the window.

"Just say what you have to say."

"The kitchen is a mess." He said.

She had half cleared up breakfast; the pan was still on the cooker, dirty mugs on the table, sink with used crockery in. Yt was not a mess – just mid-way through tidying up.

"Well you turned up."

"It's eleven o clock."

"Jacob had a restless night … we were late."

"Shouldn't he be labouring on the farm – isn't that what he does – or has he got the sack from there too?"

"He's on holiday.' She snapped.

"Jesus fuck! You have a messy little life. Who'd have thought my little sister would have ended up like this?"

"Just get on with it, Seb. You're wasting your time belittling me … I'm not listening."

"No, you never do, do you? Just go off on your fanciful flights of lust – or whatever is driving you on this time … well here's the deal. It's time to sell this house."

He raised his head and stared down at her.

"I thought we agreed six months." Marelle replied, feeling the breath leave her quickly.

'Yes, well, there have been developments – and as I said, the playing field is no longer level."

"Meaning what?"

"Meaning firstly, the house is probably at its highest value right now. This development will knock it down some, but it's halted for this heritage site crap – once it all kicks off again and your beautiful vista out here is under four feet of concrete we can kiss goodbye to a whole chunk of money. We've got a small window they reckon."

Marelle was just staring at him.

"And, secondly – I don't want *him* getting *his* hands on any of this property. I can see what he's doing. Marry you then he's entitled to half of whatever is yours – easy – and I don't want *him* being any part of that."

'That's stupid. He's never mentioned this house – he doesn't want this house!"

"Of course he does! Look at him! He has nothing – he's a farm labourer – he lived in a fucking caravan until you enticed him in like a stray animal – now he's sitting pretty – promised you he will marry you – sitting pretty, just waiting."

"Utter fucking crap!"

"Oh I've seen it many times. Is he paying rent now? Who pays for his food – the, electricity he uses? Hey? Not him I'd hazard a guess."

"He offered, I refused." She snapped.

"Then you're more stupid than I even thought you were."

"Fuck off Seb. Mum was right, you are just like our father."

He scoffed. "I'm not getting into an argument about Mum and Dad – but he is living here for nothing – you are paying for everything. He's lapping it up. He is not having this house."

"Then I'll buy you out."

"What with?"

"I have money."

"Not enough for half of this place. You had a two-bedroom semi on a housing estate … and you've got half from a hurried sale on that.'

"I'll get a mortgage."

"What with!? If you carry this through you can forget working for me ... you'd be on your own."

She sighed to herself, invisibly.

"And I'm not selling it to him." He nodded behind him to Jacob who was staring out over the airfield. He looked as if he was watching something; she couldn't see what.

"You can't just sell the house, half of it is mine."

"In value, yes."

"What do you mean?"

"Well I have never invoked it before, but the house was left to both of us, but it was predominantly left in trust to me with the agreement that you would be entitled to half its value. If I want to sell it I can, as long as I give you half."

"Well what's the difference between that and me buying you out?"

"Because that way he doesn't end up with this house for free and I'd hope to God that you would see sense with the money in your hand."

"You can't do that."

"I can."

Suddenly the conversation was quieter. Marelle looked about herself. She didn't look him in the eye.

"I'll give you a choice. Either I sell the house and split it 50/50 with you or I buy you out now at the current amount it's been valued at. You take the pick – whichever you prefer."

"You don't know what the current value is."

"Oh, I do."

"How?"

"I had it valued yesterday. It's all ready to go on the market as soon as I give them the go ahead. They reckon they have a few interested parties already ..."

"No-one valued this house. I'm not stupid. You're trying to tell me it's worth less than it is."

"It's been valued."

"How?"

"Yesterday. I came here with the agent. You weren't here so we took a look around. He's given me a value."

She almost gasped. "*You* came *here* yesterday! Without telling me? You've been in this house when we were out?"

He nodded. "I have keys, remember? And if you had been here – working, like I am paying you to do – then you would have known."

She shook her head. There was a knife on the worktop. Never before had she felt the urge to injure someone in the way she wanted to plunge that knife into her brother's flesh right now. That was why the doors had been closed, that was why things were moved.

"You're a fucking bastard."

"Listen to yourself Marelle. Just listen ... you have no answer ... you can't challenge me ... the choice is yours. I pay you now and you get out or I sell it and split whatever it makes fifty-fifty with you.

"I'll buy you out."

"Not an option as far as I recall."

"You can't do this to me. If I get the money, you can't stop me from buying it."

"I'm not selling half of it. I'm selling all of it. It's just your choice whether I pay you half the market value now or you take a gamble on half of what it makes. Either way you'd better start packing – oh and that fucking monstrosity out there has to go." He nodded to the caravan. "And what's that fucking pikey van in the drive? Looks like a bloody traveller's site!"

She stared at him, looked at him. He was the same person whom she had looked up to all her childhood; who had always been the person she ran to – who had always been there when her father left and her mother was fooling around with a new boyfriend. He'd taken her to New York on her twenty-first; he'd taught her how to drive. But right now, she only felt hate.

"But you're my brother." She said, quietly.

Seb reacted violently, angrily to that. "Well start acting like my fucking sister then and not some spaced out fucking hippy who's so hell bent on getting her brains fucked out by the village rough! Start acting your age and living up to your potential!" He spat. "He's a fucking waster, a waste of space – and what he was planning in that fucking toilet I don't even want to think about ..." Seb was very close to her, poking a finger right in her face. Marelle was aware of Jacob outside and she felt him looking in at them. "Where do you think you are going to end up with this hey? He's going to marry you, is he? Well, tell me why he hasn't then? Hey? What's he waiting for – he's fucking stringing you along. He can't believe his luck and you're stupid enough to lay your fucking head down at his bloody, filthy feet." He took a breath, turned back, wagged a finger. "I'll give you one last chance. You give all of this crap up and come down to live with me; settle down – I'll put you through Uni and you can work for me properly – make something of yourself. It's not too late."

Marelle could feel a tremble rising from within her. She wasn't sure whether it was fear, anger or sadness but it grew, flowed into her veins and down into her fingertips.

"Go." She said. "I'll tell you my decision. When is the deadline?"

"Next Wednesday." He said. "The house goes on the market on Thursday."

"Right." She replied. "I'll call you on Wednesday."

He stared back at her, expecting more.

"And what if I let you sell it. What about me? What if I stay up here – do you still want me to work for you?"

"You won't have anywhere to live. You won't have internet access."

"That's my problem. Will you?"

"I'll think about it." He replied.

Marelle glared at him.

"I'm only thinking of you." He said, quietly.

Her eyes just burned into him. She could find no more words now. She just wanted him to go. Seb blinked once, pushed himself away from the worktop. He stood there for a moment. Seb was easily as tall as Jacob – only he did not have the same presence, that charisma – that humility.

"I'll see myself out." He told her.

Seb walked past, straight to the hallway, straight to the front door. He did not look back, acknowledge her nor Jacob as he opened the door, stepped out then closed it behind himself.

The click of the door closing seemed to echo around the entire house. It reverberated from the eaves, through the bedrooms, down the stairs and rushed back to her in the kitchen. One, loud, punctuating click of the door closing.

She heard his car start. Heard him rev the engine – it didn't sound like his normal car – more sporty – more expensive. It moved out of the drive, and she heard him drive down the road.

Marelle turned her head. Jacob was standing down near the boundary fence; he was half turned looking towards the kitchen window. His hands were down by his sides, he wore skinny black jeans and a grey long-sleeved t-shirt that had an emblem of a Celtic cross on the left breast. She hadn't noticed earlier.

This house was Frankie's.

Jacob was walking back towards the house. He came up the steps and opened the back door.

Sound returned to the house, air rushed in and she felt the breath she had inside her suddenly release.

"Alright?" He asked, stepping in. His feet were bare. She looked down to them. Jacob had nice feet, good arches. She didn't know what size they were.

"Marelle?" He asked.

She looked to him; looked right into his deep, dark eyes, fell right into the unfathomable depths they represented. She felt her fingers yearn to touch him.

"He wants to sell the house." She said.

TWENTY

Jacob came in, closed the door and stood barefoot in the kitchen.

"Well, you always knew this would happen."

"But he's been in here – while we were out." She felt a sob rising. "Yesterday, while we were at the dentist's – with a bloody estate agent. He wants to put it on the market. He's going to sell it."

"Do you want to?"

"Of course I don't." She gasped.

"Well he can't then, can he?"

"Apparently, he can. The house was left to both of us but it's in trust or something, to him – he has control as long as he gives me my share … he won't sell it to me – he …" She shrugged. "He'll sell it and give me half or he'll give me half up front now, and we'll have to get out." She rambled, wiping at a tear running down her cheek. "Those are my choices – and he's given me until next Wednesday. He will put the house on the market on Thursday. He won't let me buy his half."

Jacob wrapped an arm around her. He sighed. "Do you want me to call him?"

"No!" She exclaimed. "No, I don't want you speaking to him – he's a nasty piece of work … he's going to sell it to someone else Jacob! I wanted to …" She began to cry. "I wanted to make this *our* house; I was going to ask you if you wanted to stay here – if you wanted me to buy it – if we should make this *our house*; *our ho*me. I wanted to ask you, but I was waiting – I was waiting …"

He held her to him. She felt small in his arms; he felt tall and strong today.

"I'd love that." He said, with a smile. "I can help you buy him out … it would be ours then."

She looked up into his face. An honest face that held so many lies.

"Do you want to? Do you want to live in Frankie's house?"

He laughed. "I do."

"But he won't sell his half to me. He wants to sell the whole house – he won't sell it to me because he doesn't want you to have the house. He won't sell half of it."

Jacob hugged her to him, held her tightly, kissed her on top of her head.

"Then we'll buy all of it." Jacob smiled. "No, we'll get someone else to buy all of it, for us."

"How?" She sobbed.

He laughed. "I don't know!"

"… and who? Who has that kind of money?"

"First we have to find out the value so we at least know what we are looking at." Jacob said.

"Well how do we do that?"

"Have any sold recently like this?" He asked.

Marelle shrugged. "I have no idea." She wiped at her face where there were still tracks of her tears.

"A local paper? The internet?" He asked.

"Marelle sighed. "We should be thinking about raising the money first."

"We'll think about that afterwards, we need a number first."

Marelle consulted the internet. It was difficult. This was a small village – houses didn't come up for sale much and when they did there were never two the same or even quite similar.

"When was it built?" Marelle questioned.

"Before me." He replied. 'This house has been here as long as I can remember but from the style of it, the bricks – I'd say 1940s?"

"That old?" Marelle exclaimed.

Jacob nodded.

A smaller semi-detached cottage with a large garden had sold for two hundred and forty-five thousand about six months ago but it was not really comparable.

"So we are looking at that, in the least." Jacob stated. "I'd say a lot more. You've got three large bedrooms and a large drive at the front."

"I have no idea about houses." Marelle sighed.

"Let's say three hundred thousand." Jacob said.

'Three hundred thousand!" Marelle exclaimed. "How in hell are we going to raise three hundred thousand?" Her voice broke again on the last few words.

"We can't be guessing at this." Jacob continued. "Do you reckon he has used a local estate agent?"

Marelle shrugged.

"Well, there are about four in town – I think we could go round and ask tomorrow."

"Ask what?"

He smiled. "Well, pretend we are looking for a house here – ask if they have any on the books or coming up. The won't miss an opportunity to make a sale even if it's not on their books yet – if Seb has been speaking to them, they will think it's their lucky day!"

Marelle laughed because she still wanted to cry. "You're as devious as I am!"

He grinned. "Of course I am! I didn't get to hide away here for ten years without being devious!"

And when he grinned now, that grin made her heart spin after waiting so long to see it in it's true form.

Today it was Jacob comforting her. Marelle was still angry with Seb's intrusion and his attitude. He was her brother, but he was happy to throw her and Jacob out on the street. She was even more angry at him because he had been in this house yesterday – uninvited. He had been in here, violating her space – without her permission or knowledge. And now he had topped it off with a revelation that the house had actually been left in trust to him. For him to dish out to her what he thought fit. He didn't have to do that; he could have been *reasonable* – she would have been reasonable if the shoe was on the other foot. No, Seb had turned. He was no longer the father figure or an older brother whom she could look up to. Now Seb was nothing – just a cold hearted, apathetic bully. He didn't understand love or compassion or – or *anything*. Caroline had done that. Marelle could see it now. Caroline was jealous of everyone else and as insecure as the day was long.

Jacob had caught her in intense and angry thought as she scrubbed away at a stain on the draining board with a wadge of kitchen towel. He slid an arm around her waist from behind – usually her move and placed his head close to hers.

"Hey steady on, you'll go right thorough it in minute," He whispered.

'Just wishing it was Seb's face." She replied.

Jacob kissed her neck, and she turned to look up at him. In bare feet herself she felt so much smaller he seemed to tower over her today. Marelle smiled and raised her eyes to his blackening eye and his swollen mouth.

"Does it still hurt?" She asked.

"Not so bad. Just very tight. I'll be glad when the swelling goes down a bit."

Marelle smiled, looked right into his eyes. For some reason she thought of the picture she had seen her on her phone in the dentist's waiting room. That picture that was young, innocent, naïve Jacob – before he had even become Jacob or even let that thought cross his mind. She had stared at that picture and although she could clearly see it was him – she could not believe Jacob had ever been that young with that fresh bewilderment in his eyes – still with the scars of acne on his cheeks. Marelle suddenly wanted to ask Jacob about that period in his life – how he had come from a drunken father who had beaten him, to working on the farm, to studying nuclear physics, to being in a band and then ending up being drafted under Chas' charge as eye candy for a new rock band. Just how?

But then she fell into his eyes again and none of that mattered. Now she had to worry about being chucked out of this house by her own brother. With a smile she raised her hands up behind his neck.

"We're in a fucking mess Jacob." She said, smiling but with her voice splintering.

"No we're not! It's all fine. Stop worrying." He grinned. "We'll sort it …"

She gave a little laugh. "Oh Jacob!" Placed her head against his chest. "You'll still be saying that next week when we're living in your caravan – out there!" She nodded to the airfield.

"And if we are, we are. Did me ok for ten years." He patted her back with his hand. "Fancy going for a wander over there?"

Marelle felt they should have been working on raising money and devising a plan instead of pulling on shoes and preparing to go for a walk around the airfield. Everything she looked at or touched in this house now started to gather significance by the second and the fact that it would all soon be ripped away from her quickened her heart and caught her breath at every turn.

Nonetheless they were just about to go out of the back door when Marelle's phone rang.

She sighed, fished for it, then studied the number as it rang in her hand. It looked vaguely familiar, but she couldn't place it.

"Hello?" She said.

"Oh, hello my dear. It's Mr. Wright – I'm looking for Jacob."

Now she remembered the number and dialling it to say Jacob was sick. She sighed.

"He's on holiday today ..."

Jacob looked up to her.

"I know dear but I need a quick word if he's available – sorry to disturb his holiday ..."

Marelle raised her eyes to Jacob. "Mr. Wright. Wants a quick word." She whispered and held out her phone.

He took it without hesitation and stood a step away as he spoke.

"Mr. Wright? Jacob."

Marelle watched as he listened. Staring at the kitchen floor with her phone to his ear.

"Yeah." He said. "Yeah, it will, probably – it needs to come off."

Wright said something else. Jacob listened.

"No." He listened again. "I'll come down and have a look ... I can probably sort it out ..."

Marelle shot him a glance, but he flicked his eyes away. "Yeah, give me ten minutes. I'll come down."

He handed the phone back to her with a tight little smile, expecting her to protest.

"Jacob, you shouldn't be working – you're on holiday!" She sighed.

"I know but he's decided to take a lorry to a rally tomorrow and he's picked the one that's got issues and won't start. He's cleaned it right up and polished it then decided to see if it would start – it wouldn't." Jacob explained. "I know what it is. I may as well go and sort it out."

"But Jacob, you can't go crawling about under lorries – what if you knock that tooth or something?"

He laughed. "I won't! I can guess what's wrong with it – give me half an hour and I can fix it if he's got the parts ..."

"Can't he take another one?"

"He's hell bent on taking this one!" Jacob said. "It's alright. It's bonus points for me!"

Marelle gave a crooked smile. He was going, no matter what.

"Can I come?" She suddenly piped up. "I won't be in the way – I can help – and keep an eye on what you're doing!"

Jacob sighed. "I don't know if you can come, but I don't see why not."

Marelle said she would drive but Jacob said 'no' – he would take the van. Marelle had never been in the van, and she did secretly wonder what had gone on in this vehicle over the years as she climbed into the passenger seat and rummaged for the seatbelt which didn't look as if it had ever been used. The van was old and worn and grubby but had a certain character about it. Jacob appeared more than comfortable in it; like an old friend that needed no words of introduction.

The last time Marelle had been in the workshop was the day Jacob had suffered an electric shock from a suspect piece of equipment. She'd found him here – as white as a sheet, gradually gathering composure and with a burn on his hand. She recalled her suspicion that Sam had been behind that and remembered the fear she had felt at yet another stab of the spear at Jacob for no reason. At the time, things had gradually been gathering momentum, but she had not realised when she should have – but she hadn't and hindsight was a flamboyant sidekick!,

Today Jacob drove past the workshop where that incident had taken place and drove round the back of the buildings to pull up alongside what looked like a newly erected metal building. When he got out of the van she followed and walked along beside Jacob as he strode around to the front of the hangar where a large shutter door was pushed right up.

The space inside seemed much larger than Marelle had expected but within it there were at least four old lorries and a stubby looking bus, right at the back. It was neat and tidy but had a smell of oil and diesel in the air. Jacob walked around a green and black lorry that looked as if it had just been polished. Marelle looked at it as she followed. On the door, in hand painted letters it said D.R. Wright, Farmers, in beautiful gold brush script.

There was a slight tapping noise coming from the direction Jacob was headed in, interspersed with the odd grunt and little exclamation. They rounded the green lorry and came up to a maroon and black one, the front engine flap propped up and Mr. Wright leaning in the engine bay, knocking at something. A space had been cleared in front of the vehicle in order to get it out but, so far, it had not moved. As Jacob walked up, Marelle one step behind him watching his slender legs in the ripped black jeans, a quiet but nonetheless highly audible fart escaped into the echoey building.

She tried not to laugh but failed, turning her head slightly away as Jacob walked up to Mr. Wright.

He heard him approaching and stood up stiffly, away from the engine compartment.

"Thank you. Thank you, Jacob." He said. "Good afternoon young lady – sorry to pull him in off his holiday." He smiled at Marelle then looked back to Jacob.

"Oh dear! What have you done?" He asked.

"Nothing, I had dental surgery yesterday – that's why I was off … it's fine." Marelle thought to herself that it hadn't been anywhere near 'fine' last night.

Mr. Wright laughed. "You want to keep away from them! Especially if they do that to you!" He chuckled. "Now look here – bloody thing won't start. Keeps turning it over like a mad thing!"

Jacob stepped forward. Looked in the engine bay – mostly at what Mr. Wright had been doing. Marelle folded her arms and watched. Jacob was at home here – this was his domain; he had claimed it in his ten years alone.

"It's probably the fuel tank." Jacob said. 'Remember when I brought this home and it kept breaking down? There's a lot of crap in the fuel tank – they refurbished and made it pretty but didn't sort that out."

"Oh dear. Yes, I remember ... what can we do? We haven't got time to put a new fuel tank in it."

"Haven't got a fuel tank anyway and you will be lucky to even get one – that's probably why they left it in the first place." Jacob explained. "I can fit a fuel filter?"

Wright liked that. He smiled, stepped back slightly in acceptance of Jacob's suggestion.

'Will that sort it?"

"For a bit. It's not the answer but should allow you to use it for a while. The tank will need sorting out eventually though ..."

"Oh yes, yes! I know that. We can see if we can find one but, in the meantime, – the filter – can you do that?"

Jacob nodded. "Take a little while. I'll have to see what we've got out the back as well ..."

"Oh good, good!" Wright said. 'I don't really know what I'm doing with this technical stuff. I'll leave you to it, shall I?"

"Yes, leave me to it." Jacob replied in a flat voice that encompassed Jacob.

"Ok. I'm just going up to the house for a bit of lunch then." He pointed.

Jacob nodded.

Wright smiled at Marelle in a way any old man looks at a younger female.

"Are you alright to stay here with Jacob or do you want me to give you a lift home?"

"Oh, I'm fine. If it's ok for me to stay?"

"Oh yes, of course. He might need a hand." He chuckled and began to walk away.

Jacob watched him go, out of the door and off to the right. Seconds after they heard his car start up and move off.

"Won't see him anymore today." Jacob remarked then sighed. "Why the hell has he taken this apart?" He moaned looking in the engine. "But it's ok – I'll put all that back together!"

"Can you do it?"

He nodded. "Yeah. Could have done it before if I hadn't been suspended!"

Marelle watched him work. He knew exactly what he was doing and how to do it. When she had watched him take the bike apart many times with that meticulous methodology, she felt how at home he was with anything mechanical; they didn't speak to you; they didn't answer you back – but most of all, with a little time and patience, they could nearly always be fixed.

"How come you are so good at this?" She asked, watching him closely.

"Because when I was a kid if something broke you had two choices – throw it away and be without it cause you sure as hell wouldn't get a replacement or learn how to fix it." He replied. "You make a few mistakes along the way, but you learn."

"But you didn't have to fix lorries, did you."

"No – but when it comes down to it everything is pretty much the same – it just fits together differently." He went walking off to a cupboard at the back of the building. Marelle leaned her head back so she could see where he was.

'These old things are simple." He commented. "It's just time and patience."

"How old is it?" She asked as Jacob knelt on the dusty floor and began looking beneath it.

"About the same age as you!" He grinned. "Maybe a bit older."

"Oh yeah – and who's faired the better then?" She grinned, tongue in cheek.

He sucked in air and winked. "Oh I don't know – could be a close one there but, well, I haven't had to change parts on you yet!" He stood up, rubbed his hands down his jeans and grinned cheekily at her.

"Oh, I'm not so sure. You damn near broke my heart a while back." She said, smiling then swallowed as she felt the impact of that statement in the solid silence of the garage. Marelle felt oddly embarrassed with herself for blurting that out right there. She looked into his eyes then blinked away.

Jacob smiled sweetly, his mouth still slightly swollen, marring his smile.

"But it didn't break, and it's ok now, isn't it?" He whispered.

Marelle smiled and nodded. "Just about." She said.

"Unlike this hunk of metal." He nodded to it. "I'd better get on – or we'll be here all night."

He worked on. She observed; following him as he moved around the vehicle; marvelling to herself how he could do this; how he knew exactly what to do. This was Jacob but this was also Ezza. Marelle wondered just the two people could actually be in the same body.

A couple of hours later he was walking around checking everything, tightening everything one last time.

"Nearly there." He said. "Just check this and hope we don't have diesel spraying everywhere in a minute or two."

"Is it a foreign lorry?" Marelle questioned.

"No, British. One of the last British lorry manufacturers." He stated. "All these are British – hard to come by now. He picks them up from private dealers ... pays too much for them ..." He wiped his hands on some blue tissue paper. "Be nice if he had decided to collect American Muscle or even British sports cars, but no ... it's old lorries. He's after a Commander next – that'll be fun." For a moment Jacob was off on a little verbal journey detour around his knowledge of these vehicles. It didn't seem that he actually liked them, but he respected them.

"Right." He sighed. "Let's see if she starts."

He walked round, opened the driver's door near to her then taking a hold on the side of the lorry he leapt up into the cab.

Marelle stared up at him, he smiled, one hand on the wheel – looking too at home for comfort in the old lorry.

"Stand to the front a bit. It might piss diesel everywhere!" He advised.

Marelle took a couple of steps to her side, her hands shoved into her jean's pockets as she turned to look along the side of the lorry then up at Jacob again. She drew a breath as she looked at him; God, she loved him so much and even more when he had that expression of abject concentration on his face.

He turned the key and Marelle was immensely aware of the tiny chain of clicks and whirs and small mechanical noises as that action flowed down through the vehicle. The starter clicked, sprang into life and turned the engine over. Then with a deep growl the engine started. It chugged a little then settled into a steady, rhythmical, fuel filled heartbeat. Jacob smiled as she looked up at him; he had his hand out in an open gesture.

Leaving it running he climbed down from the cab, walking around the old vehicle as it spewed diesel fumes into the enclosed space.

"Good." He said.

Then he half climbed up to the cab again and cut the engine.

"Better call him and let him know." Jacob said to her walking forwards and holding his dirty hands up to her. "He really needs to take it around the block before he goes wherever he's going tomorrow."

Marelle smiled, put her arms around him while he avoided pulling his greasy hands on her.

"You're so clever!" She laughed, on tiptoes and gently placing a kiss on his lips.

"I know.' He replied, looking longingly down at her in a way that flipped her heart through three sixty. His eyes drilled into hers and he lowered his face, kissing her in the way she wanted him to.

'So is your mouth feeling better?' She asked when he broke away.

"It is now." He smiled, sweetly.

Here in the garage, or whatever it was, she raised herself up to him as he came down to meet her.

'Hello?" A voice suddenly called. "Is everything alright? Seems a bit quiet?"

Marelle opened her eyes with a sigh as they heard Mr. Wright approaching.

They stood apart, like two guilty schoolchildren. Marelle smiled as Jacob looked guilty as charged. He shuffled and metamorphosized into Jacob.

"How is it?" Wright questioned, unaware of what he had interrupted.

"Good." Jacob nodded. "She's running now."

Wright smiled, patting the lorry. "Oh that's good news – is she all good to go then?"

"Well, do you want to take her around the block while I'm here ... just in case?"

"No, no! You've never done a bad job for me yet. I trust you!' He laughed. "Thank you for coming down ..."

Jacob nodded. "That's ok. Took my mind off this." He pointed to his swollen cheek.

"Have you had a tooth taken out?"

"No, had one repaired."

"Repaired?" Wright questioned.

Jacob nodded. "I smashed it a while back. Had a false one put in."

"Implant?"

Jacob nodded.

"Sounds painful." Mr. Wright commented "... and expensive. Must be paying you too much!!" He chuckled, walking towards the back of the lorry.

They left him to lock up. Jacob climbed up into his van with Marelle beside him. He drove home without the seatbelt on.

"Why do people judge you like that?" He asked, his jaw tight despite the swelling.

"Like what?" Marelle questioned, sensing his tension but not really understanding why.

"Saying some flippant comment like '*I must be paying you too much*' – just because I've had this done? That's what I mean. For the last ten years I've had to not let anything catch the sun or they're straight on it ..."

"I think it's just the sort of thing I would expect any boss to say." Marelle smiled. "Chill out. What does it matter anyway, hey?"

"It's like that with the bikes too. I could have one back, but tongues will be wagging ... everywhere."

"Then let them. Your life is your own it doesn't matter what they think, does it?"

He sighed. Breathed out noisily through his nose.

"It still does at the moment ..."

TWENTY-ONE

As they pulled into the drive Marelle could still feel the discomfort in him following Mr. Wright's remark, but this was immediately exacerbated when they saw the dark blue car parked in the road and catchpole walking down the path.

"Shit." Jacob sighed.

Marelle released a long, quiet sigh too. Him being here only meant one thing.

Jacob parked the van beside Marelle's car then got out. As he turned to close the door he met Catchpole walking back up towards him.

"New set of wheels?" He questioned, casually.

"No, work van, from the farm."

"You've never had it before."

"No, they said I could use it. I guess I've finally reached a point of trust – at least with some people." Jacob replied.

Catchpole stared at him. Didn't answer directly to that comment but nonetheless made it clear that sarcasm wasn't a good response.

"What do you want?" Jacob asked as Marelle walked around the large, white van to join him.

"Oh just an update." He replied. "Can I come in?"

Jacob looked to the ground for a few seconds, blinked his eyes up towards Marelle then started up to the house.

"I suppose so." Jacob answered.

Catchpole had been in their kitchen so many times he fitted in with an air of familiarity but was never truly welcome. Jacob didn't sit down, instead, he leant against the worktop. Marelle did likewise.

Catchpole remained on the opposite side of the table to them. Today he wore a cream-coloured shirt underneath and ill-fitting blue suit. The shirt may have been a white one, yellowed with time - Marelle wasn't sure. She looked up at him.

"What's happened to your face?" Catchpole enquired, staring at Jacob.

"Dentist. Yesterday." Jacob replied.

"Looks nasty."

"It's fine."

Catchpole gave a very small smile to himself paused for effect before he continued.

"Otherwise everything is alright? Work ok? No more … repercussions?"

Briefly, Jacob raised his eyes to Catchpole, made that fleeting second of eye contact which caught Catchpole slightly off guard for an equally tiny expanse of time; he wasn't used to eye contact from Jacob.

"I'm fine." Jacob stated.

Catchpole looked to Marelle but got nothing, he turned his eyes back to Jacob.

"What did you want to see us for?' Marelle questioned. She did not want him here; the quicker he got to the point, the better.

Catchpole sighed. 'Just an update."

Neither Jacob nor Marelle said anything else, so he chose to continue.

"Forensics have examined the deceased and deem that it is that of a small, full-term infant. They expect that the child was new born or at most, a few days old when they passed away. From carbon dating they would estimate that the body was buried approximately fifty years ago maybe a few years each way. He looked at them both as he spoke. Marelle looked him in the eyes; Jacob kept his fixed on the floor. "And they have identified the remains of being that of a male child."

The silence was static. Marelle could almost feel the charge between all three of them. Jacob did not move.

"So, bearing that in mind, I just wanted to ask you again if you have any recollection, any memory, that may shed some light on this. Did anyone ever say anything about a sibling, or a stillborn child?"

Jacob raised his eyes to Catchpole. There was a brief moment where he allowed eye contact but soon blinked away again.

"No." He replied, succinctly.

Catchpole stared at him, tried to lift Jacob's eyes to his own again but with that gaze. He failed.

"Nothing? No tiny inkling or spark of anything that may lead us to identify who this poor, unfortunate individual is?"

Jacob shook his head.

"He must be related to you. I believe he has to be a stillborn sibling." Catchpole stated. "You must have heard *something*." He screwed his mouth in question. "Do you want to have a think about that Jacob?"

"I don't know anything about this body! I don't know if him and I know nothing *about* him. And stop personalising him – it was a body ..."

"Not even a fleeting memory?"

"*If* it took place when I was a child then I have no memory of it!" Jacob exclaimed. "I was a child myself. Memories may have got buried away deep inside you – lost – I *knew* about Frankie – I *knew* he disappeared. I know nothing about this I don't know who he is or when he was there."

"Didn't your father ever say anything?"

"My father couldn't string two words together into a sentence most of the time; he was blind drunk, asleep or down the pub – if I tried to speak to him, he would hit me. I *avoided* conversation with him ..."

Catchpole sighed, walked a step closer to the side of the table, leant his hands on the back of a chair.

"I don't think you're telling me the whole truth Jacob. I think you know more than you are letting on ..."

"I can't help what you *think*; I *know* what I *know*."

"Exactly Jacob! You know what you know! But some things just don't add up." Catchpole explained., quietly. "I think you are lying to me."

Jacob half laughed. Looked to the side them down again.

"Because I've checked a couple of things out. You say you went to University – say you studied nuclear physics ... God knows how – but you told me that and I've checked it out. You didn't. There is no record of you ..."

"I dropped out. I didn't complete the course."

"But you would still be there. You would have enrolled there. You received funding – it would be documented. You didn't go to University – you didn't study nuclear physics." Catchpole stated bluntly. "But your brother did."

Marelle felt an ice-cold stab of fear run right through her body, slitting her open with a dagger of ice.

Jacob did not stir. She tried not to show her own discomfort but right now she wanted to tell Catchpole to shut his mouth and get out of her kitchen. She stayed abjectly silent.

"What has this got to do with *that* body being discovered in *that* garden.?" Jacob exclaimed.

"Nothing directly, just background information ... and enough to tell me that you are a liar Jacob – you didn't go to University – you just used your brother's past to re-invent your own – because it sounds better, doesn't it?"

Marelle heard Jacob exhale noisily; it wasn't a sigh, more, more an exclamation of disbelief.

"You've lied about that, and I know you are lying about this. There's something in there and there's something going on. I know. I can sense it."

Marelle felt trapped. She could not imagine how Jacob felt.

"I'm not a liar. But I can be – I can lie that yes, my father did say to me in one of his more lucid moments – he told me about a baby my mother had given birth to, before I was born. And the baby had been stillborn – and my father told me that he had buried the dead child in the garden – right where you found him. They never gave him a name and just buried him out here – safe in the hands of God!" He seethed, angry – or feigning anger – Marelle was not certain, she had not seen him like this before. "Don't you think if I knew all that then I would have told you just to get you off my back and to stop you from coming around here accusing me of being a liar – in front of Marelle – my future wife."

The icy dagger turned into a warm rod of excitement.

"And anyway." He continued. "What would I have to gain from lying to you? Why would I even want to cover that up? Whoever he is, or was, he is buried there. I did not kill him or place him in that hole. If I knew I would tell you. I have nothing to gain by lying about this."

Catchpole eyed him. 'That's understood – you would have been an innocent bystander at worst. But I still think this runs deeper; there's more to you and your story ..." He lifted a finger, almost threateningly.

Jacob stared back at him.

"Are you still agreeing to take a DNA test?"

"I said I would. But what would that prove?" Jacob asked defiantly.

"It would let us be a little more certain that the remains found in that garden, the garden of the house you used to live in, were a direct relation to you. It would be another piece in the puzzle – and believe me Jacob – it is a puzzle that I intend to complete."

He remained staring at them both for a few passing seconds like they were two naughty schoolchildren in the headmaster's office. Then he patted his hands against the back of the chair like a drum beat to signify his leaving.

"I'll leave you to have a think Jacob." He said, making a move to go. "And, once again, if there is some mighty or otherwise divine intervention which suddenly relights a memory then please let me know so we might be able to establish just who this was and how they happened to be there."

He gave them both a final glance and then turned to go. Jacob pushed away from the worktop and followed him back along the hallway. Catchpole knew his way out. As he reached up to the latch on the front door he turned back to Jacob behind him, now with Marelle there too.

"I'll sort the paperwork for the DNA test." Were his last words as he left.

He closed the door behind himself and left them both standing in the hallway, staring at the back of the closed door.

"He knows."

"He doesn't. he doesn't know anything – he wants us to think he knows." Jacob replied, looking down then moving away and back to the kitchen. With one glance back at the closed door, Marelle turned and followed him.

"It's what he tries to do." Jacob continued. "Makes you think he knows more than he does in the hope that you say something."

"Are you sure?"

"If he knew anything more, he would say more – he wouldn't keep hinting and pushing. He knows nothing."

"But he's right about University – technically – isn't he?"

"Yeah." Jacob stated. "And I'm a liar."

"You're not a liar Jacob."

"I am. I lied. I've lied to everyone. I've lied to you."

"But I know the truth now." She said. "You didn't lie – you've just hidden the truth!"

"But when you lie people stop believing you." He answered and raised an eyebrow to her. She looked at his bruised face and the look in his eyes that belied his calm exterior.

"I believe you." She told him. "Does anyone else matter?"

"Not unless it's going to land me in shit."

"Will you have to tell him?"

'No!" Jacob exclaimed. "I want to have the moment with Chas before anything gets out. I want that element of surprise. If I catch him out, he'll at least listen for a moment – if he knows it's coming he'll tell me to fuck off!"

"Will he?" She seemed taken aback.

"Probably, if he's had time to prepare. If I surprise him, I can get a finger in the crack before he manages to slam the door."

"I thought he was your friend!"

"He was. But me turning up may be a little too earth shattering for him – especially if he gets wind of it before I show myself ..."

"But what if Catchpole does know?"

"He doesn't know. He's poking around. I'm not saying that he won't start to put two and two together given enough time. He's onto it, that's for sure."

"Are you scared?" Marelle asked, looking at his eyes dancing around.

He gave a grin. "I'm not scared. Anxiety about the possible outcomes but I'm not scared."

She watched his face for a moment or two then swallowed before she finally asked the question that had been on her mind since he'd confided in her.

"What if Chas does tell you to fuck off?"

"He won't. If I get it right, he won't. But he has to be the first person to realise it's me. If Catchpole starts to sling mud around and it begins to stick, then I may well fail."

"And what if you fail?"

"I won't."

"What if you do?"

He shrugged. Turned to face her fully on. He had both hands in his pockets.

"I'll worry about that when it happens."

Therefore, Marelle went to bed that night her own worries now combining with Jacob's. He said he wasn't scared; he'd maintained that hard shell exterior that Marelle was only too familiar with. Everything was ok; everything was just fine – it proclaimed so wholeheartedly but she could look into his eyes and know it definitely was not. His ability to hide things, including the truth, was truly honed and rehearsed.

In her head she pondered on which worry was currently the most threatening. The thought of having to get out of this house in a few days' time; or the new, very real threat of Catchpole unearthing the truth about Jacob. Marelle was not sure. If they were forced to get out, then they would be destitute; if Jacob's truth was uncovered then his whole future was in jeopardy. She was suddenly filled with a fear and turned herself to him in the bed beside her, laying her head against his chest and running her hand down his arm. He was still but she knew he wasn't asleep either.

"What are we going to do about the house?" She asked, her voice softened by the velvety darkness.

"Tomorrow we will go and ask around the estate agents. Say we are looking for a property in the village. There's little that comes up for sale here so if Seb has spoken to any of them, they will fall over themselves to try and push a sale even if it's not on the market yet. We'll find out how much it's up for and we can take it from there."

Marelle raised her head and looked at him in the dark room. He did not stir.

"... and then what?" She asked.

"Then we'll think of what to do next."

TWENTY-TWO

"Put something smart on." He said, eating toast, still very gingerly.

Marelle stopped mid-way through extracting a tea bag from a mug and stared at him.

"Pardon?"

"Put something smart on." He repeated.

"Why?"

"Make it look like you've got money. If we pitch up looking like we couldn't possibly afford a house, then we won't get anywhere with them."

"I don't have anything ..." She answered.

"Of course you do! What about what you wore to Frankie's funeral? What about that navy blazer you've got?"

"Have you been going through my wardrobe?" She laughed.

'You mean like you did? In the caravan?" He replied with a smile that was still damaged by the slight swelling on his face.

"I'll find something." She sighed.

Jacob taking the lead in a public situation was quite new to her. She had experienced him dealing with developers and archaeologists coming onto the airfield and he had impressed her with his business-like demeanour which had been unexpected. Today he had preened himself in the bathroom for half an hour – pushed his hair into some weird quiff-like style and out on a black jacket and jeans with a blue and white checked shirt beneath – no tie. She had supposed that was 'smart casual' but to her it was delectable – except for the hair, which she didn't like. His final act were sunglasses which helped to cover the slight bruise under his left eye but also added a certain panache. He looked like he had a million pounds in his pocket already.

Walking down the street in a busy little market town, arm in arm with Jacob was also a new experience. For once Marelle actually felt like the person she actually was – doing 'normal' things. But as they stepped into the first estate agents she knew what they were up to was far from normal.

"Morning." Jacob smiled to the young woman in a bright orange sleeveless dress who welcomed them on their arrival.

"Good morning. How can I help?"

"Well ..." Jacob began, speaking more words in public than she had ever heard him utter before. "We are looking to move into the area and were specifically looking for a property in the village of Groveham Parfield ... we have kind of fallen in love with the place."

"That's a lovely village." The girl smiled. "Let me see ..." She tapped into her computer. "Please, sit down." She gestured as she waited. Jacob sat; Marelle followed suit but placed a hand on his thigh.

"We have a couple of properties in the villages – nothing specifically in Groveham however – what were you looking for?"

"It has to be Groveham." Jacob added. "We're not really interested in anywhere else."

"I can take your details and do some research. Were you looking for detached?"

Jacob smiled. "That's ok. We'll leave it for now. I can always give you a call to see if anything changes."

"Well let me take your number and I can call you." She tried.

"No, that's ok. I'll try a few more estate agents … thank you." He gave a little smile and was about to get up. "Oh, just out of curiosity what sort of price is the average detached house in Groveham now?"

"Well we don't have anything in Groveham as a benchmark but something like this is around two hundred and sixty thousand." She turned her screen to show them a modern red brick house – looked brand new – reminded Marelle slightly of the house she had owned with Chris – only larger.

Jacob looked, faked interest. "Ok, ok. Many thanks." He smiled. "We will be in touch."

The next two were pretty much the same. The third did have one property in Groveham and proudly showed them a pink cottage with a beautiful garden. Marelle recognised it as being down close to the pub; she had always thought it was weekend cottage for someone as there was never a car in the drive during the week. It had outbuildings and a yard to the side. He showed it to them.

"Beautiful setting." The agent said. "Cottage is grade two listed. Apparently, it used to be the butcher's shop." He raised his eyes to them, smiling at his bounty. The butcher's shop, Marelle thought to herself, wasn't that where Mrs. Avison had spoken of, that her father had owned? She suddenly remembered her conversation with the elderly lady in the village when she had first moved there. Mrs. Avison had hinted at what Marelle now knew about Jacob but at the time Marelle had not believed her, thinking it was just confused rambling of a closing mind. Mrs. Avison alone had known that Jacob was Nat – but that knowledge and whatever else she may have known had died with her and may have gone forever – until Jacob had chosen to tell Marelle. Those first, long summer days when Jacob had intrigued her. When she didn't know him but wanted to. When she had been taken in by those dark eyes, that lithe frame, that hair – and been touched to her very heart by his kind, gentle, misunderstood soul inside. Days when she had longed for a moment like the one she was in right now. Jacob by her side, and his ring on her finger. She smiled and gripped his hand in hers as her chest filled with pride and accomplishment.

"Lovely. But we were looking for something a bit more modern. I'd be banging my head on the beams in that one!" Jacob laughed.

The estate agent laughed too, just to be polite.

"I think that's all we have at the moment." He explained. "Properties in Groveham are sought after. They don't come up very often don't hang around when they do."

"How much is the cottage?" Jacob asked as Marelle's mind began to wander again.

'This is five two five. It has outbuildings and half an acre of land at the back. We have had offers, but they have not been accepted. There may be some movement if you are interested, but not a lot."

Jacob sighed. "That's ok. Thank you."

"We have properties in Spixhall, only four miles away from Groveham …"

"Er, no, we have kind of set our hearts on Groveham." Jacob said.

"I can take your details …" He offered. "We can make some enquiries."

"We would rather wait and keep an eye out … we're often driving through Groveham so we can see if anything comes up."

The guy beside the one they were speaking to put down his phone and held a finger up as he swivelled his chair around.

"Groveham?" He asked.

Jacob nodded.

"Went out there last week. Nice old house – backs onto that disused airfield – needs a bit of updating but I'm told everything works. Hold on …" He sorted through his notebook and picked a page. "Not instructed yet but the guy who owns it is keen to sell quickly."

Marelle looked up to Jacob but he didn't acknowledge her.

"I've got a few pictures here if you have five minutes …"

"Oh yes, sure … we're interested!" Jacob smiled with the grin of a reptile. He held her hand in his and just squeezed it gently.

"Ok. Hold on … "The agent replied, the guy selling it has tenants in, but it will be vacant possession upon completion – he's got to sort that with them before he puts it on the market … I think he's had a bit of trouble with them." He searched on his laptop. "It *will* go quickly however. I can guarantee that."

"Isn't the airfield being developed?" Jacob asked.

"So I'm told. I don't think it will have a lot of impact on this property however. A lot of it is being preserved as a heritage site so it's unlikely the house will end up in the middle of a concrete jungle!" He laughed." "Here you go … they are straight off my camera so it's warts and all." He swivelled his screen and scrolled through about ten images of the house; their home. The white van in the drive and all of the rooms obviously lived in.

"You can see they are not the tidiest tenants." He chuckled.

Marelle leaned in closer, looked at the pictures of the kitchen, the living room, *their bedroom* – Frankie's room and the bathroom. Violated, taken without her knowledge while Jacob was at the dentist. She felt a renewed anger rising in her directed at Seb; this was their private space displayed to anyone who asked – right there.

"And what has it been valued at?" Jacob questioned looking at his work boots in the kitchen, on the floor, down near the door.

"Well – we valued it at two eight nine, but the owner is convinced it's worth more. He may be right as it's in a very sought after area, but he wants to put it on at three oh five. At two eight nine it would go within an hour or two – it's a prime property for development. At three o five it's probably going to linger a bit. I had advised him against it, but he wants to go on at that price. He is convinced it will sell quickly."

Jacob nodded. "And when does it go on the market?"

"How long is a piece of string? Said he would call back at the end of this week when he has hoofed the tenants out, but – I don't know to be honest."

"Definitely interested." Jacob said, looking at the screen if only to avoid Marelle's glances.

"I could call the guy. Tell him you want to make an offer?"

"Erm ... not right now." Jacob returned. "Take our number and ring me as soon as it goes on the market. I'll make an offer then."

"You might miss it." The agent said, slightly sarcastically with a little shake of his head.

"I will be in a position to make an immediate decision then so, if someone calls me the moment it goes on the market ..."

The agent gave a sigh. "I would strongly recommend that you make an offer now – I can put it to the vendor and we can seal the deal."

"It doesn't sound to me like they will accept an offer..." Jacob commented.

Marelle was watching him; she'd not seen him in operation like this; in full flow. She guessed this was Nat – not even Ezza – and observing his guarded, calm negotiation she was in awe and ready to fall in love with him all over again.

"Oh, he might ... if it was the right offer." The agent said.

He won't, Marelle thought to herself.

"I would really advise you to jump the gun here and put in a subject to viewing offer."

Jacob smiled. "My way or the highway."

Marelle felt a smile break across her face that she could not control. She could not believe he'd just said that.

"Shall we leave your number?" Jacob had turned to her.

"Erm, oh yes. No problem ..." She reeled off her number and the agent wrote it down on a form.

"I will make sure either I, or one of my colleagues will call you as soon as we are instructed but please be aware that this by no means guarantees you first offer. Someone could come in five minutes after you have left and ask the same question and then decide to make an immediate offer ..."

"Understood." Jacob replied. "I'll take my chances!"

They left the premises with a calm, measured demeanour and walked up the street a few metres before Marelle could no longer contain herself.

"I gave them *my* number. What if Seb sees it an recognises it?"

"He won't." Jacob stated. "Our number won't be disclosed to him – anyway he probably speed dials your number and would have no actual idea of what it is." Jacob replied, calm as a cooling planet with a boiling, molten centre.

"But three hundred thousand!" She exclaimed, clutching his arm. "I can cover a quarter of that I can try for a mortgage but that would kind of rely on Seb." Jacob was walking more quickly now but saying nothing. "Could we get a joint mortgage?" She asked as he hurried along. "I mean … but then I suppose you wouldn't want to get a mortgage, not being Jacob. I mean …" Marelle sighed again, almost trotting alongside Jacob now, feeling short beside him today as he strode with his head held high for a change.

"I don't know of any other way to get a mortgage." She continued. "But it takes ages doesn't it … we've got four days – shall we go and ask in a bank now, while we are here?"

He didn't answer her, but he had a smile on his face when she looked up at him.

"Jacob!" She called his attention to her. "So we know how much it is – but we've got to find the money – don't we need to …"

He stopped, on the pavement in the middle of town, just stood still and waited for her to turn around and stand in front of him. She screwed her mouth and squinted in the autumn sun reaching between the buildings in the medieval grid system as she looked up at him.

"We don't need a mortgage." He said, taking her hand. "We don't need a mortgage."

Marelle stared at him. "Why?"

"Don't worry about the money." He said. "I can afford the house."

Marelle's eyes widened involuntarily. "How can you afford the house?"

Jacob stared down at her with steady eyes, holding her hand as people on their normal Saturday shopping trip passed by them. He smiled. That cheeky, humble smile she liked best; the smile when he was *truly* happy – the smile when the lights were fully on and glowing like a beacon.

"Because I've worked all my life and barely spent a penny of it." He shrugged a shoulder, almost like a child. "Never had the need to."

Marelle smiled back at him, emotion pulling at her expression as she tried to hold on to it, at least here in the street. "We won't need a mortgage." He added.

"Then why don't we just go right back in and make an offer?"

"No. If Seb finds out it's us, he won't accept whatever offer we put in. Then we've lost our only chance …"

"But how will we buy it then?"

"*We* won't." He replied. "We'll get someone else to buy it for us."

Marelle stared up at him. He still had a smile on his face that was intrinsically sublime; he almost had an aura of peace about him which was alien yet mesmerizing all at the same time.

"What?" She asked.

"We'll give someone the money to buy the house for us."

"How?" She questioned. "And who?"

"That's what we need to decide." He still had the smile, still had the excited look of a child who had just received their first bike for Christmas. "Let's get home first – we need to discuss a few things …"

They sure did. Suddenly everything was so very real and thundering along like an express train. There was a thoughtful silence between them as Jacob drove home. Sitting at traffic lights he reached across and took her hand in his, glancing at her with a smile as he gave her hand a gentle squeeze. Marelle looked at him and let the warmth of that moment spread across her face, but she soon looked straight ahead again as the lights changed to green. He drove on and she could feel the sting of tears pricking her eyes. Eventually he pulled the Mercedes into their drive next to the white van.

"This place needs a wall and a gate." He remarked. "A nice, curved wall at the front with a proper gate …"

"Well I am sure we can do that!" Marelle grinned.

Jacob sauntered into the house behind her, with that measured, leggy stride. Marelle went along the hallway to the kitchen, but he started up the stairs.

"Where are you going?" She questioned, expecting him to follow her to the kitchen.

"Get changed." He said as if it was the most obvious thing.

He arrived back downstairs in the kitchen in an old t-shirt and the ripped jeans. Marelle looked at the Yellow Son logo on his chest, faded with the years. He pulled out a chair. She was leaning in the fridge, door open, not looking at him.

"You gonna get a new Yellow Son t-shirt soon?" She laughed.

"Nah." He smiled. "I'd never wear my own band t-shirt."

"How old is that one?"

He shrugged. "Old."

His hair was still in that strange brushed back quiff, which she didn't like but he nonetheless still looked adorable standing there. She smiled, shuffled, one hand on the fridge door.

"Come here." She said quietly.

He walked forwards to her, hands in his jean's pockets. "What?"

She closed the fridge door, reached up and ran her fingers through the quiff. He had product in it and it resisted a bit but she messed it back into a more spiky style, just tipping over his forehead.

"Better!" She said.

"You really only love me for my hair, don't you?" He laughed.

"Yeah!" She smiled cheekily. "And everything that's beneath it!" She slid her arms through his and clasped them behind his back, her chest to his body.

"So if we can afford this house then who are we going to ask to buy it for us?" She enquired.

"Well ... "He paused. "We need someone we can trust, someone who will work with us and totally understands what we are trying to do."

"Well we've got such a huge group of trustworthy friends – that should be easy!" She replied, the tone of her voice not immediately sarcastic but nonetheless containing irony.

"It *is* easy."

She raised her eyebrows to him.

"Sit down." He nodded. When she did, he continued. "Think about it ..."

"Who is the only person we can both totally trust?"

Marelle looked into his eyes. He had such an intense stare if he wanted to use it.

"Bella?" She asked.

He gave her a smile with his eyebrows raised in acknowledgement.

"We can't ask Bella!"

"Why not?"

"Bella is ..." She laughed. "Bella is ... *Bella*!"

"And you trust her; you said she would never do anything to hurt you ... you told me I could trust her ..."

"Yes, but Seb *knows* Bella. If he sees her name or finds out she's involved, then he will know what's going on very quickly ... we can't ask Bella. It's not fair ..."

Marelle had deflated his balloon, poured water on his fire.

Jacob thought for a moment. "Then the only choice we have is to use a company that buys properties ... it'll cost, and I don't know how quickly they can operate or of they'll do it anonymously."

"Do you know of anyone like that?"

He shook his head. "No."

Marelle sighed. She paused, took in a thought. "What about Mr. Wright?"

Jacob laughed. "Mr Wright?! Everyone would know within three minutes – no – I wouldn't ask him. I don't trust him. Him and his family have thrown me out of my home and hired and fired me so many times I have lost count."

She took a deep breath in frustration. "Why can't we just pay the fucking money and buy the fucking house?"

"Because Seb owns it." Jacob added, for good measure.

"Cunt!" She said under her breath.

"Have a look on-line." Jacob suggested. "See if there is anyone local who is a property acquisition company ..."

Marelle got up, fetched her laptop and brought it to the kitchen table. After a few taps she turned to Jacob thoughtfully.

"What about Mae?"

"Mae?" He asked. "Mae?" Again, with a laugh. "We don't know Mae from Adam!"

"But Bella does."

"She is in love with Mae but I'm not sure how well she knows her …"

"I think Bella knows Mae a lot more than she is letting on!" Marelle imparted. "I trust Bella with my life and if she trusts Mae to do this then I do too."

Jacob made a face of unsurety. "But Mae hardly knows us. She'll think we're some kind of petty criminal trying to do something illicit … I certainly wouldn't agree to it if I was her!"

"Bella can explain it all to her. I am sure she would understand …"

He shook his head. "We're just strangers to her – no doubt weird ones at that!"

"Only one way to find out." Marelle responded, raising her eyes to his.

TWENTY-THREE

"Hey babe! What's wrong?" Bella answered fairly quickly.

Marelle had the phone on speaker, so Bella's voice came out loud and clear. "He's not run off again, has he?"

"No!" Marelle laughed, looking into Jacob's eyes as she spoke but he flicked them away. "Bella I'm here with Jacob now and you are on speaker phone – so behave!"

"Oooh sounds serious!"

"Are you on your own?"

"What? Now you're worrying me – you'll be asking if I'm sitting down next!"

"Are you?"

"No! What's wrong?"

Marelle smiled, paused. "Are you on your own?"

"Yes! I'm at Mae's but I've just come out to my car when you called. What's wrong Marelle?"

'Well, nothing's wrong but we are looking for help. Seb is going to sell the house – we'll be chucked out if he does with very little notice! We want to buy the house – we've raised the cash, but Seb won't sell the house to me or Jacob – he wants us out!"

"I thought you owned half of it?"

"So did I. I'm apparently entitled to half of the value of the house, but Seb has full jurisdiction over the property. He's given me the choice of taking half what he had has the house valued at right now – *he actually came in here when we were out and had it valued* – or wait until it sells and then have half of whatever it makes. I've got until Wednesday to decide then he puts the house on the market …"

"Shit." Bella said.

"We have a plan though …"

"But how can he not sell it to you?" Bella asked.

"If he knows it's me, or Jacob, then he simply won't accept our offer – no matter what we do."

"Well how will he find out?"

"Through the solicitor, or estate agent I suppose. As soon as he sees any paperwork he will know." She looked to Jacob – it was a good question.

"Can't you buy it anonymously?"

"Someone's name has to go on the documentation – and you normally have to prove you are who you are saying you are." Jacob replied to Bella. Those words somehow stuck with him a little. Bella sighed. "So what's the plan then?"

"We need someone we trust to buy the house for us."

There was a moment of silence.

"Who?" Bella asked, expectantly.

Marelle sighed. "We've thought about this ... we can't ask you because Seb knows you too."

"Well surely I can buy a house?"

"No. He'll realise what's going on. If we fuck this up, we will get chucked out. We need someone to buy the house who Seb doesn't know ..." She said. "*And* who we can trust!"

"Then who?" Bella asked, slightly puzzled as to why she was involved in this conversation.

Marelle looked at Jacob as she answered.

"Mae." She said.

"Mae!" Bella exclaimed. "You want to ask Mae to buy the house for you! Why Mae?"

"We don't really have any other options if we are honest, but we thought of her – Seb won't know her – the question is ..." Marelle took a breath, suddenly realising exactly what she was asking. "... Bels, do *you* trust her?"

Silence. Absolute silence from the other end of the phone. Longer than Marelle felt comfortable with knowing that it was Bella connected on the line. She took a breath, waited that moment longer than she thought was correct, looked at Jacob, into his dark eyes while he raised his brows a little.

"Oh Marelle, that's a big question." Bella finally said. "I'm head down in my car with my arse in the air and you expect me to answer that right now?"

"Well ..."

Bella continued. "I mean – yes – I do trust her but I haven't known her for very long – I trust her but I don't know *about* her ... this is a big thing ..."

"I know it is Bella." Jacob said and somehow his voice added weight to the situation. "But we've got one single chance to get this right."

Bella sighed, audibly.

"If Seb gets wind of this we'll be living in Jacob's caravan and we both want to own the house ..." Marelle added, for good measure.

"Would you trust her with three hundred thousand pounds of your own money?" Jacob asked. "And, of course, would she do it?"

"Shit Jacob! You have a real habit of muddying the waters, don't you?"

Jacob grinned at Marelle.

"Let me ask her. What's the deal then?"

"We need someone to call the estate agents first thing on Thursday and put in an offer for the full asking price for the house." Jacob stated. "Once the offer is accepted then that person will need to be the one who signs everything and is documented as the new owner. We will have the money in a bank account ready to be transferred as soon as the sale is complete. She won't need to handle the money, but she will need the details of that bank account. She will own our house at that point – on paper – we will then have to get ownership transferred to us once Seb is out of the loop. There may be a couple of phone calls and things to sign after that, but we will do all of the admin."

"And what does Mae get out if it?" Bella questioned.

Jacob looked at Marelle and Marelle in turn looked back at him. They hadn't thought about that; they had expected her to do it out of the kindness of her heart.

"Well she can tell us that. It's open to negotiation." Jacob replied.

Bella sighed. "We were all set for a cosy weekend at Mae's …"

"You can still have a cosy weekend at Mae's – we just need a yes or a no!" Marelle laughed.

"When we will be thinking about this!" Bella retorted. "She hardly knows you she *likes* you, granted but she doesn't *know* you. This is going to sound so odd!"

"Do you want us to come to you?" Jacob asked.

"No!" Bella exclaimed quickly. "Leave it … leave it with me. I will speak to her. When is it?"

"This Thursday, first thing – there may be other people after it."

"Christ alive!" Bella sighed. "Ok – I'll speak to her. I'll ring you later."

"Only we don't have long to pack if we don't achieve this." Marelle added.

"How do you two live your lives like this? Hey?" Bella mused, slightly playfully but not entirely.

"I don't know Bella." Marelle replied. "We're fine. Other people just keep putting things in the way!"

"Leave it with me. I'll speak to her." Bella said again. "I'll call you back but don't go climbing the walls in the meantime …"

"We won't! We're chilled!" Marelle laughed.

"Yeah!" Bella replied sarcastically. "Speak later. Love you both."

"Love you too Bel." Marelle smiled.

She turned to Jacob. "Bella didn't sound too positive."

He shrugged. "It's a bit too much to take in, I guess. We've lived with it for a few days."

"I guess…" Marelle mused. "If anyone can do it, Bella can but Mae is an unknown quantity to us."

"Don't be disappointed if she says no. She is a bit of a quiet one. It might be a step too far." Jacob warned, "We have talked about it a lot and have it clear in our heads. When you try to explain it to someone else it does sound a bit dodgy!"

"I wish Bella could do it.' Marelle said. "She wouldn't ask questions; she'd just do it. For us." She gave a little smile to herself at those words. "What's the plan if she does say no?"

"We'll have to find someone – a company, a solicitor – to buy it for us. It'll cost a fortune and I'd rather someone we had a bit of a stake with do it … but if it's what it takes …"

She sighed. "I never thought Seb would carry it through and be so vindictive."

"He doesn't like me. He had nothing against you but if I'm involved, then that changes everything. I know *why* but I have honestly done nothing wrong."

"I don't think he would ever have accepted you – even if he hadn't found you in the toilets. He had already formed an opinion and that was that."

"Just like everyone else."

Marelle raised her eyes to him. "Not everyone."

"The ones that count know the truth." He said. "Come on, let's go for a walk ..."

The airfield was wearing autumn now. The arid, ethereal light of the summer days had gone and there was a brightness – a *sharpness* about colour and contrast that came with the cooler edge.

The wild flowers were mostly gone; closed and brown; their pastel colours now only existing in memory as their beauty had faded. The grass was long and dried to a brittle buff colour. Burned by the sun and laid in a uniform direction as the wind had combed fingers through it. The sky was wide and consuming – like you could dive into it's wild blue and move among the small, fluffy clouds; flat bottomed but with white, billowing cumulous above. The cool breeze was strong but not invasive. It flicked her hair off her face and tousled it with a gentle touch. Marelle slid her fingers into the crook of Jacob's arm and walked with him.

The land was in metamorphosis as autumn closed the door on summer. Leaves were still on the trees – darkening in hue and drying now. The same leaves that had burst enthusiastically out of leaf buds a few months ago – bright green and fresh. Heralding spring and new life. Now they had lived and were about to die in the sacrificial passing of the season – dried by the wind then ripped from their increasingly tentative grip on life and scattered with the breath of an autumn breeze. Insects that had choroused their existence with beating wings and chafing legs were now gone. Dead by now or over wintering somewhere. A lone red admiral butterfly fluttered past them, almost hurrying. The sound of insects replaced by the noise of the breeze soughing though the grass and the rustle of it around the trees as it rattled their dry and hollow leaves. Swifts and swallows had long since departed to warmer climes and the house martins had followed them. Marelle wondered if the same birds would return next year. What would she be doing when she first heard their calls which would herald the beginning of a new summer.

Some of the fields around them were still stubble. No longer golden and capturing the evening light but grey and bleached. Green plants now growing through between the lines where the wheat and barley had once grown. Other fields were already ploughed and sown. Tiny shoots of new life ready and waiting. Acres of sugar beet, their thick, fleshy leaves in rows of emerald green – reaching for as far as you could see.

Jacob had worked in these fields beneath the blue skies of summer and the grey ones of winter. He felt the seasons coming and going in his blood. Marelle gripped his arm and they walked up the runway as the sun pushed it's yellow rays out from behind a cloud to light up their faces.

"I don't know what's going on here anymore." He said.

'They asked you to keep on as watchman …"

"Over what? The comings and goings of the machinery? If I lock the gate they'll be forever wanting it opened. They've taken a lot of stuff away this week. Almost looks like they're moving off again."

The portacabins had gone. Marelle had only just realised.

"When did they take those away?" She asked, staring at the spot where they had been, grass dead and yellow in a perfect rectangle.

"Oh the other day. I've lost track. They just turn up …"

"Isn't that odd?" Marelle questioned.

He shrugged, standing there with his hands in his pockets, near the main gates – which were closed but no longer had the chain and padlock on.

"No." He said. "It's happened before. A few years back. They put a load of stuff on then took it away again. It doesn't mean anything – only another delay – that's all."

He waked on and she hurried beside him again, stepping through the long grass just by the perimeter fence. She had not walked this far with him in a while; she assumed he had as she knew he often came across here. The grass was longer and there were jewels of blackberries, hips and haws in the shrubby bushes that were growing around the fence.

A couple of cars passed on the road as they walked then turned with the fence, taking a dog-leg away from the road as the airfield moved across the fields. Marelle walked with him, tramping through the grass towards the Thor site and the belt of trees in the distance. A hare, flat in a scrape in the ground, suddenly leapt up inches in front of them and bounded off. Marelle gasped at the sudden movement and Jacob laughed at her.

It was a while since she had walked around here with him like this. Today it felt peaceful again; in a long, slow exhale after the onslaught of machinery had threatened its existence. Out here she felt the blood in her veins and the breeze on her face. It was Jacob's escape and now she felt it was deep within her being too.

The Thor site seemed still and silent today; almost as if it was waiting for something to happen. It crouched, breath held, in the sharp light of the changing season. The old dead tree reached its skeletal fingers forever skywards and reflected a dull, silverish hue today.

"We'll go round to the top then walk down the road." Jacob advised.

By 'the road' he meant the bumpy concrete track which ran in a straight line back to where his caravan used to stand. He had told her it had been a service road on the airfield when it was functioning – it was a route they had not walked much. Marelle looked to the concrete buildings right at the far extreme of the space. They never ventured up that end very often, at least not together. Maybe a couple of times when they had been discussing searching for Frankie and she knew that was where the magenta roses Jacob had brought her grew but it was not a corner of the airfield they went to often.

"We don't come this way very often." She commented, reflecting her thoughts.

Jacob turned his head. "It's a bit rough-going up there – there's no road. It was a runoff area – a place where they stored planes that weren't in operation."

"Was it?" She asked. "What sort of planes?"

He shrugged. "Probably Marauders – maybe the odd Mustang?"

"So, this was an airfield and a missile site?"

He nodded. "But not together. It was an airfield in the second World War then became a Thor site after that – when the threat was not of invasion but of nuclear annihilation."

Marelle stared.

"You called the building a 'mess hut'?" She asked. He had, once, when he had brought her the magenta roses.

"It wasn't. I think it was a maintenance building. Frankie always called it a 'mess hut'."

She smiled.

'The roof has just about caved in. I doubt it will stand another winter. The fire all but destroyed the other building ..."

"What fire?" She questioned.

"Years ago. Before I moved on here. It was the end of the harvest and they were burning the stubble fields – it got out of control and burned the whole end of the airfield – completely black and barren. I am sure that's why the grass and wild flowers at this end are so abundant and so different."

"Did someone set fire to it then?"

"No – it caught from the stubble fields."

"Why were the stubble fields on fire?"

"They used to burn the stubble fields each year – to get rid of the excess straw and sterilise the land. It was quite spectacular – we loved it as kids!"

"What, just set the whole field alight?"

He nodded. "It was controlled – well meant to be – sometimes it got out of hand – imagine the whole field burning ... you could hear the crackling and see the smoke for miles. Sometimes the heat was so intense you could feel it on your face from a field away. It was fascinating when we were kids – we used to try and help but usually got chased off!"

"And they don't do that now?"

"No." He laughed. "I can still remember it so clearly though." For a second, he stood still and looked across to the building; obviously remembering Frankie – she could tell from his expression. He walked on again and she huddled close to him. She had stirred a memory; a moment of melancholy.

They got back to the house an hour later. Marelle had checked her phone several times but there were no missed calls. She didn't mention it and neither did Jacob. Marelle made tea and Jacob went out of the front door and into the front garden. She heard the door go and looked through. He had left it open and was right down near the road looking at the entrance with his hands in his pockets. He sauntered back.

"What are you doing?" She asked.

"Just looking. I said about the wall."

"Oh yes. It would be better." She replied. "Be a faff opening and closing a gate though."

"We could have an electric one?" He suggested. "Remote control. Drive up and it opens." He grinned. "Be cool."

Marelle laughed. "Is that one of those little gadgets you've always dreamed about?"

"Maybe!" He laughed.

They had a makeshift tea of beans on toast and were still sitting in the kitchen at a quarter to seven.

"She's not going to call, is she?" Marelle finally said quietly, standing at the sink, picking at one of her fingernails.

"You said Bella would never let you down …"

"I know; she won't but it's not Bella, is it? Mae probably thinks we are some kind of criminal now and wants nothing to do with it; Bella is probably trying to think of a way to break it to us. Christ! It might even have split them up! I can just see Bella getting angry with Mae when she said 'no'. Bella is probably driving home now – or driving here!"

"I think your imagination is running a little wild. These things take time. She probably wants to think about it a little. She's a sensible girl."

Marelle raised an eyebrow to him but made no other comment to his remark.

Eventually she slid onto the settee next to him

"So, what's the plan with Yellow Son?"

"Concert in two weeks, well, just under, we will go and I'll let Chas see me. Take it from there …"

"Where is the concert?"

"Norwich." He replied. "About an hour's drive."

She nodded.

"The last gig of the tour is about two weeks after, in Guildford. They always do the last gig there – it's where most of the band come from." He reeled it off, well-rehearsed. "There was one in between but it got cancelled – something to do with the venue. They didn't reschedule it."

Marelle nodded.

"What do you think will happen?" She questioned.

"When?"

"When Chas sees you."

He shrugged. "Honestly, I do not know." He replied, almost as a confession just as her phone began to ring, still wedged in her jeans pocket. It was Bella. That picture of her in a bright, pink, strapless top; her long dark hair over one eye. It didn't look like Bella and had probably been filtered and edited to death.

"Bella!" She greeted, after extracting the phone and hitting the green button. "Hang on, I'm with Jacob. I'll put you on speaker."

She did so and held it between them. "Go on ..."

"Ok, I've got Mae with me here too ..." Bella explained.

"Hi." Mae added.

"Ok." Bella said. "I have spoken with Mae, and she must be as mad as you two are because she has agreed to do it."

Marelle gasped quietly and beamed at Jacob as she wrapped her fingers around his arm.

"But ... Mae has a few suggestions which, to me, sound like good ones ... Mae?"

"Hi guys." Mae said. Her voice was clear and far more commanding than they had expected. Neither of them had heard her speak outside the weekender so it did surprise them slightly. "I'm happy to do this for you but I would like to involve my brother if it's ok with the both of you?"

Marelle sighed silently. If Mae's brother was anything like Seb, then this would not be a walk in the park. Mae continued.

"I'll explain. My brother is a newly qualified solicitor, and he wants to specialise in property law. I have spoken to him, and he is happy to take this on – he doesn't see it as having many complications – he just suggests drawing up a couple of documents between us just to safeguard everyone. He can also take on the negotiation and sealing the deal."

"OK –" Jacob replied, at length.

"He is actually at his wife's parents this weekend but he would be happy to speak to you first thing on Monday if you want to call him. Once everything is signed, he will go ahead."

"OK." Jacob replied again, still an amount of unsurety in his voice.

"He will want a fee – mainly for liability concerns – but he will make it mates rates – *my* mates' rates!"

"OK." Jacob repeated once more. They were both slightly gobsmacked mostly by the command of the situation by Mae and fundamentally by how the whole plan had suddenly changed.

"Does all of that sound suitable?" Mae questioned when they did not immediately respond.

"Ok, erm – yes!" Jacob eventually replied. "Yes. Thank you to you and your brother. So what is the next step?"

"Call Devon tomorrow morning and he will talk you through everything. He has my permission to use my name as the purchaser, so he won't need to speak with me." She explained. "I'll give you his number – do you have a pen?"

Marelle scrabbled, leapt up and eventually found a pen on the worktop. She passed it to Jacob, followed by an old envelope she had already started writing a shopping list on.

Mae reeled off the number and Jacob wrote it down then read it back to her.

"And he can do it all by Thursday?" He continued.

"He can do it whenever you want him to – you only need to get an offer accepted – everything else will happen after that."

She was right. Neither of them had thought that simplistically.

"And what do you want for your help with this?" Jacob asked her.

"Nothing." She laughed. "You can owe me one!"

After further small talk and profusive thank you's, they eventually said their goodbyes.

Jacob hit the red button and sat there, staring into space for a good few seconds. Marelle took his hand on the table.

"Wow!" He laughed, shaking his head. "How did that happen?"

"It's fate!" Marelle smiled. "Somebody up there wants us to have this house!"

TWENTY-FOUR

Jacob suggested that he call Devon in the morning, but that she should come down to the workshop with him when he called.

"Wright normally goes to an auction in Diss on Mondays, so he won't be around.' He explained. "If you come down about nine, we can then call him."

It was with that intention in mind that she drove to the farmyard in the morning and parked next to the white van. Marelle walked inside and found him alone, fiddling with some vehicle component on the bench at the end.

"You alone?" She asked.

"Yeah. For now. Not that anyone much comes in here anyway ..."

"Who works here now?"

"Ryan and me. Skid is still around too."

Marelle knew Ryan – wasn't sure who Skid was but she had heard that name mentioned before. She took out her phone.

"Here."

"I'm calling then, am I?" He grinned.

"Sounds better from you."

"Ok. Been thinking though – when the property is transferred to us it will have to be in your name only."

"Why? I'd rather it was in both of our names?"

"Because it can't be left in Jacob's name, and it can't be in Nat's name either. Best keep me out of it ..."

"But you're paying for it!"

"We can sort it out later. It doesn't matter anyway." He said. "You got his number?"

"Yeah." She pulled the envelope out of her pocket. "What kind of name is Devon?" She smiled as he took the phone and dialled.

Devon was precise, polite, meticulous and more than ready to take this on for them. He spoke eloquently and immediately understood what they were trying to achieve. With his thoroughness they were on the phone for the best part of an hour but left the call with a complete plan in place save for some documents they needed to sign which he said he would email to Marelle. By that evening they promised they would be read, signed and emailed back with the proviso to put the hard copies in the post the next day. Once an offer had been accepted, they would need to transfer the money into Devon's holding account but Jacob said he would see to that nearer the time of completion.

She left Jacob with a hug and a lingering kiss, alone in the workshop before she returned home. He waved her off at the door as she left and that brought a smile to her face. Every day seemed to bring them closer together and seal the gap behind them as they went – no matter what the cause was.

When Jacob came home that evening, she had already printed out the documents and had them ready to sign.

"I thought you said it would need to be in my name?" She asked.

"On the actual documents when ownership of the house is transferred. Doesn't matter for now but it is written in it that if one of us dies then the title to the house will be passed to the other party. No one will see those documents for the sale of the house.

"Oh, OK." She replied, watching Jacob sign a name that wasn't his.

Shortly after her signature joined his and they were one step closer.

As promised, she took a photograph of the signed documents and was in the process of emailing them to Devon.

"De Sousa." She said. "Devon De Sousa. That's a name and a half! Mae's name must be Mae de Sousa. She commented. "Sounds grand!"

Jacob smiled and was about to say something when the doorbell rang.

"I'll go." He said. "You finish doing that."

Marelle continued the email and attached the documents. She could hear Jacob's voice from the hallway hut not what he was saying. When a more elevated voice of a female suddenly filtered through, Marelle hit 'send' and got up quickly. She had expected it to be Catchpole – trying to catch Jacob when he knew he was home from work. It definitely wasn't him and she walked quickly towards the hallway where she could distinctly hear an emotional female voice.

"Oh my God Jacob!"

Marelle heard it gasp as she approached and stepped through the doorway into the hall, a look on her face that would have turned milk sour!

There, on the doorstep, was a young, petite, blonde girl with her arms around Jacob, her hands clasped behind his neck; he had his hands on her waist.

"Who is it?" Marelle announced to make her presence behind him known.

Jacob turned; she released her grip but he left one hand on her waist. Marelle stared at it momentarily. The girl was very young, tiny, pretty – elf-like features and a choppy blonde bob. She smiled warmly; her eyes full of emotion.

"Marelle – this is Kally." Jacob said – obvious surprise – or fear – in his voice. "Kally, this is Marelle – she is my fiancé – we are going to get married."

Kally flashed her grey-green eyes to Jacob, then to Marelle – her smile broadened.

"Oh that is such wonderful news. I am so happy for you!" She stepped around Jacob and set a foot in the hallway which Marelle looked at sternly. Kally extended a hand to Marelle; Jacob still had his fingers around her impossibly small waist.

When Marelle reached back to Kally's outstretched hand it was against every iota of energy excitedly pulled Marelle to her in a hug that was strong but felt truly happy for them.

Marelle stepped back out of her grasp. She folded her arms and stared at Jacob.

He looked mutually embarrassed, bemused, frightened – he smiled with a sigh, eyes flicking all over the place.

Kally had called him Jacob.

Marelle glared at him. He looked down, smiled, withdrew his hand back to himself from Kally.

"Marelle, Kally used to live around here. She moved away – what, a long time ago now ...?"

"Seven years!" Kally stated.

"Seven years, hey? She moved away with her parents."

Kally smiled. "I used to ride my horse across the airfield."

Jacob grinned. "She used to have a horse – Captain?" He said with a question. Kally nodded, smiling. "Have you still got Captain?"

She nodded again. "Of course I have. He's fine!" She turned to Marelle. "I used to ride down the road by the airfield – used to say 'Hi' to Jacob as I passed by. Then one day I had an incident with a lorry right by the front gate. Jacob was there and saw it. He said he would open the gates each morning so I could ride across the airfield instead of round the road." She looked up to him, her eyes bright then she laughed. "As long as I stuck to the route – because of the shafts!"

Jacob smiled.

Marelle didn't.

"Then we became friends." She smiled.

'Till you moved away." Jacob added.

"And I gave you my address and I told you to keep in touch, but you didn't!" She pointed a finger playfully. 'Then I have been away with mum and dad for a few weeks ..." she briefly turned to Marelle. "We went to the States – once in a lifetime bucket list thing for dad – and I come home to have my neighbour describe you to a 'T'." She turned back to Jacob. "They said you had come to the house twice – looking for me? Sorry, it was a few weeks ago now ... I thought something must be wrong for you to turn up ..." She told them.

Marelle's mind was in a whirl. She didn't know of this person; who she was; where she lived – Marelle didn't understand the tale or how Jacob came to go to her house. Was she mistaken? Marelle looked at Jacob. He was looking down; he looked uncomfortable.

Kally smiled, laughed. "But it's good news ... isn't it?" She put her arms around Jacob again. "You came to tell me your news, didn't you?" She closed her eyes and hugged him tightly.

Marelle stepped forward.

"What's going on?" She asked. "I don't understand any of this. Jacob!" Her voice sounded stern. Jacob looked to her. He sighed. "I did go to Kally's house a few weeks ago – before we met again in the pub car park ..." He nodded his head, trying to indicate the intent of the matter to Marelle without divulging all of the details. Marelle stared at him; stared him down as she felt an anger rising within her. He had a talent for lying – she knew that now. He had a skill for hiding the truth – even from her.

"Look." He said. "She's come a long way – why not come in for a cup of tea – we can all have a chat."

Marelle's eyes did not move from him; she exhaled hot air through her nose.

"That would be nice." Kally smiled. "Could I possibly use your loo first though? Sorry!" She laughed.

"Sure." Jacob said. "Straight up the stairs – left at the top."

Kally smiled at him and at Marelle then squeezed past.

Jacob closed the front door as Kally took her tight little bottom in skinny dark blue jeans up the stairs. He had hardly got it closed before Marelle grabbed him by the arm and bundled him awkwardly and angrily into the kitchen. Pushing him right over to the window, she placed her hand in the centre of his chest.

"What the fuck!" She hissed. "Who is she?"

"She used to live here. Just like I said …"

"An ex?" She cocked her head. An ex he said he had never had.

"No!" He exclaimed, backing away from her. "She's a kid. You can see how old she is now – it was seven years ago!"

"Why did you go to her house? You ran away from *me* and went to *her*!" Marelle exclaimed in an angry, rasping whisper.

"Ssshhh!" Jacob answered. "It's OK."

"It is not OK!" Marelle replied to him in a voice deliberately low but urging to get louder. "Now she's here! Who the fuck is she?"

There was a look of defeat in his eyes, embarrassment, bewilderment. Said he had never had a meaningful relationship then this little blonde pixie pitches up and plasters herself all over him.

"I'll explain later. She was a friend – she was someone I could talk to who didn't pass judgement on me – she took me as I was and brought a little ray of sunshine into my life. I helped her out by letting her ride through here and she became someone I could talk to …"

"But why did you go to her house?"

"I don't know. She was the only other person I'd ever really spoken to – or confided in – I needed to speak to someone then … I thought it was worth a try …"

"You had me – right here to speak to but you chose to fuck off. Damn me, damn how I felt! Do you know what it's like to feel your heart breaking in two?" Marelle blurted those words out in a faltering whisper and saw the extreme hurt in his eyes at them.

"She's not a girlfriend. She was a kid – she means nothing to me, but she has come down here and we can at least be hospitable. You can beat me up about it afterwards."

She stared into his eyes, and he stared into hers. The seconds passed by, and they heard footsteps coming down the stairs. Jacob moved away.

"In here." He called to her.

"In here" Marelle silently mocked behind his back. Just who was she to him? Whatever it was he intended to keep it quiet for now. Too true that Marelle would break all hell loose around him later. She sighed and flicked the kettle on.

Kally walked in, smiling. Jacob gestured to a chair.

"Tea?" He asked. "Milk, no sugar?"

She laughed. "Yep. I'm still as sweet!"

Marelle stared at him. He flicked his eyes away. Kally smiled at her.

"I am so glad you to are together." She said. "He needs someone to look after him."

Jacob laughed.

"Jacob used to make me tea if he was in. I would ride past his caravan and if the door was open, I would stop. He would have a chat and he used to make me tea. I'd let Captain graze beside the caravan." She smiled, then looked up to Jacob. "How come you are living here?"

"Marelle inherited the house." Jacob explained.

"How long have you two been together?"

"Oh, about a year." He answered, making tea as Marelle stood watching silently. "What about you? What are you doing? Still live with your Mum and Dad?"

She nodded. "Yeah – studying to be a vet. I took a year out as dad was diagnosed with cancer."

"Oh, I'm sorry."

"He's ok. All clear now but he came up with a bucket list on the back of it. That's why we were away – he wanted to drive Route 66!"

Jacob laughed. "Wow!"

"I moved back in with mum and dad – save up for a deposit when I want to buy a place."

Jacob nodded. "Well done on the studying. You always said that was what you wanted to do."

She smiled. "I couldn't believe it when our neighbour told us about this tall, skinny guy on an old motorbike ..." She raised her eyes to him. "I thought of you straight away. He said you came back twice; said you wouldn't say much but looked sad! It had to be you!"

Jacob grinned a little.

"So the airfield is still here?"

He nodded. "Just. They began work a few weeks ago – moved a lot of stuff on. Then it's stopped again – they're moving the machinery away again ..."

"How many times has that happened?" She grinned.

Jacob shrugged. "Looked serious this time ... so what brings you down here?"

"I came to see you!" She replied. "I figured that if something was so important after seven odd years for you to come and knock on my door then I had better come and find you!"

Jacob put mugs of tea on the table. He handed one to Marelle with a warm smile on his lips and in his eyes. She watched him move back across the room and sit down in his usual chair. Marelle sipped the tea but remained standing against the worktop.

"I drove past the airfield and stopped at the gates. I couldn't see your caravan. I asked in the shop if you were still around …"

Marelle made a face and stared straight ahead of herself. Jacob did not respond.

"They said that they thought you lived here – but were very cagey! Do you still work on the farm part-time?"

"Well pretty much full-time now." Jacob added.

"Oh well done!" Kally smiled. "You still make good tea!"

"Did you drive all the way down, by yourself?"

"Well, we took my sister to Manchester University at the weekend then dad is at some aeroplane thing at Cambridge. I said I wanted to see a friend out this way – so I drove here while Dad is at Cambridge. It's his car …"

"Is he still in the RAF?"

She shook her head. "No, he's a partner in a flying school … retired just after we moved up there …"

Jacob nodded. "So, what about you? Anyone special in your life?" He enquired. "Or are you still young, free and single?"

Marelle pursed her lips.

Kally laughed coyly. "Well, there's Kristov."

"Kristov hey?" Jacob grinned, looking briefly at Marelle.

"Yeah – he was a newly qualified vet at the practice where I did work experience and I suppose you could say we are an item! He's Polish."

"Polish! Are you going to go to Poland? It's a long way!"

'So is Scotland!" She winked, playfully.

"We were in Cambridge the other day, weren't we Marelle?"

"Yeah." She replied with disinterest.

"I was at the dentist, having an implant to replace a broken tooth – that's why I've got a black eye!" He chuckled, pointing to it.

It hadn't been funny a few days ago, Marelle reminded herself.

"Oooh!" Kally grimaced. "I did wonder but didn't' want to ask I thought you'd come off your bike again!"

"No." He laughed.

"Is it ready for the wedding?" She questioned.

"What?"

'The tooth?" she grinned, pointing.

"Oh, no – well, yes, ultimately." He fumbled for words. "We haven't actually set a date for the wedding yet …"

"Oh come on Jacob! You can't do that!" She laughed, looking at Marelle. "You can't put a ring on her finger and not set a date!"

"We will!" He exclaimed. "Give us a chance!"

"Will, I get an invite?"

"Of course." He replied. 'I know where you live."

"And I know where you live too!" She looked a little longingly at him. Marelle shuffled her bottom against the worktop.

"I like your new haircut." Kally commented. "Looks cool ..." She laughed. "You haven't changed much just the hair!"

"Marelle did the hair." He told her.

"Oh, are you a hairdresser?" Kally exclaimed.

"Used to be." Marelle replied.

"He used to shave it all off or let it grow really long.' Kelly giggled. "Looks much better like that."

"Thank you." Jacob smiled. "But that's all down to Marelle."

"Super job!" Kally commented then smiled. "Oh, I'm so glad you are happy! I was worried about you, but I can see it's all good news."

"Yeah." Jacob nodded, looking up at Marelle with a languid depth to his eyes. Marelle stared briefly back at him then lowered her eyes away.

Kally was not short of talk. She spoke about her home and Captain; she told them about her part-time work in a bar; her recent month in America, travelling Route 66 with her parents and younger sister. Until eventually she sighed, smiled and stood up.

"I'd better go. It will take me about an hour to get to Cambridge."

Jacob nodded. "About that, if the traffic's not too bad."

Kally turned her head to the back window and suddenly saw the caravan.

"Oh, you've still got the caravan!" She exclaimed.

"Yep!" Jacob smiled. "She's still here."

Kally laughed. "It needs to be left on the airfield with a plaque on it." She made a gesture with her hand. "Stating Jacob was here!"

Jacob laughed. "I doubt it!"

"Well at least I managed to find you again! I'll take note of your address – we can keep in touch.' She explained. "And you know where I live ..."

She winked.

"I do."

Kally turned to Marelle, walked up and hugged her again. "I'm glad he's got you." She smiled.

Marelle managed a smile, nodded and the hug this time was not quite so tense.

Out in the driveway Kally was about to get into the black Volvo parked there as Jacob walked along studying it. The he suddenly said

"Wooah!" And he held up his hand. "You've got a flat tyre."

He walked closer to the car, pointing to the passenger side flat tyre.

"Shit!" Kally exclaimed. "I did go in a pothole up the road. I thought it was ok."

"It's completely flat."

Kally sighed. "I'll ring the AA. God only knows how long they will take to get here though."

"You don't need the AA." Jacob stated. "I can change it – do you have a spare?"

"Yes – dad would make sure of that!"

Jacob walked forward and held out his hand.

"Give me your keys. It won't take long."

"Are you sure? You've been at work all day … I can call the AA. It's what they're for."

"Give me your keys." He grinned. "You're not calling the bloody AA to change a wheel!"

"Thank you!" she grinned. "I forgot how practical you are!"

Jacob walked around the car and opened the hatchback. Then he paused and looked at them both standing watching him.

"Marelle, take Kally out the back, let her have a look at the airfield – she can see if she thinks it looks the same …"

Dusk was beginning to oust the light, and the sun was already sinking in the sky. The last place Marelle really wanted to be was walking across the boundary and onto the airfield with this girl who had already shared some of Jacob's past. Nonetheless, she did so, feeling a slight easing of the sense of threat she had initially felt.

"Wow! It's not really changed at all!" Kally beamed. "Of course, I'm not used to seeing it from here but it's pretty much the same." She turned around herself, looking in all directions. "Is the Thor site still there?"

Marelle nodded.

"Fascinated me. Imagine missiles right here – armed and ready to go at any second!" She replied. "So you inherited this house?"

"Yeah."

"… and was Jacob still living on here in his caravan?"

Marelle nodded then decided to elucidate. "I was in the house one night in the winter and the power went off. It came on everywhere else but not my house. I'd only just moved in and was still in disarray – I wasn't sure what to do. I'd spoken to Jacob previously so took a stab, walked over here and asked him for help."

"And he was your knight in shining armour?"

Marelle smiled. "Yeah. It took a while but the rest is history."

Kally smiled, warmly. "He really is a lovely guy – I used to see him as a bit of a big brother – I used to love visiting him."

"I asked *him* to marry *me*. Then, afterwards, *he* got down on one knee at the Thor site and asked *me* properly. He's given me his mother's engagement ring." She showed Kally, proudly.

Kally took her hand. "Oh my! That's beautiful – he showed me this ring – you must mean the world to him." Kally raised her eyes to Marelle as she released her hand.

Marelle smiled. "He means the world to me."

"I'm so happy ... he seems so happy." She replied. "Because he wasn't always happy."

They walked a few steps forward, onto the edge of the concrete of the runway.

"I used to ride up here." Kally said. "In the main gate, up past Jacob's caravan then over there and through the gap in the fence!" she smiled. "I often thought about Jacob after I left. Wondered how he was what happened to him. I gave him my new address and he said he would keep in touch – but he never did and as time went on I realised he probably thought I was just an annoying kid!" She looked across the expanse before her; the golden light touching her face just as it had theirs, many times. Kally sighed. 'Sometimes he was very down – I suppose he suffered bouts of depression, but I was just a kid and you don't see that – you want everyone to see the world through the same rose coloured spectacles that you do! I'd just try to make him laugh, make him smile." She laughed gently now. "I used to bake him cakes and bring them over on Captain – then we would have a mug of tea and a cake!" She smiled. "I'm so glad he's found someone like you!"

"I'm glad I found him." Marelle smiled.

"I couldn't believe it when our neighbour said some strange guy had been knocking on our door! Said he was a tall, skinny guy on a beat-up old motorbike – said he was quiet – wouldn't make eye contact with him, polite but seemed very melancholy. I knew straight away it was Jacob, but it worried me – something had to be wrong for him to come and find me ..."

Marelle said nothing. Folded her arms around herself and looked towards the sunset.

"But I can see he's happy!" Kally looked at Marelle again who in turn was watching the setting sun. She felt Kally's eyes on the side of her head. Eventually she smiled and turned to her who immediately looked away, looked to the sun then looked down.

"Look after him, won't you?"

Marelle was a little surprised at that comment – especially from someone who knew very little of Jacob's truths as far as she could tell.

Kally sighed. "There's one thing." She said, looking back at the sun. "It happened years ago – I was only probably about fifteen – maybe ..."

Marelle turned her head to Kally. Now she was not wanting to make eye contact.

"I should probably have told someone at the time but, I was still a kid – I didn't really understand – I was worried if I said anything then I would be stopped from coming to see Jacob ..."

Marelle felt a tension in her neck; suddenly realising that her jaw was tense as she now stared at the side of Kally's head.

"I've thought about it many times and since I've been older I can see it for what it was – it was probably a one-off moment of confusion and turmoil in his mind – but it's played on mine for years." She took a moment, took a shallow breath then continued. "But, in the circumstances it's probably something you should know." Kally was staring into the distance, watching the orange glow of the sun sinking.

TWENTY-FIVE

"It was a Sunday. I remember it like yesterday. It was this time of the year – there were stubble fields that I could ride on so I hadn't been through for a few days. Anyway, the gate was open, so I rode right through and up towards his caravan. The door was open but there was no sign of Jacob. I stood and called him a couple of times – expecting him to appear at the door with a mug and that grin." She paused. "He didn't appear – so I got off Captain and walked up to the caravan. I just about managed to walk up the steps and look inside while still holding on to Captain. I shouted Jacob again, but he didn't appear to be there. It was unusual as he always closed the door if he wasn't there. I called again, waited a bit then got back onto Captain and thought that I would ride up by the Thor site – Jacob often went walkabout up that end …"

Marelle was watching her every word of the journey. Kally had come across as overconfident but now she seemed unsure if she should carry on.

"So, I rode up there … up to where the three sites were – there were low walls, we would sit on them sometimes …"

Marelle nodded. Funnily enough, she knew them well too.

"I couldn't see him up there either. It was odd, he never left the caravan open if he wasn't close-by. I began to worry that maybe he had fallen down one of the holes he always warned me about. I rode back a bit, along the top road – I shouted his name a few times, waiting to listen in case I heard him call back or reply. I remember sitting there on Captain, in the silence – just sitting there on a horse on the runway, listening. Going forward a few steps and then calling again." She stopped, almost as if she was still considering continuing. "Captain saw him first!" She finally said. "Did a massive spook and nearly spun round on me – always trust a horse when they sense something they're not usually wrong!" For a second there was small smile on her face. 'Then I turned him back, looked where he was looking – right up in the oak tree, sitting on a branch, looking at me."

It wasn't what Marelle had quite expected the revelation to be and she felt some of the tension go out of her neck – then return when she too began to ponder the significance.

"I could see by the look on his face that all was not well. It didn't look like Jacob. I hadn't been around for a few days because of the time of year, and I had the stubble fields to ride on – but it didn't look like him. His face looked puffy, dirty, grazed – I could hardly see his eyes, but they looked blank. Somehow, I felt he was staring at me, but not seeing."

She looked down and carried on. "*What are you doing*?' I asked him' I remember half laughing because I was nervous and a little scared at his behaviour – then I saw the blue rope." Kally swallowed, looked to the sun then down. When she lifted her eyes again, she looked at Marelle. Kally's eyes looked languid, tearful. "He had a rope wrapped around his neck, snaking across the grubby white t-shirt he wore before it was twisted several times around the branch he sat on. He only had to slide off the branch, or jump down – his feet would not reach the floor …"

Her eyes met Marelle's full on. There was distress in them now when she guessed there had mainly been wide eyed innocence on that day, many years ago.

'I didn't realise at the time how close he was. I realised what he was trying to do, and I realised the implications but it wasn't until I thought about it as an adult years later that it occurred to me just how close he was to sliding off that branch and ..."

Kally looked away. Fought tears; emotions, fear. Marelle was starting to collect the thoughts that were spinning in her head as Kally continued.

"He was blind drunk, sitting in the tree with a rope around his neck and I was there, sitting on a horse. The child in me wanted to squeeze my legs into Captain's sides and ride away but there was also an adult starting to grow inside me that told me to stop him going through with this. I sat and talked to him, I went on and on about all of the things we had laughed about; all of the things we had ever spoken about; I reminded him of all the things he'd told me – just kept talking to him in the hope that my words would stop him letting go of that tenuous grip he had on life at that moment."

Marelle swallowed. She knew that feeling – when he had stood on the edge of the weir looking down into it – she'd felt that fear; that grip of helplessness of not being able to stop him if his intent took over.

'What ..." Her voice was elusive in her dry throat, "How ...*what* did you do?"

"Talked and talked. For hours. While he sat there. I wondered if I had a knife with me – to cut the rope – but I knew if I made a move he would jump. All I had were words. So I just talked, and talked ... all of the time watching him, his face, looking for that twitch in a muscle that would lead to his fall." She explained. "I don't know if his intention had been for me to find him or whether the thought of me finding him had been enough to stop him ... it was hours. Hours! I started feeling tired and Captain started getting fidgety, but I thought that the minute I walked away he would let go. It was before I had a phone – I couldn't get help as I would have to leave him. My parents would be missing me – what if it got dark? I got off Captain, tied his reins to a small tree then walked right up to the oak and stared up at him. He didn't look down but continued staring at the spot where I had been. I didn't know how to climb a tree. If I tried, he could easily jump." She drew a breath, paused. "I didn't want to see that. And it took me a long time to get that image out of my head." She fought back tears and did not break, just as she had not given in on that day. "I lay my head against the trunk and just stared up at him. I stopped talking and just stared – never took my eyes off him – wondering if I could catch him if he did jump – of course I know I couldn't – but I thought about it."

The same way that Marelle had thought about trying to stop him diving into the water.

"Then he just started unwinding the rope from the branch. Didn't comment or even change his expression much but I watched him unwind the blue rope until it was in his hands and not tied around the bough. I could feel my heart beating inside my chest; I could feel the wash of light headedness sweep over me but I did not – dare not – move or even show how quick my breathing was!

I looked up at him as he took the noose from around his neck and held it coiled in his hand. Silently he dropped it down from his hand onto the dry, dusty surface beneath the tree."

Marelle could almost feel the relief in Kally, even now. Kally sighed.

"I reached forward and picked it up – almost as if that would stop it ever happening again – as if this was the only piece of rope in the world and me having hold of it made everything safe. I looked up at him; he was staring across the airfield but with a sigh he looked down at me. He looked tired, lost … '*come on*' I said to him – slowly he climbed down; so carefully, so steadily until he stood next to me beneath the tree. I walked back with him to the caravan, leading Captain. We walked in silence. I held his arm and he didn't protest – we went back to the caravan, and he went inside, closed the bottom half of the door then turned to me. '*Are you alright?*' I asked. I remember he nodded then closed the top door too." She took a breath as if to steady herself, bring herself back to the present. "I worried what he would do, and I worried what I would find the next day when I rode through. But do you know what? I rode through and he was there, bright as a button as if it had never happened… he never mentioned it again – and neither did I."

Kally stopped talking. There was a moment's silence as Marelle absorbed every word of Kally's story.

"How old were you?" She finally asked.

"About fifteen. It was before I did my O levels, so I must have been around that age."

Marelle made a painful little face.

"I never told anyone. I never mentioned it to him, and he never said anything more about it. I didn't tell anyone because, well, I thought it would be bad for him and I was scared if I told anyone then they would stop me from coming over here."

Marelle shook her head.

"I just thought it was something that you ought to know." Kally continued. 'You know – if you are going to marry him. I know, I can see how much you mean to him … I've never told anyone else, never mentioned it. As a kid you gloss over things but as I've got older, I've thought about it a lot and realised how close he came that day and what it meant … then when my neighbour said he'd been at our house – I was terrified!"

"How did you find him?"

"Just drove down here. I expected the airfield to be long gone – was surprised when it looked pretty much the same. I drove past the gate, couldn't see his caravan so I asked in the shop."

"What did they say?"

"Said they thought he was living in Valspar on the moan road. Said they couldn't be sure but that was where he was last living. Said he didn't have a lot to do with anyone in the village …"

Marelle gave a small, sarcastic intake of breath.

"And I found your house and knocked on the door. I just wanted to make sure he was ok. And I can see he is!"

She smiled, a sweet, warm smile. Kally meant no harm.

"I never asked him about his past and he never told me – we were just here – he was him and I was me and each day was a new day. I think that's how he liked it." Kally hit the nail on the head – those words explained everything. Kally was no threat; Kally was another piece of the jigsaw of his past and, maybe even a corner piece.

"We'd better go see if he's changed that wheel." Kally suggested.

Marelle nodded but held out her arms to Kally and in the slowly setting sun across the airfield she took the young woman in her arms and hugged her with a love and warmth she hadn't expected to feel when Kally had turned up on their doorstep a couple of hours ago.

"Thank you." She said.

Kally stood back with a smile. "He's special. Look after him." She said. With a look in her eyes which showed she had passed on that baton which had burdened her for so long.

Jacob was standing staring into space when they walked back. It took him a moment to snap out of it, but he did so and smiled at them.

"All done." He said. "But get the puncture fixed – don't go driving all the way home without a spare!"

She laughed. "Of course Jacob! You know my Dad would never do that!"

"Are you driving straight back tonight?"

"No, we're stopping overnight in Cambridge."

He nodded.

"OK!" Kally finally smiled. "I'd better be off then."

Jacob smiled too.

She stepped forward and hugged Jacob. In his arms she looked so small; he held her tight and she pressed her face into him. Marelle watched and this time, she smiled too.

"You take care." Kally said releasing him before she turned to Marelle.

Hugging her in the same way, fingers hard against Marelle's back. "Look after him Marelle!" She said quietly to her in the embrace. "I guess I will see you at the wedding." She grinned as she stepped out of the hug.

"For sure!" Jacob nodded. "I'll make sure you get an invitation."

Kally smiled, blew a kiss then got into the car. With a small wave she pulled away down the road.

Marelle turned her head to Jacob. He had an apologetic look on his face as he sighed.

"I'm sorry. I should have mentioned her."

Marelle felt all of the emotions that had been held at bay while she was with Kally suddenly pour through the gate that was now open. She turned to him, embraced him with twice the force that Kally had.

"You don't have to explain … I understand."

And she buried her face in his clothes as her fingers clutched handfuls of the fabric. No words passed between them as they held one another in the driveway for the moments which it took till Marelle had squeezed the tears back into her eyes and she could look back up at him without them streaming down her face.

"She's sweet." Marelle commented. "She's lovely …"

"She's grown up." He smiled. "I certainly didn't expect to see her again."

That night when Marelle lay next to Jacob in her bed, she stared across at him in the darkness. His face in profile as his head rested squarely in the pillow beside her. He was asleep; she could hear him breathing softly; her feet were just touching his legs, and she had a hand on his upper arm. For once he was asleep and she was not. With the brief appearance of Kally fresh in her mind – like a guardian angel swooped down to remind Marelle there was, and always would be, thoughts in his head that she herself would never know or fathom. She acknowledged that today had been bizarre and the fleeting visit strangely unnerving for her. Kally had disappeared back into his history almost as quickly as she had appeared out of it – with a goodbye and a wave – probably never to be seen again.

Jacob slept on. His beautiful face at peace but still holding secrets from her. A million secrets; a million reincarnations of him that she felt right now she may never know; a million iterations – all of which she was now holding in her hand and all of which she knew she had to protect. Both from the world wielding spears and from Jacob himself.

There was a new anxiety in her the next morning when Jacob left for work. She stood at the door and watched him climb into the van with a smile; his packed lunch in a bag which he took with him. Marelle smiled in return – reminding herself that he was hers now and that she had nothing to worry about. But it was all still inside her.

It peaked later when her mind wandered to morbidly wondering which tree it had been. Then her heart faltered, and her breath caught when she remembered their conversation a while ago. The old, dead tree up by the Thor site; the one she had unknowingly called 'the hanging tree'. Her words had been a comment on a childhood conversation sparked off by the skeletal remains of the tree reaching into the sky on that day. Was that the tree? She would never know unless he told her; and she would not ask him.

Marelle had to live with that knowledge – bury it away within her. It was a tale from Kally – she didn't know for sure if it had happened – it might have been a childhood tale – embellished and distorted like folklore. Somehow though, she suspected it wasn't.

One truth that could not be bent out of shape was Wednesday arriving and she did not need the reminder Jacob gave her that morning.

"Seb is calling you today, isn't he?"

She nodded, hugging a mug of tea.

"What if he doesn't?"

"He will.' She stated. 'It's Seb. He'll call."

Jacob was looking at her with a quiet smile. The bruising on his face had lessened considerably today.

"It's fine. I know exactly what I am going to say to him."

"Stall him till the end of the day."

"Why?"

"He could get it on the market before tomorrow – someone else might get in before Devon has the chance to."

She pondered on that. "I doubt it. It's overpriced – it needs updating and it's got a potential concrete jungle about to spring up behind it …"

Jacob raised an eyebrow. "Estate agent said it was in a sought-after area."

Yeah, pretty little cottages. Not 1930s red brick houses …"

He stared at her.

"I'm not putting it down. I love this place. I'm looking at it from someone else's point of view."

Seb called at three thirty. Late enough if she could keep him talking for half an hour but she doubted she could. She didn't have a lot to say. He tried to make small talk, spoke about the weather, sounded awkward.

"Sell it." She said.

"Pardon?"

"Sell the house. Get it on the market. I'll have my half out of the total selling price."

There was a silence on the line for a moment. He had obviously been expecting her to plead wholeheartedly.

"I've thought about it. If you think it's the right time to sell, then sell it." She repeated.

"Good." He eventually said. 'That's good …"

"So when …?" She added.

"Well, soon – hopefully. I'll get it instructed tomorrow first thing.' His voice was speeding up now at the concept of her agreeing with him now being absorbed. "That's good. That's sensible Marelle, well done."

"What about viewings?"

"Oh the estate agent will handle all of that – don't worry. In fact, I know there is someone interested already – they might not even want to view!"

Marelle smiled. Yeah, funny that!

"Now you've got to get that shit heap of a caravan out of the back garden, start packing as well."

"No. I'll move when contracts exchange."

He laughed. "I don't think so Marelle. You need to start packing now and get out, now."

"No, I'll go when contracts have exchanged. What if I move out and it falls through? I'd rather stay until we know that's not going to happen."

He sighed. "Oh, ok. We'll cross that bridge when we come to it, but I don't want you stalling me – trying to play any clever little games!"

"Why would I do that?" she hissed. "Half of the money is mine – I don't want to delay getting it, do I?"

He sighed. "Ok, we'll leave it at that – for now.'

Marelle didn't say anything.

"I think it will be a pretty quick sale ..." He went on. "Well done Marelle – it's the sensible decision – you won't regret it – get this sold then you can get your life back on track.' He actually laughed.

She sighed.

"Well done!" He continued. "You won't regret this."

Despite his patronising tone, Marelle pulled a smile to herself. Tomorrow he would be saying that on the other side of his face!

When Jacob came home that night there *was* an uneasiness about what the next day would bring but it went unsaid.

"Seb must have spoken to the estate agents again because he is so sure that there is someone already interested in the house." Marelle imparted.

"They probably called him, trying to push him into putting it on the market."

"So what happens tomorrow?" She looked at Jacob, he stared back at her for a second then turned to look at the darkening skies outside the kitchen window.

"Devon will call the estate agents first thing – offer the full asking price – Seb will accept because he will be so excited that the house has sold so quickly then the ball will start rolling ..."

Marelle gave a little smile. "I can chip a bit in – I *want* to."

Jacob shook his head. "No, don't worry."

"But I do ..."

"It's fine." He smiled to her. "I'm happy – it's a good investment.' He walked over and hugged her to him. "In more ways than one!"

"Take my phone." She said in the morning as Jacob was getting ready to leave. "Just in case Devon calls ..."

"I don't need to. He won't call. He's just got to call, offer the full price and say that Mae wants to buy the property – it's a done deal. If he calls it will just be to confirm he's made the deal."

She pursed her lips and sighed.

"It's ok, I'll have the other phone with me – call me if there's an issue – but there won't be."

"Where will you be?"

"Not sure. Either in the workshop or might be out in one of the fields ... you can call me if you need to."

Jacob was either keeping totally calm over it despite how he really felt, or he was just completely assured that it was all sealed. Marelle didn't have that tranquillity. As the hands of the clock edged towards nine her heart was racing. She must have glanced at the clock a hundred times as the hands hardly moved. Right now, she told herself, right now someone they hardly knew was buying this house around them. By half past nine panic had set in and her hands felt clammy. She called Jacob.

He took longer to answer than she expected, her voice was breathless when he did.

"He hasn't called." She exclaimed immediately.

"Well that's ok. He's just doing what we asked him to do. That's fine. Stop worrying!"

"Where are you?"

"Up near Twight's Corner – just ploughing a bit of set-aside in around the edge."

"Where's Twight's Corner?"

He laughed. "A bit on from the Church – where the T-junction is."

"I need to learn all of these places." She said with a small smile.

"You do!" He laughed. "Now you are going to be a property owner here."

Marelle laughed to herself as she told him to take care and that she would see him later. Then the phone rang in her hand just as she was putting it back in her pocket. She didn't recognise the number but answered it immediately.

"Hello."

"Good morning, this is Devon DaSousa – is that Marelle?"

"Yes!" She exclaimed, almost breathlessly. "Hello …"

"Hello. Is Jacob with you?"

"No, he's at work."

"We have a slight complication with the house purchase. It's ok, these things happen but we need to convene …"

"I can go to where he is – we can ring you back there – he's only five minutes away." She said quickly, her heart quickening now. "What's the problem?"

Devon sighed slightly. "I have put your full price offer to the agents, but they had a second offer of the full price after yours but before they'd told the vendor. Rather naughtily they passed both offers on to the vendor – I know why – and due to there being such interest they have advised the vendor to put the house into a bid situation …"

"What does that mean?"

"It means they are looking for a counter offer from you *above* the asking price; they'll do the same to the other party and so on until one party drops out …"

Marelle sat there in silence. She swallowed. Her breath was coming quickly now.

"What?" She asked. "Who else wants the house? Who is it?"

"We don't know that. Do you want to make a counter offer?"

"Yes!" She exclaimed. "But I need to go to Jacob."

"That's ok. Go and see him then call me back on this number."

Marelle was crying as she immediately called Jacob.

"Hi." He answered.

"Jacob!" She cried with tears in her voice. "Devon called, there's a problem."

"What?"

A sob came out first. "Someone else has offered the full price on the house. They want us to bid a higher offer."

"What! They can't do that!"

"It seems they can. Can we?" Her voice sounded small.

"Yes –" Jacob answered. "But we offered what they were asking."

"I know and we offered first but then someone else made the same offer and of course, Seb being Seb, has seen an opportunity." She gave a little gasp of a cry. "I need to come to you – we can call Devon together …"

TWENTY-SIX

Jacob had just pulled the tractor alongside the verge by the road. She'd driven up there in a blind panic. Why had this happened? She had said yes to selling and she had opened them up to this. Someone else was after their house; they had no right to it! She wished she had stalled Seb now, been awkward, said no.

Jacob opened the cab door as she approached – he held out a hand and almost lifted her up. Marelle had tears streaming down her face as he held her arm and sat her to the side of the seat in the tractor.

"I'm sorry." She sighed.

"It's ok. These things happen." He smiled. "Let's call Devon."

They both sat in the tractor cab, the phone on speaker and that house and their home in the balance.

"Hi Devon." Jacob said in that voice which he had within him for such situations as this.

"Hello Jacob. Has Marelle explained the situation?"

"Yes, she's here with me. What do we need to do?" Jacob questioned in reply, looking at her. He gave a smile.

"If you want to make a counter offer, I would suggest you make a substantial enough one to let them know you are serious. I'd go in at three fifteen."

Marelle watched Jacob's nostrils flare slightly as he took a breath but stayed calm. "Ok." He said. "We'll offer three fifteen."

"Alright. I'll put that offer to them. Stay close to your phone." Devon advised.

"We're right here. We're not going anywhere." Jacob stated.

They sat in silence except for Marelle sniffing. There were no words between them right now. Both staring at the freshly turned earth right by the tractor.

Marelle had never been in a tractor before but in the circumstances the experience was not an enjoyable one.

The phone rang. Jacob hit the green button and put it on speaker.

"Hi Devon."

Devon sighed. "I think we may be up against a cash bidder with deep pockets." He warned. 'They've counter offered three two five."

"Three fifty." Jacob said, no hesitation, not even looking at Marelle. She stared at him.

"Three hundred and fifty thousand." Devon confirmed.

"Yes." Jacob said, finally lifting his eyes to Marelle then sighed when he cut the call.

"We're going to lose this ..." Marelle said.

"No, we're not!"

"Who else wants this house?" She asked. "Hey? Who else wants our home so much?"

Jacob shrugged.

"It's *our* home!" she stated tearfully.

The phone rang. She held her breath.

"– Devon." Jacob greeted.

"Jacob." He echoed. "I'm sorry, they've countered three seven five."

There was silence in the cab. It seemed to last forever; Marelle had to take a breath.

"Ok." Jacob said quietly.

"Four might be a limit – might be enough to fend them off. I sense it would be their next bid."

Jacob pondered on it for at least two seconds then spoke while looking at her.

"Four hundred thousand." He said.

"Are you sure Jacob?"

"I'm sure. Four hundred thousand." He repeated to Devon.

"Shit!" Marelle remarked as they waited. "Why the fuck did I do this?"

"It's not your fault." Jacob replied, reaching over to place his hand on hers.

This time the call from Devon did not come back as swiftly as it had done before. After a few minutes Marelle sighed, very audibly.

"He hasn't called." She stated. "What does that mean? And how do we know this is genuine – how do we know that?"

The phone rang. Jacob answered.

"Hi."

Devon sighed. "I'm sorry, we have a serious bidder." He answered, pausing.

Marelle raised her tear-filled eyes to Jacob. Neither of them said a word.

"They've gone up to four fifty." Devon said.

Marelle sobbed; Jacob sighed.

"This is extraordinary behaviour. I'm not sure what is happening here …" Devon continued.

"How do we know there is another bidder?" Marelle suddenly asked in a tearful and elevated voice. 'What if it's just the vendor pushing the price up?"

"We don't, to be truthful but I would be surprised if that was the case it would be more than the estate agent's business was worth to engage in practises like that. Devon explained. "However, do you want to continue?"

'Yes!" Marelle exclaimed. Jacob did not reply immediately but he was staring at her when she raised her eyes. It suddenly felt very hot in the cab, and she realised that she had no idea how much money Jacob actually had or where he was getting it from.

"Yes." Jacob finally said, but quietly.

"What's your offer?"

"Four seven-five." Jacob said.

Davon paused. "I'm not sure it's enough, their last bid was fifty k. It may have been a last-ditch attempt with whatever they had left – it might just be a gesture to let you know you're fighting a losing battle. We can't second guess I'm afraid. Do you want me to propose four seven-five?"

"Yes." Jacob replied.

'OK."

The phone clicked and he was gone again.

'It's too much, isn't it?" Marelle asked.

"It's a lot more than this house is worth."

She sighed. "I wouldn't put anything past Seb. He's greedy and he's self-centred."

"Something is going on." Jacob stated quietly.

Then Marelle was suddenly struck by one point. A smile almost came to her face.

"Hey! Remember, I get half of whatever the house makes – so whatever we bid, we will get half of it back. So, effectively we will only pay half of what we bid!"

"Good point." Jacob agreed.

"So we could bid up to six twenty?"

"Marelle." He shook his head. "The house is not worth six twenty. We could get somewhere much better for that amount of money …"

But it wouldn't mean anything to us! This house is *our* house." She emphasised. "It was Frankie's house …"

Jacob sighed again. He was digging deep. Marelle shivered. The phone rang. Jacob answered. Devon sighed.

"They have bid five hundred." He stated. "I'd advise you to stop."

Neither of them spoke. Marelle looked away and stared out if the window. The sun was glinting off the freshly turned earth, still in the smooth, flat shape that the plough had carved. The earth violated, all laid open; a scar that would not heal. She felt like that right now. Her hopes and dreams were disappearing like the dead straight lines of the ploughed soil, running into the distance, along the headland, past one of those white posts that were dotted about. What were those white posts? They had numbers on them. Jacob had not explained and she had not noticed until now.

"Five fifty." Jacob said.

She snapped her head round and stared at him. He was not looking at her.

"Are you sure?" Devon asked. "I don't know when they will be prepared to stop."

"Five fifty." Jacob said again.

He didn't raise his eyes to her as they sat in silence after that call had ended. Marelle felt hot, then cold. She shivered. Her stomach rumbled.

Devon called.

"I asked the estate agent who the other bidder is. They have said they cannot tell me but have assured me they are genuine – they've countered five seven five."

"Well they're reining it in a bit more now. Six hundred!" Jacob said.

Marelle took an intake of breath.

Devon paused.

"Jacob, Marelle – maybe it's time to bow out. That's twice the value of the house." Devon told them, his voice stern. "My advice is for you to stop now. This is over half a million pounds. Please do not get carried away with numbers or bidding – remember those numbers represent money – money you will have to find and pay – it is the best part of a million pounds. Please, stop and reconsider ..."

"Six hundred thousand." Jacob said immediately.

Devon sighed. Marelle looked at her feet.

"Are you sure?" Devon questioned. "I'm sure." Jacob said.

"I'm happy to bid for you but I want to make it clear that this is against my advice." Devon added.

"I understand. Six hundred." Jacob answered.

"OK." And he was gone again.

Marelle looked up at Jacob. She sniffed as her eyes met his. He looked serious.

"I'm scared." She said.

Jacob smiled. "What of?"

"Losing this."

"We won't lose it." He replied.

There was a prolonged pause. Jacob sat staring out of the window of the cab; pretty relaxed, one leg up, one arm hanging casually down. As relaxed as you like with the best part of a million quid hanging over his head. They would get half back, but they still had to find it first. And Devon had spoken to them like they were two teenagers – he'd told them to stop! He didn't understand. He didn't have to understand.

The phone rang. Jacob answered.

"Hi."

"Hello." Devon replied. 'They're not lying down over this. Six fifty. They've got deep pockets and long arms! Are you sure you fully understand what you're doing?"

"Yes, I understand." Jacob had laughed. "We want this house. It's *our* house!"

Marelle watched. Sometimes he looked so young and wildly innocent; sometimes he looked so old and wise. He flitted between the two. She felt her lip tremble and tears well behind her eyes.

"Try six sixty." Jacob said.

"Six sixty?" Devon repeated. "They have been countering in fifty thousand handfuls."

"Six sixty. See what they say." He replied.

"Ok." Devon answered and was gone.

"Jacob ..." Marelle sighed. "It's a lot of money ..."

He nodded.

The phone rang.

"Six seven five." Devon said.

Jacob laughed. He laughed. Marelle began to wonder if he was truly of sound mind and for a second looked to him, stunned. She saw Jacob; steady and true as ever.

"Six eight five."

Devon was done with warnings and questions. He went off again.

Not a word was exchanged between them in the cab as they waited.

Devon replied. "Ok, they've countered six nine five."

"Then we'll bid seven hundred." Jacob said.

Marelle furrowed her brow and narrowed her eyes at him. The numbers were scaring her now. The wait was much longer. The two of them sat there. Five minutes passed. Nothing. Ten minutes passed.

"What's happening?" Marelle said, worriedly.

"They're considering why they are having to pay over seven hundred thousand pounds for a house that's worth three hundred." He quipped.

"Are you?"

"No." He replied succinctly.

The phone rang. Jacob looked to her before he answered with an intense, deep stare which told he may not be able to go on. It was the first time she had seen that in his eyes.

"Hi." He said.

Devon paused. He sighed. "That is probably the most extraordinary thing I have been involved with. I don't totally agree with this or understand what is going on, but I promised you I would help you with this strange request – which, may I add, also involves my sister – who talked me into doing this. I don't know you two; I don't need to know you – you are clients – but, with hindsight, I would not take this on again." He stopped talking. Left a few seconds of silence. "It's yours." He stated. "They can't go on. Seven hundred thousand pounds – the final and winning bid."

Jacob stared at nothing; moved his eyes to her and appeared to flicker back to reality. He swallowed.

"Your offer has been accepted. The house is sold subject to contract. Once contracts are exchanged you can officially take possession of the house – well, my sister can!"

"And when will that be?"

Devon laughed. "Hold up. I need to let this sink in! It's a cash sale, no chain, no complications – maybe three or four weeks."

"So what now then?"

"We'll sort that out with the agents and the vendor ..."

Jacob nodded. "So it can't be taken away from us now?"

"Until contracts exchange, the deal is not done. But I suggest you get that seven hundred thousand and my fee together into the bank account so we can move as fast as possible once it starts going through."

Once the phone call had finished, they sat there in silence, a kind of weariness about them both. They had been there just over an hour. Finally, Jacob sighed, Marelle shifted her bottom on the hard plastic she was sitting on.

'Well, I'd better get on." He said.

"We've been through all that and it's still not ours."

"It is!" He smiled. "We're not going to pull out, are we? And I'm sure Seb is not going to turn down that amount of money …"

"I don't trust him. Until that contract is signed, I don't trust him." She said.

"As long as he doesn't find out we're behind it. Play it cagey …"

She sighed. "He'll call in a minute. He won't be able to contain himself. He'll be looking forward to that phone call – and so will I!"

"He'll probably try to make us move out"

"I've told him already. I'm not moving until contracts exchange … it's part of the deal."

"Hmm!" Jacob laughed softly, sarcastically.

He reached across and took her hand, guiding her to stand up. "I'd love for you to stay here but I'll get in trouble if I do."

He touched her face, smiled to her. He kissed her with that tenderness that was so inexplicably Jacob.

"Hey, we just bought a house!" He whispered.

"There's no turning back now …" She smiled.

"I was never going to anyway." He told her.

Going back to the house was strange. Everything seemed different. It *felt* different; she didn't know why but suddenly found herself staring at random things – a plug socket, a light switch and reminding herself that this was theirs now.

Then, at ten past three, the call came. Seb's number popped up on her phone – she had never saved it under his name, but she knew his number by heart. She paused, composed herself and answered.

"Hello?"

"Well for once in your life it appears that you made a good decision." Seb said straight away.

"What!"

"Your decision to take half of the price of the sale."

Marelle did not reply.

"The house is sold – subject to contract – but I am confident it will all go through quickly. I accepted an offer this morning – it's great news Marelle! Guess what I've managed to get for that pile of bricks?"

"I've got no idea." She replied dryly to his overly happy voice.

"It's unbelievable!" He laughed. 'Totally unbelievable! I knew we had one party interested but wow! Someone popped out of the woodwork, and I let them slit each other's throats! Seven hundred thousand! There are some very rich and very stupid people out there – and we were lucky enough to find one of them!"

"Seven hundred thousand?" She asked, surprised that he had not told her a lesser amount.

"Seven hundred thousand!" He repeated. "And you can have your share of that ... to make a decent life for yourself instead of dossing around with that fucking waster."

Marelle paused. Could Seb have possibly got more insults into such a short space of time? She knew however, that she had to bite her tongue – sharply.

"Now you, young lady, need to start packing and get your bottom out of that house."

"Not until contracts have exchanged."

"No. Now! I want it all out as soon as possible."

"No Seb. When contracts exchange. I'll move out on that day."

"No, no, no. get packing now – we don't want to jeopardise this in anyway."

"No! I'm not going through all of that in case it falls through. It's not done until contracts have exchanged. I'll move out on that day. I've not much to move ..."

Seb sighed. "And that fucking pikey wagon too!"

"I'll make sure the caravan is re-located."

Seb laughed, sarcastically. "Where are you going?"

"What do you care?"

"You can come to ours – you know you can." He offered, plaintively.

It was her turn to laugh. "No. Not ever again Seb. I'll find somewhere – don't worry about me."

"You should be happy. This is unbelievable – it's over twice the value of the house!"

"I haven't got the money in my hand yet and I've got to find somewhere else to live."

He gave an unpleasant little laugh. "Your choice."

Marelle chose to ignore before it angered her further.

"Who's the buyer?"

"Single female, cash buyer apparently – must be rolling in it – had some highfalutin lawyer bidding for her. God only knows why she wants to live there."

"Who was the other bidder?"

Seb laughed. "The developers! Got shot up the arse though and we filled our pockets!"

"The developers?" She asked.

"Yes. They approached me a little while back – so I knew we had a buyer … didn't go to plan for them though! This other bidder kicked them right out of the ballpark!" Seb was chuckling.

"Why did the developers want this house?"

"Access." He said. "I don't suppose you know … since this heritage site thing has reared its head they have had to make a few changes to their planning application – the only access they will have is where the main gate to the airfield is. There has been a lot of objections to the new plans and the prospect of having all that heavy traffic right through the village. They needed a new access off the main street – a "back" way in …"

"But there wouldn't be room to get access past the house." Marelle commented.

"The wouldn't go past it – they would demolish it and make a new road going in. They offered me two fifty straight the other week but I told them I wanted to put it on the market – they could make me a better offer … seven hundred thousand was obviously a bit too much – like chucking good money after bad."

"Demolish this house?" She mumbled.

"Yeah."

"No!" She gasped. "You nearly sold this house to someone who was going to knock it down?"

"Yeah." He laughed.

"Why?"

"Their money is as good as anybody's – what does it matter? We've sold it, it's not ours anymore …"

"I care!" she exclaimed.

"Grow up!" He reprimanded. "I might still sell it to them if this falls through."

"This place has history!" She almost cried. "They can't knock it down!"

"Well hopefully the new owner won't be tempted to sell it on to the developers – then it will be a happy ending! Won't it? I don't know how you get so attached to inanimate objects."

She sighed. It would not fall through, not over her dead body would it ever fall through.

"Talking about inanimate objects …" Seb was continuing. "I don't want any of his stuff or him in that house as from right now. I'll let you stay until contracts exchange but I want him and everything he owns which is obviously very little – out of that place right now!"

"Don't worry, I promise. Any of Jacob's possessions will be in their rightful place by the day contracts exchange."

"What's that shit about! No, now. I want him out, now – and that bloody caravan – and that big fucking white van … it's an eyesore!"

Marelle sighed. Leave it. She would say too much if she let him keep goading her. And now she knew both how the house had made such a stupidly high price and what the consequences would be should Seb find out what they had done. The very bricks and mortar around her ears was at stake.

"Make the right choice in this Marelle. Don't waste this opportunity. Do something worthwhile with the money." Seb was lecturing. "I'm sorry it had to come to this but it's for the best. It was a blessing being left this place, but it has turned into a curse. Now it's done, it will give you a chance to move on."

"Yeah." She replied. "I guess so."

There was a pause from Seb, a kind of virtual fist pump in the air from him. Marelle sensed it. Deep inside there was one from her too but it had to remain hidden.

When Seb finally went off the phone Marelle immediately wanted to call Jacob. There were tears in her eyes and a sob in her throat. She stood looking around herself – out to the garden ... and beyond. They wanted to raise this place to the ground – this house, this place where Frankie had lived – and disappeared from – this place where she had first made love to Jacob – albeit angrily! This place where he had sat in the kitchen in their early days and she had cut his hair. All of those moments and memories reduced to dust and rubble. Lost; forgotten. No. It would not happen, ever, as long as she was alive. And she would not call Jacob now; she would wait until he returned home this evening. He was off work again on Friday for the final dental appointment and he had spent a large proportion of his working day negotiating the future of this place – just as she had – so she would not disturb him further.

All day she looked at the house. Looked out at the driveway and the access to the airfield at the back. It was the perfect position to run a road through. She, and Jacob, had obviously not had the foresight to see that and it made her shudder. To think if they had not been able to bid – or worse, not been able to match and shake away the other bidder – then within weeks, days, it would have been gone. Flattened, destroyed, tarmacked over and in years to come no-one would have ever known it had been there. She sighed, tearfully, felt the house breath and live around her; heard it settle and creak against the earth and felt the happy spirits of Frankie's family, and Jacob as a child, reside here from the time many years ago.

While thinking about that she looked out across the airfield. That wide, open, beautiful space. That too had once been in the same position. That had been a bustling hive of activity – an enclosed village within a village. Right there, lives, deaths, laughter, tears. Vehicles racing around, people going about their work – silent decisions. There would have been planes originally – Jacob had said – taking off and landing. Deployed on missions during the war – in defence of this country, this village, Jacob's family, ultimately her family too. Thor missiles had been placed there – reaching into the sky with yearning fingers, wanting to fly. All of that now gone, half forgotten. Forever.

Did Jacob sense that and feel that way too? Was it not only Frankie he had sought to protect but also the flickers of the past?

TWENTY-SEVEN

Still staring out of the window with thoughts swooping around her head like the swallows over the airfield in the summer, her phone vibrated then rang in her pocket. Her own picture and phone number from years ago appeared. It was Jacob. She had to change that picture!

"Hi." He said. "OK?"

"Yeah, fine!" She replied brightly, keeping her thoughts to herself.

"I'll be a bit later than usual so don't worry. I'm just finishing something off and I did spend over an hour on the phone this morning!"

"Oh, OK! No problem. I'll wait till you get here ..."

'Heard from anyone?"

She sighed. "Only Seb."

"Oh?"

"Yeah, well ... there are a few *interesting* things that came out of that conversation but nothing for us to worry about – as long as he doesn't find out who has really bought the house."

"He won't. I promise." Jacob said with a calm and level voice. "See you in a bit."

"Love you!" She called as he rang off.

Marelle sighed. Looked out of the window again, still holding her phone. She brought it up to her face once more and called Bella. She would be just about home by now.

"Hiya!" Bella replied.

"Hi Bella."

"What's up?" She asked, slightly surprised that Marelle had called her.

"The house?" Marelle said, a little blankly.

"Oh shit! Yes! I'm sorry – I've just come out of work – well?"

Marelle paused, took a breath, let cool air pass through her nostrils. We bought it!" She finally said. "Well, technically Mae bought it!" And could not help a smile from finally breaking on her face as those words and their meaning passed from her lips.

Bella squealed in delight. "Oh wow! So it's all yours!"

"Yes, well, will be, when contracts have exchanged – as long as Seb doesn't find out before."

"Was Devon ok?"

"He was brilliant ... only someone else was after the house and Seb, being Seb, had us bidding for it ... it was horrible but eventually we won! Cost a lot more than we anticipated though!"

"Oh wow! But that doesn't matter, does it? It's *yours* now!"

"Nearly. Is Mae there?"

"No, no. She's at work. I haven't spoken to her today. We don't live together you know!" Bella laughed. "She'll be glad though ..."

"I'd like to thank her."

"I probably won't see her until the weekend." Bella replied.

"Want to come down? You can both come and stay?"

"Erm ... I think she's working this weekend. Her shifts change on Sunday – anyway, I'm not sure we are at that stage in our relationship yet – you know – going away for the weekend ..."

"Oh." Marelle answered, slightly confused. Bella was normally a fast worker. "Is everything alright?"

"Yes! Great!" Bella smiled. "Just *different* – If you know what I mean!"

Marelle smiled. In a way she did; in a way she didn't. "Good." Marelle said. "I'm glad she could help – I think we may have lost it otherwise."

Marelle nearly poured her heart out about the developer but stopped short. Maybe it was wrong to let on she knew that. This was such a tense and tentative moment that she did not even want her breath touching the words to have any implications.

"I'm so happy for you both." Bella laughed. "That house means so much to you, doesn't it?"

"It does." Marelle confirmed but they were small words. It meant so much more.

"Maybe we can come the week after next?" Bella added, sensing she may have sounded too hesitant before, now she sounded enthusiastic.

"OK." Marelle smiled. "Oh hang on. I think we are going to a Yellow Son gig that weekend."

"What!" Bella exclaimed with a laugh.

Yes, what indeed? Marelle also thought to herself. The very night which Jacob hoped to reveal his existence to Chas and throw himself upon the ensuing shit storm.

Marelle swallowed as her mouth became dry.

"What's going on?" Bella grinned. "There's no stopping him now!"

"No. I know." Marelle replied. "It does feel like that."

"I searched some more ... on the internet." Bella continued. "There's a lot. He was quite a little superstar, wasn't he?"

"A bit." Marelle smiled, "You haven't ....:

"No!" Bella exclaimed. "Not a soul. I *promised*."

Marelle sighed.

Bella laughed. "I don't know! You're marrying a rock star and I'm a lesbian!"

They both laughed together but Marelle still felt that stab of anxiety racing through her. The more she learned about Jacob, the more she worried.

"One step at a time." She said, more quietly, almost to herself.

Bella heard it nonetheless. "Huh!" She exclaimed. "I'm trying!"

Marelle was trying too. Trying to stop that awful dull ache of anxiety which seemed to be with her so much lately. It never used to be like that. She had wanted for so long to capture this butterfly, now she had it safely in her possession she worried constantly about it beating it's pretty wings against the sides of the jar. The downside of possession was the fear of loss but one could not be enjoyed without the other clutching at your heart.

It was seven before Jacob walked in. She had heard the van come into the drive and had turned to await his arrival as she stood in the kitchen. It was virtually dark outside – a long way from the heady days of summer when they had walked among the golden, bobbing heads of flowers and laid in the long grass on the airfield. She sighed as the front door opened and closed, leant her bottom against the worktop as his footsteps made their way along the hallway.

When he walked out of the dark hallway and stood in the kitchen doorway with the light on his face, his beautiful dark eyes raised to her with their utter kindness and humility portrayed in their velvet depths she felt the fragility of that butterfly again, beating its wings against the glass.

His face was smeared with oil or grease – or dirt, and he looked tired; in his hand he had the rucksack she had packed him lunch in that morning.

He smiled, his lips just flexing.

"Yeah." She sighed.

He walked in, twisted his mouth away, dropped the rucksack down by the door just as he always did. His eyes were on her the whole time. She watched him, flicked her eyes away, flicked them back again. Then she was suddenly overwhelmed by a wave of tears and sadness that had been residing, waiting within her since that telephone call with Seb.

Marelle covered her face with her hands, let the sob rise inside her. Jacob sighed, moved over to her, placed his hands on her upper arms.

"What did Seb say to you?" He asked, holding her.

She shook her head.

"Nothing." She removed her hands from her face, took a shaky breath, looked away. "It's not what he actually said – it's what he told me."

"What did he tell you? What's wrong? What's he done?" Jacob asked quietly.

"The other people ..." She began. "The other people who were bidding for the house – I know who it was."

Jacob gave her a small smile, tilted his head back a fraction. "Does it matter?"

"No ... well, yes!" She exclaimed, alert in her voice.

"Why? It's ours now ... it doesn't matter ..."

Marelle swallowed.

"It does because, the other bidder was the developers."

"The developers?"

She nodded. "We were bidding against them because – do you know what they wanted to do?"

"Why did the developers want this place?"

She looked directly to him. "Because they are having issues with access to the site – they wanted this place so they could demolish it and make a new way in." She swallowed, sobbed.

"Knock it down?" He questioned.

"Yes." She nodded. 'If we hadn't have won then they would have flattened this place; demolished it and everything with it ... everything – all those memories ... Frankie's memories ... our memories ... it would be gone and we came so close Jacob, we came so close to losing this house, this place, forever ..."

Jacob shifted, stared at her, looked down at her, his head bowed. "No, we didn't." he said with a little smile. "We didn't, I could have gone higher ..."

"Higher?"

He nodded. "I wasn't going to let them win – whoever they were. You wanted the house – I was going to buy it."

She stared at him as she spoke in reply, his hands on her arms, a glint in his eyes and a smile on his face.

"They had already approached Seb apparently – that's why he put it on the market because he's greedy. They had offered him a price, but he thought he could get more if he put it on the market and was trying to push them up ... and he did."

"And so did you."

"But it cost *you* more."

"Doesn't matter." He said.

Marelle sighed and slid her arms around him. He was so quiet and gentle; she felt him and held him in her arms.

'I've been upset about that all afternoon – I can't imagine what would have happened if we hadn't been able to buy this house – I thought it was safe; that it would be here forever but so easily it could have been smashed to the ground."

"But it won't be. It *is* safe. Soon it will be legally and totally ours."

She lay her head against him with a sigh and realised there was a new facet to him that she had not seen before. Marelle had witnessed it rising. She had glimpsed it standing in the shadows at the periphery. Now it had stepped out into the open, revealed its strength right in front of her – flexed it's muscles and showed Marelle. Jacob could be amazingly dismissive at times – now he could ignore what he did not want to believe and run away from it with flags and streamers flowing brightly behind him. What had filled her own heart with fear and anxiety all afternoon was simply not worth thinking about in his eyes right now. It simply did not matter because soon the house would be theirs – end of.

He held her, gently kissed the top of her head and stroked her hair while she sensed him gathering himself into an arrowhead, forging forwards, towards what he perceived to be his pot of gold on the distant horizon. She felt his body metamorphosising from Jacob to Ezza – and she still had to get to know Ezza.

She lay in bed next to him later that night and worried about this new delusional level of confidence that Ezza was gleefully projecting ahead of Jacob. She could feel it seeping out of him – but at the same time, when he raised himself up on his arms above her and bowed his head down to her, there was still a gentle innocence portrayed on his face that reminded her of the teenager he had once been. The young adult she had never known but whom she could so clearly see in him now. She reached up and kissed him, staring into those bottomless, bewildered eyes.

"Love you." She said.

It was that anxious teenager that she sat beside in her car on their way to the dentist again on Friday morning. The last experience had been enough to avoid going back. Jacob was happy with the temporary tooth and had skirted the idea of not attending.

'It won't be like last time." Marelle reassured him. "The nasty bit is all done – it'll just be swapping over to your bespoke tooth ... surely?"

"This one is fine ..."

"But you've paid for the other one – this one may not last, it's only a temporary one – plus you need after care just in case something goes wrong."

"Nothing's going to go wrong, is it?" He worried.

"I doubt it. But if you don't go back, they won't be willing to help ..."

"They'll be willing if I pay them!" he exclaimed. 'I don't want it to be bruised and swollen next week."

"It probably won't be." She said. "I doubt he's going to do much more than take one out and put a new one in!" Marelle looked at him as he drove. He was looking straight ahead. His forehead looked tense.

"Anyway, if there is any bruising, we can cover it up with make up."

"I'm not wearing make up!" he laughed.

She smiled. "I don't think anything is going to get bruised today. Do you want me to ask if I can come in the room with you?"

"No." He replied. "You'll have to cut my hair – before next Saturday – I need to make it look like Ezza's."

She grinned. "Well, there are plenty of photos, pick one and I'll do my best."

"It needed to be a lot longer really ..."

"Then you shouldn't have made me cut it all off!" She exclaimed remembering that day before Frankie's funeral where he had insisted. She had shed tears as she'd cut it close to his head and taken away that look which she now knew was purely from Ezza. "It'll be perfect. I'll make it look right." She added, not wanting to add in any way to his anxiety today.

"I need to go to the storage unit as well – I need to dig out some clothes." He said, almost thinking aloud.

Marelle glanced at him, smiled then glanced away. She hoped he was right in what he was thinking and doing.

When he pulled up in front of the dentists in Cambridge, both of the parking spaces were taken and there was nowhere else to park. Jacob pulled across behind the two cars and glanced at the time. They had been held up slightly on the road just before Cambridge and were on time but not by enough to allow them to go looking for parking spaces in a city that was so very car adverse.

"I'll go in. You drive round the block. They'll probably come out in a minute or two." He suggested looking across at her.

Marelle sighed a little, not really wanting to be forced into doing that.

He stared at her.

"OK." She finally said. "Are you ok going in on your own?"

"Yeah, yeah." He nodded, undoing the car door and beginning to get out.

Once round at the driver's side, Marelle stood face to face with him for a second. Then she tiptoed up and kissed him once, on the lips.

"I'll come in as soon as I can park."

"Ok." He nodded.

"Well go on then!" She smiled, wanting to see him actually go into the building before she got into the car and drove away again.

Driving around the block was a nightmare. The avenue where the dentist was located was relatively quiet but at both ends it led onto a busy thoroughfare. There was a roundabout at one end with multiple exits and a complicated set of traffic lights at the other. To 'drive around the block' meant sitting at the traffic lights for about five minutes, turning right, travelling down a busy dual carriageway to the roundabout then negotiating three lanes of heavy traffic to get back up the avenue again. On her first pass nothing had changed so she frustratedly drove around again. On the second pass it was the same but as she approached for the third time there was someone at one of the cars parked in the two parking spaces at the front. Marelle stopped double yellow lines to wait so she could drive into the space the moment they pulled out, However, it was an elderly couple who took forever to get into their car, sat for ten minutes thinking about it then had problems getting out of the space – especially with her parked where she was as they obviously could not see down the road to their satisfaction to pull out. Moaning to herself, she moved her car back a little. They also reversed, stopped again. There was no way Marelle was going to drive around again as you could guarantee someone would slip into that space before she returned.

She sighed as they edged out inch by inch. It was a quiet road and if they had been paying attention, they would be aware that anything coming along was unlikely – but they continued to move at a snail's pace, glaring at her when they finally moved out of the space. Marelle ignored them and swiftly drove the Mercedes into the empty space. Finding her heart was beating a little fast and her head was racing, she took a moment to gather herself then grabbed her handbag from the opposite footwell and got out of the car. She locked it as she ran up the steps and turned the shiny brass doorknob on the green door as she entered.

There was a different receptionist on duty today. Quiet background music ameliorated the silence as she looked up to Marelle.

"Can I help?" She smiled.

"I'm with Jacob Frost." Marelle replied. "He just came in – I've been parking the car …"

The way the young woman looked at her screen with a slightly puzzled expression for a few moments suddenly struck fear into Marelle. About to sit down, she took a step back towards the desk. What if he hadn't come in here? What if he'd doubled back and gone off? The receptionist didn't seem to think he was here.

"He was having an implant completed." Marelle added, now leaning on the counter.

"Erm …" the girl said, still searching her screen.

"He's just come in here – five minutes or so ago – maybe ten?" Marelle repeated and wanted to add 'you must have seen him' but didn't because the fear in her voice would have been obvious.

"I've literally just come down here. Angela has had to go upstairs …" The receptionist said as she looked at her screen.

"I've just dropped him off, right outside. I watched him come in. I've been trying to park the car!" Marelle explained slight panic just clawing at her voice.

The girl studied the computer, her eyes flicking across the screen as she sensed Marelle's rising anxiety.

"What did you say his name was?"

"Jacob Frost." Marelle stated. "He had an implant a couple of weeks ago – he was coming back today to have the proper one fitted. I just dropped him off – he's got to be in here!" She insisted, leaning further over the counter.

"I can't see his name here – what time was his appointment?"

"Nine thirty." Marelle replied, an edge to her voice now which was verging on tears. "If he didn't come in then I need to look for him – he was worried about coming here today – he may have gone off somewhere …"

"It's OK. Don't worry." The girl said.

"It's not OK!" Marelle exclaimed a little more forcefully than was appropriate. "If he's not here I need to go and look for him!"

"Hold on." She finally said and went to get up as Marelle gave an exasperated sigh and ran her hand through her hair just as the door to their side opened and the receptionist that had been there before appeared.

"Angela!" The new, blonde receptionist called. "Have you checked in a Mr. Jacob Frost?"

Marelle looked at her as she walked round behind the reception desk and leaned over to look at the computer.

"Yes." She finally said. "He's upstairs."

Marelle released a breath of relief and put her head in her hands with her elbow against the counter.

"You've deleted him!" Angela said with a chuckle. "Look …" And clicked the mouse a few times.

Marelle stared at them and their frivolity of the situation while she was standing there with her heart in her mouth and her knees weak beneath her.

The blonde woman finally looked up to her, with a smile.

"Sorry, yes. He's upstairs with the dentist. I deleted him apparently!" She obviously found it amusing.

Marelle stared at her almost in disbelief until she finally said. "Please take a seat. I am sure he will be down shortly."

Stepping back to the vacant chairs, Marelle tried to slow her heartbeat and stop the adrenalin from pouring any more into her blood stream. The two behind reception disappeared around the side out of sight.

She sat, watching and waiting while she was overwhelmed by the feeling she had felt only moments ago. Just one little mistake like that had pushed her into a moment of panic. She took a deep breath, dried her eyes and thought about Jacob walking back down the stairs any second now in order to dispel the other thoughts that she knew were bound to follow.

Last time Jacob had come down those stairs he had been as white as a ghost and drenched in sweat. That had been his first visit to a dentist, and he was not a good patient. Today, she prayed, it would be different.

The sound of footsteps on the stairs caught her attention and somehow, she instantly knew it was him. It was a kind of collected knowledge – a *feeling*; she just *knew* it was him from the footfall she could hear and the sense of him approaching.

The door opened and Jacob walked through, his hands in his pockets behind the navy-blue blazer he wore. He smiled to her – an open, warm smile that was both confident and happy.

"Alright?" She asked.

He nodded and walked forward to the desk. The dentist walked across behind him. Marelle clutched her bag to herself and stood up, quickly stepping to his side and sliding a hand into the crook of his arm.

Jacob was happier today and walked outside with her filled with a new confidence.

"I'll drive." He said.

"You sure?" She asked, remembering how he had been the last time they were here.

"Yeah, fine." He replied with a little smile.

She got into the passenger seat beside him; he took his jacket off and put it in the back.

"Let me see." Marelle asked.

He lifted a finger and pulled up his lip to expose the new tooth. It was a perfect match and fitted in completely with his existing teeth. She hadn't minded the gap, but this was so much better.

Marelle smiled. "So you are all perfect again now!"

TWENTY-EIGHT

"Hey!" Marelle said to Jacob as he sat at the table in the kitchen drinking a mug of tea right after breakfast on Saturday. "For you!"

The postman had just delivered mail and along with the normal brown envelopes which were either bills or junk mail, was a white envelope with black handwriting on the front. It was addressed to Jacob.

"For me?" He questioned, looking at it. He turned it over in his hands and looked at the writing. "Nobody knows I'm here ..."

"Well somebody does!"

He sighed and continued staring at it in puzzlement.

"Unless you've got x-ray vision you'll have to open it." Marelle laughed. "Or I suppose if you stare at it long enough you might work it out!"

He gave a small, tight smile then slid his finger into the opening and ripped along the seam.

He pulled out a folded piece of blue paper and what looked like a photograph. Marelle watched as he looked at it; a larger smile forming on his lips. With bright, warm, eyes he turned it to her.

It was a picture of a grey horse, eating hay, looking happy.

"It's Captain." He said, passing it to her. "From Kally."

Marelle took the picture, looking at it as he opened the folded blue paper. He gave a little laugh as he read it to himself; then eventually aloud.

'Dear Jacob and Marelle, thought I would just send you a picture of Captain, just so you can see he is fine! So glad I came down and managed to see you both. You are a wonderful couple, and I am so pleased to see you both so happy. Looking forward to the wedding. I didn't leave my phone number but here it is if you need it. And Jacob, you know where I live! All my love Kally.'

He smiled. "Aah, that's sweet."

Marelle smiled. "You've never mentioned Kally to me ..."

"No, I didn't expect to ever see her again."

"So you only tell me about people you think you will see again?" Marelle asked, playfully.

"No." He laughed. "It's just – she'd gone – I'm not saying I'd forgotten about her but ... I'd lost her in the past – with that period of time. Just one of many passing through. She had been here then, she left and she was gone. I thought she would keep in touch, but she didn't. She was young – moved to a bright, new world with so many other things to think about ... I don't blame her. You kind of leave those people and memories of them at that place in the past ..."

He was staring at the letter. Marelle stared at him, but he chose not to look at her.

"But you went to her house ..."

He shrugged. "Probably a mistake."

There was silence for a moment.

"I missed her when she left, I missed seeing her – and seeing Captain."

"She must have been very young?"

He nodded. "She was but mature beyond her years. She never judged me, just accepted me being here – doing what I was doing." He said. "She got it that if I didn't want to talk then she wouldn't talk. Sometimes she would just sit there with me, staring into a bonfire or just listening to the birds." He sighed then smiled. "But you know she has stuck to her dream. She wanted to be a vet, and she had become a vet. How many people do that – stick to their dream and see it through?"

"You did." Marelle smiled sweetly to him.

He laughed sarcastically. "No I didn't!"

"But you got to be a singer in a band! Surely that was a dream?"

"It wasn't my dream."

Marelle glared at him with a perplexed expression.

"The band thing came about as an accident. Some guys I was at college with started a band for a laugh – persuaded me to sing – I have no idea why!" He gave a little laugh. "Didn't expect to take it anywhere but we played in a few pubs and clubs, and I loved it. I liked that amount of love and adoration that I could drum up from an audience. Then one Friday one of the guys comes to find me – I was on my way back here – says to get my stuff together as we had been asked to stand in for a band that dropped out of a live TV performance. Don't truly know why, or how but suddenly we were in a TV studio, getting poked and prodded – about to play with no rehearsal or much of an idea of what we were actually doing!"

"How old were you?"

"Don't know really. I was happy at college, doing what I was doing but someone contacted Fabian to get in touch with me and next thing I know I'm speaking to Chas …"

"Sounds like a dream come true to me." Marelle smiled.

He gave a little grin then got up. He took the picture of Captain, stood up and attached it to the freezer door with a fridge magnet in the shape of an apple. Then he stretched his hands above his head and looked out of the window. Jacob looked thoughtful. Like he had only half finished a conversation but had chosen not to continue it right now.

He spent the morning outside. Initially he had been in the back garden but disappeared after a while which gave her a few moments of anxiety until she spotted him at the front of the house. Marelle watched him for a bit, her arms wrapped around herself in secret solitude. He walked about the front garden area – paced it out; stood at different corners, surveying it.

It had probably once been a pretty garden, but Marelle surmised it had long since been made into a driveway and as it had, then the garden had disappeared. The high hedges around the property needed a trim. Her car was parked in front of the house to the right, with the white van to the left. The garden sloped gently down to the road and off the dropped kerb. She looked at it. The area was actually larger than you first realised and her mind wandered back to the threat of this place being made into an entrance to the development on the airfield. It was an ideal space and an ideal position – she could understand why they had fought for it. But she was glad they had lost.

Jacob occupied himself until lunchtime then came in and filled the kettle. Marelle took it as a cue to start thinking about lunch too and walked through to the kitchen with him.

"You know, if you cut that laurel hedge back a bit you would get another five- or six-feet extra space each side." He said.

"Would we?" She asked. "Do we need it?"

"Well …" He mused. "It would give us enough room to build a garage."

She looked at him, a little puzzled.

"There's a lot of space out there – if it was cleared and tidied up, we could put the wall and gates in *and* build a decent garage at the end."

"If you want … it's up to you …, do we need a garage?"

"I could keep the bikes here then.' He answered. "In fact, I could get rid of the lock-up."

She shrugged and nodded. Not really bothered but happy if he wanted to do that.

"I'd like to get the wall and gates done first …" He continued. "I might make some enquiries …"

"Be careful! We don't want Seb getting wind of anything and I don't trust him not to have spies!"

Jacob laughed. "Don't worry. No-one needs to know."

"What?" She asked.

"I'll just work it out in my head for now."

Marelle smiled. It pleased her that he was thinking about the changes he wanted to make to the house – to make it *his* – *theirs*.

It turned into a bright, crisp autumn day and after lunch Jacob announced he was going for a walk around the airfield.

"I'll come!" Marelle piped up, rushing to get her jacket from the living room. With her hand crooked in his arm she walked down the back garden path and stepped over the fence onto the airfield. Jacob walked with a long stride an eager look in his eyes and a smile on his face today in the bright sunlight. Marelle looked up at him.

Autumn was beginning to touch the hedgerows and the tops of the trees. It's golden flush was beginning to colour the leaves; soon it would rob them from the very branches that had nurtured them for the previous year – but for now the foliage remained in that passing, colourful state – oblivious to that fact.

They walked up the runway and crossed the grass at the end towards the main gate. The grass had grown and now reached up the sides of the portacabin that remained. The long grass was now brown, dry and spiked with the deep red of dead docks and the warm buff of teasels still drying in the autumn sunshine, their pale purple blooms now a vague memory. They walked together through the grass to the chain link fence at the end. The main gates were closed, padlocked, and he gave them a glance as they passed by. Then he stopped, turned to stand staring back in the direction of the house.

"Imagine." He said. "Imaging if all of this was ours now – right from here to the house. We could leave it just like this!"

Marelle smiled. "Would you, if you could?"

"Yeah." He sighed. "I would – but it's all way beyond my reach. It's prime development land in waiting …"

"According to Seb, it's prime development land without adequate access."

He laughed. "It's got access they'll just have to work a bit harder. They'll always find a way – change the plans – or in the end, somebody will sell them some land."

"Well, it won't be us." She replied, tightening her hand on his arm.

He walked on. Stepping through the long, tangled grass, yellow and white flowers still blooming up this end where the sun had an unabridged view of the land. Then suddenly, as their feet fell into one more step there was a flash of wings and a pained alarm call as a pheasant, waiting under their feet until the very last moment, flew up vertically and unexpectedly. Marelle let out a small scream of exclamation and turned into Jacob, clutching at him in that moment of fright.

He laughed. "It's a pheasant!"

She sighed. "I know." Then chuckled.

"Beautiful creatures. He commented. "So vibrant – with their white collars in their Sunday best!" He watched the bird alight away from them and scurry across the concrete of the service road. "There he goes. He's safe over there."

Marelle slid her arm tighter through his, held herself closer to him and felt his lithe, muscular frame against hers.

On the corner up towards the Thor site they passed under the low, spreading branches of a horse chestnut tree, one of the first to adopt the rust of Autumn and already its leaves were falling. Jacob stooped down and picked up one of the fallen conkers that were scattered at the foot of the tree.

"Have you ever thought about this? It's one of life's wonders that could so easily pass you by but if you take a moment to stop and think about it for a second, pause in this life that you are racing through at a million miles an hour, you realise that the moment the green , spiky case of the horse chestnut is broken open and you catch the first, fleeting glimpse of the shiny, plump, mahogany brown chestnut inside, you realise that you are the very first person to ever see that! The very first person in the whole wide world. No one before you has ever seen that conker!"

As he spoke, he manipulated the conker in his hand until the green case opened along the centre and, just as his words had described, the bright redbrown of the new born conker, patterned with swirls in the sunlight, it rested in his hand.

"Most people don't. It passes them by." He handed her the conker.

She looked at it, turning it in her fingers. Feeling the still waxy coating on it from it's safe, warm swaddling of the green case. "Can you eat them?"

"No!" He exclaimed with a laugh. "You can eat sweet chestnuts – these are horse chestnuts – conkers – didn't you ever play conkers?"

She shook her head. "No!"

"Jeez!" He laughed. "Bloody townie!"

Marelle slid the conker into her pocket as they walked on.

"Season of mellow fruitfulness." He said after a while – pointing to the bramble bush that was clutching at the perimeter fence. "We could have picked some – you can eat those."

"I know." She replied. "You told me before – they're black currants."

"Blackberries." He corrected.

"Aren't they the same thing?"

"No." He laughed.

Their path took them to the Thor site. It was in full sun with shadows cast by the belt of trees behind it. Jacob climbed deftly up onto one of the low walls. He stood upon it, his legs slightly astride, looking up into the sun, still high in the sky above them. Over their heads it was a pure, azure blue without a single cloud. He held out a hand to Marelle and raised her to his level. She stood beside him, arms folded, staring at the sun.

'Yellow sun!" She said, with a grin.

He laughed. "I like that!"

"I know." She smiled, sarcastically and took his arm again.

"Why are they called Yellow Son? Do you know?" She asked.

"Yeah, I know." He replied. "Chas is a bit of a cold war buff … his father used to work as an engineer on the Vulcan bombers – Chas always said he as actually involved when the Cuban Missile Crisis nearly took us to the brink. Yellow Sun was the name of the thermonuclear weapon that the planes would have carried at the time. Only Chas changed the 'u' to an 'o' to make it 'son' in memory of his father and him being his son …"

Marelle looked to him as he recalled that story inexplicably.

"Oh, so they're named after a nuclear weapon?" She questioned in surprise.

He nodded. "That's what Chas always said …"

"Wow!" She said, moving closer to him beneath the clear blue sky and the sun beating down on them.

This was the place. This very spot where nearly everything in her life for the past year connected to. It was where she had enticed him for that picnic on her birthday; the spot where she had stolen the first kiss and made her intentions clear to him. It was the place he always came to when he needed to clear his head; where she had mentioned Black Shuck which had ultimately led him to locate Frankie's body and it was at this spot that she had watched Sam lay into Jacob in that final, awful tirade before Jacob had disappeared –

possibly never to return if his plans had come to fruition. And right here was where he had proposed to her.

Marelle looked down at her feet. She was surprised there were no remaining bloodstains on the concrete beneath her feet. But the rain must have washed any traces away.

"Sam nearly killed you here." She said, almost to herself.

"No, he didn't." Jacob laughed.

"He tried."

Jacob made a little noise; Marelle was not sure what it meant.

"He knocked your tooth out!"

"It's mended now." He replied.

Marelle smiled to herself and shook her head at his resilience.

"Why did Sam hate you so much?"

"He didn't hate me. He didn't understand me. He couldn't understand me or the way I lived my life, and it frustrated him – and his frustration manifested as anger – or fear ..."

"Well that might be your belief. I think he was just a bully – a nasty one – along with his father."

"Well they've both gone now." Jacob continued staring at the sun.

Marelle sighed, turned her head, pivoted slightly. She smiled to herself and looked across the space where her eyes settled on the silvery form of the dead tree to her right. The '*hanging tree*' she had called it, and a shudder passed over her as she wondered if was *that* tree? It had to be. She stared at it, stoic and pale in the bright autumn light and she sensed it pulling her gaze. Denuded and exposed; a signpost. She drew a breath and turned back to Jacob, clutching his arm and holding close to him.

"Could we get married here?"

"What?"

"Here. On the Thor site? Could we get married right here?"

He seemed taken aback by her suggestion, snapped his head back in puzzlement. "Why?"

"Because it's special here. Because it's *our* place."

He paused. "I'm not sure. We may not have access very much longer – probably not."

She sighed. "What about the church? Would you want to get married in the church?"

"I don't know." He replied, turning to her, taking her hand in his. "But we'll sort it. We'll see – there are other things to sort out first." He smiled that gentle smile, wrapped his arms around her and hugged her to him; swaying as he embraced her on top of the low wall, the sun above them in it's clear blue sky and a buzzard calling mournfully across the airfield.

"Come on." He said, and hopped down from the wall, reaching up to her. She went to take his hand, but he gripped her around the waist and lifted her back down gently, like a child. Then he took her hand and they walked on.

They took a path around the perimeter all the way back. The Heras fencing was in place around most of it, but the foliage and grass had already begun to grow through it, claiming it as their own. Nearly back to the gap at their house, Marelle stopped and pointed to a bush, growing against one of the original concrete posts – it was adorned with a mass of blue-black berries.

"Look!" She said, stopping Jacob. "Are those blueberries?"

He looked at them, then at her. "No." He replied.

"What are they then? Can we eat them?"

He paused for a second. "You can eat them ..."

Marelle walked forward to the shrub, leaving his hand lingering behind her as she did so. She reached out and held her hand against one of the branches, cupping the berries and turning to look at him. 'They're beautiful ..."

They were. Shiny black berries, tinged blue with a film of condensation on them in the sun.

"They're sloes." He said,

"What?" She asked.

"Sloes. Blackthorn – watch it they're quite spiky with those thorns ..."

Marelle carefully plucked one berry from the dark, prickly branches and popped it in her mouth. Jacob stood and watched until she screwed her face up and looked back at him. She waited for a moment then turned her head away and spat it out as he laughed.

"Christ! I thought you said they were edible!" She exclaimed, wiping her mouth with her hand.

"They *are* edible! I didn't say they tasted nice though, did I?"

"What the hell do you use them for then?"

"People make sloe gin with them." He answered. "Well people used to – I don't know if they still do. It involves an awful lot of sugar if I remember ..."

"It bloody well needs to!" She commented, still making a face. "Don't let me eat things if they aren't going to be nice!"

"Did it draw your arse up to your eyebrows?" He laughed, grinning.

She slapped his arm lightly in jest.

"You have to learn." He said, still with a grin. "I did!"

They laughed most of the way back about his escapades as a child – eating things he probably shouldn't have as she recounted games of do-dare-double-dare with Bella that had mostly involved eating less than delectable items.

They eventually stepped over the fence and into her – their – garden, laughing playfully until Jacob silenced her with a brief embrace and kiss in the garden.

"Well good afternoon young lovers!" A voice said from the side of the house.

Marelle jumped and Jacob looked up as Catchpole sauntered around the building.

"Excuse me." Jacob said to him. 'This is a private garden."

"No gate." He gestured. "Knocked at the door but no answer. I heard you out here." He explained. "I'll shout knock-knock next time."

Jacob sighed as he tucked Ezza away again and lowered his eyes to the floor.

"There's a saying around here that says to let sleeping dogs lie." Jacob said, stepping forward and standing a couple of metres away from Catchpole as he leaned on the wall of the house.

"But it wasn't a dog, was it?" Catchpole replied. "It was a child. Someone had created that child; someone had carried that child inside them for nine months and given birth to that child. He was someone's son – possibly someone's brother …"

Jacob did not reply. Just stood and looked towards the floor as Marelle moved close to him and slid her hand into his arm.

TWENTY-NINE

"Anyway." Catchpole continued. "I don't think that's an exclusively local phrase. I've used it in my neck of the woods too, together with 'there's no smoke without fire … have you heard that one?"

Jacob sighed, raised his eyes to Catchpole for a split second then looked away again.

"Are you still the caretaker then?"

"Yes." Jacob said.

"What's happening over there?"

"No idea. Work has stopped. They've asked me to carry on …"

Catchpole nodded. "You surprised me with your sudden outburst of laughter back there!"

So he had been there a while if he had heard them laughing.

"She ate a sloe." Jacob replied, no laughter now, looking at him again.

"A what?"

"A sloe." Marelle replied. "I thought it was a blueberry!" She smiled but neither Jacob nor Catchpole mirrored that.

"What did you want?" Jacob questioned.

Catchpole gave a smile. "Why do you think I want something?"

"It's not like you to make social calls …"

He smiled sarcastically at Jacob. "Well, I could stand here all-day trading proverbs and sayings with you but, I won't. I've come to request a DNA test with you."

Marelle felt herself tense. She was sure she pulled herself closer to Jacob, but he didn't say anything. Disappointment touched her after all she had said to Catchpole; she had been wrong to trust him.

"You did say you would be willing?" Catchpole questioned. "They are confident they have a sample from the deceased."

"What will a DNA test on me tell you?"

"Well a good reason will be to confirm that the deceased may be a relation to you …"

"And what will that prove?"

"It won't *prove* anything Jacob. It will allow forensics to identify the deceased as being a close match to your DNA – a brother maybe? We would at least know that much, and he wouldn't be an abandoned body, uncared for and unloved. We could at least close that part of the case and we would just be left with working out how he came to be there."

"Why do you think it's – he's – related to me?" Jacob asked, stalling, she knew.

"Well he was buried in the garden of the house where you and your family lived …"

"So was Frankie – you didn't suspect him to be my brother?"

"You told us who Frankie was – we didn't have to discover that ... but anyway – who knew who's brother was whose around here in those days?"

Jacob exhaled noisily in exclamation at Catchpole's last remark.

"So how about the DNA test. I've got the paperwork – of course, we are only requesting this. You can still refuse ..." Catchpole added.

"I know." Jacob answered. "How long will it take?"

"The test? Half an hour of your time at the station."

"And the results?"

"Well it won't be priority – couple of weeks maybe. Why, do you have plans?" Everything Catchpole said today stank of sarcasm.

"No." Jacob answered but Marelle could see his thought process. "I can't come down this week – I can't take time off work. I've had a bit of time off for dental surgery, so I need to make that time up ..."

"Not a problem." Catchpole replied. "When are you free?"

Jacob shrugged. "Week after, maybe?"

"Shall we put it in the diary?" Catchpole enquired – with more than a touch of patronisation in his voice.

"Can't say yet. Not until I know about work."

Catchpole stared at him. Paused for a moment. "Jacob. It's better for everyone if we get this over and done with. As you said, it won't *prove* anything, but it will take us partway at least to some sort of identification ... how about Wednesday next week? Just pop into the station and let them know at the front desk – they can get the test sorted for you and send it off. Take half an hour – you can do it in your lunch hour." He explained. "If I'm there I'll even come and hold your hand – how's that?"

"We are in a sarcastic mood today, aren't we?" Jacob muttered.

"It gets to me through the day. Dealing with people who don't really want to speak to me." He stated. "So Wednesday then?"

Jacob shuffled his feet, looked to the floor. "OK." He said.

"You don't *have* to." Marelle exclaimed to him.

"No, I know. But Wednesday is OK. Lunchtime." He said, looking up at Catchpole.

"Good!" He smiled. "It makes sense. We will know and you will know. Put everyone's mind at rest ..."

Jacob said nothing. Looked to the side of Catchpole and twisted his mouth a little.

"Thank you." Catchpole said, with a nod. His eyes moved to the caravan. "Is that your caravan?" He asked.

Jacob nodded.

"Putting down new roots?" He asked.

"Needs must." Jacob replied.

"What's in it?"

"Nothing. It's empty." Jacob replied.

"Did you live in that before you …" He looked to Marelle. "Moved in here?"

"Yes, for ten years." Jacob said, succinctly.

"Wow!" Catchpole replied. Paused, stood there staring at the caravan then to Jacob. "And you say you've had some dental surgery this week?

Marelle heard Jacob sigh.

"Yes." He said, inertly.

"What have you had done?" Catchpole enquired.

"I lost a tooth, remember? I had it repaired."

Catchpole nodded in acknowledgement. "Can I see?"

"No! I'm not a bloody horse!" Jacob exclaimed.

Catchpole held a hand aloft at Jacob's response. "OK, OK. I just wanted to see – my wife has broken a tooth – we were looking for someone to fix it – wanted recommendations, that's all."

Jacob stared at him but said nothing.

"Was it an implant?" He finally continued. "Or a bridge?"

Jacob shrugged. "Don't know. It's just *repaired*."

Marelle felt Catchpole's glance on them, steely and cold, trying to make an incision.

"Well, that's good." He said with a smile. 'Toothache is just about the worst pain as far as I am concerned."

Marelle gripped Jacob's arm

"Not cheap though, is it? And I doubt you can get a repair like that done on the NHS, can you?"

"I don't know." Jacob replied.

"So it *was* private?"

"I paid." Marelle piped up.

Catchpole raised his eyebrows to her. "That was a very kind gesture." He let it come out somewhat sarcastically.

"Well. I didn't want him with a gap in his teeth in the wedding photos." She quipped, equally sarcastically.

"Ah yes.' Catchpole said. "Plans underway, I take it?"

"We're in no hurry." Jacob answered before her words came out. Marelle felt her eyes widen but she refrained from any other outward sign of her anxiety at that remark from Jacob.

"Wednesday then." Catchpole said.

"Next Wednesday." Jacob reiterated. "I can't do this Wednesday."

He nodded. "Next Wednesday." And he stood up from the wall, grinning as he made a move to depart. "You know …" He began, then paused again. "The DNA test may tell us if you are, or are not, related to the deceased but I won't let go of this until I get to the bottom of you! Because, you know, nothing is … everything is just a little skewed off centre, isn't it? Not enough for most people to really notice but when you see it over a period of time, it kinda looks a bit wonky? You know?"

"No. I don't know." Jacob answered. "I am what you see."

Catchpole chuckled. "And what exactly is that, hey? A born and bred local lad who has worked on the village farm from an early age but who speaks with the eloquence of a poet, received pronunciation – and you always manage to look as guilty as hell!" He stated. Stared at them both then laughed before he turned and walked away.

Jacob followed him, slowly, with Marelle tagging behind. They watched him get into his car and leave.

"Need to get that bloody wall built." Jacob said. "As soon as we can."

They went inside, through the back door. Jacob was quiet except for his comments about the wall. The Jacob level was turned full up at the moment.

"You didn't have to agree to the DNA test.' She said, breaking the silence he had surrounded himself with as she didn't want it to fester.

"Yeah." He sighed. "I know but I wanted to get rid of him. I can call off if I need to but to be honest, we may as well just do it. Get it over with …"

"Are you sure?"

He nodded. "It may eventually be a blessing in disguise – depending on what I decide to do … but I want to get to that gig first. See what Chas has to say."

Marelle glanced at him, then looked away in case he saw the fleeting uncertainty in her eyes.

"Why did you say that *'you weren't a bloody horse'*?" She questioned because that line was still in her head.

Jacob smiled. "He inferred that he wanted to look in my mouth – it's how you tell the age of a horse – you look at their teeth."

Marelle gave a little laugh. "Do they?"

"Yes." He replied. "His eyes are everywhere, and he's got his fingers in everywhere too …"

Marelle made a face to herself at that comment, but Jacob saw no humour in his words.

"He can't work you out." She said.

"No, but he's having a bloody good try!" Jacob answered.

Marelle lay curled in his arms that night. He held her protectively, a gentle embrace that wrapped itself around her and said, '*this is mine*'. She smiled and liked it. She had claimed him long ago and it pleased her when he staked his claim too.

Admittedly, she had forgotten but Jacob announced the following morning that he wanted to go to the storage unit. *Get some clothes*, he'd said but when she had driven him there, he was unusually interested in the bikes.

"Shall I take on home?" He grinned with a glint in his eye.

"If you want." Marelle shrugged unsurely. "Won't that fire up even more suspicion from Catchpole? He's having a go at you for having private dental treatment – what's he going to think when he sees that?"

Jacob grinned. "He won't see it!"

"He seems to have his eyes and spies everywhere?"

"Well, so what? Hey?" Jacob smiled.

He said he would think about it for a few minutes while he searched for clothes, but Marelle knew it wouldn't take much deliberation to come to a decision. He had already made up his mind.

The clothes he had in the other storage unit were unbelievable. He opened boxes and uncovered rails of clothes she had not seen before. As he flicked through them like a teenager at Top Shop Marelle got the sense he was looking for something specific.

"You must have spent a lot of time buying clothes!" she commented. "Or did someone buy them for you?"

He smiled as he sorted through a rail of jackets. "I didn't buy most of them – most of them were given – or loaned to me. If we did any publicity stuff in the old days – we would often get given clothes to wear – sometimes we got to keep them, sometimes we just didn't give them back!"

"What are you looking for?"

"Ah! This!" He said in reply, pulling out a garment from the rail.

It was a black waistcoat, simple upon first glimpse but as he freed it from between the other tightly packed items Marelle could see it was far from that. It was tailored, hand stitched, impeccably finished in a gentle concave curve to each of the sides but as he lifted the hanger to his hand it exposed a flash of pure scarlet silk both in the lining and on the back of the waistcoat.

"Just hope it still fits!" He grinned, pulling it out fully.

Jacob searched more and found a shirt, an off-white, pin tucked dress shirt with long, turn-back cuffs. As she watched him pull together parts of Ezza, she got a feeling that this was a moment of resolution in his life – taking out those clothes that had been packed away forever because now he had a reason to wear them again.

Marelle watched him. He knew exactly what he was looking for – obviously had a certain appearance in mind and in his usual, wholly meticulous way, compiled it from the boxes and racks of memories he stored here.

He found a suitcase and carefully folded everything before putting it inside and zipping it closed. He looked up to her and grinned.

'I'm going to take a bike home." He said, mischievously.

'What, now?"

He nodded. "Why not?" He took the case and stood it by the door to the room. "I'll have to get changed though."

"Changed?"

"Yeah, I'd rather put my leathers on – those two out there can bite back." He chuckled while she glared at him.

"Maybe, after all, it's not the best idea?"

"Why?" he laughed. "You've never seen me in leathers – nor on either of those. I'll give you the choice, which one?"

"Neither of them." She replied.

He laughed. "It's ok. I'll go off in front and meet you at home."

"No Jacob. Please!"

"It's fine." He reassured her. 'They'll both be at home anyway, once we've built the wall – and a garage …"

"Garage!" She exclaimed, then sighed, realising he had said '*home*' so matter-of-factly and that meant so much more.

"Which one?" He asked again, fire glinting in his eyes.

"I don't know." She finally replied, quietly.

Jacob laughed to himself and began looking at a rail again, searching through items with protective plastic covers on them.

"Well if you won't choose then I will." He said. Half to himself, pulling out a garment and peeling the plastic off it.

It was a full leather motorcycle suit. White with black and lime green accents. With the enthusiasm of a child promised something spectacular he stripped down to his pants and t-shirt them climbed into the leather suit. It fitted perfectly, like everything he owned and he looked good in it – as he did in everything! He looked taller in the leather as he stood in front of her, her eyes wide with anxiety but held in the knowledge that she could not stop him doing this.

Five minutes later he was getting onto the blue bike. Marelle didn't know what they were, nor the difference between the two machines. She only knew the old white trials bike he had rescued from a ditch and renovated. At that time she hadn't realised he had this well-hidden need for an adrenalin rush whilst seated on what she would consider a lethal weapon. She could see it in him now, eyes all aglow and bristling with excitement.

'I'll see you at home.' He said. Sitting astride the bike with his feet on the floor.

This was a different kettle of fish and Marelle's mouth felt dry as she looked at him, folding himself into the bike so they were one – built and designed for speed.

"Please don't try and keep up with me." He warned. "I'll be fine."

"You had better be!" She answered as she stared into his eyes before he dropped the visor and hid himself completely from her view. It no longer looked like Jacob, with the suit, the helmet and the way he moved with the bike – it was someone else. Both feisty and fearless. She didn't like it.

He sat and waited while she got herself into the car, rode slowly with her until they got out of the compound and onto the short, paved area leading to the slip road. Marelle looked across her car to him, he nodded his head, gave a thumbs up and moved in front of her. With a glance over his shoulder, he moved confidently forwards. Marelle watched, heard, felt the bike leap into life – literally, as he floored it. Holding a wheelie for a couple of seconds as he disappeared before her. Marelle almost stopped the car, her legs and arms seemed to have stopped working as she glared at him – fastly disappearing up the slip road and into the traffic. She saw him weave between two cars and he was gone. Literally gone. She accelerated to sixty, thrashing through the gears but as he had already stressed, the car was no match for his two wheels and higher octane.

"Fuck." She said to herself.

She drove the ten or so miles home along the dual carriageway with sweating palms and her eyes constantly scanning the scene ahead for the carnage which she expected to fid at any moment. Around the last, sweeping, shallow bend she spied blue lights approaching fast behind her and fear gripped her guts so hard she thought she would have to make an emergency stop the moment she turned off. All at once she felt cold and hot as the police car approached with full lights and siren, dopplering past her, almost shaking her car with it's speed. She gasped a shaky breath to herself, expecting to see the police car brake in front of her on the bend as it curbed away from her, expecting to see wreckage. The road curved away and around and ahead the police car disappeared into the distance. There was no wreckage, no carnage, no destroyed motorbike or damaged Jacob. With racing heart and arrested breath, she gripped the steering wheel and turned off the road.

The last image of Jacob pulling the wheelie and weaving between the traffic at excessive speed filled her mind as she guided the car back home along the sheltered country roads back to the village.

There, in front of the house sat Jacob. Leaning against the bike, helmet off, waiting for her. Marelle alighted from the car, her knees shaky and her hands wet. Jacob gave a little laugh as she walked up to him.

"What kept you?"

She stared at him. "Don't do that ever again! I thought you had had an accident – there was a police car screaming up the road …"

"Probably chasing me!" He grinned.

"That was too fast!" She exclaimed.

"No, it was fine! Sharpens the reactions!" He said. "Oh, it's been a while … but that was good!"

"What if the police had stopped you, hey?" She asked, walking up and wrapping her arms around him. The leathers creaked, they smelled new.

"Oh they won't do that!" He laughed. "Being on the bike is like being able to fly – it's a third dimension of freedom."

"What!" She shook her head and looked up at him. "I don't like you riding like that. It's dangerous."

"It's fine!" He laughed. "One question now that I've got here though …"

"What?"

"Where shall I put the bike?" It's spent its life wrapped in bubble wrap."

She looked at him. "I don't know. Will it go in the caravan?"

He laughed. "I don't think so! Is it ok if I bring it in the house?"

Marelle was a little surprised but not particularly bothered. She shrugged. "It's your house too now – it's up to you."

"I don't want to park it round the back though – it's a bit of a risk squeezing it up the side passage."

"You used to take the other one up there."

"I know, but I wasn't too bothered of that got scratched. I don't want any scrapes on this one from something as silly as that."

"Take it in the front then leave it in the living room – I don't mind." She replied. 'In fact, it would be quite cool!"

Cool wasn't quite the word that came out when he tried to get it up the steps and into the house. Jacob had taken a sheet of plywood out of the van and made a makeshift ramp over the steps. It was quite steep and he took a run-up at it, struggling slightly to get the bike right to the top and finally over the ledge of the step. With the front wheel over the step and in the hallway he halted. Half to get his breath, half to instruct Marelle to lay newspaper down first just in case it leaked anything.

"I'm not taking it into the living room." He said. 'I don't want to make that tight turn through the doorway. I'll leave it in the hall, up near the kitchen – is that ok?"

She nodded. "Wherever you want it is ok."

Parked in the hallway, on a carpet of magazines rather than newspaper, the bike looked much larger than it had outside. Jacob wiped it down, polishing it a little and obviously admiring it as he did so.

"Did you buy that or was it a gift too?" Marelle asked, leaning in the kitchen doorway, watching him.

"No, no. I bought this one." He answered with a pride in his voice.

"Was it new?"

He nodded. "I bought the other one too but that wasn't new – I bought it off a friend of a friend of one of the road crew. He needed some cash." He looked a little pensive as he looked at the bike. "It's the first time I've ever brought one here – back home."

That was the second time today he'd called this house 'home'. Until now he had rarely referred to it as *home* in that way. It had been 'the house' or 'your house'. Now twice today, he had called it home.

So, in their house, with the bike parked in the hallway he now stood in the kitchen looking out of the window. The night was clear and sharp. Marelle stood beside him; clouds were just clearing the moon which was illuminating precisely from behind. Jacob reached over and flicked off the light switch, plunging the kitchen into darkness and strengthening the light and impact of the large, pale-yellow moon now exposed as the clouds before it parted.

"Hunter's moon" He said.

"What?" She asked, beside him, her face illuminated by the reflected light on earth's satellite.

"It's a Hunter's moon." He repeated. "You saw the Harvest Moon before – well this is a Hunter's Moon."

Marelle looked at the huge yellow moon, clouds parting around it like curtains. She recalled his explanation of the Harvest Moon and it's significance in this rural landscape, rising like a lantern above the golden and vast stubble fields of a month or so ago. Now they were gone and the large, full moon she now looked at reflected its light over the freshly toiled plough lines.

"What is a Hunter's Moon then?" She asked.

He looked at her briefly then moved a hand to the back door, nodding his head to her, he went outside.

The night was still and mild. A gentle breeze just touched their faces. It was a clear night with a velvet sky, dotted throughout with stars and the odd gently moving cloud which were caught by the yellow light from the large full moon.

They stood together; he placed an arm around her.

"A Hunter's Moon." He explained. "Marks the change of the season, the darkening of the days – a herald of change and new beginning." His voice was soft but clear. "It also signifies to us that it is time to hunt and gather for the coming winter."

Marelle looked for a while. "There are so many rules we don't know." She said after a pause. "Rules generations have lived – and survived by."

"And they are being lost." He added. "Old wives' tales which are now seen as quaint – but were actually markers and waypoints throughout the year that we lived by." He sighed. "Simple days when Mother Nature ruled us."

Marelle reached up a hand and folded her fingers around his arm. They stood together looking at the moon, silent and constant in the sky. During moments like this Marelle could see the struggle within him; could understand what was inside his head. He so wanted and loved the simplicity of being Jacob; of being by himself, keeping quiet – maybe even just being with her; but ripping at that side of him was Ezza – now alive again, kicking and screaming to get out and be the person he had been over ten years ago.

As they stood there in the back garden, looking out over the airfield, staring at the moon in the black sky, it's given light on their faces, she understood. For all of that time he had suppressed the person he really was, held it firmly down with the dark gaze of Jacob looking out on the world. Until the advent of her arrival and the epiphany in the car park where Ezza had re-awakened and started clawing at the body bag, Marelle understood the turmoil that was raging inside him and the fear with which he was now living. Her fingers tightened on his arm, held him, claimed him as her own and tethered herself to him.

'The Hunter's Moon is also a light for the predators to hunt and make their kill as the season changes." He added. "The barn owl will be out there – stretching her silent wings across the airfield ..."

THIRTY

By morning the moon had gone. The day was grey but over the airfield was a thin layer of mist like dry ice, settled into a level strand of white vapour. It was eery and she'd not seen it that way before.

"Is that normal?" She asked.

Jacob looked out of the window. "What?"

"That mist? Is it mist or is it smoke?"

"It's mist." He replied. "Yes, it's normal – does that sometimes when the temperature drops quickly."

"Oh." She said.

"It'll burn off soon."

Within half an hour Jacob had climbed into the van and driven off and by nine the mist had gone too.

Marelle tidied a little until she got bored, spent half an hour fiddling with her hair in the bathroom mirror then came back downstairs. Walking through the house she felt it sigh around her. She felt a warmth from it that she had never really felt before. Marelle looked at each wall, each corner, each doorway and now saw them as an intrinsic part of her life with Jacob – no longer just a place to lay her head anymore and suddenly she felt a need to start caring for it because it also signified the root of her life with him too. This home had history for him. If it wasn't for this house, she would never have met Jacob; it was *meant* to be their home and in a few days, it would be theirs, completely, forever.

Marelle sat down to work, thought about Jacob, wondered what he was doing, imagined his gentle hands working on the vehicles, driving the tractor, touching her. She got up and made tea – a longing within her for him the more she thought about him. Jacob with Ezza rising. She smiled. She did not know Ezza but was ready to embrace him too; she just wasn't sure that Jacob could control or had a full understanding of what the implications of setting him free may be.

The doorbell rang. She instantly looked at the time. It was ten past ten. With a sigh she got up – it may be the post, but she wasn't expecting anything. It was probably Catchpole – although she could see no reason for him to be here unless something else had come to light. She could see a shadow behind the frosted glass as she approached. As she reached up to open the door the shape of the visitor dawned on her. Marelle sighed as her eyes fell upon Seb, standing on her doorstep; a long black overcoat on and his BMW parked right there in her front garden. Marelle stared at him, felt angry.

"What do you want?" She asked.

"Contracts are likely to exchange pretty quickly – you need to be packed and ready to ship out."

"I'll '*ship out*' when contracts exchange. Not before. What if it falls through?"

"It won't fall through ... it's a single female, cash buyer – sounds foreign. It won't fall through."

"I'm not packing up before that day." She stated. "I'll pack on that day. Not before."

Seb stared at her. "If this falls through because of your stupidity ..."

"You just said it wouldn't fall through ..."

"Not financially, I'm sure but if you fuck about when they want vacant possession ..."

Marelle tilted her head backwards as she answered – almost defiantly. She had him here; he couldn't argue.

"I won't fuck about." She replied. "Anyway, once contracts have exchanged, they've exchanged – they can't pull out – the sale will have gone through – if they have to wait a couple of hours for me to pack up a few bits and bobs, well, then they'll have to, won't they?"

"That's a stupid and inconsiderate attitude. You need to be packed up and out on that day."

"I will be – once it's gone through – what day is it going to be?"

"I don't know yet. It's in the hands of the solicitors. Couple of weeks? There's no chain. Apparently, we've struck lucky – no chain, cash buyer and someone stupid enough to pay well over the odds – you've fallen on your feet, but you still can't see it, can you?"

"See what?" She folded her arms.

"A way out of this! A decent life for you instead of shacking up with this fucking no-hoper."

Marelle stared at him.

"Where will you go?"

"What is it to you? Does it matter?" She snapped.

"Not really." Seb replied. "I told you, you're on your own ..."

"No." she said. "I'm not on my own. I'm with Jacob."

He gave a sarcastic little laugh. "So he's still stringing you along?"

"He's not stringing me along!"

"Where is he?" Seb asked.

"What's it to you?"

"Nothing." Seb replied. "Nothing at all."

She stared at him; looked into his eyes and saw her own.

"Can I come in?" He asked.

"Why?"

"To make sure you're not wrecking the fucking place or growing cannabis in the loft." He stated dryly. "I don't trust him – or you."

"Well come into the bloody house then!" She exclaimed, standing aside and opening the door. "I'm here, on my own – there are a few sticks of furniture and that's it." She spat. "You're a fucking idiot!"

Seb looked at her with the derisive expression of a controlling father as he walked casually up the steps and into the house. He had hardly set foot in the hallway when she suddenly remembered the bike in the hallway.

Too late. He was in now; she felt her heartbeat quicken and a wave of nausea pass over her. Seb was already peering into the living room, trying to look casual but taking it all in with narrowed eyes.

"Nothing sinister." She laughed, walking past him and giving a sarcastic smile – going into the living room herself in the hope that he followed her. He looked in the room them looked at her.

"What's that smell?"

She shrugged. "What smell?"

"Smells like petrol." He said.

"Petrol?"

He ducked back out, sniffed, looked along the hallway.

"Jesus! Marelle! What the fuck is that thing doing in here?" He exclaimed, turning back to her with an outstretched hand in the direction of the bike. "How long has that been in here? For fuck's sake – you'll burn the whole fucking place down – get it out, now!"

"I can't get it out."

"I'll fucking get it out!" He said, angrily.

"You do not touch that bike!"

"It's in my house and by definition, my property."

"You lay a finger on that, and I will knock your head off your fucking shoulders." She shouted.

He laughed. "Shut up Marelle!" Seb replied. "What else has he stashed away in here? Hey?"

"Nothing. But even if he had it's none of your business."

"Oh, I think it is." Seb stated then moved off towards the kitchen. "And that fucking caravan is still there. I told you to get it moved."

"We will, when contracts exchange."

Seb flew towards her. Stopped short. She didn't flinch. "No. You'll move it now! You'll move that death trap out of the hallway – or I'll sell this house and I won't give you a single penny."

"You have to. It's in Dick's will."

'Then take me to court and fight me for it." He hissed.

"You really would, wouldn't you? You would totally go against Dick's wishes as written in his will – defy his wishes when he has been so generous to leave this house to us, when we didn't even know him or visit him. We've gained from this – from what he left us – what he worked hard to buy and to make his home. It was important to him, and he wanted us to have it so we would look after it; keep this house in his memory. But no! To you it's just a money pot – just pound signs – just change in your pocket …"

"Well that's all it is at the end of the day. Bricks and mortar, pounds and pence. It's no use to us – the money would be more useful and give you a chance to start again."

"I don't want to fucking start again!" She shouted. "You have no fucking idea Seb. No fucking idea!"

"Oh yes I do! You can't see the wood for the trees – you're obsessed by him – fuck only knows why – probably because you fancied getting a bad boy – a bit of rough – a bit of dirt under your fingernails for once." Seb pointed at her. "He's using you. Can't you see that? He's a fucking low life … and …" Seb pointed in the hallway. "And how does he even get a bike like that? It's probably stolen – is he planning on selling it? Raise a few quid – for a few more beers, a couple of hits? Hey?"

"It was his brother's bike." She offered.

"Yeah, whatever." Seb snarled. "That's why it's stashed away here …"

He turned back to her, chest to chest, looking down at her.

"You are from a good family, you have been brought up correctly – I never thought my little sister would get herself into this situation with some fucking waster – not to mention that he was eyeing up kids in the toilet – you'll have more than me to fucking deal with if that gets out – you think this is shit now – just wait until you are wading knee deep in it and people are hounding you too – labelling you with the same warped, twisted accusations…"

"You know nothing! Nothing!" She spat, looking up into his face, angry energy bristling through her fingertips. "You have no idea who he is or what he is truly like."

"I don't need to know – I can *see*. I can see exactly *what* he is!"

'You know nothing!" she repeated. "Stop putting words into people's mouths and totally unfounded ideas into their heads."

He laughed into her face. "I don't need to Marelle – it's all playing out right in front of their eyes and everyone can see. It will only take that child in the toilet to recall that fucking paedophile staring at him in there; he'll say something to someone and then it will all come spewing out! All of that vile, corrupted, dirty little existence of his. I'm only trying to protect you – walk away before it happens – uninvolve yourself while you still can …"

Marelle stared up at him. There were tears pricking the back of her eyes but she sure as hell was not going to let them fall. Seb believed this. He really, actually believed this – that from that moment when Jacob had mistakenly taken refuge in the toilet, to take a few moments where he could be quiet and alone – Seb had been hell bent on him being a paedophile. Jacob for God's sake! And he knew nothing; Seb knew *nothing* – only that split second when he had seen Jacob in there because some stupid little brat of a child had told Seb '*there was a strange man in the toilet*'. He would have said the same no matter what; some little runt of a child who had been conditioned into always looking out for perceived danger lurking around a corner – a paranoid, molly-coddled, over-fed child who had been on this planet for no time at all and understood *nothing*. But Seb believed that child; he believed it above her, his own flesh and blood!

"There's nothing to walk away from Seb. There's everything to walk towards. It's all in your stupid, little deluded head!"

"We'll see. I'll be proven right. I always am. I've got a sixth sense over this. You wait; you'll be destitute and out on your arse – when he's fucked off, or dead ... you wait." He raised an eyebrow.

"Get out!" She said. "Get out or I'll call the police an tell them you are harassing me ... how will that look, hey?"

"I'm your brother you stupid little bitch!"

"Get out. Don't come back. When contracts exchange, we'll go and leave this place to the new owners – I don't want to ever set eyes on you again!"

He laughed. "You are so unconvincing when you try to be angry!"

Marelle pushed him with her hand on his chest.

"Oh, am I? Just get out. It will all be over soon, and you can fuck off back to your big house in Surrey with your selfish wife and your conceited children. One day Seb, when you're kids have grown up, they'll look back at their family tree and ask you why you treated me so badly; why you ex-communicated me – because in the future this will look far worse on your part than you can even try to make me look. Now get out; your tenure here is over ..."

Seb stared at her, gave a horrid little smile and a tiny laugh.

"And I'm fucking glad it will be.' He said. "I'll take the money for damages to this place out of your share. I don't see why I should have to pay for them out of mine."

"You do that Seb. Because you know, I don't fucking care!"

He left, his hands in his pockets and a self-satisfied smile on his face. As she closed the door, she felt she had done the wrong thin. Had she said too much? They just had to hold their breath until the sale went through; play it cool and not let on in any way that they had pulled a fast one on Seb.

If he delved, if he got an inkling then he would for sure, stop the sale. Her head was pounding as she tried to remember what she had said, what she had inferred because he would sure as hell go over it word by word in his head now. She panicked, took out her phone and called Jacob.

"Yup." Jacob said. It was an unusual greeting for him but he was obviously in a frame of mind where 'yup' seemed appropriate. Now she had called him, she started to wonder why she had.

'Hi." She said. "Sorry, I just had to call – Seb just turned up. We argued ..."

"Are you OK?" He asked, concern in his voice.

'Yes." She laughed. 'But it got a bit heated – I don't think I said anything to him which may impact on the contracts being exchanged."

"What do you mean?"

"In the heat of the moment, I just blurted things out – he was being very mean about you."

"What's new? You should be used to that!"

Marelle sighed. "He threatened to chuck your bike outside – I stopped him – but I virtually told him to fuck off and not come back because it was nearly all over and soon he wouldn't have any hold over me – or words to that effect. I didn't actually say that I didn't say anything that may lead him to the correct conclusion but, well, you know what he's like – he'll go off and replay the conversation in his head ..."

Jacob sighed. "But dd you actually say anything?"

Marelle paused. She had already divulged Jacob's past to Bella a little too easily only to have Bella cover up for her. It made her just stop and think. This time she hadn't; she was sure she hadn't.

"You've got to keep this under your hat! You can't let Seb know or he will sell it to the next highest bidder – and we know who that is ... just keep quiet." He said. "God I'll be glad when this is done."

Marelle sighed. Felt like she had been told off but knew, in this instance, he was right.

"I didn't say anything." She confirmed, almost just to herself. "He just made me so angry ..."

"Don't rise to him. Turn the other cheek."

She lowered her eyes to the floor as he spoke to her. Those were words from someone who used 'turning the other cheek' and that action had got him through the years of secrecy.

"But he was saying some horrible things about you – I'm not going to stand there and let him do that!"

"He'll say those things whatever you do. Just smile and let them go. I'm used to it, day in and day out ... it doesn't matter."

It most certainly did to her! She drew a cold beath through her nose. "Where are you?" She asked.

"In the yard at the moment. I might have to go out with Mr. Wright to pick up some vehicle he's bought – he's waiting for a phone call from the owner."

"Where's that then?"

"Down south somewhere – if we go today. If I do, I'll let you know, I might be late – later if the damn thing breaks down!"

"Do you have to?" She asked,

"Yes, I have to. It's my job." He said, solemnly.

Marelle smiled to herself. Maybe not for much longer.

She busied herself. Decided to tidy the kitchen then went upstairs where the boxes in the third bedroom reminded her that she hadn't ever really moved in properly yet! She walked back into the middle bedroom – Frankie's old bedroom – and stared out over the airfield.

The view from here was wide open with the huge flat space yawning before her. A piece of land Jacob had intimately got to know over the past ten years and whose very material infiltrated him. He was part of it, and it was part of him. Yet he had no hold on it, no right of possession to it. He had no right to this land, but it called and held him every day of his life. He would never truly leave it and whatever happened it would never truly leave him.

Marelle sighed and leaned her elbows on the red tiled windowsill. She cared about this place as much as Jacob did now. It had gripped her with a hold that was strong yet sensitive, loving yet controlling. And to think when they had inherited this house she had planned to only stay here for a short while; she'd thought she would hate it after living in an urban environment all her life and that being away from the people and places she had loved would never be for her. But look what this place had laid before her – and how she could never have resisted it. This place, had changed her – mentally, spiritually and completely. The things she had cared about so deeply before hardly mattered to her anymore. She believed there were invisible threads connecting everything, pulling them in the direction that fate wanted them to go. There was something higher at work, all of the time, completely. She had always said there was no such thing as coincidence – only really because she had heard it on a TV show and thought it was cool – but now she knew there really wasn't such a thing and that fate moved constantly to write your history,

It was almost dark when Jacob returned after work. Marelle was now used to the sound of the van pulling into the drive but tonight the headlights were illuminated and they swept across the dark hallway as he turned in. He had started to walk around to the back door rather than her rushing to the front like an excited school child and tonight he did the same. Walked in the back door, dropped his bag on the floor and gave her a bright-eyed smile.

"Hey." She smiled back. "Alright?"

"Yeah." He replied, going to the sink and filling a mug with water. He drank and looked out of the window.

"So you didn't have to go and pick up that car?"

"It's a van." He answered. "No, not yet ..." He stared into the semi darkness. "We change the clocks at the weekend ..."

Marelle looked up at him. "Already?"

He nodded. "Already."

"Does it matter?" She enquired.

He turned to look at her, took another mouthful of water. "Matter?"

"Yeah. If we are going to the Yellow Son concert – will changing the clocks make any difference?"

"Nah!" He laughed. "Just get an extra hour when we get home." He gave a little grin. "If we come home ..."

"What do you mean? *If we come home?*"

He smiled, looked out of the window again but the darkness just gave him his reflection in the glass. He turned back to her with a cheeky grin pulling at the edges of his lips. "Well, you never know – we might get invited back to Chas'."

She may have glared at him with eyes that were a little too wide and a little too vacuous.

"What!" He asked.

She sighed quietly to herself. He was buoyant; she didn't want to sink him. For a second she thought about saying nothing and letting it go – but it had been rolling around the perimeter of her mind for a bit too long now.

"What if Chas doesn't recognise you?"

He laughed. "Of course he will recognise me! I stood next to him on stage for over twenty years!"

"He didn't recognise you on the beach."

"I didn't *want* him to. I didn't look at him. I didn't speak – he wouldn't have known me from Adam – I made sure of that!"

"What if he doesn't believe you?"

"Of course he will! He'll see it's me!" Jacob exclaimed, laughing at her as if she was being stupid in a cute way again.

She wouldn't sink him. Not tonight.

"What if he doesn't want to speak to you. After all they've been playing without you for well over ten years – why would he want anything to do with you?" She rolled her eyes to his and saw a flicker of disappointment – not at the thought of rejection – to him that was an absolute impossibility – but to the fact that she had chosen to ask such questions. Jacob smiled a small, warm smile, put the mug down then walked over to her, wrapped his arms around her and pulled her to him.

"Because they still talk about me, because the fans still love me. Why wouldn't they want to speak to me and welcome me back?"

She looked to him. "Because you walked out on them – over ten years ago ...?"

"There were reasons for that. I wasn't well, I was ill ..." He replied quickly, still a laugh in his voice.

Marelle drew a breath in through her nose. She was trying, really, really hard to keep positive but his take on this was worrying her and his refusal to accept it was going to be nothing less than a perfect outcome was troubling to say the least.

"... you pretended you were dead ..." She finally said.

"I didn't pretend I was dead. It was forced upon me!"

"But you could have said something – you could have spoken up – contacted Chas?" the words left her lips, but she felt harsh in saying them – but he needed to entertain this possibility.

He shook his head. "I had a mental breakdown – I didn't – *couldn't* – then it went on too long to go back. Or maybe I lost my memory, maybe I've only just remembered!"

He looked down to her, a grin on his face like the smile of a crocodile. Marelle looked into his eyes but today he was not listening. Just as he would not listen in the past when he was so dark and troubled, he would not listen today either when he was sky high on this dream. Sometimes, when he was in that frame of mind, she wondered exactly how much he had – or hadn't – really told her.

Marelle sighed and laid her head against his chest. "I just worry." She said.

"Don't worry. It'll be fine. I can imagine Chas' face when he realises it really is me!"

Marelle closed her eyes and felt his body, warm and firm against her. His heart beating inside and the blood running through it.

"There's a guy coming to look at the wall tomorrow." He suddenly said.

She lifted her head. "Wall?"

He nodded. 'The wall at the front with the gates."

"But it's not officially ours yet, is it? What if Seb finds out. I don't trust him not to have spies everywhere!"

"It's fine. He's only coming to look. I've spoken to him, told him what we want – he needs to have a look. You don't have to be here ..."

"I'll be here." She replied.

"He does some building work around the farm now and again. I spoke to him the other day ...as soon as we complete I want him to get onto it."

Ok." She replied. 'So I don't need to show him anything?"

"No. he knows all about it.' Jacob smiled. "The sooner we can get gates on this place the better."

True, she thought. It would be better and would stop people coming up to the door so casually.

"... and ..." He continued. "I need you to cut my hair."

She smiled. He had said the magic words. Marelle leaned back slightly in his arms, looking up at him. She lifted a hand and ran her fingers through it.

"How?" She asked, slightly nervously following the time before, just in advance of Frankie's funeral when he had forced her to cut it all off. That had broken her heart; after all, that first ever time she had cut his hair had gone a long way to cementing this future.

"I've got a picture ... I know of a picture ..." He corrected himself.

"Like I did it before?" She asked, hopefully.

He nodded. "Pretty much – it's not as long on the top as I would have liked it but, well – you can work wonders, can't you?"

She grinned and hugged him. Somehow, she knew she already had.

"Tomorrow?" He asked.

"Of course!" She nodded.

THIRTY-ONE

The guy in the blue van had knocked on the door. He was older than she had expected, smaller and walked with a stooped, hurried gait. To be honest he didn't totally look capable of much menial work, but Jacob had said that he came with recommendations, so she was happy to trust his judgement.

"I've come to look at where the wall and gate needs to be built." He had announced in a thick Suffolk accent when Marelle had answered the door to his knocking.

"Oh, OK. Help yourself." She had replied with a smile.

So she was now watching him from behind the curtain in the living room as he studied the entrance, took a few measurements and scribbled something down in a little yellow notebook.

It would be odd to look out from here to see a wall and a gate but at the same time it would affect a feeling of security. She was still peeping at him when her phone rang. Thinking it was probably Jacob checking if the guy had turned up. She studied the screen and saw it was not Jacob. It was Devon.

Her first thought was that Seb was spying on them and had seen this guy surveying their front garden. Her heart was in her mouth when she answered.

"Hello?"

"Oh good morning, Marelle. Is Jacob there with you?"

"No." She answered, with emptiness in her chest. She could not gauge his intent from those few words. "No, he's at work. Do you want me to get him to call you?"

"Erm, no. It's OK, but ..."

He had said 'but'. 'Buts' were never, ever good. She took a breath shakily as she looked out at the man with the blue van, standing looking at the drive.

"But the vendor is pushing for completion this Friday."

'This Friday!" she exclaimed, at first panicking then realising it was a good thing.

"Do you want to speak to Jacob to make sure he is happy with that. Obviously, we will have to have the money transferred by then. If he needs more time I will attempt to push them back a bit."

"I think it will be fine."

"Can you call him and let me know as soon as you can?"

She nodded. "I'll see if I can get hold of him." Marelle was watching the guy get into the blue van now, getting ready to leave.

She guessed this was Seb's vindictive, conniving self wanting everything played *his* way? She dialled her old phone number. It rang. She counted the rings; eight times and her old voicemail sprang into life. Marelle sighed. She would have to get him to change that – and her picture which always came up when Jacob called her. Five fidget filled minutes later she called it again. Still no answer.

Sometimes Jacob was the worst person in the world at answering the phone! She wondered if he heard it ringing and chose to ignore it, whether he had left it somewhere where he couldn't hear it or if he was genuinely busy and did not know it was ringing. She was not sure. If he knew it was her, she was sure he would have answered – especially with the things that were happening right now.

She went into the kitchen, opened a packet of crisps, stood there and ate half of them then dialled the number again with greasy fingers. He did not answer.

"Fuck." She cursed to herself. She needed to let Devon know, and she had no idea of what arrangements Jacob had to make for the money. Marelle grabbed her car keys.

She drove down to the farmyard – this time without hesitation, going through the gateway and driving across to the workshop. The white van was not there, and Ryan was coming across the yard on a small tractor with a trailer attached. As she climbed out of the car, he looked towards her but looked away quickly as he passed and before she could visibly try and attract his attention. She sighed, then rattling her keys in her hand she went into the workshop.

It seemed deserted, eerily quiet and still.

"Jacob?" She called even though she knew he was not there.

Everywhere looked tidy, nothing was out of place today – he probably hadn't been working here. Maybe he was out on a tractor in a field – but then, the van would be here. She walked back out of the door and a breeze picked up dust from the yard, throwing it in her face and blowing her hair back from her forehead. What now? She stood by her car for a moment, thinking. Maybe call him again?

She remained beside her car, took out her phone and dialled her number again. She did wonder if she may actually hear it ringing somewhere here, but she didn't and as she held it to her ear it rang once, twice then she was alerted to the sound of a vehicle approaching. She looked up to see the white van swing into the entrance and cross the yard to where she was. Jacob was in the driving seat, and he looked slightly puzzled as he pulled up alongside her car. She put the phone back in her pocket and walked to the driver's door of the van as he got out.

"I was calling you!"

"I know, I'm sorry. It was in my jacket on the floor of the van." He closed the door and turned to her. They were close together in the space between his van and her car.

"Where have you been?" She asked.

"Up to the airfield. They were taking the portacabins away."

"Were they?" she asked, inquisitively. "Are they moving out?"

He shrugged. "No idea. They've done all this before so who knows? What's wrong?"

"Wrong?" Her mind was elsewhere for a moment.

"Why are you here?" he questioned, raising his eyebrows.

"Devon called." She replied quickly, urgently. "He says the vendor is looking for completion this Friday."

"Friday!"

She nodded. "I told him it would be fine – but he said I needed to ask you because you will need to transfer the money ..."

"Yeah, yeah ..." He answered, thoughtfully. "Friday! Wow!" Jacob looked up and a smile broke on his face. "That means the house will be ours!"

"Yeah." She smiled in return.

And for that fleeting second or two they stood smiling at each other between the vehicles like a couple of teenagers at a school disco.

"Shall I call him?" She asked. "He wants us to confirm Friday is OK?"

"Yeah.' He gestured limply with his hand.

They spoke to Devon, on loud speaker, in the gap between the cars and agreed Friday. He told them what they needed to do and when they would need to do it. On Friday the contracts would exchange, Mae would own their house and Devon would then start the process to transfer ownership into Marelle's name. Jacob handed her back her phone, gave her a little glance and ran his hands down his thighs; his palms were sweaty.

"Done." He said. "I'd better get on – I'm going to have to take a bit of time off to transfer the money in the next couple of days, so I don't want to be seen shirking – I've already been up the airfield for an hour."

Marelle clutched her phone, looked up at him. How had she pulled this off? How had she wheedled her way into this man's life – not only got him entangled with her but woven herself so intrinsically into his past, present and future? She clutched his arm, pulled him to her and gave him a tender little kiss.

"Love you." She said.

He grinned, pulled her in and hugged her tightly, swaying to and fro.

"I gotta go." He whispered. "Love you too!"

Duing her time with Jacob, Marelle had learned that sometimes with him things had to be very precise. That evening when he announced he was ready for her to cut his hair she knew it was much the same demonstration of that trait. He said he had a particular photograph in mind that he wanted to emulate and had her searching through hundreds of images of him on her computer to find it. Eventually he said

"There!"

Pointing to the screen and landing upon a picture of him in a dark top, standing on stage, holding a microphone, about to say something.

It wasn't one of the oldest images of him, but it wasn't one of the latest ones either. Neither was it one of her favourites.

'That one?" She asked, a little surprise creeping into her voice. "Are you sure?"

"Well, I can't have it exactly how I'd like because it's not really long enough on top, so I think that would be the next best thing." He explained. "This one here is how I'd really like it." He scrolled back a few images and settled on one of him in a white shirt, kneeling on stage. The haircut he had here was perfect; it was much longer on top, almost falling into a spiky quiff with the back and sides so beautifully graduated.

"I can do a cross between the two." She offered.

"Nah. I don't want to look like someone trying to be Ezza." He answered.

She eyed him a little strangely at that comment. "That's very short at the back and the sides – you can see your scalp through it!" She commented on the picture he had chosen.

"I know but it's the most likely 'real' Ezza haircut I think we can manage ... can you do it?" he smiled to her with a glint in his eye.

"Of course I can do it!" She grinned. "So, you want it *exactly* like that?"

"Exactly." He nodded.

Marelle sat him on a chair in the kitchen just as she had the very first time she had offered to cut his hair. It had kind of been payment for his help on that very first night when he had come over to assist her during a power cut. She knew now how reluctant he must have been to do so, but as he'd said, and demonstrated many times since, he was a sucker for a pretty face or a damsel in distress. He had allowed her to cut his hair in any style she chose and she had used the skills learned as a teenager when she had dreamed of such creativity. She had provided him with a haircut very similar to Ezza's significant one without any knowledge of his past. That first time had drawn her to him with a lust that had initially surprised her and at the same time opened his eyes to the image and the lost life of Ezza again.

Something so simple had released the possibility of so much. Neither of them had known at the time.

Now she had the clippers poised again and hoped to God it was the same.

"Who used to cut your hair, in those pictures?" She asked as she worked.

"Oh, loads of different people. There was one guy in London who was really good. He did the haircut in the other picture – old guy in a dirty little backstreet barbers shop but his work was so good. Did all of that with scissors – no clippers – took him ages but I would honestly say it was one of the best haircuts I've ever had. I went to him when I could ..."

"Better than mine, hey? Are you really going to say that when I've got the clippers in my hand!" she laughed.

"Oh I thought that went without saying!"

Marelle smiled, pushing his head forwards slightly. "I'm surprised you managed to sit still for that long for someone to cut it with scissors and comb." She remarked.

"I guess I used to have more patience!" Jacob answered.

"You didn't the first time I cut your hair – you were like a five-year-old who didn't want it done!" Marelle laughed. "It's a wonder it looked so good."

"I wasn't sure what you were going to do. I'd given you a free rein … but I figured it would be better than what I would do to it myself!"

"Well thank you!" She laughed. "Are you sure you want it *that* short around the back and sides?"

"Just like the photo." He reminded her.

Marelle did as he asked. She would have preferred a more graduated cut, not so short at the back but this was how he wanted it, and she felt part of his journey and his dream as she created the style in the image from a good few years ago. Nearly finished, she stopped, comparing the image on her laptop and him before her.

"What do you reckon?" She asked. "I don't think we ought to take any more off the top. It's shorter on top in the picture but I think this looks better."

"Well I can't see what you've done." He reminded her that she didn't ever let him look in the mirror while she worked. The perfectionist in him would cause too many issues.

"Hold on." She put down the clippers and went to get a mirror. It was the one she often used to put on make-up or do her hair. She placed it on the worktop for him to see. Jacob observed himself. Turned his head, ran his hand over it. Recounted Ezza and every point was ticked off.

"Yeah, leave it." He said, still looking, still musing.

"Sure?"

"Sure." He replied, turning his head and running his hand up the back of it. It was much shorter now than it had been when he had made her cut it all off for Frankie's funeral. Marelle had cried at the time but now understood why he had made her do that.

"Wow." He said in a quiet voice. 'That's really very good. He turned and a truly genuine smile of excitement broke on his face.

"It's very short at the back and sides." She said.

"It's perfect!"

Marelle smiled.

He looked at himself in the mirror again. He spiked the top with his fingers, looked straight into his own eyes. Ezza looked back.

Watching him the next morning, Marelle wasn't sure she liked the new haircut. It was perfect and he was happy, but she didn't like the extremely short back and sides. The graduation was good, and the top worked delightfully but she just didn't like it being so short.

"You'll feel the cold!" She smiled.

"Hm?" he turned back to her as he was about to go out of the door.

"With your hair that short, you'll feel the cold!"

He laughed. "Shut up!"

She smiled. In two days', time this house would hopefully be theirs and in three Jacob would be eye to eye with Chas.

Friday had the potential to be fraught. She knew that Jacob had taken the day off, they had spoken to Devon and knew what they had to do. The very large fly in the ointment was going to be Seb. He had not been in contact since earlier in the week, but she knew he would be there.

"I'll deal with him." She said. "I'll fend him off until you come home with the keys."

It would be symbolic; they already had keys – but she needed Seb's keys in her hand to be sure.

"Don't say anything until I am back here with the keys in my hand." Jacob told her.

"I won't. I can keep him arguing, don't worry!"

The day before, Jacob had placed the funds for the house, plus fees, into a holding bank account to which a virtually complete stranger had access. A case of mutual trust was a big ask but Jacob had conceded to do it without so much as a moment's thought. Marelle remembered the day she had purchased a house with Chris. It had been snowing and there had been a delay. She had moved out of a rented flat and had a car full of stuff – he had still been at his parents. They'd sat in her car for over three hours, running back and forth to a telephone box to check if the sale was going through. That had been fraught too – but not like this.

Devon had said he expected completion to be around midday. Jacob went off mid-morning, leaving her in the house. Ten minutes after his departure there was a knock at the door. Marelle readied herself, wiped her hands and walked through, prepared for the verbal onslaught she was about to receive.

"Oh." She said when she pulled the door open and saw Catchpole standing there.

"Morning." He greeted. "I take it he's not here?"

"Er no, he's busy.' Marelle answered. "Why?"

Catchpole stood with one foot on the bottom step, looking up at her slightly. "I heard you were moving?"

"Us?" She asked, buying time while her mind sought to work out this scenario; one they had not planned.

"Yes. You. A little bird told me this house was on the market and it's little friend also told me it's been sold … where are you going?"

She dithered. Stuttered, didn't know what to say for the best. "Er, well …" Her mind wouldn't find words which were appropriate to say. What should she say? If she said yes then he would want to know where – if she told him the truth it would lead to even more questions and suspicion plus it might get to Seb. After all, how did Catchpole know about the sale?

"Not far." She eventually said, in a quiet, small voice that did not seem like her own.

"Were you going to tell me?"

She laughed. "It happened quickly."

"Why?"

Marelle was about to fabricate an answer when her attention was drawn to a figure striding up the driveway; a beige trench coat flapping behind him. Seb, as expected.

Catchpole had parked his car across the entrance to the driveway so Seb would have been forced to park slightly up the street.

"What the hell are you doing?" He bawled from halfway down the garden. "What are you doing?" He reiterated as he moved closer. "You should be out! Your stuff should be out of this house ... I trusted you and I knew it was a mistake ... and you're standing here gossiping on the doorstep. Contracts exchanged half an hour ago – I got delayed in traffic and get here to find you as if nothing was happening! What the fuck are you playing at!"

Catchpole turned to him. "Good morning!" He said.

Seb glared at him.

"DCI Catchpole." Catchpole said and held out a hand. Seb didn't take it but eyed him for a moment, wanting to continue with his verbal tirade at Marelle.

"And you are ...?" Catchpole questioned.

"My brother." Marelle stated.

"What are you doing here?" Seb asked him in frustration.

"Private matter. Same as it seems to be between you and your sister?"

"There's nothing private about this mess!" Seb exclaimed. "You!" He pointed to Marelle. "Are squatting!"

She laughed. "Calm down Seb. No one told me contracts had exchanged. Keep calm – it's alright."

"It is not alright. You need to be out of this house now! I will give you an hour then I'm locking the door."

"So you still have keys then?"

"No, but you obviously do. Give them to me now." He held out a hand.

Marelle stared at him; her arms folded across her chest.

"Is that fucking caravan still there too! I'll fucking smash it up if it is!"

"That would be criminal damage, wouldn't it, Mr Catchpole?" She questioned, quietly.

"It certainly would." He answered.

"In that case then, if we are talking about criminal damage, we should be looking at what these two have done to this house! There's that bloody eyesore in the back garden and he's got a fucking motorbike parked in the hallway leaking petrol everywhere!"

"No need to swear sir. I'm sure if there is criminal damage to the house, as you suggest, then the police at the local police station would be happy to assist if you contacted them." Catchpole replied. "Personally though – I can see no evidence of criminal damage here."

Seb stared at him. Catchpole smiled and Marelle did her best not to laugh.

Seb turned back to her. "You are not entitled to still be in this house!"

"Seb, calm down. Look the purchaser is not here – are they –no-one's beating down the door – are they? If it's exchanged then it's not your house anymore, is it?"

"And it's not yours either!" He snapped.

"So why are you worrying about it? And you owe me my half of the deal."

"You're lucky any deal has taken place with your behaviour!" He pointed, angrily.

"I can assure you it's fine. We spoke to the Estate Agents – the purchaser is not in a hurry to move in. It's perfectly fine for us to stay on here for a bit."

"You spoke to the Estate Agents! And they said that!" His anger was bristling.

She nodded.

"What right have you to speak to them; you have no right to speak to them!"

"Well, we did. It's fine. Stop getting your knickers in a twist …" At that point she saw the white van pass by the drive. Jacob looked up at her from the driver's seat as she stood on the doorstep with both Catchpole and Seb in attendance. He too would have to park further down the street due to Catchpole blocking the drive.

Marelle wasn't entirely sure what was going to happen in the next few seconds or if Jacob would even appear or wait. She tried not to focus her eyes on the van or the end of the drive, so she looked back to Seb who was in full flow again.

"This deal was vacant possession, upon completion. That means you move out. You have not, so officially, you're squatting."

Marelle laughed.

"This is what that fucking paedophile has done to an intelligent, bright, young woman!' Seb exclaimed in exasperation to Catchpole.

Catchpole eyed Seb. "Paedophile?" He asked.

"Yes! A fucking paedophile. That waste of space she's taken up with and with whom she is illegally occupying this house!"

Marelle went to say something, remembered Jacob was just outside the drive, and paused.

"Why do you say that?" Catchpole asked.

"Because he is; because he's not right in the fucking head – because I found him loitering in the toilets at my daughter's – my *twelve-year-old* daughter's – birthday party!"

Catchpole looked a bit puzzled; there was an expression on his face Marelle wasn't sure she liked.

"He was going to the toilet Seb." She said. "You jumped to conclusions – you know that!"

"He was banging his fucking head against the wall in the toilet! One of my friend's kids came up to me and said that there was a strange man in the toilet!"

She felt the air seep out of her. "You know what was happening Seb!" She stated, staring into her brother's eyes.

"Did you want to report this?" Catchpole interjected.

Seb stared at Marelle.

"You've got no grounds to accuse him of that." She said. "You jumped to the wrong conclusion because you were mad at me. Jacob is not a paedophile!"

"Sir." Catchpole said again. "Is this true? Do you want to report this?"

Seb stared at Marelle. He wanted to; she could see he *so* wanted to trouble their waters even though he knew there was no evidence except for Jacob being in a public toilet at the wrong time. But she also knew the consequences and the mention of *that* word in Caroline's perfect little life was enough to prevent him pushing this. He flicked his eyes away. He shook his head. Marelle stared at him and felt just the tiniest taste of victory in her mouth. Her eyes focussed over his shoulder as Jacob rounded the corner of the drive and began to walk towards them.

THIRTY-TWO

Marelle looked over Seb's shoulder, towards Jacob as he walked up in his usual unhurried way. He was wearing the jeans with the rip in the knee and his work boots. Marelle watched the rip open and close as he walked, showing a little glimpse of his bare flesh each time he took a stride. He was looking at her as she watched him approach over Seb's shoulder.

Catchpole turned to Jacob slightly but said nothing. Jacob continued walking, past Catchpole and into Seb's peripheral line of view. Marelle watched Seb lock his eyes onto Jacob, turn his head and follow his approach with those cold eyes until Jacob placed an arm around Marelle's shoulders and she moved close to him. Jacob raised his head and stared straight into the eyes in front of him. He raised his hand slightly, a set of keys dangling from his middle finger.

"Well we are officially living here now, so I would prefer it if you left the property." Jacob said, clearly but quietly.

Seb stared at him, shocked for a second, stupefied that Jacob had confronted him this way. Then he laughed.

"You!" He laughed. 'You?" He shook his head. "Don't make me fucking laugh ... I know you haven't bought this house. Just get the fuck out!"

"No." Jacob stated. "We haven't bought this house. A friend of a friend has bought it, and the agreement is that we stay here. Indefinitely. I've just picked up the keys on the purchaser's instructions – we are the official tenants here now. You don't own any part of this house any longer – you have no say in it anymore so instead of asking us to leave, I suggest you go."

Marelle rolled her eyes to her brother; resisted the urge to stick her tongue out to him.

"Bye Seb." She said instead.

Seb stared at them both. Knowing that he had been beaten this time. He narrowed his eyes.

"You are on your own young lady. I told you; I *warned* you! And when this piece of shit has bled you dry and dumped you on the street then you'll realise I was right." He hissed, was about to turn and leave but decided to turn on his heel and speak again. "And I'll tell you – I won't let this go because I *know* ..." He took a step towards Jacob and lifted a finger to him. "I *know* you're not some innocent fucking hick, I know you are nothing more than some fucking, dirty, scheming criminal– you think you can just slide around in the shit of your own life, but I can smell it as much as I can see it written all over your stupid fucking face. And I won't let it go. I will unearth what you've done, and you will receive whatever punishment is coming to you when I do ..."

Jacob stared at him but gave no expression. Marelle's eyes mirrored his.

Seb finally turned and strode away. Marelle knew he was angry, and it was an anger she had not seen in him before. It seemed final this time.

Jacob's fingers tightened slightly on her shoulder as Seb disappeared. Catchpole stood there, casually, one hand in his pocket. He turned his head back to them.

"It's a long story." Marelle said.

Catchpole gave a little smile. "Is there anything I should know?" He questioned.

Marelle shook her head. "No." She said.

Catchpole stared at her for a few seconds, waited but he said nothing. Eventually he moved his eyes to Jacob?

"Is that true?"

"What?"

"That you are tenants in this house? I thought it was your house." He turned to Marelle.

"It was, well half of it was. He's just tried to sell it from beneath me." Marelle exclaimed. "But it's been bought by a friend of a friend, and she has agreed we can stay here."

Catchpole nodded, his hand still in his pocket. "You two have a complicated life, don't you?"

"No." Jacob stated. "Our lives are simple – if we are left alone to get on with it!"

"I just wanted to check …" Catchpole asked, continuing. "Your brother – what was his full name?"

Marelle felt Jacob deflate next to her; the air rushed out and tension rushed in.

"Nathaniel Ezekiel Frost." Jacob replied. "Why?"

"Did he use any other names, or did he go by any other names?"

Marelle fixed her eyes on Catchpole, fearful of what he may ask next.

"Not that I am aware of.' Jacob replied. "As I said, his life took a very different path. We weren't close; I don't know much detail of his life before he died."

"But you inherited all of his estate, did you not?" Catchpole replied with a question, looking up at Jacob, a smile on his face.

"I was the only living relative." Jacob confirmed. "Why?"

"Why what?" Catchpole asked although he knew only too well what Jacob meant.

"Why are you asking about my brother?"

"Oh well, you know – just looking into things to establish some facts about the deceased child …"

"But my brother is dead."

Catchpole nodded. "But he wasn't when that child died, was he?"

Jacob shrugged. "I don't know. He didn't live with us."

"No." Catchpole said as if humouring an insistent child.

"Why are you dragging up things about my brother? What has any of this got to do with him?"

"Families." Catchpole said. "You never know, just looking for clues. Somebody, somewhere must know something about this poor unfortunate individual."

"Somebody probably does. But it's not me." Jacob stated.

Catchpole remained staring at Jacob for a few brief seconds as if waiting for him to say something else. Marelle imagined Jacob looked away not maintaining the eye contact as she could not see from her position alongside him. Eventually Catchpole moved his eyes away, looked down to the road. 'And you are going to come down to the station for that DNA test on Wednesday?" He questioned, trying to be 'by the way' about it.

"I said I would." Jacob confirmed, quietly.

Catchpole looked back to them. "Good." He said. "We can at least tick that box then."

They went into the house as Catchpole drove away. Jacob closed the front door with his back against it and remained there for a second. Marelle, realising he had not followed her to the kitchen, stopped and turned. Jacob stood there, still against the front door. He sighed.

"Did you do biology at school?" He asked.

"Pardon?" Marelle questioned, wondering where his train of thought was going.

"Did you study biology?"

"No." She smiled.

He nodded. "Well I did." He said. "I did and there was this flatworm that lives in water. Tiny thing, they are essentially a very basic organism. They are blind but if you put one in a tray of water and a piece of food at the other end you can sit and watch that tiny, blind flatworm work in a pattern, seeking out the food, back and forth, zig-zagging until it finally homes in on the item of food. I don't know if it is intelligence or instinct – or if their rudimentary brain can even cultivate intelligence ... but nonetheless ..." He sighed and finally strode towards her. "Nonetheless, it eventually works it out and achieve it's goal ..."

He walked up to her; she reached up and took his face gently in her hands.

"Ssshh." She whispered. "This is our house now – let's think about *that*."

The timing of the purchase of the house couldn't really have been worse. Yesterday they had achieved a huge step in their journey together but now Catchpole's visit and the upcoming Yellow Son gig were consuming Jacob in such a way that the house being in their hands fell by the wayside. Jacob was intense today, painted with colours so bright yet bounded by solid black outlines. Marelle sensed that one eye which stared out of his soul was Jacob but the other was definitely Ezza.

The whole day was planned around his perceived perception of how it had to be that night. He had it all in his mind in a rigid timetable – knew exactly what he needed to be doing every minute of the day until they arrived at the venue that evening. Marelle felt that drifting with it was her only option, pulled long by the strength of Jacob's tide.

For some reason he spent a lot of time on that day staring in the mirror. Marelle didn't question him or ask why – she had learned enough to let him be. From mid-afternoon, one hundred percent of his attention about getting himself ready. His intention was to be a bold and obvious reincarnation of what he presumed to be typical Ezza, as he had said, he had just one chance to get this right. He had to get Chas' attention enough to make him want to ask questions. Jacob had no intention of proclaiming himself or waving a flag – he just wanted Chas to see him and recognise him. Fate would do the rest.

But she feared that fate would do nothing. Marelle feared that fate would give him one quick glance from Chas, who would hardly notice him and life would move on beneath their feet. That was what she feared because in Jacob's mindset that was simply not an option.

Marelle watched him preen himself, play with his hair, put clothes on, look at himself in the mirror. Ezza *was* a vain bastard, and Jacob had done well to hide that streak.

"What shall I wear?" She had questioned, standing in the bedroom, watching him.

"Hmm?" He responded, flattening the sides of his hair with the palm of his hand.

"What shall I wear?"

"Anything you want. Whatever you're comfortable in ..."

"Well as the fiancé of such a rock star I want to look the part!"

He grinned, gave a little laugh. "Just be yourself ..."

"Well if I put-on six-inch heels and a strapless dress I'm going to look pretty silly, aren't I?"

"Put the dark jeans on with your cowboy boots and that pink shirt." He suggested.

Marelle stared at him. She wasn't even aware he took much notice of what she wore or even what clothes she owned. "Shall I?" She asked.

It had been what she had worn the night when she had stolen that very first kiss from him at the Thor site. It had been her birthday and she had decided to make her move and make it clear to him just what she wanted. She wasn't sure if he even remembered that or if what she had worn was all she remembered!

It was an odd feeling seeing Jacob in the clothes he had selected to wear. She had seen him in the lock-up when he had chosen the outfit, and they had been hanging in the bedroom since. Admittedly she would have considered it a little over the top but it was Ezza and was what he was wearing in many of the old pictures. But when Jacob put those clothes on and stood in front of her it was an odd feeling. She wasn't sure why, but it made her feel ever so slightly uncomfortable. Used to seeing him in ripped jeans and a fleece, she knew how good he could look when he dressed up – but this was a whole new look; a whole new persona – but which she somehow felt intimidated by.

His hair was perfect and sharp, placed to an exact style – today with enough product in it to make sure it stayed there. Marelle could smell whatever he had put in it from a distance away! He looked tall and thin; the shirt he wore was oversized anyway – and she had never seen him in a waistcoat before. It was Ezza alright but it was not Jacob;. It may have been once, but now with Jacob running through him he looked like the result of a rummage in the dressing up box. She smiled to herself as he stood playing with the car keys, looking in the mirror in the hallway. Tonight, she was with Ezza; Jacob was somewhere else right now – she didn't know where.

"I'll drive." He said.

Tonight he drove faster than he normally did. There was an urgency about him. It was at best a two-hour drive and he had it all planned. The timings were waymarked in his head – he knew what time he had to leave, what time they should arrive at the venue, where they would park and the very minute he planned to be at the entrance. Marelle let him take the lead and followed him, hand in hand.

The venue was a newish building. All glass façade with a large space and a café at the front. They were early but there were a few people milling about. She noticed two guys in Yellow Son t-shirts chatting close to the café as they walked in. Over to the far left was a flight of stairs with a door beside it at the bottom. There stood a gathering of five or six people in a group, laughing. A security guard stood at the door behind them. Jacob headed in that direction. As they approached the small group, one member at the front raised her eyes to them. She had been chatting quite animatedly to the person beside her– they didn't seem overly interested in her words so did not notice now that she had stopped. Ellen. Of course. Right at the head of the queue. She wore a navy blue 'Yellow Son' hoodie, but they could see the image of Ezza just visible on her t-shirt beneath. Ellen stared at them; stared hard at Jacob but did not say anything to them. Marelle knew Jacob had flicked his eyes away, but she still saw Ellen mouth '*for fuck's sake*' to herself then turn back to her conversation.

Marelle tightened her hand on his, involuntarily squeezing it as they stood together in a haphazard kind of queue. Jacob certainly looked the part, certainly stood out from the other people there but as is normal with the British psyche – no-one visibly gave it any attention. Ellen chose not to speak to them and apart from a woman a couple of places ahead of them who gave Marelle an uncertain little smile, no-one tried to make conversation with them.

People began filing into the brightly lit foyer in twos or small groups. Soon there was a buzz in the air– everyone excited to be here – groups forming around the entrance. Marelle leant against Jacob and looked over to her left. There was a makeshift stall set up selling t-shirts, hats and various items with Yellow Son's logo printed on them. The logo was basically the same as the one on Jacob's old t-shirt but obviously less faded. Most of the shirts were black or white with the logo large on the chest and the tour dates beneath.

A mix-match of Yellow Son clothing adorned those around them. Some in brand new, just purchased t-shirts, others in an array of colours and styles and which marked various tours and years throughout their history. There in the middle stood Jacob – Ezza – dressed in his white shirt and his black waistcoat, red lining blazing where it was visible. Right there, among them all walked their beloved Ezza – but no-one even suspected it. Marelle clutched his hand then moved her eyes to the right as the doors began to open in front of them and the crowd began to shuffle in anticipation. A female employee stood inside the open doorway and a security guard on the other side. She checked tickets and the security guard stamped everyone's hand. Ellen made her first place in the queue obvious to everyone and was the first to disappear into the darkness of the dimly lit auditorium. Then they too were in the doorway, tickets being checked, and hands held out in anticipation of the numbers being indelibly stamped into the backs of their hands. Marelle had put hand cream on in the car and doubted the ink would hold, she was checking it when Jacob dragged her forward. He took her hand, and they passed through the doorway into the open space of the auditorium too. Nodding to her to follow he strode across the still empty, wooden floor to stand right at the barrier, slightly right.

Marelle leant her hands against the cold steel. This seemed oddly familiar after being at the previous gig with Bella and Mae. This time they were on their own; there was no Bella to hide behind. This time Jacob's plan was to be here at the front and stare right into the eyes of Chas. In under three hours Jacob may well have a better idea of what the future held for him.

He wasn't saying much, just staring at the stage – his face devoid of any hint of expression. She knew that tension in his jaw; that thousand yard stare in his eyes. Here, on a stage like this – well much bigger than this – he had walked out and lost it; lost the ability to be Ezza and to do what she now knew, he truly desired. Who said it would be any different second time around? Who said that he could walk out and still be that person whose clothes he wore and whose haircut he had calmly instructed her to reproduce? He didn't know. Nobody knew – just as the very first-time mankind had tried to harness the power of nuclear energy, nobody truly knew what the consequences might be.

Marelle looked up at him. His eyes were hollow and dark, black pools of insecurity. She felt his heartbeat.

"Is there a support band?" She asked.

He suddenly looked to her, like he had forgotten she was there.

"I don't know." He answered. "I assume so ..."

The place was filling up behind them – many people made straight for the bar at the back but gradually gravitated down on to the floor. Ellen was four or five people along to their left. She appeared to be with an elderly balding guy but was staring at Jacob when Marelle looked across. Then she obviously made a comment about him to her companion as both of them stared. Maybe, in a little while, she would have something else to say.

Jacob didn't notice. Consumed in his own world; staring blankly at the stage – not happy to be here like everyone else around them but resigned to it.

The minutes and seconds ticked away unbelievably slowly as the buzz of the crowd around them grew. The weight of people behind them increased with the noise until the crew had finished checking everything on stage. Eventually the lights dimmed, and two guys walked on to the stage to muted applause from an audience who had not come to see them.

They were two older guys, both with a guitar. Weatherworn from a lifetime of performing and never having made it, they were comfortable on stage – not fazed by the lack of response or adoration from the crowd – not from their own confidence or presence but through the years of having endured this, time after time. The guy singing had a nice smile, but he did not direct it at anyone, looked right through the crowd and beyond to his own horizon.

They played well. Their songs were catchy, and they were both completely competent musicians. The crowd were half watching, standing through something they wished would hurry up and end. Many people were engaged in conversation, looking at their phones. Behind them, Marelle heard a whole conversation about the price of drinks in the bar they had been to before the gig. She held on to Jacob as he stared up at the performers on stage, dead fish eyes as he tested the waters. No-one made eye contact with him.

They played for forty-five minutes to an audience that wasn't in the least bit interested in them. Then they left the stage, Marelle watched them walk off. They did not look back at the audience and most of the audience didn't even notice – or care – that they had gone.

Jacob remained staring at the stage while the crew raced on to start moving, checking and placing equipment. Behind them people moved and jostled for places. Marelle wrapped her hand around his arm and lay her head against him. She raised her eyes along the barrier and caught Ellen staring at them again.

Jacob didn't move. For the thirty minutes they stood there, not moving an inch. He didn't speak and Marelle didn't ask any questions but there was a thread of silent communication between them. She knew he was deep in wrangling thoughts with himself and with what he was about to do.

Half an hour later the lights dimmed and the walk on music that Marelle recognised from the previous gig started up. The lights had dimmed down to darkness and the crowd was buzzing with a rising anticipation.

Then the four of them walked on. Marelle still couldn't remember all of their names – but the drummer was first on and took his place behind his drum kit. He was followed by the other two with Chas coming out last. He walked on with his hands in the air, clapping as he smiled to the cheering crowd. Jacob's eyes were fixed on him as Marelle raised hers to look at Chas too. All four of them took their places with their instruments. Chas walked to the front, looked to the guitarist on his right and they started up a now familiar tune which Marelle remembered from before. The crowd cheered, Chas laughed, everyone looked happy and Jacob stared.

At that moment Marelle was hit with a rushing realisation of what that moment when Jacob and Chas finally made eye contact would mean.

It would signify the end of Jacob and the rise of Ezza. It would mean that Jacob would no longer need the existence that he had carved out of nothing. It meant he would shed that skin and leave it like a discarded item of clothing that was no longer required.

In that moment her life would change as much as his. He would be opening himself up to a tsunami of reality which would mean all of his closely kept secrets would suddenly be out there – being picked through by everyone who thought they had an interest.

It would not be a simple glance but a collusion of their sight which would amount to just a fleeting second. This would be a look of utter depth and conciliation, of reunion and reincarnation.

Once he'd made that yearned for eye contact with Chas their lives may never be the same again.

Marelle looked up to Jacob and gripped her fingers around his arm but his eyes were fixed on stage. There was an urge within her to tug at his arm and almost guide him away from here; take Jacob away with her while he still remained but the expression on his face and the absolute depth of the gaze in his eyes told her it was probably too late to turn back now.

Chas did not look into the crowd; he took up his guitar and the other group members followed cue with a familiarity between them gained from the years together. With an unrehearsed synchronicity they launched into the track they had opened with at the other show. A couple of bars further in Chas stepped up to the microphone and sang the first line of the song.

Marelle could hear his voice better tonight. It was clear and precise above the music. He played and sang with a polished edge, an accomplished, time-served performer.

They moved smoothly from the initial song into the second track without a pause or any word from Chas. Around Marelle and Jacob people were cheering and clapping, animated like water moving around a stationary rock in a stream while Jacob stood there with his eyes fixed on Chas. In turn Chas was a master at this. He knew not to stare into the crowd for too long; he knew not to allow himself to make eye contact with anyone however, at the same time, offering each individual his total attention. Marelle found her own eyes carefully watching him too and, she thought, there was a fleeting moment when he did look at Jacob and a tiny flash of unease passed over him. But as quickly as Marelle thought she witnessed that, it had gone, and Chas was directing his attention elsewhere.

As the set progressed, Marelle was sure she noticed Chas' eyes straying in Jacob's direction again. Very subtle, you would not notice it if you were not looking for it, but his eyes moved that way – hardly settling at all, hardly even a glance but nonetheless a tiny moment before they looked away again. Then she watched it happen again – there was no mistake this time. His attention had been spiked in passing and now he had returned to have a subtle second look. It wasn't that long, lingering look of utter realisation that Jacob was maybe hoping for; it wasn't even a snippet of eye contact – it was the looking away and looking back again. *That* was the indication that there was *something* there – even if nobody was entirely sure of what.

After that song, they let the music die down instead of ploughing straight into the next track. It was the point where Chas would address the audience – like he had at the other concert. Marelle felt her fingers tighten more on Jacob's arm, but she doubted he could feel or even notice. Chas held an arm aloft and shushed the crowd.

THIRTY-THREE

"Thank you!" He said. "Thank you all for coming tonight. I can see a few familiar faces in the crowd ... and you know that's what keeps us coming back again and again ..." He looked to his right, at the guitarist who smiled back at him.

"Remember this one?" Chas laughed and they launched into another song to rapturous whoops from the crowd.

Marelle watched Chas as he stepped up against the microphone, legs straight and strong, astride as he belted out the lyrics. He was good, he'd done it for years and years but from what she had seen he did not have the finesse of Jacob – or rather, Ezza. Chas did not look like that unassuming bloke they had seen walking along the beach with his dog a few weeks ago. From that encounter Marelle would never have guessed he stood up there and did this for a living. But he did – and he was a consummate professional. The crowd loved him. But right now, Marelle felt that he was avoiding eye contact with Jacob.

Marelle got the impression that the crowd loved him. Maybe they had got used to Chas by now. Maybe they would not want Ezza back. She raised her eyes to Jacob again, but his stance and his gaze were unmoving.

They played on, and as before the slotted one of the 'big' songs into the set early, getting the crowd going, wound up the frenzy with one they could all sing along to. After that Chas stopped the music again, laughing and absent-mindedly – or not – playing with his guitar.

"Jeez!" he laughed. "How good was that. Hey? How fucking good was that?" He looked out to see the crowd, looked at Ellen. "No, no I've got the boss here tonight, so I've got to be on my best behaviour, or I'll get the sack!" He smiled. He had a nice smile. "She's watching me. I can feel her beady eyes on me!" He laughed, patted his guitar. "Mind you – if I was sacked there's a fella here who I think could take my place. Have you seen him, hey? Have you seen him?" He turned his head and looked in their direction. Looked right at both of them. By sheer luck and determination, he looked Jacob right in the eyes. "I'm afraid Ezza isn't with us anymore – where have you been fella – he went swimming with the fishes and never came back." Chas stared at them, held out a hand. "God bless Ezza. We all miss Ezza, don't we? Right down to his cotton socks – and everything that went in them ..."

The crowd mumbled a unified acknowledgement of Ezza. Chas continued.

"Still – you look good. I didn't know they made an Ezza fancy dress outfit!"

The crowd laughed and so did Chas. He smiled towards Jacob. "I'm not taking the piss ... good on you fella ..." and he held a thumbs up to Jacob as he laughed and turned away to pick out an intro that Marelle was now familiar with.

Jacob laughed, lifted his hand in the air but the moment had passed. Chas had moved it on.

Yellow Son launched themselves into another succession of four or five songs which moved from one to the other without any pause for words. The crowd went with it, loved it, cheered, jumped up and down at Chas's lead.

At a couple of points, he looked Jacob's way and recognised that undying stare that Jacob had fixed on him. Once, Chas held the stare, looked directly back into Jacob's eyes. Neither blinked and it was Chas who turned away first.

Gradually, she was realising that Chas knew there was something going on here.

They played the same set as before and she half remembered what was coming. Jacob was in his own little zone so did not really notice. Marelle began to sense Chas avoiding looking in their direction now. When – and if – he did, it was just a quick glance as if to see whether Jacob was still staring. Each time he was – because Jacob's eyes never moved away from Chas – never lost an opportunity to clash eyes at every available moment.

They played '*the last one for tonight*' which, of course, everyone knew wasn't the last one. When they returned to the stage for the encore Chas strode on, this time staring straight at Jacob across the distance between stage and barrier. Then he pointed a finger right at them, mouthed something and made a gesture of indeterminable meaning. Marelle felt Jacob shuffle his feet slightly in acknowledgement, but his stare never faltered. The song struck up to a clapping, cheering crowd around them as they stood like two rocks in a stream of broiling water. Marelle took a deep breath and wrapped her fingers tighter around his arm.

As that song came to an end she felt Jacob tense. He knew this was the last song, but he did not know if he had succeeded in attracting Chas' attention in the correct way to elicit any contact with him beyond the glances on stage.

The music died down and Chas walked up to the microphone.

Thank you." He smiled. "Thank you. See you all soon … goodnight!"

The four of them came together at the front of the stage, waved, smiled.

The crowd cheered. The band waved. Jacob shuffled. Chas turned away, said something to the other guys in the band. Marelle still could not remember their names.

They appeared about to walk off. Jacob leaned over the barrier, Marelle held his arm. She was not totally sure he would not go over it as this precise moment. Then Chas turned back, looked right at him – held the haze for a moment then turned on his heel and walked over.

Jacob turned to meet his eyes as the house lights came up. For a few seconds their eyes were locked, Jacob's head turning as Chas approached a parallel spot on the stage to them. He stopped, pointed a finger.

"Hey fella. Nice try. Don't go eyeballing me again at a gig hey? I've enough ghosts to bear …" He paused, grinned in consideration then stood upright.

"Chas, it's Ezza!" Jacob shouted. "It's me!"

His words sounded more than pathetic as Marelle gripped him and turned her face to Chas as well. Chas made a face that was a little painful, a little sarcastic.

"Come on fella. Get a grip …" Chas said.

Someone beside them realised that Chas was conversing with the crowd and leant over the barrier, pushing into them, screaming at Chas – congratulating and thanking him profusely. For a moment Chas smiled and spoke to them politely.

"Chas. It's me. It's Ezza. I'm still alive!" Jacob cried again.

The other person was still yelling at Chas. Jacob was pleading. Chas stood up again.

"Chas!" Jacob shouted. "Give me five. I can prove this!"

Chas stared at him, right into his eyes, lingered and held the gaze but then he turned his head and walked away, exiting the stage on the far side.

Marelle felt Jacob tense. She felt his muscles solidify as he raised himself up slightly on his toes.

"Chas!" He shouted, urgency in his voice as Chas disappeared.

That was it. This was the moment Marelle had dreaded and the one which she knew would shape both hers and Jacob's lives from this moment on.

"Chas!" He shouted urgently again, moving slightly along the barrier as people began to depart from their positions at the front of the stage.

Marelle moved with him, they came face to face with Ellen, placed dead centre.

"Chas!" Jacob yelled again but he had gone.

Marelle looked at Ellen who was in turn staring at Jacob – or Ezza unnoticed by him.

"Idiot." She said, as she too moved away. If she was moving away, then she knew Chas was not coming back.

Jacob." Marelle called to him, but he was pulling away from her.

"Chas!" He shouted again, desperation clawing at his vocal chords. He stood, holding on to the rail, staring at the exit Chas had left through.

People were moving off, walking away, laughing – happy – discussing the gig. Jacob wrapped his hand around the metal rail, leaned back a little, raised his eyes to one of the crew who had begun stripping down the leads and cables. Their eyes were in contact for a second or two but then Jacob blinked away, dropped his gaze as she still hung on to the barrier.

Marelle held his arm tightly, laid her head against him.

"Are you OK?" She asked.

He didn't answer. He shuffled, rocked slightly against his grip on the rail. Marelle looked to his face. He looked as if he was about to cry and she tightened her hold on him.

'Jacob?" She asked again but he wasn't listening. She could almost see the sound going on in his head right now. A cacophony of screaming, wailing ghosts from his past and her future. He lifted his head slightly, looked at the stage where members of the crew were scurrying around like ants, laughing and joking with one another. Marelle sighed. She didn't want to drag him away like a reticent two-year-old but the room was emptying around them. The floor was strewn with plastic cups and pieces of paper. Marelle looked down and kicked a couple away with her toe. As she looked up again at Jacob's face, she wondered what would truly be the right thing to do here. She sensed someone approaching them on the left side of the barrier. It was security, all in black with a hand held radio and a fluorescent trimmed tabard on. She sighed. They were about to be moved on, and she was not sure how Jacob would react. Marelle had experienced his emotional and anger filled erratic behaviour before – although at that time it had also been alcohol fuelled. At least tonight he was sober. She placed her fingers securely around his arm and prepared herself.

"Excuse me sir." The security guard said, walking up and standing next to both of them on the stage side of the barrier.

"It's ok." Marelle answered pre-emptively. "We're just leaving.' She tugged slightly at Jacob's arm."

"Excuse me sir." He said again. "But I've been asked to see if you could possibly come backstage – the guy in the band wants to speak to you …"

She felt Jacob's head snap round to him before she even realised what the security guard had said. Marelle raised her eyes to both of them seeing the none too subtle stare as Jacob's eyes also engaged with his.

"If you could follow me." He continued.

Jacob went from static and sessile to suddenly moving quickly and striding along the front of the barrier towards the right-hand side of the stage. At the far end, the security guard moved the barrier out of the way to let them pass through.

"Follow me." He said.

They walked down a narrow passageway alongside the stage then turned right along a dimly lit corridor at the back of the stage to another corner which obviously ran back down the other side. The walls were painted breezeblock, and it felt cold. All along the back wall were brown laminate doors. Marelle noticed they were numbered and as they turned the final bend, they stopped in front of number eight.

"I just need to do a security check." The guy informed them. "Are you happy for me to do a quick search?"

Jacob looked at him blankly for a second, then nodded and raised his arms to shoulder height. Marelle didn't understand what he was doing or what this meant but as the guard took a moment to search and 'pat' him down, Marelle realised what was happening and that Jacob seemed used to this. She could feel the adrenalin running through him as he stood aside, and the security guard turned to her. She heard Jacob's stomach gurgle.

"Are you happy for me to search you?" He asked.

Marelle wondered what would have happened if she had said no, but did not want to hold anything up so she nodded and copied what Jacob had just done a few seconds before. She hardly felt him touch her and was aware of all the places she could easily have concealed something that would not have been found from that search but she raised her eyes to Jacob and caught a broiling distance in them she had not seen before. He shuffled from one foot to the next as the guard stepped past them both and tapped gently on the door.

"What?" A voice shouted from inside, not angrily, just abruptly.

"It's Dave from Security. I've brought that guy round ..." He announced, his face against the door.

Jacob stood there, his eyes wide and fixed on the door. Marelle could see his nostrils flaring slightly as he breathed. There was a pause – a moment where all three of them just stood there in the corridor, dimly it, quiet, except for the muffled sounds from the auditorium. Someone laughed closer to them, Marelle supposed from another room. Surreptitiously the smell of fear perfused her own nostrils. She suspected it emanated from Jacob.

The door clicked and opened an inch. There was a light on inside which was brighter than where they stood. The inch widened and there, in the arc of the open door, stood Chas.

He looked smaller standing there, older. There were lines on his face she hadn't noticed before. His eyes were bluish grey, quite dull, but quite piercing at the same time. He raised his eyes to Jacob, stared hard at him but Jacob did not blink or look away.

"Thank you." Chas said to Dave from Security. "It's OK. Just hang around ..."

Marelle stared at him. Was there a genuine concern here for someone to be carrying a weapon with the intent of harm? *'Just hang around'* Chas had said. He obviously didn't feel safe with Jacob.

Chas looked back into Jacob's eyes. "So fella, what's the game?"

Jacob sighed. "It's not a game. I'm Ezza... I didn't kill myself ..."

Chas laughed. "No, you're not. It's a nice try ... it's close – it had me fooled for a second but ... I don't think so!"

"But it's me! I can explain everything. Listen to me – ask me anything ... I can prove I'm Ezza!"

Chas exhaled noisily, holding on to the door. "Nice try ... you got my attention ..."

"No!" Jacob suddenly exclaimed loudly. The security guard took a step closer. "No!" Jacob repeated, more quietly. "Give me five minutes – please ..."

Chas stared at him. Marelle could see uncertainty flickering in his eyes. Uncertainty as to whether he should listen to this weird, pleading man but she could also see a shadowy glimmer of recognition in them too that seemed to be desperately trying to hide itself behind the cloak of uncertainty. It was that which she knew Jacob had seen too and was now trying it grasp its slippery form in his hands.

'Five minutes.' Jacob repeated. "It's me. It's Ezza. I'm not dead."

Chas sighed again. He stared at Jacob, looked over his shoulder to the security guard, then back to Jacob.

"Five minutes." He said. "Come in."

He opened the door and stood aside. Jacob walked in, past Chas. Jacob looked so much taller when he was actually next to him and passing by.

Marelle followed closely, hoping she would not be excluded. If she was she would argue to stay. As they filed in, Chas leaned out and said something to the guard. He closed the door behind them both.

The room was small – probably twelve by twelve at the most. It had mirrors along one wall with a long counter beneath them. There were four chairs along that side; a table in the middle had bags and cases on it. A laptop was open on the table with an email screen open. Chas walked past them and sat himself down. He had changed his t-shirt and now wore a faded orange one. A denim jacket with a sheepskin collar was draped over the back of a chair and an opened bottle of Budweiser stood on the counter at the far side.

Jacob stood in front of him, Marelle slightly behind. She looked at the back of Jacob's head, thought that his hair was too short at the back.

'So, what's this all about?" Chas asked.

"You saw me out there. I know you saw me!" Jacob began.

"Yes, I saw you. Some idiot dressed like the ex-lead singer of the band ... the *dead* ex lead singer of the band ..."

Jacob exhaled noisily in exclamation. "I wasn't *dressed* as the ex-lead singer of the band. I *am* the ex-lead singer of the band."

Chas smiled. Marelle was unsure if it was sarcasm or warmth. He had a nice smile. "Do you think Ezza would still look like you if he was here today? We are all older. We all change. He'd probably be fat and bald – or have a beard and long hair – not look like he's just stepped off the stage from over a decade ago."

Jacob stared at him. Stood there in that silent room and stared at Chas.

"I swear to God Chas, it's me. It's Ezza. I did not kill myself. I did not drown. You identified someone else as me all those years ago – you cremated someone else as me ... I'm still here ..."

"Then where have you been for nearly twelve bloody years? Why didn't you come forward at the time and let everyone know?"

Jacob made a little exclamation; shook his head. "I was in a bad place. You know I was. I wanted to be alone. I wanted to keep my head down and take a break until I could see my way straight again. I went home ... I shut myself away ... I spent a couple of weeks in bed, hardly moving, sleeping, eating, waking – while my head took the lead. I listened to voices and played non-stop movies in my head. My intention *was* to come back – then I heard on the radio that I had been found dead. That I had taken my own life. At first, I was angry and upset but I soon realised that this was a chance to start again ... to be someone else. It meant I had to turn my back on Ezza but at least it meant I had freedom to carry on in a way where I at least stood a chance of having a life ..."

"So what happened then? Why are you here now?" Chas asked him in a way that suggested he wasn't in the least bit interested anyway.

"I met Marelle." Jacob replied. "And she showed me that I am living a lie; that I have a real life to reclaim – I want to come back Chas."

Chas laughed. "You what!"

"I want to come back to Yellow Son."

"Jesus!" Chas exclaimed under his breath. He laughed again. "Yeah, that's fine ... yeah, just go ahead ... some fucking weirdo just appears at a gig and I believe his cock and bull story so – yes – I'm just going to let you walk right in and take over what I have left of Yellow Son and my *own* livelihood ... what the fuck are you ... apart from someone with monumental balls for coming up with this and having the gall to go through with it!"

"I'm Ezza. I'm Nathaniel Ezekiel Frost. Look at me Chas! You can see it's me!"

Chas turned his head to Jacob. Marelle could feel Jacob's need to be animated but he was wholly restraining himself.

"Yeah, yeah, yeah. You *do* look like him – granted. You do have a touch of his mannerisms and raw desperation ... and you do have that fucked up look in your eyes. I can see the craziness in there – I always said you would end up topping yourself – you know I did. You were always a fucking headcase anyway! What if this were true, hey? What if you *are* Ezza ...?"

"Then I want to come back."

"Prove to me that you are Ezza then." Chas said.

"Ask me anything ... there must be things that only I could know ... let me sing ... let me show you!"

Chas made a noise, a grunt, an exclamation of the strange situation he found himself in.

"Come on. You *know* it's me. I can tell you know." Jacob stated.

"I don't know!" Chas replied. "It's a fact that I could never know, and you expect me to lay it all on the line for *you*? Why?"

Jacob sighed. "The crowd still acknowledges me – they still remember me – they all still *love* me. Just think what it would mean if I came back."

Chas sniggered. "Yeah! Just imagine!"

"I can prove to you that I am Ezza!"

"How?" Chas snapped.

"Ask me some things that only I would know ..."

'What's my real name?"

"Patrick Charles Symonds." Jacob answered without hesitation.

"What was the rejected name for the album that eventually went out as 'Nightshift'?"

"Flare." Jacob said.

Chas grinned.

'What sort of car was I driving when we first met?"

Jacob glared at him. Paused, then said. "A petrol blue Range Rover."

"Registration?"

"Fuck off!" Jacob replied.

Chas laughed. "No, I don't know it either! But all of these things – you could have got them off the internet – you can get *anything* off the internet – they don't *prove* anything."

"Chas. You know it's me. I know you – I stood beside you for nearly twenty years – I *know* you know it's me so why keep pissing around?" Jacob exclaimed.

"All of this stuff." Chas said. "You might have learned. People are weird you know …"

"You know it's me. You've known all along that it wasn't me that you identified."

"It looked like you. Same height, build – been in the water for three weeks though so there was no guarantee from the facial features – wore your jacket – still had your car keys in the pocket, your wallet …"

"It wasn't me." Jacob stated.

"So what do you want? Coming here to this gig?"

"I want to come back as Ezza …"

"No, no, no." Chas replied. "That's not happening!"

"Why?"

"It's not happening." Chas stated. "If – and that's a massive *if* – you were Ezza – which I don't know for sure, either way – if you really *were* Ezza and I let you come waltzing back, like nothing had ever happened – well apart from the legal and other implications around that – it would be one big fuck off to me and to the rest of the band who carried on and have worked damn fucking hard over the years, taken all kinds of shit – to keep this going and scrape a living from it. Think how the others would feel. Their share of everything reduced to accommodate a fifth member – and I still have no bloody idea who you are …"

"You know it's me. You wouldn't have given me time of day if you didn't know it was me …"

At that point someone banged on the door.

"What?" Chas shouted.

"Wondered if you were alive. Are you coming with us?"

"I'm fine. Jog on. I've got my car here."

"We were going to get food."

"I'm OK. Jog on." Chas shouted back.

"'K."

Jacob turned his eyes to Chas. "Marty?" He said.

Chas nodded.

'They would know it was me."

"No, they fucking wouldn't!" Chas answered. "And I don't want you pestering any of them. If you do, I'll get a restraining order …"

"What!" Jacob exclaimed.

"You're just some stranger who's waltzed in here tonight, dressed like Ezza – looking like Ezza ..."

"I *am* Ezza!"

"Who knows? Who knows, hey?"

"*You* know." Jacob said.

"No, I don't." Chas replied. "Look, I said five minutes. You've had more. Best be on your merry way now fella."

"But Chas! It's me! I'm not dead – I'm still here ..."

Chas stood up, picked up the denim jacket and went to put it on. He shook his head. "I'm going home."

"Chas! *Please*! This is my last chance. This means so much to me ... I just want to come back ... you *know* it's me. You *know* it is ... what are you scared of?"

"Scared of? Nothing fella!" Chas slid into his jacket.

"Then listen to me." Jacob pleaded.

"I've listened. I'm not convinced. You know, fans know more about the band than I do! They never cease to amaze me! Nothing is beyond the impossible!"

Marelle was an observer, watching this passive aggressive game of chess unfold before her. She could see Jacob's desperation but at the same time she could see Ezza right there, up front, screaming silently for his life. She wanted to help him but had nothing she could add which would help. Jacob stepped closer to Chas. Chas stood himself upright but did not back away.

"Look." Jacob sighed. "Look into these eyes and tell me you don't know who I am ... look!" He leaned forward, pointed to his eyes.

"I never liked looking into Ezza's eyes. Always too much fucking darkness in them."

"Look!" Jacob exclaimed. "You know! *You know*!"

This was getting heated as Jacob – or Ezza – sensed it slipping through his fingers. Marelle felt a rush of fear pulse through her – how far would he take this?

"I don't fucking know! I'll never fucking know but that's a risk I'm prepared to take right now!"

"Chas! Please!" Jacob lowered his voice and pleaded. His eyes now closed.

"No." Chas said.

"Is Mya here?"

"No."

"You said she was – during the gig."

"She's not. I was making things up to say. You should know what it's like ... she's not here."

"She would know it was me."

"Maybe she would but we are not going to find that out, are we? We're going home." Chas stated.

"You were right. I will end up topping myself. I will, this time – and it will all be down to you!"

"Nah, nah, nah – don't pull *that* one. I'm done. I'm not playing your games …" Chas said, quietly but angrily.

Marelle wanted to reach out and drag Jacob out of this now, but she was frozen to the spot.

"Well fucking listen to me!" Jacob cried now. Desperate, he actually *cried*. Thrashing about in the water of this terminal conversation, fighting for his very life right now.

"I've listened. You can't prove to me who you are!" Chas remarked, sternly but quietly. "Go now or I'm calling security."

"No."

"Come on. Out." Chas ordered.

"Chas, it's Ezza. It's me! Please!"

Chas walked towards them; one arm raised to usher them out.

'Stop!" Jacob yelled, reaching out and grabbing Chas' arm. "Just stop!"

"Hey fella!" Chas said calmly, quietly.

"Just fucking stop this! You know who I am!"

'I don't."

"You do!"

"No, I don't!" Chas exclaimed, really raising his voice for the first time. "I don't fucking know. Maybe I don't want to fucking know!"

'That's it! You don't give a fuck about me! You did this to me – you pulled me into this and now you don't really give a fuck! You bastard – you fucking bastard!"

Chas was staring into his face, holding him off, bracing himself against Jacob's grip.

"Then tell me this!" Chas retorted. "Tell me this! Tell me the name of the girl you got pregnant and who I had to arrange for her to get rid – tell me that because there's only you, me and her who would know that."

THIRTY-FOUR

Jacob stopped. His face lost all expression. Marelle watched the colour drain from it. He suddenly looked defeated and small against Chas. Chas waited, raised his eyebrows.

"Well?"

Marelle watched Jacob blink twice, swallow, fight with the words in his mouth.

"Isabelle Dorftt." He finally said.

Chas stared at him, shrugged his hands off him and stood a pace back.

Chas didn't say anything, just stared at him for a good few passing seconds. Then he nodded, gestured to a chair.

Jacob stepped sideways, did not raise his eyes to either Chas or Marelle but sat himself down, staring at the floor.

Chas sat down again, nodded subtly for Marelle to do the same. She was glad to, her legs felt abnormally weak and her mind was off somewhere else right now.

Chas raised an elbow on the countertop, rested his head on his hand.

"Fuck me!" He said.

There was silence now. She could hear Jacob breathing, but he would not look at her. Chas was staring at him.

"I always knew it wasn't you." Chas finally imparted. "I expected you to turn up when that body was identified. When you didn't, I began to wonder …"

Jacob suddenly had no words. Ezza was curled up tightly deep inside him and Jacob had reverted to not making eye contact with anyone.

"Where've you been?"

Jacob shrugged reminded her so much of how he had been in the beginning.

"At home." He finally said.

"What, for nearly twelve years?"

Jacob nodded. "I got chucked out of the house – I've been living in a caravan on a disused airfield … working as a casual labourer on a farm."

"Well you look good on it." Chas smiled.

"That's partly down to Marelle."

"So why now?" Chas asked.

"I told you. I want my old life back. I can't go on hiding and living a lie. We want to get married, and we can't do that until I get my identity back …"

"Well, how have you lived for the last twelve years?"

"I assumed the identity of my brother who died at birth."

"Shit." Chas said.

"I want my life back."

"But why this here. Surely you can do this without involving me?"

"I want to be Ezza. I want to be with the band again." Jacob answered, his voice quiet now.

Chas shook his head. "No lad. We're not going to do that. Not now."

"Why? Tell me why? Imagine how good it could be if I came back!"

"Imagine the shit storm!" Chas added. "You don't want to do this to yourself – I'm glad you're still alive and I'm sorry for whatever happened to you but, just go and marry her – have a nice life, forget about this."

"I can't. This is part of it. This is Ezza – this is *me*. It's what I need to do – *again*."

"You don't Ez." Chas said. "You don't need this."

"Let me sing – let me sing, just once. I can do it now. It's all fine now."

Chas shook his head. "No."

"Please!"

"I can't. I won't. Not now." He repeated. "I'll tell you this Ez – we're calling it a day next year. We're all getting on a bit, we love it but it's hard work, and it's tough. We're old men – we can't do this forever. It will be announced officially in due course … we've got a few dates next year as a final tour for the fans then that's it."

"No." Jacob shook his head. "You can't stop! You're still filling venues – they still love you!"

"They do. But our fans are as old as us. They're dying too. Yes, we still fill venues but, well, we want to quit on a high note – not wait until we start dying ourselves and have to knock the band on the head." He explained. "You've got ten plus years on us lot remember – you were a spotty youth when you turned up … there's no point in you coming back just to end it next year."

"But I can. I don't mind."

Chas shook his head.

"It's all sorted." He slid the laptop towards himself, punched the keys then turned it to Jacob as it showed their logo on a blue background. Underneath it said 'Sunsetting Tour. The End.' "Have merch sorted, dates sorted, venues sorted."

Jacob stared at the screen, then looked to Chas.

"It's over." Chas said.

"But I could come back for this tour." Jacob suggested.

"And create a massive shit storm for everyone. No let's leave it as it is."

Jacob stared at the screen.

"Go solo." Chas said.

Jacob made a face. "I'm Yellow Son. I can't, don't want to …"

'Then just go home, marry the girl and live happily ever after. Forget about us. You had good times –and at least you're still alive and good looking!"

"Would you think about it?" Jacob persisted.

"No. I won't think about it. It's done." Chas said.

"I'll give you my number. Marelle, give Chas your number – write it down." Jacob turned to her, barking orders.

"I don't have a pen." She said.

"Have you got a pen?" Jacob asked Chas.

"I'm not taking your number. I'm not playing these games with you. It's over Ez."

Jacob looked around the room hurriedly, looked on every surface, every corner. On the table in the centre was a sheet of A4, printed with the set list they'd played tonight and a black marker pen. He grabbed it, thrust it at Marelle.

"Write it down!" He ordered again. Then he turned back to Chas. Marelle wrote her number in thick, black numbers on the A4 sheet behind him.

"Just take my number. Think about it. Call me." Jacob suggested.

"No." Chas stated. "I'm not getting your hopes up and I'm not pretending this is even a possibility. I'm not taking your number."

There was another knock on the door.

"Yes!" Chas shouted.

"Mr Symonds. We want to lock up in five minutes."

"OK." He shouted back. "I'm coming."

Jacob took the piece of paper, thrust it at Chas. "Take my number."

"I'm not taking your number." Chas replied. "Now they're locking up. It's time to go." He stood up, gestured for Jacob to do the same. He stood; Marelle copied. Chas held out a hand. Jacob stared at him. Chas held an open hand out to him. Reluctantly Jacob took it in a handshake which to him, looked akin to a Judas kiss.

Chas shook his hand.

"Glad you're ok. Nice to see you. Now go home, marry your lady and have the best life. You don't need me nor Yellow Son to do that." He dropped his hand, gathered his things, picked up a case and ushered them towards the door.

'Take care of yourselves.' He added for good measure as they came up against the door. He opened it for them and waited for both of them to step through. Chas in the doorway, case in hand, gave Jacob a smile.

"Ezza." He said, finally looking to Marelle. "Look after him. He's a special one."

"I will." Marelle said in a voice that seemed so tiny and insignificant as she wrapped her fingers around Jacob's arm.

Chas stepped out, closed the door behind him with a click.

"I'm going home." He said.

The walk back to the car was very similar to the night she had walked back from the Thor site when Jacob had been hit with the realisation of what had really happened to Frankie – except there was no screaming or wailing but a growing, dangerous silence. It frightened her more than any bestial noise he had made that night.

Their car was the only one left in the car park and as they walked up to it the lights went off one by one in the venue behind them. Once in the car the dash lights lit up his face.

"He didn't take the number." He said.

The drive home was silent. Jacob had made no move to drive or even go towards that side of the car. Marelle wasn't quite sure if she was thankful for that or not. He gave no instruction as she drove and she had to rely on road signs and her own memory as they traversed the dark and virtually empty roads in the now, early hours of the morning.

There were questions in her head. Battling round and round, bumping up against her lips but never finding their way out. All of the things Chas had said, all quite derogatory even though they weren't conveyed like that. All mentions labelling Jacob as crazy, unstable, dark – suicidal. Thrown into the conversation randomly like a cornucopic pick and mix of his past – but all eventually jostling to point in one direction. The same direction that Kally's visit had led her. And now, with that knowledge in mind together with the conversation with Chas and the blocking, red flag he had waved – made Marelle fear that her love and her love alone, would not be enough to find him; or to save him.

Right now, he was withdrawing beside her. Sat there, staring into space with his tongue in his teeth. She knew he was processing the information – but the outcome would only ever rest at one option.

Then, overarching it all was the elephant in the room which Chas had happily let loose. Isabelle Dorftt had conceived Jacob's child; had carried his child – once – albeit it only for a brief period. Marelle didn't feel jealousy, or anger about this. She understood, as she had previously conveyed to Jacob, that people had previous lives. She felt empty.

All along, Marelle had known he had a previous life that she was not aware of. He had told her snippets, hinted at things, described his past and laid out a picture for her. Now the picture he had painted seemed but one tiny piece in the disproportionate jigsaw of his life which, she was beginning to wonder, even fitted together at all. Right at the centre of it she was beginning to sense a gaping chasm of a black hole which the pieces were constantly teetering on the edge of.

This was meant to be a happy time – they were engaged – Jacob was focussed – they were buying the house – the Thor site was saved and work had stopped again on the airfield. Tonight, should have been the cherry on top; should, in his eyes, have been a black slapping, man-hugging reunion and a welcome back into the fray. Instead, his hopes had been wiped away, dashed – made finite. And, according to Chas, time had run out.

And here he was now. Slumped beside her in the seat. She almost expected him to bring his knees up and curl up in the seat. He didn't. She thanked God it was late and the pubs were closed – whatever he demanded there was no way she was stopping.

Marelle drove on for an hour and a half. He never said a word and neither did she. The house was dark and felt cold when they arrived home. Marelle flicked lights on, turned heating up, headed for the kitchen to make a mug of tea. He followed slowly, stood in the doorway – hands in his pockets still looking every inch Ezza.

"I'm going to bed." He said.

"Don't you want a cuppa first?" She turned to him, slightly surprised.

"No. I'm fine." He replied.

She put down the tin of tea bags, walked up to hi and folded her fingers around the lapels of the waistcoat with the scarlet lining and looked up into his face. It was straight. Totally straight. Not happy, sad, disheartened, fearful – just straight.

'Do you want to talk?" She asked.

'No." He replied, quietly.

"Anything you want to tell me?" She enquired.

"No." He whispered.

Marelle looked into his eyes. Something flickered in them for a second. She smiled and tiptoed up to place a kiss on his lips. He was cold and although he did not shy away, he did not respond to her. The vivid dream she had experienced of him in the morgue came back to her – and she remembered the feel of his cold, dead lips.

"I'm going to bed." He repeated.

"Ok." She replied. "I'll leave the tea. I'll come up with you."

He sighed, looked to the floor briefly then turned away from her and headed for the stairs.

At some point during the night, the rain beating against the window, Marelle awoke. She heard a roll of thunder in the distance and a brief white illumination of lightning. Beside her Jacob was asleep, on his side, turned away from her. Silent.

In the morning, after a fretful night's sleep she sat up in the bed. The rain fell from the leaden sky like heavy tears. This day was not one for celebration. Neither did it appear that there was any reason for one.

Jacob was asleep. He had the covers pulled right over him so only his hair was visible. He was quiet, unmoving, curled up on his side like a child beneath the covers.

Last night seemed so far away. The conversation in the room with Chas seemed like it had been alive only in her imagination. All of the words rolling into one; the angst; the fear; the desperation. Chas had not given him what he wanted. He had been pretty cool, pretty controlled, pretty amicable in the circumstances, but he had not given Jacob what he craved and offered no hope that it would ever be the case now. It was over. His dream was over.

Marelle didn't know how to approach this. Normally she had words and could help in some way. But this was a dead end, and she was not sure what solace she could offer, if any at all.

She sat herself up in bed, trying not to disturb the covers around him. Rain was tapping at the window and she could see the sky was steel grey. It made her shiver but somehow seemed appropriate today.

She climbed out of bed, wrapped a dressing gown around herself and went downstairs. She adjusted the heating as the whole house seemed cold and damp. The kettle and mugs were still poised on the worktop from last night. She flicked the switch on the kettle again. Slowly she raised her eyes to the clock in the hallway. The day was hardly light yet she was surprised to see the hands showing a quarter to ten.

"Shit!" She whispered to herself. On a Sunday it would have been normal for her in the past but since Jacob had been around that time could be construed as being halfway through the day.

As the kettle boiled and subsequently, the tea brewed, she stared out of the window. Rain was driving across the airfield in misty sheets – chased and folded by the wind. In the distance the branches of the trees were animated by gusts; their branches slowly being stripped of any leaves that remained. Marelle completed the tea and started back up the stairs with a mug in each hand. With the weather outside and last night's events, today was going to be a long one.

Jacob hadn't moved. Marelle put the mug down on the table next to the bed and walked around the bed where she carefully climbed in again while holding on to hers. Beneath the covers she playfully traced a toe down his buttocks and legs. He did not move. She snuggled closer to him, still sitting up in bed, sipping tea.

"Jacob." She finally said. "There's a mug of tea waiting for you."

"Yeah." He replied inertly from beneath the bedclothes.

Marelle looked at him – or what she could see of him which was essentially his hair. For a moment she stared, then blinked her eyes away and sat there drinking tea.

Half an hour later her tea was cold, and he had not stirred.

"Jacob." She said. "Your tea will be cold."

"It's OK." He mumbled.

Marelle sighed. "Well, I'm going to have a shower – be back in a minute …"

It took her ten. She didn't hurry but returned to the bedroom naked, with her hair in a towel, smelling of lavender shower gel.

In the knowledge that it was now after eleven she walked around and gently ruffled his hair with her hand. He had plenty of product in it and it felt stiff. She smiled.

"Hey sleepyhead. Are you getting up?"

He didn't reply so she gently lifted the covers to look upon him. He kept his eyes closed and did not move or acknowledge her. "Jacob?"

"Just … leave me be …" He said quietly, not opening his eyes.

"It's late. The weather is awful." She replied. "Aren't you going to get up?"

He made no attempt to answer straight away – paused long enough to worry her. The adrenalin had already kicked in when he finally spoke.

"No. Leave me be today. I just need today. I'm fine here."

Marelle stared at his still form, curled on it's side, eyes closed.

"We can talk about this Jacob."

"I don't want to talk."

She sighed. Looked at him. He needed a shave; he needed a shower; his hair was thick with whatever he'd plastered into it yesterday.

"You know …" She started." Anything Chas said … it hasn't upset me …"

There was not a flicker of acknowledgement from him until eventually he decided to reply.

"Good." He said, very quietly. 'Thank you."

Marelle held the cover up, looking at him. Then she leaned forward and kissed his forehead, gently.

"Don't you want breakfast?"

"No."

She smiled at him. "Ok." She stared a moment longer. "Is there anything I can do?"

"Just leave me today. Go and get on with your day. I need time."

"OK." And she put the cover back down over his head.

"Close the door." He muttered.

The truth was that her whole day revolved around Jacob – if he wasn't around, she had no day to get on with. She was fearful but at the same time she was grateful that he was here, in the house and he had not taken off anywhere. She would hear him if he made a move.

Marelle tidied the kitchen, made some toast, dried her hair and stood staring out of the window at the grey rain falling relentlessly. It was still windy but had dropped intensity from earlier. She picked up her phone and dialled Bella's number.

Bella took longer than expected to answer but did so eventually, and the background was noisy with chatter and clattering.

"Hi." She said.

"Where are you?"

"I'm out. Are you OK?" There was concern in her voice.

"Yes. Why?" Marelle asked, wondering.

"The storm! That's why I'm out. Bloody power went off – couldn't even make a cup of coffee!"

"Storm?"

"Yeah, last night. Absolutely crazy – rain, gale force winds, thunder and lightning…"

"Oh we didn't get it that bad. It's awful weather but nothing like that …"

"Well you were lucky – Mae is on days this week – she's ok but we thought it was a bloody hurricane!"

"But you're both ok?" Marelle asked.

"Yeah, fine. Hopefully the power will be on when I get back. There are a few branches off here and there, but I've survived! It's presence was akin to that of a lingering fart – it was pretty unpleasant but a bit of a dark aftermath!" She laughed and Marelle chuckled too. Bella had the knack of making light of everything and finding a smile in there somewhere.

"What are you doing?" Bella questioned. "Thought you would have been up to no good with lover boy at this time on a wet and windy Sunday!"

"We went to a Yellow Son gig last night."

"Oh wow! Getting the bug now, hey?"

"Well …" Marelle paused. "It didn't exactly go as planned …"

She told Bella even though up to now she had not shared Jacob's ultimate intention. Some points she deliberately left out but ended with the fact that he was now in bed, refusing to get up.

"Well is he alright, shut in there on his own?"" Bella questioned.

"Oh I don't think he'll come to any harm in there – anyway I'll hear if he gets up – the floorboards creak on his side of the room …"

"Has he done this before?"

"Well, no – well, yes, sort of. He's slept for nearly a whole day before when something has got to him."

"So, for Jacob it's normal behaviour?"

Marelle sighed. "I suppose it is."

"Just keep an eye on him. I'm sure he'll be fine. After all, he's got you *and* the house now, hasn't he?"

"Hopefully that's enough …" Marelle answered.

Hopefully, it would be.

The day hardly got light and darkness fell early. By evening the rain had eased off but there was still a stiff breeze. Thankfully they had not lost power today. Not that Jacob would even have noticed. She had remained in the house with one ear to the floor above. She heard Jacob get out of bed once – listened intently as he went to the bathroom and then straight back. He'd not eaten or drunk anything all day. She wanted to go and check on him but from their brief and strained conversation that morning she knew he did not want to be disturbed. So she bided her time, waited – she herself had hardly eaten either but did not feel hungry. At the end of a long day, she went back upstairs and into the bedroom.

It was dark. The curtains were still open, but it was a moonless night, so any light afforded into the room was minimal. She tiptoed around the room, undressed, went to the bathroom and then back to the bed. Jacob did not stir or say a word. When she slid gently into the unmade bed beside him that situation did not change. Lying on her back she wanted to reach out to him but feared rejection – at least indifference. She felt uncomfortable in her own bed, like there was stranger beside her and she was afraid of awakening them.

Sleep was elusive and she lay stiffly, listening to the wind off the airfield whistle around the corners of the house. She was cold too and needed the warmth of his arms to take that away. Marelle had expected not to drift off but realised that she had when she felt Jacob get out of bed.

"Where are you going?" Her voice cut through the complete darkness. It was silent, the wind had dropped.

"To the bathroom."

"Hurry back." She said.

"I'm getting up. It's six." He stated. "I'll have a shower then go to work."

"Is it! I'll make you breakfast …" She scrambled to get up.

"I'm not hungry."

"Jacob, you've got to eat something!"

He sighed and wandered out of the bedroom in the darkness.

Marelle got up, pulled on clothes, switched lights on throughout the house and made her way to the kitchen. As she boiled the kettle and made toast she heard him in the bathroom. She heard the shower then the toilet flush. At least this all looked more positive and normal. Maybe he'd got his head straight now and was back on the right track.

His appearance in the kitchen however did not add anything to enhance that hope.

He walked into the bright light of the kitchen squinting. His hair was wet, and he'd brushed it back from his forehead, flat against his head. He wore a tatty old jumper beneath a holey navy-blue fleece hoodie. As he walked over to the door where his bag and boots were standing, he unrolled a black woolly hat and put it on his head. He was pushing his feet into the unlaced boots as she stared at him. His face looked gaunt, his eyes sunken and dark beneath – none of which was helped by the two-day growth of stubble on his face. His skin looked grey and dry. He did not look like Jacob, but an old man today – stooped, shoulders slumped.

"You need breakfast." She said blankly, staring at him.

"I'm fine."

"Jacob! Just a slice of toast." She held the plate out to him. He took a slice and place a corner in his mouth as he stamped the boots on and picked up his bag.

"Tea?" She held out a mug.

He took it, drinking the tea as he put keys in his pocket and pulled the hoodie over the woolly hat with his free hand. Putting the mug down he turned to the back door, thought for a second then turned back to her.

"See you tonight." He said.

She looked up at him, walked forward, placed her hands on his chest.

"You'll need lunch."

"I'll find something."

"You'll *find* something!" She laughed. "I'll bring lunch down. Will you be in the workshop?"

'I suppose so."

"I'll come down; we can have lunch together."

He glanced at her, glanced away then back to her eyes. He gave a little nod.

Marelle smiled. Reached forward and kissed him. "Be careful."

He nodded. Looked her in the eyes then looked away again. With his head bowed he took her in his arms and held her tight.

"See you later." He whispered then turned, unlocked the back door and left. Seconds after she heard the van start up and reverse out of the drive.

She was left standing there alone, half wondering what had happened in the past half an hour where she had gone from being asleep to this. Should she should have actually let him leave the house? There had been meaning in that hug. His appearance worried her too – he looked like someone who took no care of their appearance – which was so unlike Jacob. He reminded her of when she had first met him and did wonder if it was the same hat that he had worn then.

She had always worried about the consequences of him finding Frankie, but she had also worried equally as much about him never finding Frankie and how either would haunt him forever. In many ways this was the same – she had worried about him being Ezza again but also worried deeply about the implications of being rejected by Chas. Jacob had not, for one second, entertained that idea, nor even considered the possibility that Chas would not welcome him with open arms. The truth was that had been the case and now Jacob was on his knees.

What made it worse was the truth that there was nothing she could do. Nothing. Before she had helped him, made plans to search and look for Frankie – laid out a path, courted possibilities. Now she had nothing to offer – she had thought about trying to contact Chas but knew it would be futile at best and embarrassing at worst. He had said no, and he had given his reasons. She held no weight with him and neither, it appeared, did Jacob – or Ezza.

What could she do but hope her love could pull him through this as unscathed as possible. For a start she would focus on making lunch.

THIRTY-FIVE

Marelle breathed a sigh of relief when she pulled into the farmyard just after midday and the white van was there. It was with an almost joyous spring in her step that she took the bag she had filled with food and walked into the workshop.

Ryan was just inside the door. He had green overalls on and appeared to be wet. Marelle gave him a small smile which he acknowledged.

"He's over there." He pointed to the back of the space.

He had his back to her. Stooped over the workbench, fiddling with something. He'd lost that presence, those straight shoulders, that positive stance.

"Hi." She greeted.

He turned, looked at her. "Hi." He said, then turned back.

"I've brought lunch." She walked up beside him and placed the cool bag on the bench, leaning forwards and smiling up at him. He still had the hat on, his eyes didn't move from the object he had in his fingers for a moment or two. Then he placed the small, round, metal and rubber object on the bench and looked at her. His eyes only lingered for a second before he moved them away again. That worried her. She had spent a year gaining his trust and attention and now it seemed to have flown. Whatever Chas had said should have made no difference to them.

"Alright?" She questioned.

He nodded. "I'll stop for a bit ... do you want tea?"

I've brought a flask!" She smiled, not wanting him to waste time making tea. The door she had entered through slammed shut as Ryan left.

"He's all wet!" She laughed.

"I know." Jacob sighed. "I've warned him enough times." But he didn't elucidate as to what it was.

Marelle smiled. "Give me hug. I need a hug."

He stepped forwards, opened his arms and she folded herself into him. He smelled of oil and diesel. She closed her eyes and he placed his arms around her. Then he rested his chin on her head – just as he had always done.

"Don't be so sad." She said, her face against him. "Please ..."

"I'm not sad. I'm disappointed." He replied.

"Well don't be disappointed. We knew this may be an outcome – in the same way that we didn't know if we would ever find Frankie ..."

"But we did find Frankie." He stated.

"It doesn't make any difference Jacob ... it doesn't change our plans – we've still got everything we ever had."

He didn't reply, just held her. After a while he sighed. "So, what have you got in the bag?"

It was a start. It was enough today. He was speaking to her, he was eating and drinking and still breathing. She chatted with him as they stood in the workshop, eating cheese sandwiches and drinking tea from the flask. A couple of times she raised a smile from him and that pleased her. It wasn't that endearing cheeky grin, but it was a smile, and that was good.

He was standing leaning against the workbench, drinking tea from a mug with a picture of a tractor on it. Right now, he looked less troubled, less despondent but still a mess. She smiled at him, bright eyes and warm love in them – she moved in for a second hug. Maybe tonight, now he felt better, he would clean himself up a bit. She had elected not to say anything, not wanting to shatter any improvement in his mood that she liked to think she was responsible for lifting.

When she finally leaned away from him and looked up into his eyes, she grinned then reached up and removed the hat. His hair, having been wet when he had out that on was dried flat against his head.

"Are you cold?" She asked, grinning again then running her fingers through his hair to release it. Against her hands it felt soft and shiny. 'That's better!"

He gave a tiny smile, took the hat from her and replaced it after running a hand over his hair to flatten it again.

Marelle smiled but felt a pang of sadness inside. She clasped his hands in hers once the woolly hat was back on his head.

"I'd like to stay ..."

"No point. It's cold in here, I'll spend most of the afternoon under that lorry and Ryan will be back shortly. You'd be sitting there doing nothing and getting cold ..." He replied. "Go home in the warm. I'll see you tonight."

She sighed. "I've nothing to do – I don't think I'll hear from Seb again."

'Do you want to?"

"Not really. But now I've got no income ..."

'Then you'll have to get used to being a kept woman – won't you?"

She raised her eyes to him. "Oh, I can take it if you're there ..."

"I'll be there later." He said.

At home she sat looking at emails for a while. Seb had warned her he would cut her off and he had. She didn't think she would care, but she did. Marelle cared because it had been good money. She missed it, but she did not regret her move, even though it had not gone to the plan in Jacob's mind.

At six, as promised, he came home. She heard the van pull into the drive and resisted the urge to runout to meet him. Minutes later he came in through the back door. He still had the hat on, and the hoodie. He gave a small indifferent smile as he entered and kicked his boots off.

They ate dinner and talked about the day; they discussed the house and when they should contact Devon but there was a stilted edge to all of it; a lack of enthusiasm, an effort. To Marelle it now seemed that every word was rehearsed, considered, placed. It made her recall days in the past when he had been so distracted by whatever was going on inside his head that he would be unreachable, non-communicative – like someone had flicked a switch and turned Jacob off. Tonight, it was as if that switch was half on, half turned up, half listening. She wasn't sure if this half existence he seemed to be courting now was better or worse than those times in the past when he had been unreachable. Was it an act? Was it him? Was this how it was going to be? There was no passion in his eyes – be it for life or death. No focus in his mind. No positivity in his movements. They went through the motions and retired to bed when he, unusually, said he was tired. They slept. He woke at six again and repeated the process of the day before with him rushing out of the door after she had forced tea and toast on him, leaving her alone in the dark house with only her echoing sigh for company.

He had gone out of the door looking pretty much the same – or worse – than he had yesterday. She did not like the stubble – now almost a beard – and she did not like the hat whch he seemed to be constantly wearing. There was nothing intrinsically wrong with either but they were just *not* Jacob.

During the day she wanted to call Bella but knew she would be at work. She picked up the phone. Maybe text her – maybe she would call at lunchtime? She was just about to do that when her phone rang and her picture appeared. Jacob.

With that fear driven anxiety as to why he was calling, Marelle answered with some hesitancy.

"Hi?"

"Hi." Funnily enough, his voice on the phone sounded the same. She smiled.

He continued. "I won't be here at lunchtime – probably. I may need to go and pick a van up for Mr. Wright ..." He sighed. "I might be late."

"How late?"

"Not sure."

"Where is it?" Marelle questioned.

"Hampshire." He answered.

"Well, where is that?" Marelle exclaimed, then her mind reminded her. "Hey, wasn't that where we went to Frankie's funeral?"

"Yeah." He said, with a vague hope she had not remembered that disappearing.

"Are you ok going down there?"

He gave a small laugh that was nervous. "Of course I am. As far as I know I haven't been banned from the county – only banished from that graveyard ..."

'Yes, but, well – last time you were there ..." She sought her words. 'It was awful ..."

"But I'm collecting a van."

"Do you want me to come with you?"

'No. I can't take you – I'm in the car with Mr. Wright ... look I'd better go ... it's going to take long enough as it is."

Marelle sighed. "Ok." She was worried about him doing this and especially with the mood he was in. She wanted to be with him. "Be careful then. Phone me ..."

"Of course I will. But I won't be back until late ..."

That conversation threw her day into array. Marelle didn't want him doing this alone. He'd not been down there since that awful, disastrous day of Frankie's funeral; that day when Frankie's sister had accused him of everything under the sun and told him to keep away from Frankie's grave. At that point Jacob had been at his lowest but no-one had realised just how close to the edge he had been then. Not until the day he had confessed to her his intentions on the night Bella had stumbled across him singing karaoke in a pub.

Now he would be back down there, in that same area, with thoughts of that day in his mind too. He would be driving back, alone, thinking about Frankie.

There was nothing she could do but wait. The hours dragged by and by late afternoon the sun was low in the sky with the clouds rippling away from it in pale, luminescent pink. It was a beautiful beginning to the sunset, and it played out to her over the airfield but she wished Jacob was here to share it with her. Alone, it was nothing. Marelle watched the sun sink lower in the wide sky until her phone rang again. And she pounced on it.

'We're just leaving." Jacob said, almost before she could get a "hi" out.

"How long will it take?" She questioned, looking at the sunset then the clock.

"Took us just over three hours to get here – it will take longer to get back. I'm driving something that was made in the 1940s!"

She sighed. "Is it a lorry?"

"No, it's a small panel van – he's convinced it was one his father bought new and had on the farm. Someone has restored it – thankfully to a pretty high standard – but it's going to be quite a slow drive home."

She sighed. "Well, be careful!"

"I will." He answered. "Might be home by midnight."

"Midnight!" She exclaimed.

"Hopefully before. I'll stop and give you a call when I'm about halfway."

"What about dinner?"

"Oh, I'll grab something when I get back. I'll be fine, see you later."

He arrived home just after eleven, dead beat and looking like death warmed up. Despite her protests at him needing to eat he drank a quick cup of tea, showered then went straight to bed. Marelle huddled close to him, but he was asleep long before her.

Marelle found sleep difficult with the day's – the week's – emotions bottled up inside her. She needed to talk even if he didn't. She needed to understand what was going on inside his head and what his plans were. His behaviour was frustrating the hell out of her, and she felt like she was being punished for Chas' rejection. She didn't know why; she didn't understand why and once again Jacob had slipped into a new skin that she felt she had no experience of.

Him rising at six again the following morning and bundling off into the darkness of the Wednesday morning did not help. She sighed and watched him reverse down the drive. The pale-yellow headlights of the old van sweeping across the front of the house before they illuminated the street ahead and moved off.

This façade could not continue. Why had he changed so much just because he had been rebuked by Chas? And he hadn't even been rebuked; it had been a gentle but persistent 'no' – and with good reason. Yellow Son was nigh – decision out of their hands – made long before he had probably even decided to come back – there was nothing they could do about that. Nothing had changed in their lives. *Nothing*. Everything was the same now as it had been when they had travelled to the concert on Saturday night. The only thing that had changed was the outcome of Jacob's wild speculation. Obviously this whole Ezza thing meant more to him that she did?

That left her cold; made her feel used and discarded. Is that why he was punishing her with this behaviour? Was it conscious behaviour? Did he realise what he was doing or how it was making her feel?

She took lunch down to the workshop but found Ryan there on his own. He was standing outside, smoking.

"Where is Jacob?" She asked.

"Out cutting hedges, somewhere. Went out first thing – haven't seen him since."

"Where?"

He shrugged.

"Will I find him if I drive around?"

"Probably – unless he's in the middle of a field ..."

Marelle sighed, went to leave then turned back. "Has he spoken to you?"

"What about?" Ryan seemed taken aback.

"Well – anything?"

"About work, yes ... not much else. He doesn't talk much."

"Do you think he looks ok?" Marelle questioned.

Ryan shuffled, uncomfortable at her questioning. "How do you mean?"

"Well, he doesn't look like Jacob ..."

He shrugged. "Thought it was a new look ... he changes a lot. You know, long hair, short hair, no hair – scruffy clothes, smart clothes – smart haircut. It's him ..."

She sighed, looked at Ryan as he took a drag on the cigarette.

She gave a smile, headed back to her car and left the yard.

She drove up the road, down by the Church, around the top lane and back to the crossroads near the pub but could see no sign of him. She wasn't totally sure what she was looking for – his van was still at the yard so she guessed her would be in a tractor. She looked across fields and along roads ... he could be anywhere. She pulled her car into the side and took out her phone.

Marelle dialled her old number. Waited and stared out of the windscreen as she did so. It rang and rang.

"Jacob." She cursed, feeling her heart begin to race and that familiar fear set in. She had told him she would pop down at lunchtime – but he had obviously forgotten – or absorbed himself in something so mundane that time and existence were mere inconveniences.

With a resounding heartbeat pounding in her head, she pulled away again and began to drive around the perimeter of the airfield. Marelle checked each field she passed as far as she could see – she was not sure these fields were farmed by Mr. Wright, but she looked anyway. Eventually, passing by the main gates of the airfield she noticed one was swinging open. It caught her attention enough for her to take a second look and it was then she saw the tractor parked just inside the gates.

All tractors looked the same to her with the exception of colour, but this one had a red and yellow contraption on the back. She indicated quickly and swung her car into the gateway. She parked, tentatively looking up at the tractor but not quite able to see who was inside. It had to be Jacob.

She got out of the car and walked through the open gate, arms wrapped around herself as it was a chilly wind today and she had no coat having expected to be in the workshop. Turning her head to look up she could see it was Jacob, sitting in the driver's seat, staring out over the wide expanse of the airfield.

She walked around looking up at him. He didn't see her and was staring straight ahead of himself, looking back towards where the caravan had stood and the house. Marelle waved to catch his attention, smiled when she saw him move. He rubbed his face with his hands and paused like that for a second or two before she saw him sigh and reach across to open the door. She had climbed up onto the step and into the cab on previous occasions but today he stepped down before she had the chance to. He descended backwards, rubbed his face again then turned round to her.

"What are you doing?" She smiled.

"Taking a break. I'm tired after yesterday ..."

'I've been ringing you. I've brought us lunch. Ryan was at the workshop. He said you were out somewhere cutting hedges?"

"Yeah." He answered, sniffing. He still wore the hat, still hadn't shaved, still flicked his eyes about instead of looking at her. Fiddling in the pocket of his hoodie he pulled out her old phone.

'It's dead." He said.

She tutted softly. "That's why then!"

"Sorry." He apologised.

"Come and sit in the car – we can have a picnic!" Marelle grinned, holding out a hand to him. He took it limply, allowed her to lead him to the car.

Once inside, with the sandwiches she'd made shared between them, she looked at him.

"Are you alright?"

He side-eyed her as if she had asked a stupid question.

"I'm OK."

She sighed. "But you're not ..."

He paused. Chewed. Looked straight ahead. "I'm pretty fucking disappointed."

She sighed. "But that won't change anything will it? Chas has made that decision – he'd made it long before you showed yourself ..."

"Had he?"

"He said he had; he had it on his computer – said dates and stuff were sorted."

"I can't believe he is actually finishing Yellow Son. What the hell is he going to do with himself – he knows nothing else ..."

"It's his decision."

"He *knew* it was me. He knew it wasn't my body he identified ..."

Marelle paused and ate, thinking of *anything* she could do.

"Just think what me coming back could do for Yellow Son! Everybody in the crowd would have Ezza back tomorrow if they could – *everyone* – and he's turning that opportunity down. Closed door. Blank. Finished."

"Well if that's what he's decided to do then that's what he's decoded to do. Seems everyone is in agreement ..." She explained. Paused for a second. "Look Jacob, I know it's not what you want to hear but just let it go. It's not going to happen – it shouldn't affect us though, should it? I fell in love with Jacob – I want him back." She smiled, placing a hand on his thigh, squeezing it gently. "We don't need Yellow Son; we don't need Chas. We have everything we need – we have the house now ..."

"You fell in love with Ezza" he replied.

"Don't be silly. I didn't even know Ezza, did I?"

'This is Jacob." He stated. "What you see here is Jacob. I'm being Jacob!"

She stared at him, shook her head, went to speak.

"You lit a fire in me which gave life to Ezza – you fell in love with Ezza ..."

She felt tears behind her eyes. "What does it matter. I fell in love with *you* ... I want to marry *you* but this ... this *disappointment* is eating away at you and it's a waste of time because there's nothing we can do."

He took a while to reply.

"I need to think it through. I need to get it straight in my head ... it's all whirling around at the moment."

"Well talking about it might help instead of moping about on your own ..."

"Maybe." He replied.

The conversation hadn't gone the way she would have liked but it ended with him hugging her beside the tractor. Holding her tightly for a second or two as if it meant more than he was letting on.

"Sorry." He whispered.

"Sorry! What for?" She asked gently.

"Getting in this mess." He said.

She smiled, left him with a hug, held his face in her hands and told him not to be silly. At least he was acknowledging it.

Jacob arrived home earlier than normal. Dinner wasn't ready so he decided to go and shower while she finished it off – which pleased her. Because it meant she wouldn't have to sit and look at him wearing that woolly hat all through dinner.

He seemed to be gone a long time, but she refrained from worrying too much as she could hear him moving between bathroom and bedroom a couple of times. In her heart she wished that he would appear in the kitchen clean shaven, and with his hair in its usual style, but that little fantasy was dispelled when he came down with his hair wet and flat and with the best part of a week's stubble on his face. It didn't suit him, and she didn't like it – it made him look older, thuggish. He had put on jeans and an old grey v-neck jumper with a hole in one elbow. It looked too big and his shoulders beneath it's fabric looked bony.

He sat down at the table, ate slowly, didn't say anything for a while.

"I was thinking." He finally said. "Maybe Chas was right. Maybe I should just stay as Jacob …"

Marelle raised her eyes to him. 'Why do you say that?"

"Well maybe I should just keep my head down – remain as Jacob. Live that life."

She stared at him. "Well, I'm fine with that, you know I am. We were fine before you told me about Ezza."

He looked at her, head slightly down, eyes raised. "But that would mean keeping a low profile – I could never be found out."

"Well, you wouldn't. I told you; I'd be happy to marry Jacob – I don't care if you get found out anyway … I just want the old Jacob back."

'This …" He pointed to himself. "*Is* the old Jacob. I told you – you awoke Ezza in me. It's Ezza you've fallen in love with."

She shook her head. "Of course it isn't."

"Well it must have been. You don't seem to be so happy with me as Jacob."

She gasped to herself in utter exasperation. "What! How can you say that?"

"Because I can see the way you look at me. You disapprove of me dressing like this, not shaving, wearing the hat …"

"I do not."

"But you don't like it! You cried when you cut my hair!"

"It was a shock! You looked so good but you insisted.' She replied, feeling emotional at the turn of the argument.

"And this is a shock too? Seeing Jacob as he really is?"

"*Why* though? I don't understand why you're doing this – why you aren't taking care of your appearance, why you aren't shaving, why you are wearing that hat all of the time?"

Jacob looked her straight in the eye. "Well maybe I don't want to see Ezza every time I look in the mirror. Maybe I don't want to be constantly reminded of that dream which has been shattered."

Marelle looked away, felt tears welling. She drew breath and fought them but they were stronger than her. She looked down and shook her head. He slid his chair out, stood up and went upstairs. She heard him in the bathroom.

Marelle sniffed as tears rolled down her cheeks. Why was he being like this? Why couldn't they just carry on as they had been. He had never been Ezza – he had always been Jacob and always would be to her. She had begun to think she had a good grasp of what was going on in his head now but this recent behaviour had thrown all of that out of the window. In one day, one evening; one *hour* – everything had changed, and she felt like she was walking through a debris field of their relationship right now.

He lumped about upstairs, moved from bathroom to bedroom noisily. She tried to ignore it, wondered what he was doing but sat defiant like he was some misbehaving child that she was choosing to ignore. Then it went quiet and *that* worried her. She sniffed, listened, didn't like the total silence. Wiping her face with the back of her hand, she sighed to herself and started out of the kitchen.

At the foot of the stairs, she suddenly heard a noise that she was only too familiar with. A noise that animated her and she ascended the stairs two at a time until she reached the top two steps. Her eyes immediately settled on the plug socket easily within her reach. Without a second thought she ripped the plug from the socket, on her knees on the carpet of the upstairs landing. Silence.

The long lead snaked and whipped slightly as he stepped out of the bathroom, looking at her as she had to plug to the extension lead in her hand.

Jacob had her hair clippers poised; a second later and he would have completed an initial pass through his hair with no guard on the blades. She could see he had managed to take a tiny patch off just at the front but nothing more.

"What are you doing?" He asked.

"You're not doing that." She replied. "I'm sorry, you're not."

"Plug it in."

"No. They're mine. I didn't say you could use them!" She retorted childishly.

"You do it then." He held the clippers out to her.

Marelle stood up, walked up to him, went to take them but he would not release them to her.

"Give them to me!" She asked.

"No, not unless you agree to shave it all off – or I will."

She stared at him as they both gripped the clippers. He'd taken a tiny patch, half an inch deep but about two wides, right down to the skin. Already she was thinking that was ok – she could cover that up.

"I don't want you to," she replied.

"You're not telling me what I can or cannot do."

That sentence was probably the most hateful he had ever said to her – mainly because he actually meant it.

"It's hair." He said. "It doesn't matter."

"Well evidently it does!" Marelle exclaimed. "If it didn't matter then you would leave it. Why this childish stupidity? Why are you intent on making yourself look like an idiot?"

The words left her lips. Instantly she knew she shouldn't have said them.

"An idiot! Maybe it's because I feel like an idiot! I don't want to look in the mirror every time and see Ezza – Ezza's gone – that part of my life is over – *finished* – Ezza ain't coming back. I don't want to see him every time I see myself – reminded for being the idiot that believed he was loved and wanted and could have all that he had before!"

"Jacob you're not an idiot." She sighed.

"But evidently I am!" he shouted, sarcastically. "Evidently I look like one – and you only care about the way I look – you just like the candy on your arm, the picture on your phone ... you cried before when I cut my hair – you cried!" He laughed as he shouted. "Before, when I didn't want to look like Ezza, and was trying to avoid it – you *cried*. If you really loved me, you would let me do what I need to do – you would *support* me!"

Suddenly, in the hallway, the doorbell rang. They both ignore it.

"Let you do what you need to do! Don't insult me, Jacob! I've supported you through every second of this last year. I've chucked away everything I had to be with you and I don't regret it; any of it – I just don't understand why you are acting this way ..."

The doorbell rang again. A long, urgent press. They were both still face to face, clippers between them.

'You don't, do you? You really don't." He grinned maliciously.

"I don't understand why this changes things between us ..."

"It hasn't!" He snapped. "It hasn't changed anything between us – you just won't accept that I have to do certain things to get my head straight ..."

The doorbell rang again – calling, *demanding* an answer.

"You've got to let me do what I need to do."

With the doorbell ringing and Jacob acting so out of character, Marelle allowed anger to override her fear. 'Like go jump off a bridge or try to hang yourself in front of a fifteen-year-old girl! Is that what you need to do to get your fucking head straight?"

His eyes drilled into her. She stared back. Scared at what she had said and indeed what he may now do. The doorbell buzzed; this time backed up by a loud knock on the fabric of the door.

He threw the clippers at her, ran a hand through his hair and pushed by to head down the stairs. Clutching the clippers and trailing the lead, still plugged into the extension socket behind her, she turned and followed him. Two steps behind as he opened the door.

There, in the dim evening light, one hand against the wall stood Catchpole. He looked Jacob up and down.

"DNA test." He said.

Marelle walked up behind Jacob. He looked skinny from behind, but normal. She watched him jiggle one leg.

"I forgot." Jacob said. "This isn't a good time."

"Neither was this morning, was it? Or last week – or, I suppose, any time I care to make for you to come down and take the DNA test, is it, Jacob?"

"I forgot!" He reiterated. "I don't see what difference it makes anyway. The child is still dead, it won't tell you who did it."

"Doesn't matter? It might have mattered to that child. That child that did not have a life – nor any identity ... cast away like rubbish ..."

"I know nothing about it." Jacob stated. "I'll come down tomorrow."

"Will you?" Catchpole questioned. "It's always tomorrow – you're being evasive. When it comes down to it, you're being evasive, and you know what that tells me?"

Marelle's phone rang in her back pocket. It was extra loud; she had turned it up in case Jacob had called her back earlier she that she wouldn't miss it.

"That tells me that you are reaching a point where you have run out of ideas. Where you've backed yourself into a corner ..."

Marelle looked at her phone. It was a withheld number. She pondered as it rang loudly. Normally she would not answer a withheld number – no number, no answer – was her rule but, it might have been Devon. She pressed green.

Catchpole was continuing. "So you start getting evasive, forgetting things – trying to hide yourself in your self-made pile of lies ..."

"Hello." She said.

THIRTY-SIX

"Who's that?" A voice asked, slightly cheeky, slightly over familiar.

"Marelle." she replied, confused.

"That's right. I couldn't remember it!' The voice laughed.

Her mind sought for an identity as she thought '*who the fuck is this*?' but heard Catchpole continuing.

"What you've got to remember Jacob Frost, is that this is a murder investigation – you might have been a child at the time, but I think there's a lot more going on here than you are telling me ..."

"Who is this?" Marelle asked, plugging a finger in her ear.

"I'll do the test tomorrow." Jacob stated again. "I've told you all I know."

"Chas." The voice on the phone said.

"Chas!" She repeated to herself, her mind a whir with Catchpole's conversation, Jacob's behaviour and this phone call. 'Oh! Hi!" She finally exclaimed, walking away from the ensuing argument in the doorway, the clippers were still in her hand with the phone against her ear, lead trailing behind her.

"Hi sweetie. Is your man there?"

"Jacob?" She asked, stupidly.

"Ez babe." He said.

"Ezza, yes, sorry. I don't call him that ..." She laughed.

"I can hear him." Chas said.

True, he probably could. Jacob was raising his voice to Catchpole, telling him his accusations were unfounded.

"... was a bloody child myself! What every other fucker was up to I had no idea! I was trying to fucking survive!" He was raising his voice and swearing; she knew the odds were beginning to stack.

She tapped his arm. "Jacob."

Catchpole pointed a finger. "I always knew you were not that meek and mild little mouse of a man you liked to portray "

"Jacob!" Marelle moved in front of him, looked up into his face which probably looked the craziest she had ever seen it look; a week's worth of stubble, eyes glaring, skin sallow, hair flat with a bite out of the front of it. "It's Chas." She said.

Those words opened a vortex, sucked everything away with a diminishing image that span away into oblivion the moment their eyes met, and he realised what she had said.

"Take it!" She shook the phone.

He looked bemused, confused, frightened. "Take it." She urged.

Jacob took the phone, turned away. "Chas!" She heard him say.

Marelle raised her eyes to Catchpole. Her feet were bare, and she still clutched the clippers like a comfort blanket.

"Where's he going?" Catchpole asked as Jacob walked back along the hallway.

"This is not a good time." Marelle repeated. "You can see the state he's in and he has been waiting for this phone call. I need to calm him down and he needs to get his head straight. he genuinely forgot – *I forgot* – there's no ulterior motive. I'll bring him down there in the morning. Will that be convenient?"

Catchpole stared at her as Jacob disappeared towards the kitchen behind her. He sighed. "I've never met anyone like you two before." He said, shaking his head. "I don't know why I keep giving you a second chance." He drew a breath slowly. "Ok, tomorrow."

She nodded. "Tomorrow, I promise."

Marelle could not close the door quick enough and run back down the hallway, still gripping the clippers to her chest. Jacob was sitting on a kitchen chair, knees apart, phone to his ear, one hand on top of his head, fingers in his hair.

"Yeah." He said, unsurely.

She stood and stared at him. Chas was speaking, Jacob stared at the floor.

"I understand that." Jacob said.

He would not look at her as he listened to Chas, flicking his eyes here, there and everywhere.

"Of course." He said.

She watched. Chas obviously spoke more than Jacob who instead punctuated the conversation with several "yes'" a couple of "I understands" and a "I can find it." As Chas talked on, and Jacob listened.

"Mya" Jacob asked after a while and a smile broke on his face like a burst of sunshine from behind a cloud. "Of course I will."

Suddenly he raised his eyes to Marelle and gestured for a pen and paper. She scrabbled around the kitchen and eventually found one, placing it before him with a used envelope, on the table.

"Ok Chas." Jacob said, gave a little laugh. "Yes, you know that, I will." He swallowed, listened then said. "Can I have your number?"

She watched as he listened but did not write anything down. Chas talked on for a bit as Jacob continued to listen.

"I won't." Jacob stated, listening again until he finally scribbled a number on the envelope and write 'Chas' above it. "OK, Yep. Yeah." He said to Chas. "I will. Ok, Bye."

For a second or two he sat there, looking at the floor, Marelle staring at him, the clippers still in her hand. It was like he didn't want to breath or move or take himself out of that very moment but eventually he raised his head, lifted his deep, dark eyes to her.

"Chas." He said.

She nodded.

"He told Mya what happened – she said he was fucking stupid and told him to call me back."

"Mya, his wife?" Marelle asked.

He nodded. "He wants me to meet him next week. Wants to hear me perform with a view to letting me come on for the encore at the gig in a couple of weeks.y"

He spoke the words like they were not his, like he was quoting from someone else's fantasy. Marelle stared at him, not sure what to say herself. Things like this simply didn't happen and Chas had seemed so adamant. He must have gone back for the telephone number which meant he was having second thoughts even before he left the building. Jacob was holding in a smile; she could see it, pulling at the edges of his mouth, lighting up his eyes. She allowed a smile to break on her face too, stepping forwards and throwing herself against him, ending up sitting across his lap with her arms around his neck. He hugged her and she heard him chuckle behind her back. He squeezed her so tight she almost had to tell him to stop even though she didn't want him to.

"Hey!" She sat back a bit, looked him in the eye. "You won't be needing these then?" She held up the clippers that were still in her hand.

"No. I won't." He replied with the welcome return of a grin she had not seen flourish in a while.

Jacob was in orbit. She had never seen him this buoyant. Hope had been restored where despair had lived, and he could not believe that a single phone call had come at that moment and suddenly his whole future – and hers – had changed. From having nothing he had everything and the path he stood upon was well lit and clear for as far as he could see.

"Shit!" He kept exclaiming to himself in between hugging Marelle and pacing the room.

"It's kind of scary now it's real." He laughed. "And this will truly stick one right up Catchpole's arse!"

"You've got to go for the DNA test tomorrow. I placated him by promising you would go."

"Well I'm not going now! They'll find out soon enough who I am …"

"Jacob! I promised him. He wasn't very happy as it was."

"What are they going to gain from it?"

She shrugged. "What have you got to lose? It'll get him off your back for a bit."

Jacob sighed. "Means I'll have to take time off work *and* I'll need a day next week …"

"Where have you got to meet Chas?" She asked.

"Some rehearsal studios near him. Won't let me go to his home – but I suspect he's got his own studio there … didn't want to give me his phone number either but he finally relented." He explained. "I think I know where he means – it used to be called something else years ago."

"Can I come?"

"Of course you can!" He grabbed her and hugged her again.

He went on to tell her more of what Chas had said to him. How he had finally mentioned the encounter to Mya, his wife, and how she had been aghast that Chas had considered walking away. Mya had seen the opportunity.

"Chas said that I will have to deal with any fall out though. He said anything that comes about after I show myself is my problem and I'll have to deal with it ... I can. I'm not scared of that shit!"

When he climbed into bed next to her that night, he was warm and soft from a shower. He laughed and buried his freshly shaved face against her. His hair flopped over his forehead. She kissed him and cradled his face in her hands.

"Pinch me!" He laughed. "I can't believe this is happening! It's a dream come true!"

"I know it is. Believe me!" She smiled and nestled against him. She sincerely hoped it was and it didn't turn into a nightmare.

Marelle slept well but awoke with a splitting headache the following morning. She was standing in the kitchen taking pain killers when Jacob came down, walked up behind her and wrapped his arms around her. She stayed there for a moment then turned to him, looking up at his face. He smiled and she slid her arms around him.

"Nice t-shirt." He grinned.

She looked down at herself. She hadn't realised it was the old 'Yellow Son' t-shirt she had put on. "Maybe you'll get a new one soon."

He laughed. "I like that one!"

Marelle hugged him, glad to have him back – not cast to the seven winds as he had been heading over the past few days. She squeezed him, felt his ribs against her arms and his lips warm and inviting against hers.

"What time do you want to go to the police station?" She asked.

He sighed. "Shit! I'd forgotten. I really don't want to take a morning off – I haven't asked ..."

"Go at lunchtime – I'll run you down there. Catchpole said it won't take long – he did suggest you could do it in your lunch hour?"

"Mmm." He said. "I'll go down in the van."

"I'll take you down. We can spend lunchtime together. I'll bring sandwiches..."

He gave a little smile, rested his chin on her head like he always did. "Ok." He grinned.

She picked him up from the workshop as promised. He was ready, waiting with a grin that warmed her heart. His happiness was a fragile thing, it walked along a line so thin and fragile but once he had a secure footing and a balanced step it could be timeless. She watched him now, his face, his eyes, his straight shoulders, his hair. This was the man she loved and the flame she had to nurture.

He climbed in, pulled the seatbelt around himself and they started off. They chatted. Both knew things had been said over the last few days that both needed explanation or had been said in haste. Now wasn't the time to bring those up but, in the end, she knew they would come into the conversation.

Today however, for someone so close to the next step in his life – which was a big one – Jacob was happy.

By now Marelle pretty much knew her way to the police station and pulled around the grand stone building again, to park at the side of it.

"Shall I come in?" She asked.

"No, I'll be fine. Hopefully won't be long." He replied, getting out of the car. Turning back in to her, he smiled. "We'll stop somewhere on the way home and eat lunch, shall we?"

"Sure." She nodded, smiling back into his eyes – no fear in them at the moment.

Marelle watched him walk away from the car towards the entrance to the police station. She observed his walk, his shoulders straight, his head high, legs sturdy and a slight spring in his step. Walking ultimately towards one of the most significant moments in this life he had taken upon himself. Jacob disappeared inside and she settled into the driver's seat, pushing her bottom deeper and laying her head back. The sun was streaming into the car window but there was not a bit of strength or warmth in it now. Like diluted lemon squash where before it had been intense. Right now, she sensed, they had turned a corner, and their path together slipped through a narrow opening onto a track that would eventually meander its way back towards Ezza's existence.

And right now, she realised what Ezza was and why being Ezza meant so much to Jacob. He filled that hole in his life which, left unplugged, would lead to his ultimate exsanguination. A hole that had opened in his infancy, which had bled him out day by day, year by year until the apparition of Ezza had manifested itself and fitted so perfectly into that gaping hole.

Then one day he had picked at the scab, he had dislodged it and Ezza lost the ability to fill that gap. Once again blood had poured from the wound and he could no longer plug it with Ezza. In those bleeding, fearful moments he had existed in the shadows, filling that gap as best he could with whatever he could – Jacob, searching for Frankie – *her*. But he knew, and she knew, the one thing that could and would plug that hole and stop the blood leaking and oozing out of the edges of the ill-fitting stop-gap. And to be Ezza he had to let Jacob go; he had to become Nat again and then, only then, he could allow Ezza to manifest himself once more.

This was the first true step to letting Jacob go. And she was right here, smiling and handing him over to that retribution.

The sound of the car door opening made her startle with surprise as she snapped her eyes open to see Jacob, sliding into the passenger seat and smiling to her.

"Done." He said.

"Already?" She asked, composing herself and sitting up. She had expected to be sitting here for at least an hour.

"Yeah." He answered, putting his seatbelt on.

"That was quick. Was it ok?"

"Yeah, fine. I was expecting a lot more ceremony but it's just a process to them."

"So, when will they know the result?"

He shrugged. "Don't know. But it doesn't matter. We both know what it will be."

"And then what?" She questioned.

"Nothing." He answered "It makes no difference. Until I decide to tell them about Jacob. Until then it makes no difference …"

They stopped the car in a lay-by on a back road and their way home to eat the sandwiches she had made. The fields beside them were flat and wide – just cultivated and sewn – hedges at the far horizon as she stared back towards the industrial spectacle of the local sugar beet factory – belching expanding white clouds of steam into the blue autumn sky.

He was relaxed and happy – laughing and chatting with her. Two days ago, she feared she had lost him – but that now seemed so far away she had almost forgotten it.

He paused in the conversation, thought, then said

"What Chas said …" He began. "I admit I wouldn't have told you – but it's not something I want to hide from you. But Chas played a tough game – he threw that in and I'm sorry. I probably wouldn't have told you but at the same time that's not the way I would have wanted you to find out …"

Marelle looked to him briefly, looked away, looked back. She smiled.

"I'm not ashamed but I'm not proud – I didn't do anything *wrong*."

"I know." She said. "It's alright. As I said, we all have a past …"

He grinned. "We do … but I don't want you wondering about it …"

Marelle smiled, patted his thigh.

"She was German." He said. "Spoke perfect English. Just sixteen … it was my first tour with Yellow Son – I was young and stupid. Suddenly I had all of these girls eyeing me and reaching out to me …she came to a couple of gigs we did in Germany. Right at the front, looking at me with *that* look in her eyes. Then she follows us back here, turned up at a few more gigs – right at the front … came to the stage door afterwards. Long story short she ended up hanging around with me, coming with me on the bus to gigs and, of course, I was young – she was younger, but she was really fucking attractive in a quirky kind of way. She had to go back to college at the end of the summer… then a couple of weeks later she turns up and says she's pregnant."

"How did she manage to get in contact with you?" Marelle asked, that very question at the front of her mind.

"She had been to my flat – a lot. She knew where I lived." He replied with some acknowledgement of his stupidity.

"How did you know it was yours?"

"Truthfully, I didn't but she was pretty straight, and I had been with her for the previous six weeks. Her mother was staying over here for the summer, and she was planning to study here later on after school." He looked a little distant but continued. "She wasn't making any claims or trying to be clever – she turned up at my door genuinely scared ... not knowing what to do."

"What did you do?"

"Called Chas!" He half smiled.

"Did she want to have the baby?"

"No." He answered quickly. 'Said she didn't want to have a child but was too shit scared at her father finding out. If she was scared then God knows what he would have done to me if he had found out!"

"So, what happened?"

"Chas sorted it all out – well I suspect Mya was involved but she didn't show herself. Paid for her to go to a private clinic, gave her a lump sum and apparently got her to sign some legal document ... she went home afterwards, and we never saw her again."

"What was her name?"

"Isabelle Dorfft." He replied.

"What was she like?"

"Very young!" He laughed at himself. "Bit of a tomboy, long skinny legs in leather trousers, black cap sleeve t-shirt – dyed red hair ... looked more of a pop star than I did! I was flattered someone like her was interested in me!" He said, coyly. "Chas gave me a proper bollicking. Put me straight." He pondered then then gave a little smile. "Sorry you had to hear it like that and sorry it happened."

She shook her head. "It's fine. I understand ... as you said, you did nothing wrong, and you saw her right too ..."

He gave a loose shrug with one shoulder. "I don't feel good about it, but I don't let myself feel bad about it either ..."

"Did you ..." Marelle corrected herself. "Do you want children?"

"Hell no." He answered quickly.

Marelle smiled and looked away momentarily.

He sighed. "Sorry. I should have asked you before my mouth ran away with me ... do you?"

She laughed. "No – well yes – well no!" Marelle stuttered. "No." She reiterated. "There was a time when I thought I did – when I was with Chris – but I wouldn't have wanted them with him ... then I decided I didn't. Anyway, it's too late now." She placed her hand on his leg again. "I want to enjoy the rest of my life with you ..."

He grinned, took her hand in his, kissed her fingers gently.

"We'd better get back." He said.

Alone in the house she felt she was walking on air, delightfully happy yet strangely unsettled. She didn't know whether it was elation or fear or the heady mix of the two. She had watched him walk back into the workshop with that leggy stride and he had turned back to look at her with a grin. It was like she had fallen in love with him all over again.

She felt the house breath around her; come to life with her happiness and the new life they were embarking upon. Were they truly leaping off the edge of a cliff hand in hand and casting off the vestiges of this life – leaping to safety – a place where there were no lies, no shadows, no secrets.

If she looked back, she could see the meandering path they had followed – the breaks and rocky patches on it – but she left that behind her as she knew she was experiencing the last days of Jacob. Then soon, he would be gone.

When Jacob returned that evening and walked through the back door, she had to retrain the urge to put herself upon him the way she had on that very first night when she had made it clear how she felt about him. He came in, dropped his rucksack on the floor and kicked off his work boots.

"Need to get that wall and garage built." He commented. "The bike can't stay in the hallway forever."

She smiled, walked up to him, placed her hands flat against is chest and gave him a peck on the lips – which was a lot less than she really desired right now. "Well I'll leave that up to you. You know what yiu need – just go ahead …"

He smiled. "I've never owned a house before."

She grinned. "You don't own it yet. Mae does."

"Good as." He replied. "Anyway, it's going to be in your name to start with, not mine."

She gave him a warm smile, wanted to kiss him but refrained, her hands still flat against his chest. She could feel the warmth from him convecting through his clothes; she could feel the gently rise and fall of his chest.

"You know Mae must think a lot of Bella to do this for us. I thought it was a bit of a joke when Bella first told me."

"Why?" He laughed.

"Well, it's Bella!"

"We owe Mae … we owe both of them."

Marelle hugged close to him. "Oh I'm sure they'll find some way for us to pay them back." She laughed. "Bella usually makes sure she gets her pound of flesh in the end! Shall we invite them over – we could take both of them out for a meal?"

"Sure but wait until it's all gone through – I don't want to tempt fate!" He answered.

Devon called them a few days later. He said he would transfer the house unto Marelle's name over the following days.

"I can send the paperwork and we will all be done and dusted – except for my fee, of course." Devon explained.

Jacob had smiled wryly. Of course." He looked to Marelle as they hovered over the phone on speaker, then lowered his eyes. "Thank you, Devon."

"It's been a pleasure." He replied. "It's been *interesting*. Good luck with the house."

THIRTY-SEVEN

"What shall I wear?" Jacob asked.

They were both sitting at the kitchen table, just having eaten. He had come home from work and still had his work clothes on. It was Tuesday evening and tomorrow then would drive to this meeting with Chas at the rehearsal studios.

Marelle laughed. "You're asking *me* what *you* should wear? You're a regular clothes horse – I should be asking you! Well, I don't think it's a formal affair, is it?"

"No." He laughed.

"What will Chas be wearing?" She offered.

"Probably jeans and a t-shirt, probably a leather jacket – or a denim one ..."

"Well, you do the same." She suggested. "Hey, why not wear the Yellow Son t-shirt?"

"That's too corny!"

"No, it's not. It's kind of, well, showing respect ..."

"Is it clean?"

She nodded.

The doorbell rang. Jacob looked at the clock. The nights had drawn in now. It was completely dark outside despite it being only just after seven. They had already resigned themselves to the night. Marelle looked to him; he sighed and got up. Only one possibility was in both of their minds.

She followed behind Jacob as he opened the door. He flicked the outside light on at the same moment, rendering Catchpole squinting in a pool of light in the darkness.

"Aah, you are in. I thought you would be ..."

"I've just come home from work." Jacob stated.

"Great that I managed to catch you then. I've got some news for you." He looked up at Jacob in his elevated position on the top doorstep. Marelle moved closer and placed a hand in the small of Jacob's back as he looked down at Catchpole.

"Ok." He said.

"Can I come in? Catchpole requested. "Might be more private that having this conversation on the doorstep?"

The kitchen was in a mess, dirty plates still on the table, pots and pans in the sink – but Jacob stood aside and let him enter. Catchpole knew the way and followed the light at the end of the dark hallway as they walked behind him.

"Sorry, were you eating?" He asked, but with little actual apology.

"Finished." Jacob told him.

"Well." Catchpole began as they came into the kitchen and stood staring at him. Jacob did not gesture for him to sit. Standing a good couple of inches taller than catchpole and today with his back straight and shoulders square he had a slightly commanding position over him.it was the first time Marelle had been aware of that. Jacob was usually stooped, or slumped, or sitting down when Catchpole delivered his rhetoric. Today was different.

"I have the results of the DNA test." He announced.

Jacob stared at him; Marelle clutched his arm. Nobody said anything in reply. Catchpole gave a tiny smile, put his hands in his pockets and raised his face to Jacob.

"It's a 48.4 positive match." He said. "That's a confirmed match for a full sibling."

Again, Jacob said nothing nor made any gesture of response. Marelle felt no tension in him as Catchpole spoke. Jacob had been well-aware of what was coming.

Catchpole continued. "That means he is your brother."

Jacob bobbed his head slightly, pursed his lips for a second, lowered his eyes to the floor. Catchpole stared at him, waited. Marelle looked to Jacob then to Catchpole.

Eventually, he took a considered breath. "It must have been another child I knew nothing about. I didn't know my parent's had another child." He spoke with the distance in a voice that was purely and clearly Jacob.

Catchpole stared at him. "No memory then?"

"No."

"Is it a shock?"

Jacob paused, blinked a couple of times. "Yes." he replied. "But no, not a shock that there was another child."

"Buried in your garden?"

"Well, yes. I didn't expect that, of course. Must have been before I was born …"

"Obviously, due to the fact that your mother died giving birth to you!" Catchpole reminded him, sarcasm in his words.

"Well, how am I supposed to even know about him. He is my brother, maybe, but I have no knowledge of him even existing …"

"Nobody ever said anything?"

"No." Jacob looked towards him. "My mother was dead; my father was descending into grief fuelled alcoholism … it could have been years before I was born. And to be honest, had both of my parents been there I doubt it's something they would have told me about."

"What about your 'other' brother?"

"What about him?" Jacob snapped.

"Did he know?"

Jacob made a noise which was half amusement, half exclamation. "How would I know?"

"He was your brother. You must have spoken to him at some point and, as they say, blood is thicker than water."

"I don't know if he knew. If he did, he never said anything and we will never know now, will we?"

Catchpole smiled. 'This unknown child, this long-lost sibling of yours will need to be registered ... and you are the only living relative. Effectively next of kin ..."

Jacob nodded slowly.

"When the body is released to you the deceased will need to be registered and then cremated or interred in a cemetery. That is up to you. I don't think you have to give the deceased a name but there are laws that have to be followed – which should have been abided by all of those years ago. Now that may be down to you as the only living relative of this unfortunate individual."

Marelle slid a hand around Jacob's arm. He seemed slightly more tense now.

"So what happens with the investigation now?" Jacob questioned.

"We will investigate further as much as we can, but the bottom line appears to be that this child was probably stillborn – or died very soon after birth – to your parents who then decided to not to register the birth or the death – or give the child a name – and instead to go ahead and bury the child in the back garden of the property. That looks to be the course of events that took place." Catchpole explained. "Unless, of course, you know something different?"

Jacob shook his head. "I told you. I have no knowledge of a third child – another brother."

"Well with that degree of matching DNA it's a pretty conclusive confirmation that the deceased was from the same mother and father as yourself – and presumably, your older brother – Nathaniel, wasn't it?"

He nodded. Marelle felt tension pull tighter in him at the utterance of that name from Catchpole.

"It's a shame." He continued. "How one family was befallen by so many tragedies, isn't it? This child, probably their first born dying so early only to be buried in an unmarked, unregistered hole in the ground in a back garden; your mother dying during your birth; your father falling into alcoholism due to his grief at losing his beloved wife and then your brother – Nathaniel – or as I believe he used to be referred to as Nat – taking his life after your own father had succumbed to the effects of a lifelong addiction – leaving just you. Jacob."

Marelle daren't move; she felt every breath, every twitch of muscle, every movement of an eye was being analysed. Catchpole was working around frantically, trying to dislodge a keystone which he knew would bring the whole thing tumbling down.

"When you summarise it like that, it does seem quite tragic." Jacob uttered quietly. "But when you are living it, you don't see it like that."

"No?" catchpole asked. "I suppose not. After all, you were just a child, weren't you? Just an innocent, young child. How old were you when your brother died?"

"In my thirties." Jacob replied. "I hadn't seen him for years."

"No. So I understand. He worked for a record company, you said?"

Jacob nodded.

"Well, I suppose, in a way, he did ... he was a singer, wasn't he? In a band, I believe?"

Marelle could almost *feel* Jacob's pupils' contract at that.

"He was, but I don't know much about that."

"Quite a rock star you know ..."

"Was he?"

Catchpole laughed. "You could have been twins!" He exclaimed with a grin.

"So I've been told ..." Jacob replied.

"Mmm." Catchpole mumbled. "But, well, he's not here either, is he? Cremated and scattered to the four winds by his friends, is that correct?"

"As far as I know." Jacob said.

"Well. You know now. You had another brother, another sibling, another family tragedy." He looked right at Jacob. "The body will be released to your undertaker of choice. It may be a little while longer in case we need to revisit anything, but we will be in touch shortly."

"Ok." Jacob replied blankly.

"He could still have a proper burial. A proper identity at last ..." He straightened himself up. "I'll see myself out ... I know the way." He laughed. 'I trust that you are alright following that news. You can speak to a counsellor if you need to ..." He began to walk out of the kitchen and along the hallway. He paused for a moment by the motorbike. "Nice." He said. "Yours?"

Jacob nodded. "Mid-life crisis."

Catchpole grinned sarcastically. "Of course!" He moved on and went to the door. "If anything occurs to you – comes back to you – however small, please let me know." He turned back and said "You never know. This might trigger something in the back of your head which makes a little more sense after all these years. It's amazing sometimes how something can jog a memory ..."

Jacob reached up to hold on to the open front door as Catchpole left.

"I'll be in touch." He imparted as he did so.

Jacob closed the door. Stood looking at it with his back to her for a second or two. Then he turned to face her. He looked pale in the dim light.

"It's not a shock but I didn't want this right now. I was hoping to stall it for a bit ..."

"Stall what?"

"Having to register and bury him." He replied.

"I didn't realise you would have to do that." Marelle commented. "I thought the police would deal with it ..."

"They would have to if I wasn't here. But I am, so it's down to me. I don't want to have to register him until I can say he is Jacob." He looked to her. "And I don't know when that will be."

The rest of the evening was tense after that, but he was not totally consumed by the prospect as much as such instances had affected him in the past. At least it appeared that way to her – but she was still aware. Mentally, she shortened the leash.

Her own thoughts wheeled through scenario after scenario. Heard Catchpole's words again and again. Words that scarred deeper each time – unsheathed blades within his voice – just glinting their menace in the darkness.

"Jacob." She asked, calling his attention. "If the body was released to you, and you registered it as a third child to your parents – not Jacob – then you could continue as Jacob, couldn't you?"

He sighed. "No." He stated. "No. I want this straight – I can't go back to Yellow Son *and* still be Jacob. That won't work …"

She sighed to herself. This was a a *get out of jail free card* as far as she was concerned.

"But couldn't you get away with it? Just for that one gig? You don't even know for sure if Chas is going to let you actually sing yet, anyway."

"No." He stated. "I want this straight. I want to walk out of this knowing who I am and where I'm going." He gave a smile at the end as if to placate her – equivalent almost to the time he had told her to shut up and go away because she was asking too many questions! They had been walking with him over the airfield in the very early days. This time however, his tone was slightly more diplomatic.

"He mentioned Nat." She said.

Nat – Jacob, Ezza. She said it as if in the third person when she knew, although the idea was still alien, that Nat was actually standing in front of her.

"I know." He nodded. "He's been fishing – been looking. He's got no proof … brothers look alike, it's a fact of life."

Marelle looked to him; he wasn't looking at her. Maybe not quite that much alike she thought to herself. Catchpole knew something was going on – it was obvious. He just needed the final piece to make it all fit.

Catchpole's visit that evening had been the last thing they needed and the epitome of bad timing. It could have affected Jacob in a far greater way if his mind had been in a different place, but he was focused and this meeting with Chas; channelled solely into that which coloured his mood in the brightest, truest colours imaginable.

He wore the old Yellow Son t-shirt and slipped a leather jacket over the top. Marelle had not seen that before – it was nice, black but suitably distressed, soft as ever, a perfect fit for him. There he stood, looking at himself in the mirror, running his hands flat against the sides of his head. The top was long, spiky – beautiful. Marelle walked up behind him and stood at his shoulder – she looked to his eyes in their reflection.

"Quite the rockstar!" She laughed.

"Sssh!" He smiled. "Don't go quoting Catchpole, he'll have enough to say soon as it is!"

Jacob drove, holding out his hand for the key as they stepped out into the driveway. Without protest she handed them to him and sat herself in the passenger seat.

"Do you know the way?" She asked as they started the journey.

'Pretty much." He replied.

"Have you been there before?"

"I'm not sure. It may have changed its name. I assume it's down near where Chas lives – I can't see him travelling far."

"Will anyone else be there?" She questioned.

"I don't know – he didn't say for sure, but I got the impression it would just be him." Jacob replied.

He drove on, calm, collected, quiet. The radio was on quietly, but neither was listening to it. Marelle's mind wandered as she watched the landscape pass by. Green fields, industrial areas, tractors working on the land, houses.

"Do you remember Jacob being born?" She suddenly asked – her thoughts spiralling so the question seemed out of context but he caught her train of thought. Truthfully, he was probably thinking along the same lines himself.

"No." He replied. "I was too young ... I don't really remember much more than just being in that house with my father. It was cold and dark; he was drunk, and I was hungry ... nothing changed until I was old enough to earn money and make my own decisions."

"You don't remember your mother at all?"

"Not really." He stated. "I remember Frankie's mum – it kind of gets mixed up in my head and sometimes the memories of Frankie's mum seem like memories of my own mother."

Marelle smiled sweetly to him, but he did not respond.

"Maybe there are tiny, fleeting glimpses where I think of her, and I can almost see her in my mind's eye – just like the glimpse of the shiny flank of a fish in a dark pond. I remember a purple taffeta dress, the faint smell of lavender soap ... but I don't know. It might be something I've made up that has turned into a memory ..." He stopped talking, drove for a bit but was obviously still thinking. "I do get the impression there had been light before the darkness, sometimes." He added.

Half an hour on and they were driving through a small town which led out into the countryside, narrow roads and high hedges on each side.

"We should be getting close." Jacob commented.

"I thought it would be more built up." Marelle said.

"Doesn't look like it." Jacob replied, leaning forward and looking down a long gravel drive to their left. "Looks like it's here."

The drive opened up to a square gravel car park. It was a 'U' shaped courtyard of converted farm buildings. Black wood, small areas of landscaped borders around them, low, perfectly clipped box hedges. The car tyres swooshed across the gravel as he pulled her car into park beside a dark grey VW camper van.

"Is this the right place?" She asked, expecting something different.

"I think so." He answered, reversing the car perfectly.

In front of them a figure appeared, walking up a narrow pathway opposite to head across in front of them, mug in hand. It was Chas. He stopped and waited for Jacob to park. An average unassuming middle-aged guy, sipping coffee, watching them.

"What the fuck is that?" He asked when they both got out, nodding the car. "Bit of a grandad car?"

Jacob raised his hands. "Not guilty. Not my car!" He grinned.

"Didn't expect you to be driving something like that." Chas commented., walking towards Jacob.

"It's Marelle's car." Jacob held his hand out to her.

Chas stopped, sipped from the mug. "That's a big car for a girl." He smiled.

"Hey!" Marelle piped up.

Chas laughed, walked forward and held out a hand to Jacob. Jacob took it and they shook hands with a smile. Then he turned to Marelle and held out his hand to her.

Marelle came around the car and for the first time, took Chas' hand. It was warm and surprisingly fleshy. He gripped hers in a handshake that felt both secure and full of warmth.

"Well done." He said to her. "You got him here!"

"He got himself here!" She replied.

Chas nodded his head towards the narrow path leading down to the large central building. "This way. Got the place to ourselves ..."

"Nice place." Jacob commented, walking alongside Chas, Marelle holding onto his arm.

"Yeah. Handy." Chas said.

"Do you live close by then?" Jacob enquired.

"Yeah, not far." Chas answered, opening a door and holding it for them to go through into a central vestibule with corridors spanning off on each side.

They followed him off to the right, into a large space with a wooden floor and one whole wall of windows looking out over farmland. There were thick navy-blue curtains pulled two thirds of the way along. At one end, near the door there were cupboards and worktops – a kettle, microwave – sugar had spilled all over one surface.

At the other end was a barrage of travel cases, chairs – equipment that Marelle had seen on stage and cables snaking everywhere. Chas closed the door behind them.

"Make yourself a drink if you want." He gestured to the cupboards but walked towards the other end of the space.

Marelle followed with Jacob. She watched Chas as he progressed forwards, mug in hand, no hurry about him. He had quite a bumbling stride and looked smaller than she remembered – more subdued today than he had been when they had spoken with him after the concert. Very calm, very confident, very unassuming. So much so that Marelle began to question if he was indeed, the same person!

"You can thank Mya for this. You know that. As always, I defer to her seeing sense in any situation. She was pretty angry at me for letting you go – I had to go back and find that bit of fucking paper with your number on!" He explained.

"So you're convinced it's actually me now!" Jacob asked, smiling.

Chas turned to him. He gave a grin. "I always was!" He stared at Jacob in a way that almost, *almost*, suggested there was a brotherly warmth in his heart for Jacob. "Just didn't really know if I wanted to go there."

"I'm glad you decided to." Jacob replied.

"Yeah, well. We'll see, wont we?" Chas answered. "So, you two, married?"

"No, not yet." Jacob answered. "Engaged …"

"When's the big day then?"

"We don't know yet." Marelle added this time.

Chas laughed. "Tie him down, claim this one or you'll still be waiting in twenty year's time. I know *exactly* what he's like!"

'It's fine." She smiled, looking at Jacob. "So do I!"

Chas spoke as he wandered between the boxes, putting the mug down on one, fiddling with things, checking connections.

"You're a fucker, aren't you!" He exclaimed. "I knew you'd turn up one day, one way or another! So all this crap with solicitors and this elusive 'brother' who never wanted to speak to anyone – that was you?"

"Yeah."

Chas laughed. "Jesus! So where have you been?"

"In Suffolk, working on a farm."

"A farm! Didn't you used to do that before?" Chas asked.

"Yes, same farm." Jacob confirmed.

"For all that time?"

"Yeah." Jacob nodded. He was being surprisingly forthcoming with Chas but then she supposed, he had nothing to lose here.

"You got a house there then?"

"We have now, but no. I lived in a caravan on an old airfield …"

Chas was not surprised, not particularly reactive to anything Jacob said – either he was that cool and ambivalent to it, or he wasn't listening. After a few more minutes of fiddling and small talk he sat down on a stool, gestured to Jacob to sit opposite. Marelle joined them.

"Now." Chas stated. "You are here because I have been persuaded, by Mya, to give you the chance to sing with Yellow Son again."

Marelle saw Jacob shift his position slightly on the chair as Chas said those words and she saw that burst of excitement shimmer through him.

"But." Chas said, "I'm not prepared to jeopardise Yellow Son in any way if I think it's not going to work." He stared sternly at Jacob. "You've got to understand that. If I think you're crap, or you're not going to be able to do it – or I think having you there is going to fuck things up – it's off."

"I understand." Jacob replied earnestly but Marelle suspected he didn't.

"This isn't an open invitation – yet." Chas added. "Right, I'll play, you sing. Get your arse over there."

Jacob looked to where Chas was pointing. He didn't move.

"Come on." Chas beckoned, getting up. "This is your one chance, don't blow it. I for one am still not sure I should be doing this ..."

With a sigh Jacob stood up, followed Chas slowly and unsurely to the far side where Chas picked up a guitar and Jacob walked up to the microphone. He stood behind it, lifted a hand and placed it on the mic in the holder, tapped it.

"It's on." Chas said, his head down as he fiddled with his guitar, played a few notes.

"What are you playing?" Jacob asked Chas.

"Catch it." Chas replied. "You know it ..."

Chas began playing. Marelle had not recognised it but not being a full band, or the recording she knew, it was not a hundred percent in her head. She looked to Jacob, but he was not looking at her, he had his head down, nodding gently to himself. Chas turned his head and looked to him in anticipation, but Jacob remained with one hand on the mic and his head bowed.

Then he raised it, looked straight ahead of himself for a second the delivered the first line of the song, perfectly, exactly where it should have been. Hearing his voice coming through the microphone, set up so perfectly for him, and in total harmony with Chas' playing Marelle looked to him as he continued with the rest of the verse. His voice was perfect, but he looked stilted, static, slightly uncomfortable.

Marelle saw Chas lift his eyes to Jacob and a slight smile came to his lips as he played on. Marelle smiled broadly to herself, swung her legs on the chair she was seated upon. This was good, he sounded good.

Then Jacob suddenly snapped his head back from the mic, stopped singing and stepped away. Chas continued, staring at him but Jacob made a gesture for him to stop.

"I can't." He said. "I can't do it like this ..."

"Like what?" Chas exclaimed and by the tone of his voice in those two words she sensed this slipping between Jacob's fingers.

"It's not right. I just can't do it – I need an audience ..."

"You've got a fucking audience." Chas pointed to Marelle. "If you can't sing in front of one person then how the hell are you going to sing to a few thousand?" Chas questioned, tersely with the guitar on his lap, gesturing at Jacob in frustration. "Just get on and sing the whole song!"

Jacob sighed. Closed his eyes for a second. Marelle watched him gather himself.

Chas began the intro again; side-eyed Jacob whilst doing so until he finally stepped up to the microphone again. He closed his eyes, belted out the first line – louder, richer with even more passion. Two lines in he had found that sweet spot as the music came to him. It wound its way through his memory, grabbed Ezza's hand and dragged him right up to the front and kicked Jacob right out of the ballpark.

Suddenly he was animated, taking the mic out of the stand and walking the 'stage'. He was in a world purely inside his own head, one where there were two thousand people in the darkness. Chas laughed to himself. Ezza strode the stage, captivating every molecule of air in the room, held each one then expelled it on an excited mission to spread his presence far and wide.

Chas went straight on to a second track. It did not phase Jacob in the least. He was focused to the point of singularity; he was performing for his very existence but not a single word he sang or a single movement he made looked contrived. He walked the floor, handled the mic, he played the crowd that wasn't there with such a natural ability that Marelle began to wonder if he was indeed two people in the same body with one very large switch waiting to be flicked on, or off, at any time. And as he moulded into the role, he interacted with Chas in a way that warmed Marelle's heart beyond belief. There was a bond here that had been rendered dormant but was now warming, stirring, waking and coming to life once more.

THIRTY-EIGHT

She sat there and watched him – Jacob – her fiancé, the man she was going to marry – become Ezza right before her eyes. She observed him singing, interacting with Chas like they had never been apart and perform to an audience that was all in his head.

Seamlessly Chas launched into another tune straight after that one finished and by the glance Jacob gave him it appeared to be the butt of a joke or a testing one. Chas laughed as Jacob's mind was worrying furiously but finally with a smile he leaned into the microphone and the first line of the song was delivered perfectly. Chas laughed and a smile broke on Jacob's face as the second line flowed just as smoothly. It was a song Marelle did not recognise – a harsher, bounding tune with Jacob's voice raw and cutting throughout it. As he sang and went through the accompanying motions Chas stood up and wandered closer to him. He too leaned into Jacob's mic and sang the chorus in perfect harmony with him. A grin broke across their faces which was sublime. Jacob laughed and became more animated with the second verse which flowed from him so easily.

Marelle laughed with joy at the looks on their faces; let herself warm with the happiness and she shrugged her shoulders up to her ears in glee and gripped the edge of the seat she sat upon just as someone placed a hand on her shoulder.

Marelle spooked violently, snapped her head round to see a woman standing close to her, staring in awe at Chas and Jacob performing together.

"Oh my! There he is!" The woman said, patting Marelle's shoulder gently.

At that moment she recognised her from the beach on that morning …

"I'm Mya" She leaned in and said in Marelle's ear. "Chas' wife." She clutched one hand to her chest and didn't take her eyes from them. She seemed in total awe; like she was watching a ghost right in front of her eyes like she had waited her entire life to see this.

Marelle could feel her standing close; she could sense the anticipation and excitement in this woman – as Chas' playing quickened and Jacob stepped up to the mic to deliver a verse, almost acapella in a voice he mustered from the old days – full of angst and sadness. He was word perfect and pitch perfect; beside her Chas' wife gasped audibly. Chas shook his head – not in disbelief – but in *belief* of exactly what he was hearing next to him.

The song ended with Chas going for it on the guitar while Jacob drew the very last line to a crescendo. Then it stopped; just stopped and there was a second of silence where everyone seemed to be holding their breath.

Then beside Marelle Chas' wife suddenly produced a high-pitched full-on whistle with her fingers to her mouth – a celebratory whoop to what she had just seen. Chas looked up; Jacob turned his head – gave one of the warmest, most loving smiles Marelle had ever seen him portray. He held it momentarily then turned back to the microphone. He began singing, alone. Chas looked to him, a little surprised that he had made that move.

Marelle recognised the words. It was the same song that Jacob had played her on the CD player as they had sat on the airfield by a bonfire one day; the same CD that he had purposely thrown into the flames and watched burn. And it was the same song that Yellow Son had played at the first gig she had seen them in. When they had unknowingly dedicated it to Ezza as he'd stood in the audience.

Beside her, his wife gasped again as Chas began to pick along with the tune Jacob made. Marelle had heard Chas sing the song at the weekender; unknowingly she had also heard Jacob sing it on the CD he had thrown into the fire – at the time she had not known or even suspected it was him. Now she heard his voice singing it, right in front of her – each word laden with emotion; cast from him and set free to alight on the ears of those who would listen. And as Marelle listened properly to the words again, she realised what he was saying.

She had been stunned by the beauty of the song that day as she had sat next to him on a pile of breeze blocks alongside the caravan. The bonfire in front of him, smoke curling lazily into a late summer sky. On that day the song had seemed to be about the loss of a loved one. She had wondered at the time – not convinced it was a lost lover; she assumed it to be about Frankie and the impact of the loss of his childhood friend on his life. Now, as she watched him sing it and watched Chas respectfully accompany him and listened to the same lyrics she was struck by the realisation it was about Jacob, Ezza himself. It had been a very obvious comment on the state of his emotions at that time and how he felt he was losing grip. It had been a cry for help even then; a cry for help when he had played it to her – in his usual veiled and covert style. No-one had noticed it; according to him Chas had poo-pooed it. She herself had not picked up on it. It had just been a pretty song.

His voice wrapped itself around the words of loss and Marelle felt a lump in her throat; felt a shiver caress her spine and fixed her eyes on him as she felt a tear escape and fall silently down her cheek.

He finished and stood with one hand on the mic for a second and his eyes closed. When he opened them, they were warm and full, he turned his head to look at Chas and in turn had his head turned to look at Jacob. The most beautiful smile broke on Jacob's face and in that moment Marelle felt something wrap its fingers around her heart.

As Jacob and Chas looked at each other he finally moved away from the mic and as they held out an arm to one another Marelle wiped away the tear with a fingertip, not wanting to ruin her make up or make herself look like an idiot in front of Chas and his wife.

"Oh my God!" Chas' wife suddenly cried beside her. "Oh my!" She said, her voice breaking and emotion filling her.

Marelle turned to look at her and there stood a woman, possibly late fifties, dressed elegantly in black, her short, sharp platinum blonde hair perfect but her face a mess of emotions and running mascara.

"Oh my!" She sobbed again, suddenly embracing Marelle like a lost child and hugging her tightly.

"You don't know how much I've loved and missed that man of yours!" She cried. Then released Marelle as quickly as she had grabbed her, scurrying across the floor to Jacob who, still in a brotherly hug with Chas was pulled into his wife's arms so completely. Marelle watched her clutch onto Jacob like a mother re-united with a child, crying and holding on to him so as to never let him slip through her fingers again.

"Oh Ezza!" She sobbed. "Oh Ezza! My boy is back. I knew you'd never gone ..."

Marelle stood up. Her legs felt weak – half from sitting so tense on that stool and half from whatever hormones were racing around her body right now. She walked over. Chas' wife was still holding Jacob, still crying and blubbing. Jacob had his head against her shoulder, his eyes closed. It was like he had truly been reunited with family; a family he didn't or had never really had.

Marelle swallowed. These were the people he should never have left; these were the people he belonged with – who could have held him steady in choppy waters, who could have kept him on course. But instead, he had set himself adrift; rendered himself lost forever. Lived a life of lies and fear and isolation – learned to embrace death as much as he had embraced life and found the door closed on the end of the tunnel he had chosen to travel along.

Chas patted her on the shoulder as he stood to put his guitar on a stand.

"Mya. Stop crying." He ordered but not as a retribution. "Can we all stop blubbing – for God's sake!"

Mya gave Jacob a final squeeze then pushed herself away from him, looking up into his eyes as he looked back at her. It was a brief but intense moment, then she turned to Chas. "You shut it Symonds! My boy is back and he's not going anywhere!"

"Stop walking all over this. I told you how it would go ... the decision is mine. No-one else's. Stop grabbing hold of it ... it's not as simple as that ... it's a fucking shit storm so stop making fucking promises ..."

"Ignore him." She said to Jacob, finally letting him out of her grasp.

His eyes immediately turned to Marelle. They focused and looked into hers and she had him back again. He walked forward, opened his arms and she fell into them, felt complete again.

He held her. "Mya is very emotional." He whispered in her ear. "Don't worry about her ..."

"I'm not. It was beautiful." Marelle whispered back to him.

Jacob hugged her, kissed her cheek them stood away.

Chas was busying himself but putting stuff away. Mya turned back to them with a smile.

"Looks like I've gained a new daughter too ..."

Jacob laughed. Marelle smiled, his arm warm and heavy around her shoulders.

"You don't know how much I've missed him." She repeated, reaching out and taking Marelle's hand. "I'm a stupid old woman, don't mind me ..."

"We played that song a few weeks back you know ..." Chas said from his fiddling without looking at them.

"I know. We were there." Jacob replied.

"You were there!" Chas exclaimed, momentarily looking up at Jacob.

"Yes, I was hiding." Jacob added.

"Not surprised. That was a fucking dog's dinner." Chas commented. "Said that we would do this gig thinking we can do the same set on each night then fucking Luc pipes up and says he's got to go to some wedding or something ..."

"It was a christening ..." Mya added.

"Whatever." Chas said. "I didn't want to pull out cos I've blah, blah, blahed my way into this but I've got no fucking drummer! Thought it would be a laugh to cobble some kind of semi-acoustic set together then fucking Marty isn't available in the run-up. Leaves me with Jem sticking some fucking mish-mash together in the hope that Marty can keep up and join in on the night! Jesus!"

"It was ok." Jacob said. "A bit odd, but ok. Crowd liked it!"

"They would have liked anything. Load of pissed up girls – they didn't care. Was it you behind that fickle finger shit?"

Jacob laughed. "Yes."

"Fuck's sake. I didn't wonder how that got brought up. Jesus! How long have you been planning this, *stalking* us?"

Jacob smiled. Chas meant it in humour. "Not long. It took the last ten plus years and Marelle to make me want to come back."

"As I said to Mya – it's not that easy though, is it?"

Jacob kept his smile, looked at Chas, looking away for a moment. She felt him squeeze her shoulders gently. "Let's have a coffee ..." Chas said. "Mya!"

Mya went over to the far side and began making coffee. Chas kept fiddling and didn't make much conversation. Jacob nodded to him with a covert little grin to Marelle as he took her hand to walk over to Mya.

"How much coffee has he had?" She asked so matter-of-factly as if they had spent the last ten years in each other's pockets.

'He had a mug of something when we arrived ..." Jacob answered with a shrug.

'How much coffee have you had already?" She shouted across to Chas in a loud voice that was a little unexpected.

"Not enough." Chas shouted back with his head down behind a speaker.

Mya tutted. "You know he had bypass surgery a couple of years ago ... I tell him, he's not getting any younger – he has to look after himself."

"Did he?" Jacob questioned, a little surprised.

'Yes, he did. Kept it pretty quiet. The other guys know but it didn't get out. He's fine – caught him before it got too dangerous."

Jacob looked briefly to Chas, then back to Mya.

"Only don't say anything – he doesn't like anyone knowing. God only knows why!" She lowered her voice as she made the coffee. "First couple of gigs straight after were a little bit scary but, well, he's ok – as you can see. He doesn't change much." She said. "And neither do you!"

Jacob grinned. "Oh I've changed a lot."

"Nonsense!" She laughed, reaching out and touching him briefly with a smile. "So, you two are engaged? When is the big day then?"

"Not decided yet." He replied.

She tutted. "Not good enough Ez. Sort it. You can't keep a pretty young lady like her hanging on forever …"

"He can do whatever he wants as long as I'm with him!" Marelle chipped in, clutching to him, sweetly.

Mya turned and beamed at them both. "Oh yes, you've changed Ez. Look at you. You're in love!"

Shortly after Chas wandered over. He had run out of excuses to keep from joining the conversation and looking Jacob in the eye.

"You know." He said. "I can't remember what your real name is! I just keep calling you Ez – I know we always did – but that wasn't your name, was it?"

"It's Jacob." Marelle smiled, not thinking as she smiled at Chas.

"It's Nathaniel – Nat." Jacob corrected. "Marelle calls me Jacob."

"Why?" Chas asked, making a face of incomprehension.

Jacob grinned. "It's a long story!"

"Oh no!" Mya suddenly exclaimed from beside them. "We didn't film it or even take pictures – the first time you and Ez performed together in all those years and we didn't take a photo!"

"We didn't want a photo Mya!" Chas replied.

"But it's momentous!" She protested.

"No photos." He stated.

"Nice little place here." Jacob said.

"It's my brother's!" Mya laughed. "Well, half of it – he joint owns it with Danny Hart …" She said it as if they should know who Danny Hart was.

"Really?" Jacob commented.

"Yes." She smiled. "It's only two minutes down the road from us."

"My sister was convinced she saw you a while back …" Chas added.

"Did she?"

"Was it?" Chas asked.

Jacob shrugged. "May have been?"

Chas looked at him knowingly. Marelle just widened her eyes and smiled.

They talked small talk for a while longer and drank coffee. Mya had that bright glint in her eye the whole time and a loving smile on her face. After a while, and when she could contain herself no longer, she chose a break in the conversation and said

"So, are you going to ask him back? Meet the other guys?"

Chas kept a straight and neutral look on his face as he moved his grey eyes to her.

"No." He said. "We are not going to let him meet the other boys." There was a moment of still disdain from everyone listening to Chas' words at the moment. Mya was about to say something but he continued.

"This is what we are going to do ..."

The journey home was a buoyant one. As Jacob drove Marelle was thinking of the time she had driven home after they had spent that tortuous and disastrous day at Frankie's funeral. Jacob, drunk in the passenger seat, stopped by the police due to his out of character, and perceived to be aggressive, behaviour towards her in a pub on their way home. Now, when she reflected on that she could see Ezza punching furiously at the plastic bag which was suffocating him – trying to escape but being restrained forcefully. Today, as they drove home, Ezza was out; Ezza was sitting in the driving seat beside her in control of her car with a smile as wide as the horizon before them. Marelle smiled, actually smiled as his happiness infused itself into her – more than ever before with its giggling, chuckling infectivity.

"It's genius!" Jacob laughed, shaking his head.

They had been driving for half an hour before he had not been able to contain all of this within himself any longer.

Chas had very carefully explained his plan in the way Marelle now knew Chas explained everything. It was not off the cuff; it was a well and long thought - out scenario he had obviously been turning over in his mind since that first moment Jacob had sat in the dingy little room at the back of the venue that night. A plan that was pure genius but also a plan that relied on a knife edge of possibility.

"You can come on for the encore." Chas had said. "Two songs – Too Close and Lucky ... I'll put them into the encore that night. We normally play Too Close in the set, but we will push it into the encore. I want you there two minutes before – not hanging around attracting attention to yourself. You be there, ready to come on – I'll tell you the time, and the whole thing will rely on you being there at that precise moment. Don't fuck it up." Chas had warned.

So his plan was for them to do the normal show – he would sing throughout but when they came back on for the obligatory encore he would say something along the lines of needing a rest from singing – and he had someone to stand in. At that moment Jacob would be backstage and would walk into the spotlight Chas normally occupied. The music would start up and he would start singing.

"When are you going to tell the others?" Jacob had questioned at that point and Chas had sat back and laughed.

"I'm not." He said. 'That's part of it; I'm not going to pre-warn them about you – I'll tell them to keep playing whatever happens ...you'll come on, sing the two songs then I suggest you get away pretty pronto ..."

Marelle had been trying to imagine the scene – the utter chaos that could well ensue but at the same time the utter genius that could well be played out on that stage if it all fell into place. Chas had drummed the importance of timing into Jacob.

"You are to be there. Right at that moment. Ready to come on – and then just sing." Chas had reiterated. "If you're not, or you don't turn up you're going to make me look stupid."

Marelle smiled to herself at that point, sitting on the worktop, swinging her legs against the cupboards. There was not a snowflake's chance in hell that Jacob would not turn up.

Chas had then gone into minutiae; explaining how he wanted things doing; how it should sound – told Jacob not to get 'too shouty' and ended – after telling him he would phone with updates and timings throughout the next couple of weeks, by saying

'This is your one and only chance. Don't fuck it up!"

Right now, Jacob was laughing as they drove home.

"He's thought long and hard about this." He smiled. "Just as Chas always does. It's all worked out, it's all planned. It's all fucking genius!"

"But it's only the encore." Marelle stated warily.

"Only the encore!" Jacob exclaimed. "Only the very last thing that everyone remembers – only the time to showcase your very best tracks …"

She smiled and looked kindly across the car to him. Somehow, he looked different – looked lankier, younger sitting there in the driving seat. Different to the person who had driven up there a few hours before. He had turned the sleeves upon the old Yellow Son t-shirt and his arms looked thinner – muscular, tense. He was leaning forward in the car seat – not laid casually back in the way he normally did. Going home he leaned into the drive, hanging over the steering wheel like an excited child as he drove, his right foot also slightly heavier than normal. Marelle found her eyes lingering on him before she blinked away and looked out at the road ahead.

"What did you think of Chas today?" Jacob smiled.

She shrugged. "I still find him a bit 'prickly' to be honest."

He chuckled. "He acts out as a wily old fox but he's as soft as shit – if not opinionated."

Marelle found Chas difficult to read. In some ways she agreed with Jacob's summary but in others she was constantly aware of his 'key holding' status and in her eyes, so was Chas.

"Mya's a different kettle of fish though, isn't she? You can't really have any *bad vibes* about Mya." He was smiling.

Mya. Marelle smiled slightly. Yes, she was lovely, but she also had a historical and obviously very strong link to Jacob. The way she had looked at him, touched him, hugged him' it was like a mother's eyes on her only son – it was no threat, she felt, but it was nonetheless a link which Marelle did not, as yet, feel part of.

"She's very emotional." Marelle commented.

'Mya has always worn her heart on her sleeve. She's like a mother hen and we are all her babies – she has always been the same but especially so with me. I was the infant of the group, and she took me under her wing as a spotty, naïve youngster." He smiled. "Mya was the only person I was worried about when I decided to keep my head down and become Jacob. I worried she would blame herself for what happened to Ezza. If I could have just contacted someone and said '*hey, it's ok. I'm not dead*' she was probably the person I would have been in touch with. But I couldn't ..."

"Why would she blame herself?"

"Because she always looked out for me; I know she was watching me and was aware of what was happening ..."

'How old is she?"

"About the same age as Chas."

Marelle nodded.

'Always tried to get me to go to theirs for Christmas – she worried about me being on my own – but I never did – not with my father there ... and it's down to her that Chas has let this happen ..."

"Do you think so?"

"Definitely." Jacob said. "She's a tough cookie despite the way she loves everybody – don't be fooled. She wears the trousers, and she steers the ship that is Yellow Son through the choppy waters of their existence."

THIRTY-NINE

As the next few days passed Marelle couldn't help but constantly see someone else was now inhabiting Jacob's skin. He *looked* the same, he *talked* the same – he *was* the same but there was a *difference* within him. An existence of a second being, just shadowing the first – just occasionally metaphorically pushing his skin in a different direction – placing his feet on the floor in the even stride he took, filled with a new solidity that had not been there before. Everything about him was alive. Buzzing and bristling with intent, vibrating with the frequency of a life he lived now.

Here he was – just about as far as he could possibly be from the dark days of anguish, confusion and struggle; days when she thought she had lost him forever mentally, if not physically. But days when she had loved him just as much as she loved him now.

He was surrounding himself with a circle of people who loved him rather than the disparate crowd who were all ready to hate. Oh, they were still out there, and they were still haunting their future but right now he didn't care and subsequently, neither did she.

He went to work with a spring in his step; returned home the same. Buoyant from more than one telephone call from Chas at moments when he had thought of some other instruction to add. They talked; Jacob laughed – convened like friends who had never been apart.

With no work from Seb anymore Marelle courted boredom and found herself trawling the internet a little too much in search of pictures of Jacob she had not seen before. Most she had looked at many times but still marvelled at how many images of him existed with such access, but no one had ever called him out while he had stayed here. Testament indeed to the way he had carefully planned and lived the life of Jacob.

Then she turned to the house to do what her initial intent had been when she had moved in here under Seb's duress. The place needed life and personality breathing into it. Room by room she sought to tidy and clean; rearrange, plan for new furniture and decoration The guy started building the wall; said he could do it a bit at a time between other jobs and Marelle watched each brick join the construction and one by one make small foundations to their future she now knew they had together.

Marelle called Jacob's phone. She was bored and needed something to break up the day. The builder wasn't even here to watch, and she had reached the threshold of boredom with cleaning. The call connected but she was met with an engaged tone. That was odd. She took the phone away from her ear and looked at it in disbelief. Jacob didn't give that number to anyone – he always gave her number. Maybe something was wrong with the phone – maybe he was trying to call her at the same time?

She waited and watched her phone, expecting it to ring. It didn't. Half an hour later she called it three more times but on each occasion it was still engaged.

She sighed, not knowing whether to be worried if it was engaged. If he didn't answer – which was fifty percent of the time – she worried if he was ok; worried that he was hurt, or ill or ... back into his old games.

Engaged was different. It meant he was speaking to someone else – but who and why? It could also mean that he had called someone but not ended the call – she asked herself why that would be the case and came to the same conclusion as him not answering the phone. Fear washed over her. Being engaged was as bad as not answering.

Just about to grab her car keys, she stopped and dialled it one more time. This time it rang. He answered virtually straight away.

"Hi."

"Hello." She said. "Your phone has been engaged for ages ..."

He laughed. "It was Chas. Sorry."

"Has he got that number?"

"Yes, I gave it to him the other day ..."

Marelle made a little face of surprise to herself. "What did he want?"

"I don't know really." He chuckled. 'Think he just called for a chat! Mya has gone away with a friend and he is obviously at a loose end!"

Marelle kept the smile, but her mind wandered how in such a short space of time Jacob had gone from being *persona non grata* to best friend.

'Where are you now?" She questioned.

"At the farm, why?"

"I was going to bring lunch down – we could have it together?"

"We could do. I'm meant to be moving stuff out of the old barn but I keep getting stopped either by having to go back to the workshop or by Chas!"

"Where is the 'old barn' then?"

Up behind the farmhouse – big black barn, you can see it from the farmyard." He explained.

"Can I come up there?" She questioned, wondering if she should be seen stopping with him so close the farmhouse.

"Yeah, there's no-one in today. Ryan should have been doing this but he's gone home because he says he feel sick."

"Leave it for when he comes back ..."

"Nah. It's alright It's quite interesting."

"*Interesting*?"

"Yeah, they've got a lot of old stuff stashed away in here ... there are old pictures of the farm – some of my father ..."

"Are there?" She asked. "Can I see them, any of you?"

He laughed. "I don't know if I can find them again – I've moved those already and put them away ..."

She knew that wasn't exactly the truth; Jacob wouldn't forget where he had put them.

"OK." She said, not wanting to push it. He didn't want to share. "I'll be up in half an hour."

Strange. She had seen the black barn behind the house from a distance many times but hadn't really dwelled on or thought about it. Quite an imposing building, stained black like a lot of barns in Suffolk she realised, red tiles roof, huge, double-doors at the front which were propped open today. She drove right up to the entrance, parked to the left of it just as Jacob walked to the aperture with a large box in his hands. He stood and waited until she got out, lunch bag in her hand, and walked up to him with a smile. Jacob paused, stopped and waited with the box in his hands until she strode up, raised herself on tip toe and kissed him on the lips. Then he walked to a nearby tractor and trailer and placed the box in the back. Marelle walked into the barn.

The floor was a herringbone pattern of red stone tiles, they looked like they had been swept recently. There was a dustiness inside, motes dancing in the air where the sun was shining through the numerous gaps in the wood which comprised the entire structure. She looked up, pivoted round.

The barn seemed immense inside. Like a huge, wooden cathedral of a space from the dry-stone tiled floor up to the very top of the pitched roof above her. Where the naked oak beams criss-crossed in a structure that was time scarred and well worn. It had the modern intrusion of electric lighting to detract from the whole medieval feel of the place. Three single bulbs suspended from the cross beams along its length, providing a pale-yellow light which was immediately devoured by the place itself.

"Wow!" She smiled. "This is amazing!"

Jacob stood beside her in the centre of the space. This part of the barn was clear, to their right and towards the far end was a clutter of boxes and old furniture – several generations of three-piece suites and various brown wooden pieces.

"It was completely cleared out and refurbished about twenty years ago. It was collapsing and stuffed full of old junk then ..."

"What do they use it for?"

"Storage .... Mostly. They had some big party in it a few years ago ... so I'm told ..."

She nodded, still looking around herself.

'That's why they want it cleared again now ... his cousin's coming over from Australia, they want to have a big family bash in here." He walked over to the clutter. "He's getting on, I suppose he's taking the chance to come back to what was his father's and uncle's family farm years ago ..."

Marelle wasn't listening. She was still looking around.

"Ryan was meant to be helping. I can't lift that furniture until I get another pair of hands."

She followed him over to the stack he was moving. Some was covered with dust sheets, other items were exposed to the dancing shafts of light shining through the gaps, dust playing and swirling in their beams.

'It would make a great house." She commented.

"Yeah, that's what most people thought about all of the old barns around here – most of them have been converted by now."

"It's incredible!" She said, still looking around herself, into every corner and space that seemed to lead off from the main vestibule.

The pile of boxes right in front of her looked like someone had cleared a house and just dumped it here. Probably exactly what their third bedroom still looked like back at the house! Right at the front was an old wooden tea crate, full of leather straps and buckles, snaking out of it like wires out of the back of a sci-fi nightmare.

"What's that?" She asked.

He walked over to it, touched the leather before he spoke.

"Old horse harness." He said. "Left over from the days when horses worked the land instead of tractors."

"Horses, here?"

He nodded. 'I don't remember them being here, but I know my father worked with horses in the past ..."

"Wow!" she smiled.

He was looking at the box of straps and buckles "... and that's all that's left ... I've been leaving that box ... it's been stacked and moved around a few times now, been out in the rain at times, it's slowly rotting away – they've no use for it, no value to it anymore ... soon they'll tell me to throw it on the bonfire – but imagine what that has done – the work, the horses, the sweat ... an era gone and almost forgotten."

Marelle stared at it for a moment, the same as he did. It was true. Soon it would just be resigned to history, or at least to those who remembered it.

"It's sad." He said. 'I don't want to throw that away."

"Well don't. Take it home – if it's worthless to everyone?"

"What for?"

"Preserve the memory." She suggested.

"You're good at saving life's waifs and strays – aren't you?" he grinned.

"Marelle smiled back, walked up to him, placed a hand on his chest. 'Sometimes, if I think it's a case worth saving ..."

"And what are your criteria?"

"Oh, need, want, love ... I weigh it up against how I would feel if I lost the chance to take it home with me ..."

He smiled. She was close to him, her face only millimetres from his. Marelle stared into those velvet brown eyes and for once saw peace, saw calm, saw no evidence of the writhing worm of doubt and fear she had always observed in them. She wondered; did *he* see *that* in hers?

"Well, you certainly saved this one." He said quietly, almost challenging himself to actually allow the words to pass out of his mouth.

She slid her hands between his arms and his torso and kissed him with an appetite. Marelle never looked into his eyes or felt his body against her without that desire igniting within her.

He cupped her face, ran his fingers through the back of her hair and she shivered as her own hands settled on his back, his body warm and vital' She spread her fingers and felt the hardness of his ribs beneath them.

With the sunlight filtering dusty beams of pale lemon light through the gaps and the arid, complete dryness of the ancient stone floor, he took her hand and led her around a monumental 'Y' shaped upright beam. Behind that and an old trailer covered with a tarpaulin was a brown leather four-seater settee. Old but serviceable, cushions well stuffed, plump and shiny – horsehair from those old horses filling their contours.

Outside the day was a crisp, bright October one, a little breeze but not overly cold. The birds sang in celebration of another day in the sun, the trees stood and the white fluffy clouds traversed the baby blue sky. The world turned as Jacob reclined her onto the supple leather seat, pinned her with his hip bone and proved to her that she really had saved him, every inch of him. He was alive and blood was coursing through his veins.

It was always like the first time for her. Always that endless, animal want in her for him, and she prayed to God that it would never go away, or she would never tire of his lithe, hard body against hers. Now she wrapped her arms around his neck and held her to him, her bare bottom against the leather of the settee.

"It'll stain you know." She grinned.

"What?" He asked with his face against her neck.

"The leather ... if it's wet. It will stain it."

He raised his face, stared at her, then laughed.

"Don't worry about it. The whole thing will probably end up being burned – or moved to another shed for the next twenty years!"

She smiled and clutched his head back to her breast. "Jacob."

"What?"

"We need to set a date."

She felt movement from him, wasn't sure if his ribs expanded in a sigh or in momentous pride and love for her.

"I know." He finally replied.

Marelle didn't want to say the word, but it slipped out nonetheless. "When?"

He rubbed his face against her neck, held her tighter. "Just as soon as ... as soon as I can take back who I really am. I don't want to marry you masquerading as Jacob only to have someone catch up with us ...we're so close now ... very close." He answered.

She wished they were. Right now, she felt a distance. A road winding into an oblivious future that always had another turn, another corner, another twist. Jacob had proposed to her, actually gone down on one knee at the Thor site and placed his mother's engagement ring on her finger. She knew he meant it;

she trusted him but she just wanted it to happen because the threat of Jacob not being there would always be a very real one. And all of the 'what ifs' the 'buts' – Jacob simply wasn't paying attention to them right now.

They ate the lunch she had brought with her, sitting together in the barn where they had just made love in the dancing, dust filled sunlight.

She sighed.

"What?" He asked.

"Nothing."

'What?"

Marelle raised her gaze to his. "Is Chas still calling it a day on Yellow Son?"

He laughed. "What?"

"He said it was over. He's letting you sing but he said he was packing it in."

"What! With me back?" Jacob grinned. "He won't."

Marelle stared at him.

He laughed.

"Don't you worry your pretty little head about that! I've got Chas eating out of the palm of my hand."

Maybe he had but that didn't guarantee he wouldn't bite back. She wasn't sure; Marelle knew she had to let Jacob flex his wings and fly free – she knew he had to soar and feel the cushion of air beneath him – but she feared him doing it. She feared him moving away from her, mingling with a crowd of people from his past who had known and loved him long before she had. Now she knew he had a past and she knew what that involved she wanted that ring on her finger more than ever.

He came home that evening, a knowing little smile on his face which lit up his eyes from lunchtime.

"We owe Mae and Bella." He said. "Shall we ask them out for a meal?"

Brave Jacob now, Marelle thought to herself, remembering the time she had persuaded him to go out for a meal with her when they had first met. How reluctant he had been, how nervous he had acted ... and the woman in the red dress, who had later said she was the sister of someone who used to work with Jacob ... she would have to ask Chas about that too.

"We can. I'm not sure when they are both free as Mae works shifts, but I can ask ..."

"Give her a call. I don't want them to think we're just going to suck it up and not thank them properly."

Marelle called Bella after dinner, curled up against Jacob on the settee with the phone to her ear.

"Hi Marelle!" Bella greeted. "What's up?"

"Nothing." She laughed. "Jacob asked me to call ..."

"Oh yeah? Why? Need advice on finding your g-spot?"

Marelle laughed. "No, he's got that down to a 'T' – no he wants to take you and Mae out as a thank you ... you know, for the house ..."

"Oh cool. What about you?" Bella was obviously in a very buoyant mood tonight – or she was drinking already. She giggled.

'You're not getting him to yourselves." Marelle glanced to him as she said it. He grinned but did not make eye contact. "When are you both around?"

"Well Mae is down here for the next four days ... we are around for this weekend."

"This weekend?" Marelle turned to Jacob; she took his inactivity as confirmation that it would work.

"Tell you what." Bella offered "Why don't you come down here for a change – you both might enjoy the culture shock – we can have a meal then hit a club – the old haunts!"

Marelle sighed. "Erm, not sure Bella ..."

"Nonsense. Don't pull that one on me – we all know Jacob is not the shy little shrinking violet you make him out to be!"

This time it was not Jacob she was worried about. "It's not that." She said. "It's just being in close proximity to where Seb is – especially with the reason we would be there anyway."

"Stuff it Marelle! Seb's not going to be in a club, is he?"

Marelle smiled. "No, but ..."

"But what? Anyway, fuck Seb. You're Scot free now!"

Marelle wouldn't have exactly used that phrase for the way she felt right now. "Erm." she said. "I'll ask Jacob."

"Just come down. Stop fannying around."

Marelle laughed to herself. "He might not want to do that."

"Do what?" He asked, beside her.

"Go to Bella's for the weekend, have a meal then go to a club."

He shrugged. "That's fine. The weekend is on me so if that's what they both want to do than that's cool ..."

'That's cool!" She laughed. "Since when did you start saying '*that's cool*'?" She turned back to Bella on the phone, she had heard and was also laughing now.

"Ok Bella. Looks like Jacob is up for it ... not sure he knows what he's letting himself in for ... not sure I am. But ..."

"What's wrong with you? It'll be fun!" Bella exclaimed.

Marelle had one day, just over twenty-four hours to prepare herself, and Jacob, for a night in the old town with Bella and Mae. Nights from the past came back to her – alcohol fuelled behaviour in 'Avenues' and extreme girly behaviour and flirting in 'Phz'. Manic, crazy nights, pissed and stumbling, laughing, single. Now both attached and five years older it just wouldn't, couldn't, be the same.

Jacob left for work. The guy in the blue van turned up – today he had brought a younger helper with him. She watched for a bit as he set up to continue with the construction of the wall, glancing in passing, watching them work; slowly and with a precision as the bricks were placed one by one.

Mid-morning she made tea and, feeling unusually benevolent – or bored – ventured outside to offer them tea as well. The sunshine had some warmth to it, and she pulled the front door to and started down the garden, past her car to the front. Both of them were on the other side of the half-built wall, out near the road. She could hear them talking. With that structure and still quite overgrown laurel hedge, they were out of her sight. She pondered on calling so as not to make them jump but decided against that and wrapped her arms around herself as she got closer. She could hear a third voice in the conversation.

"You know he's involved with the bodies of those poor children, don't you?" A female voice said, quietly. "Prime suspect but they just can't pin it on him."

Marelle stopped, paused, hugged herself as she heard the words and her blood began to run cold.

"I don't know anything about that. His money is as good as the next blokes as far as I'm concerned ..." the builder replied.

"... and that's questionable too ... where has he suddenly got all of this money from? Building this, flash bikes, prancing around in new clothes ..."

The voice was Jill. She knew it was!

"He's a delinquent who works on the farm ... it'll come out ... something will give soon ... you'll see ..." Jill continued. "I wouldn't want to be alone with him – wouldn't want my kids anywhere near him either ... he was abused as a child – or so they say – and that kind of thing usually turns them into an abuser themselves – just for revenge ... you two need to watch yourselves." She carried on. "And what does he want this bloody wall for anyway, hey? Turning this place into a bloody fortress – behind closed door you know, and all that ..." Jill paused.

Marelle heard the builder working, scraping, knocking.

"She's no better." Jill continued. "Foul mouthed, nasty piece of work."

Marelle felt her breath catch painfully in her throat; she wanted to expel it – perpetuate the myth further in self-defence but held herself. Screaming in the street right now would not be wise.

"I don't know." The builder said.

"Is he a murderer?" A young male voice joined in.

"... and worse." Jill added.

"We don't know that, Billy." The builder offered.

"I think we do." Jill added. "We all do!" She continued. 'He's weird ... he's banned from the shop and the pub you know. He's why Tricia's house is on the market ... it went up yesterday ...had to wait for the police to give her the go ahead ... he's driving people – good people– out of the village!"

Marelle looked across the road, she couldn't quite see Patricia's house from where she was standing.

"No one will want to buy that unless they're some twisted psychopath – like him. With those poor little children buried in the garden ..."

"I don't know anything about it, Jill. I'm just building a wall, as long as I get paid, I don't want to know …"

"Not until he turns on you, or your kids – he's dangerous you mark my words."

He made a little noise in exclamation; denoted he was not going to get involved in her conversation. Wise man.

"He needs locking up. I'd question about this wall too, and why he wants it." She added, thoughtfully.

There was a moment of silence. He sniffed.

"You'll see." She said. "I'd better be off; I've got to go to the doctor's."

FORTY

Marelle loitered until she was certain Jill had moved off, not knowing whether to run back inside before he came back around this side of the wall and discovered her. She stepped backwards.

By the time 'Billy' rounded the end of the half-built wall she was back a way – enough to allay any suspicion she had heard. He looked to her with youthful, wide eyes and for a second made her think of Jacob in those early photos.

"Morning." He said.

"Morning." Marelle greeted in reply. "I'm making tea. Would you both like one?" She smiled.

The older guy also appeared from around the corner as she asked.

"That would be very nice." He said. "Thank you."

Marelle smiled back and over his she should just see the new 'For Sale' sign outside Patricia's house. Jacob's old house.

Marelle made the tea, realising she had, in fact, made a rod for her own back because she really wanted to get online and search for Patricia's house but she went through with the task first and carried two mugs of tea out to the builder and Billy.

"How's it going?" She asked.

"Fair. Fair." The old guy replied. "Got someone to help so we should get on great guns!"

Marelle looked at the wall. It had grown slowly, course by course and as she stood next to it, she realised it was actually higher than she had realised.

"Soon be able to get his gates on."

"Are you doing the gates?" Marelle enquired.

'No." He laughed. "That's too technical for me. I think he's got the gates organised though. Be nice and secure soon ..."

Marelle smiled back, struck by his choice of words – but perhaps that's all they were – his choice of words. She lifted her eyes to him, but Billy was staring directly at her, his interest obviously piqued by the conversation with Jill. She wanted to defend Jacob to the builder... months ago she would have without hesitation but instead she smiled, bit her tongue and returned to the house.

It only took Marelle a few seconds to find the house on-line with a local estate agent. It wasn't the one they had dealt with and the presentation of the house for sale looked much more professional. Seb, she surmised, had chosen the one with the lowest fees. What did it matter, he knew he already had a buyer – but not the one he had ended up with!

The picture of the little yellow cottage had been taken in full sunlight and it looked extremely attractive, nestling in a perfectly manicured front garden, on an early autumn day.

'Idyllic village setting.' The headline read. Marelle scoffed to herself and read on. 'Attractive family cottage has been completely and sympathetically refurbished to present a stunning family home in the quiet village of

Groveham Parfield. Set squarely on. a plot of just over one third of an acre (STS) the property offers a perfect setting to enjoy the idyllic village life of this pretty and much sought after Suffolk village.'

It went on to describe the interior as Marelle scanned through the photographs. She had never seen the interior of this house before and, although being aware that it had changed considerably since Jacob had lived there, she eagerly looked at each room and imagined Jacob's childhood and young adult life in these spaces.

The interior of the house was very light– and bright which she expected but she also doubted it had been like that in Jacob's time. The kitchen was modern, cream cabinets, butter yellow walls – quite open plan with a central pedestal – immaculate. It made the images of their house, which had been taken furtively while she and Jacob were out, look a total mess. The image she looked at was far different to the one Jacob had described. She continued through the pictures, each room bright and pretty, homely – but always in her mind was the time Jacob had lived there – alone and neglected by his father. Hiding, shivering – watching in that kitchen while his father had struggled with that bundle in a blanket on that fateful night.

Rooms and spaces which had undoubtedly shaped Jacob completely. It was surprising how a lick of paint and modern furniture could erase any memories that resided in a property.

And as she stared, visited rooms she did not know yet connected to, it struck her that his father had also died in that house. Where? She didn't know – nor which of the bedrooms would have been Jacob's – not the one he was probably conceived in.

Maybe Jacob should have bought that house instead, maybe it was more ingrained in him than the fabric of the one she now sat in and which he now owned. Maybe he wouldn't want that house in a million years, maybe his memories there were too bitter to perpetuate.

Curiously she looked for images of the back garden, but the ones included had been carefully cropped and curated.

Jill had said that Patricia had been forced to wait until the police gave her the go ahead to put the house on the market. Did that mean the case was closed?

She looked at the pictures for too long. Pondered on what Jacob would say – he would likely see the sign on his way home. Idyllic village life? Maybe it would be for the next owners.

Jacob arrived home on time. He looked tired. Not a good sign when he had agreed to go on a full-on Bella fest for the coming weekend. He walked in, dropped his bag and sat down to kick off his boots.

"Wall looks good." He commented.

"Yeah. He says he's nearly finished. Says it will soon be ready for the gates to be fitted ..." Gates she knew very little about.

"Good." He replied but didn't elucidate further right now.

"Did you see the sign?" She asked.

"What sign?"

"Patricia's house. It's gone up for sale."

He raised an eyebrow, rubbed his eyes, closed them. "Has it? She obviously can't wait to get out of this place!"

Marelle pursed her lips. "I had a look online, do you want to?"

"Why?"

"It was your childhood house. I thought you might be interested. It's very *yellow* inside!"

"Really?" He commented. "I always remember it as grey."

Jacob didn't seem to want to see the pictures; he wasn't interested. That house obviously held memories but not ones he particularly wanted to be reminded of.

Over dinner he ate in his usual determined way then halfway through, said

"Guess what I heard today?"

"What?" She looked up at him, sensing he had been holding on to this until the weight of it became too heavy to bear alone.

"One of the guys taking stuff off the airfield said that the whole site is going up for sale. Developers have had enough of it; it's a money pit and a white elephant ... his words ... not mine." He twisted his mouth, avoided eye contact. "Might just be a rumour of course ..."

Marelle stared at him. "Is that good or bad?"

"Depends on who buys it." He stated.

Driving back to her old haunting grounds with Jacob at the wheel the next morning seemed strange. The last time they had ventured this way had been to her niece's twelfth birthday party and the fateful night when Seb had decided was not fit to walk the earth let alone reside with his sister. That night would always haunt her, that word always haunt her, and it still threatened to manifest each and every day when nothing could have, in fact, ever been further from the truth.

Marelle was worried; worried people may recognise him, may point or whisper behind their hands that here was that weird stranger who had been found in the toilets at a kid's birthday party. She feared that and if it was going to happen, then this was exactly where it would. Also, she was now in Seb's country. True, he wouldn't be in a club, but he may be walking down a street, driving in his car or, God forbid, eating in the same restaurant tonight.

Jacob was oblivious to her thoughts, and she intended to keep it that way. Marelle looked across to him driving, smiled and placed a hand warmly on his thigh.

Marelle had not been inside Bella's house for a couple of years. It looked the same outside – maybe there was a new shrub in the front garden? She couldn't rightly remember. Bella's car was parked in the drive, behind it was a black sporty little model – not brand new but not that old either. Marelle guessed it was Mae's.

Jacob stopped the Mercedes by the kerbside in front of the modern house on the new, recently completed development. It was quiet, perfect, very regimented and residential.

They hadn't even got out of the car when Bella burst out of her house door and came running up to greet them in white jeans and a pink sweatshirt with 'babe' written on the front. On her feet were huge, pink, fluffy slippers. She ran up whooping, her arms wide to gather them both into an embrace.

"Finally!" She exclaimed. "Finally, I've got you here for a proper night out!" She squeezed them both to her as Mae also emerged, walking up with a cute smile on her face; slim and slight in navy jeans and a pure white t-shirt' her long mousy blonde hair straight as a poker and glistening in the sun. She reached their little huddle and stood before them smiling.

'Hi." She greeted.

Jacob took one hand from Bella's embrace and held it out to Mae. She smiled sweetly and took it.

"Thank you." Jacob said.

She smiled. "No problem."

Bella's house was as immaculate as it had ever been. Everything looked brand new and pristine. It was minimalist with no clutter. The hallway was long and airy – pale colours and a black onyx mirror tiled floor. That was new. It had been a wooden laminate floor before. Marelle hardly drew breath in the space for fear of disrupting the entire perfection of the place.

"Do you want me to show you your room – you can put your stuff up there." She tuned and dashed up the stairs, almost two at a time.

"It's not big but I think you'll manage." She grinned, leading them into a pale blue and white themed room, baby blue carpet on the floor and a view out of the small window over the roofs and back gardens of the adjoining houses.

"We'll manage." Jacob smiled.

"It's a king size bed so you'll be ok for …" She winked. "Or whatever!" She grinned and led them back out. "Marelle knows where everything so don't stand on ceremony – just treat it like your own. Now! Shall we crack open a bottle – no sense in waiting– we've only got the rest of today and a bit of tomorrow and I intend to get well steamed – at least if lover boy is up for it?"

Bella certainly was. Mae was intent on holding on to a single glass of wine, Marelle had accepted a couple before she realised where this was going and Jacob clutched a bottle of beer with the intention of making it last all evening. By mid-afternoon Bella was amusing everyone with pictures of her and Marelle as kids. It was more awkward than amusing, but Marelle prided herself that she hadn't changed much and she did look good in the pictures even if she said so herself. Then Bella moved on to pictures of Mae which she had obviously recently been graced with. Mae by all means had been a chubby child who had only metamorphosised into the way she looked now in her early adult years.

"Where's that one of you in the nurse's uniform?" Bella laughed, now holding Mae's phone and scrolling through it. Marelle looked over her shoulder, seeing glimpses of picture of Mae taking selfies, selfies together, pictures of a dog.

"Look!" Bella said, "There's Mae with Devon!"

She held the photo towards Marelle and Jacob. It looked like a graduation photo, Mae smartly dressed in a pale jacket and beside her a stall statuesque coloured guy with the most beautiful, chiselled cheekbones.

"That's Devon?" Jacob commented.

"But he's ..." Marelle exclaimed, two glasses of wine sloshing in her.

"Black!" Mae finished. "Yeah, he's *very* black!"

Marelle stared at her as if examining her. "But he's your brother!"

Mae smiled that pretty little forgiving smile that would melt the heart of any human, male or female, "Yes. We are both adopted. My parents were unable to have children so they adopted us. Devon was born in Nigeria. I was born in the Czech Republic."

"Really!" Jacob exclaimed. "Wow!"

"Adopted as very young babies so we are pretty much as English as someone born here."

"You *are* English!" Bella interrupted. "You've got an English passport."

"I am." She replied, looking at Bella in a way that was both warm but charged with love. It was the first time Marelle had caught that kind of glance between them but there were other moments in the day when the two of them flashed their eyes at each other in a longing, lustful way. It went over Jacob's head, but Marelle caught Bella's eyes a couple of times too and sensed their relationship had moved on. Was that what Bella had seen in her eyes with Jacob?

Mae was quieter, had a total serene demeanour about her and seemed the complete opposite to Bella but maybe that was why it was working.

Later Bella insisted on ordering a taxi even though both Marelle and Jacob offered to drive.

"No! Everybody is drinking tonight!" Bella announced. "No excuses!"

You didn't need excuses. You just needed an iron will and a robust enough attitude to stand up to Bella – Marelle knew that.

They had chosen a newly opened small Italian restaurant tucked away down a very Victorian side street in the centre of the town where Marelle had grown up. She had commented it had once been a branch of a bank but inside it was totally stripped and refurbished in a modern style. It was nicely busy but not overcrowded; the buzz of chatter was enough to get lost in but not too much as to be overwhelming. The exact type of place she would not have got Jacob near a few months ago!

Tonight however, he was totally comfortable – sat opposite Marelle at Bella's instruction because '*she didn't want them shamelessly canoodling all through the meal*' next to Mae on the bench seat. Marelle smiled to him as she nestled next to Bella but slid a foot beneath the table to rest against his.

Marelle wasn't sure if she felt underdressed or overdressed. Bella was beside her in a short, shocking pink, body hugging dress teamed with impossibly high heels and full make up. Mae was less adorned but nonetheless turned out to perfection in a sparkly blue lurex, mid-thigh dress – covering more than Bella's did but teamed with matching high heeled shoes and her poker straight blondish hair she looked stunning. Marelle couldn't compete in her smart jeans, boots and a pretty little puffy sleeved top – but then, she didn't have to. She was here with Jacob– long gone were the days in Maxies Nightclub when her sole aim had been to catch the eyes of the best looking guy in the place. She had him now!

Jacob made easy conversation. He looked fantastic in his black jacket, white t-shirt combination which looked so good on him due to its impeccable cut and his impeccable frame.

They ate, laughed, drank and joked their way through the meal until they left the restaurant at ten thirty – heading for a nightclub a couple of streets away.

The club had changed name and décor since Marelle had last been in it but was essentially the same. When she had been eighteen or nineteen it had been fun; when she had been in her twenties it had just been the place you went – now in her thirties it seemed tedious to say the least. Bella just threw herself into it; Mae joined in with some restraint, but Marelle found it difficult. Keeping an eye on Jacob was a habit – especially in these situations – but tonight he appeared fine and, astonishingly, enjoying himself more than she was. He was drinking but conservatively and seemed happy. Marelle was spending most of her time holding on to Jacob, dancing with him, hugging him. It was fine. Pretty soon they could go home.

"Marelle!" Bella shouted in her ear. "Get your arse on the dancefloor – and get some alcohol down your neck. You're spoiling it for us!"

"I'm fine Bella." She smiled.

"Maybe, but I'm not. Where's your drink?"

"I'll get one in a minute."

"I'll get you one – we're doing cocktails –get you something to get you pissed quicker – come on!" She shoved her towards the bar.

"Bella!" Marelle protested weakly.

"No-one's driving and you don't need to keep a hold on him all night. Loosen up!" She began to frog march Marelle to the bar but was soon joined by Jacob.

"I'm buying." He said.

"No. I'm buying these ones. Your wife is bringing us down ... I'm getting her something to catch up, fast!"

Jacob grinned. "Ok, Sounds good. I've never seen you drunk!"

"I'm not getting drunk!" Marelle protested.

That was how the night went. An hour or so in Marelle was being dragged about on the dancefloor by Bella despite her desperately trying to cling to Jacob. He had laughed and pushed her towards Bella again. Shortly after she was piggy backed on Bella, being swung around the dancefloor, screaming at the top of her lungs. Bella had yelled to Jacob to get everyone a refill which he had obligingly done. Marelle remembered watching him from her vantage point on Bella's back as he shimmied through the crowd and Bella whirled around. Mae was standing watching, laughing.

When Jacob returned, Mae was face to face with a guy in a dishevelled shirt; he looked worse for wear but was in an avid one-sided conversation with Mae who was just staring at him. As Jacob walked closer, he caught the end of the conversation.

"... fucking lesbian or something ..." He was sneering.

"Yes. I am." Mae replied, succinctly.

He sneered as Jacob sauntered up.

"What a fucking waste. Dirty bitch!" He remarked, stared up at Jacob was about to say something else but decided not to.

"Everything alright?" Jacob asked, handing her a drink.

Mae smiled. "Yes. Thank you. I'm used to it." She looked across to Bella, still with Marelle on her back, spinning around on the dancefloor. Mae smiled.

"Look at them." She said. "She has something with Bella that we don't have – yet."

Jacob grinned. "She has something with Bella that we don't have either! They grew up together – that's always going to be a strong relationship."

He slid the three remaining drinks he was holding onto a table he was standing by. "Come on, let's make Marelle jealous!"

He smiled, held out his hand for her. Mae placed her drink down and took his hand in hers, following him onto the dance floor until he took her in his arms and danced right next to Bella and Marelle with a wink to them both.

"Thank you for what you did." He said to Mae again, his mouth close to her ear to speak above the music.

Mae smiled. "It's ok. Honestly."

"Hopefully I can return the favour to you one day."

"I'm sure there'll be something.: She answered with a coy little nod of her pretty head just as Bella slapped Jacob playfully, but nonetheless, quite sharply, on his shoulder.

"Hey!" She exclaimed. "Hands off! You'll be turning her straight!"

Astutely, Mae managed to persuade Bella to head for home before the club closed and threw everyone out. In the crisp night air of the early hours, they all felt a little more sober.

"We will need to find a taxi." Marelle said as they stood in a group on the pavement. She had hold of Jacob's arm and Bella was locked onto Mae.

"No, we can walk." Bella replied. "It will only take ten minutes – we'll never get a taxi now ..."

"Bella it's a good twenty minutes' walk when you're not drunk and in those shoes." Marelle reminded her.

"It's ten minutes, believe me!" She laughed. "Hey, let's get a kebab, we can eat it on the way home! Who's up for a kebab?"

Marelle was sure she saw Mae roll her eyes but still allowed herself to be dragged across the market square to a dubious looking kebab van with more flashing lights on it than it probably had hygiene ratings. There was queue; a drunken queue and the person at the front was having a heated argument with the vendor.

"Let's not get a kebab." Said Mae.

Bella huffed. "We *have to*. We *have* to get a kebab! Jacob wants one – don't you Jacob?" Bella protested.

"I don't want a kebab." Jacob replied with a laugh.

'There's another down on Bells Hill!" Bella suggested.

"And that's a good ten minutes in the wrong direction!" Marelle piped up.

"Come on, we can get something at home." Mae added.

Bella glared at her.

"Remember what we've got in the fridge?" Mae said quietly to her.

"Ssshhh!" Bella out her finger to her lips then took Mae's arm again and started walking.

Half an hour later they were still making their way home. They had been held up by various stops to adjust clothing or to take a shoe off because there was a stone in it. Bella decided she had to stop for a wee in the bushes near to a modern, grey brick-built church. Jacob declared that he may as well go too while Bella crouched in the bushes and Marelle stood with Mae, waiting.

Shortly after they had started off again, they came to a square of grass, a brief respite of green in a red brick housing estate. In the middle of it was a dark green, telecoms cabinet.

"Oh boy! Remember that!" Bella shouted. A dog barked in a nearby garden at her voice in the night. "Hey! Hey!" She laughed. "We used to 'joust', do you remember – with the boys – we were on their backs like horses!" She stopped, letting go of Mae's arm. "Get on" She turned her back to Mae. "Marelle, you get on Jacob ..."

"You'd better take those shoes off." Mae pointed to Bella's feet. "You'll sink in on that grass."

Bella tutted, kicked her shoes off and grabbed Mae.

"Get on." She nodded to Marelle.

"Pardon?"

"Let's joust! Get on!"

Marelle looked up at Jacob; he was grinning. "We'll have an advantage." He said. "I'm taller."

Marelle hopped onto his back, wrapped an arm around his neck at the same time that he hooked her legs through his arms. Bella, already barefoot on the grass, had Mae astride her too.

"Charge!" Bella yelled, spinning and running full pelt at them.

Marelle gave a little scream as Jacob stepped sideways to avoid Bella. And so for five minutes abject, silly crazy behaviour ensued in childish abandon. Even

Jacob was laughing as he lined himself up to run at Bella again with Marelle leaning over his shoulder to extend an arm to fend off the oncoming attack from Mae.

Bella giggled, ducked to the side but slipped on the wet and now slightly muddy grass – enough to unbalance her so that she ended up doing the splits and depositing Mae down, thankfully feet first but sending herself onto her hands and knees. Bella was laughing, rolling over onto her back on the grass, her knees drawn up and her shocking pink dress pretty much all up around the tops of her thighs.

Mae stood over her, hands on hips. "You satisfied now hey? Never truly satisfied until you've ended up on your back with your legs in the air, are you?" Mae joked, finally stooping and offering a hand.

Jacob put Marelle down carefully. He was out of breath, bending over with his hands on his knees as he laughed. Marelle smiled and walked forwards to Bella too.

She sat up, looking at Jacob as he tried to catch his breath. "Hey old man!" She laughed.

"I was carrying an extra ten stone!" he quipped standing up and turning away from Marelle's playful slap.

Bella took Mae's hand and levered herself slowly up. Just as she approached fully upright there was a loud ripping sound.

"Shit!" She exclaimed, feeling around her backside then turning as her hand went into the seam that had ripped completely open and exposed her bottom and yellow thong to the whole world.

Mae laughed and covered her mouth with a hand. Marelle gasped, then laughed "Fuck." Bella moaned.

Jacob walked up and placed his hands on Marelle's shoulders. "Whoops!" He said.

"Fucking hell!" Bella whined. "It was meant to be stretch!"

"Not enough though." Marelle laughed. "You have better walk in front, we'll walk behind you."

"Can't you turn it round?" Mae suggested.

"Of course I can't. I'm not taking it off in the street to turn it around."

"You may as well, you're pretty much flashing everything anyway!" Marelle grinned.

"Here." Jacob suddenly added, stripping off his jacket. "Tie this around your waist so that it hangs down the back …"

Bella took his jacket. "Thank you, Jacob. See a true gentleman. He's not just standing there laughing."

"You'll be cold." Marelle told him as he stood there in just a fitted white t-shirt now.

"I'm fine." He shook his head.

Bella slid her feet into her shoes again then took Mae's arm as before. They started off again with Jacob's jacket covering her modesty and him with his arm around Marelle.

It took them another ten minutes to get to Bella's front door. She let them in and switched on the lights. Once inside she removed the jacket and handed it back to Jacob. Her pink dress was smeared with both mud and grass stains.

"Go into the lounge." She said. "I'll just go and change and then I'll be in ..."

"It's a quarter to two!" Marelle exclaimed with a laugh.

"The night is young. We've not finished yet!" Bella replied. "Not by a long chalk!"

FORTY-ONE

Mae switched lights on and found a music channel on the large TV. She smiled to them both as they sat down on the sofa together. Marelle slid a hand around Jacob's arm and rested her head on his shoulder as she thought that Mae looked very at home here.

It was literally only seconds until they heard Bella charging down the stairs again – this time in a black, scoop-neck stretchy dress, no longer than the other one but at least whole. Her feet were bare, but she had pink toenails.

"Ok." She said. "Mae come and get the glasses – we've got a bottle in the fridge …"

"Bella, I don't want any more – coffee or tea will be fine …" Marelle piped up.

"Tea! Are you fucking joking?" Bella laughed as she went towards the kitchen with Mae following.

Marelle sighed. "Don't drink too much." She whispered to Jacob.

He laughed quietly. "I won't."

"We've got Champagne!" Bella sang as she walked back into the room, holding a magnum of Champagne aloft. Mae was behind her with four glasses. "Look at this little baby!" She laughed.

"It *is* a bit late to be opening that, Bella!" Marelle remarked.

"Shut up Marelle! Stop being a party pooper – we are opening it, and you are drinking it. End of." She clutched the bottle to her. "Mae." She called and Mae came and stood beside her.

"We've got some news!" Bella announced, initially nervous.

Marelle suddenly snapped her head round to her.

"Mae and I are engaged. We're getting married!" Bella exclaimed. "You are the first to know!"

Mae smiled. Took Bella's arm and cuddled close to her. There was a brief moment of awkwardness – probably so on Marelle's behalf until Jacob shifted himself on the squishy sofa beside her and went to stand up.

"Congratulations!" He laughed. "Give me that bottle!"

He took the bottle from her as at exactly the same moment Marelle leapt up and threw her arms around Bella. For some reason she felt tearful but held them back. Jacob popped the bottle and began filling glasses as Mae held them.

"Wow!" Marelle said. "I didn't expect that!"

Jacob and Mae were thrusting glasses at them and suddenly all four were in a huddle.

Bella laughed. "So … as you can see … it's party on until the sun rises!"

"Hey, when is the big day?" Marelle asked.

"When is your big day?" Bella grinned.

"Soon." Jacob repeated. "What's your excuse?"

"We only decided two days ago!" Bella answered quickly.

Jacob laughed. "This is your night, not ours – cheers." He raised his glass.

"Stop changing the subject!" Bella poked Jacob. "Come on set a date. You've got a whole year next year to choose one …"

Jacob grinned. We want to think about it."

Bella turned to Marelle questioningly. "Do you?"

Marelle smiled. "I'm good with whatever date we choose …"

"There you go. Pressure's on you lover boy!" Bella winked. Mae chuckled.

Jacob sighed. "This isn't the time or the place – it's gone two in the morning, we are all a little worse for drink …"

"You're not drunk. I've been watching you all night." Bella pointed.

Jacob laughed.

"But you will be by then end of the night!" She continued, grabbing the bottle back and sloshing his glass full again. "Go on. Say a date."

"You say a date." He replied.

Bella turned to Marelle. "He's a slippery one, Marelle."

Marelle smiled. "You set a date first." She suggested, trying to take the heat off Jacob.

"The third of August." Bella said quickly.

"That's your birthday." Marelle informed them.

"Good enough. You ok with that Mae?"

Mae raised a hand in gesture. "Sounds good…"

"Easy!" Bella said. "Done. Now you set a date. She opened a hand to Jacob.

He had a smile on his face but flicked his eyes across to Marelle. "Twentieth of June." He said.

"That's my birthday!" Marelle exclaimed.

He smiled and nodded, tilting the glass to her. Bella drunkenly and flamboyantly pointed a finger to Marelle "OK?"

Marelle laughed. "OK." She said. "Right. Sorted. Let's get legless!" Bella exclaimed, whirling around and topping up everyone's glasses. "Drink up, there's more in the fridge."

Marelle felt cold. She drew her legs up and arched her back, snuggling against his warmth. Where were the covers? Had Jacob cocooned himself in them again and left her exposed. She stretched a toe out to feel for them, reaching across the space near her feet. Suddenly her foot hit something hard, knocking it until it moved out of the way.

The ensuing crash and the sound of smashing glass suddenly brought her back to her senses – took her back to wakefulness with a jolt as she reflexly reached out to grab whatever had fallen and sit up at the same time.

Marelle sat bolt upright. Found herself starting right into the eyes of Bella who she seemed to be cuddled up against, one hand still against her breast, the other now returning from its grasp into mid-air to run through her hair.

Bella blinked. Stared back at her. Marelle turned and looked to the smashed Champagne bottle on the floor and Jacob, half asleep, now stirring to her other side, one of his arms draped around Mae's shoulders. The TV was still on, a music channel with 70s pop ringing out across the dark room only lit up by the garish colours worn by the performers on the screen. It looked like it was starting to get light behind the drawn curtain.

"What the fuck!" Bella exclaimed. "Jesus Marelle! What are you doing?"

Marelle was staring at Jacob, wondering what he was doing. He came to his senses suddenly, realised the position he was in and sat away from Mae so quickly it she collapsed behind him on the settee with a yelp.

Bella stood up, pushing Marelle's leg off her.

"Shit!" She said, going over to put the light on.

"Careful!" Marelle shouted, voice a little out of control and louder than she expected. "There's broken glass!"

Bella tutted, doubled back and walked around the back of the settee to switch the light on. They were already on, just dimmed down to a very low level but it took a few moments of tutting and swearing, flicking the switch on and off to establish this in Bella's sudden rousing.

In the now very bright light everyone was looking at each other in a stupor that was no doubt partially alcohol fuelled.

"Shit!" Bella said again. "What the hell is the fucking time?" She checked her watch; Jacob was squinting at his.

"Quarter to nine." He said.

"It's a quarter past seven!" Bella corrected as he looked at his watch again.

"Nobody move!" Bella ordered. "Broken glass everywhere thanks to our good friend Marelle who can't even fall asleep without causing chaos!" She said, then grinned. "Been a while since we've woken up cuddling each other babe!" She laughed.

Mae sat up next to Jacob and smiled at him, he looked away. Marelle glared at hum, he shrugged.

"We must have fallen asleep." Marelle said, pushing her hair back from her face. "All together."

"Or maybe you fell asleep, and we all partied on!" Bella grinned. "Any memories, anyone? Who knows what happened, hey? Must have been a good night ... what do you reckon Jacob – have you fathered Mae's love child?" She joked, laughing wickedly. "I'll go and get a dustpan."

They all slowly came to their senses. Bella swept up the glass, Marelle watched and did her best to point it all out. Mae stood up, smoothed her clothes down and began to tidy bottles and glasses up. Jacob sat forwards, had his head in his hands for a few second which Marelle noted and observed. He then composed himself and began wiping at a wet patch on his t-shirt where he had been dribbling.

"Start a queue for the bathroom." Bella announced. "Then we'll get breakfast going."

"Breakfast?" Jacob muttered.

"Yes. You've got to drive home, and I can hear the Champagne sloshing around inside you from here – you'll need something to soak it up."

An hour later the room was tidy, and they were all sat in Bella's kitchen around the breakfast table. Jacob had been last to use the bathroom as he had let everyone use the bathroom before him. His hair was wet and ruffled.

"I can't believe we all fell asleep!" Marelle laughed.

"I told you. *We* didn't. *You* did! We all had a party!" Bella winked.

"A party so good I can't remember any of it!" Jacob commented.

"We must be getting old." Marelle added.

"Ah shut up!" Bella retorted. "Speak for yourself. Me, I'm still eighteen."

"So was that your official engagement then?" Marelle asked, widening her eyes to Bella. "And where's the ring, hey?"

"Hell no." Bella said, eating a bacon sandwich she had just made. "We've not started yet. We only decided on Thursday and told you yesterday!"

"So is the date a firm one? I will need to plan ...?"

"Is yours?"

Marelle looked to Jacob.

He raised one shoulder and one eyebrow.

"Yes." Marelle confirmed.

"Wel, you had better start planning – you've not got long." Bella warned. 'I trust it's going to be a massive do?" She looked to Jacob. "None of this sneaking off and going to a registry office."

Jacob smiled. "We'll see. It's a long way off ..."

"It's not. It's definitely not. Not in wedding terms! It's positively shotgun!"

"We'll sort it. There are other things we need to sort out first. Anyway, don't worry you will both be invited."

"Jesus! I should think so – without me you wouldn't even be getting married."

Marelle gave a small smile, let her eyes linger on Jacob for a second. He held her gaze until she blinked away.

"Hey, we can have a double wedding!" Marelle suddenly piped up.

"No we could not!" Bella exclaimed. "That would mean just one party – two weddings equals two parties. Get with it girl! Tell you what though ..." She looked Jacob right in the eye. "You could sing at our wedding." She winked.

"What?" Jacob asked.

"Do your little karaoke act." Bella smiled.

Jacob laughed but there wasn't too much humour in it, more relief. "I told you, that was a one off."

Bella stared cheekily at him. "Really?" She asked. "That's not what a little bird told me. You know Mae he's really rather good. He's every inch a rock star!"

Marelle pressed her foot down hard against Bella's under the table. Bella kicked her off but missed and ended up slamming her foot into the table leg which sent tea slopping out of an overly full mug right in front of Mae. She looked at Bella and tutted. Bella glared at Marelle.

"Hey stop playing footsie with me under the table. I'm spoken for!"

Jacob's phone suddenly rang. All heads turned his way as it was an old, less heard ring tone to say the least lost on Marelle but not on Bella and Mae.

"Oh no! It's a steam driven one." Bella commented as Jacob fumbled in his pocket.

Marelle didn't even know he had brought the phone with him, but he was not making eye contact with anyone. He got up, walked a couple of paces as he put the old phone to his ear.

"Hi." He greeted then realised he wasn't at home and could not slip out of the back door. Trapped, he paced the kitchen, getting as far away from everyone as he could, his finger in the other ear.

"Hi Chas." He said, his back to them.

Bella gestured to Marelle, making sarcastic faces at the fact that Jacob had got a phone call.

Marelle sat tight but felt her insides twist into an agonising knot. Why was Chas calling Jacob at this time on a Sunday morning just about a week away from the promised performance. She kept her eyes front, tried to smile at Bella but was listening intently to Jacob's half of the conversation.

"No, I'm not at home." He said.

Pause. Seconds ticked away.

"Why?"

A longer pause. Bella said something and laughed. Marelle smiled but wasn't listening to what she had said.

"Well, no. I wasn't planning to ..." Jacob had his back to her, shuffling against the kitchen wall.

"Yeah.' Jacob said in confirmation.

Marelle waited. She couldn't gauge the tone or intent of the conversation.

"Yeah. That'll be fine.' He said. "Ok." He gave a sarcastic little laugh. "Trust me!"

There was a long pause as Chas spoke.

"OK." Jacob said. "Yeah. Take care ..."

He turned around. Walked back and sat down. Marelle looked at him. He fumbled to out the phone away. She thought his hands were shaking.

"OK?" She asked.

He nodded. "Chas."

Bella looked up and laughed. "Chas! Who's Chas?"

"A friend." Jacob said quietly, sheepishly.

"Oooh, a friend. Didn't think you had any friends though you were the classic loner. Bit different to that guy I met in the pub that night – all fingers and thumbs, embarrassed but fire burning in your eyes for her." She nodded to Marelle.

"... and about to get beaten up by the village bully." Marelle added, quietly, thoughts escaping audibly again.

Bella grinned. "Yeah, I remember. I thought he was a gonner!" She laughed.

Marelle looked wistfully at Jacob. He was different. Bella was right – as much as he was trying to cling to Jacob, Ezza was breaking out second by second.

"Sounds like a bit of a shady deal going on there." Bella spoke as she ate. "All sounds a bit furtive!"

Jacob laughed.

"What did he want?" Marelle took her chance and asked.

"Nothing." Jacob said.

"Oooh, dodgy sounding friend called 'Chas' calls on a Sunday morning and it's *nothing*!" Bella teased. She took a sharp intake of breath.

"I used to work with him." Jacob stated, hoping it would halt the conversation.

"On the farm?" Bella asked.

"No." He said, blankly, not looking at her.

Marelle watched him. Jacob was like a swan. Rock solid calm at the surface but everything going a million miles an hour below. Why had Chas called? What had he said?

Marelle continued to stare at him, but he would not make eye contact with her. Inside she could feel adrenalin bristling. Itching at her fingers and toes to liberate itself and come screaming out yelling 'what did Chas say?'. But she quelled it, let it dwell within her for a later outburst. Fight or flight, she thought, and guessed it would be.

FORTY-TWO

It wasn't until they finally escaped the bonds of Bella and Mae and were in the car together, just pulling out of the end of a road Marelle had walked along many times as a teenager, that she asked the question.

"What did Chas want?"

The words pierced the air, waited, hanging there for attention as he steered her car around the mini roundabout that was a new addition.

"Nothing." He replied.

"Nothing! He calls you on a Sunday morning about *nothing*?"

"Pretty much." He replied. "Nothing important."

"Well, *what*?"

"He wants to come down to see me – us – before the gig – Mya probably wants to assess my mental state before she lets her husband commit himself to anything. They wanted to come today but obviously, we aren't there."

She sighed. "So what's happening then?"

"They're coming on Wednesday – asked if they could bring their dog – they're going to make a day of it – see us then take the dog for a walk somewhere..."

"Coming to the house?" She enquired thoughtfully.

"Yeah."

She didn't say anything but looked a little pensive.

"That's why he called when he did. They were about to set out."

"Does he know where we live then?"

"No – he knows roughly where; I'll give him instructions before Wednesday."

"So he's never been to your house before?"

Jacob shook his head. "No, never wanted any of them knowing my home address ..."

"Well why now?" Marelle asked.

He laughed. "Things change!"

Jacob took Wednesday off work. He had taken more day's holiday in the past few months than he had taken in his entire life. Marelle had spent Monday and Tuesday vainly cleaning the house – no, tidying the house. It was lived in; they lived in it – it couldn't be helped. Jacob didn't seem to know where Chas lived but she bet it was a much larger, more salubrious dwelling than this one. She could not imagine Mya living anywhere tired and tatty. At least they could improve this place now; they could gradually make it their own but in two days there was not much hope of much improvement beyond at least making it tidy! She'd raised it with Jacob, and he had almost laughed in reply.

"It's Chas!" he exclaimed. "He won't care!"

"I bet Mya will!" She answered. "She must be used to a big fancy house – she probably has a cleaner."

"Nah!" he scoffed. 'They're not like that; they're both just normal, down to earth people."

"But ..." she paused, only momentarily. "But he's famous!"

Jacob laughed. She didn't normally see him actually laugh like that; it was normally when she had said something stupid. It appeared to him that her last statement fell into that category.

"It's Chas!" He said, shaking his head. "It's fine. Just make him a cup of tea and give him a slice of cake or something ..."

"I haven't got any cake!" She stated.

"Well, we can get some. Stop worrying." He assured. "It's fine."

It was fine. They waited, like children expecting a visit from a favourite uncle and whatever gifts they hoped he would bring. Jacob periodically preened himself in the mirror, flattened the sides of his hair, spiked the top. Marelle smiled to herself but felt slightly uncomfortable sitting around in the house in clothes she would normally wear to go out in. Jacob had no idea of what time Chas was going to turn up and despite Marelle's urgings would not call Chas to ask.

"It will be around mid-morning I would presume." Jacob explained. "Chas is an early person rather than leaving things late."

Then when her phone rang they looked at one another before she answered it.

"Hello?" She said, expecting it to be Chas but knowing he would have called her old phone which Jacob used.

"Good morning, Marelle. Is Jacob available or is he at work? It's DCI Catchpole."

She knew it was. She recognised his voice now. His tone, his accent, his syntax. She raised her eyes to Jacob, considering whether to lie. He caught her staring at him.

"Who is it?" He whispered.

"Catchpole." She mouthed.

He sighed then he held out his hand for her phone.

"Yes, he's here." She said before she handed it over.

Jacob took the phone. There was a look on his face which suggested he half liked the cat and mouse conversations he had with Catchpole.

"Hi." He said.

It wasn't the longest or the most evasive conversation and ended with Jacob saying he would 'sort something out' and Marelle looked at him with the proverbial question in her eyes.

"He's pushing me to make arrangements for the remains of ..." Suddenly a word stuck in his throat like its presence there had suddenly grown barbs which pierced him as on its passage out. He swallowed it back. "Him." He said instead. "Forensics have released it now; they have retained samples but as official next of kin he is asking me to make arrangements." He shrugged. "I guess I'll have to, but not today."

Not today. Not the day when Chas in a bright yellow t-shirt and a black denim jacket pulled into their driveway in his camper van and walked up to the front door with a warmly smiling Mya, complete with bright red lipstick and Chip, a lively bundle of furry brown hair that ran in circles and sniffed at everything as they approached.

Marelle stood back and let Jacob take the lead – opening the door before they knocked and standing there on the doorstep to greet them.

Chip ran into the house, straight past Jacob and up to Marelle just behind him. The dog whipped around her legs, leaping up and furiously wagging his stumpy tail. She stopped to pat him awkwardly then looked back up to the scene in the doorway. Mya was already in an embrace with Jacob.

"If he's too much I can shut him in the van." She heard Chas say and suddenly realised he was speaking to her and referring to Chip.

"Oh no, no. He's fine." She laughed but, if she was honest, she would have preferred him being safely inside the van. Her eyes moved to Mya as she finally released Jacob then pushed forward towards her. Seconds later Marelle was in Mya's arms too.

"And how's my lucky girl?" she enthused, squeezing Marelle. "Been looking after my boy I can see he looks fantastic!"

Marelle smiled. He had not looked so good a few days ago!

"What a pretty village!" Mya continued. "What a beautiful place to live!"

Marelle held her smile. It was.

"Come through." Jacob was leading the way. Chip followed then overtook him; he was already in the kitchen when they all arrived.

"Chip! Here!" Chas called the dog as Jacob pulled out chairs and gestured for them to sit.

"We normally sit in here." Jacob explained. "It's brighter – the sun shines in here most of the day."

Funny, Marelle had never thought about that before. It did. The front rooms were always darker.

"And we've got this fantastic view across the old airfield." Jacob pointed. "At least for now."

Marelle smiled. "It's a very special place." She commented.

They made small talk which Mya was exceptionally good at. She also had a propensity to take over any situation – including making tea – or coffee – which Chas insisted on despite her trying to discourage him. All of her intentions were inadvertently good though and she came across as very warm and friendly, almost as if she had known Marelle for a number of years and not a number of hours.

Mya talked all of the time too. This was disconcerting as Chas was speaking to Jacob constantly as well which Marelle wanted to listen in on. From what she could hear they were speaking about the airfield and the Thor site, but Mya's chatter was intrusive.

"So how long have you lived here? In this village?"

"Oh only about a year – I didn't really know it existed before that!" Marelle laughed.

"So why did you choose to move here?"

"I didn't. I inherited this house from an uncle I barely knew. My brother and I were his only living relatives and it was left to us ..."

"Oh that's sad." Mya said but moved on quickly before Marelle had a chance to ask why it was sad.

"... and then you met Ez and bagged the most eligible bachelor in the village?" She winked.

Marelle grinned and nodded. To cut a long story short, she thought.

"He hasn't changed!" Mya continued. "I can't believe he looks exactly the same – and I can't believe he lived here all of that time, and nobody noticed him!"

"Oh I think he was quite careful about that, and he didn't look like that when I met him." Marelle explained.

"Well he certainly looks good now. Still as skinny as he ever was though – he needs to share his secret with all of us. Both of us!" She flicked a hand between herself and Chas. "Both of us have a gym membership and we walk miles with Chip but just can't keep the pounds off – him especially!"

Neither of them looked unfit or remotely over an ideal weight. Maybe Chas had a bit of a belly on him but nothing out of the ordinary for someone around his age.

"I guess it's ninety-none percent genetic." Mya was saying as Marelle glanced back to her.

Mya was a formidable woman; white-blonde hair in a magnificently sharp bob style, bright red nails and lipstick perfectly coordinated with a deep red jacket that she wore. Teamed with black skinny jeans it was still a casual look but nonetheless smart and stylish. She generously sprinkled a sugar coating on everything, but Marelle sensed that inside there was a shrewd, intelligent person who emanated confidence with a heart of gold. Marelle studied her in snatched glances, wondered on her age and surmised that she had to be late fifties or even early sixties. Mya had an eye on everything and an ear to the world at all times and Marelle wondered how Jacob had ever slipped through the net she gathered everything together in.

"It's such a pretty village." Mya repeated. "Driving here there's so much space; so much sky!" She enthused. "All of those wide-open areas going on forever...it's beautiful. Reminds me of my childhood!"

"Jacob works on the farm. He's usually out in the fields." Marelle said, then felt immediately stupid.

"Why do you call him Jacob love?" Mya questioned. 'I know Ezza isn't his real name but it's not Jacob, is it?"

Marelle smiled. "It's what he told me his name was when we met. He's always Jacob to me ..."

"... and he answers to it!" Mya laughed.

"Oh yes. All of the time!"

"You must have him well trained! None of the guys use their own names –it's strange calling people by a name you know is not theirs!" She went on. "I'll admit I sometimes come out with their proper names! God, it's so confusing!"

Marelle smiled. Glanced at Jacob and Chas who were laughing and talking about something to do with the airfield. No, it wasn't confusing. He was Jacob; she loved Jacob. End of story.

It was only after Mya made the first move to sit down at the kitchen table that Chas casually walked over while still in conversation with Jacob, pulled out a chair and quietly sat down. He was sitting in the chair that Jacob normally occupied, and that fact disturbed something in Marelle a little. Jacob sat in the spare chair in a place reserved for visitors but did not say anything or look as uncomfortable as she felt!

"So." Chas said, sitting back in the chair with the air of a reclining God. "You all set? You know what you're doing?"

"Of course!" Jacob replied.

"You know where you've got to be; when you've got to be there; what you are going to do?"

Mya was smiling at them both.

"Yes." He confirmed.

Chas stared at him for a few seconds. "Then tell me."

Jacob laughed a little. "Tell you? You've been through it with me a number of times!"

"And I want to make sure it's lodged in your head; I don't want you going off on one half-hearted tangent."

"I won't." Jacob laughed.

"You hadn't fucking better!" Chas reiterated. "There's more at stake for me in letting you do this ... you fuck up and it will be all anyone remembers. This is the last encore of the last show of this tour. If you fuck it up wrong, it will be their last memory of Yellow Son – they remember what you leave them with ..."

Jacob gave a small smile, she could see the look in his eyes which suggested there was possibly more at stake for him, not Chas. "I won't fuck up. I'll leave them with the memory of Ezza being back, singing with Yellow Son."

"Yeah." Chas answered with a hint of sarcasm.

"What about the other guys?" Jacob enquired.

"They won't know." Chas said. "They're not expecting it, but they'll just keep playing. I can't guarantee what shit they'll sling at you – or me – once we come off though." He added.

Chas was insistent. He grilled Jacob far more intensely than Catchpole had. Threw question after question at him in quick succession and demanded answers – and the right ones. He was fearful of handing such a precious breakable thing to Jacob when he was only too aware of just how butter-fingered Jacob could be at times, but Chas was also enamoured by the bright, resonating light that glowed like a halo from him – attracted like a moth to a flame craving death or redemption.

And all of the time Mya watched with bright eyes and a warm smile.

"Don't let me down" Chas said with a finality to his questioning and a finger, pointing at Jacob.

"I won't." Jacob said, with a smile.

Chas had an easy rapport with Jacob – borne from years together – years that Marelle knew nothing about. There was a kind of 'mentor' attitude from Chas and a willing pupil attitude from Jacob which partly amazed and partly charmed Marelle. But, behind it all there was still an uncertainty, a residual amount of mistrust in Chas. He remained visibly aware of that latent history of emotional crisis and the propensity to bolt which was apparent he had always mitigated along the way. Chas welcomed Ezza back, but he didn't trust him.

"Is there a pub around here we can get lunch and take the dog?" Chas asked. "Want to join us?"

"Erm … "Jacob replied. "There are pubs but I'm not sure you can take him in … it's a bit cold to sit outside and eat …erm …" He thought. Looking at the clock. "The chip shop will be open."

"Where's that?"

"Over the road.' Jacob pointed. "Only for another twenty minutes though. Why not get them and eat them here – we can go for a walk around the airfield afterwards? Chip would like that …"

"Do you want to do that?" Chas asked Mya. They obviously had plans for a cosy pub lunch.

"I'm fine with that." She smiled.

Chas nodded. "Well you'd better get down there if it closes in only minutes …"

"Well tell me where I'm going and I'll go." Mya asked. "Can I walk or do I need to drive."

"It's quicker to drive." Marelle replied.

"You go Marelle …" Jacob nodded.

She glared at him. He knew that they were both probably banned from the fish and chip shop. Last time she had sent Bella this time it was doubtful she would be able to send Mya.

'I can't get the car out." She protested. That was true; Chas had parked his van behind her.

"I'll drive!" Mya chipped in quickly. "Come on Marelle, you come with me."

Marelle found herself ushered out of the house, down the drive and into the camper van. Chas had to hold on to a wriggling Chip as he could not understand why he could not go as well. Marelle glanced back ay a laughing Jacob, turning towards Chas who was holding on to the struggling little brown dog.

'Which way?" Mya asked.

Marelle directed her, feeling conspicuous next to her in Chas; van, driving through the village.

"We haven't had fish and chips for ages. This will be lovely!" she laughed. "I don't normally let Chas eat a lot of fried food!"

Marelle smiled.

Mya laughed. "But once won't hurt! Is this the place?" She stopped in the road opposite the shop.

"Er, yeah, the one next door. That's the shop." Marelle explained.

"Such a pretty little village. I bet that shops sells everything you could possibly need!" Mya grinned.

"I don't go in it much." Marelle replied. "I tend to use the supermarket – or the garage in the next village." Her voice sounded incredibly nervous.

"Really! Oh my child! You have to patronise these places ... I would love a village shop like this right on my doorstep – I bet all life happens in there!" She patted Marelle's knee playfully. "You're missing out girl!"

Marelle gave a knowing smile. "We had better get the fish and chips, they'll be closing up."

Mya led the way, striding into the shop, speaking loudly, intimidating the person behind the counter in a friendly way which moved the attention away from Marelle.

"Shit!" Marelle suddenly exclaimed as they stood there after ordering.

"What?" Mya asked.

"I haven't got any money! I forgot!"

Mya smiled. "Don't worry, it's on us. We had planned to take you to lunch anyway."

"Are you sure? I can pay you back when we get home ..."

"Oh ssshh!" Mya laughed.

The packages were placed in a large bag with a blue fish printed on the front and Mya handed over cash at the till. Marelle stood there, feeling like a child being treated by a favourite aunt. She smiled and followed Mya out of the shop.

Jill was outside. She was rearranging flowers on a stand outside the shop. Her eyes immediately flicked to Marelle and she stared.

"Let's get these back before they get cold." Mya said, smiling and heading for the van. Marelle stared straight ahead and walked by, relieved that she had just got away with this until she heard Jill mutter behind her.

"You only build a wall if you've got something to hide."

For a split-second Marelle's stride faltered, and her anger raged. She felt it pulse in her fingertips. She had heard the conversation the other day as well and he didn't have to guess what the village gossip was. Mya was a couple of strides in front, unlocking the van and getting the door for her. Marelle took a breath, looked straight ahead and joined Mya.

They ate the fish and chips out of the paper sat around the kitchen table. Marelle had made sure Jacob had sausage and chips and he sat there now, smiling and laughing with the company – looking so happy. Far happier than she had ever seen him before. Far, far happier. Reunited with Chas, he was basking in the afterglow of being here and of what Chas had agreed to let him do. Jacob wasn't treating this as a one-off chance to perform with Yellow Son again – he was seeing it as the next step to the rest of his life. That was what fuelled his happiness – that single thought.

And his elation scared her.

"What the hell are you eating?" Chas asked, nodding to Jacob.

"Sausage – battered sausage." Jacob answered.

"You go to a fish and chip shop and have a bloody battered sausage!" Chas commented.

"I don't like fish. At least not whole fish."

Chas laughed. "What! You're an awkward bastard, aren't you?"

"Try to be!" Jacob smiled in reply.

"Always fucking did!" Chas said, shaking his head.

Chas liked to goad Jacob and Jacob seemed to enjoy it. It was a friendship that has been put on ice, right now it was beginning to warm again.

"Better take him for a walk." Chas told Mya after lunch and further round of tea and coffee.

"Get your coats on, we can all go for a walk around the airfield." Jacob suggested.

Mya and Chas had thick coats in the van, and wellies – all brand new and pristine. Chip ran around them in circles barking as they left the house and stepped through the gap in the fence.

The land spanned out before them, wide, open. A union of pale blue sky and the bleached brown grass, interspersed with new green late autumn growth which was in perfect harmony with the grey of the worn concrete airstrip and service roads.

Chip ran off, sniffing a trail, disappearing into the long grass.

"Just mind him; there are still holes and open shafts over here. We are alright for the moment, but I would put him on a lead when we get up the runway a bit ..."

Marelle smiled to herself when he said those words; it took her back as they were some of the very first words he had said to her as well.

Jacob told Chas all about the airfield as they walked up the runway towards where his caravan used to be.

"What aircraft were here then?" Chas asked.

"Liberators and then fast jets before the site became a Thor base." Jacob explained.

"Fast jets?"

"Sabres." Jacob replied

"Here!" Chas asked, a little surprised.

Jacob nodded. "Then it was designated one of the Thor Missile sites in the region."

"Until Yellow Sun was commissioned." Chas grinned.

Jacob laughed and nodded.

Mya sighed. "Listen to them." She said to Marelle. "Like kids with a train set – I don't know why they are both so interested in something with such a legacy of destruction." She walked alongside Marelle. "Hard to think of what went on here in the past when it's so beautiful now." She sighed.

"Until they build on it.' Marelle added."

"Build on it?"

"Yep." Marelle nodded. "It's on the cards but as Jacob will tell you ... it's been on the cards for over ten years, and nothing has happened yet."

"Well hopefully, it never will." Mya replied.

"That's what we hope too." Marelle whispered.

They walked on. Mya made small talk, but Marelle tuned in to Jacob's conversation with Chas. They were speaking quietly but she strained to hear.

"Mya blamed me you know. Blamed everyone – blamed herself." Chas was saying. "But you were unreachable – I knew you were free falling and half of me suspected you might not survive the landing; I still don't know what was happening to you at that time – you said your father's death didn't affect you – you said to me that you hated your father, and his death was a release. You said you were fine, but it was all at this time. I wasn't surprised by your actions, let's put it that way ..."

Marelle wanted to hear more. It was part of his story he had never really said much about. He didn't seem to want to talk about it now.

They came to the top end of the runway and the main gates came clearly into view. Jacob's head shot up at the sight of a large white van parked in the gateway. She too could see people on the grassy verge beside the entrance – they seemed to be erecting a sign.

FORTY-THREE

"What's that?" Jacob exclaimed, almost to himself and began to stride ahead in that long, lanky stride she knew so well. He stopped against the gates, one hand on the wire.

'What's that?" He was asking as the three of them walked up behind him.

It was pretty obvious what was happening just outside the gates, but he had asked the question anyway.

It was 'V' shaped construction. Two large four by four wooden posts, driven into the ground. '*Brough, Self and Topham*' it proclaimed in white letters on a navy-blue background. There was a little logo of a bird beside the words. Underneath it said '*Land Agents*' in small block capitals. '*For sale on behalf of a client. Industrial Development Land. Approx 640 acres STS.*'

Marelle stared at it and read the words three times to herself.

"Site is up for sale. We are erecting the board." One of them men with the said, turning briefly to Jacob before looking back to one of the other guys up a stepladder, banging a nail in.

"Are you the landowner?" He turned back and asked.

Jacob hung on the fence, one hand above his head, gripping the wire.

"No." He said. "I'm the caretaker. Nobody told me about this."

The guy shrugged. 'I don't know the ins and outs of it Sir. We only put the signs up where we are told to."

Marelle stood and watched, Chas to her left and Mya to her right. It was the same old story – their job was just this little bit; no-one knew anything else. Jacob had mentioned this a short time ago, but it had just been a rumour from a contractor. The whole site was up for sale. There was no element of that which would be good.

"Is that here?" Chas asked.

Jacob stared for a moment longer then leant away from the fence. "Yeah." He sighed and nodded. "Looks like the developers have had enough – selling it to someone else now." He walked back to Marelle, placing an arm around her shoulders. "Who knows what that will bring?" He questioned, moving her on. "Come on, I'll show you the Thor site ..."

It remained on his mind, she could tell, but he covered it well in front of Chas and Mya. Leading the way to the Thor site with Chas's enthusiasm and fascination for apparent, it eased the burden a little. Mya took a picture of Chas and Jacob standing on one of the low walls, staring into the distance – the first one together for twelve or so years but it came with a warning from Chas not to share it or show it anyone. Mya tutted and shook her head at him as Jacob began to explain about the Thor site being preserved and made into a heritage site.

"So how will that happen if they sell the whole site"' Marelle questioned.

"Whoever owns the whole site is responsible for the Thor site I believe ..." Jacob told her. "It's probably part of whatever deal is eventually made – whoever buys it will have to make provision to protect the Thor site and make a contribution to its preservation. With any luck that alone will put everyone off!" He grinned without.an iota of humour in his words.

That was a possible speck of hope on the horizon – who would want to buy a site and then stump up a percentage to preserve four stone walls. That was one thing but the overriding thing in Marelle's mind was that their purchase of the house and effective block of a new access to the site had been enough to tip the developers over to sell it. She hoped it wasn't.

They walked back to the house. Chas had plenty to say and to ask about the airfield. Jacob answered but Marelle could tell his mind was not entirely on what he was saying by the time both of them got into the camper van the sun was dipping in the early winter sky.

Chas said that they had better get on the road and he turned to shake Jacob's hand before he climbed into the van. Mya was already sitting in the passenger seat, Chip on her lap. She had hugged them both and hugged them again. Now she was smiling at them as Chas shook Jacob's hand.

"I'd get that bike out of the house as well." Chas commented. He had moaned to Jacob about it being in there – said it was a fire hazard and he would not have it in his house as they had left. Jacob had laughed. "And don't fucking let me down." Chas pleaded quietly.

"I won't.' Jacob stated.

"I know you won't, but don't – or we will never speak again ... dead or alive." He drilled his grey-blue eyes intensely into Jacob.

"I won't." Jacob repeated.

"Who in their right mind would buy the site with the Thor site on it – *and* having to pay for it ..." Marelle offered to Jacob's obvious brooding.

"That's my thoughts too." He confirmed. "They're kind of stuck with it ... been sitting on it for years, there have been problems in the past, access issues and now they've also got to put up for the Heritage site or something. They don't want it anymore so who else will? Any developer is going to have the same issues ..."

She gave a little smile. "So hopefully, we've got it for another ten years?"

"Hopefully. If we're all still here then."

She glanced at him. Marelle didn't like it when he said things like that but right now she was confident this was just a manner of speech.

"How much is it up for?" She asked.

He shrugged, stirring a spoon in a mug as he stared out of the window. "Millions, probably. Development land around here is about three thousand an acre. That might be cheaper due to the issues but it's still a lot of money ..."

Marelle worked it out in her head. "Christ over two million, there or there abouts ..."

"Yup." He replied. "Be more use putting it back to farmland."

"Would Mr. Wright ...?"

He laughed. "I doubt it."

"So, it may be a while then?" She smiled.

"Who knows? Someone might be waiting for it – or have other ideas for it. It could be sold right now ..."

She sighed.

"But I'm here until they tell me otherwise."

Jacob was amazingly calm over the next couple of days. That surprised Marelle. She had expected anxiety at best, manic behaviour and peeling him off the ceiling at worst but he remained calm. He went to work, came home, slept. She had expected phone calls to and fro with Chas but there was nothing. The only thing she was aware of playing on his mind was the 'for sale' board at the airfield but he seemed to have that in rational perspective at the moment too. Jacob had everything worked out, everything laid out in his mind and the plan honed and rehearsed. He was focused on that moment in his life. He knew what he wanted so completely, and he knew he could not fuck it up in any way. That focused him – at least, visibly.

On the Friday evening Marelle had sat down with him and gone through his plan. She needed to know so she could be ready when he was. The venue was a two-hour drive. They had passes so could park behind the venue. Chas had told him to be there at ten – ready to walk on at about ten fifteen. But Chas had told him not to be there much before that – he didn't want him hanging around and getting seen. He wanted him there five minutes before. Mya would look out for them and usher them through so he could literally walk on at precisely the correct moment.

So the whole day was planned around that moment. He wanted to leave at six, get there then hang around in the car close by. That would allow for traffic hold ups and unforeseen delays. Jacob would drive; he would get ready beforehand and just tart himself up in the car (his words) then go straight on. His last day as Jacob was simple; at ten fifteen he became Nat again and would walk on stage as Ezza. It chilled Marelle to the bone.

Not quite as much however as him calmly announcing he was 'taking the bike out for a spin' at lunch time on Saturday when they had already started getting clothes and stuff ready for the evening.

"You can't!" She exclaimed. "Why the hell are you going to take *that* out now?"

"I need to." He laughed. "I need to blow some cobwebs away, get an adrenaline rush I always used to!"

"No Jacob. You've too much at stake. I have got to be the voice of reason this time. You scare me on that bike."

He laughed. "Sssh!"

"No." She stated. "You are not doing it. What if you come off – it would all be over ..."

"I won't come off!" He replied, reaching out and pulling her to him.

"What if someone hits you then? It might not be your fault but it can still happen. It's a stupid thing to do."

"It's what I always used to do. It's fine, I'll be careful."

She shook her head. "There's only a couple of hours before we've got to think about leaving."

"I won't be long. I'll just go for a blast up the dual carriageway …"

"What if you get caught by the police?"

Jacob laughed at that.

"Jacob. It's a stupid idea. You are putting everything in jeopardy!" She cried.

"I'm not!" He exclaimed, grinning.

She stared at him. This was it! He'd been so calm and focussed and now it was unravelling.

"It's fine!" He said again. "I'll be half an hour. That's all."

She refused to watch him as he set off; and didn't hang around while he manoeuvred the bike out of the house and climbed aboard dressed in his leathers and the snake's head helmet. Marelle didn't even tell him to be careful. The bike started up and he was off. She gritted her teeth as she heard him accelerate away noisily.

Marelle took a deep breath, walked through to the kitchen and glanced at the clock.it was one-thirty; she would hold him to that half an hour and promised herself that she would not spend the next thirty minutes panicking or listening for emergency sirens. He'd be fine; he said he would be fine; he had too much to throw it away. He knew that; he would be fine. In half an hour he would be back, full of life and ready. She sniffed. It would be fine.

There was a pile of just washed clothing still on a kitchen chair. Miraculously they had dried outside. On the top was his old Yellow Son t-shirt – clean and ready but he would not be wearing it tonight. She walked forward and began folding the clothes – if she folded them carefully and put them neatly away, they would not need ironing. Marelle hated ironing. As she folded his t-shirts, her t-shirts, his jeans and her underwear she smiled at the early days when she had discovered he had some woman in the village doing his washing and ironing. That had amazed her with its sheer decadence at the time until she had realised that he was in fact just being treated as one of the infirm or mentally retarded of the village who were unable to do their own laundry! Now his washing was with hers; it probably didn't get ironed as well as it used to, but he hadn't complained.

Soon she had a neat pile in front of her and scooped it up carefully to transport it upstairs to the airing cupboard on the landing. With that in her arms and the scent of the fresh air outside, mingled with the fabric conditioner Marelle started towards the stairs. Four steps up her phone rang.

Panic hit her like an express train and she leaned forward to dump the clothing on a step two or three risers above her and ran back to the kitchen where her phone was ringing and vibrating on the table. She should have taken it with her and cursed to herself as she grabbed it. Already, her heart was arresting when she saw her old number. It was Jacob.

"What?" She gasped, answering breathless and scared, half expecting it not to be him and ready for someone else's voice to ask, '*is that Marelle?*'

"Hah!" He laughed. 'Thought you would be worried. I'm fine – just letting you know – now coming back."

For a moment Marelle was lost for words. Was this a joke? Was this Ezza escaping out of his every orifice ... it wasn't normal behaviour for Jacob.

"Shit Jacob!" She exclaimed. "You fucking terrified me! Don't make it worse!"

He laughed. *Actually laughed*. She could hear the adrenalin in his words. "Stop worrying. I'll see you in minute. I hit one hundred and twenty on the way in!"

"Don't tell me that!" She gasped. "Just get back here in one piece!"

He laughed again. "OK. Be back shortly. I'll be as quick as I can!"

And he rang off with a laugh before she could say anything more.

It took her a few seconds to compose herself, for her legs to feel firm again and ready to carry her back toward the stairs. Two steps into the hallway her phone rang again.

"Fuck!" She said to herself and turned back. If he was pissing about further, she would be angry.

It was Bella.

"Hi Babe. How's it going?"

Marelle drew a breath. "OK." She said.

"Doesn't really sound 'OK." Bella questioned. "What is it?"

"Nothing." She shook her head.

"When you say nothing, I always know it's *something*! What is it?"

Marelle sighed. "Jacob." She said. "On that bloody motorbike!"

Bella laughed. "What's he doing?"

"Don't you laugh too!" Marelle reprimanded. "He's gone off on it, roaring about – scares me half to death then rings me to tell me he's just done 120 miles per hour!"

"Boys will be boys."

"He's not a boy! He's a fucking grown man!" Marelle answered.

"He's a rock star." Bella laughed.

'He's not a rock star!" Marelle said. "I'm not talking about it. How are things with you?"

Bella gave a little chuckle. "All good. Mae is working this weekend ... I just wanted to check – is that date going to be totally firm for your wedding?"

"Yes. I suppose so ... we haven't made any plans yet ...but well, yes, I assume it is."

Bella sighed. "Marelle!" She said. "You two are completely unbelievable! You set a date then kind of forget about it... it's not long away – big weddings need a lot of organisation you know. You can't leave it until the last minute ..."

"We'll be fine. Why do you ask?"

"Oh, sorting out holiday etcetera. Mae wants to book hers well in advance – we were looking at the calendar last night."

"Oh wow! Super organised." Marelle commented.

"That's Mae for you. To be honest, I quite like it!" Bella grinned. "We just need to know."

"Well. Yes." Marelle replied. "Unless he kills himself on that bloody bike!"

"It's good you are saying that in jest, not as a genuine concern." Bella commented.

"Oh believe me. It *is* a genuine concern. He has been fine lately then today it's just pow! Like '*I need an adrenalin rush*'!"

"Hmm." Bella laughed.

Marelle sighed, realising she was probably being unreasonable – he'd gone out on a motorbike and she was moaning. Bella didn't know about the gig tonight – she completely wanted to tell her, but she couldn't, not even Bella. Not yet.

"Maybe just ease up a little on him Marelle. I think he's pretty safe now." Bella advised.

"I know but, well, I can't say anything but he's doing *something* tonight that he needs to be totally focussed on – it's been ages in the planning and now he's gallivanting about on some souped-up fucking motorbike!"

"Doing *something*?" Bella repeated.

"Yes." Marelle replied succinctly. "I can't divulge anything but it's big."

Bella laughed. "What?"

Marelle sighed loudly.

"Oh, *that* big?" Bella answered. "Really? And you weren't going to tell me?"

"I'm not telling you now …"

"Where is it?"

"Bella, I really can't tell you. The whole thing is balanced on a knife edge anyway."

"Wow!" Bella grinned. "So, what happens after tonight?"

"I don't know." Marelle confessed.

"Is there more?" Bella laughed. "Shit! You're living the dream, babe!"

"I wish I bloody was! I know there's going to be aggravation in one way or another."

"Tell me where it is."

"Bella, I can't."

"Go on. I can easily find out anyway." Bella smiled.

"Find out what? I haven't told you *anything*!"

"You've told me enough." Bella chuckled.

"I've told you *nothing*! OK?" Marelle stated. I know you know but I've not told you."

Bella giggled. "Oh my! How good is this?"

"Don't breath a word of what I've not told you to anyone. *Anyone*!" Marelle warned.

"Of course not babe!" Bella replied.

Marelle suddenly heard a noise, the bike, returning. It was not as familiar as the old trials bike he used to ride but she would always know it was him.

"Shit!" She said to Bella. "He's just come back. I'd better go!"

"Well at least he's all in one piece!" Bella smiled.

"Thank God." Marelle replied walking to look out of the window as he landed in the driveway, astride the bike, removing his helmet.

"I'd better go." Marelle gasped.

"Go on then." Bella told her. "And Marelle ..."

"What?"

"Break a leg!" Bella laughed.

"Oh Sshh." Marelle replied as she cut the call with Bella still chuckling to herself.

Jacob knocked at the front door. She opened it. Staring into his dark eyes, they were twinkling, effervescing with a latent excitement. Marelle wondered how much longer he could contain it.

He went back to the bike and began to guide it towards the door, He gad hefted it up the steps as it pinged and cracked, cooling as it smelled incredibly hot.

"Hang on." He said, stopping then carefully guiding it down the steps as she watched. He pushed it to the side, up near the hedge.

"It's a bit hot." He said with a grin. "Leave it there a bit. I'll get it in just before we leave." He turned and walked back towards her, helmet in hand just like he had that night at the Thor site as the sun was setting and she had randomly mentioned Black Shuck.

But today there was no fear or darkness in his eyes just that boyish glint that screamed Ezza at her.

FORTY-FOUR

He walked up the steps, lanky and tall in the leathers, his neck looked thin and his hair was dishevelled.

"Don't you dare do that again." She said, scornfully, yet warmly.

"What?!" He laughed.

"It was just the close proximity of you doing that to what's happening tonight. You were courting fate – if it was going to happen, you knew it was going to happen then. I was terrified you would hurt yourself ..."

"But I didn't." He smiled.

"Then you call me when you full well know I'll be shitting myself! Don't you dare do that again!"

"Oh, I can't guarantee that." He said, walking up the top step and into the house, safe and sound.

And so began his preparation. "Is it seriously going to take you three hours to get ready?" She grinned when he said he was going upstairs to shower.

He nodded. "I'd rather get ready and *be* ready. I don't want to arrive all flustered and in a rush."

Point taken. She wondered if he had set that much time aside in the past or whether he just turned up. Somehow, she could not imagine Chas taking two hours to get ready.

As he prepared himself Marelle also put on make-up, did her hair and pulled on her best cowboy boots. She wasn't on the stage, but she wanted him to see *her* when he came off, not a barrage of screaming female fans.

He had decided to wear an ivory cream shirt, pin-tucked with long, turn-back cuffs. It felt like silk as she stood and ran the cuffs through her fingers while it hung on the back of the bedroom door. He'd got what looked like a brand-new pair of dark wash jeans, narrow but not skinny legged and the pointy-toed boots he had worn out with her once. Over the back of a chair was a deep navy coloured jacket with brass buttons that she had never seen before. It was cut impeccably, almost three-quarter length with two box vents at the back. It was beautiful.

This had always been there, but she had never noticed. Maybe she had been the first to see the re-blossoming of Ezza within Jacob. The change from the hoodies and the woolly hats into the smart, sharply dressed alter ego he had surprised her with in those early, heady days when just the tiniest breath of Ezza was starting to escape. Others had commented, it *had* been noticed but they had all pointed towards her as the reason. Maybe she had been part of it but now, when she looked back and understood everything, she knew she was far from all of it.

And the night she had peeled that blood-soaked t-shirt from him while he had been in a state of semi consciousness, only to be stunned there was a designer label inside it, came back to her now. Bella had commented that it was probably fake. Obviously, it hadn't been. It had been irrecoverable, and she had thrown it away.

And soon he would be inside the clothes which hung on the back of that door. He would be up on that stage, performing, like he had all of those years ago in those pictures she had seen so many times. And with that he would become Ezza; the truth would be out, and he would be exposed to face whatever came out of it. Ultimately, he would no longer have that excuse not to marry her.

Marelle smiled, turned to him as he walked, semi naked into the bedroom; skin taught and pale, sinuously muscular.

"What?" He asked.

"Nothing." She smiled but her gaze lingered. "I was just admiring the shirt."

An hour later he was beginning to get an edge about him. Fully dressed and ready he was going through an invisible list in his head. Staring into space and asking her if she had random items that he wanted to take.

"Have you got the passes?" He questioned, tension now growing in his voice.

"Yes!" She responded. "In my bag."

"What about the bag of stuff?"

By 'stuff' he meant the bag of a change of clothes, hair products and deodorant he had put into a holdall and handed to her a while ago.

"Yes. It's in the car... don't you want anything to eat or drink before you go, there's time?"

"Good Lord no!" He shook his head. 'I wouldn't have got dressed if I was going to eat or drink!"

"Well, then, I think we are ready." She smiled with a little sigh and a shrug.

He screwed his mouth, stood there for a second. Then he closed his eyes and placed a finger on his forehead in concentration as he went through his list again.

"Have you for you jacket?" Marelle suddenly asked.

He opened his eyes "Shit." He whispered and turned to go up the stairs.

Marelle chuckled to herself and went back into the kitchen. Maybe she would take a packet of paracetamol with them; she may need a couple by the end of the night! She went to the cupboard, pulled out the plastic box with half empty packets of throat sweets and hay fever tablets in and sorted through until she found a mostly full box of the painkillers. She popped them into the bag on her shoulder, then returned the plastic box. She was just closing the cupboard door again when there was an enormous thud from the hallway direction followed by a resounding crash and a noise that sounded like shattering glass. She felt the house creak and momentarily jolt around her.

Standing up she widened her eyes and started back towards the hallway, one hand outstretched to pull the door open. What the hell was that, she thought to herself. Her mind was whirling between something having crashed *into* the house; something having fallen *on* the house or something having been thrown *at* the house. She hurried down the hallway, one hand on the newel post as she expected to see Jacob descending with an equally perplexed look on his face as she already had on hers.

Instead, her eyes fell on Jacob, on his hands and knees at the foot of the stairs. He was rising slowly, awkwardly. Surrounding him was scattered glass in large, vorpal shards on the green carpet, reflecting light that was passing in through the hole smashed in the glazed top of the door. As her eyes flicked between him and the broken glass, further pieces lost their hold, toppling and tinkling onto the carpet too.

"What's happened?" She asked, still pretty stunned by the whole incident and discovering this scene so unexpectedly but the words hardly left her lips before her attention was immediately grabbed by the jagged arc of what looked like fresh, red blood on the hallway wall.

"Shit!" She exclaimed as time began moving again and she started forward urgently, finally realising what the noise had been and exactly what had just happened. Guiltily she kicked the strewn, once neatly folded clean washing out of the way.

Jacob was on his knees. He was clutching his left arm to himself with his right hand clamped around his left forearm. There was blood tracking between his fingers and dripping off his knuckles.

"Bloody hell!" Marelle gasped, dropping onto her knees in front of him.

"Mind the glass!" He warned, his voice breathless and racked with adrenalin.

"You're bleeding!" She reached out, but he struggled to stand without using his hands. Marelle sprang up and assisted him, her own breathing beyond control.

"Grab a towel." He nodded in a broken voice, leaning himself against the wall.

She picked up the white hand towel near her feet and handed it to him. He didn't take it but lifted his eyes to hers. "When I take my hand away, immediately press the towel onto the same spot. Then I'll put my hand back on, ok?"

She nodded. His voice was hoarse, quiet, scared.

"Ready?" He asked.

She nodded again, towel in hand.

He unclasped his hand, let go of his arm which dropped as he did so appearing to be floppy and beyond his remit. As it did so he gasped, screwed his eyes shut and took a breath. As he did Marelle looked back down to the small spurt of blood arc from his arm and splatter onto the carpet.

She made a noise, unsure whether it had erupted as a scream, a gasp, or a swearword but the sound that came out of her mouth paralysed her as she watched the bleeding wound until he leaned forward and grabbed the towel from her with a bloodied, trembling hand. He pressed it against the wound hard, grasping his hand around it as he lifted a leg to adjust the position of the floppy arm. He grimaced as he did so and chugged out a ragged breath.

"Oh fuck! Oh fuck!" Marelle panicked. "I'll call an ambulance …"

"No!" He exclaimed. "Get something to bind around this – a bandage or something …"

"I don't have a bandage …"

"Make one, anything long that you can wind round ..."

He was propped against the wall, skin becoming paler as he spoke, eyes closed in either pain or fear, his hand clasped around the injured arm. Already, Marelle could see the blood starting to show through the white towel.

"You need an ambulance!" She sobbed.

"Find a bandage ... we've got to try and put pressure on this – we can't wait for them to get here – anything – tear that sheet up ..."

He nodded to the sheet, still folded, laying near the bottom stair. There was already blood spattered across it.

Marelle, glad of instruction, grabbed the sheet and immediately tried to tear it but the edge was too strong to yield. She tutted and ran back to the kitchen, grabbed scissors and made a cut in it. Running back to him she was ripping a four-inch strip down the length of the cotton sheet. She completed the tear and trailed the makeshift bandage towards him.

'Wrap it around.' He said. "As tight as you can get it." His voice was tired, quiet, resigned. "Tighter!"

He felt hot to her touch. "It'll cut off your circulation." She said, remembering her mother telling her off for putting a plaster too tight onto her finger so that the end started turning blue!

He rolled his eyes to her. "That's the idea."

She drew a breath sharply, winding the strip of sheet around and around as tight as she could pull it.

"Split the end and tie it.' He said.

She looked up at him, unsure what he meant.

"Cut the strip up the middle for the last six inches or so then tie it around my arm to hold it in place."

Marelle did as he had said, tying it then looking up at him.

"What are we going to do?"

He looked at her with fear in his eyes. "Hopefully, it will stop ... if it does, we will get on our way."

She made a noise at him in despair, in disbelief. "We can't ... you can't go on stage like that!"

"I've only got to sing ... I can sing like this!"

"Jacob!" She exclaimed. "We've got time, I can take you to the hospital – they can check it out, patch you up ... I can drive fast ..."

He shook his head. "Once I get in there, they won't let me go ... come on, let's get in the car ..."

Marelle felt tears rising. She stared at him. He looked as if he was about to cry, holding on to both pain and emotion – and probably anger, but also there, in his eyes was desperation. His very last chance was right there but he was losing it now, falling through his fingers, slippery with blood and pain. Marelle could not deny him that. There was no way she would allow him to lose his grip on that dream.

She picked up the keys. "Ok." She said. "We'll clear this up later."

He walked to the car, cradling and holding his arm, unsteady, still trembling. He stood, hunched, and waited for her to open the car door for him before lowering himself in, maintaining his tenuous hold on pain and clarity.

"I'll put your seatbelt on." She said, quietly leaning in and over him. He sat back with his eyes closed. She pulled the belt over him, looked down at his arm.

There was blood seeping through between his fingers again.

"Jacob." She said, staring at it.

"What?" He asked, opening his eyes. His pupils were large and dark.

"It's still bleeding."

He looked down at it, sighed. "Go and get another bandage."

She didn't move, just stared at the slowly penetrating circle of red.

"Get another bandage!" He urged, shrilly.

"Jacob." She stated. "It's not stopping, it's still seeping through the towel *and* the bandage – there's blood all over the house. It's not going to stop."

He sighed. "Just get in."

"No. This is stupid. Call Chas, tell him what's happened, and I'll get you to a hospital."

"No." He stated. "I'll be there. I *promised* him."

"You can't."

"I can't miss this." He said in a voice that was verging on tears.

She stood up and stared down at him with a sigh. This was her fault; she had left the pile of clothes on the stairs, and he had tripped on them coming back down as he rushed. He had fallen down the stairs, he could have broken his neck! And she had worried about him going out on that bike! He'd smashed his arm through the glass panel on the front door – an old door and it was obviously *not* safety glass. His arm looked broken; he was in severe pain, but he had obviously damaged a blood vessel – maybe even severed an artery. She was watching him bleed to death in front of her. There wasn't time to panic.

"Look." She said. "I'll take you to the hospital – they can stitch it up – we can then dash down to the gig ..."

"No." He said. "It will take too long – we'll be there hours ..."

"No, we won't. They're not going to leave you bleeding like that – you will be a priority and once they've stopped it bleeding, we'll go. You won't have to wait – you are the emergency ..."

"We won't make it." He replied.

"We will. The sooner we go the better. We've got a few hours in hand." She kept calm but lowered her eyes to the expanding circle of blood, almost saw it spreading as she watched it. "Trust me." She whispered to him before closing the door and running around to the driver's side.

She had seen the signs to the local hospital when they had driven into the police station and had an idea of where to go.

"It will be fine." She said to him as she put the key into the ignition.

He writhed slightly in the seat, had his eyes closed and his hand around the forearm. She could see his knuckles were as white as his face. Marelle started the engine. She sincerely doubted he would make it tonight, but her first priority was to keep him alive; just as it had always been.

"Would it be better to raise your arm?" She asked suddenly.

"Can't." He replied.

"Let me help." She leaned over and began to try and lift his injured arm.

The sound he made was unearthly, like some guttural beast prowling hungrily.

"Don't!" He gasped. "Just don't!"

Marelle drove. Reversed out between the newly built walls and down the road, accelerator to the floor, faster than she had ever driven through the village before but not too fast to notice the board outside Patricia's house now had 'SOLD STC" slapped across it. Marelle noticed but it hardly went in – now was not the time to share that information.

Foot down she checked road signs as she went. Occasionally she snatched a glance apprehensively across at Jacob in the passenger seat. He had his eyes closed, face slack, pale, grey.

"OK?" She asked, hardly daring to hope for an answer.

"Yeah." He said, just to appease her but he was not.

Gently she reached across and placed a hand on his thigh. "We're nearly there I think." She whispered but had to take back her hand to drive. It felt damp when she took it off his leg, she looked at it, fearing the worst. There was a dirty, rusty red stain moistening her hand. It felt cold; not fresh blood but obviously soaked into the dark fabric of his jeans from when it had happened. Working her own bottom deeper into the seat with a pang of burgeoning discomfort at the way this was panning out, she pushed her foot down harder.

It was that time of the day when people were moving around so the traffic was heavier than normal. They exited a roundabout and sat in standing traffic for ten minutes, intrinsically metres away from the hospital entrance as far as she could tell. Marelle sighed noisily, looked at him; looked at his hand still clutching the injured arm. He was too quiet; she would have expected him to be in full panic mode – not slumped silently in the passenger seat when they were only hours away from what he had spent the last twelve years yearning for. He would not be on that stage tonight, maybe she should call Chas?

The traffic started moving and she quickly pulled the car forwards again. Now able to see the entrance to the hospital, maybe two or three hundred yards up ahead. The red 'H' sign loomed but traffic was a slow-moving serpent, twisting its way along then coming to a halt again, literally a moment away from the left hand turn.

"Fucking hell!" She said to herself.

There appeared to be temporary traffic lights some way ahead. They were red, she could see the light and the line of traffic moving through from the other side.

"Come on! Come on!" She repeated to herself, then looked across at Jacob.

"Nearly there." She said, staring at him. His head was against the passenger window, eyes closed.

"Jacob!" She said again. "Jacob!" Then she thrust out a hand and tapped his thigh.

He sighed. "What?"

"Stick with me!" She panicked, trying to sound as bright as she could but darkness was picking at the edges. "We're nearly there ... if these fucking traffic lights would change!" She clutched his thigh for a moment then saw the light change from red to green up ahead. She placed her hand back on the wheel.

"Come on ..." She sighed, edging forward barely two inches. Nothing moved. The lights were green, but nothing was moving.

"Fucking hell! What are you doing! Just fucking move!" She hissed, looking quickly at Jacob. He was not holding his arm so tightly. The bandage was blood soaked now. Marelle banged the wheel. *Why* was nothing moving? She needed to move fifty metres at the most; she could *see* the turning. Nothing was coming the other way. They had to let her through; it was an emergency!

"Fuck it!" She exclaimed, turned the wheel through her hands as much as she could and moved the car out of the line, travelling on the wrong side of the road, avoiding a central traffic island and arcing back round to the same line of traffic. There was a small gap over the entrance to the hospital but not quite enough to get a car through. They should have left a gap, but they hadn't. The white estate car to the left and the red four-wheel drive to the right would need to part. She came in at an acute angle, pushing the nose of the Mercedes towards the gap between the front of the white car and the back of the red one – and kept going. Her car was still half over the other carriageway now – anything coming the other way would not be able to pass either. The person in the white car elected to ignore her, staring straight ahead at the line of traffic.

"I'm not going to push in you dickhead!" She snapped, edging forward but the driver ignored her.

The red car shunted forwards, having seen what she was trying to do but they were not able to move forward enough. A gap opened slightly and to her disbelief the white car began to pull forwards into it.

Marelle bipped her horn. The words of her driving instructor came back to her, the horn is a warning, not a rebuke. Well, this was warning; she was coming though, like it or not. Marelle edged forwards, got the front of her car in such a position that it would be hit if the white car moved forwards any further.

She pointed to the hospital entrance, furiously stabbing her finger in gesture. She bipped again. The red car edged an inch backwards to her right. Moving slowly on towards the entrance road to the hospital, grateful that the red car was at least trying to let her get through. Not really knowing if the space was enough, she crept onward, waiting for crunch but it never came. Then, just as she was about to clear the space the white car began honking it's horn at her, together with a hand gesture which denoted they were not too happy with her manoeuvre.

"Fuck you!" She flipped the bird and angrily raised a finger but accelerated aggressively. If she took their bumper off, she was past caring. Horns blared as she slipped through the gap and drove up the tree lined road into the hospital car park.

"Fuck you." She repeated to herself, driving around and under the barrier which opened as she approached. She wanted to drive right up to the doors of A&E and leave the car running while dashing in, screaming for help like they did in movies – but she didn't want to run the risk of not being able to drive up there or find a place to leave the car. Instead, she drove through the car park, took the first space she found and parked responsibly. Luckily it was an end one which made it easier to get into and enable her to open the passenger door fully because it looked like she would need to do just that in order to help Jacob out.

She cut the engine and sighed. Her heart was racing, her hands were clammy.

"Let's get in there." She said, turning to him. "The sooner we can get in the sooner we can get out, hey?"

"I'll be OK." He mumbled. "Maybe we should just go ..."

"I've just nearly elicited a road rage incident!" She gasped. 'I'm not just going – come on!"

The fact that he said he would be OK and that maybe they should just go would have been a laughable one in the circumstances. With the shakiness of his hands and the unsteadiness of his feet as he walked Marelle suddenly began to feel herself slipping beneath the surface of hopefulness as she walked with him towards the main door of the A&E department. Her growing fear was exaggerated by the simple fact that he was not panicking about being here and was willingly heading into the hospital. He looked ashen, not just pale, but grey.

The doors slid open for them and they walked into the department; she glanced at him. There was resignation on his face. Suddenly she herself felt trapped, as the doors hissed closed behind them. How many people entered here and never left? Marelle was hot and felt panic rising in her, but a chill rippled down her spine.

FORTY-FIVE

She had never been in the emergency department of a hospital before but headed towards the red sign which said 'Reception – all patients to report here'. She wanted to take Jacob's arm but daren't in case she made anything worse. Instead, she turned, let him catch up to her then placed her hand around his back as she stopped at the reception desk. A thought occurred to her that calling an ambulance would have taken this step away, but it was too late now.

"Hi." She smiled sweetly.

The girl at the desk smiled back.

"Erm ..." Marelle mumbled. This was all too *nice*; too civilised. Marelle was aware of Jacob beside her, she remembered the panic and fear in his eyes and felt the rising sickness in herself. Her knees were suddenly weak. She took a breath.

"He's fallen down the stairs and put his arm through a glass door – it won't stop bleeding and I think it's broken." She said.

"Could I take the patient's name and date of birth?"

"Jacob Frost." Marelle said, then swallowed. Jacob Frost who had spent his entire existence hiding from ever exposing himself to registration or recognition. She reeled off his date of birth – and suddenly wondered too if it was his actual date of birth. Her mind was whirling around that thought in the vacuous sterility of this area; she could feel the heat coming off his body against her and felt a sudden weight fall towards her – swaying against her hand at his back. She looked to him.

He staggered slightly, shaking his head as if to clear it, unable to reach out an arm to right himself he stumbled a step backwards and leaned against the wall next to the reception hatch, leaning his uninjured arm against it. Marelle kept her hand against his back, looking to him as he moved and feeling in that second that he was going; losing his grip on consciousness he'd held tentatively on to during the last half an hour. Whether it was a faint or his body closing down she did not know but Jacob was suddenly very heavy against her. In reaction she held him against the wall to keep him upright but feeling her hold failing. She let out a yelp of a scream, struggling to keep him there.

"Shit! Help!" She shouted. "Jacob!"

He was pretty much unresponsive to her but seconds later came to a bit and had to reposition himself, twisted sideways a jagged step as Marelle just, *just*, managed to hold him upright.

Then there were other hands, other people around her, their hands on Jacob.

"Ok." Someone said. "He's OK love, we've got him." She didn't want her fingers to leave her touch on him and kept her place. There was a chair and a buzz of people around them. Marelle touched his shoulder; touched his hand. Jacob was floating between awareness and unresponsiveness – at moments he had his eyes open, raised a hand, helped himself, groaned a bit and complained when his left arm was moved but generally he was falling into unconsciousness.

"Jacob!" She called, holding his hand.

"If you could give his details to reception then we'll take him through – he'll be fine – we'll look after him." A man in a green uniform explained beside her.

There were four other people there; three in green uniforms which she guessed were ambulance crew or paramedics who had been passing at that moment and a young woman in blue scrubs. Three of them crowded around Jacob, now in a mobile chair but totally out of it. The fourth guy stood with Marelle.

"He'll be ok." He repeated to her. "Do you want to finish giving his details to this lady."

Marelle looked towards Jacob; they were moving off with him; taking him away from her.

"Erm." She worried. "I need to go with him – he's …. I can't …" She stuttered, flailing with words.

"He'll be OK now. He's just through there in safe hands … if you can give his details we can get you back to him. What happened?" He started a distracting conversation with her, sensing she was ready to run after Jacob.

"He fell down the stairs, put his arm through the glass in the front door. It won't stop bleeding." She answered.

"Oh nasty." He replied. "Well he's in the right place – he's probably just fainted – it happens a lot." He reassured. "Let's get him booked in."

"He has to be on stage in a few hours." She rambled. "He can't stay here …"

"Well let's get him seen to first – have you told the lady here his name?"

Marelle nodded, turned back to the desk, realising she was crying and wiped her face with her hand.

"The receptionist reeled back his name and date of birth."

Marelle nodded.

"Is he a UK citizen?"

She nodded again.

"Who is his GP?"

Marelle stared at her. She didn't know. He didn't have one, did he? "I don't know." She sniffed.

"Ok, don't worry, we can find that out."

Marelle drew a cold breath. They could try.

"I'll leave you to it." The ambulanceman said, moving off.

'Where is he?" Marelle called after him.

"They'll give you a shout in a few minutes." He smiled as he left.

She turned back to the receptionist; her eyes were full of tears and she felt bemused and lost. One minute he had been with her, now he was gone – that quick; that sudden. She felt a sob rising.

"If you would like to take a seat through there, I will ask someone to come and speak to you ..."

Marelle looked towards the waiting area – it looked busy and chaotic. She looked back.

"How long will it be?" She questioned. "He can't stay. He's got to go on stage at ten o clock."

"I can't say how long he will be. The department is very busy – and it depends on his injuries ... if you could take a seat, I will get someone to speak to you as soon as they are available."

Marelle sighed. They had just under six hours until he had to be there, stepping onto the stage – how could it take that long? But growing within her was that shaggy head of doubt, telling her this was not going to work out.

She sat down on a red plastic chair. On her right was a young guy and girl. It wasn't obvious what was wrong with either of them, but he sat staring into space beneath a white baseball cap while she chewed furiously on a piece of gum. To Marelle's left was a woman with a number of disparate, out of control children – spread around the floor and the department; their fingers in the vending machines or playing noisily with the toys in the corner. Everyone looked morose but no-one looked ill. No kids with saucepans on their heads or people wiling in pain. Then, she supposed that was why they were all sitting here, and Jacob had been taken straight through. Marelle noted there was no clock in the area, but a red digital display constantly scrolled that the waiting time was 'up to four hours'. If it was, they were stuffed – but luckily Jacob had slipped the queue. Surely he had been taken through as a priority and had been treated as such?

Nonetheless, as she watched the department function around her, she felt panic growing as the minutes ticked by. She really ought to phone Chas – it would be better to let him know what had happened than to just not turn up. In the circumstances, if she told him up front he may be sympathetic enough to give Jacob another chance – Mya would certainly want to. This was nobody's fault; it was an accident – he would understand. She wished she had Mya's number as she would be easier to speak to. She tapped her pocket and suddenly realised she had left the house without her phone nor Jacob with his. She had no way of calling Chas unless she went home and she didn't want to leave here without Jacob and anyway, would there even be another chance?

It had been nearly an hour. Marelle had sat there fidgeting between the walking wounded and misbehaving children while Jacob had been whisked away. Out of her sight, somewhere deep in this building. She had no idea what was happening or where he was, if he was awake or unconscious – alive or dead. She took a long hard breath, shaky and unfulfilling for her racing heart as she tried to push away the thoughts that always seemed to be waiting in the wings just to haunt her.

She had let him out of her hands; something she swore she would never do again and now, once again, she had no idea where he was or what condition he was in. Suddenly a child on the floor let out a blood curdling scream which made her jump, the mother immediately shouted at the child as it fought with what was probably a dirty, sticky sibling and the child screamed more. Marelle looked briefly then looked away. She did not want to be part of this.

"Marelle!"

She shot her head round, not so much surprised by someone in this alien place calling her name but more by the fact that it was Jacob's voice calling her. Sharp and clear, strong and alive. Her eyes fell to him, appearing from around the jutting out half-wall at the far side of the department where patients were taken when they were called.

He stood there in his skinny dark jeans and cowboy boots, bare to the waist but with a flimsy hospital gown half wrapped around his torso. There was a fresh, clean, neat dressing on his left arm, but he was still clutching it with his right hand, gathering the gown in a bundle around himself as he did so. He looked impossibly tall and thin standing there – his hair hardly out of place and his dark eyes solely focused on her.

Marelle leapt up, strode across towards him. Got to the wall just as a member of staff in blue scrubs appeared at his other side.

"What's the time?" He asked, tension in his voice and in every muscle she could see.

She looked to her watch. "Twenty past five." Her hand reached out and connected with his right arm, her fingers wrapping around his skin and confirming he was still alive. He felt hot.

"Mr. Frost, if you could just come back in here ..." The other person asked.

"No, no, we've got to be off ..." He replied, half turning, caught between them and Marelle.

"I don't think the doctor has quite finished with you yet – we need to look at that arm ..." Her voice was sympathetic and calm.

"It's fine. It' stopped bleeding now." He commented, 'I'll just get my shirt then we can go ..."

"The bleeding has stopped for now but that's just a temporary measure Mr. Frost ... if it starts bleeding again you will need medical attention ... the wound still needs to be examined ... your shoulder joint is also dislocated ... we can't let you leave like that ..."

He looked to Marelle, looked back to them, hovered.

"I can come back tomorrow ..."

The member of staff sighed. "You can. But a dislocation is very painful and it's also probably compromising that arm ... if it's not reduced it could possibly lead to permanent nerve damage and at worst amputation ... I would strongly advise you remain here and let us at least see if we can make you a bit more comfortable ..." She looked around Jacob to Marelle. "Are you his partner?" She questioned.

Marelle nodded.

"You can come through with us ... come on lets go back so the doctor can come and speak to you ..."

He looked to Marelle; he was in pain. She could see that. "We've got time." Marelle said to him.

He sighed.

"Come on, come this way ..." The nurse nodded, "We'll be done real soon ... you can't go walking around with your shoulder dislocated, can you? At least there are no bones broken ..." She led the way back to a cubicle on the right, The curtain covering the entrance was open and there was a trolley in there that he had obviously just left. His shirt was draped across the foot of it. "Take a seat and I will let the doctor know you are in here ..." She gestured.

Jacob walked slowly, holding the injured arm against himself. His back was completely exposed, and Marelle could see his ribs as she followed behind him. There was a definite deformation of his left shoulder, she could see that now. He propped his backside against the trolley and hunched himself around the pain he was feeling from the arm.

"Can you get onto the bed." The nurse laughed, "It's not safe with you half on it like that – we don't want another accident, come on, relax ... it will be OK."

That was easy to say but hard to envisage right now. He followed instruction stiffly, getting onto the trolley, allowing her to set the back into an upright position and then gently lowering himself against it. He winced as he sat back.

"It hurts less standing up." He protested.

"Yes, until you fall down again. You passed out in reception, remember?" She turned to Marelle as she went to leave. "Keep him under control! I'll go and see what's happening." As she left, she pulled the curtain across.

"It's stopped bleeding, we may as well go ..." Jacob said straight away.

"And go on stage like that?"

"I don't need two arms to sing!" He exclaimed.

"Just give it five minutes ... get some pain relief at least ..." Marelle suggested. "We've got time. If we left now, we would still have at least an hour or so to spare.

"What if there's traffic? I always built in at least a couple of hours ..."

"Then we'll find a detour ..."

He shook his head, stared into space. She could feel the sparks flying off him, the static built in his veins and ready to snap. He was wired, maybe he had already been given something that had heightened this state of excitement. He jiggled one leg, either in pain or impatience.

"Were you out for long?" She asked.

"I wasn't ever out." He replied. "i went a bit dizzy, but I could hear everything."

"What have they done so far?"

"Took the dressing off this and it spurted blood everywhere, wrapped it up, took me to x-ray, took it off again and it spurted blood everywhere. Brought me back here and put this bandage on. I was on a drip, but I disconnected it." He said, bluntly. "If they're not back in five minutes we'll go."

"How bad is the pain?"

"About eleven if I move it." He said. "I can't feel my fingers though."

She sighed. "I think maybe we had better wait a little while …"

He jiggled his leg again, shifted slightly, yelped then decided to sit forwards. "Fuck!" he said.

"Shall I call Chas?"

"No, don't fucking call Chas!" He stated, "Chas doesn't need to know. He won't answer his phone anyway." He seemed to be in intense pain for a second, closed his eyes briefly. "I get there or it's over."

She wanted to ask what was over but didn't want to hear his answer.

"What's the time?" He asked.

"Quarter to six."

He shuffled, swore, shook his head.

"Did you just pull the drip out then?" She asked, going back to his earlier comment.

He nodded. "This is next …" he turned his hand to her. There was still a cannula inserted and taped to it."

"Maybe you needed it?" She questioned.

"I need to get out of here." He responded. "Pass me my shirt …"

She walked to his feet and picked it up. It didn't look so pristine as it had hanging in their bedroom.

"Come on, let's go." He said, bring that with you. I'll put it on when we get there …" He shuffled forwards, kicked his legs off the bed and slid onto the floor. His top half was virtually naked, but he still clutched the gown around him. He had one arm in it, the rest loose and the back open.

"Are you sure?" She questioned, looking sternly at him.

He nodded. Took a step away as he turned, faltered and staggered the step back again until his bottom touched the bed. Marelle immediately shot out a hand to him and held his upper right arm. He shook his head.

"Got up too quick." He added, taking a step forwards again and lunging uncoordinatedly sideways until he crashed into the chair and the wall, unable to put out a hand to save himself he hit it bottom first, and she thought for a moment he was going to hit the floor.

"Jacob!" She yelped, now next to him, holding him by the arm.

"Come on." He said, nodding and rolling away from the wall.

Marelle slid a hand between his good arm and his body, holding on to him like a child, steadying him as he stood away from the wall. He was in no fit state to be walking let alone leaving here and getting to the venue. When he had called her across the waiting area, he had looked better than he did now – maybe she had just been so happy to see him that she hadn't noticed but he had been moving slowly and with the aid of the wall. Nonetheless he pulled away from her now, heading for the curtain, pushing his way through it but getting tangled. Marelle reached out her free hand, still holding his shirt and pushed the blue material away and came face to face with two doctors about to come in.

"We're leaving." Jacob said. "If you need me to sign anything then get it and I'll sign it ..."

Marelle held his arm, pulled him slightly to her to steady him.

"If you want to go, you can but I would not advise it." The doctor said, not panicking, not trying to push him back in. "The wound on your arm may start bleeding again at any moment and you have a complete dislocation of the shoulder joint – it won't get better on its own and if it's left for a few more hours, you may not regain full use of it." He stared at Jacob and Jacob stared back at him. "We can attempt a closed reduction – if you want to remain here for a little longer?"

"How much longer?"

"Depends on how long it takes. The sooner we try, the sooner we will know."

"What does it involve?"

"We can give you some pain relief and some muscle relaxant and hopefully, manipulate the ball back into the socket. Have you dislocated your shoulder before?"

"No." He replied.

"It could be back in in five minutes ..." The doctor bargained. "Come back and sit down, let me show you the x-rays ..."

"Can you just get on with it?" Jacob asked.

"That was our intention." He smiled, holding out a hand for Jacob to return into the cubicle. "If you get yourself as comfortable as you can on there, I'll go and get my colleague and the required medication ..."

"I don't want any medication, just get it over and done."

The doctor laughed. "You need to be totally relaxed; you won't be if we don't give you something ... trust me you will thank me afterwards ..."

He lay on the bed in a sitting position, as tense as tense could possibly be. Marelle could see vacillations in the muscles in his injured arm, his jaw was tight and clenched.

"Let's just get it over and done with ..." Marelle said quietly, stroking his forehead and feeling how stiff his hair still was.

"I'm not hanging around anymore." He stated. "Let them do this then I'm leaving ... do you want to go and get the car?"

"No, I'll wait with you." She smiled. "It's OK, we'll make it. I'll drive fast!" She joked. She would, if it meant getting him there, she would break every speed limit on the way if she had to. He sighed again, closed his eyes, rolled his neck. Sighed again.

There in front of her was a different person the one she had berated earlier for going out on the bike. The one who had laughed like a giddy schoolchild when he had phoned her on his way back. Joking, relaxed, funny. Now here was a ball of tension about to unwind itself or at least start climbing the walls. Marelle surmised it was pain and fear pushing his personality in that direction, but she had not seen it before from him. He usually went quiet and silent, slipping away into shadows. She hoped it wasn't yet another manifestation of Ezza; as it was one, she felt she had little control or recall over.

The doctor returned with a colleague. Jacob moved up a notch further and anger kicked in. He swore at the doctor and told him to '*fucking get on with it!*'

"Hey, hey, calm it down." She had said to him, as her mind flicked back to the time in the pub when he had got drunk after Frankie's funeral and turned on her. That had not been Jacob either.

"It might be best if you go and sit in the waiting area." The doctor suggested.

Marelle wanted to stay, knew she stood more chance of calming him down than anyone did, but she also knew her presence would possibly inflame the situation more. Her emotions were wildly swirling around inside her even though she was holding on to an external calm. It wouldn't take much for them both to be screaming.

"I'll just be outside." She told him, kissing his cheek. He had his knees drawn up now and felt like he was about to shatter into a million pieces. "I'll see you in a minute."

He nodded and for a moment she saw that spotty teenager staring back at her with big soulful eyes. By the time she got the other side of the curtain her eyes were so full of tears she could hardly see where she was going.

It was well over an hour later when she walked back in behind the curtain. The cubicle looked dishevelled. Things were pushed and piled out of the way; there were pieces of plastic packaging on the floor and Jacob was sound asleep on the bed. His hair was messed up at the front, his injured arm folded across his bare torso. Marelle walked up to him. His eyes were closed, and he was breathing gently. Propped up in a sitting position he looked totally relaxed. So different to how he had been the last time she'd seen him.

Gently, she touched his right hand. There was a cannula still in place, but Jacob did not stir. She played with the front of his hair and put it right again, looking into his face. There was an eery silence and stillness about him she was unsure of.

"It's looking good." The doctor suddenly said behind her. He was wearing soft soled shoes, and she had not heard him approaching. "It's back in the socket where it should be – he just needs to keep it in a sling for the next few days – I'll get the nurse to sort that out, but we would like to admit him tonight anyway." He explained. "He'll take a little while to wake up fully but we have given him some pain medication so that should help when he does ..."

Marelle turned to him sharply. Jacob could not stay here the night – he had to be away. They'd done this now so there was no reason why he had to stay here. She chose not to voice that opinion yet, however.

He started coming-to forty minutes later when a nurse arrived with a sling for his arm and started trying to put it on. Initially he resisted her trying to lift his arm, then shrugged her away and turned onto his side, pulling away from her. At least he seemed to be using the arm now.

The nurse spoke to him as if he could hear and understand her, which he evidently could as he suddenly uttered

"Fuck off."

"Now. Now." She said, half humorously. "I'm trying to make you more comfortable – can we just get you sat up a bit?"

He resisted, moaned, fought her a little but eventually sat up on the bed, his eyes closed and head dropping forwards. For a few seconds he was compliant and drowsy. Then he opened his eyes.

They opened with a snap, suddenly wide and awake – there was a fire in them that appeared to be raging as it took a few seconds for his brain and body to reconnect completely. By now the nurse had got the sling on and stood away from him.

"Does that feel comfortable?" She asked.

He ignored her, gave an exasperated little gasp and swung his legs off the side of the bed, landing his feet on the floor and standing up – twisting himself in the bedcover as he did so, pulling it from the bed together with the pillows he had been propped up in. He proceeded to step forwards with it still wrapped around him. The nurse grabbed it before he tripped and with that in one hand and the other gently against him, she stopped his progress.

"Steady on. Take it easy." She warned calmly. "It's alright ..."

He looked at her in bewilderment, stared for longer than what would be considered normal. Then he turned and looked over his shoulder to Marelle, stiffly. He sighed; she watched his rib cage expand and deflate slowly as he stood there. He shook his head.

"I've got to go." He said.

"No, you haven't, come back onto the bed – you need to rest and take it easy." The nurse replied, her hand wrapping around his upper arm as he staggered slightly.

"I'm going.' He said, not really to anyone, turning away from the nurse.

"Where are we going?" He asked Marelle.

"We are not going anywhere." The nurse reprimanded, her hand still on his good arm. "Now just sit back down here for a moment." She pointed to the bed.

He stared at her, eyebrows furrowed, staring down at her as if he was trying to determine exactly what she was.

"She's, my wife." He said, just staring at her blankly.

He wasn't looking at Marelle when he said it, or even gesturing on her direction so she hoped it was her he was referring to.

"I know she is, and she wants you to sit down on here too – just for a minute, just to get your bearings for a moment or two ..."

He sighed, almost stamped his foot. She pushed gently with her hand turning him towards the bed. He shrugged her off angrily.

"She was my wife! It's your fucking fault she died. You fucking little piece of shit!" He exclaimed with a definite violence and anger behind it, pushing her away with full strength and frustration.

"Hey!" She exclaimed. "You don't want me to call security – it's alright ... calm down. You're feeling a bit strange following the medication you've had. If you just sit down here calmly and rest you will feel a whole lot better, I promise."

He glared at her. His eyes were wild with confusion and terror. Marelle had seen it in him before – when he had suffered gut wrenching nightmares. They had now faded into the past, but Marelle feared their resurgence here. She had dealt with it many times– he had even hit her once, purely accidental, but nonetheless scary. Right now, she could see that same look in his eyes.

"Jacob." She stepped forwards. "Just rest for five minutes, come on sit on here with me. It'll be alright ..."

He had said strange things on those nights of terror too, things that still didn't make sense in the same way this new outburst didn't. Words muddled in his head around thoughts that weren't quite straight.

He turned to her, tearful, shaking his head.

"I'm really thirsty." He said, almost crying.

"Well sit down for a minute. I am sure we can get you a drink." She looked to the nurse. He was between them. Marelle one side, the nurse on the other. He reluctantly stumbled backwards and sat his bottom on the bed, exhaled slowly then placed his good hand up to his forehead as if trying to squeeze reality back into place.

The nurse disappeared. Marelle sat down next to him. He sighed.

"Bloody hell." He whispered.

FORTY-SIX

Marelle leant into him, placed a hand on his thigh. "It's alright."

"Feels like my fucking head is about to explode." He whispered, screwing his eyes shut. By his voice Marelle felt he was back in the room at least.

"It's shock. There's been a lot going on. They've obviously given you something to knock you out and for the pain. Just sit for a minute."

"What's the time?"

Marelle barely dare look at her watch.

"Twenty past eight." She said.

"We won't make it!" He gasped, looking up at her. "We won't make it!"

Marelle was in complete turmoil inside. Ever since the moment she had gone to him in the hallway it had been an alternating fear of not making it versus making it. Now the needle had settled. The time had gone. There was but a single choice.

"We could leave right now." She offered.

"We won't make it." He repeated, suddenly as lucid as he had ever been.

"We can try." She said. "It's probably just do-able. We can go straight from here?"

He stared at her, stared into her eyes with those big, brown childlike ones of his, just fraying around the edges of his massively dilated pupils. She heard him exhale calmly.

"Let's go then." He said.

She stood up, took his arm, bunched his shirt up beneath her arm.

"Just keep walking." She said as she pulled the curtain back and they stepped out of the cubicle together.

The nurse was returning as they turned the corner.

'Hey." She called. "You can't just leave – the doctor needs to see you …" She had a plastic cup of water in her hand. "It's not safe for you to leave just yet – you could be putting yourself in danger – if you wait, I will get the doctor to come and see you …"

"We're sorry but we've got to go." Jacob said.

"He'll be OK." Marelle added. "I'll look after him."

The nurse sighed in exasperation. "Can I not persuade you to stay – you really are taking a serious risk here …"

"No, thank you for everything but we need to go."

"If that starts bleeding again then get medical help straight away." She advised. "And be careful with the shoulder, it could easily pop out again."

"I'll be careful." Jacob said.

He urged forward, Marelle holding on to him. His steps were firm enough, but she could feel he was a little unsteady. She held him close and used her weight to keep him upright. They moved out through the reception area where they had entered. The outer doors opened slowly with a quiet his and they were out of the building. Marelle suddenly felt able to breathe again.

The night was clear, and moonlight washed the cars in the car park before them. It was cold and Marelle shivered, clutching his arm. Jacob was still bare chested.

"Do you want your shirt?" She asked as he walked beside her.

"No." He replied. "Let's just get to the car." There was a shiver in his voice. Walking more quickly beside her now, her arm in his, half naked, striding across the car park at night, looking every inch some kind of out of his mind, under the influence, lost soul. In the dark, cold, blue moonlit winter air Marelle looked to him. He looked fearfully like he had in her dream of him being on the slab in a mortuary which had haunted her then and still haunted her now. But instead of it being an apparition in her head, this time it was real, and he was alive, right in front of her, but that still didn't settle her mind.

By the time they reached the car they were virtually running. His teeth were chattering and he gave a little laugh as she opened the door for him.

"Home James.' He said with a grin that wasn't entirely his. Marelle chose to ignore. When she got in he was shaking his head with his eyes closed.

"What's wrong?" She asked, pausing for a moment before she turned the key in the ignition.

"Nothing." He answered. "Clearing the demons."

Marelle side-eyed him. Not sure whether it was a sensible comment from him or a fired off random one.

"Ready then?" She asked.

He nodded, staring blankly out of the windscreen.

Marelle drove to the car park exit and remembered the trouble she had experienced getting in. Jacob certainly didn't.

"Shit!" She said,

The whole road to her left was now closed. The only way out was to go right but she didn't want to go right. If she turned right, it would take her half an hour to get to the road she wanted to be on. It would add time to their journey that they didn't have. They wouldn't make it. Every minute, every second counted now. She hesitated, stopped at the junction, dithering, spending precious moments deciding what to do.

"I'll have to go right." She muttered. "Is there a quicker way?" She asked him.

"If you go right then double back through the housing estate you can get out on to Downham Road – that will take us to the A14 slip road at Worsley Village."

"You'll have to navigate." She said, swinging the wheel through her hands and moving the car to the right.

"Shall I drive?" He asked.

"No!" Marelle exclaimed. One thing she did not want was him driving; she was not sure how together his brain was right now and doubted he could safely drive a car. "Just tell me where to go."

He directed her right, then left, then right again along streets of gently curving residential properties, not dissimilar to where Bella lived. Marelle had never been here before and was surprised there were so many houses in an area which she had assumed to be open countryside behind the hospital. Jacob was humming to himself, interspersed with the odd single word of direction. It was odd but she didn't question it as it seemed to be working. Then, after taking a sharp left-handed turn they were confronted with the road being blocked by three wooden bollards with reflective markers on them that twinkled in her headlights. A sign beside them proclaimed 'New Road layout. No Through Road.'

"What the fuck?" Jacob exclaimed.

"How do we get through?" She asked, stopping the car and staring straight ahead as if it would make the bollards part, and the signs disappear.

"We can't." He said with a sigh. "Tt's a rat run. They've permanently closed it off. Turn around."

"We can't!" She moaned. "We've just spent ten minutes winding around here – it'll take us ten minutes to get back. Can't we squeeze through somehow ... we can't go back now! We won't ..."

"Stop!" He suddenly shouted. Just one word, very loud and very sharp.

Marelle stopped mid-sentence and stared at him. She probably had the same look on her face that she'd had on the day he'd told her to get off the airfield; the day he'd told her she talked too much and asked too many questions. That day seemed so long ago now yet remained so freshly with her. And those questions, they had led her here.

"Go home." He said.

"What?"

Go home ..."

"If we ..."

He interrupted. "Go home. I've got a better idea."

Marelle turned the car around in the narrow residential street.

"What idea?" she asked.

"Just go home." He replied in such a wildly calm voice that she didn't question it.

Adrenalin was already pouring into her bloodstream as she eventually accelerated until they were on the dual carriageway. She felt slightly jittery; like she'd drunk too much coffee without enough to eat. Unsure of Jacob's mood she didn't ask any further questions but halfway home he started singing quietly to himself. After the third repetition of the same words over and over Marelle glanced briefly at him. He had his eyes closed and sang the same words again in a hushed tone.

"Still the moon rose and the news at ten said never again but I can't move you out of my heart ..."

She recognised the words and sought for their place in her head. Finally, she realised they were the first line to one of the songs Chas had told him he would be singing tonight. Marelle turned her head back to the road and put her foot down harder. She drove as Jacob sang softly on.

Marelle no longer knew what was going on. They were only a couple of minutes from home and just over an hour from when he was due walk on stage at the venue. She was unsure what was going to happen, what his plan was or even if he still had any kind of grip on reality. Turning into the main street of the village in the darkness of the early winter evening, the street was eerily quiet and empty, silent and still beneath a blue moon. Arriving home, she turned into the drive, now bounded by the two tall, curved walls, wondering what plan he had in his head to transport them that distance at warp speed. It was just over an hour until the exact time Chas had told him to be there waiting, ready to lay the rest of his entire life unashamedly in front of a crowd and the rest of the band which would lead him to slaughter or salvation. Marelle knew not which but as she pulled the car up closer to the house her eyes settled on it.

Her heart skipped a beat, and she suddenly feared she knew exactly what Jacob was thinking.

He stirred as the car stopped, opening his eyes, ceasing the repetitive chanting and instantly animated to get out. Marelle looked to him then to the shiny blue motorcycle still parked at the end of the driveway.

"Keys?" He demanded, leaning back in.

She stared at the bike but handed them to him across the car.

"No Jacob!" She suddenly shouted, getting out of the car herself and following him up towards the front door as he discarded the sling.

"I'm just going to get on the bike and go." He announced. "I should just about make it."

"No!" She placed her hands on him, his skin still bare. He felt hot. "No, you can't."

"I'll just grab my helmet and jacket." He told her, going through the front door stepping around the glass from the smashed window, neither of them turning an eye to the blood spattered across the wall.

"You can't!"

"I can. Or I'll die trying." He muttered, running ahead and up the stairs. "Follow me in the car."

"How can I? You'll be gone. Go in the car. I'll drive really fast; the roads will be quiet."

"We won't make it." He replied calmly as she followed him into the bedroom. "Anyway.' He added. "Your car is nearly out of fuel. You would have to stop and fill up. There's no time. I'll go ahead. You follow."

He had taken his shirt from her which she was absent mindedly still carrying. He put it on. There was blood very prominently up the front of it. He quickly did two buttons up as he turned to grab his leather jacket draped over the back of a chair.

"Jacob you can't. What about your arm, does it still hurt?"

"Nothing hurts at the moment." He said quietly, slipping into the leather coat.

"Take me on the back." She pleaded.

"No." He stated, picking up the snake's head helmet. "I can't go so fast with you on the back."

Marelle sighed. "Please!"

"I don't have another helmet – or a leather jacket. I'm not putting you in danger like that."

"Jacob." She cried. "Please! I can wear your black helmet."

"It's scuffed; it's damaged."

"It's better than nothing." She explained.

"It's too dangerous." He said. "I just need to get there."

She raised her eyes to him. For a second, she paused in the mania, his eyes met hers and he could see her thoughts.

"Above me?" They implored.

His eyes did not answer her – she feared she did not want them to as she worried what their reply might be.

"The whole point of everything we have ever done together is pointing right to this. The compass is only showing one direction." She said. "Take me with you. I'd rather die with you than be left here, alone." This time she voiced it; many times, she had thought it.

He tutted. "Get the black helmet then – and put a couple of coats on you'll be cold."

Jacob was outside ready when she ran out to him. She had put two padded coats on and gloves.

He turned to her.

"This is a much bigger, faster bike than the other one. Hold on to me at all times. When I accelerate you will be pushed back – be aware there's nothing to stop you flying off the back – except me. When I brake you will be thrown forwards. If you need to keep one hand on me and one on the tank in front of me to brace yourself. Then do so. Lean down with me, mirror my movements, keep everything in and tight." He said quickly. "Now put the helmet on.

Not totally sure of how to do that she squeezed her head into it. It smelled strange and deadened her senses. He reached over and did it up, turning her to face him.

"Just make yourself part of me – and don't scream."

She nodded as he turned and put the snake's head helmet on. Turning back, he looked briefly at her – a look in his deep brown eyes that was almost apologetic. As he turned back to the bike he staggered and looked slightly unbalanced, steadying himself with one hand against the house wall. He shook his head then climbed astride the bike, a little more awkwardly than she had seen him manage it before. He nodded to her to climb aboard behind him. Marelle took a breath, steeled herself and cocked a leg over. Somehow it fitted around her quite comfortably and she wrapped her arms around him, her head close to his back. Even before the engine growled into life, she could feel him trembling beneath her hands. Then his stomach muscles tensed, and he was off.

The noise, the speed and the sheer vulnerability of it hit her in one rush of anxiety and she gripped him harder. He was going too fast, braking too little, too late and throwing the bike about with little care for anything except the ground he was covering. Marelle closed her eyes and lowered her head against him, preparing herself both physically and mentally for the moment that symbiosis of balance and speed broke down. She felt he was pushing every second to the absolute edge of sanity and when she didn't think it could possibly get any worse, he hit the dual carriageway and accelerated.

There was a constant scream in her throat, but she pushed it down each time it rose. Her eyes were closed tightly, her arms stifling him, as close to his body as she could get – as close as she had ever been – becoming one as he had said. It was unnerving in the dark with no control or communication – travelling at a speed she doubted she had ever travelled at before so close to the ground – pushing herself against him as she feared the acceleration and wind rushing past them would tear her from the bike. Her fist gripped at a handhold of leather at his chest, squeezing her knees in and lowering her head – it was a relentless head-down, onward charge south into the night. The clear parts of the road were opportunities for Jacob to push the bike even harder, faster and she felt the power of the machine fill every one of her senses.

The approached a large multi-lane roundabout. With four lanes going into three, she felt the boke brake and Jacob sit up slightly as they folded into the traffic. Marelle could feel the latent urgency in the bike as it burbled; she could feel the crouched anticipation withheld as he waited behind the cars. Ahead the road opened up to its full three lane width again but Jacob immediately started to accelerate before there was space, coming too close to a yellow car in front, flexing the bike to miss the bumper by microns, weaving to the left, to the right between cars where there was barely room to pass but he slid through, skimmed left, leaned right, passed the final white four wheel drive then crouched low with her against his back and she felt the bike take hold and lunge forward like an animal to rip up the unlit road ahead. With her hands against him he felt what she could only think was a ripple of fear pass through him until she realised he was laughing.

Marelle was not laughing. She was wishing for this to end, to be there, at the venue, and not to die tonight. Death crossed her mind many times – wondering if she would feel pain, wondering if it would be constant darkness or rebellious light. She concluded she did not fear death itself if it was quick – although at this moment she wanted much more life – she was too young to die – but the feared living life half dead. So she prayed; if they didn't make it then it was to be the end.

She closed her eyes, immersed herself in the sensory pool of darkness, cold and speed. She blocked out everything except the feel of his body in her arms. '*I will go to my death with my eyes closed and my head down*' she thought to herself.

The journey seemed endless. Her mind kept thinking that they must nearly be there; she dare not move a hand to look at her watch but it seemed like forever since they had stood in their driveway at home. Jacob just kept accelerating, ripping through the night with little consideration for speed limits or other road users. Normally he was calm and unflinching when he drove; tonight, he was rampantly belligerent with all around him on the tarmac.

An hour so ago he had been in a hospital bed, confined, being abusive to a nurse – now he had her life in his hands at a million miles an hour. If he spoke, she could not her him and if she said anything he would not hear her. They just travelled.

With her eyes closed and her heart beating violently along with Jacob's, she allowed her mind to flip-flop between being nearly there and having only been travelling for a short time that felt like an eternity. She didn't know. Marelle didn't know where they were, where they were going or how far away it was. She just had to trust Jacob and that was one thing she had never had a problem with. If her life needed to be in anyone's hands, then it was his she would have chosen. She had trusted him throughout – to trust her; to always come back to her – and he always had.

And suddenly she felt the bike veer left, Marelle opened her eyes and realised they were descending a slip road. She felt him brake, pushing her into him. She wanted to release a hand to steady herself but she daren't. Jacob was braking harder now as the white lines approached; she felt the back of the bike shimmy slightly, feel loose. She shifted, which didn't seem to help, pushed her knees into the back of his legs. The bike wobbled; he slowed and balanced it. Marelle gripped him. At the give way markings he stopped, put a foot down and turned to her.

She thought he asked if she was OK. Marelle was not sure, but she nodded. With that he kicked off and floored the bike once more along a more urban looking street. There were streetlights and the road led into civilisation and the outskirts of a town, a city. Jacob had slowed but was still going faster than he should have been. She sat up slightly with him, feeling every muscle in him twitch and move. He had been alone on this bike as long as she had been alone on the back of it, with only the road and the night for company her mind had wandered; she wondered what his had boundered to.

Suddenly overwhelmed by the situation she found herself in, the time, and the fear that they were going to be too late she tightened her arms around him and lay her head against his back. They came to a junction, a large roundabout. He looked right then accelerated smoothly away into a built-up area. There was now more traffic around them, bright car headlights and Illuminated signs on commercial properties. People on the pavements, pubs open without people outside, fast-food takeaways. There were sandy coloured stone buildings – grand edifices from centuries ago. Jacob turned left sharply down a narrow street of back entrances to shops, past a chain link fenced off area to the back of a grey concrete building with a small car park behind. The space was crammed with cars and vans, haphazardly parked like a jigsaw puzzle. He stopped the bike.

Jacob hopped off quickly, just catching her as he swung his leg over. He nodded to her to follow.

Jacob took an unsteady, giddy step sideways then he turned, and he was gone – between the cars, squeezing sideways, removing his helmet and leather jacket as he went.

Marelle trotted behind him. She was struggling to undo the helmet but finally freed herself and took it off. Sound flooded in and she could hear a band playing and people shouting as Jacob headed towards a grey door. He reached it and pulled it open. Pale yellow light flooded out and Marelle could hear Yellow Son playing. Jacob was a silhouette in the doorway, helmet and jacket in hand, a security guard in front of him.

"Do you have a security pass Sir?" The guy asked Jacob. Without hesitation Jacob turned slightly and showed him the laminated AAA pass he had tied to the belt loop of his jeans. Marelle gasped to herself and wondered for a split second where hers was then she remembered it was on a lanyard, around her neck, where Jacob had placed it before they left with the words *'you won't get in without that.'*

She fished it out from beneath her two coats, swinging it towards the security guard. He took it in his hand, studied it in his fat fingers and nodded to her to go in behind Jacob.

Jacob was running along a passageway to the right in semi darkness. She heard the band stop playing and the crowd start cheering and shouting. Were they too late– she hadn't looked at the time – had they got here just as it ended after all of that effort, all that pain and anxiety?

In front of her Jacob suddenly crashed into the left-hand wall, he corrected himself, stepped to the right, staggered and had to put a hand on the wall to steady himself. Marelle got to him and reached out a hand to him, but he rolled off the wall and continued.

There was a buzz, voices, laughter and the crowd in the venue cheering and stamping their feet. Jacob stepped around a left-hand blind corner and there was Mya.

FORTY-SEVEN

Mya stood at the back of the stage watching the band come off in a huddle. She turned towards them and stepped forward; one hand extended to them.

"Oh my. Where have you been?" She gasped, her hand going to Jacob's shoulder. "They had a power failure at the start, they're running a few minutes late – luckily." She looked up to Jacob, he was looking over her head. At the very end of the corridor were Chas, Marty, Jem and Luc – chatting. Waiting, just out of the line of sight, to return onto the stage for the encore. Mya kept her hand on Jacob, keeping him back enough to prevent them seeing him in the shadows. He was staring towards them, transfixed, head high and proud but a ragged look in his eyes and a sad solemness to his mouth. He swallowed.

"Are you OK?" Mya asked.

He nodded, running his fingers through his hair after wearing the helmet. It wasn't perfect but it was ok.

Suddenly he turned back to Marelle, clutching his helmet and jacket to himself he fished in a pocket and held money out to her.

"Go to Merch and get me a white t-shirt extra large." He said.

"What?" her mind was switched half off at her behest. She had not fully engaged it yet.

"A white Yellow Son T-shirt – extra-large – I've got blood all over this one ..." He said.

Mya stared at him then at Marelle.

'That way." He pointed then turned his eyes to Mya.

"What happened?' She asked, clutching at him.

"Long story." He answered.

The noise from the crowd rose, filled the space around them as one-by-one the band returned to the stage, Chas last of all.

Jacob moved forward, placed his jacket and helmet down on the floor. Mya had a hand on his arm.

"Are you ready Ez?" She asked, looking up and smiling at him.

He looked straight ahead and nodded.

Out on stage they heard Chas over the quelling crowd.

"OK. OK." He announced. "You knew we'd come back – but ..." He paused with the crowd right in the palm of his hand. "But, you know, I'm tired of singing tonight. Let's make it a bit different for the last couple of songs. As you know this is our last gig for this tour and this year and I'm done now. I'm tired so I've asked someone else to come along and sing on these last two songs ...let's see how it goes." He started playing the intro and as he predicted everyone else joined in, just as they normally would,. Mya eased Jacob forwards, her hand in his back.

"Go on." She said. "That's your cue."

He paused, raised a finger, counted into the music, waited for the exact moment then turned away from Mya and walked briskly onto the back of the stage.

Marelle came running up just as he disappeared, still clutching the black helmet and now a brand new, neatly folded white Yellow Son t-shirt.

"Where is he?" She gasped.

Mya nodded towards the back of the stage as lights danced and just touched their faces at that end of the corridor. The music was building, and the crowd suddenly let out an enormous roar.

'The moon still rose and the news at ten said never again but I can't move you out of my heart ..."

She heard the words he'd whispered in the car bellow out across the auditorium. It was undoubtedly his voice but how strong and how beautifully clear it sounded.

She stood there, transfixed, t-shirt in hand, breathing in gasps.

Mya took the helmet from her and placed it on the floor next to Jacob's then did likewise with the t-shirt.

"Come on, let's go and watch at the front. I want to see this ..." Her hand grabbed at Marelle's and drew her along. The noise got louder. Jacob's voice got louder. The screaming of the crowd intensified as she went down a passageway and through some black curtains at the end to find themselves in a small cordoned off area right in front of the stage. The wild crowd was behind the barrier on one side and the stage on the other.

Marelle looked up. Picked out by a spotlight standing where Chas would normally be, was Jacob. Lit up like a beacon himself, light playing around him as he leaned into the microphone. He looked so different, so relaxed, so perfect.

"He's as high as a kite." Marelle murmured, not really to anyone but Mya snapped her head round.

"What?"

"He's as high as a kite." Marelle repeated. "A short while ago he was in hospital, he fell down the stairs while he was getting ready ..."

Mya placed a hand on her arm. "Tell me after, I can't hear you sweetie ..." She smiled.

Marelle grinned and nodded. Mya pointed up to Jacob and smiled to her. Marelle turned her head back and looked up to him.

Animated, alive, rippling with energy and on the edge of leaving his skin Jacob suddenly had the whole place right in his hand. Hanging off his every breath he took, pulsing with every beat of his heart every single person in this place was solely captivated by his presence. Whether they had known Ezza, loved Ezza, mourned Ezza or never even known his story or the fact that he had ever existed, were in complete awe of the figure who had walked onto the stage a moment ago and now moulded the atmosphere purely around him.

Marelle had never seen him truly perform – she had never experienced the static charisma he really did possess when he got up there. Yes, she had seen the pictures and the videos, but you did not understand it's power until you saw it, and felt it, right in front of you. Chas had said "He's a God on stage." And bloody hell, he was!

Mya was watching the crowd watching him. Marelle looked along the front row. There was a unanimous chorus of the lyrics, people were singing, jumping up and down, hands in the air, moving with the music and the energy. A single entity awakened by the reincarnation of a sleeping hero. Her attention moved to one particular guy a few feet away from her. Probably Chas' age, wearing a Yellow Son t-shirt, hanging over the barrier as far as he could – arms outstretched as he sang the lyrics with tears streaming down his face.

And suddenly the emotion and the energy in the whole building touched her. It stared her in the face at first then dived deep into her chest and wrapped fingers around her beating heart, squeezing it just enough to hurt as they seamlessly moved on to the second track of the encore.

Marelle stared up at Jacob. He was in full flow – something finally released to fly free. It was the same man she had been captured by – that quite, vulnerable innocence no more; this was the same man she had slept with last night and would climb into bed with again tonight. The same heart, same blood and muscle – but tonight she knew it would not be Jacob she lay down next to; tonight, it would be Ezza, or Nat. The only Jacob that remained was the body of his dead brother in the police morgue.

Halfway through the second song there was a part where Jacob sang out a *'woh-ho'* – drawn out into a cry. She had heard it many times and would have confessed this was probably one of her favourite songs to hear him sing. He had sung it at the studio with Chas but tonight, when he took a breath and sang that it was the clearest and loudest, she had ever heard. A chill rippled down her backbone as that sound echoed around the place – like the final vestige of Jacob leaving his body – proclaiming he was back and leaving an indelible mark on everyone.

It was beautiful but chilling; it was sanctity but terrifying. Her eyes filled with tears as she looked up at him – at what she had lost, but what she had gained.

Mya gripped her arm from her side and gave a little jump in sheer excitement. Marelle turned her head and looked at Mya, there were tears glistening in her eyes as she stared at Jacob.

He interacted with Chas on stage like he had never been away, he grinned at the other guys in the band, and they grinned back and made little gestures like they had been expecting him to be there all along. They were all professionals; they all knew how to act and how to make it look like sheer perfection itself but Marelle could sense there would be a lot of words afterwards. Chas was laughing, nodding to himself, being far more animated than he usually was when he had to sing himself. The whole stage presence had suddenly become effervescently dynamic; somehow like there was a loose stick of fizzing dynamite rolling around on stage amongst them. Marelle smiled but sincerely hoped it didn't explode.

They were coming to the end of the second song that Jacob had been instructed he would be singing. The end of his resurgent fifteen minutes of fame in the spotlight and he had certainly burned the brightest he ever could right here, right now in front of her. The band played out the final few bars, Chas came up to centre stage with him and took the lead in the outro with lead guitar as Jacob stepped back very slightly ready to take a bow and say thank you.

Chas however, played the final note of that song but immediately launched into an intro she was very familiar with and so were they crowd. They had already played this track in their set earlier; it was their most famous and most rousing one. Chas had said two tracks, two tracks only and the ones he had specified and grilled Jacob about so many times – now he grinned, turned to the rest of the band who instantly understood him and fell into the track again in full flow. Chas turned to Jacob and for a split second they looked at each other, then Chas nodded as if to say 'go ahead' and Jacob did.

"Shit!" Mya said beside Marelle. "They are going to go over time."

Marelle looked at her but didn't understand what she meant. She suddenly seemed a little edgy, staring at Chas.

There was no edginess on stage, just enthusiastic performance as Jacob strode the area, one side to the other, leaning down to be closer to the crowd at one point dropping to his knees as he was pictured in so many of the images on line and holding a hand out to the crowd in front of him as each and every one of them looked only at him. He replaced the microphone in the stand, stood there while the band played around him and with eyes as full as the atmosphere in this place he looked out to the crowd and took it all in by the bucketful.

Marelle looked up to him. She could see his chest heaving, the shirt looked wet and clingy, he hung on to the mic stand not this time in sheer terror and confusion but this time to steady himself and his heart as it filled with pride and emotion at being here. The front of the shirt was blood spattered a lot more than she had originally realised and it, being screwed up either in the hospital or in her hands did not look the best but she doubted tonight anyone would mind. With her eyes raised to him she suddenly felt the distance and the journey she had travelled with him, this felt like a culmination, and end.

Where would he go now?

Her eyes misted a little, but his voice cut through in the final verse of the song. She watched, felt Mya breathing close beside her. This track had an abrupt end, little outro, it finished on the last word and with that crescendo it stopped. Jacob bowed his head and held up his right arm, half in acknowledgement to the crowd, half as a wave. Chas played the last note with absolute aplomb and intensity but already the other guys were holding up their instruments or throwing drumsticks into the crowd. Jacob leaned forward, went to say something into the mic but Chas came between him and it, nodding for him to step away. Chas waved nodded, raised his hand too but at the same time turned Jacob and ushered him off stage quickly.

The crowd roared, cheered, knew it was the end this time and released themselves from the barrier, relaxing, moving away. Marelle stood staring at them as already the crew were running onto the stage. The cheers turned into a buzz, people laughing, talking about what they had just seen as they began to move away.

Mya tapped her arm. She nodded her head for Marelle to go with her, Marelle hesitated, looking at the stage, at the crowd, feeling the emptiness now they had left. She shivered but still had two coats on. She turned to follow Mya but was alerted to someone yelling at her from the barrier.

"Hey! Hey!" A woman called to her, leaning over the barrier, her long auburn hair swinging as she did so. By her side was another female, blonde spiky hair, wearing a Yellow Son t-shirt. "Can you get me the set list?' The woman continued shouting, pointing to the front, waving her hand frantically between Marelle and the edge of the stage. Marelle looked to her then to the stage.

She gestured again.

Marelle looked to the curtain where Mya had exited then stepped forward to the two women.

"Pardon?" She asked.

The woman was leaning right over the barrier, Marelle wondered if her feet were actually touching the floor.

"Can you get me the set list?" She asked again in an accent Marelle wasn't sure of, but nonetheless she understood. "Like that?" She pointed to the other end of the stage where one of the crew was handing a piece of paper that had been stuck to the floor of the stage to someone else hanging over the barrier. "Please!!" she pleaded.

Marelle turned her head towards the stage, it was just below her head high, but she could see the sheet of white A4 taped with black tape at the corners, just in front of her. She didn't know if she should give it to them, or if she would get into trouble for doing so but the woman was pleading with her constantly so she stepped forward, reached into the surface where Jacob had been standing moments before and peeled it away from the dusty wooden surface. Holding it in front of her she stepped back to the woman and passed it to her.

She smiled broadly as she took it. "Thank you!" She grinned. "Thank you so much. Weren't they just bloody bleezin!!"

Marelle smiled. It was language she didn't understand but the two of them seemed ecstatically hap;ıy at being there, at having seen the performance and at having the sheet of paper given to them.

"It's OK." She said, not truly knowing if it was.

"Is he permanent?" The woman asked. "He needs to be!"

Marelle laughed slightly. "I don't know." She said with a smile that almost, almost broke as she thought of the idea.

"Just bloody bleezin'!" The woman said again. Marelle smiled and nodded, turning away and looking towards the black curtain where Mya had left. She strode forwards with an outstretched hand and pushed it aside, she could still hear them laughing and squealing behind her.

It was dark behind the curtain, and she had to orientate herself for a moment or two, one hand against the cold wall, then progressing forwards, along the corridor Mya had led her down a short while ago.

At the end it opened up to the backstage area and the corridor leading away that they had entered by. It was chaos.

Mya stood at the end, looking at the mêlée ensuing before her. All members of the band where crowded together against the wall. She could see Chas with a hand extended holding one of the guys away from him and subsequently Jacob who was cornered against the back wall by the other members. Everyone was shouting or pointing and speaking at once. Jacob being taller than most of them was visible in the middle of the huddle – at least he was laughing, speaking, shouting trying to answer a million questions at once.

Marelle walked up to Mya.

Chas was mediating with arms outstretched, one hand trying to push Jacob away and along the corridor.

"Get in there!" He nodded, pushing him along then putting himself between that door and the rest of the band.

"I'll talk to you all tomorrow." Chas was saying." Keep your fucking hats on, nothing changes ... go home." He gestured but they kept crowding in on him, Jacob was still hovering behind Chas, smiling, standing in the corridor, stepping backwards slightly, saying something and running his hand through his hair. He looked so tall and thin in here, silhouetted slightly in the pale-yellow light.

"Tomorrow!" Chas shouted at them, half turning and pushing Jacob towards a doorway just behind them. "Go!" He turned fully to Jacob and ordered.

Jacob grinned, laughed, staggered a little at Chas' slight push but moving backwards as Chas turned his back on the rest of Yellow Son and opening the door for Jacob.

The three of them stood for a second looking at each other in confusion,

"What the fuck?" The one she remembered as being the drummer said as they all looked towards Mya and suddenly realised, she was there too. They advanced, all talking at once again.

Mya raised her hands flat to them. "It's OK!" She reassured.

"Who the fuck was that? Is that who I think it is?" One asked, half drowned out by another joining in. "Why? He can't just do that – we should have known ... makes us look pretty stupid!" They continued to fire questions and explanations at Mya as she responded back by shouting over them and shaking her head.

"I don't know." She stated to them, smiling and raising her hand. "Chas said he will speak to you all tomorrow so he will speak to you all tomorrow. There's nothing to get excited about ..."

She grabbed Marelle's hand as they did not relent and dragged her through the middle of them in the direction Chas had pushed Jacob.

"Fucks sake!" Marelle heard as she ducked her head and passed through.

Mya dragged her to the door, turned the handle but it was locked. She knocked. "Chas, it's me!"

Seconds later Marelle heard a bolt sliding across, Mya turned the handle and this time the door opened inwards. She pulled Marelle behind her, entered the room and closed the door.

FORTY-EIGHT

Jacob laughed. He had a bottle of water and chugged it down in one go, tossing the empty bottle into a bin at the far side. It was a hole in one as it landed in the bin precisely. He cheered and congratulated himself childishly for the act.

"Yes, you were fucking excellent!" Chas said to him, sitting himself down on a plastic chair. "If I'm honest I thought you'd fuck it up one way or another!"

"Me. Fuck it up?" Jacob laughed.

Mya walked across the room towards him, Marelle hovered, feeling strangely distant.

"Is that blood?" Mya asked, picking up the bottom of his shirt and holding it out to make a show of it.

"Blood, sweat and tears!" Jacob smiled.

"What have you been doing?" Chas asked.

"Nothing!" He laughed, letting himself fall back to lean against the wall.

"Calm it matey." Chas commented.

Jacob held out a hand, flat in front of Chas. It was trembling.

"Sit down" Chas said.

"Can't!" Jacob laughed, picking up another bottle of water.

"Sit down, save your energy. You're going to need it to sort all of this shit out!"

"Ezza is back!" He proclaimed before raising the bottle to his lips and drinking half of it.

No-one either confirmed or denied that statement.

Mya was staring at him.

"What have you taken Ezza?"

"Nothing!" He scoffed at her. "I'm high on that. That's all."

Mya sighed.

Jacob looked across and caught Marelle's eye, finally. For a moment he calmed, he gave her a small smile and a smouldering stare – evidencing he was still in there, among the fog of excitement whirling around him.

"You got that t-shirt?" He questioned.

"It's out there, with your jacket and the helmets." She replied. "Shall I go and get it?"

He nodded, drinking some more of the water then standing up from the wall and walking over towards Chas. He began unbuttoning the shirt paced back with it flapping.

"I'll go and get it." Marelle said, quietly, turning to the door.

"No!" Mya suddenly exclaimed. "I'll go. You'll get eaten alive out there…" And she exited through the door.

Jacob shrugged his shoulders rolled his neck. "Fuck." He said then grinned.

Marelle stared at him. This was not Jacob; this was not Nat nor Ezza. This was some weird, mouthy, apparition riding on the back of whatever they had pumped into him at the hospital and the sheer exhilaration of the three songs he had just delivered out there. Some weird cocktail had produced some weird creature. At least she hoped that was the case.

"You are fucking wired man." Chas moaned, still sitting down. "What the fuck are you on? I'm not tolerant of any of that shit. You *know* that."

"Never were, were you?" Jacob uttered. "I'm drinking water you dickhead!" It came out quite aggressively.

Chas sat upright, turned to him with a pointed finger.

"I did you a fucking favour. Don't start being an arsehole!"

Jacob smirked at Chas but didn't answer back.

Marelle looked between Chas and Jacob. She felt tension, nothing serious but a bit of disappointment in Chas at Jacob's attitude. He was flouting devil horns, and she wanted to explain.

At that point Mya returned with the t-shirt, both helmets and Jacob's leather jacket.

"Quiet?" Chas asked, picking up a bottle of beer.

Mya nodded. "Quite enough." She placed all of the stuff on a table. "You two came on that bike then?" She asked.

"Yes!" Marelle said quickly. "It was a bit of a dash wasn't it, Jacob?"

"Why do you fucking well call him Jacob?" Chas asked, shaking his head.

Marelle stared at him, she felt reprimanded. Chas didn't know. Chas had not been around for the past twelve years.

"Because that's what she calls him!" Mya interjected. "I call you a few names that aren't your given ones sometimes!" She turned to Marelle. "What were you saying? You said something to me out there about hospital?"

Marelle nodded. She raised her eyes to Jacob. "Do you want to tell them?" She asked him.

He gave a little flick of his hand as if to tell her to go ahead.

She sighed. He stared at her. No doubt he would add to it as soon as she started.

"He's been in hospital; he fell down the stairs a few hours before we needed to leave and smashed his arm through the half glazed front door. It wouldn't stop bleeding... and he had dislocated his shoulder ..." She told them as he stared at her like a sullen teenager with his chin dropped and eyes raised. "They wanted to keep him in, but we walked out – the bike was the only way to get here in time. He's had a lot of medication ..."

"So who rode the bike?" Mya questioned.

Marelle looked to him and raised her eyebrows. "I don't have a bike licence."

"Jesus!" Chas exclaimed.

Jacob laughed, a childish giggle. "We made it." He said, standing the half empty bottle of water down and slipping out of the sweaty, bloodstained shirt. He screwed it up into a ball and laid it on a chair. Walked over to the table and picked up the Yellow Son t-shirt. He lifted it by one corner and shook it out from it's neat folds.

Marelle smiled at him, admired him.

Chas was staring at him. Mya was too, she swallowed. He put his head through the neck of the t-shirt; his dark, stiff, spiky hair popping through first then he pulled it down. It was too big, made him look even thinner.

"Nice." He said. "I can go out and meet my fans now."

"You are not going anywhere." Chas remarked

"Is that where you cut your arm?" Mya nodded to the bandage that was, surprisingly still in place and still clean, now visible with the short sleeves of the t-shirt.

Jacob looked at it as if he'd not noticed it before.

"Yes." Marelle replied. "It was that shoulder he dislocated too ..."

"Aren't you in pain." Mya questioned.

"No!" He exclaimed as if it was a stupid question. 'They did a remarkable job."

"They did." Marelle agreed. "But we left when they wanted you to stay ... you might have to go back. I don't think I dare take that bandage off ..."

Mya looked at Chas. She sighed.

"So how are you getting home?" She asked.

"Same way." Jacob replied. "Pass me a Bud ..."

Chas shook his head.

"Mya, book them into a hotel somewhere near here ..." He said.

She sighed and took out her phone.

"I can ride home ... it's quicker." Jacob explained.

"No, you can't sweetie. It's freezing out there tonight ... and you are going to be tired!" Mya said. "I'll find somewhere ..."

"I'm not tired. I'm ready for anything!" Jacob stated. "I'm still buzzing – get me on the bike and I'll get home in no time." He grinned.

Marelle looked sideways at him Her eyes were wide. Mya looked at her then back down at her phone. 'They're all fully booked." She sighed. 'There's a golf spa place about forty-five minutes away – it has rooms as they're so bloody expensive!"

"Don't put him anywhere where they've got a Jacuzzi – you know what happened last time – and especially in the state he's in."

Marelle wanted to know more. She daren't ask.

"I can't bloody believe you came down here with no plans for staying or getting home!" Chas commented.

"The plan was to drive down earlier then I would drive home. Because of what happened we ran out of time ... the important thing was to get here ..." Marelle explained

"I knew you would fuck it up." Chas said, shaking his head and drinking from the bottle.

"I didn't fuck it up." Jacob added.

"Get them a cab." Chas suggested.

"Give me half an hour and I'll ride home." Jacob replied, finally sitting himself down on a chair opposite Chas. He sat with his knees apart and his elbows resting on them. He looked jittery and was wobbling one leg up and down.

"You're not riding that thing home tonight!" Chas warned. "I've got a degree of responsibility in this, and I don't want my name being associated with you killing yourself – again!"

Jacob gave a little chuckle.

"Shall I call a cab?" Mya questioned.

"No. I can't." Jacob turned to her. "I'm not leaving the bike here." He sounded the most lucid he had for hours, and Marelle hoped it was wearing off. Then he laughed. "Take me to the fucking cleaners!" And she supposed it wasn't.

Mya looked at Jacob, then turned to Chas. She was thinking before she spoke.

"We could drive them home." She suggested.

"I live bloody twenty minutes away – it's a two-hour drive!" Chas exclaimed.

"It would be the safest ... in the circumstances ..." Mya replied.

"And then drive back? What bloody time do you think that would be woman? Hey? I've just been on stage for two hours, I'm not a bloody kid anymore!" Chas said to her – there was no anger in it. Marelle sensed it was the way they conversed most of the time and somehow, there was affection in it.

"Or they could come back to ours?" Mya said quietly.

Chas sighed, shook his head. "Bloody hell. See what I mean. I shouldn't even be having this conversation. Let him back in and suddenly I'm his surrogate fucking father ... what bloody state is he going to be in to drive that thing back tomorrow? Hey? For fuck's sake – here we bloody go again. Drive him home then – you'll have to drive ..." He said to Mya.

"You've only had half a bottle." She nodded to it.

"Because I'm fucking knackered!" He said loudly.

"You can stay at ours for the night." Marelle offered.

"We can stay in the van." Mya smiled. "We often do, it's not a problem. I'll just need to send a message to Susan to tell her she will need to keep Chip a bit longer ..."

She got up and walked past Chas, looking down at him with a knowing glance. "We had planned to go that way anyway ..." She raised an eyebrow to him.

He sighed and stared back at her with a look that was both knowing and daring her to continue. She didn't.

Jacob had gone quiet. Marelle looked to him. He was staring into space, a blank expression on his face.

"What about the bike?" She asked.

"What?" He said, as if he had not been in the room for the last ten minutes of conversation.

"The bike. If Mya drives us home, we will still have to come back and get the bike." Marelle told him.

He sighed, shook his head quickly as if to wake himself up. Then stood up. "It's ok. You go with them; I'll ride back behind you ..."

"What the point of that!?" Chas exclaimed. "You – are a fucking liability!"

"No, you're not riding the bike tonight." Marelle told him. Can't we put in inside here?" She looked to Chas as if he would know.

"I'm OK!" Jacob laughed.

'Then I'll come on the back with you ..." Marelle added.

"Stop!" Chas shouted. "Put the fucking bike in the back of the van – will it fit in? I don't know ... Mya go and have a look outside to see if the lads have gone home ..." Chas stood up, started collecting things together. "You know for the past twelve years I've not missed wiping your arse and doing your shoelaces up ... not one bit!" He warned. "Looks like I'm going to have to start getting used to it all over again ..." He swore under his breath and brushed past Jacob who was standing there with one arm slid into his leather jacket. Marelle saw a ripple of laughter just play on his lips.

The bike just fitted in. Chas was not happy with it being in there and even less happy after the struggle it took to get it in. A security guard assisted, Jacob instructed, loosely and Chas did a lot of swearing.

The journey home was much slower than the one there and Marelle felt grateful for being in the front of the van instead of on the back of the bike. She wasn't sure if they would have made it home alive. At least on the way down Jacob had been wide awake. Now he was fading fast, told by Chas to go in the seat behind and perpendicular to the driver's seat. Ten minutes into the journey he was fast asleep.

"Is he OK?" Mya questioned; aware he had gone quiet.

"Yes! Don't bloody well wake him up!" Chas stated, in the middle seat in the front. Marelle turned her head to look at Jacob. The figure in the seat was relaxed, tall and lean with his legs out before him, head on a cushion, peaceful. He was Jacob again in all but name. She smiled.

The cold light of day was an hour or so away when Marelle woke in their bed, at home, and felt a cold space beside her. She reached out a hand, then a foot, searching for him in the empty bed util her foot reached the far edge. She sat up with a gasp in the darkness.

"Jacob!" She asked, into the silence.

Suddenly her heart was racing, accelerating so fast it robbed her of breath and her lungs felt like a vacuum. It was that night again; that night when she had woken to find him gone. Panic grabbed at her, drilled into her knees in its dull, painful way and loosened them as she stood up, heading for the door which was closed. Why was the door closed?

"Fucking hell!" She cried to herself as she ripped it open and stood out on the landing.

A noise from downstairs grabbed her attention, familiar enough but drumming fear into her with the sound of it now. She heard the back door click and open.

She started down the stairs, forgetting what had happened yesterday but remembering on the last step that Chas and Mya were here, in the spare bedroom ... and that there was still a hole in the glass of the front door. She swung around the stairwell, heading along the hall to the kitchen.

"Jacob!" She called, breathing hard with panic terrorising any breath she tried to take. It had been second, he couldn't have got far by now, she could catch him, she could grab him, barefoot in the back garden.

The back door was open, and he stood there in it's aperture. The night was cold and frosty – on the way home the air had been sharp and the grass white with haw frost and now she could feel the cold air penetrating the house like a cold damp blanket gently alighting over them.

"Jacob." She said. "What are you doing?"

"I couldn't sleep." He answered. "I couldn't think straight ..."

She walked up to him. He still had the Yellow Son t-shirt on. She wrapped herself around him from behind.

"It's cold." She said.

"Dawn is an hour or so away." He replied, looking out into the night, along the path he now owned, past the caravan he had lived in to the airfield which had been his world. "When the sun comes up it will be a new day. I wanted to see the sun rise because today ... today ..." He paused. He sounded so unsure, as unsure as he had been when she had first known him. "Today I am Nathaniel Ezekiel Frost. The person I was born as, and I can't go back on that now."

She laid her head against his back.

"I'm scared." He said.

"What of?" She asked, speaking against his back, feeling his warmth radiating through the t-shirt, smelling him.

He paused. Shrugged limply.

"Was I OK?" He asked with a tentative edge to his voice.

She squeezed him, her arms around his middle. He felt cold at the front, warm at the back with the cold air creeping into the house. "You were amazing!" She grinned.

"Was I?"

"You know you were!" She laughed.

"No, I don't." He sighed. "It's a mess of images in my head. I can't remember much of it. I don't even know if I really did it! There are catches of memories but I'm not sure if they were from last night or years ago ..."

She hugged him. That was odd. But well, the whole thing had been odd.

"What did Chas say?" He questioned.

Marelle laughed. "He said you were 'fucking excellent'." Then she added, "You were a bit rude to him afterwards though, but I explained you might have been under the influence of the medication!"

"Shit! What did he say?"

"He was fine ..." Marelle replied. "Anyway, you can ask him yourself, when he wakes up."

"Wakes up?" He asked, half turned into her. She ducked around the side of him and looked up into his face. "Yes, he's here, with Mya ...

"Here?" Jacob seemed tense at that.

"Yes!" She laughed. "They drove us home because they didn't want you riding the bike home with me on the back as you were acting so oddly ... they brought the bike home in Chas' van."

"The bike?"

She placed her hand on his upper arm. "You *really* don't remember?"

He shook his head.

"And you don't remember the ride down there either?"

He continued shaking his head.

She exhaled. "Shit!" It was no use feeling scared after the event, but it didn't stop her body going through the motions nonetheless and she didn't want to make him feel worse. "It doesn't matter." She smiled. "The main thing is – we got there – you did it and you were fucking awesome!" She looked up at him, he gazed down briefly then avoided eye contact, his hair was a mess and needed washing, he looked pale, thin. He clenched his jaw and swallowed.

Chas was not a morning person. He wanted coffee; Mya didn't want him having coffee but relented only to find the coffee they had was in his terms 'warmed up cat piss'. He drank two cups, however. Marelle made toast and they sat in the kitchen. Mya was chatty and smiling as normal. She helped Marelle with breakfast, taking over as 'mother' and hustling around them. Jacob looked tired. He had showered and changed but complained of a headache. When Marelle asked him about his arm, he said it was sore but not much else. Their conversation avoided the obvious. Mya kept staring at Chas as if goading him to say something, but he was not biting. Marelle was gradually learning the language that existed between them; gradually becoming aware of the intensity of their well-worn relationship; the banter and beration between them which had a sweetness she found touching – and the words unspoken between them but conveyed with the most modest of glances and gestures.

"I see Patricia's house says sold." Jacob said as he ate. "That was quick." It was a passing comment, but he had obviously seen it from the window upstairs.

"I noticed last night." Marelle told him. "I wonder where they're going?"

"Who knows?" He said quietly. "Places don't come up in the village that often."

No, Marelle thought to herself, just their house and Patricia's house, inexplicably linked. It seemed like the end of something. She wondered if the new owners knew about its history, no doubt they would soon be informed.

Chas and Mya left mid-morning. He and Jacob managed to get the bike out of the back of the van between them, but it proved to be a struggle. Chas swore at Jacob a couple of times but in the end, he patted him playfully on the back.

"Good job Bud." He said as he walked around to the front of the van where Mya was standing with Marelle.

"I'll be seeing you then." Chas smiled, fastidiously avoiding saying anything about last night.

Mya gave him a reprimanding little nod of the head.

"Thank you for bringing us home." Marelle smiled. "You can stay anytime – if you want to …"

Mya patted her arm. "That would be a pleasure … I will never tire of you two's company!"

Chas fiddled with the keys in his hand as Marelle stared at him.

'Thank you." Jacob said. Feeling the end of the thread pulling through his fingers and as yet there was no knot to stop it. "For letting me sing last night. It meant a lot, you know …"

Chas stared at Jacob, pulled the keys through his hands a couple of times, didn't reply in a time frame that made them all think he wasn't going to say anything.

"Yes, well … it was a leap of faith – on everyone's parts – on the surface it worked out. I'm not making any promises, but you brought something back last night which we haven't had for a long time. I've got to speak to the guys – if, of course they're still speaking to me!" He imparted. "And you've got to deal with whatever shit comes out of this for you." He laughed. "Good luck with that!

"I'm up for it." Jacob said with a nod.

"Yeah, well. We'll see, hey?" Chas replied.

Jacob nodded slowly. "I could do the final tour – it would be a fitting end …" His voice was quiet, but desperate.

Chas smiled at him, raised both his hands in an empty, non-committal gesture. "Take it easy …" He pointed to Marelle. "Take good care of him."

Mya looked at Chas in that way she did when she thought he wasn't saying enough.

"Let's tell them." She said.

"We said we wouldn't." Chas replied to her squinting in the sun.

"Ah go on!" She pleaded. "Let me tell them …"

By now Jacob's attention was spiking right in front of everyone, it extended its spiny tines out from him as they probed the air for any inkling of what this revelation may be. Marelle was caught between a breath and a heartbeat and felt the blood rush to her fingers.

Mya smiled, stood beside Chas, leaning against the van. "Well." She said. "Say hello to your new neighbours."

They both stared at her. Not quite understanding what she was saying straight away but Mya continued.

"We loved this village the very first time we came here and then we saw that pretty little yellow cottage for sale … we put in an offer, and it was accepted!" She grinned widely. "We are going to be your neighbours, right here!"

Jacob pointed to the house.

Mya nodded excitedly. "Isn't that wonderful? We will probably only come down for the odd weekend to start with … but it's perfect!"

Chas gave a small smile. "Mya's idea." He said.

"Oooh come here!" She stepped forward and hugged Jacob. "I told you; I'm not letting you out of my sight again! This is the best; it was meant to happen."

Jacob winced slightly when she released him. Mya noticed and kept a hand on his arm. "You need to get that looked at – Marelle make sure he does …" She pointed as she moved to her and hugged her in the same way. "We'll see you soon. Very soon!"

FORTY-NINE

Jacob walked into the kitchen, turned and stared at Marelle as she followed him in. He stared her right in the eye and sighed. He went to say something but changed his mind, obviously not able to find the exact word for how he felt right now.

"Shit, maybe?" Marelle asked.

"Bloody hell." He whispered.

"They don't know, do they?" Marelle questioned, tipping her head to one side.

"No. No." He answered.

"Are you going to tell them?"

"Tell them what?"

Marelle looked up at him. "Everything. They are sure as hell going to find out sooner or later. Mya won't keep her head down that's for sure!"

He sighed. "Bloody hell! Why did they have to go and buy *that* place! I should have said something then – the longer I leave it the worse it will look. I've got Yellow Son at stake too here – right when I've got him thinking about it ... that place is destined to be the bane of my life!"

Marelle's phone rang. It was on the worktop and vibrated against an empty mug and spoon as it rang. She reached for it.

"Bella." She said. She put it to her ear. "Hi Bella."

"Babes you ok?" She asked.

"Yes, fine, why?"

Bella sighed. "You don't do Facebook, do you?"

Marelle laughed. "No, I told you, couldn't stand it, too much bitching and wastes so much time ..."

"It's moved on Marelle – you need to get yourself on there. Is this on speaker?"

"No." Marelle answered, looking at Jacob and suddenly being alerted to the fact that Bella wanted a private conversation.

"Fuck!" Bella said. "Get yourself on there – your rockstar of a husband has just lit it up like a beacon!"

"He's not on there." Marelle replied – or was he? Marelle didn't bother with it now – in the beginning, when it was new and fun, she had made herself a profile - posting selfies and pictures of her and Bella but when so called friends started leaving stupid comments or just sharing inane videos of their latest meals or dogs doing stupid things she had quietly retreated.

"He doesn't need to be! Go to Yellow Son Unofficial – you may have to follow, or join or something – I had a look a few times when we were seeing them so I'm in the group ..."

"Unofficial doesn't sound too sharp ...:"

"It's the fan group. Went nuts last night. His performance made an impact and started a huge debate ... they are all laying into one another arguing whether it was, or it wasn't!"

"I don't need to see that."

"Oh I think you do." Bella suggested. "Just for information or ammunition ..."

"For what?" Marelle questioned.

"For when they start knocking on your door ... it won't take long to get around you know. Just think about it – everyone thought he was dead then he turns up singing at a concert out of the blue. Jeez a body was cremated which everyone thought was him --- there are regular outpourings of grief for him on this fan page, *all of the time* ... it's going mental. It's a great story ... they're going to be picking at the bones ..."

"Of course they're not!" Marelle scoffed.

"Well is he ready for this?" Bella asked, "He's not going to be able to mope around being Jacob now, is he? It's out there, there's no going back ... did he realise what this would do?"

"Of course!" Marelle replied, a little tersely, flicking her eyes to Jacob – not wanting to alert him to this conversation when he was standing there worrying himself sick over how he was going to tell Chas that he had just bought the very house that had both spawned his unhappy existence of a childhood and the suspicious death of two children who had ended up buried in *that* garden.

Bella sighed. "And this is just the very tip of the iceberg. This is just fans arguing – what's going to happen when they start asking who the body was that they cremated, when they find out he's been pretending to be someone else all that time ...what about ..."

Marelle interrupted her. "Bella, we know, ok. *We know.*"

Bella was quiet. She didn't like being interrupted.

"It's alright." Marelle said and felt a little odd that she was telling Bella it was alright. "How's everything with you, and Mae?"

"Fine." Bella replied. "Not as complicated as your life for a start."

Marelle sighed. "It's not complicated. It's simple." Jacob walked past her with a sniff and went along the hallway, she watched him go upstairs and heard him go into the bathroom. "He planned this. He knows full well what will happen but it's something he has got to sort out or he would have been haunted by that for the rest of his life. That's why we haven't got married yet – this all needs to be sorted first. It's one step at a time and we'll get through it."

"So, what's happening with Yellow Son? Is it a permanent thing?" Bella questioned.

"We don't know. It was a one-off last night ... obviously he wants it to continue but nothing has been said ... yet."

Bella sighed. "Just be careful Marelle ... and tell Jacob to be careful – it was less than a year ago he was in a real bad place, wasn't it?"

"It's what he wants Bella. It's all he wants – you should have seen him up there on-stage last night. He was *so alive*! It was a different person!" Marelle smiled with unbridled enthusiasm.

"Mmm." Bella mused. "Doesn't mean it's the right decision though, does it?" There was a short pause before she continued. Not enough for Marelle to think closely on those words. "Just keep an eye on him and look after yourself. I'm just warning you – don't think it's all going to be plain sailing from here …"

She didn't expect that at all. Marelle had never *expected* plain sailing at any point in her life but when there was a loud knock at their front door just after lunch, she raised her head and stared at Jacob with a look of horror on her face. No-one they knew banged on the door like that and right now they couldn't actually see who was there without opening the door as Jacob had boarded the hole up. He got up and walked through, Marelle trailing. Jacob had obviously not been party to the conversation with Bella and didn't hesitate when he opened the door, but Marelle peered around him timidly.

A guy with a grey beard and smiling grey eyes stood there. He had a ruddy complexion and bowed forwards as Jacob open the door.

"Gates." He said.

"Pardon." Jacob questioned.

"Your gates, I said I would pop over and fit them today if I had time – I've got them on the trailer …"

"Oh, God, yes, I'm sorry …" Jacob exclaimed. "Hang on, I'll get a coat."

"It's a strange day to fit gates … it's Sunday!" Marelle commented, still wary that there was an ulterior motive somewhere in the man who had come to fit the gates. Jacob grabbed his hoodie and took a final mouthful of the mug of tea he had been nursing after lunch.

"No, I forgot – he did say he would come and fit them on a Sunday if I wanted to pay him cash … you haven't seen them, have you?

She hadn't. Marelle had left that up to Jacob, after all she had little or no knowledge of gates or what contributed a good one. However, they were not as she had expected. For some reason she had thought they would be like a five-bar gate, open woodwork so you could see but what he had on the trailer were two enormous, six foot high solid, dark oak gates. They were shaped so they were slightly lower in the middle when they met. Stained a dark brown they were very solid and very impressive. Jacob admired them, ran his hand along them as they lay on the trailer.

"Beautiful." He smiled.

By darkness, the gates were in place and Jacob was excited. He took her outside and showed her how the gates would open, and close to demand from a remote fob they could put on the car keys. It worked from indoors as well but, he said the guy would come back and install a proper button in the house so they could open them remotely, this would also have an intercom so anyone wanting to come in could buzz them and announce their arrival. He loved it and was like a kid with a train set but Marelle saw it as a hindrance – before she could just get in the car and drive away. Now she had to wait for the gates to open. He laughed as they returned indoors another piece in his plan finally in place.

That evening she took her phone while Jacob was in the bath. She had vowed that she would not venture on to social media, but curiosity was getting the better of her. Maybe it would have died down by now – after all, Yellow Son were hardly the ultimate musical sensation that were on everyone's lips; they were a time served, well-worn old rock band – they had fans but it was a loyal following. Ask most people in the street and some may know the one song from their heyday but would know little else.

Amazingly she logged in to the site with little problems but then was faced with her profile from a few years ago. Her profile picture was one of her when she had experimented with lightening her hair; it made her look pale and she had too much make-up on. The very first post she saw was a picture of her and Chris, smiling beside the new car he'd bought. She stared at it – this was her old life – it didn't seem like it had ever been part of her now. Scrolling she looked at pictures of her and Bella, mostly drunk. One of Chris with his parent's dog and one from her that just said "WTF". She hit the search button and typed in Yellow Son.

Sure enough their page popped up – their logo and a picture of the band looking moody. She had seen that picture before. The last post was advertising the gig last night, saying tickets were still available and that it was the last date of the tour this year. Other posts were just gig dates. She hit the search button again and keyed in Yellow Son once more, in the list which came up was Yellow Son Unofficial. She hit the name.

The page opened. It was not private and she could see everything straight away. First up were pictures of last night's gig – of Jacob. There were hundreds she guessed; post after post, various pictures but all of the same thing. Jacob. Close-ups, shots from the back of the room, Jacob just standing there, Jacob in full flow, Jacob on his knees. This felt strange. These weren't picture from years ago when she had not known him; these were now, yesterday, *her* Jacob.

"*Is that blood?*" Someone had posted and those words caught her attention. She scrolled down, read the replies.

"It can't be. Who would perform on stage with blood splattered over them?"

"Chas' blood. He must have been held hostage. There's no way he would let an imposter into the group."

"From bleeding us dry and taking us for idiots."

"Blood or not blood. He was very good."

"Some two-bit clown dragged in because Chas obviously thought it was funny. This could be the shape of things to come."

"It's a betrayal. Bringing someone in totally out of the blue, no mention of it beforehand, not telling the loyal fans. This is Chas quitting the band. This is the end of Yellow Son."

"Look at the pictures. It doesn't look as if the rest of them knew about this either."

"Rift."

"It's not Ezza. How could it be Ezza. He's dead."

"It's an insult to the memory of Ezza. Bringing in a look-alike in this way. Who the hell is he?"

'This is terrible. This is slap in the face to all those loyal fans who have supported the band since Ezza died. It's distasteful and taking us for idiots. Were we actually meant to believe this was Ezza? I am disgusted."

"Nice try but a mile off. You can never sing like Ezza; you can never look like Ezza. There was only one Ezza, Don't treat the fans like this"

"I think it was Ezza!"

'This will be the shape of things to come. You wait and see."

And so it went on. The people posting on the page were not happy about it but the reaction of the crowd at the venue didn't not emulate those feelings. The crowd had loved it, had loved Ezza … no-one Marelle had seen had seemed this disgruntled.

Then it got nasty when they were discussing whether it was Ezza or not.

"It's NOT Ezza. Look at him. He's a fucked-up streak of piss. God only knows where he came from, but I suggest he goes back there."

"Was he drunk?"

"I don't know who you are, but you are NOT Ezza. Stop pretending to sing like him and look like him. You will never be him."

"Our beautiful Ezza died. You have no right to stand in his place and sing those songs pretending to be him. I will not go and see Yellow Son with this imposter up front."

"WTF is going on?"

It was endless and none of it happy. She had expected to see posts full of happiness and excitement – with the same feeling that the crowd had shown last night. But it was hate – for Chas and for Jacob. Outright hate. She stared at the words of derision over and over again.

"What are you looking at?" Jacob suddenly asked, in front of her. She had been so absorbed she had not even heard him coming downstairs.

She visibly panicked, looked suspicious and said 'nothing' in a very small, unsure voice, immediately getting rid of the page from her phone.

"Well you were pretty absorbed!" He commented.

"Yeah, well, you know it draws you in sometimes, doesn't it? Just crap." She shrugged.

Did he access social media platforms? She had no idea. There was no evidence that he ever did although in their early days when she had given him her old phone to use she had worried he was just some reclusive country bumpkin who would have no idea to how to use a mobile phone – there were times she had even wondered if he could read – but now she knew he was as capable as anyone, probably more so. Their words hurt her; they would hurt him even more.

He walked up to her and presented his left forearm. He had removed the bandage. The arm was pale up to the point of injury then it was fading into a maroon-coloured bruise around the two inch laceration. It was jagged, looked deep but had formed scab while the skin pulled together. Thankfully it looked dry.

"Oooh, is it ok?" She asked.

"Yeah, it's a bit tender if you touch it but, well the air will do it good ..."

"I thought they would have stitched it." She commented.

"Mm." he replied, looking at it and turning his arm into the light. "I'm not sure what they did. I don't remember."

Marelle stared at it. A two-inch hole in his arm that had nearly ripped his chance with Yellow Son away from him. It looked insignificant but she wondered if it had been fate fighting so hard for his corner? Marelle raised her eyes from his arm up to his face and stared into his eyes. He sensed it and looked down at her. In those eyes she saw the same person she had fallen in love with, the same person who had needed so much coaxing and persuasion to let himself fall in love with her. The same person that she had watched last night, in the spotlight in that stage, flying free at last.

All at once, she scrambled to her feet and threw her arms around his neck. Burying her head in his chest and feeling his warmth, his flesh and bones.

After that weekend normal seemed like a bit of a let-down. Jacob went to work on Monday morning. The weather was grey and cold, the steely skies spit light rain most of the day with a cold wind blowing from the east. No-one knocked at their door – not that they could anymore – and as far as she knew Jacob had no communication with Chas. He seemed settled which surprised her.

She didn't know his plan from here. Marelle had thought he had one but now she wasn't so sure, he had walked out on stage as Ezza a few nights ago – an action which she thought would set the world on fire – but in reality, it appeared that no-one was prepared to believe it was him. The fans on social media did not like what had happened, but it had not caused any major ripples in the fabric of his existence. Chas had let him perform with them then gone off without much of a word about it. It was like the firework had fizzled out and no one wanted to return to it. Jacob was working on the farm, probably in a tractor or under a vehicle – Jacob again. She thought he wanted this, but he was being very quiet about it Once again he confused her and his action was not as she expected. He went to work and came home each day. Marelle waited.

Just after six on a cold, dark and wet Friday evening. Marelle was washing up; she had just asked if he had heard from Chas when her phone rang.

She picked it up with a wet hand. The number looked familiar, but she couldn't quite place it.

"Hello?"

"Hello, Marelle?" It asked. She knew the voice now and felt herself deflate. "It's DCI Catchpole."

"Oh, hello." She replied.

"What's with the gates?"

"Pardon?"

"The gates? I'm sitting out the front in my car. I can't get in. I needed to speak to Jacob." He explained.

Marelle smiled, she looked to Jacob. 'Catchpole' she mouthed.

He looked resigned but gave a small smile. "I'll let him in."

"Jacob will open the gates." She replied to him.

They both watched the gates open slowly and the headlights from Catchpole's car manoeuvre into the drive. He didn't normally come into their drive. He normally parked across the entrance to it. The gates closed behind him, and he climbed out of his car. She heard Jacob sigh as Catchpole walked up to the door.

"You've got it like Fort Knox." He commented standing on their doorstep in the pale-yellow glow from the light on the wall. The top of the door was still boarded up. For some reason Jacob hadn't rushed to mend it. Catchpole nodded to it.

"Not vandalism again." He asked.

"No." Jacob replied but didn't go into detail.

"Can I come in?"

Jacob stood aside. He looked Catchpole directly in the eye with a calmness that worried Marelle. Catchpole made his way to the kitchen.

"Sorry." He said. "I always manage to come round at a mealtime." Tonight he seemed oddly mellow.

"It's OK. We've finished." Jacob answered. "What do you want."

Catchpole gave a little laugh. "Very forthcoming Jacob. It's almost as if you have been expecting me." He smiled at Jacob then Marelle. "Your sibling." He continued. "You need to make arrangements for his remains to be either buried or cremated. A death certificate will be issued and you need to register his death. Is there a name to go on it?"

Catchpole raised his eyes to Jacob and stared right at him with those pale grey green eyes. For once Jacob held his stare and did not flinch away.

"I think there might be. I think we know who he is now, don't we?"

Jacob nodded.

Marelle felt her heart lurch. The moment had not been at that concert the other day, it had not been afterwards when they were with Chas, it had not been when she read those comments on Facebook. The moment was now. None of those other things mattered because Jacob could be whoever he wanted to be but right now was his moment to tell the truth. A breath away, a heartbeat away, a millisecond away. This would be the moment when Jacob died and Nat was resurrected and now she understood he had been waiting for this.

"His name is Jacob William Frost." Jacob said quietly.

Catchpole nodded. "So, who are you then?"

"Nathaniel Ezekiel Frost." Jacob said.

The silence in the house was viscous and tangible. It curved around every corner, every doorway, sucking out any little sound it could to make the whole house a noiseless vacuum.

"I think you need to come to the station with me." Catchpole said. "We can be civilised and go in my car, or I can call a van to come and collect you."

"Now!" Marelle exclaimed. "I can drive him down there tonight – or tomorrow…"

"Not this time." Catchpole replied. "I am arresting you for fraud, perverting the course of justice and as a suspected accomplice to murder. You do not have to say anything. But, it may harm your defence if you do not mention when questioned something which you later rely on in court. Anything you do say may be given in evidence."

"No!" Marelle shouted. "*Murder* – he's not a murderer! Jacob tell him …" She pleaded reaching out to him and taking his arm.

Catchpole moved between her and him.

"It's OK." Jacob replied but his voice was shaky. He had obviously not been expecting this either. "Can I get a coat?" He asked Catchpole.

Catchpole nodded as Jacob walked back to the kitchen to pick up his jacket from the chair. Catchpole followed him, watched him.

"This is unfair!" Marelle shouted at Catchpole. "He hasn't done anything wrong. He just used his brother's name – that's all. He hasn't *murdered* anyone! This is a mistake …" She followed them as Catchpole took Jacob's arm.

"Jacob!' She cried after him. "Please, this is a terrible mistake … I'll come with you …"

Catchpole stopped her.

"You can't come with us. "Wait here and he will be able to call you tomorrow …"

"Tomorrow!" She yelled. "No. No. Please! Jacob …"

He gave her a glance and a small smile as Catchpole walked him out of the door and into the rain. He opened the car door and Jacob got in.

Marelle stood on the step and sobbed, she wretched her guts in anger and frustration that he had been ripped away from her. He had only posed as his brother – he had not done anything else – *anything*. How could he be arrested for murder? This was stupid. This was a mistake! She watched the car drive away in the rain.

She ran in, grabbed her cars keys and intended to follow no matter what, but then she paused with them clutched in her hand. Following him would not help, it would waste time. Instead, she grabbed her phone. Maybe there was someone who could help.

FIFTY

Marelle did not sleep. She watched each hour come and go, wondering if Jacob was still awake too. Wondering what was going through his mind right now. He had been terrified; he had not expected that – it was obvious. Fraud yes, he had mentioned fraud to her but not murder! Murder for God's sake – what if they framed him, what if he ended up going to prison? What would Chas say when he found out? That would be it! With all the best will in the world he would not tolerate a murder suspect. She reckoned it would even be a stretch of faith with Mya.

In her desperation last night Marelle had called Devon. He was a solicitor! Wasn't that what you did? If you were questioned by the police, you needed a solicitor. He hadn't answered his phone at first, but her tearful and desperate message had elicited a response five minutes later. He said he did not specialise in criminal law ... more words which drove even deeper into her heart but words she had to contend with ... but he knew someone who would be in a position to help.

He asked questions and took details as she gave them.

"Did they have a warrant for arrest?" He asked.

"I don't know." She shook her head realising with each passing second how much if this she didn't understand.

"What were the charges?"

"Murder!" She sobbed. "Fraud, murder and something else ..." the very word hit her harder each time.

Devon did not react or say anything to placate her.

"Ok." He replied, took further details and said to leave it to him. Marelle asked if they could call her, let her know what was happening. Devon sighed again.

"The lawyer's primary responsibility is to represent the interests of the client, who is Jacob. I am afraid that discussions about the case will be with the client only and not a third party, even if that third party is you, his partner. I'm sorry. They will speak to Jacob. Hopefully he will then get a chance to call you ..."

She thanked Devon but felt in an even darker place. This was getting serious now; she had never expected it to come to this. What had appeared like a small, even if difficult, hurdle to get over was now a yawning great chasm and each passing second she felt her fingertips losing their grip on that safe ledge where she had placed herself.

Now it was morning. His side of the bed was cold, quiet, unslept in. She reached across it and felt tears begin to prick her eyes. The only consolation she had was that he was safe, and she knew exactly where he was.

It was far too early to call anyone on a Saturday morning, so she paced the house. She daren't shower in case her phone rang, she couldn't face food but drank a mug of cold water as she stared out into the darkness towards the airfield. When he had stood at that door the other day, he had said he was scared; she thought he was meant he was scared of what him performing with Yellow Son would bring. Maybe it was this he had been scared of.

She wondered how Catchpole had found out. She wondered if indeed he had or had been lucky enough to pick the exact right moment when Jacob was ready to confess. Jacob had been duped; he'd walked into it with his eyes wide open, thinking that telling the truth now would solve everything. He could not have known this was coming; not in a million years. She waited for it to get light in the hope that she would get news soon.

It was Jacob's phone which rang. With hers right in her perfect for quick access he leapt up from the settee where she had curled up with a cushion to stare into space. His phone was still on the table in the kitchen, she flew across the floor, scattering chairs to grab it before it rang off.

"Hello?" She asked breathlessly.

"Ah Marelle, sorry I thought I called Ezza's phone."

She felt the air move out of her lungs and the little sparks of anxiety begin to dance again. Chas. Chas had not been in touch since they'd left a week ago, he'd picked a bad time to call.

"You did!" She replied with a smile that she pulled from somewhere. "He's not here at the moment."

"Not working, is he?"

"No..." Marelle said immediately but realised that was the wrong. "Well, he's at the farm, he wanted to borrow some tools ..." Why was she lying? Soon she would be so deep on that she would forget how to find her way out.

"Always a bloody early bird!" Chas remarked. "*Does* he sleep, *ever*?"

"Yes, he does!" Marelle replied, trying to keep humour in the air. If it started faltering, she would cry.

'Will he be back in about an hour or so? We stopped overnight at a campsite about thirty miles away. We were coming up – Mya wants to measure something in that cottage. The owners have said she can pop in and do that..."

"Oh, erm ... I'm not sure. He hasn't got his phone with him so I can't call." She rambled

'That's ok. I'll come and give him a look anyway while she's gossiping about curtains or something." Chas replied. "I'll catch you later ..."

"Ok." Marelle answered thinly but he had already rung off.

That was not what she needed right now. Suddenly she found herself right at the centre of the dial with one big, pointed stick bearing down on her. Marelle had never felt so alone in her entire life.

Marelle got dressed, tidied herself, brushed her hair and ventured outside. The sun made the occasional appearance but soon ducked behind a cloud. The easterly wind was dry and cold, it bit at her cheekbones as it whipped her hair away from her face. The dark, wooden gates looked imposing in the daylight. She had the remote control in her pocket and took it out. The icons on the two buttons were not entirely clear as to which button did what but trial and error soon told her the top one opened, the bottom one closed. She pressed the top one, waiting until the gates finally gave a little shudder then began opening. They were slow, she imagined sitting there in her car waiting for a big enough space to go through – she would get impatient. The same as she did for everything.

She left the gates open. If Chas was turning up, she would prefer him to be able to just drive in. In her deepest thoughts she hoped he wouldn't notice the gates. The wall had been there and with the gates open it didn't look that much different to the last time he'd been there.

She decided she would tell him Jacob was still at the farm. He'd been called out to help Mr. Wright. She didn't know when he would be back, but should she get Jacob to call him? That would work. If Jacob was home later then he could call him, if he wasn't and if he was charged, then – well, it would all be academic anyway.

Jacob had started clearing the front garden space, making it wider by cutting the hedges back. He did little bits here and there without saying anything or even her noticing some of the time. His bike was parked up near the house, he'd covered it with a new, green tarpaulin for now, putting stones around the bottom of it to keep it in place.

Trying to keep her mind occupied about anything else except Jacob's face when he had been taken away, she went back into the house. She checked her phone, checked Jacob's phone. She glanced at the clock in the hallway. It was a quarter to twelve, nearly eighteen hours since Jacob had gone. She wasn't sure of the process but if he was charged and remanded in custody, she may not see him again for days, weeks – God forbid, months. Marelle would have to visit him in a prison. Like in the programmes she watched on the TV – separated, not allowed to touch each other in a room with a number of other people. It would kill him; he would not survive that. Her thoughts got the better of her and she suddenly caught her breath, rolling into a gasp and then a sob. And what for, for *nothing*! He had done *nothing*, only used Jacob's identity for the last twelve years – who had that hurt, except him?

She had her hand to her mouth and tears filling her eyes when she heard a vehicle in the drive. With a vain hope that it was catchpole's BMW bringing Jacob back with an apology for making such a stupid mistake she hurried to the window to look. It was Chas' steel grey minibus. He was stepping down from it, looking at his phone. He put it to his ear and she could see him talking, laughing. Maybe Jacob had called him?

She went to the front door and opened it. He was standing there talking on his phone.

"No." He said. "It's a shitehole." He looked up at her. "I'll call you later."

"Is he here?" He asked.

While Marelle's inner self screamed, she kept composure and pulled a smile. "No, sorry. He's on an errand for Mr. Wright – the farmer who owns the farm …"

"He's a right little lackie isn't he?" Chas grinned. "Loves it, doesn't he – always said he wanted to keep working there when he could …" He shook his head. "I don't know. Your mans is an odd one …"

"Do you want me to ask him to call you?" She offered.

"Yeah." He nodded. "When he can. Not urgent. There's plenty of time ..."

She smiled slightly. He may need it.

"Is Mya over the road?" Marelle questioned.

"Yeah, talking about bloody curtains – I told her we haven't even exchanged contracts yet, stop worrying about the fucking curtains!"

"Sorry, do you want to come in? I can make a cup of tea – or coffee – if you want."

"No, no that's fine. As soon as the boss gets over here, we had better be on our way. Just though it was a convenient time to pop in and see his Lordship ..."

She wanted to ask him about the social media pages, about what feedback he had from the other night but she daren't and was in full knowledge that he probably wouldn't tell her anyway.

"Do you think he'll come back?" Chas suddenly asked.

She narrowed her eyes and stared at him. How did he know? Had he worked it out – no, that was unlikely. Had somebody told him, and if so who. If anyone else knew about Jacob's arrest, then it had not been passed on by natural progression.

"Come back?" She repeated, buying time to think.

He nodded. "What's your gut feeling? You live with him day-to-day; I can see you are pretty close. Do you think he'll come back?"

Marelle stared at him, didn't know what to say. "Well ..." She stuttered. "I would like to think so, God I hope so. We knew there would be issues, but we didn't expect this ..." She breathed out noisily, realising she'd said a little too much.

Chas stared at her, with a fatherly, puzzled expression. "What?"

"You asked if I thought he was going to come back ..."

Chas was staring at her like she was stark raving mad. Maybe she was, perhaps this was what a first dip into madness felt like.

"To Yellow Son ..." He explained.

Her eyes widened; she gave a laugh that was half a sob realising he had just asked her if she though Jacob would come back to Yellow Son. "Oh God!" She gasped. "Oh my God. Of course he would ... oh please, yes! He really would ..."

She felt like she was going to cry. Chas had come here today to ask that, the one think Jacob wanted to hear more than anything else.

"Well keep it under your hat. Not a word. I can't say anything for definite yet but there's a very good chance it's on the cards – if of course he wants to – for next year's tour ..." Chas winked. "Keep shtum. Scout's honour!"

"So where's my boy?" Mya was suddenly striding up the drive with a bundle of yellow material in her arms.

"He's not here. He's out with the farmer." Chas said, turning to her. "Playing haystacks – or whatever they do round here. I guess we'll learn all these country things soon enough. What's that?" he nodded to the bundle in her arms.

"Oh she's given me an old curtain so I can see what size they are ... odd couple!" She commented with a little shake of her head. "So, what are you doing with yourself all day, with Ez gone off with the farmer?" She giggled.

Marelle managed a smile although inside her whole being was curling in tightly on itself wanting to cry. "Oh there's always something to do."

"Well, we'll be neighbours soon – we can keep each other occupied!" Mya smiled. "When is Ez back?"

"Er ... "Marelle said, and she could just feel her voice breaking on her. She pulled back. "Not sure, sometimes he can be gone all day when he gets commandeered into one of these little trips!"

"No point in us hanging around then?"

Marelle shook her head. "Probably not. I don't even know when he'll be back ..." She felt her lip wobble, looked down and folded her arms to try and hide it. She sniffed.

'Well, that's Ez for you!" Mya smiled. "Shall we go then – we can get back to take Chip for a walk."

"Yes, tell Ez to give me a call when he gets back." Chas said with another wink and a little wave. Marelle returned the wave and watched them get in the van. Inside was turmoil, outside she stood there with a limp smile on her face as she waved them off. Mya grinned, waving frantically from the passenger side. Maybe she should have told them.

She closed the door, walked up the hallway into the kitchen and was immediately hit by all of the emotions she had been suppressing in the conversation with Chas and Mya. Marelle hugged her arms around herself and closed her eyes tight as the tears began to fall. There was an open invitation for Jacob to go back to Yellow Son, to do the whole of the tour with them next year – it was obvious this was already discussed and prepared for just so long as he wanted to go back. Jacob was the one mitigating factor that the deal hung on. For once it had worked out for him, he had planned it to this day, but he was in police custody, facing charges which although complete lie, nonetheless life changingly serious. He was out of her reach; she had no influence on what happened to him; she couldn't even speak to him even though she knew exactly where he was.

So, why was she standing here?

Grabbing her cars keys and both phones she strode out of the house, about to get into the driver's side she looked up and saw the gates were closed. Why were they closed? She had left them open – Chas had driven through them and they had been open. Did they close anyway after a certain amount of time? She tutted. Patted her pockets to see if she still had the remote control on her. She found it in her jacket pocket. Now, should she drive up to the gates and then open them or open them now and drive out. They took an age to open so maybe that was the better option. She could start them opening and then turn the car around to drive out, save her getting impatient on top of her heightened emotions. She held the remote up and pressed the top button. Nothing. For some reason she shook it and pressed the button, *hard*. Nothing. She walked closer and pressed the button. Nothing.

"Fucks sake." She sighed and pressed the bottom button. There was an odd little click from the gates but no movement. Marelle pressed the bottom button again. There was a small whine then nothing. She sighed. Maybe they had blown shut and not closed properly. Maybe she had to close them properly before they opened. Maybe that was what the click and the whine were. With an index finger tightly on the top button she pressed again. Nothing. Not a click, or a whine, or the tiniest movement. The bottom button only brought silence this time too.

"Bloody hell!" She exclaimed and strode up to the gates, pulling at the right one in the crease where they met. It felt like it was locked and wouldn't even open manually. She folded her hand around the shaped top and pulled hard. Pitted her weight against it and jiggled it back and forth. There was minimal movement, and inch or so either way. It seemed stuck. She shook it more, angrily, wiggling it until it moved a little more and she could get an arm around the other side. With brute force she forced the gate open, enough for her to slip her body between the two edges, pushing with every ounce of strength anger and frustration she had bottled inside her against the gate until there was a click and it began to scratch its way in an arc across the gravelly surface, not under its own power but by her own forceful volition.

"Fucking gates!" She gasped under her breath as she lowered her centre of gravity to push it the final few feet against the wall then stood back, gasping for breath with her hands on her hips. The gate didn't look right. It seemed to have dropped in position and the lower edge was hanging down towards the floor at one point. She looked up at the hinges. The gap at the top was much wider than the gap at the bottom. Something had gone wrong with the gate, *that* was the problem. With a sigh she looked at the gap the one open gate left. To push the other one back as well was feat of strength she didn't feel she had right now. The gateway was wide – it always had been, you could get two cars side by side in it. The open gate was right back against the wall. She looked at the gap. If she got dead straight her car would fit through, no problem. So, she walked over got in and did a three-point turn in the drive between the white van, the hedge and Jacob's bike the with the car facing the right way and straight with the gap she drove forwards.

Marelle had opened the right hand gate so the left-hand side of the car had to pass against the gate that was still closed. If she got as close as she could to the right, then she knew the left would be ok. Looking at the right front corner of the car and the back edge in her wing mirror she proceeded forwards.

Something banged immediately and she felt resistance to her progress, she went forwards a little more and together with the loud scraping and cracking sound she could see the outer edge of the left hand gate coming with her.

"Oh fuck!" She gasped. Went into reverse but the gate seemed stuck against her and went back with her. She hit the wheel, went to get out of the car and realised she was too close to the left-hand gate and the wall to open the door. She stopped, put her elbows on the wheel and covered her face with her hands. Why this, why now? There were tears streaming down her face, but she wasn't actively crying. If she wanted to get out if would have to be through the hatchback and she didn't even know if she could do that from inside the car. And anyway, she had to go backwards or forwards to get out of this. Either way would cause damage to the car and the gate. There was no point going backwards. She took a breath, sat up and gripped the wheel, depressed the right-hand pedal and went forwards. The gate scraped the whole length of the car until it cleared the back wing then fell, haphazardly at an angle on what remained of its hinges. Marelle didn't look back; she looked straight ahead and drove on.

Truthfully, she didn't know why she was driving to the police station. They wouldn't let her see him and she had no influence over what was happening but she guessed she wanted to be near to where he was. Even if she just sat in the car park. She knew he was in the building next to her and if he came out, well she would be there.

Marelle parked in the car park where she had parked before when she had waited for Jacob. She stopped the engine and sat back in the seat. What damage had she done to the car? She hadn't cared when it had happened but now, she worried about it. She wouldn't get out and look; she didn't want to be seen here if Catchpole happened to be looking out. There would be time later to assess the damage. Now she would just sit and wait.

She watched people come and go. Some were laughing and happy, others looked troubled. A white police van passed by her car and went to the side of the building where two large, grey metal gates slid open. She had not noticed that before but realised it was probably where Jacob had been taken last night. The entrance for criminals. She hoped he wouldn't be leaving by that way too. He couldn't be. She told herself. He simply couldn't be. OK so he had posed as his dead brother for years, he had a driving license and other documents in his name but that was it! He hadn't murdered anyone! He had been a child, barely more than a baby when anything had happened – how could this even be a consideration? But sometimes these things happened, sometimes people were mistakenly accused of something they did not do, they spent years in prison for a crime they did not or simply could not have committed. These things *did* happen.

She shivered. Reached forward and turned the radio on. The music seemed familiar and she turned it up, incredulously it was Yellow Son playing on a national radio station. Their biggest hit, the only one they ever played on the radio but nonetheless it was Yellow Son. She heard Jacob's voice; she turned it up louder, but her lip and felt new tears fill her eyes.

Was this a good sign or a bad sign. She didn't know which but there was no such thing as a coincidence.

The November sky soon began to darken. Lights popped on around the car park and in the street running alongside the station. People started to go home for the day or go out for the evening. How long should she stay here? She had nothing to go home for, no reason to be there. He wouldn't just 'go home' this time, he wasn't at large, lost out in the world – free to roam and do whatever he wanted. He was captive, in this building, right next to her.

She heard a clock striking the hour in the distance, in the town centre back up in the centre of the medieval grid system. It was six o clock. Maybe she would be here all night. Then her phone rang. She grabbed it from the dashboard.

She did not recognise the number; it was not a local code nor appeared to be a mobile. In the circumstances however she had no choice but to answer.

FIFTY-ONE

"Hello?"

"Hello is that Miss Marelle Buckleigh?" A standard unemotional voice asked.

"Yes!" She exclaimed.

"Oh hello, I'm calling from Southern Contracts – we have been advisers in the area would like to discuss with you how we can save you money on your energy bills ..."

"Oh fuck off!" She exclaimed angrily and hit the red button. It was six o clock on a Saturday evening for God's sake. She sighed, trying to slow her heart beat a little.

Her phone rang again. She looked at it. Another weird number. No doubt he had got his friend to call to wind her up even more. They had done that before when she had been rude to a cold caller. She stared at the number. But, what if ...

She pressed the green button but said nothing. Waited. She could hear people talking in the background. Yep, that was a call centre. Someone laughing in the distance, the sound of someone's phone ringing an somebody calling 'Mike' across a room. She maintained her silence, waited.

"Marelle?"

That voice was familiar. That voice filled her heart with a soaring joy all at the same time as her throat with a sob.

"Jacob!"

"What are you doing?" He asked,

She laughed, sobbed spluttered. "Nothing. I thought this cold caller was calling me back because I was rude to him ..."

"I've just got to sign some paperwork then they're letting me out ..."

"You can come home?" She cried.

'Yes ..."

"So they are not charging you?"

"Not at the moment. I'll explain later ... can you come and pick me up? If not it's ok, I can get a taxi ..."

"I'm here!" She said, joyously.

"Where?"

"Here, at the police station!"

"Why?" He asked. His voice was flat. He sounded tired, empty.

"I was waiting for you ..."

He sighed. "I'll be out in fifteen twenty minutes. Where are you?"

"In the car park. I'll come in ..."

"No, no, wait there. I'll come out." He said.

"Ok." Marelle smiled. "I'll be here!"

Those twenty-four minutes were the longest of her life. She sat with her neck twisted so she could see the entrance to the police station. Every time someone came out, she looked to them expectantly, the way they walked, their silhouette against the sodium lights. But he did not appear.

Then, stood at the top of the concrete steps, by the handrail was six foot one of muscle and flesh that she so desperately wanted to hold. He was looking about but soon spotted her car even before she had thrown herself out of it and was running towards him. She watched his lanky unhurried stride bring him to her.

He stopped and let her come to him. She took his hands and pulled herself into his body, closed her eyes and placed her head against his chest. There were no words, she just wanted to feel him, to smell him, to be this close to him. He hugged her back.

"It's OK." He said, quietly, "Let's get home. Give me the key's I'll drive."

"They're in the car." She replied. He walked towards the driver's side letting his hand cling to her for as long as he could but finally parting as she trotted round to the passenger side.

It was at that point that she remembered the gate and the damage. Marelle had not got out to look at what she had done but now as she stood at the passenger side it was horribly obvious. Along the full length of the car was a wide scrape, denting the bodywork as it traversed the once red, shiny side of the car. Paint was missing and there were streaks of white and bare metal, darker streaks where paint from the gate had been deposited. The wing mirror was half missing – it had been bent back when she had squeezed through past the gate, knocking the colour coded back off it. The mirror was pretty much all that was left having sprung back into place but with a crack right across the glass. Her heart missed a beat as she looked at it, but she did not want to convey it to Jacob just yet – they had too much time to make up to worry about cars. Slowly she walked forward and put her fingers out to the door handle – that too, was missing. There was just a flat metal plate left where the handle had been. She slid her fingers under the edge of that and to her amazement it worked, lifting so she could open the door. It all looked bad in this light; in the day light it would be much, much worse.

She slumped down in the passenger seat and closed the door, hoping it still would. Jacob was in the driver's seat, he still had the door open and the inside light was on. She smiled across to him.

"Are you OK to drive?"

"Yeah, I'm fine ..."

He looked tired, grubby. He needed a shave and there were dark circles beneath his eyes; his skin looked dry and dull.

He closed the door and started the car.

"Did you see a lawyer?" she asked,

He nodded. "Yeah – he was good, but pricey!"

She felt a stab of regret. She hadn't thought about cost. "I called Devon." She confessed. "I didn't know what to do."

"No, that was a good move." He said. "Lawyer was pretty much there before I was even processed through custody!" He grinned. "Did you speak to him?"

She shook her head. "Devon said he wouldn't be able to speak to me."

"I think I may have still be in there if it wasn't for him ..."

"Have they dropped the charges then?" Marelle asked.

"No." Jacob replied. "The accomplice to murder one *has* been dropped – but perverting the course of justice and fraud still stand but I have been released under investigation."

"Well that's good isn't it." Marelle smiled. "The murder one was stupid! That was the one to worry about, wasn't it?"

"Well, yes, but fraud and perverting the course of justice can carry heavy sentences too." He told her. "My lawyer thinks they probably don't have a leg to stand on with the perverting one, but he thinks fraud may be one we have to fight ...it depends how they view it."

She sighed. "So we are not out of the woods yet?"

He shook his head as he pulled on to the main dual carriageway. He looked in the mirrors.

"What's wrong with your wing mirror - has somebody clipped it in the car park – it's cracked." He commented.

"Is it?" She asked. Marelle didn't want this conversation right now; she would rather get him home and face this in the morning

"Yes, look ..." He nodded to it.

She looked. The crack showed up in the headlights of the other cars as a black line right across the mirror.

"Was it like that when you parked?" He asked.

"No, well, maybe ... I don't know ..." She struggled. "It's broken."

"Well if it happened in that car park, we need to tell them they might have it on CCTV."

Marelle sighed. "I don't think it happened in their car park. I didn't leave the car."

"Well it wasn't like that when I left ..." He looked at it again.

Marelle gave a little sob to herself, took a breath. "I had a bit of trouble with the gates!"

"Gates?" He asked, his mind full of questions and lawyers and custody suites – just as she had hoped it would be, so he may not notice the damage to the car or the gates straight away.

'The new gates." She said, looking out of the window and making herself small in the seat. "The wouldn't work; they got stuck..."

"Stuck?"

She nodded. I opened them to let Chas come in and left them open ..."

"Chas?" he interrupted.

"Yes, he came round. They went to Patricia's house, something about curtains and he came round to see if you were there. Wants you to call him when you can – not urgent, he said ..." She explained but a smile broke on her face in her reflection as she thought of their conversation. "I should call him as soon as you can ..."

"Did you tell him where I was?" He questioned.

"No. I lied. I said you were out with Mr Wright, and I didn't know when you would be back."

He sighed. "Was he ok?"

"Yeah, fine ... just Chas .... and Mya ..."

He paused for a moment, she watched his jaw clench and unclench as he stared at the road ahead.

"So, the gates ...?" He continued.

"I'd opened them and Chas went. I decided to drive down here and when I went to go out, they had closed, by themselves, but they wouldn't open again."

"What did you do?"

"I don't want to talk about the gates ... I want to talk about you ... are you ok? Did Catchpole treat you alright?"

"I don't really want to talk about any of that." He said. "It's an experience I don't really want to repeat – ever ..."

She sighed.

"What happened with the gates?" He persisted.

"They were stuck. I couldn't open them. They wouldn't open or close, just clicked a bit. I forced one open as best I could, but the gap wasn't big enough. I caught the car as I came out ..." She told him, quietly. "I was worried about you, I was upset ..." She defended immediately.

"You *forced* one open?" He repeated.

She nodded.

"How?"

"Brute force and ignorance."

He sighed. "Bloody hell! They lock with a solenoid – if they're stuck you can disengage the motor ... you shouldn't *force* them open..."

"You didn't tell me that!" She protested. "I was stuck in there and I wanted to come here. I would have knocked down the walls of Jericho with my bare hands if I had needed to ..." Marelle exclaimed. "Anyway, they're gates! They don't matter. *You* matter!"

He didn't say much else all the way home. He was disappointed with her; she could tell but in the circumstances that's all he could really be. If his life was at stake in anyway then he knew she would do whatever was necessary to get to him, even if it meant damaging inanimate objects. They could be replaced. He could not.

When he pulled into the drive the right-hand gate was almost flat to the floor. It was hanging on the top hinge so had twisted downwards and lay in front of them at an angle. The car's headlights scanned across their dark, wooden surface – it had a sheen to it.

"Fucking Hell Marelle!" He exclaimed. "That's not damaged, that's *destroyed*. What is the bloody car like?" He almost shouted.

"It's damaged, all along the side, the wing mirror is broken, and the handles are missing … it was stupid, I know, but I was worried …"

Jacob sighed. He was too tired to get angry with her – and she wondered if he even could. He got out, moved the gate enough to get in, looked at the passenger side of the car and shook his head to her.

"I'll deal with that tomorrow." He said.

Tomorrow was another day, and it dawned with a bright, frosty start. Last night he'd been hungry – he'd eaten zealously, drank two mugs of tea straight off then had a shower. By ten he had been in bed asleep with Marelle curled protectively around him. Now, this morning, he was staring out of the sitting room window at the carnage in the front garden with another mug of tea in his hand. He had already been out and surveyed the damage more closely. Both gates were salvageable, he reported but the mechanism may not be. The best he could do was open them and stand them against the walls for now. The car would need a body shop.

"I'm sorry." She said, walking up beside him. "I was scared."

"I know." He replied. "So was I. I still am … but I can't do anything about it. It is what it is now. I have started this journey and I have got to finish it – whether it's here or in prison we have yet to find out."

"Don't say that!" Marelle gasped. "It won't come to that not now … *will it?*"

Jacob shrugged. "Who knows. My fate is in someone else's hands now …" He stood there for a moment'. "You said Chas wanted me to call him?"

"Yes!" She smiled. 'Yes! Go on and call him!"

There was a smile on his face when he came off the phone with Chas. Marelle had left him to it; she knew what was going to be said and that grin when he walked back to her in the kitchen was worth all the treasures of the world.

Jacob walked up, hugged her to him, kissed the top of her head.

"Ezza is back!" He said.

Marelle lifted her head, looked up at him. His skin was glowing now, there was light in his eyes, his hair caught the frosty cold sunshine streaming in through the kitchen window and the tips looked red.

"Back?" She smiled. "What back with Yellow Son, properly?"

He nodded. "That's the plan. That's Chas' plan. He's spoken to the other guys, and they are prepared to give it a go. There's just paperwork to sort out, contracts etc. Forty dates in the UK next year …" He smiled.

She grinned widely up at him. "We're a good team, aren't we?"

"The best!" he smiled. "Wouldn't have done it without you. I can *almost* forgive you for the gates …"

She hit him hard on his chest, laughing but soon laid her head back down and hugged him again.

With despair still hanging over them in this cloud of happiness they ventured out in the low sunshine of a cold November afternoon to walk around the airfield. She felt that it was a moment he wanted to take to re-engage himself with it. Maybe walk around it for the last time, who knew? It had been a while since they had done this together and right now it reminded Marelle of that very first day she had climbed over the back fence and set foot in this sacred place.

The air was cold and crisp. The sky was a pale icy blue with long streaks of filamentous cloud winding around the edges. The trees were bare and waiting, the grass was dull – or still brown from summer, the sun was pale yellow and dropping. The birds of summer had gone but there were blackbirds calling, a small murmuration of starling skeined and twisted in the winter sky above them, settling in the cold dead, bare branches of the trees. The lonesome call of a buzzard pierced the air, but they could not see him today. Marelle had a woolly hat on, gloves and a fur trimmed jacket. She locked arms with Jacob and skipped along beside him. He wore his work boots, the ripped jeans and the black hoodie with the hood up. His hair poked cheekily out of the front and spiked around the edges. The Jacob she knew and loved and recognised so completely. But today his eyes were more alive than she had ever seen them before and his whole being had a vitality to it she could almost touch.

They strode up to the Thor site. Three deer scattered in front of them and raced off through the long grass and brambles, one turning as they left to look back at them before it too joined the others. Marelle wondered if it was a family, with one being the fawn they had seen earlier in the year. She liked to think it was.

The Thor site was desolate today. Grass and vegetation here where it was not so sheltered burned back to the bare minimum for over wintering. Jacob walked up to one of the low walls, opened his arms for her to stand in them, against him. They stood with the sun in their faces just breathing in what was here, letting it touch and infiltrate, relax and revitalise them. To their left a male pheasant in vivid winter plumage walked by slowly, making a little "whoop whoop" noise quietly to himself as he passed. His feathers were a riot of autumn colours, he looked plump, and his tail feathers were long and beautiful.

"He's a survivor." Jacob said. "Been here a few winters I believe. Stays here and avoids getting shot down when they shoot."

They watched him until he disappeared around the far wall.

Marelle looked along the tree line. Most were conifers that retained their foliage but in the middle was a gap where the deciduous trees had lost their leaves. In the summer it had been a thick green wall of bobbing leaves in the breeze. Now it was clear and suddenly she spotted something she had never seen before.

"What's that?" She asked.

"What?"

"That hut."

Jacob laughed. "It's not a hut, it's a watchtower, from when this was Thor site."

"I haven't seen it before?"

"You can't really see it in the summer as it's covered by the trees that have grown since then. It's pretty intact. Good place for birdwatching …"

"How do you get to it?"

The steps up and watchtower were mostly metal. It had been protected by the trees that had grown around it and was in pretty good shape.

"Just be careful.' Jacob warned. I think it's solid but keep your hand on the rail just in case …"

Marelle went in front of him, slowly, taking each step carefully, rising up above the airfield until they both ducked through the hatch at the top and stood on the wooden floor of the watchtower looking out over the airfield and the flat farmland for as far as they could see. Their breath was gathering the moisture and condensing in the air which was just above freezing.

"Wow!" Marelle smiled.

The scene was ethereal, heavenly, unworldly. Countryside as far as the eye could see, flat and expansive. Pale golden in the afternoon sunshine, still and ringing with the quietness and tranquillity of this place.

"This is amazing." She gasped, turning and looking out at all angles. "What was it used for?"

"Look-out tower to make sure there were no intruders on the site." He replied.

"Didn't spot you though, did they?"

He laughed.

She looked around the space. It was open all round with a wooden waist high barrier circling the platform. It had a pointed, cone shaped roof which overhang the edge slightly. It felt solid.

"How high is it?"

"About seven metres." Jacob replied.

"How many people can you get in here?" Marelle suddenly questioned, looking around herself.

"I don't know, maybe six – it was only built for one or two at a time. Why?" He was watching her.

She turned to him. "It's perfect!" She laughed. "We could get married up here!"

He shook his head. "I don't think so!"

"Why? You can get a licence as long as the person conducting the service is allowed to do a marriage … could we?"

He shrugged. "I don't know. It's a bit impractical."

"Since when has that ever been a bar to us doing something!" She laughed. "Imagine it – it would be brilliant! Oh, can we …"

"Depends on what happens to the airfield. It might have been sold by then." He replied

"But this will still be the Thor site – it will still be here, won't it?" She enthused.

"That's the plan as far as I know. But if someone buys it and it goes ahead it will probably be shut off ..."

She sighed. "Can you ask?"

He looked at her and gave that lopsided grin. "I'll see ..."

"Well, we know the date, don't we?"

He nodded. "Well ... yes, but we might have to see when the tour dates are ... we haven't set anything up yet but those will be planned. It's easier for us to change our date ..."

She looked at him, silhouetted against the sunset. "You're not back pedalling on me, are you?" She questioned, raising an eyebrow.

He shook his head. "No. But there are other things to consider now." He smiled.

Marelle sighed, with a smile. "Maybe I need to do this?" She asked.

"Do what?" He cocked his head, staring into her eyes, still smiling.

She grinned, gave a cheeky little smile, lowered her eyes then looked up to him again. She reached forward and took his hands in hers.

"Nathaniel Ezekiel Frost – *will* you marry me?"

EPILOGUE

Marelle had the Christmas with Jacob she had always longed for, Just the two of them, cosy in the house that was now theirs with a fire in the grate and a Christmas tree in the corner. They had agreed on no presents but on Christmas Eve Jacob received news from Catchpole that following investigation all charges had been dropped against him. He had committed fraud, but the case had been thrown out before even getting to court due to the circumstances and the only person who has lost out due to his actions had, ironically, been himself. On Christmas Eve he became a free man again. It was up to him to recover his own identity and that would be the next struggle.

Jacob's remains had been buried in the cemetery, in the same grave as his parents. A new stone had been erected to replace the one which Jacob himself had smashed and at the bottom the words 'also their son Jacob William Frost' with the dates of his birth and death. Three days apart.

They had visited the day the stone was put in place. Marelle had bought flowers and placed them on the grave. Seeing Jacob's name on a gravestone brought back many fears to her and she guessed she would always think about those moments when she looked at it. Jacob had lived, and Jacob had died and now he had claimed that name back but, Marelle knew, the man standing beside her would always be Jacob to her.

Patricia moved away. Chas and Mya moved in, piece by piece. Jacob did not tell them the full story – no doubt, in time they would find out or they would hear something and as at the moment they were flitting in and out like moths round a flame but the relationship between Jacob and Chas only strengthened day by day and Marelle felt a loyal and strong ally in him.

They had turned up on New Year's Eve, planning to spend their first night in the cottage. Both of their kids had hoofed it up to Edinburgh for Hogmanay, so they were left alone and came down with Chip. Jacob invited them round and they found themselves around a bonfire at midnight in the middle of the airfield.

"Is this what you normally do?" Chas asked, looking cold.

"I don't normally do anything." Jacob replied. "I'm usually on my own. Usually asleep, probably."

"So, you made an exception for us?" Chas laughed, sarcastically.

Jacob shrugged. "Just wondered what it was like out here, at midnight on New Year's Eve."

"It's fucking cold!" Chas exclaimed just as a while barrage of fireworks went off close by in the village. "Oh bloody hell!" He said with a flinch.

Mya laughed. "Hey, how about a chorus or two of Auld Lang Syne?"

"Give over woman!" Chas retorted.

"Well we've got two singers and no volunteers – I'll start you off."

"Oh don't start that! It's the same every year!" Chas exclaimed.

"Oh shut up you party pooper. It's tradition! Ready – *Should old acquaintance be forgot, and never brought to mind …"* She began singing as the bonfire cracked and a few later fireworks split the air behind them. Marelle joined in although she knew only a few of the words. Jacob sang along too beside her – he knew the words and Mya winked at him at one point. She began a second verse and Chas started da-da-da-ing along with her and then grabbed her hand and Marelle's the other side of him and swung them up and down in time to the music. Mya leaned forward and slapped his hand away. Jacob laughed. Mya stopped singing.

"No!" She said, "You don't do that, not till the last verse – everybody thinks you do it from the start but traditionally, you don't …" She explained.

Chas laughed, "She's flexing her Scottish heritage!" He nodded. "She does this every New Year with her Auld Laang Zyne routine …"

"Shame on you!" She gasped, but with a smile. "I was born in Edinburgh; I *have* Scottish heritage …"

"And you moved down to London when you were a month old!" Her interrupted her.

'I did, But I still know how to say it properly. You're doing it on purpose. You know it's Auld Lang Syne …you know it winds me up!"

"Oh, I do. I do because we go through this every fucking New Year!" He nodded.

"Oh sssh. You grumpy old git!" Mya laughed.

"What does it mean?" Marelle asked?

"It means I've fucking had enough and I'm bloody cold!" Chas exclaimed, rubbing his hands together and jumping up and down.

"Thank you, Marelle!" Mya said, kindly. "It means *Long Time Since …* it's about remembering and cherishing old friendships and past times … so you can see why it's appropriate and timely tonight." She took Marelle's arm and squeezed it. "And here's to the future too!"

To Chas' pleasure they eventually walked back to the house, went into the light of the kitchen blinking away the darkness.

'That was beautiful Ezza!" Mya said. "It's one New Year's Eve we will always remember!"

"Who's for hot chocolate?" Marelle asked.

Chas sat himself down. Jacob took off his coat and turned to him.

"Chas." He said. "Do you fancy buying an airfield?"

Printed in Dunstable, United Kingdom